EMERGENCE

BOOK TWO OF THE SAGA OF RUINATION

RAMÓN TERRELL

TAL PUBLISHING

For you, Moms. For you, Pops.

Khatal
Marai
Shetar
Shatteredlands
Sandlands
Mt. Blood
Shiedra
New Dama
Delaini Village
Valraga
Lal'eshma
Jietar
Altarra
Sleeping Morghan
Nassak
Carlayn
Border Highlands
THE RIDGELINE
Desiden Isles
Port Syara
Terratoma
The Triplets
Barbaros Island
Dokayuk
Werewood
Drylands
Vyne
Frostlands
Glacier Bay
The Black Glacier
Nogth
Port Tryphlan

…rain becomes fire, the air is crushing, the breath of darkness blots out the sun, and mountains bleed crimson tears. Thus the Incursion. Thus the Ruination.

—Unknown Author

PROLOGUE

Malkiem stood atop one of a forest of mountain peaks, each separated by miles of river snaking its way through the valley hundreds of feet below. He looked behind him to see the blue glowing figure of Zeraphal standing atop her own mountain peak. On yet another, further away, stood Typhirelli, his red, blue, and brown glowing figure blazing like a beacon.

He looked back ahead, not bothering to note the locations of the other Illuminarians. Malkiem knew his comrades were there, waiting for his call. Miles separated him from his fellow Illuminarians, as miles separated him from his former comrades, barely distinguishable in the distance ahead. Those miles might have been mere inches, for every one of them, Illuminarian and Fallen alike, could reach each other in the span of a few breaths.

The humid air sat thick and charged, coursing with static electricity. For three days Malkiem and the Illuminarians had battled Devrin and his Fallen, hurling massive amounts of essence at each other. Despite neither side having slept even a moment during that time, they had to take brief moments to stop, lest they rip the world apart.

Cold, callous, and evil to the core Devrin may be, but he wasn't stupid. He couldn't endlessly bathe in the power of the essences with the world at his fingertips, if they destroyed the world first.

Malkiem narrowed his eyes. The distant peaks stood tall and majestic, shrouded in a palpable darkness where seven dots glowed in the various colors of the essences. He wondered if Devrin truly understood those who followed him. Did he have even an idea that his group of once noble essence wielders were like him, selfish, cruel, and twisted by their own ambitions?

Well, almost like him. The Fallen shared many of the same traits with varying degrees of extremity and personal ambitions. The corner of Malkiem's eyebrow twitched. To anyone who knew him, that subtle movement would be the equivalent of an audible snort from anyone else.

The leader of the Illuminarians didn't miss the irony of his thoughts. Whatever Devrin and the Fallen might be, Malkiem and the Illuminarians were a mirror image. How thin was the line they walked? How well balanced were they to walk upon it?

Malkiem closed his eyes and opened himself. The essences rushed to his call, flooding into his body, the blood in his veins, his mind, his very being. The weight of the world flowed around his body, inside his soul. Less than a flicker of the power of creation touched him. It would have been enough to disintegrate the most powerful of essence wielders with lesser knowledge and abilities than he and the others, spread about this cluster of peaks.

When Malkiem opened his eyes, he saw seven distant blots of light flare to life, and felt the five behind him also filling themselves with the power. This needed to end now. The world could not endure the continuous clash of these two groups.

Air came to his call. The essence swirled around him, lifted him from his perch, and sent him speeding across the land as if they were but a handful of running strides.

Devrin's arrogant and ever-confident smile came into view as Malkiem closed the distance between them. With a mighty leap, the Fallen flew straight up.

The air crackled with electric energy as Devrin summoned and launched down on Malkiem, a bolt of lightning larger than an entire city.

Malkiem stopped over the peak where the Fallen had been standing, crossed his arms over his chest, and commanded *air*. The enormous bolt of lightning split around him and shattered the mountain below. He heard Devrin's voice above the thunderous explosion.

"Seriously, Malkiem," the Fallen leader shouted. "How long do you insist on playing this game? You know as well as I that the world cannot sustain our antics forever. We should come to an agreement before we break our toy, don't you think?"

Malkiem's face tightened. That's what the world was to Devrin. A toy to be used for his amusement. His glowing body pulsed between silver and blue as he called forth *water*, combined it with *air*, and sent a raging river of ice shards streaming at Devrin.

The Fallen commanded *fire*. An inferno encircled Devrin that stopped most of the twenty-foot shards, but not all. Devrin moved left to right, using *air* to navigate around the spears that were too hard and moving too fast for his fire to completely melt.

Somewhere he heard the distant scream of Mycia. It wasn't a scream of pain or rage, but bliss. Sebanavick's answering laughter preceded an explosion that rattled Malkiem's chest cavity. Those two were more similar than Malkeim was comfortable with. Explosions, raging fire, and screaming winds lit the mountainous valleys as the Illuminarians and the Fallen fought in their endless battle. Neither gained advantage, and the world suffered every moment of it.

"Nothing to say?" Devrin shouted from above.

Malkiem commanded *air* and shot straight up for the taunting Fallen. Devrin narrowed his eyes and sent a column of fire spinning down on him. He then commanded *earth*, grabbing boulders from the destroyed mountain and pulling them up to his call.

Fire met Malkiem from above while thousands of tons of rock

met him from below. The Illuminarian met both in an explosion that rocked the region. Trees shuddered and fell, rifts tore the ground open, and the river far below jumped as though a giant hand had smacked its surface.

Like the bolt of lightning Devrin had thrown at him, Malkiem shot out of the fiery cloud of dust and debris, rushing straight into Devrin's rapidly diminishing smile. The Illuminarian drew *air* and *water* to his left hand, closed it into a fist, and struck the Fallen with a lightening infused uppercut to the chin that erupted in a blinding shower of sparks. In the air far below, Typhirelli drove his knee into Revdrak's stomach. He then delivered a chop to the back of the Fallen's head as he doubled over, then used *air* to stop a falling boulder and launched it toward Devrin. The boulder pulsated between all the colors of the essences as it sped toward the leader of the Fallen, who tumbled backwards, head over heels, through the air.

The boulder struck with a mighty explosion. Typhirelli shoved Revdrak away and kicked him in the side for good measure. He turned and looked above, toward Devrin, and worked his hands in a quick pattern. The energy and debris from the explosion stopped and drew back in toward the Fallen leader. Devrin's eyes widened, and he crossed his arms across his chest curling himself into a ball.

Typhirelli flexed his arms and punched his fists downward. The explosive energy compounded on itself and exploded with concussive force. Fallen and Illuminarian alike tumbled away from the massive burst of energy.

Devrin uncurled himself and glared down at Typhirelli through the smoking wisps slithering away from his singed body. Typhirelli winked at him just before Mordayne flew into him. The two sped through the air and crashed into the side of another mountain. The impact sent a spray of rock and dust falling to the river below.

In the distance, flashes of light preceded the audible explosions of Udorian and Dyrge clashing over and over again, while Amadon battled Lenara on one of the distant mountain peaks.

Malkiem commanded *air* and ascended toward Devrin. In his right hand, he created a spear of ice, while his left hand glowed red like living magma. Just as he was about to strike, he saw a great darkness in Devrin's eyes, like a void of nothingness threatening to swallow him.

"I've learned something new, Malkiem," Devrin said in an *air*-enhanced voice. "I told you I've had enough of this back and forth game. Ascend!"

The Fallen disengaged from the fight and flew higher into the sky. The Illuminarians gave chase even as Malkiem finally reached Devrin. Within a few dozen feet, he saw the grin on the man's face as he felt the essences retreating from his body.

Malkiem gasped at what felt like numerous hands clawing and grabbing at the power flowing around and through him. Something snatched away the power at his command, and he began to fall.

He heard Amadon's surprised shout, as well as Mycia's enraged scream. They'd stripped the others of the power as well, but how? Helpless and falling to his death, Malkiem could only ponder this new development in the last moments of his life. He looked around and noted his fellow Illuminarians also falling, speeding headfirst to the ground like spears falling from the sky.

Malkiem felt a tingle deep inside his being that lit afire. The essences had returned to him! Perhaps the effect was temporary, or only effective within a certain range. Whatever the answer, Malkiem would find it later. He summoned *air* and arced his descent until he was flying upward again. All around him, the other Illuminarians did the same. As one, they sped back toward their enemies.

"Stop! Everyone stop!" It was Dyrge who'd spoken.

Malkiem looked across the distance and followed her horrified gaze toward an area of sky beyond Devrin. The sky darkened, while silver, blue, red, and green, the colors of the four essences, flowed into it.

The darkness greedily drew in the power, the colors disappearing into the black void as if they'd never been. Across the valley, each of the Fallen hovered in place, backs arched, as the essences were pulled through them and into the black patch in the sky.

"Stop them!" Malkiem shouted. "Knock them out of the sky!" He'd barely gotten the last word out of his mouth as he launched an enormous column of fire toward Devrin. From below and on every side, his comrades did the same. Six raging columns of flame at least a hundred feet wide flowed toward the Fallen. Off to Malkiem's left, Typhirelli split his column in two and sent one toward Udorian and the other toward Mordayne.

The flames engulfed each of the Fallen, but instead of immolating them, the fires flowed right into them and out, blending into the essences streaming into the darkness.

Hovering below his ancient enemy, Malkiem watched in helpless indecision. Given what had just happened, he was convinced that if they got too close, the essences would be stripped away from them again and fed into whatever it was in that darkness. He ground his teeth as he searched for an answer. "What in the name of the Creator are you doing, Devrin?"

"Ha! Funny you would mention such a thing, old friend."

"We ceased being friends a long time ago," Malkiem spat.

Devrin shrugged. "As I said before, I'm tired of this back and forth game. Surely you must be, as well."

"By feeding essence into the sky?" Malkiem asked. He frowned at the ever-darkening area above. It felt alive.

"Malkiem!" Typhirelli called from the side. "What are you *doing*? Take that freak down!"

Devrin smirked. "Yes, Malkiem. Put me down. Put us *all* down."

Malkiem commanded *earth*. Far below, a massive chunk of rock dislodged from the wall of the valley, broke apart, and reformed into a stalagmite. Once formed, it aimed toward Devrin and sped upward in a straight line for the Fallen. Malkiem kept his eyes on Devrin to keep from tipping his hand.

"You can't, can you?" Devrin taunted, even as Typhirelli shot toward Mordayne. Before Malkiem could shout for him to stop, Typhirelli got too close. His ascent slowed, and he roared in anger as he began to fall. Amadon flew down and grabbed him. She held him aloft until the essences answered his call again. That gave Malkiem an idea. He retreated from Devrin, who laughed at him.

The black blot in the sky continued to grow, and somehow Malkiem knew it had indeed become a living thing. An evil thing. Below, the stalagmite sped upward, almost close enough to be within view.

"Both of you," Malkiem said once he reached Typhirelli and Amadon. "Combine your efforts with *air* and throw me at him."

"Sounds insane," Amadon said.

"Sounds fantastic," Typhirelli added as they both summoned *air* to their command.

"Wait until I say," Malkiem said. He turned toward Devrin, stealing glances at the ever darkening cloud in the sky. He thought he saw two red slits open side by side and focus on him. He felt more hate than could be possible emanating from those slits.

The stalagmite shot into view from below and behind Devrin, speeding straight for the Fallen leader. "Now!" Malkiem shouted. Amadon and Typhirelli launched him at his old nemesis, who turned his lazy gaze on Malkiem and slowly shook his head. Malkiem blinked away the tears streaming from his eyes from the speed of his ascent.

The essences winked out as soon as Malkiem reached the dead space surrounding Devrin, but his momentum carried him through. The smugness on the Fallen's face fell away when the stalagmite ran through his lower back and out of his abdomen. Less than a heartbeat later, Malkiem swung his elbow into the side of Devrin's face with the full force of his speed behind it.

The impact broke his elbow, but it would have shattered his

hand, had he used his fist. Already focusing on healing his elbow, Malkiem twisted himself around as he began to fall. If the impact hadn't broken Devrin's neck, the stalagmite surely killed him.

Dyrge commanded *earth* and *air*. "A little over the top, don't you think?" she yelled, as she broke the rock apart and reformed the pieces into smaller spear-like weapons. She sent them straight for each of the remaining Fallen.

Malkiem didn't answer, for he knew Devrin better than any of them. When the essences returned to him, he commanded *air* to hold himself aloft once more. He watched Devrin's body fall from the sky, his line of essence that fed the black cloud died away. Whether it was in shock from the apparent death of their leader, or the lack of his guidance, the lines of essences winked out from the other Fallen as well, who began to fall from the sky in exhaustion.

Dyrge followed through, and each rocky spear aimed for its respective target, aimed for hearts that had long ago gone as black as pitch.

Malkiem looked to the blackness in the sky. The blackness glared back at him. It was the most hateful, baleful gaze he'd ever seen, and it threatened to wither him where he floated. Two swirling appendages sprang from the cloud while an enormous claw formed on each end. If mist could growl, it would have been the same hideous sound that came from the cloud of blackness.

Their dead enemies forgotten, the Illuminarians attacked as one, hurling every physical form of the essences they could imagine. Ice, fire, stone spears, and lightning bolts assaulted the thing, but it absorbed the attacks; drank it all in. Malkiem nearly screamed when he felt the essences reach the thing. It was as if the essences had *died* upon reaching it.

The cloud extended its arms out to its sides and curled them around the group of floating Illuminarians. Malkiem and the others fled, easily outpacing the extending arms. But the creature wasn't reaching for them, but around them, toward those who'd created it. Every one of the Fallen slowed in their descent, then began to rise.

"What in the name of the Creator *is* that abomination?" Mycia shouted.

The enormous cloud focused its withering gaze upon her and all of them at the same time, and Malkiem heard a terrible voice infect his mind. It took every bit of his will to keep it from driving him mad as the sound ground against the inside of his head. The last thing he heard as he watched in dismay, the hole in Devrin's torso closing, were the words torturing his mind, his very soul.

I am Shurza.

1

BROTHER AMERUS

Brother Amerus Layun ran a hand over his mostly bald pate. He gently slid a stack of books aside and cupped his hands over mouth. He'd been doing that a lot as of late.

He looked at the stack of books again, as though they might speak to him. The literary pile stared back at him in uninformative silence. Not a single one of those tomes held any information beyond superficial accounts regarding the monsters that had attacked Vyne. He'd been researching for weeks, trying to find anything that might point him in the direction of a solution to the bigger problem he knew was coming.

Amerus took a deep breath and exhaled through his nose. As much as he hated to admit it it, it had come down to himself and that first magus, Selvetar, to find a solution to this problem. Arch-minister Decius had doubled down on his uselessness, refusing to believe the attack was anything more than an isolated incident caused by the imprisoned wilder.

While the timing might have made for a suspicious coincidence, only an idiot would pass the matter out of hand. Decius, of course, fit that description far better than he fit his actual occupation, much to the misfortune of Vyne.

The senior monk reached for the solitary book on his right, the remaining book he hadn't yet read. The spine creaked as he opened it and flipped through the pages. He hoped Selvetar was having better luck, and simultaneously hoped he'd never hear from the man again. Magi in general weren't a group Amerus trusted, but that man made him especially uneasy.

Amerus stopped at an interesting passage regarding creatures of the underworld. As with every book in the stack to his left, the amount of information was lacking, but there were a few notes that caught his attention.

"Hmm. Bipedal beasts with four arms, skin like cooled lava rock, and blood like magma. Tall, hulking, relentless, and brutal. The creatures cursed their enemies even as they swiftly cut them down. The fist of the underworld. The Drauk." Amerus sighed yet again at the perfect description of the horrid creatures that had attacked Vyne. He found more troubling images as he flipped through the pages, some monsters even more horrible looking than the drauk, but with even fewer details about them. Each image had the same quote underneath; "they precede the blight. They herald the Ruination."

"The Ruination." Amerus knew that story all too well. Most of the populous knew the word, and that it related to some apocalyptic event, but little more than that. A myth from ages past that may or may not have happened. The most studied scholars and monks from the Brotherhood of the Source knew the history.

Brother Amerus had studied extensively about a group of powerful magi breaking into two factions. One faction had remained dedicated to the study of the essences while the other faction had studied the power for its own sake. Amerus had studied the War of the Immortals, the many battles between the two factions that came to be known as the Illuminarians and the Fallen. The latter had created a beast that supposedly absorbed the essences themselves.

Amerus grunted and shut the book with a resounding thud. Part of him thought it nonsense. Monsters popping up from the under-world preceding a great evil that brings about the end of the world? Who wouldn't scoff at such a notion? But how many books could he ignore about it? The average Marailander might not have read many or even any of the ancient historical texts, but Amerus had read all that he could get his hands on. Were these books all filled with nonsense? Were they just fanciful stories originating from different parts of the world that all validated each other? Or was there something to it?

A knock on the door brought a welcome interruption to the senior monk's dark thoughts. "Come."

The door creaked open to admit an ashen-faced Brother Krusp. The man was pale as moonlight on the best of days. Now, standing there with his hands clenched together so tight the veins were showing, he looked like a ghost. "My apologies for the interruption, Senior Brother Amerus. But I have news of the brothers you sent to investigate the dead patch of land northwest of here."

News of the *brothers*? A stab of ice settled in his stomach. He kept his features neutral. "Why isn't Brother Landon here to deliver his report himself?"

Brother Krusp somehow managed to clasp his hands together tighter. "He … can't, Senior Brother."

Amerus frowned. "What do you mean he can't?" At this point he knew the answer, but hoped for some small chance he was wrong."

"Brother Landon barely survived, Senior Brother."

The senior monk slowly pushed his chair away from his desk and stood. "Survived. Survived what, Brother Krusp? I wasn't aware the mission I sent them on contained an element of danger to survive."

"I would urge you to hear it directly from Brother Landon, Senior Brother." Krusp's hands were clenched so tightly they were shaking. "As soon as I saw his condition and he told me that only he had returned, I came straight here."

As senior monk of the Vyne branch of the Brotherhood of the Source, Amerus had a responsibility to be a beacon of strength for the brothers. Through sheer force of will, he wrestled down his alarm and nodded. "Then, let's go see him." He swept out the door and heard it close behind him, followed by Krusp's footsteps.

They left the main building of the brotherhood, crossed in front of the Temple of Contemplation, and moved swiftly through the gardens. The fragrant roses and flowers normally could sooth his most dour mood, but so grim were the possibilities swirling in Amerus's mind, he smelled none of it. For a mercy, Brother Krusp didn't feel the need for pointless chatter, and so left him be.

He did smell the infirmary, however. The pungent odor of therapeutic insense found his nostrils, as did the sharp scent of boiling kava root. Amerus followed the agonized grunts until he finally came to the room housing Landon. He gave a knock, then gently opened the door.

Brother Landon lay squirming on a bed with three nurses holding him down. A fourth nurse was in the middle of administering a cold balm to several angry burns on the man's legs and arms.

Amerus clenched his teeth to keep his mouth from hanging open. The nurse applied the cold balm on Landon's left arm, but avoided touching his right, which lay slack on the bed, dusty brown and cracked like parched earth. The poor man's arm looked so fragile that it might simply break apart into dust if the nurse breathed too heavily on it. Perhaps the nurse thought the same, for he took extra care not to touch anywhere near the limb.

"What's happened?" Amerus moved beside Landon's head, earning a disapproving frown from the lead nurse. He ignored the man and repeated his question. "Brother Landon, what happened to you?"

"D ... dead. All ... d ... dead. N ... no chance. All together, still ... no chance."

Amerus lay a hand on the man's forehead and closed his eyes.

He reached his other hand into the pocket of his robes and closed it around the corlite stone inside. He wished he were better at healing. "Keep talking, Brother."

He concentrated on grabbing hold of *earth* and *fire*, bending and molding the essences, then grabbing *water*. As Amerus molded the three essences into an ethereal blanket to settle over the wounded monk, he listened as brother Landon spoke of the most awful things he'd ever heard.

A man with skin like charred tree bark leaving disease in everything he touched. Despite being outnumbered seven to one, the man easily dispatched every one of them.

"M … moved too fast. No man … should move so fast. Essences … in … in … ineffective."

Amerus had done all he could do for the agonized brother. He stepped back with a tired sigh. "Send word of any change in his condition," he said to the lead nurse. "One way or the other."

"Of course, Senior Monk," the nurse replied.

Amerus swept out of the room, Krusp on his heels. The other monk trotted to keep up with his swift gait. "What was all that, Senior Brother?" Krusp asked.

Brother Amerus didn't reply until they exited the infirmary and were alone again in the gardens. As much as he disliked admitting it to himself, First Magus Selvetar had been right. They needed to work together on this, which meant he would have to speak to the man as soon as possible. Which, unfortunately, meant he would need to be in the man's presence, and often. Too often.

"Go to your chamber and speak to the Creator, Brother Krusp. Beseech His wisdom, courage, compassion, and strength. Beseech his guidance on the times to come."

The tiny bit of color that had returned to Krusp's face drained away. "What do you mean, Senior Brother? I will heed your words, of course, but what—"

"Brother Landon's words speak of dark times to come. Go and pray, and fortify yourself. We have lived in comfortable times under the Creator's blessings. Uncomfortable times approach, and faith will be tested true."

Krusp's mouth fell open at that, and Amerus knew he wanted to ask what in all the world that meant, but the monk knew better than to question Amerus further. With a deep bow, the man hurried away.

Amerus blew past the many people who greeted him with a bow or a quick blessing. So occupied with Landon's fragmented account of what befell the party, he barely noticed they were there. He didn't see the path in front of him, the steps he took two at a time to enter the temple, nor the hallways he navigated.

Without realizing when he'd gotten there or how long he knelt, Amerus found himself on his knees before the Altar of Creation. At some point he'd lit several incense sticks and placed them in a bowl of fertile soil.

There could be no doubt about what was coming. The appearance of drauk might be passed off as an isolated incident. There were, after all, monsters and evil in the world. All sorts of phenomenon, good and bad, occurred across every land. But Brother Landon's account of the attack and subsequent decimation of his party chilled Amerus to his core.

The senior monk said a prayer of thanks to the Creator on Brother Landon's behalf. That he had escaped with his life was no small miracle, for few could claim to have survived an encounter with a droughtlord.

2

EMIEL

Emiel watched Amoura Xanna's floating and rotating body. Her eyes were closed, but he knew they glowed as silver as her shining essence ring. He glanced about, hoping the levitating magus hadn't drawn any unwanted attention, whatever that might be.

Beside him, Lief also looked around. He hadn't seen her this nervous since their escape from those horrible mountains, the Triplets. Her dark brown eyes were open wide with fear, and it seemed to Emiel that her sandy, almost translucent glowing skin had dulled and gone pale. Even her clay-red hair had gone dim.

"Got any words of wisdom, Tinfar?" Bone asked.

Lief stared at the mercenary for a long time before she finally spoke. "Don't sleep."

Bone blinked several times as a snarl crept up his mouth. "Don't sleep. What in the name of the Fallen is that supposed to mean?"

"I suppose you could go to sleep and find out," Lief snapped.

Emiel glanced at her. That was unusually sharp, even for her. "You okay?" he asked.

Lief hugged herself and shivered. "Whoever sent us here is cruel. This is a place of endless torture."

"Torture?" Bone replied. His teliak bone armor made a muffled squeaking sound as he turned this way and that. He indicated the vast expanse of nothingness populated only by seemingly infinite elevated pathways snaking their way into the darkness. "Endless, maybe, but what is torturous about this, other than the possibility of wandering endlessly until you starve?"

"Sounds tortuous enough to me," Emiel replied.

"You'll find out soon enough, Bone man," Lief replied.

Bone glared lazily at her. "Bone man."

"She is right," Amoura said.

Emiel turned back to see that the magus had finally settled back to her feet. The silver glow of her essence ring, signaling that she'd been manipulating *air*, pulsated a few heartbeats more before reverting back to its simple marble color.

"I'll take a wild stab at this," Bone said. "The Maze is a place of endless dangers at every turn. No one who's ever entered has left, and it's only a matter of time before you die in a futile attempt to find your way out. And there is no way out. Does that cover it?"

"Mostly," Amoura replied. "I know of no one who has escaped the Maze, but I also know of no one who's ever been in it. There are only books and legends, and I hadn't believed any of them until this moment."

"That's fair," Emiel said as he turned a circle, gazing out at the innumerable pathways stretching into the endless nothing. "I wouldn't have believed this existed, either, if I wasn't here."

"Because most humans can't seem to believe anything they haven't already seen or touched," Lief added.

"Humans believe in the Creator," Bone said absently as he, too, looked around. "And I can't think of anyone I know who's ever seen or touched Him."

"You believe in the Creator because you want something from Him," Lief replied. "Or, you're afraid of Her, or think it's only through Her that you can be happy. He is either your salvation or damnation, but despite all of that, every human I've ever seen seems to always want something from everything around them."

"So much scorn from such a small person," Bone remarked.

"Did you just refer to the Creator as male *and* female?" Emiel asked.

Lief waved a dismissive hand and didn't even bother to look in his direction. "You call the Creator Him, the people of Khatal say Her. You're both right and wrong." She looked over her shoulder. "Which seems to be the case more often than not. Or, you're just wrong."

The one and a half foot-tall woman was clearly in a mood, so Emiel let it go. Fortunately, Bone picked up on it as well, and dropped the subject.

Amoura had been staring in the same direction during their discussion. "The air brought no smells to me of any dangers that might be lurking beyond our vision. I heard no footfalls or moving bodies. But I heard whispers; promises."

"Promises?" Bone asked. "Do I want to ask what those promises are for?"

"It was only an impression that I got," the magus answered. "I'd wager you don't want to ask, but you do want to know."

Bone nodded. "Aye. I'd rather know what's coming for me, even if it's something terrible."

Emiel glanced at the young mercenary, wondering if his accent slip was an indication of how nervous he was. "Okay, so we've got no indication of monsters around here, at least not in the immediate area. And, we've got something like a promise waiting for us, somewhere. Given the situation, it's safe to assume we won't like it." He shrugged. "Might as well get moving. Do you know which way to go, Amoura?"

She shook her head. "No."

"Ah, okay then." Emiel raised his hands and let them drop. "I guess, let's just pick a route and get going. I've got my girls to get back to, an archminister to throttle, and if I'm not too exhausted, I'd like to find the Fallen-cursed bastard who dropped us in here."

"And do what?" Amoura asked him.

"Maybe hug his neck really hard with my hands," Emiel replied.

"That would be difficult," Amoura replied. "The Maze isn't accessible via a doorway or any location you can just walk into. Whoever dropped us in here is capable of opening a gateway from one plane of existence to another. That is no small thing."

"You can't do that?" Emiel asked.

"I would have had us out of here the instant we arrived if I could," Amoura answered. "In all the order of magi, in all the branches residing in all the many cities and regions in the world, I only know of one man who can open a gateway."

"Well, that narrows the list of suspects down," Emiel replied with more enthusiasm than he felt. The look Amoura gave him suggested she either missed the sarcasm or wasn't in the mood for it.

"Despite our differences or the situation that led us here," she said, "I doubt the first magus would have dropped us here. Also, if it was him, the best you could do against Selvetar is amuse him before he uses a number of creative ways to dispatch you."

"Thanks for the confidence," Emiel replied.

To his surprise, the woman's face softened. He found himself drawn into her beautiful, steel-colored gaze when it wasn't glaring at him. Emiel gave himself a mental slap. What in the world was his problem?

"Other than Magi Master Vladrick himself, I can't think of anyone who might match Selvetar," she said.

"What about you?" Bone asked. "You've done some pretty handy stuff with that ring of yours. I'm sure you could outsmart him or whip up some sort of surprise to catch him off guard long enough for me to run a blade through his back."

Amoura's responding sigh showed her growing impatience.

"Whip up a surprise. I am not a baker, mercenary. He would likely incinerate you, after him," she pointed at Emiel, "while holding me off long enough to do it. You would die, both of you, in short order. And before you tell me how we survived Vladrick, Selvetar is probably a match for the master, but is far more crafty. Now, as for this Fallen-cursed place." She turned her back on them and went silent. Emiel glared at Bone, but the mercenary just shrugged.

"The minute we take a step, it will change," Amoura said. "If the legends hold true, as they have thus far, the Maze is a pathway to and through the void. The void exists between this realm and our own."

"The void?" Emiel asked. His heart pounded in his chest, and his hands went clammy. "You mean *the* void, as in the prison of the Fallen, "the void"?"

"Precisely," came the reply.

"And … there's no other way out?" Emiel asked, trying to keep the desperation from his voice.

"I'm sure I would have suggested another option were it available," Amoura replied. "Or we could continue this discussion indefinitely and just remain where we are for the rest of our lives."

"Almost sounds like a better option," Bone muttered, but he went about checking the gear on his person, then punched his fist into the palm of his other hand. "Okay, let's get this over with."

"The first step is hope," Lief said.

Emiel was about to ask what the tinfar meant when the black surroundings shifted. Colors and sounds assaulted them from everywhere, coalescing in a whirlpool of randomness that Emiel had to close his eyes to escape from, less it scramble his mind. When he opened them again his heart leapt.

Not more than a dozen feet away and smiling at him, were his twin daughters. Nandi's hopeful expression glowed in typical contrast to Amiya's hint of sarcasm. The woman standing between them broke his heart. Aunya, his beloved wife, dead since the birth of his girls, stared at him with eyes filled with love.

Emiel bit his bottom lip. It wasn't real, he knew. It wasn't real and it couldn't be real. But it looked real; so real. They were standing within reach, right in front of him. His mind screamed at him to look away, but his heart pleaded with him to take a step and grab them all in a crushing hug. Was this where his wife was trapped after she'd died? Had the girls died and were trapped here with Aunya? His heart nearly stopped just to think it. Maybe he could get them out.

He shook his head. Of course not. They weren't there. This was some sort of trick …

"Hey, Dad, you just gonna stand there staring?" Amiya asked. "You look as sick as that time Nandi showed you her drawing of us standing in front of the house."

"Shut up, Amiya," her twin said. "We just barely found him and you're already mouthing off."

Emiel looked from one to the other through the entire exchange and laughed. It was them. It had to be. This wasn't like that trick Vladrick had pulled on him. These were his girls and his wife. They weren't simple images like the one the Fallen-cursed magi master created as a trick. These were his girls. They actually spoke!" He hesitated. The girls had spoken, but not Aunya …

"Both of you, hush," Aunya said.

The pieces of Emiel's broken heart melted when he heard his wife's husky voice, so filled with love, matriarchal warmth so typical of a Barbarosian mother. "Aunya," he whispered. Emiel forced himself to look away from his family at the others. They, too, stood transfixed, staring at his beautiful family."

Emiel focused back on the three ladies. "I don't know how we ended up here, and I'm sorry I failed you all, but I'm getting you out of"—he waved a hand—"whatever all *this* is." Aunya and the girls smiled at that, and Emiel took a step toward them.

"Emiel, no!" Lief hopped and grabbed his hand. "It's not real!"

"Yes, it is," Emiel argued. "Let go of my wrist, Lief. I've

finally found them and you want to take me away from them? What are you, jealous? You don't have a family of your own?"

As soon as he said the words, he regretted them. When Lief's hand slid away, he felt even worse. "I … I didn't mean to …" the stricken expression on his friend's tiny face nearly undid him. He looked back to his family to see all three of them scowling at her. They looked up in unison from the tinfar to meet his gaze, and their smiles returned.

Emiel felt a flicker of doubt that grew when he noted how horribly they'd looked upon his tinfar companion, the only friend he'd had for the whole journey to Altarra. His family simply stood there, silent as if waiting.

"Get away from the edge, Emiel," he heard Amoura say.

The magus's even, ominous tone stopped Emiel mid-step. When had he started walking? He looked down and shuffled backward with a gasp. One more step and he would have walked off the edge of the path and fallen into infinite blackness.

He looked back up to see his family silently staring at him. "Nothing to say?" he asked with a mixture of nerves and hopefulness. *Please don't say the wrong thing, my girls, my lady. Please.*

"We're held where we are, my forever love," Aunya said. She'd called him that since the day they'd met. Despite his doubts, Aunya had always known they would marry. "You have to come get us, and then we can leave here with you."

"In death," Amoura said.

Emiel rounded on her, but when he saw her stepping back as well, also dangerously close to the edge, it gave him pause. The magus was staring somewhat in the same direction as his family. Her fists were balled and anger burned in her eyes. Beside her, Bone had drawn his sword. Lief sat on the ground a few feet away, cross-legged with her hands folded in her lap, head hanging.

"Emiel." Aunya's voice drew him back. She and the girls raised their hands in unison and beckoned to him. "Help us be free."

"Yes," Amoura said. Emiel glanced at her. "Yes, I will help you. I will deliver you." In the time he'd spent traveling next to the woman, he'd never heard such danger in her voice. It chilled his blood.

Amoura's ring flared red with such intensity Emiel had to shield his eyes. She opened her fists, and blue fire erupted from her curled fingers. The fires engulfed whatever was in front of her and a piercing scream broke the silence.

Aunya reached an impossibly long arm out and grabbed Emiel's shoulder. Despite her hideously long arm and the painful grip on his shoulder, whatever had grabbed him still looked like Emiel's wife.

He struggled to free himself, but the grip was far stronger than he. When he drew his knife, the concern on Aunya's face gave him pause.

"We just want to be with you, my forever love."

"Don't call me that," Emiel growled. "Don't ever say those words again.

"Dad?"

Emiel looked at Nandi. No, not Nandi, Whatever it was disguised as Nandi.

"Dad? What's wrong?"

Emiel looked into her earnest brown eyes, filled with uncertainty. This wasn't real; it couldn't be. But they were standing right in front of him. They even sounded like his family.

"Dad, you …"

Without realizing it or knowing how he did it, Emiel's body erupted in flame. The flames blew out from his body to engulf his "family". All that remained of the three figures was now indistinguishable burning creatures.

Before Emiel could even begin to digest what had happened, the ground beneath them rose. Emiel dropped to his hands and knees. All around them, other pathways rose and fell.

"What in the armpit of the underworld *is* this place?" Bone asked.

"Your home and your tomb," a voice said from somewhere below. "Convenient."

Everyone turned in the direction of the voice just as several bipedal creatures crawled over the side. Emiel's skin crawled as five gray-skinned creatures straightened and grinned at them. Their eyes glowed white in contrast to the endless blackness surrounding the path. Seeing those things crawling from over the side made him move towards the middle of the path.

One of the creatures looked directly at Emiel and favored him with a toothy smile. "Aw. Upset about your dead family? Worry not about your failure. Their suffering ended. Eventually."

Emiel lit afire again and sent a wave of flames over the creature, immolating it where it stood. He similarly dispatched the other monsters just before Lief appeared beside him, her hands balled into little fists. The ground beneath the creatures exploded and sent them spinning away and falling back into the infinite darkness below. Emiel looked down at the glowering tinfar. He'd never seen her truly angry, before.

"They know your hopes and fears, your losses and your loves. Everything." Lief continued to glare at the place where the creatures had been. "And they will use it all against you."

"Who's they?" Emiel asked.

"This entire place," Amoura answered. "It is a place of torment. Creative torment. Keep moving."

They moved along the path, keeping a wary eye on the sides. Sometimes the path was rock, sometimes tiles, sometimes dirt. Everything about the Maze shifted with random frequency. A gust of freezing air would pound into them for a few moments, then sunlight would appear just long enough for them to feel the warmth before turning into a freezing torrent.

There were voices as well. An endless assault of whispering and laughter, giggling, growling, moaning, weeping. In the distant blackness Emiel thought he saw a large, winged creature that looked like a mosquito, only big enough to carry a person away. It was naive to even hope it would stay where it was.

"Ya know why I left when ya were still a boy, lad?" a voice said from over the side of the path.

A tall, barrel-chested man with a thick red beard that covered a good portion of his freckled face pulled himself over the side and climbed to his feet. The man wore loose-fitting breeches and a long leather coat that hung open over his red-haired chest. "Ya were just sa damn *soft*, lad. Couldn't take a right good if it came from a leaf in the wind."

The man crossed his massive arms, towering over them with a scowling grin. He looked over the rest of the group and snorted the same snort Emiel had heard from Bone throughout their journey. "Still can't be a man, boy. So weak ya need a scrawny islander," he snarled at Emiel, who snarled back, "a little toy girl," he jerked his chin at Lief," and a *woman*," he favored Amoura with a disgusted expression. The magus merely arched an eyebrow at him. "Pathetic, boy. I always knew you'd never—"

Bone unsheathed his sword and moved between the others so fast, Emiel barely had time to react. The big man who could be no one other than Bone's father, or rather, something mimicking him, reached over his shoulder and drew a huge axe. By the time he'd gotten it over his shoulder, however, Bone had disemboweled him from left to right and back again.

The thing that had mimicked his father dropped to its knees and let out an inhuman scream just before Bone lopped off its head and kicked it over the side. "Come on," he said, stalking past the others. "Which way, magus?"

"Forward!" Lief yelled. "Anywhere but here, run." She darted past them, waving for them to follow.

"What's her problem?" Bone grumbled.

"Dramatic?" Emiel replied, then he felt it. The party froze when the ground rumbled beneath their feet.

"Run, fools!" Lief turned away and heeded her own words.

Emiel turned and saw the ground breaking apart and falling away behind them. "Run run RUN!" He took off after Lief, Bone and Amoura falling in around him.

"What *is* this place?" Emiel huffed.

"Why don't you shout it into the nothingness," Bone answered. "Maybe something'll answer and the two of you can sit down and whittle wood while you discuss it."

"You're an ass," Emiel replied. Despite the situation, the boy laughed. Emiel thought he heard Amoura mutter "idiots" under her breath.

Lief kept the lead, taking one path after another. Her decisions seemed random, but the pathways all around them, except the ones they took, had started to crumble away. She *was* an earth tinfar, Emiel reminded himself. Perhaps even here, she intuited where the safer paths were.

"Wait, wait." Lief skidded to a stop and looked around. She closed her eyes, then popped them open and darted to the right. "Hurry."

The pathway to the left crumbled and fell away before they got a dozen feet away from the juncture. Lief continued to lead them along the paths, seeming to read each intersection like a sign only she could see.

Emiel thought he caught sight of a tiny red glow on Amoura's essence ring. He wanted to ask about it, but his breathing was labored. Better to concentrate on keeping up.

A figure faded in and out of view on one of the pathways in the distant darkness. It looked to be keeping pace with them, despite taking far fewer steps. It also looked slightly bigger than them, despite the distance. Emiel felt a shiver down his spine. "Anyone see that off to the right?"

"Maybe it's the thing coming to tell us about this place?" Bone said, unsheathing his sword.

"We'll have to face it," Lief said from ahead. It's the only path that won't fall away."

"Of course," Emiel muttered. He tried to grab the essences. He succeeded only in sensing that they were there, like being in pitch darkness and feeling something brush up against him.

As the two paths came closer together, the creature pacing them grew bigger. Its giant bat-like wings flexed with anticipation, and it flexed arms as thick as Emiel's body. It curled its fingers, extending claws that could surely cut him to ribbons. It narrowed its glowing red eyes above a wide mouth filled with cracked and yellow teeth, with tusks protruding from its lower jaws.

"Oh good, a friend!" Bone said with mock cheer.

"Is your inappropriate sarcasm a fear defense mechanism?" Amoura asked as her essence ring flared to life.

The hulking winged beast came fully in sight, each step a resounding thud that vibrated beneath their feet. As it drew closer, its claws flexed open and closed in anticipation.

Emiel strained to grab any one of the essences. Physically, he could do nothing to harm that thing, but he might make a difference if he could grab the essences. Maybe he could burn it, or freeze it, or … he felt whatever flicker of the essences he'd felt a moment ago slipping away. *Too ambitious. Keep it simple.*

The winged creature stomped closer, and Amoura Xanna sent a stream of fire into it. Flames spread over its body but it kept stalking toward them like a living torch. Emiel wrestled with his growing fear as the thing made a straight line for them. Amoura blasted it again and again, but it kept coming as if it felt nothing.

"You've *got* to be kidding me," Bone growled over his shoulder.

"Do I need to guess?" Emiel replied. "Another one behind us?"

"You win," came the answer.

Amoura blasted the flaming monster with long spears of ice that barely punctured the thick fiery hide. Her efforts did little more than cause it to stumble, but it kept coming. Behind him,

Emiel heard Bone's rushed footsteps as the mercenary engaged the new foe.

A piece of the ground exploded. The debris raised into the air and crashed into the face of the monster. When it raised its arm to shield against the assault, Lief raised her hand, turned her palm toward the monster, and thrust it forward. Another blast of rock assaulted the beast. It hunched forward, inching its way forward.

Good idea. Emiel reached for *earth* and it came to his call. He gestured toward the ground in front of the monster, and it erupted in a blast angling at its midsection. The assault threw it off balance long enough for Amoura to blast it using a similar tactic.

"Hey, friends!" Bone called. "Mind splitting some of that essence action over here?"

"Oh, sorry." Emiel turned and grabbed *earth* just as Bone dove out of the way of a pounding fist that would have flattened him. He broke the ground around the monster and hit it from every direction. The feel of wielding *earth* essence was exhilarating. Emiel had never experienced such a sensation, such a feeling of being so powerful, and this was nothing compared to what Amoura and Lief were doing to the monster they fought.

Emiel shoved the thoughts out of his mind and focused on the task at hand. He concentrated on grasping the other essences, but found them more elusive. Bone stabbed the monster in the side of the leg, retracted, and rolled aside. The monster bellowed and punched the ground where the mercenary had been. Bone rolled behind it and cut it across the hamstring.

What should have been an agonizing and debilitating injury only caused the monster to drop to one knee. The injury might have slowed it down, but not enough for Bone to finish it.

Emiel gave up on trying for the other essences and grasped for *earth* again. It came readily to his call and he channeled another wave of solid stone fragments speeding at the monster again.

A huge chunk of rock floated over their heads and stopped over the monster. Bone hollered and sprinted away. He dove the last few feet to get out of the way as the giant rock dropped on top of the monster's head. As large as the creature was, it went down so hard and so fast, its wings twitched upward as its body crumbled under the weight of the boulder.

Bone's armor creaked as he hurriedly climbed to his knees, then feet. He glared at Emiel.

"Don't look at me," Emiel said, holding up his hands.

The mercenary angled his glare past Emiel down to about knee-level.

Emiel turned to see Lief shrug. "You're fast. I knew you'd get away in time."

"And what if I stumbled, or fell, or it hit me?" Bone asked through gritted teeth.

"But it didn't, did it?"

Bone looked like he wanted to throttle the tinfar, but she turned her attention back to the monster Amoura fought. The thing was still afire, and still trying to get ahold of the magus. Amoura blasted it from every side with exploding rock, then shot it with a barrage of ice spears. Nothing she did caused more than superficial damage to the thing.

Lief broke apart another large chunk of the path behind them, moved it over the monster, and let it drop. The boulder-sized chunk of rock fell on the monster's head, but instead of collapsing into a dead heap like the other one, this one fell, shook its head, and climbed back to its feet. It arched its back and let out a roar that made Emiel's chest cavity vibrate.

"Of course that wouldn't work twice," Bone remarked. He took measured steps back as the beast took another step forward. "Hey, magus," he said over his shoulder. "Maybe put the fire out so I can attack it."

"No," Amoura replied. "Step back."

Emiel thought the mercenary would offer some kind of retort, but he complied without comment.

Amoura blasted the thing with ice, rock, and flames, one after the other. The only effect it had on the monster was to slow it down as it shielded its face and continued forward.

The party continued to give ground until they came to a juncture. "Left then right," Lief said.

"Get it off the path," Bone said. "Not much can hurt that thing, so just knock it off."

Since the ground behind the monster wasn't crumbling away, Amoura broke pieces of it apart and hit the it from the right, repeatedly bombarding it with giant rock after giant rock. Lief helped as well, and Amoura, having given up on ice spears, formed ice boulders instead.

When the winged beast began to lean against the assault from that side, Emiel grabbed *earth* and made the ground explode toward it from the other side. Amoura quickly added to his efforts by hitting it with a powerful gust of wind. Lief swung a boulder around and hit it from that side as well.

Having been balanced against the assault coming from its left, the monster easily fell over the side under the attack from the right. It fell into the infinite blackness below, bellowing in rage all the way.

The group didn't bother to look over the edge. They continued on, jogging behind Lief. The paths rose and fell, angled upward, forcing them to climb, then downward, causing them to scoot on their backsides or risk sliding right off the edge.

They picked their way down the rocky path to the bottom, then ran on, stealing wary glances in every direction. The rock pathways were still crumbling all around them, but Lief led them true. They turned right and saw a circular portal.

"I'm sure that's not where we have to go," Emiel said dryly.

"Let's just get this over with," Bone replied. I'm sick of this place."

Amoura held up a hand for them to stop. Emiel was about to ask what was wrong, but she just stood staring off into nowhere. Emiel frowned at the woman until he realized she was listening.

After a few tense heartbeats, he heard it, too. A long, distant roar that grew progressively louder.

Emiel sighed. "Not again."

The path in front of them exploded as the giant winged monster burst through. The pathway shook under the weight of its landing. It stood between them and the final turn to the pathway leading to the portal, heaving hatred with each breath.

Amoura blasted it repeatedly from one side until Lief struck from the other. However savage the bat-winged creature might have appeared, it wasn't stupid. It lowered itself against the assault, barely moving as the magus and tinfar hit it from both sides.

Emiel joined in as well, hitting it with everything he had to little effect. He shook his head. No matter how much he threw himself into it, he couldn't even approach the power Amoura wielded, and she did little damage to the thing.

The monster lifted it fists and pounded the path. The quake threw them off balance, and it charged. Amoura wielded all four of the essences at it, one after another or combining them.

Emiel could feel everything Amoura was doing. He could feel when she grasped a single essence or combined them. He felt when she successfully wielded them in harmony versus bending them to her will.

Without thinking about what he was doing, Emiel grabbed *earth* and, with some strain, *water*. He combined their physical namesakes and sent a stream of mud into the creature's face, then its feet. Bone snickered from behind, but he paid him no mind. It was working.

Emiel had hit the beast square in the face, and now its huge mouth fell agape as it coughed up mud. It stepped too heavily just as Emiel had hit its feet as well, and it slipped and fell.

Amoura followed Emiel's lead and kept it stumbling, while Lief pounded it from above with debris from the destroyed section of the path.

The beast suddenly shrank down to the size of a small human.

Emiel frowned. It was a girl now. Nandi. The sight of it lit him with white-hot anger. "You played that trick," he yelled. "Didn't work then and won't work now."

The thing that looked like Nandi lifted its head and looked on him with tormented brown eyes. Emiel steeled himself against the sight. It was a lie, but the sight of his little ladygirl's face twisted in pain made his heart shudder. "Dad," it said. "Please, help me. I don't know what's happening. First I'm back home, now I'm here. Something keeps changing me into this big monster with wings." Tears spilled down her eyes. "What's going on?"

"Ignore it, Emiel," Amoura said. The uncharacteristic softness in the magus's tone made Emiel look at her. She looked back at him with compassion in her silver eyes, the first he'd ever seen. "That isn't your daughter, you know that."

"What's she talking about, dad? I'm your ..."

"You're not my daughter," Emiel said. That thing didn't need to hear the words, but he did. He needed to hear himself say it. "You're the same monster that attacked us, and I'm going to kill you."

The thing wearing Nandi's face grinned. "Maybe I'm not. Or maybe I'm what lurks inside both of them." It shrugged and stood up. The smirk, and the way the thing moved now was decidedly not Nandi. It chilled Emiel just to look upon it. "Well, then. Since that little situation is over, let me welcome you to the end of the Maze. I admit my surprise that you've made it this far. Come."

Emiel stared incredulously as the monster—still using Nandi's form—turned away, fully expecting them to follow it. Amoura shared a look with Emiel and fell in behind it; many paces behind.

"And I'm going to kill you," Bone whispered in his ear. "Flare for the dramatic, eh spicetrader?"

Emiel snarled at him. "You pick the most inappropriate times to joke, kid. You know that?"

The Nandi creature looked over its shoulder. "Why so far back? I promise not to kill you."

Emiel started to respond with some sort of retort, but when Amoura didn't bother to acknowledge it, neither did he.

When no response came, it shrugged and turned back. "Of all the unfortunates who have found themselves here, only two have survived the pathways. I'd be interested to know how that is." It looked over its shoulder. "Nothing to say? Are you sulking? I'm not the one who brought you here, remember. It was either through your own stupidity in playing with space warping, or someone truly powerful doesn't like you very much." It laughed.

"Mind wearing something other than that appearance?" Emiel asked.

"You prefer my previous appearance?" the thing asked.

"You don't want to know what I prefer," Emiel quipped.

It led them through several turns, each time, the party covertly glancing to Lief, who confirmed it was the safe path. Emiel stole a glance at Bone and Amoura. They must be thinking the same as he. However Lief was able to determine the safe paths, there was no need to let this thing know that.

The final turn brought them through what Emiel guessed must be the end of the Maze. They stopped at the end of the long pathway, just before the threshold to a circular platform. On the far side stood two figures in long, loose-fitting pants, with nothing but a flowing cloak covering their torsos. Blue flame danced where their heads should have been. The strange beings stood on either side of an upright disk that was larger than the platform it sat on. A yellow current of some kind occasionally streaked across its surface.

Emiel opened his mouth to ask what in world those things were, but he looked at Amoura instead. The woman stood still as a statue, only her eyes darting left to right as she took in the situation.

"I feel like a lamb right before the slaughter," Bone said.

The Nandi-thing stopped in the middle of the platform and half turned. The grin on its face, so uncharacteristic of his daughter, sent chills down Emiel's spine and made him want to throttle the monster. "So wary," it mocked. "Why the hesitation? You know this won't be pleasant. Of course it won't be!" It beckoned to them. "Come. Wouldn't you rather get to it quickly, or waste your lives standing there?" It placed a finger to its lips in thought. "Well, I supposed you might hesitate; prolong these last moments of life?"

Emiel ground his teeth. The taunting bothered him less than this monster wearing his daughter's visage while doing it. He wanted to crush it under a mountain.

The Nandi-creature beckoned to them. "Come. I give my word that you will not be attacked upon joining me here."

Emiel laughed at that. "Your word?"

It shrugged. "Or, you could stand just beyond the threshold for the rest of your short lives. It makes no difference to me."

"Solid point," Bone muttered.

Amoura stepped onto the platform first, and the others followed her lead. Emiel felt a tap on the side of his leg when the creature turned its back. "You're going to need more than just the *essence* you're good at," Lief whispered. "You'll need all of them."

"What?" He looked down at her. "What do you mean?" The only response he received was an impatient frown before the Tinfar stepped away.

Emiel stared at the flame-headed figures. They stood with feet shoulder-length apart, the fingers of each hand curled like claws and crossed in front of their chests. For some reason he couldn't explain to himself, Emiel felt the nearest one turn its focus to him, though it didn't move.

"What are the terms?" Amoura asked in a tone so casual, she might have been inquiring about the price of a meal, or lodging.

"Straight to business eh?" the Nandi-creature said. "Well, terms can be a private thing. The stakes of any given situation can vary. So let's give each other a little privacy."

The world around Emiel vanished, leaving him in darkness.

3
____

EMIEL

No up or down, no left or right. Emiel shouted, but he couldn't hear his own voice.

A tiny blue dot appeared in the distant blackness and grew larger. As it neared, Emiel realized it was a blue flame. He figured it to be the head of one of those creepy cloaked figures. Fear welled in his chest and he grasped for *earth*. A voice spoke in his head with such power, he froze where he was.

"To reach your greatest potential, you will sacrifice. To achieve your greatest ambitions, you will sacrifice. To achieve that which your heart desires above all." Two figures slowly came into view. Nandi and Amiya. They were running from an unseen threat. Cuts and bruises covered their arms, their faces dirty and hardened with pain. *"You will sacrifice."*

"Sacrifice what?" Emiel demanded, though deep in his heart he had a feeling he knew where this was going.

The images of Nandi and Amiya faded to be replaced by Bone, Amoura, and even Lief. Why hadn't she disappeared like she had several times before? Was she not able to, here?

"Two will remain, one will go. Make your choice now, for they will make theirs."

Emiel closed his eyes. "You won't play this game with me. You're not going to play us against each other so you can have two of us to do with what you please." He snarled at the flame-headed creature. "What do you plan to do with the ones left behind, eat their souls? You look like the sort of thing that does that."

"Does the fate of your companions here concern you, or theirs?" The image of his friends faded to be replaced once again with his daughters. Emiel didn't know if what he was being shown was true, but deep in his heart he knew that despite the truth of the conditions, these were his daughters. Had this already happened, was it happening now, or had this yet to come? Seeing his ladygirls like this tore at his heart.

"A life for a life, equal trade. Make your sacrifice, and you will be returned to their side. If you do not, others will make your decision for you." Again the image faded, and he was shown Amoura, who no doubt faced the same decision. The magus's expression was unreadable. The image faded, and Lief came into view. The tinfar woman looked on the verge of tears. What were these things showing her?

The image faded again, and he saw Bone. The young mercenary stood with his sword in a tight grip. His brow pinched together in an intense scowl. *"Will he sacrifice for you? Will he sacrifice you? Make your decision in his hesitation, before he does the same."*

"Make my decision." The icy fear gripping Emiel's heart started to melt under the heat of his building anger. "Make my decision; a decision to condemn my friends."

"Do your daughters not matter?" the thing said into his mind. *"Do they matter less than two strangers who kidnapped you, separated you from your daughters, and are the reason for your presence here? You would not be in this place were it not for them. They are the catalysts of your struggles, they are the cause of your separation from your family, they are the reason your daughters are in*

peril while you are here, helpless to save them. Do they truly deserve your compassion; your loyalty? Be done with them, and reunite with your family."

"Just like that?" Emiel asked. "I decide to leave, and I'm returned to my family?" Emiel thought about everything that had happened since that fateful day he'd returned home to an empty house. What normally should have been a warm home filled with the smells of food and the banter of his twin daughters, had been an empty shell with a note from a man he despised.

Emiel's face tightened when he thought about the trip to the mansion, and his subsequent conversation with the archminister, Decius. He remembered how the man had toyed with him, the condescending tone, speaking of his family as if they were of little consequence. He thought of his first encounter with Bone, and how the mercenary had knocked him out, and how he'd awoken on his back in a wagon.

Then came the endless dangers of the road, the jarku, the shrikes, the appearance of Amoura and their flight from the four-armed monsters. Their journey through the mountain range known as The Triplets.

Emiel's hands curled into fists as he remembered it all. The sudden appearance of Lief, his only friend during that journey. The tinfar had saved his life, *their lives*, on more than one occasion. Amoura, beautiful, graceful, and deadly. Bone, skilled and courageous. They'd fought and bled, together, argued, and saved each other's lives.

Amoura, Lief, and Bone had freed him from Magi Master Vladrick. "Just like that?" he asked, his voice low and even. "I make my decision and I'm gone?"

"You have but to speak the words and your trials here will be little more than a memory of your struggles that returned you to them. Speak the words. Make your will known, and return home."

Emiel nodded. "Oh, I'll return home. I'll be reunited with my girls again." Quicker than he could have thought possible, the essences raced to his call. He hadn't grasped them and wrestled them to his will, they had come to him as if of their own will. In his anger at the thing that sought to manipulate his fears and greatest desire above all, his determination to do whatever it took to find his girls again, the power came to him.

The essences, all four of them, flooded into him, wrapping and twisting themselves inside his body, outside his body, like a raging river. The flame-headed being made no sound, but it recognized the danger. It invaded his mind and pressed down on his will like a heavy, poisonous cloak. It bore into his mind and sought out his will. He felt it trying to crush him from the inside.

Emiel focused the massive amounts of power swirling all about him and released it in a torrent upon the creature. It crossed its arms and braced itself, but the sheer volume of *earth, fire, water,* and *air* essences crashing into it was too much. It broke apart under the force of the onslaught, the tatters of its remains drifting away into nothing.

The isolating darkness separating the group abruptly fell away. Emiel heard the others gasp at the sudden change, but he held his focus. The creature wearing Nandi's visage changed into the same type of being with the blue flame head as the other. "Impossible," it hissed.

"I agree," Bone said. He stabbed the nearest robed being through the chest. "Given the chance, I thought I would choose to be rid of you all in a flash." He wrenched the sword free and stabbed it again through the abdomen. "Don't know what's come over me."

The flame-headed being flinched as Bone stabbed it multiple times, but gave no indication of whether being impaled even hurt. When the mercenary tried to cut it across the waist, it grabbed his sword and pulled him in close. Once he was in range, the being smacked him with a backhand across the face. The slap spun the young warrior around and he crumpled unconscious to the ground.

It kicked him so hard his body lifted into the air and fell back to the ground in a roll.

Bone's body would have rolled right over the side of the circular platform, but Lief lifted part of the ground up into a small wall. His bone armor creaking with every revolution, the mercenary crashed into the wall and lay unmoving.

The being whipped its hands out to its sides and they lit in blue flame. It sent that fire speeding toward Bone, but another wall of rock rose up to stop it. The being kept one hand focused on the wall and turned its other hand toward Lief.

Emiel hollered and drew *air* and *water*. The essences charged to his call and he created a wall of ice half as thick as the platform upon which the combatants fought. The blue flames hit the wall of ice and began to melt through the center. Emiel replaced the ice as quickly as the fire melted it.

On another end of the platform, Amoura threw spears of ice and stone at her adversary. She buffeted it with powerful gusts of freezing air and once again launched pieces torn away from the path connected to the platform. The being fended off her attacks and countered. It sent gouts of blue flame at her; left, right, right right left. It lit the black air overhead with a ceiling of blue fire and dropped it down on the magus.

Amoura swept her arms in an inward arc over her head, then down to her sides. What could only be described as flaming ice met the ceiling of blue fire and burst it apart.

"You will never leave here," the being hissed into Emiel's mind.

Emiel thought of Amiya and Nandi. They were already forced to grow up without one parent. Now, they had to survive in an ever more dangerous world without him to protect them. He narrowed his eyes at the flame-headed being.

"You will fall, here," it said, *"and be banished to the underworld forevermore."*

"Then I'll kill anything between me and the way out," Emiel

said, his voice barely audible even to himself. "I'll break the damned underworld if I have to. I'll rip it apart on my way out and if you, any monster, or the Fallen themselves get between me and my girls, I will *obliterate* every single one of you."

Without realizing it, Emiel had felt what Amoura had done to create the strange ice fire. He'd internalized it, adapted it, and turned the thick wall of ice into freezing flames. He walked to the glacial blaze and stepped inside it.

Bone forgotten, the being focused its efforts on Emiel. It attacked his mind with images of his daughters being beaten, falling, stabbed, burned. It showed him endless images of their torture, and whispered into his mind that their agony was eternal.

Emiel clamped his eyes shut, gritting his teeth against the mental assault with each image of his daughters' torment, he felt himself grow hotter as his anger grew. His insides lit ablaze in a molten wave of rage, then the cold.

He opened his eyes. He drew the ice flames into himself and charged the being. It lit him in an inferno of blue fire, but he charged right into it, right through it, and punched it in the chest. The being stumbled backwards and made a sound that could have been a gasp.

Emiel grabbed its robes, yanked it forward, and punched it in the chest again. He held his fist against it and growled as the being lit like a torch from the inside out and burst into thousands of tiny cinders that floated in the air and winked out.

Amoura still battled her adversary. She hit it with wave after wave of freezing air carrying lethal spears of ice. When it knocked the projectiles aside, she assaulted it with more chunks of rock.

It shattered the rock and retaliated with fire. A piece of the ground behind it suddenly thrust upward and speared it in the back. Another spear shot out of the ground from the side and impaled it from the right.

Fire lit in Lief's narrowed eyes. She continued to impale the being with stalagmites every time it broke one apart. Amoura feathered it with so many ice spears Emiel could barely see it. He felt the power inside diminish with his fatigue, so he thought of his girls again. He thought of how this thing wanted to keep him away from them. He remembered how it had tried to tempt him into trading his friends for his freedom. Whether he'd have been returned to his girls or not, he would have been an empty shell of his former self. He'd have had to live a lifetime of guilt and shame at his cowardice.

He curled his hands into fists as the heat of his anger grew again, and with it, the essences flooded to his call. He drew them in, and they flowed his body, a raging river of living destruction. He bombarded the impaled being with fire, wielding massive amounts of the essence's physical namesake. He combined water with that fire, then air.

Emiel lifted a huge chunks of bridge and set them drifting around the embattled creature. He combined fire and water and burning air with it. Somewhere he heard Lief yelling his name, but her voice sounded tiny in his mind. With a final thought of what this thing tried to do to him, to his friends, to his daughters, he focused on the destructive creation before him and it collapsed inward onto the flame-headed being. In mere heartbeats, he encased the creature in a ball of rock.

Everything went quiet as Emiel walked toward the giant pulsating ball of stone, glowing red, blue, silver, and brown. He placed his hand on the rock and released all the pent up anger and rage in a slowly increasing growl that erupted into a roar of defiance.

The ball of rock exploded, causing quakes in the ground beneath his feet. Debris flew in every direction and Emiel thought he heard a curse behind him. When the rain of debris cleared, nothing remained of the flame-headed being. Emiel stood there for a time, just breathing. When he turned back to the others, he saw that Bone was awake and staring openmouthed at him. Beside the mercenary, Lief also looked at him with an expression Emiel couldn't place.

They were all inside a dome of *air*. The silver glow in Amoura's eyes faded out, and the dome dissipated. The magus stared at Emiel with a mixture of confusion and what looked like trepidation.

Emiel frowned. "Why're you all looking at me like that?"

Bone placed a hand on his knee and pushed himself up. "This is how people stare at someone who looked like they lost it and were going to destroy everything around them."

"What in the name of the Fallen are you rambling about?" Emiel asked.

Amoura approached the standing disk. "This is our way out."

"I hope you know how to operate it, then," Bone said. "Seeing as how our guy over here disintegrated the only creatures who knew how to use it."

"I doubt they would have told us," Lief said.

"That's a really big word, Bone," Emiel said. "Did it hurt to use it, or have you been waiting your whole life for the opportunity?"

Bone rocked back on his heels. "Woah hoo! Our spicetrader's growing a spine."

Emiel opened his mouth to answer the jab, but bit it off when Amoura muttered something about leaving the two of them behind. He moved beside the magus and studied the wall, stealing a glance at her here and there. Despite the situation, he couldn't help being captivated by her smooth dark skin, her delicate eyebrows, her round full lips and neatly platted braids. The contrast of that to her silver eyes added a haunting quality to the beautiful woman.

Amoura flicked a glance at him then returned her attention to the disk. It was such a quick thing Emiel would have missed it if he'd blinked.

"I think the spicetrader is going to profess love," he heard Bone remark from behind, followed by tiny chuckling. Emiel felt heat rising to his face to mingle with the betrayal he felt from Lief's laughter.

He pretended not to hear and focused on the disk. Lines wove in various patterns across the gray stone. This close, he noticed runes lining the outermost rim of the disk. They were so smooth and perfect, Emiel couldn't imagine the level of expertise needed to carve them.

"I wouldn't," Amoura said when he reached out to touch the polished stone. Another yellow streak whizzed across the surface only a heartbeat later. "There are wards on this disk that we need to disable."

"Can you do it?" Emiel asked, trying to keep the desperation out of his voice.

Amoura stared at the disk for a long time before answering, "I don't know."

"Those runes are old tongue," Lief said. "They're from what you call the Second Age."

"You can read that?" Bone asked.

"Somewhat," Lief replied. "If it was language from the First Age, I could read it easily."

"There's that much of a difference?" Bone said.

"Blame your species," Lief replied. "You're always changing things. The tongue you spoke during your First Age shared enough with other tongues that there could be understanding. But by your Second Age, humans began to change the words you spoke and separated yourselves."

Emiel looked down at Lief when she came to stand between him and Amoura. "Other tongues?"

Lief snorted. "You're not the only species that knows how to talk, you know?"

"No," Emiel sputtered. "No, I didn't mean ... I wasn't saying—"

Lief waved him off. "Be quiet. I'm concentrating."

Emiel reared back at that. "Well okay, then."

"It's saying something about the Maze having no beginning, but," a tiny frown creased her brow, "but, only one end."

"That's useful," Bone said.

"Feel free to come have a read," Lief said absently, still studying the runes.

She began to read in a language Emiel didn't understand. When he looked to Amoura and Bone, they both wore the same uncomprehending expressions as he. "Is that Khatalese?" he asked.

Lief let out an irritated sigh. "Yes. Yes, it is ancient Khatalese, not much different from all the variations they've created to complicate it. Their language, even today, hasn't changed much since the First Age, and is the most similar to this. Now will you please stop asking me questions?"

Emiel held up his hands in a warding gesture. "All right, sorry. Wow." Behind him, Bone snickered.

"To reach the terminus," Lief read, "is a testament to your strength and connection to the one aspect that is your savior. To best the keepers testifies to your cunning, skill, and indomitable will. To open the gate, test the might of your mind."

Amoura stepped back and looked the disk over. She pointed to a symbol at the top, then the left and right sides, and finally the bottom. "Those are the ancient symbols for each of the four essences, or "aspects", as the Khatala call them."

"Aspects," Emiel repeated. "It says that to reach this platform was a testament to our connection with the one aspect that was our savior." He looked at Lief. "You're an *earth* tinfar. That's why you knew which way to go on the paths?"

Lief nodded. "It was luck that the pathways are stone. I don't know why, or even how tall they are, since it looks like there's no ground below."

"Whoever or whatever created this place probably hadn't anticipated a tinfar ending up here," Amoura said. "Let alone *e'ta* tinfar." She gave the one and a half foot-tall woman a nod of appreciation.

Bone pointed a gloved finger at the disk. "That last part. What was it again? To open the gate, test—"

"Test the might of your mind." Emiel shared a look with the mercenary. "Didn't we do that already?"

Amoura stared at the disk while the others talked. She squinted at the disk Emiel wondered if she, too, was considering the potential implications of what the next and—hopefully—final challenge might be.

"The toughest battlefield," Amoura said, "is never in a place against a physical foe."

Bone nodded. "The most difficult battle anyone can ever wage is in their own mind."

Emiel turned a look of mock surprise on the young warrior. "Very good. Sounds like there's more than porridge between those ears after all."

Bone snarled at him. "It's true, spicetrader. I'm not sure how strong a will it takes for you to sit through the mighty challenge of mixing spices every day, but I've trained with the sword since I was old enough to hold one. My da pounded the lessons into me verbally and physically.

"You ever get punched by an adult before you reached your tenth year, spicetrader? How about twice? Three times, four, five, until you stop counting? Until you've woken up with a swollen face and have to keep going until your da says it's enough?

Emiel's mouth slowly fell open a little more with each word the mercenary said. "That sounds ... pretty awful."

The boy shrugged. "It was, for the first several weeks. Thought my da hated me; wanted to kill me. Then one day I saw him chopping wood. Man could easily split a log as wide around as you with one chop of his axe. That's when I realized he could'a killed me a long time ago if he wanted to.

"So I kept getting up. I kept wiping the blood outta my mouth and nose and kept going. My da punished every mistake with a lot of pain, but he never broke me physically. Never broke a bone or broke my face. But he broke my spirit over and over again until he couldn't, because I stopped letting him."

Bone off into the distance as though looking through a mental portal into the past. "I learned that only death could break me before I reached manhood, because my da forced me to forge my mind into an unbreakable thing."

"That's really dramatic," Lief said. "Why would your own father harm you so? What could be so bad about the world that you need to suffer in preparation for it?"

Bone lowered his icy blue gaze to meet the tinfar's. She looked up at him with pure innocent curiosity. "The world is a cruel and merciless place, lass," he replied, bits of his accent slipping through. "It's filled with monsters and if yer not strong enough, they'll run you down and feed on yer carcass, leaving only yer bones to bleach in the sun."

Lief took a step back, horror twisting her tiny features. "That sounds terrible. Just … dreadful!"

Emiel looked at the tiny woman in confusion. He might not have been raised as brutally as Bone, but he agreed with the younger man's perspective. The world was indeed a hard place filled with those who would cheat, lie, and steal from you; or even kill you. It was filled with lethal animals and lethal monsters, sickness and disease. "Is the world not the same for tinfar?" he asked.

Lief frowned at him with an emphatic shake of her head. "No! Not at all. I can't imagine a world like the one you just described. I wouldn't want to live in it. I couldn't. It sounds like a dark and terrible place."

"So, nothing goes wrong in the little piece of the world tinfar huddle in?" Bone asked.

Lief's responding glare made Emiel fear she was going to do something painful to the straw-headed mercenary. "No, boy. Our lives aren't perfect and we certainly don't *huddle*. What we *don't* do is create horrifically difficult lives for ourselves that we must then struggle to thrive in. We live with the world, not against it."

"You mean you let the world run your lives," came the boy's retort.

"I mean we are not so disconnected that we continually suffer for it," the tinfar shot back. "Monsters and great evil don't plague us, boy. They only plague *you*."

"My apologies for interrupting your argument," Amoura said. "But I'm ready to leave. Let us activate this portal and be gone."

Lief spared one last glare for Bone then whipped her head away and spun on her heel. Bone looked helplessly at Emiel as the tinfar woman stalked away.

"You're an expert at making friends, you know that?" Emiel said.

Bone shrugged and lifted his hands. "What?"

"My best guess at this," Amoura said, "is that we may each be forced to face our greatest fears. Whatever this thing is, when we try to pass through it, I think we'll have to go through our own personal torments to escape."

"Sounds like fun," Bone said dryly.

"What *is* this place?" Emiel asked. "And how in the name of the blasted Fallen does it know so much about us?"

"Why does the sun rise in the east and set in the west, Emiel?" Amoura replied. "How did humans learn to talk? Why does the underworld exist and why doesn't the Creator personally reach down and pluck us out of danger whenever we find it, or it finds us? We could ask questions for several lifetimes and it would bring us no closer to getting out of here."

Emiel sighed. "It was a rhetorical question, Amoura." He clenched his teeth as the magus continued to study the disk. *I'm getting tired of being snapped at.*

"Think you know how to activate this?" Lief asked, to which Amoura shook her head.

"It's nerves," Bone said in a low voice, surprising Emiel.

"She's as anxious as us to get out of here, and is probably nervous about facing whatever she fears as much as we are."

Emiel felt his rising anger fade. "Yeah. I guess we're all a little tense."

Bone looked around the infinite labyrinth of rocky pathways zigzagging out of sight in every direction. "Let's just get this stupid trial out of the way and get out of this creepy place. We hang around too long, there's no telling what else'll show up to play."

Amoura pointed to four runes positioned at each corner of the top and bottom of the disk. "Lief. Can you read those?"

"*Ushaa*," the tinfar said, pointing to the large rune on the left corner. She pointed to the bottom left, top right, and bottom right in turn. "*Olayem, naara, tinu*. Water, earth, fire, air. The four essences. I think, once you feed all of those runes, it will activate the disk."

Amoura moved back until she stood with the others in the middle of the platform. "Remember, your mind is your power. Master it. Do not let it master you."

"Whatever this thing throws at us is all in our minds," Bone said.

"And our mind has the ability to strengthen us or poison us," the magus replied.

Emiel stared at the disk, taking in the words of his companions. If what Amoura and Lief said was true, the disk would know his deepest fears and bring them against him. *It's all in my mind*, he reminded himself over and over again. *Whatever happens, it's not real*. Emiel's palms started to sweat. If those things they'd fought to get here were all in his mind as well, he was in trouble. He glanced at Bone, whose chest rose and fell as he took a deep, steadying breath. He looked at Lief, who closed her eyes. As always, Amoura Xanna stood perfectly still and composed, patiently awaiting her challenge.

"Everyone ready?" the magus asked.

Lief opened her eyes and gave a sharp nod. "Ready!"

"Let's get this over with," Bone replied.

"Let's do it," Emiel said. He felt Amoura accessing the essences. She raised her hands and sent a gust of air into the rune bearing the essence of its namesake. She sent a gout of fire into its respective rune, then water, then a small chunk of rock into the final rune.

As she activated each essence rune, the line of runes on the outer rim following it lit up as well. Each of the runes pulsated in the respective colors of their essences. Several moments passed and the party watched as the runes continued to pulsate while nothing happened. They stopped glowing and the light inside each of them died away, leaving nothing but complete darkness.

Emiel froze. He lifted a hand in front of his face but may as well have had his eyes closed. "Is this part of the test, or did we do something wrong?" When no answer came, he reached out to his right, where Bone had stood barely an arm's length away. Nothing.

He lowered his arm and concentrated on willing his pounding heart to slow down. *In my mind. All of this is just in my mind.*

A pair of red slits split the darkness a few dozen feet in front of him. Emiel crouched and took a half step back, his arms out at his sides. He looked from left to right, but of course he saw nothing. The slits looked like they were moving closer.

Near frantic, Emiel reached for the essences but they ignored his call. He tried again and again, but nothing. He forced himself to stop panting and wiped his sweaty palms on his legs. *Calm down, Emiel. This is in your head. You're doing this.*

A row of white split the darkness below the approaching red slits. The white line quivered as it thickened, and he heard a low, deep growl.

Uh huh, Emiel thought. *Those are indeed teeth.* Of course. Of course this Fallen-cursed Maze-thing would know that being eaten alive topped his list of fears. *Gotta face this. Amiya and Nandi are depending on me.* He used that thought to bolster himself. He stopped backing away and took a deep breath, reaching again for the essences.

A trickle of the power came to him, like the last drops of water from a nearly empty waterskin. Emiel grasped at it with desperation just as the red slits closed the distance. The thick white line of teeth rose and tilted sideways, split in two, and opened wide in front of his face.

4

THE TWINS

Nandi awoke to the sound of snoring. She cracked an eye open and saw Joga slumped in a chair on the far corner of the room, his head hanging over his left shoulder.

She started to get up, but just the thought of it drained her energy, so she closed her eye and lay there. She grinned at the sound of a frustrated sigh on the right side of her bed. Amiya grunted and muttered something about the Khatala man sounding like a congested walrus.

Nandi pressed her lips together to keep from laughing as her sister continued her griping. A bony finger jabbed her underarm and she rolled across the bed in a jumble of sheets. "Hey!" Nandi said just before she tumbled over the side of the bed. "Oof."

While she fumbled to extricate herself from the covers, Nandi heard Joga's rhythmic snoring sputter. "You could have hurt me," she said, finally sliding out of the tangled mess.

Amiya rolled her eyes. "The covers softened your fall. Don't be a baby."

"Sama still not understand how sisters love each other, but push and shove and argue."

Nandi looked to the windowsill where Sama sat cross-legged

halfway in. The sun filtered in around the tatamble girl, setting her green hair and—currently—brown skin aglow. She briefly wondered if that was the girl's normal skin color, or if she even had one. "Hey, Sama." She looked at Joga, who stretched and yawned in his chair. "Hi, mountain man."

"Not you, too," Joga said. "First sister, now you. North Frostlands where I'm from are far from mountains."

"I know, I know. It just … fits you." She giggled at his responding sigh. "How long have I been asleep?"

Sama looked over her hunched shoulder out the window. "A long time, girl has slept, since three days when the sky wept."

Nandi's mouth dropped open. "Three days?"

"Yup," her sister said. "You even slept through the stink."

Nandi blinked. "Stink?"

"First three nights we sleep in barn," Joga said. "Man call it haloft."

"It's pronounced hayloft," Amiya corrected. She looked back to Nandi. "We're not exactly rolling in money, so we got the guy who owns the barn out at the stables to let us sleep there in exchange for free work and mountain man, here, going out and hunting dinner for everyone."

Nandi pretended not to hear another sigh from the Khatala man. "So, we stayed in a barn for two days, then paid for this room?"

Amiya nodded. "It took some serious talking, though. The innkeeper did *not* like the idea of him"—she jabbed a thumb at Joga—"sharing a room with two young girls."

Nandi started to correct her sister about it being three girls before she remembered how Sama couldn't bear to be inside any structure for long. She figured the nimble girl probably climbed up to the window and sat with her back halfway out so she could feel the open air. "How did you convince the innkeeper?"

"It was the fact that we didn't look abused," Amiya said. She smirked at Joga's responding snort. "And … I told her that if he had been abusing us, I'd have dumped a burning log from our campfires in his boy-place while he slept." Joga snarled and snorted again. Amiya giggled. "That convinced her."

Nandi's suddenly growling stomach quieted the room. Everyone stared at her until it ended, quite a while later.

"Girl is hungry after three days of nothing but sleep," Joga said. "Should go eat, then find what news we can."

The Khatala man's words brought the world back into focus for Nandi. In the span of a few heartbeats her mind raced across time and many miles. She remembered their captivity at the orders of Archminister Decius, and their dad being forced to complete some task to free them. She remembered the lessons they'd received from the mysterious man named Selvetar, the attack on Marai, meeting Joga, and their subsequent flight from Marai.

Pursuit, the leapers, running to keep from being eaten or stomped to death from on high. The volcano, the lavakhan, and the man with the lava rock skin. She shivered at the unwelcome memory of the time she'd been captured and used as a conduit of the essences by the ant-headed creatures called ghuza. Thinking about all those pinpricks in her skin had her hugging herself and rubbing her arms.

Joga left to get a table and food in the common room while Nandi dressed. Amiya filled her in on all the chores they'd done while she slept. She went into extra detail about the musty smell of the mountain moles, and how they were even more smelly in New Dama than the ones Dad had out back, behind their home in Vyne."

Nandi felt a jab of homesickness at the mention of their house. It seemed impossible that so much could have happened, and that they had traveled so far.

The twins left the room and went downstairs to the sparsely populated common room, leaving Sama to climb out the window. The tatamble girl had no desire for human civilization and would find them once they left town.

They found Joga at a round table with a basket of steaming

buns in the center. Nandi thought her growling stomach might hurl her at the table. She snatched a bun out of the basket and shoved it in her mouth before she'd even sat down. She swallowed and reached for another, but stopped when she noted Amiya and Joga staring at her. With a crinkled grin, Joga indicated the basket with an open hand, that she continue. Amiya just called her a pig.

Nandi snarled at her sister and shoved another bun in her mouth. Since they were currently the only patrons in the common room who were eating, the innkeeper personally delivered their food. She stopped at the side of the table as Nandi finished off the last bun.

"You're a hungry one, aren't ya?" the woman said as she sat down the first plate, then reached into the crook of her arm where the second plate was balanced, and sat it down in front of Amiya. She gave Joga a suspicious look. "He not been feedin' ya? You can tell me, girl. No need to be afraid while you're safe, here."

Nandi snickered when the khatala man squirmed in his seat. "Thank you, ma'am, but he is our friend. I was hurt and he helped us."

The innkeeper nodded and placed the plate in front of Joga, who stared at it as if he might dive headfirst into it. Apparently hunger outweighed indignation. "Nothin' against you personally, understand," the woman said to him. "But you can't be too careful these days. Girls get snatched from their parents all the time and raised as laborwives or worse. Boys get snatched away and sold as laborers, servants, or forced to become bandits by all manner of outlaws. And all of that added to the news of horrible things happenin' everywhere since the local volcano blew its top."

That got everyone's attention. "Please, dashan," Joga said when the lady turned away. "Can you tell us more of these things you say happen after volcano erupts?"

The innkeeper tugged at her apron. "Dashan. That's that pretty word you Khatala folk say to women, right?" She gave him an approving nod. "Your ma raised you right, young man. As for the stuff happenin', they're probably just rumors. You know how folks like to gossip. But folks from both sides of the border are talking about great big monsters with four arms spitting foul curses and hacking people to bits."

Nandi, Amiya, and Joga shared a look that the woman didn't miss. "So, you've all heard the same, then? Well, that's only part of it. Folks've been rambling on about creatures leaping impossibly high in the air and flattening anything they land on, including people. Folks from all over Marai and Khatal are talkin' about it." She shook her head. "If even a little of what I've been hearing is true, it makes the war sound even more stupid than it already was."

"Any news about Altarra, ma'am?" Amiya asked.

"Altarra?" The innkeeper shrugged. "Not much coming from there, but I imagine if any of them supposed monsters did show up, there's enough power in that place to blow 'em back where they came from. Nah, only news filtering through my inn about Altarra was some sort of situation within the Order of Magi, but those folks keep everything to themselves. Any group of folks that secretive must be up to no good, if you ask me."

The innkeeper looked over her shoulder and spotted a couple of new patrons entering. "Enjoy your meal before it gets cold. And stay in New Dama. Here and Altarra are two places I've heard of that ain't had trouble."

Yet, Nandi thought.

Everyone shared a long silent look as they digested the information. When the hunger threatened to tie her stomach in a knot, Nandi dug in. After a three day fast, she practically inhaled her food.

"I guess it's good news that nothing's happened in Altarra," Amiya said around a mouthful. "Maybe Dad is there and safe."

"Yeah, maybe," Nandi replied, shuffling green leafy vegetables and some sort of roasted root into a sweet and spicy sauce. It smelled like a dream and tasted like bliss, though the spice wasn't strong enough to Nandi's inherited Barbarosian palate.

"Food is good," *cough*, "but spice is too much," *cough cough*. Joga held his fist up to his mouth, took a deep breath, and coughed some more.

"You've got to be kidding me, mountain man," Amiya said. "Big and tough as you are, and you can't handle a pinch of spice?"

"More than pinch," came the muffled reply. *Cough*. He wiped his tearing eyes and sniffed.

Amiya leaned back in her chair and laughed at him.

The Khatala man looked to Nandi for support in between coughs, but she shrugged. "If you can't eat this, you'd starve in Barbaros, Joga."

"Can't" *cough* "be possible. *Cough cough cough*. Glaring at Amiya, he reached for her mug of water and took a long draw. "Ah! Argh! Make worse!"

Amiya had put her spoon down, she was laughing so hard. "That's what you get for drinking my water. Drink your ale, tough man. It'll help better than water. Or I can get you some milk and a bun?"

Ale sloshed over the rim of his mug when Joga snatched it up and took a long draw. He finished the drink in one go, and sat the mug down, staring at the table in concentration. "Helped a little," he said. "Mouth still on fire, but helped."

"That has to be the funniest thing I've seen in a long time," Amiya said, earning another glare from Joga.

Nandi's ravenous appetite had overridden her sense of humor. She shoveled the last spoonful of hot food in her mouth and washed it down with her water. "Oooh, that was good."

"Must've been," Amiya said. She waved her spoon in the direction of Nandi's empty plate. "You gulped it all like it was air. Did you even chew?"

"Did you even *chew*?" Nandi echoed. "Yes I even *chewed*, thank you. If you're done roaring like a beached seal, think you can finish eating so we can go?"

Amiya leaned away from her with a frown. "Beached *seal*? At least I don't *eat* like one!"

Joga reached across the table and patted the air between them. "We finish food and go. Must find news before continue on to find father."

Amiya pressed her lips together and nodded. After a few moments of swirling her spoon around in her food, she shoveled in a mouthful. Nandi took another sip of water and stared into the mug.

"You think he's … okay?" Amiya asked.

Nandi lowered her mug and looked at her mirror image. Amiya rarely let her feelings show, especially when she was scared. Seeing her now, looking at Nandi with an expression that said she needed to hear something good, made Nandi's stomach twist into a knot. "Of course he is," she said with more confidence than she felt.

Amiya forced a grin on her face. "Good. Now say it like you believe it."

Nandi let out a half snort half laugh. Of course her sister would know what she was thinking.

"I'm sure father is fine," Joga said. When they looked at him, he responded with a determined nod. "Two of you able to wield great power. If you, then him too."

"We've never seen him use it," Nandi said. "And we didn't know we could do it until recently."

"Like you, probably forced to learn," Joga replied. "When danger come, life or death, you learn fast. He learn." With one last regretful look at his food, Joga pushed back from the table and stood. "Come. We get news and continue to this Altarra. Find your father."

"Go ahead," Nandi said, sliding Joga's plate in front of herself. "I'll be right there."

"Piglet," Amiya said as she pushed away from the table. "You keep that up, you're gonna end up like bigbelly."

Despite her loathing of Archminister Decius for putting them all in this situation, Nandi giggled. She lowered her face to the plate and inhaled the sweet and spicy aroma, then shoveled in another mouthful.

❧

AMIYA ELBOWED the mountain man in the hip as soon as she exited the inn and came up beside him. "Hey, which way is Altarra?" she asked, ignoring his responding grunt.

Despite it still being morning, the air carried a comfortable warmth to it. Late spring had begun to chase away the last bit of winter's bite. Birdsong flitted through the air, as did the rattling drone of the cicadas.

Amiya wondered if any color other than brown existed in the whole of New Dama. From the gravely ground to the wooden and clay stone buildings, brown. Even the clothes the locals wore were brown. After three days here, Amiya could easily pick out the locals from the visitors, despite New Dama's diverse population. Locals wore brown clothes. They may be different shades and patterns of brown, but brown nonetheless.

"Not sure," Joga replied. "Not travel much in Marai. Maybe north of here?"

"Don't ask me," Amiya said. "I just asked you. Maybe we should go back in and ask the innkeeper.

"Wait here," Joga said.

Amiya followed his gaze and saw that he had spotted a group of Khatala walking by. They were tall like him, but bigger. While Joga had long hair, the two men wore theirs cut short. Amiya saw only a few inches of the women's ponytailed hair, as they had it wrapped in simple, dark green cloths.

The group stopped when they noted Joga's approach. Unlike his blue-green orbs, these Khatalas' eyes were a solid green that seemed to sparkle in the sunlight. His back to her, Joga performed some sort of gesture Amiya couldn't see. As one, the group clasped their fists into their palms, then slapped their right hands over their hearts.

"He find some friends?" Nandi asked.

Amiya glanced at her sister, who was still chewing. She swallowed and stretched with a contented groan. "All full?" she asked, giving Nandi a pat on her now round stomach. "Ready to go roll around in some mud?"

Nandi thumped her behind the ear before she could dodge. "You'd eat more too, if you hadn't had anything for three days, so shut up." She jerked her chin at Joga and the other Khatala. "Who're they?"

Amiya shrugged. "Don't know. All I got so far is 'wait here. See my people. Talk and make friend.'"

Nandi snickered and hit Amiya in the arm with the back of her hand. "Don't make fun of his accent. How well do you speak his language?"

"I'm not in Khatal," Amiya countered.

"Beside the point," came the reply.

"Not really."

Nandi sighed.

Joga executed what Amiya figured to be the same gesture he had when he'd first approached the group, to which they reciprocated. *Must be some sort of greeting.*

"Making friends?" Nandi asked when Joga returned.

"News," the big man said.

A tiny frown creased Amiya's brow when she noted the concern in his eyes. "Looks like bad news."

Joga responded with a solemn nod. "Is my homeland. Your king still make war."

Amiya rolled her eyes. "Our king. You say it like we personally sat him on the throne. What's going on with the war? Dad never told us much about it other than how he wished Alyn would learn how to talk instead of throwing weapons at the problem."

"Father sound like wise man," Joga said. "Those I talk to," he indicated the departing Khatala, "say possible that war reach Frostlands."

Amiya felt her stomach lurch. "That's your homeland."

Joga nodded. "My homeland not involved in this, but it spreads. Other tribes might get involved. Might expect Frostlands to fight." He let out a long sigh and looked to the southwest, the direction of his home. "My people not a large people."

"You look pretty large to me," Amiya said. "I mean, you're not as large as them"—she pointed in the direction the other Khatala had gone—"but you're still bigger than most Marai-landers."

"No," Joga replied. "I mean big, like numbers. My people not have big numbers."

"Oh." Amiya chewed her lip and glanced to her side to see Nandi doing the same. "They'll probably need you to fight, won't they?" Joga didn't respond, but Amiya saw the muscles in his jaw tighten.

"It's okay," Nandi said. "You have a responsibility to your people. We can make it to Altarra on our own."

Despite her reservations about that, Amiya nodded. "Yeah. If you need to get back home, we understand."

"What?" Joga furrowed his brow. "Never do such thing. What kind of man I be, if I leave two girls alone to find father. You help me fulfill bloodmark. Could not have done without you. You think I abandon friends? Never!"

Amiya wished she didn't feel such relief, but she had to admit to herself that the thought of trying to make it to Altarra to find Dad on their own felt daunting.

"Is more," Joga continued. "Big city Altarra. Is not north, but south and east."

"We *passed* it?" Nandi said. "How could we have passed it?"

"Easy," Amiya said. "Constantly running for our lives, traveling underground, and headed toward that volcano to kill the lava lizard-thing. That, and the fact that we've never been far from Vyne before now."

"You think Dad's still there?" Nandi asked, a bit of trepidation creeping into her voice. "What if he's already finished whatever it was he was supposed to do and already started back?"

"Ugh. That would stink like a mountain mole," Amiya replied. "Let's hope not."

"We need to get moving," Nandi said, trying to take charge, as usual. "If we miss him, we'll have to backtrack all the way home and hope we catch up."

"Either way, we've got to head back home," Amiya replied. "And we'd be headed back toward your home, anyway, right?" She looked up at Joga, who nodded.

They spent the next hour replenishing their supplies with as little money as possible and gathered up their gear. Before they were half a mile outside of the borderland town, Sama found them. The girl seemed to appear out of the ground itself. Amiya envied the tatamble's chameleon-like ability.

In between Sama's complaints about them taking too long to leave the confines of the town, they shared with her their plans to turn back south.

"Leave one cage for bigger cage? Why Sama would do this?"

"It's where they sent our father," Amiya said. "We don't know if he's still there, but we have to go in case he is."

"What if sister girls not find father?" Sama asked. "Then they ask Sama to go farther. More big cages with more humans who take and not give."

"Oh, Sama," Nandi said. She tried to wrap her arm around the tatamble girl's shoulders, but she shrank away, her black eyes going wide.

Nandi took a step back and held up her hands in a warding gesture. "You okay?"

"Why try to strangle Sama?" the girl demanded. "Sama help girls with same face to find each other. Sama help fight beast in lava, fight man in lava. All when she not have to, but Nani girl try choke Sama."

Nandi was waving her hands through the whole thing. "No, no, no," she chuckled. "Sama, it's a show of affection."

Sama narrowed her eyes. "What is affession?"

"Affection," Amiya said, moving beside her sister. "See?" She wrapped her arm around Nandi's shoulders and gave her a squeeze. "Like this." She yanked Nandi in close and gave her another squeeze, then yanked her again, and again."

"Stop it," Nandi growled. "Will you stop it?"

Amiya's grin widened. "See? This is how we show love for each other, Sama. It's affection." She continued to yank Nandi around until her sister almost lost her balance. "Hey!" she cried out when Nandi grabbed her by the arm and pulled her around.

They tripped over each other's feet and tumbled to the ground. Nandi grabbed Amiya's wrist, but she twisted them and broke her sister's grip. They rolled around in a dusty ball of entangled limbs, feet, hands, and grunts.

Somewhere Amiya heard Joga's exasperated groan right before his large, powerful arm wrapped around her waist and lifted her off the ground. "This how sisters behave?" he asked. "Attack each other like this …" he trailed off when Amiya, staring across him at Nandi, burst into laughter. Nandi's chin wrinkled with repressed mirth until she, too, erupted.

Joga practically dropped them on the ground and walked away. Sama tilted her head and stared at them with the most confused expression on her face. She finally left them, muttering something about strange human girls.

"Guess we should get going," Amiya said, dusting herself off. Her mood sobered when she thought about Dad. "I guess we've wasted too much time, already."

"Not really," Nandi replied. "If we're grim all the time it won't do us any good."

Amiya rolled her eyes. "Quit repeating Dad."

"Is he wrong?" Nandi asked.

"I hope we're not walking the whole way," Amiya remarked once they caught up. "Otherwise it'll take forever."

"Town another hour away," Joga said. "Sandlanders tell me."

"Oh, those Khatala people you were talking to?" Amiya asked.

Joga nodded. "Yes. Caravans stop through all the time. Can maybe get ride if we work."

"I wish we had more money," Amiya grumbled. "Then we wouldn't have to work all the time to get stuff."

"Must always work to get anything," Joga said. "If already had money, means worked for it when at home. If not have money, must work for what you need. Doesn't matter."

"Ugh. You sound like Dad too," Amiya muttered.

They reached the town just after midday and had little trouble finding someone that needed work done. Whether it was someone's Fallen-blasted fields, or repairs done to a barn, or some other menial task someone didn't want to do, "opportunities" came aplenty. Amiya wondered if people saved these tasks specifically for when people like her came along.

Joga's appearance alone got them on a caravan. A woman with three mule-driven wagons took one look at him and agreed to grant them passage as close to Altarra as she was traveling in exchange for Joga's service as a guard. The girls, however, would help with cooking meals and feeding the animals.

Late into that same evening, they huddled around a campfire finishing the last of a pot of boiling stew. "Dangerous times come on us these days," the woman who'd introduced herself as Anna, said. She sat cross-legged and used a stick to draw in the dirt. "Used to be I'd only have to worry about a pack of wolves, shrikes trying to tear through the wagon covers to steal food, or even the occasional jarku pack. Now there's word about four-armed horrors cutting people down, giant monsters nobody's ever seen before bursting out of the ground right in the middle of cities." She sighed. "Something dark is happening in the world. I got a feeling this is just the beginning."

"You sure you're not being dramatic, Anne?" one of the two other caravaners asked. He was a slim man with a thick beard and calloused hands. "We ain't seen anything like what people been buzzing about. Probably bored rich folk out of Altarra wanting to spread rumors to add some excitement to their lives. Get everybody riled up and such."

"You're a cottonhead, Darry," Anne said. "Altarra is one of the few places that hasn't been attacked yet, and you know just like I do that there's people from all over saying the same thing. Only a fool would ignore it."

"Guess we been lucky," the man named Darry said in a quiet voice.

"Uh huh," Anne said with a nod. "That's exactly what we been. Lucky."

Amiya looked from her sister—who seemed deep in thought—to Joga. He sat across the fire, staring into the flames as though he hoped to divine some information about what, she could only guess. Amiya thought about Dad, and it sent an ache through her chest that made her heart hurt. He *had* to be okay. He didn't have the essences to protect himself like she and Nandi did. Hopefully whomever he traveled with kept him safe.

She looked into the campfire as well, enjoying the heat on her face and losing herself in the dancing flames. Her jaw tightened, and a frown slowly creased her brow. One thing Amiya knew for certain; if something did happen to Dad, no place or person, or legion of soldiers, could protect Decius from her.

5

SELVETAR

The tower of magi loomed over not only the great sprawling city of Altarra, but the land beyond. Tall and imposing, reaching nearly to the clouds, one could see the surrounding landscape for miles in every direction. Because it was the oldest structure in the history of Marai, various rumors circulated throughout time about its creation. From master stonemasons brought from around the world, to the Creator Himself erecting the structure, the rumors only grew more varied and often ridiculous.

All of the stories and rumors, however, led back to one actual truth. The tower of magi had indeed been erected by essence wielders capable of feats most magi today wouldn't believe possible.

Selvetar knew the history taught to acolytes and beginning magi, but his knowledge of the fortress—for that's what it actually was—went much deeper. Its creation held no small bit of irony, in that its beginning signaled the strengthening of a bond between humans and tinfar that weakened towards its completion.

Hovering over the highest point of the tower, the first magus kept warm air swirling about him. This high up at this time of year, the air carried a lethally cold bite. Selvetar tried to think of the last time anyone had seen one of the diminutive people. So many generations had passed that the tinfar were largely forgotten. They were even excluded from the history of the tower and their hands in its creation.

The first magus floated up and down on the breeze like a fisherman's bobber upon a gently rippling lake. Selvetar's dimly pulsating essence ring gave a little silver flare, and he rotated until he faced the opposite direction. Across many leagues sat aggressive Jietar, known for its fearless warriors. Selvetar could just make out the tops of its tallest buildings beyond the hills and trees separating it from Altarra.

As of yet, no reports of drauk attacks had come from Jietar, but it was only a matter of time. The appearance of drauk and other monsters of the underworld heralded one thing only.

Those who knew even a smattering of history referred to it as the black cloud. Others called it the plague force. Others still, referred to it as simply the great death. Most thought it an evil force that had been locked in an eternal battle with the Creator, defeated and sealed away until it could escape again. Selvetar narrowed his eyes at that last thought. Pass enough millennia, and people forget. The thing wasn't eternal, but in fact, had been created by the Fallen.

A rare sigh escaped the stoic magus before he could stop it. What was coming had two true names, and only two. Shurza, the blight essence. He didn't know how it had been freed from its void prison, but Selvetar had to find out quickly, for if Shurza had indeed been freed, so too would those tied to it. The Fallen.

Selvetar closed his eyes and allowed the swirling warmth to part in front of his face. He drew in a deep breath of crisp fresh air. Floating up here, hundreds of feet in the sky above the fortress always helped him to clear his mind and gather perspective.

He opened his eyes as the warmth closed in front of his face again. Amoura Xanna was missing. Not only that, but she'd taken the hybrid spicetrader, Emiel Dharr with her. Also of interest was that the mercenary with the unique armor forged from the bones of the rare and dangerous teliak beast had accompanied them. That last bit convinced Selvetar that he needed to speak with the—now former—apprentice. Vladrick had been incensed that Amoura had defied him. It didn't help that the magi master had been dealt injury during the confrontation.

A tiny smirk stretched the corner of Selvetar's mouth, pulling at one of the sides of his inky black goatee. Vladrick claimed to have heard a tiny voice behind him before being assaulted by a powerful blast of rock. That sounded suspiciously like a tinfar, and given the particular projectiles, he suspected an earth, or *e'ta* tinfar.

Strange times indeed. A man and his twin daughters, all hybrids, a tinfar making contact with humans—something that hadn't happened for many generations—and a magus who possessed the qualities of a hybrid. Selvetar thought it cute that the young woman thought she could hide her abilities from him. That she was able to understand the old teachings was in itself remarkable. The fact that she could apply those teachings, committing the techniques and unique properties of each essence to memory, and manipulate them with such variety was practically a shining beacon to the first magus as to what she could do. It also warned him to be careful.

Vladrick may or may not be the most powerful magus in Marai, but he wasn't the most knowledgeable. If he was, he would have been able to sense the finer details of when someone wielded the essences. Amoura possessed the beginnings of what made a master magus easily on par with Vladrick and himself. The pragmatic first magus even admitted to himself that she had the potential to surpass him.

Selvetar descended alongside the highest tower. When he'd first been promoted to the rank of first magus, he'd been pleased, thinking himself closer to one day becoming magi master, once Vladrick retired. The years of watching the master in his position and all that it entailed had altered Selvetar's perception of the prestigious title.

The position of magi master meant that one must preside over every magus in Marai. He was responsible for leading the way, ensuring that those who were elevated to the level of magus were properly educated and stayed on the correct path.

Selvetar found it more work than he desired just to keep track of things in Altarra, much less everywhere else. Traveling back and forth from here to Vyne provided enough of an annoyance and interference to his studies.

Vladrick had become stale. The responsibilities of his station were a heavy weight to bear, but it didn't change that fact.

"Mmm." Selvetar rethought that. Stale wasn't the correct term, and thinking of the dangerous master in such a way could lead to unfortunate circumstances. No, the man hadn't become stale, more than static. The man possessed more knowledge than any hundred magi combined, and could likely battle and defeat a host of magi by himself. But he wasn't constantly improving, constantly learning, as Selvetar and Amoura had been.

His feet gently touched down on the hard-stone balcony of the highest spire. He needed to find the apprentice. The more Selvetar thought about it, the more convinced he was that he needed to have a lengthy conversation with Amoura Xanna. The woman didn't like him, but that mattered little. At worst, he might convince her to work alongside him while he learned more about what was to come. At best, she might join him.

Selvetar chuckled as he passed a group of acolytes walking up the spiraling stairs. The group went silent and quickened their pace. He had that effect on new arrivals. It was why Vladrick made it mandatory he attend the welcoming of every class of aspirants. His presence alone intimidated the weakest of the hopefuls that they dropped out before the true testing began.

He didn't give the acolytes another thought. The source of his mirth came from the thought of Amoura joining him in his search for likeminded magi across Marai. The headstrong apprentice would most assuredly balk at the idea of working in close proximity with him.

Selvetar finally reached the main level of the fortress where buzzing acolytes laden with books scurried here and there, talking excitedly about the day's lessons. The newly elevated magi also mingled about, carrying the typical air of superiority of being raised above those who occupied the same probational status they themselves just recently escaped.

When the first magus entered, acolyte and magus alike parted before him. The room didn't, however, go quiet. Instead, conversation morphed into choppy, nervous chatter, as if everyone feared what would happen if the room descended into total silence.

Selvetar turned toward the wing of the fortress that held his personal study, then stopped. He half turned and looked over his shoulder at a group of magi so recently elevated that they still wore the neutral sand-colored robes of those who have not yet become part of a sect. The first magus locked gazes with one of them, and the young man scurried to Selvetar's side and bowed.

"May I be of service, First Magus?"

"Nial Orensia Red," Selvetar stated. "Tell him to come to my study immediately."

The young man's mouth bobbed open and closed a few times as he likely started to say that he didn't know anyone named Nial Orensia. Selvetar arched an eyebrow at him, and the boy offered another series of awkward bows and hurried away.

Selvetar continued toward the hall. He passed magi bearing the brown, silver, red, and green colored cloaks of each sect, as most of the fortress existed in a neutral space. The only areas specific to each sect were each of the four towers dedicated to its given essence affinity.

He passed through halls adorned with life-sized busts of historic figures in the Order of Magi. Long flowing carpets muffled his footfalls in some hallways, while polished stone floors in others carried his steps in crisp reverberations.

The smell of sweet or pungent incenses thickened the air near meditation chambers, while intense heat or freezing cold hinted at training that commenced beyond other doors.

Selvetar passed by chambers resplendent in stained glass windows with depictions that varied from beloved figures of the past, to depictions of nature, or human civilizations. One circular room, the largest of them all, held long flowing canvas paintings depicting the previous ages, legendary magi, and the symbols of each sect in their respective colors. He thought of the stained glass dome roof of that room. The most magnificent piece of art in the fortress by far, and certainly the most impressive Selvetar had seen in all his travels across Marai.

The Room of the Immortals. As with every other time he passed by the massive chamber with only one door, he looked up at it with a hum of approval. Composed of a ton of stone, six feet thick, and encased in another three-foot-thick layer of ice, the door stood twenty feet overhead with no stairs or ladders for access. Entrance to the Room of the Immortals must be earned, and only a magus proficient in all four of the essences was able to access it.

Once again, Selvetar wished he could have lived during the age of the immortals. How much could he have learned? What secrets lost to time might he possess if he'd lived in that time? Perhaps the same secrets and the same knowledge and unfathomable power the immortals had attained that made them immortal in the first place?

One thing Selvetar knew for certain. Regardless of being one of the most powerful magi in the world, his knowledge and use of the essences was likely infantile compared to the power the Illuminarians and Fallen had wielded.

The stray notion led him to thoughts of the Illuminarians. While he felt certain that recent events were a sign that the blight essence had been unleashed once again, and with it, the Fallen, what of the Illuminarians? Every book on the subject spoke with confidence on the fate of the Fallen once the blight essence had been contained. But the fate of their counterparts had been obscure.

The brightness, color, and opulence of the fortress gradually faded as Selvetar reached the east wing. He descended the stairs and walked down the final corridor leading to his private study. The door creaked in protest as he pushed it open, then once again when he closed it.

Selvetar lived in this room almost as much as his own personal chamber, so he needed no light to navigate the dark room and find his desk. He rested his elbows on the desk, pressed his palms together in front of his face, and intertwined his fingers. Chin resting on his extended thumbs, he sat in the darkness with his thoughts.

If he catalogued every magi known to Altarra, the number would be in the range just north of possibly three thousand. Of those three thousand, there were probably several hundred who had attained a high level of skill. Of those several hundred, only a handful might attain the level of mastery and be capable of merely gaining the attention of an immortal in battle.

"Mmm," the first magus rumbled thoughtfully. "He held no illusions to his abilities. If it came to a fight between himself and Vladrick, Selvetar would have had to rely on his cunning to defeat the more powerful magi master. And Vladrick would be no match for the weakest of the Fallen.

A knock on the door cut through his thoughts, but he continued to consider everything he knew about the immortals, the blight essence, the war of the immortals, and the ages past. Outside the door, he heard a foot shuffle, but only once. Nial knew better than to knock twice. If Selvetar had summoned him, the young magus would wait until the first magus was ready to receive him.

"Come," Selvetar finally said.

The door hesitantly creaked open and Nial's face came into view, torchlight from the halls dancing across his nervous features. Selvetar frowned. How long had he been sitting here thinking?

Nial stood in the open door, studiously not meeting Selvetar's eyes. "You summoned me, First Magus?"

Fingers still entwined like crisscrossed knives in front of his mouth, Selvetar silently looked at Nial until the man finally looked up to meet his eyes. Selvetar's piercing gaze flicked from the young magus to the door behind him. Nial turned and gently closed the door, engulfing them in darkness once more.

A tiny flare of red light pierced the darkness from Selvetar's essence ring, and four torches in wall sconces lit the room in a soft golden glow. Nial remained where he stood, parchment-thin lips pressed together. His left hand twitched in an effort not to run his hand over his oily slick black hair. A nervous tick.

Selvetar indicated the young man take a chair sitting against the wall. Nial went to the chair and started to sit, then wisely stopped and turned to face the first magus again.

"This will be a conversation," Selvetar said. "Such are held face to face, are they not?"

"Of course, First Magus," Nial replied. He picked up the chair and placed it on the other side of the desk. He sat down with his hands folded in his lap, and stared at the middle of Selvetar's desk, occasionally looking up when the first magus didn't speak.

The boy squirmed under Selvetar's steely gaze, but in truth, the first magus stared not at Nial, but through him and into his own distant thoughts. *Enough.* He needed to puzzle out the mystery of Amoura's disappearance. "You were present when the master apprentice fled with the hybrid man and the mercenary."

Nial flinched under the weight of the statement. "I ... was, First Magus. I did my best to stop them but they ..."

A look from Selvetar quieted him. "Did you see her leave? Did you witness her leave the fortress with your own eyes?"

"I did not, First Magus."

"How not?"

The young man flushed the same color as his sect. "I ... was incapacitated, First Magus."

"Incapacitated," Selvetar echoed, no emotion in his voice one way or another.

Nial chewed his thin bottom lip until a trickle of blood ran between his teeth. He licked it clean. "To my shame, I was unable to defeat the master apprentice and bring her back to face the justice of you, First Magus, and Magi Master Vladrick."

Selvetar chuckled. "If you had been able to stop Amoura Xanna and bring her back, even if she had no companions to aid her, either she would have already been sorely hampered in some way, or I would be congratulating you on your new path to replace her."

The hopeful look on the fool's face almost made Selvetar regret his words. "You show great promise, Nial Red. But I haven't called you here to discuss your possible ascension, nor the fact that the master apprentice could reduce you to glowing embers should you try to engage her again."

That sucked the wind out of the ambitious red's sails. He nodded and looked down at the table again.

"I need you to recount everything that you saw and experienced," Selvetar continued.

Nial took a deep breath. "I confronted her about why she had removed the magi master's guest and where she was taking him, as it was in the opposite direction of the master's chamber and meeting room."

Selvetar didn't move or speak. Nial wisely took it as a sign to continue. "When the confrontation turned aggressive, myself, Jonrick, and Sanda tried to stop her."

"And she overwhelmed you all." Again, not a question, but a statement.

Nial's mouth screwed up as though he were being forced to dine with a dung beetle. "She did, First Magus."

Selvetar responded with a barely perceptible nod. If it weren't for the current circumstances, he would have felt pride that Amoura—his student more than Vladrick's—had so effectively defeated three capable magi that she'd left them unconscious. "Is there anything else?"

"When we woke up …"

Selvetar couldn't help enjoying this.

"… we were in the infirmary. Sanda is confined to his room with regular checkups. He suffered a concussion. Jonrick has a twisted ankle, a broken nose, and lost a tooth."

"You walked away unscathed?" Selvetar prodded.

"They had to reset my dislocated shoulder," Nial murmured, "and I bruised the side of my face when I hit the floor."

Selvetar nodded, noticing the bruise now that the boy mentioned it. The healers must have done something for that as well, for it was largely gone but for the little blemish that shown in the crackling torchlight. "Have you spoken with Magi Master Vladrick?"

"He has not summoned us, First Magus."

Selvetar imagined not. Having suffered a defeat, it would be difficult to imagine the highest-ranking magus in Marai summoning three subordinates to lick his wounds with. "Very well."

Nial took the hint and stood. He replaced the chair against the wall and moved toward the door.

Selvetar reached for a tome at the corner of his desk and opened it at the marked page. There had to be something in these books he'd missed; some bit of information that might provide an answer or advantage in the conflict to come. And it would come.

"First Magus, if I may?"

Selvetar didn't lift his head from the book, only his eyes. "Yes?"

Unable to hold the first magus's gaze for more than a heartbeat, Nial swallowed and lowered his gaze. "Some speculate that she'd used a technique where she walked through one space and arrived in another, far away." He dipped his head apologetically. "I know it sounds ridiculous, but I thought perhaps it might help."

"Thank you, Nial," Selvetar said. "You've been most helpful."

Nial repressed the tiny grin creasing his thin lips, bowed once more, and left.

Selvetar stared at the door long after the opportunistic Red had closed it. Amoura, *bridging*? Unlikely. That ancient technique had long slipped into obscurity during the Second Age. He knew of no one other than himself possessed of that knowledge, and history dictated that only the immortals had known how to do it back then.

He pursed his lips. When Amoura had been tasked with assisting in bringing the hybrid spicetrader to Altarra, Selvetar had bridged her into the general area the mercenary and his charge had been, without having to be present. Could there be someone else in the fortress capable of the same?

"Mmm. Unlikely," Selvetar thought aloud. Not that he ruled out the possibility of any other magus in the world being able to bridge, but he assessed every acolyte the day they were elevated to the rank of magus. Of course there were plenty of powerful senior magi in the fortress, but unless they were keeping such an ability secret, he knew nothing of anyone possessing the ability to bridge.

Selvetar dipped his feather pen in the inkwell and began recording his thoughts. He stopped mid stroke and looked up from the parchment, a frown creeping across his brow. He replaced the pen in the inkwell and slid back from his desk, crossing the room to a bookshelf at the far end of the room. He passed the several empty spaces where the normal occupants now resided on the corner of his desk, and came to a black volume with a red TF on the spine.

The first magus slipped the book off the shelf and quickly returned to his desk. After he sat the book down, he ran his finger along the spines of the stacked books and stopped at a gray one. He removed the pile on top and picked the book up. *History of the Magi*, the title read. He looked down at the black book. As with the spine, the cover had the same two letters only; TF. The Fallen.

There wasn't much in the world that could shake Selvetar.

Indeed, even the appearance of the drauk in Vyne hadn't invoked more than a mixture of curiosity and urgency to dispatch the underworld monsters.

He opened the book and scanned through the text within; text in his own handwriting. The order of magi was the most powerful organization in the world, yet in its heart sat foolish superstition. Only the most studied magi knew that the Illuminarians and the Fallen had once belonged to the first Order of Magi. While the Order might consider it a thing of pride that the Illuminarians had been of the first magi, the Order spoke of the group that had turned to the pursuit of power to be shameful.

Selvetar knew better. Shame did not keep the senior magi from teaching the earliest history of the Order. No, not shame; fear. If a magus, trained, educated, and held to the highest standard as an essence wielder could fall to the temptation of unlimited power, what would it mean? What would the world of non-essence wielders think? What would the members of the Order itself think?

These were the fears of the highest-ranking magi. They weren't unfounded or foolish fears in themselves, but the fact that magi feared these possibilities themselves was the failing. Selvetar continued to page through the book of his own writing. No one in the Tower of Magi would have entertained the idea of digging into the history of the immortals and notating every known fact. They would rather bury their heads in the sands of their own ignorance and fear.

Selvetar knew differently. The triumphs *and* failures of the past, particularly the failures, held the keys to growth. The origin of the Fallen, and how they manipulated the essences was vital information. As he flipped through, scanning page after page, Selvetar felt the growing sense of foreboding that his personal philosophy was about to be tested.

He found the section he'd been looking for and carefully read through. He reached a particular passage, took a deep breath to steady himself, and read it again. His face darkened as he re-read it once more. The Tower of Magi, a beacon of power, a steadying presence to those who would study and wield the essences for the betterment and protection of all, was compromised.

Selvetar's eyes hardened as he read the passage a fourth time. His lips compressed into a line, his hands balling into fists at either side of the book. *One of the main differing traits*, he read, *between the Illuminarians and the Fallen rested in the cunning of the latter. Why do all the work when those hungry for power and immortality were in infinite supply? One need offer only a taste of such power. If the hopeful proves capable, perhaps a meal, with the promise of the full course when one proved worthy.*

No matter how much he wanted to deny it, every time he read that passage, the truth grew clearer. He forced himself to read on. *Such is the cunning of the Fallen. While the Illuminarians knew the temptations of power and saw theirs as a burden of responsibility, the Fallen embraced all of it, the light and the dark, and exploited the darkness in others to do their bidding.*

Fascinatingly, my studies have found that while ascension is typically slow, there was one who had been granted the "blessing" of the Fallen and ascended rapidly from the lowly rank of under-lord to droughtlord due to his tenacity and focus. So skilled and powerful did he become, that he even learned to manage the side effects of the power granted by the Fallen known as the "curse".

In my extensive studies on the subject, I've found through piecing various bits of research together that no death or withering rot dogged this man's steps. The space around him did not wither to the telltale illness exhibited by lessers who came after him. I've discovered that he even learned a technique through the manipula-tion of the essences fire, water, *and* air, *that he was capable of temporarily altering his visage to hide the cracks and creases indicative of those bearing the "curse". This afforded him the ability to infiltrate the order of magi and move about as he chose.*

I've come to learn that this man's name was Demerog, and the above listed talents made him as dangerous as the Fallen simply by his subversive abilities alone. Though his power was not equal to that of the Illuminarians or the Fallen, of whom his creator was apparently Devrin, the power he wielded eclipsed all but the most powerful magi. It was even mentioned that he had mastered bridging, an ability that possibly only the immortals possessed.

Selvetar pursed his lips. The magi of history were far more powerful than their current brethren, yet even among their ranks, Selvetar had seen nothing to indicate they had mastered bridging. With Shurza free, and the Fallen undoubtedly so as well, so too, would the servants of the Fallen be free.

The more he thought about it, the more convinced Selvetar became that it was Demerog who'd bridged Amoura out of the fortress. He didn't understand why, but it hardly mattered. The presence of Demerog in the Tower of Magi was upsetting enough, and the more the first magus thought about the implications, the worse he felt.

Selvetar closed the book, summoned *air*, and blew out the torches with its physical namesake. He sat in the darkness of his study for a long time, considering how he would go about the task of rooting out of their midst the most powerful of droughtlords.

6

MIKUNA

The cold breath of Frostland sighed through the snow-dusted trees, across frozen lakes, and between the white hills and mountains farther south. It slithered across all of Frostland Khatal, a soft greeting in the ears of the smallest bird to the largest mammal. That frosty whisper found Mikuna's ears, as well as the ears of every other Frostland Khatala. The whispered welcome of home.

She ran her fingers through the ends of her long hair, back to its normal white now that she and her people had finally returned home. She took a deep breath and filled her lungs with the cold crisp air. The cold, here, would likely burn a Marailander's lungs and send them into fits of coughing, but this air was a comfort, crisp and fresh. Life.

Mikuna looked down at her bloodmarked visage staring back at her from the surface of the frozen lake. She looked at the top left side of her forehead, where she had been cut. The light brown skin was smooth where a scar should have been. The making of a bloodmark never scarred.

She visually traced the bloodmark from her forehead down the left side of her face. One stream flowed around the inside of her left eye, along the side of her nose, around the corner of her mouth, and down her chin. It kept going all the way down her neck, and met the other stream that snaked down the side of her face and down her shoulder.

Mikuna continued to follow the bloodmark down her arm. The streams splintered into four more, twisting around her arm to the top and inside of her hand. Hers was the only bloodmark in the tribe to have two meanings. The two streams were the first part. The stream down the inside of her face was Joga, while the longer, thicker stream was herself. The meeting of the two streams; her and Joga being linked as adoptive siblings. Them intersecting and parting ways signified Joga going off on his own until they met again.

Her breath clouded in front of her face when she sighed. That had been when Joga went off to battle the Mulgin, while Mikuna remained with the tribe to assist the Ancients in completing their business with the Sandland Khatala, and the return home.

Mikuna considered the rejoining of the streams. She and Joga would meet again, and soon. The crisscrossing streams foretold it. The lower part of her bloodmark, however, interested her the most. She and Joga's fates were inextricably tied. While Mikuna had already committed feats that would be told in stories of the Frost-lands for generations to come, Joga was just coming into his own. His life would depend on hers in a way she wasn't sure yet, and possibly the opposite as well.

The streams met again at her elbow, where they splintered off and formed what looked like flames that ran down the rest of her arm to the back of her hand and her palm. The dream had been vivid but incomplete. Still, it had been enough to tell her that she and Joga would play a part in the battle to come; not the petty battle between the Khatala and the fragile easterners, but some-thing bigger and darker.

She closed her eyes and opened herself to the earth. She smelled the sweet and refreshing scent of the surrounding stoutgreens that stood tall and green year-round, home to the eagles and hawks. The scent of a nearby snow fox, and a herd of elk, filled her nostrils. She felt the curiosity of the inquisitive animal and realized it was observing her from a nearby mound, camouflaged almost perfectly against the white powder it crouched upon. Yes, it was good to be home.

Mikuna allowed herself to bask in the crisp vitality that was her home until the call finally came. The call rode the whisper of the Frostland air that glided out of the stoutgreens on the other side of the frozen lake. The Ancients were ready to speak.

She stepped onto the frozen lake without hesitation. Her entire village could have fit on the frozen body of water twice over. During the summer when Father Alyu held sway and the lake thawed, and the Frostlands became as warm as a Marailander winter, the water would be fresh and clean, and the hibernating fish and plants inside would wake again.

When she reached the other side of the lake, Mikuna entered the trees, listening to the subtle call upon the air and following it to the source. She passed by the first Ancient, eyes closed and sitting cross-legged with her back against a tree. Mikuna's gaze inadvertently went to the woman's bloodmark, which began on her right cheek and flowed upward to surround both eyes. It was when Ancient Uloa closed her eyes, that she truly had sight.

Mikuna continued on, passing another Ancient as snow began to fall again. The large white flakes fell and melted on his bare shoulders and chest. His bloodmark began in the middle of his sternum and traveled up both sides of his chest. The bottom end traveled down his abdomen to form the branches and roots of a great tree. The tree of the Frostland family. Ancient Oama.

The sound of crunching footsteps from behind indicated the Ancients had risen to follow. Mikuna wove her way through the trees until she finally came to a snow-covered stoutgreen whereupon a woman sat cross-legged with her back against the base. The woman had been looking at Mikuna the moment she came around the tree and into her line of vision.

Mikuna let her eyes follow the woman's bloodmark, which began at her left shoulder. It flowed like veins carrying precious lifeblood down her left arm as well as across the top of her chest and down her right arm. The veins ended in each palm, connecting to half a heart. The two halves of the heart of Frostland Khatal; the two tribes of the Frostlands.

The woman looked into Mikuna's light brown eyes as she placed both hands, both halves of the heart together. Mikuna, born of the southern Frostland Tribe and welcomed as a child of peace into the northern Frostland Tribe, placed her hands together in turn. She held the Ancient's gaze until the older woman indicated she sit. Ancient Nami, bearer of the bloodmark of a uniter. In adopting Mikuna, the orphaned child of the southern Frostland Khatala, Nami had united the north and south.

Mikuna ignored the cold beneath her when she sat. The crunching steps ceased as the other two Ancients took their seats behind her on either side.

"You are thinking about your brother," Ancient Uloa said from behind and to the left.

A tiny smile flickered across Ancient Nami's face. "It doesn't require your Sight for that to be obvious."

"You worried for his life, but no longer," Uloa continued.

"If she does not worry, she has dreamed," Ancient Oama said from behind Mikuna's right side.

"Your brother lives?" Nami inquired.

"He does, Ancient," Mikuna replied. "But danger surrounds him. It surrounded him before, and continues now that he's completed the task of his bloodmark."

"Your dream gift is not always simple to interpret, child," Nami warned. "Are you sure he has completed his task? Are you sure he lives?" Despite her neutral tone, Mikuna didn't miss the hint of hopefulness in the Ancient's voice.

"Of that, Ancient, I have no doubt. He has killed the mulgin and he remains in this life." Ancient Nami's expression didn't change, but her eyes betrayed her relief, the same flicker of relief Mikuna herself had felt when she woke from her dream to realize Joga had survived. She still didn't understand exactly what the two balls of fire orbiting him meant, but she suspected they had played some part in her adoptive brother's triumph.

"Have your dreams revealed his path?" Ancient Uloa inquired. "If he has completed his bloodmark task, his path should lead him back to the Frostlands."

Mikuna wondered if any of the Ancients believed that. It didn't take special sight or dreams for one to see the spark of adventure in Joga, even if he didn't see it in himself. If she were honest with herself, Mikuna felt it, too. Maybe that was why they were destined to become siblings through her adoption into the northern tribe. "I don't have the answer to that, Ancient," she replied. "I feel that he's left the borderland city, but I saw nothing that gave the impression he intended to return home."

"Of course he would return home," Uloa said. "Why would he not? His people need him, especially in the days to come."

Mikuna frowned, but quickly smoothed her features. *Days to come?*

Nami nodded in agreement. "His people need him, yes. But his life is not for us to control. Creator *Amyadali* will send him back to us if and when She chooses." She looked back to Mikuna. "Your curiosity plays as brightly across your face as Father *Alyu* on a midsummer day. It is time to speak of why we've called you here."

The eldest of the Ancients bore into Mikuna with her unblinking stare, yet the young woman felt as though Nami were looking someplace far away. "The Terratoma and Dokayuk battle the king of Marai," she said, her voice deep and contemplative. "As the conflict escalates, it will draw in the Nassak and Sandlands, no matter their desire to remain uninvolved."

Mikuna's confusion deepened as Nami continued. Every tribe

of Khatal knew of the ensuing hostilities between the Dokayuk and Terratoma, and the Marailander king. The conflict was between them alone, and Creator *Amyadali* willing, it would resolve soon, and both sides would stop and raise their eyes to Her, and sing their apologies, proclaiming their blindness to be cured.

"This is unlike the conflicts sometimes fought between our peoples, child," Ancient Nami said, reading Mikuna's expression. "While the Terratoma and Dokayuk forces seek to beat the Marailanders back into their senses, that they see the foolish war for what it is, the eastern king strives to blast our brothers and sisters from the land and send our warriors back to the True home."

Mikuna sucked in a breath through her pursed lips. "Please excuse me, Ancient." The woman indicated she continue. "How can this be? Even the worst fighting between our nations, we did not strive to eradicate each other. How can a people think this way?"

"They do not necessarily seek to kill every one of us, child," Nami replied. "But the Marailander king would take the spear from the hand of Khatal, that it not be raised against him again."

"All of our warriors," Mikuna breathed.

Ancient Nami nodded. "Every one, until only children and elderly remained."

Mikuna lifted her chin. "Then, he does not truly understand us."

"This is truth," Ancient Oama agreed. "The land of Khatal is hard, and makes its people harder, tougher, stronger. This king of Marai thinks only the young are strong."

"Pray he does not recognize his mistake," Uloa said. "For if he truly understood the truth of us, he would rally every warrior from every civilization of the east against us."

"But unlike Marailanders, every one of us are trained to fight," Mikuna said, her blood growing hot with every word. "If he tries, every one of us will rise up—"

"And die in huge numbers," Ancient Nami interrupted.

Mikuna's mouth fell open. "Ancient—"

"We are bigger, stronger, and connected to the aspects by our very nature," Nami said. "While they require the sacred corlite to experience the glory of Mother *Illyu*. But they have great warriors as well, and the power their sightless wield is undeniable. And, there are more of them. It could be that we would win such a great and terrible war, but the cost, child. The cost would be devastating."

"Their numbers would only take them so far, should we unite," Ancient Oama said.

"Again, at great cost," Nami reiterated.

Mikuna's determination evaporated. Nami was right, of course. She was always right. But, there was something else in her tone; something the Ancient was holding back. "What will we do, Ancients?"

"The Nassak and Sandlands have refrained from entering the war," Oama said from behind. "It has strained relations between them and the Dokayuk and Terratoma. Eventually, they will be forced to enter the war. The Drylands will be next, and after them …"

Oama left the thought hanging, but Mikuna finished it. "Us." Hearing it spoken as it was, the outcome seemed inevitable. All of the Khatala nations would be pulled into a war with foolish beginnings. Many had already gone back to the True Home, and more would join them. She felt a great disdain for the Marailander king. She wished she could personally challenge the man and run a spear through his heart.

"You are here because you are as important to the survival of Khatal as Joga," Ancient Nami said.

Mikuna blinked. "My dreams do not come at my bidding, Ancients. And I can only interpret them as best I can."

"Not because of your dreams, child," Nami said. "Though they are important. You have the mind and heart of a leader, and you are strong."

Mikuna felt her heart skip a beat. No. She didn't want this. "I've led no one, Ancient."

"Yet there are those who follow you," came the reply. Nami favored her with a knowing grin that made Mikuna wish she could sink through the snow and into the ground.

"There are others with more experience than me, Ancient," Mikuna argued. She unconsciously glanced about. The surrounding trees loomed over her, closing in like the walls of a Marailander building. "I've not even completed my bloodmark, and there is much left for me to learn."

"Some bloodmarks have a conclusion," Ancient Uloa said, "others are lifelong. Yours is such, girl. There are many with more experience with you, and would lend their experience to your cause, as we lend ours to the chief of the tribe. Do you think Chief Maia knows everything? She is but twenty years your senior, not more than a child, herself." The elder chuckled. "She is aware that she doesn't know everything there is to know in order to lead us, and that is one of the assets that makes her a good leader. She needs others with equal sensibilities."

"Do not despair over our words, child Mikuna," Ancient Nami said. "We did not bring you here to compel you to leadership. It will come to you when it does, and you will rise to the challenge. We have called you here because the Terratoma are already pressuring the Sandlanders, while the Dokayuk are leaning on the Nassak. Their meetings grow as heated as the sand under the summer gaze of Father *Alyu*. Soon the southern tribe will arrive to discuss these events, while you will go and observe the conflict. Study the mood of our sister nations, Mikuna. It is important that we know how strained the Terratoma and Dokayuk are, and how aggressively they call upon the closer tribes for aid."

Mikuna fought back her panic. "Ancients," she raised her eyes to look at the space several feet over Nami's head, a gesture to address them all. "Would not my presence only turn their eyes to us sooner?"

"Observe from afar," Nami answered. "If you feel compelled to speak with them, we trust in your discretion to do so."

"When do I leave," Mikuna asked. The time for anxiety, and wishing she were not in the position thrust upon her was over. The Ancients had given her an important task, and she would see it done without complaint.

"Go to Jista's hut," Nami answered. "Plan tonight and leave tomorrow. Learn what you can of this lingering battle, and relations between the four tribes."

Mikuna bowed at the waist in obeisance, unfolded her legs, and stood. Ancient Nami's voice found her as she wove through the trees. "Go with the blessing of the Ancients. Be with the protection of Creator *Amyadali*, and the love of Mother *Illyu* and Father *Alyu*."

SHE FOUND Jista's hut to be crowded and buzzing with the din of conversation, mostly between the woman and Akrim. Mikuna patted the wall of the hut with the flat of her hand and waited.

"Come and be welcome, sister Mikuna," came the answer from inside.

Mikuna entered to see Jista sitting cross-legged on the floor, a grinning Akrim sitting to her left. Bayaku leaned against the wall off to the side, the veteran warrior's arms and legs crossed. Mikuna slapped her hand over her heart and bowed. The others returned the gesture and she moved to sit across from the host.

"Would you like tea?" Jista asked. Not waiting for an answer, the tracker stood and went to a pot sitting over a small flame. "We hope to keep this meeting short," she said as she poured the steaming hot liquid into a bowl. "If we can keep the jokester on task long enough that Bayaku or myself don't skewer him out of annoyance. She returned and handed the bowl to Mikuna, who accepted it with a nod of thanks.

The bowl warmed her hands, and Mikuna closed her eyes and allowed herself to enjoy the sweet scent of winter rosebud drifting into her nostrils.

"You look like you want to bathe in it, Mikuna," Akrim remarked.

Eyes still closed, Mikuna replied, "would *you* like to bathe in it, Akrim?" She opened her eyes and turned her head to look at him. She lifted the bowl and arched an eyebrow.

"Always so serious," Akrim replied. "No, thank you. I like my skin on my bones, but you're too kind, really." He looked over at Bayaku. "Think that tea is hot enough to melt that icy sense of humor?"

Bayaku, who'd had his head lowered in thought, flicked his gaze up to meet Akrim's. It wasn't exactly a hostile response, but Akrim still shifted uncomfortably and looked away.

Mikuna found that Akrim tended to joke too much, but she didn't blame his nervousness around Bayaku. Unlike most Frostland Khatala, the seasoned warrior wore his snowy white hair close cropped, providing a clear view of his hard, hazel eyes, large pores, and the fearsome scar from the top right side of his head, angling across the bridge of his nose to end at his left chin. If that hadn't made the man's appearance unnerving enough, his bloodmark made him positively frightening.

Like every other Khatala, he'd been given his mark at the onset of adulthood, which was determined on an individual basis rather than the number of years lived. Joga had told her the story of how Ancient Oama had cut Bayaku on his right jaw. The blood had flowed down as well as up the right side of his face, and continued down the entire right side of his body. The streams of blood had branched out, thickened, and taken on the image of blood veins made of flame. The bloodmark of a champion with an indomitable spirit and unbreakable will, forged in blood of fire.

Mikuna looked away and sipped her tea. The sweetness of the winter rosebud was just right as it warmed her insides on the way down. The warmth of the tea combined with the presence of these three who would accompany her, calmed Mikuna. Having Bayaku alone by her side would have been enough. With the expert tracker, Jista, and Akrim—who despite his constant humor was a great fighter in his own right—Mikuna began to feel better about her assigned task.

"The presence of you three gives me the impression that this task isn't going to be as easy as it sounds," Mikuna said.

Akrim crossed his arms over his chest with a smirk. "Don't know what you're talking about. All we have to do is slink around the fringes of a warzone in hopes of learning more than the delicious recipe for disaster King Delicate Flower has cooked up for his people."

"I'll be sure to borrow some of your overconfidence when I'm ready to return to the True Life," Jista replied. She looked Mikuna in the eye. "I take it you've met with the Ancients already, since you're here."

"Just left them," Mikuna replied. "They suspect it's only a matter of time before all of Khatala is drawn into the war."

"If that happens," Akrim said, "it's going to go bad." Mikuna glanced at him. A dark expression replaced the smirk on his face from a moment ago. "The Terratoma lust for blood the moment they taste it from their enemies, and the Dokayuk revel in shedding it, when provoked."

Jista nodded. "Those two nations alone have been enough to keep the superior numbers of Jietar at bay. If the rest of Khatal enters the fight, there will be much death."

"The Ancients believe the Marai king will rally all the forces of Marai to his side to sweep over us and render every nation of Khatal defenseless and vulnerable, every warrior sent to the True Life."

Akrim snorted.

Jista looked up at him with raised eyebrows. "You think the Marailanders so easily defeated?"

"I think such a prospect unlikely," Akrim answered. "Such an endeavor would take time, communication, and organization. If the delicate king of the east were to even try it, we would know. Any hesitance the rest of Khatal might have about joining in the war would disappear, *and* he'd be bringing the fight to our environment, on our terms."

"Hmm." Jista pressed a finger to her cheek. "For an annoying thorn, you sometimes make sense."

"Thanks," came the dry reply.

Mikuna wanted to be as confident, but the Ancients' words were still fresh in her mind. "I'm not so sure."

"How not?" Jista asked. "Akrim is right. Our numbers are smaller, but we can mobilize quicker and Khatal is our home. It would take weeks, possibly a month or more for every force in Marai to come to their king's call. We could assemble in a manner of two weeks and form a spear to run right into the heart of Marai before that happens, or simply wait for their foolhardy march into our lands."

"The Ancients think that would not be a good thing," Mikuna said. "The forces of Marai uniting, that is. They weren't at all positive about such a prospect."

"That confuses me," Akrim replied.

"It would awaken our fury," Bayaku said. The stoic warrior's low, gravely voice broke through the conversation like a blade through the snow. "If the Marailander king brings the entirety of the land to rise against us, it would awaken the fury of Khatal." He passed his hard hazel-eyed gaze over all of them. "What happens now is not war. If all of Marai rises against us, it will truly be war."

Mikuna felt an involuntary shiver go down her spine. The fury was something no one spoke of. The elders and the Ancients kept the history in their minds and passed it on as a warning. There was a reason the easterners called them wilders, though most of them didn't truly know why their ancestors had coined the term.

"Well," Akrim said, breaking the silence. Despite the lightness of his tone, Mikuna heard the fear beneath it. "If *that* happens, we may as well all just return to the True Life." He chuckled nervously. "What would be left?"

"Scorched earth, charred bones, bloodstained hands, and broken souls," Bayaku answered.

Akrim responded with more nervous laughter. "My question was more rhetorical, but of course you're right." He looked at Jista, then Mikuna. I'm safe to assume that no one else in here wants to lose themselves in the fury?"

"That is an accurate assumption," Mikuna answered. It felt like someone had draped a sheet of ice on her back. To enter the fury was to push her humanity aside and surrender to the primal. Mikuna thought of the ceremony that every Khatala must complete once they reached a certain level of mastery of the aspects. She remembered doing a different jahaka dance, only once, and being told by the Ancients and the elders that she was forbidden to do it again. The dance had taken her to the edges of the fury.

Sitting across from Jista, Akrim to her right, and Bayaku out of sight against the wall behind her, she saw in the faces of the other two that they were remembering their own ceremonies as well. She saw in each of their faces the same feelings twisting inside her.

"Seems that's a perfect excuse to head back to my hut and sleep," Akrim announced. "We rise before dawn, correct?" Mikuna nodded absently. "Great. Gives me plenty of time to host all the nightmares waiting for me in my sleep." He slapped his hand over his heart and bowed at the waist. He stood and repeated the gesture to Bayaku.

Mikuna heard the other warrior return the gesture, then Akrim left. The man might be annoying on occasion with his perpetual sarcasm and misplaced humor, but at the moment, she appreciated Akrim's levity.

"I detest agreeing with that man," Jista said, breaking Mikuna out of her spiraling thoughts. "But I fear my sleep will be no less unpleasant."

"Nothing's happened yet," Mikuna said. "It hasn't gotten that far, and there are no signs of the Marai king rallying his entire land against Khatal. It is all speculation at the moment."

"At the moment," Jista echoed. "Marai is prideful."

"We are no less so," Mikuna countered.

The tracker conceded the point with a nod. "Perhaps such a confrontation is inevitable."

"Our return to the True Life is the only inevitable," Mikuna replied. "Everything else is flexible."

Jista stared at her. "Your dreams speak differently."

"Not always." Mikuna resisted the urge to look over her shoulder to see if the ever-silent Bayaku was still there. "I have had dreams that come to pass exactly as I saw, others coming to reality in a different manner, and some that didn't happen at all. We have our purposes for which Creator *Amyadali* has brought us here to complete, but the paths we take are many and varied."

"Your words are seasoned with elder wisdom," Jista replied.

Mikuna thought of Joga, and her dream of him and the two balls of fire. Somehow, deep inside, she knew that he would have perished without them; whatever or whoever they were. Varied paths. She looked into the tracker's eyes and saw the subtle approval there. "It might be that we can go to this war and find a way to de-escalate it."

"That is not our mission," Jista said.

"No," Mikuna agreed. It's not." Now she did look over her shoulder. "What do you say, Bayaku?"

The warrior's gravely response hung heavy in the golden torch-light. "Our paths are many and varied."

7

EMIEL

At the very last instant before the gleaming teeth bit off his face, Emiel grasped just enough *air* to swat it aside. Whether through panic or his lacking knowledge and abilities, the blow wasn't strong enough to completely deter impact.

Emiel felt the hot breath of whatever creature had lunged for his head as it passed by his face. The teeth snapped and dealt him a cut along the cheek. He cried out and dove aside, quickly scrambling back to his feet and looking around. Nothing.

Crouched in pitch darkness, he tried to control his panting as he spun about, searching for the animal. Nothing. Emiel gritted his teeth and strained for the essences. He reached for them with all his will, but the power slipped through his grasp every time. He might have been frustrated if not for the terror.

He heard the pit-pat of something moving in front of him, then to the side, then behind. It was circling him. Emiel turned with the sound while reaching for the essences that ignored his desperate call. Something large slammed into his back and sent him sprawling.

Emiel grunted in fear as he scrambled back to his feet. A snarl rumbled in his ear right before something crashed into his back again. As soon as he regained his footing, a paw that must have been the size of his head smacked him in his upper back. The blow knocked him off his feet and sent him face first to the ground.

A long, low growl split the silence and steadily grew louder. Emiel got up and ran. He didn't know where he was going or if the end of the platform lay right in front of him. His next step may well be open air, where he would fall to his death. At that moment it didn't matter. Fear had taken over and he just ran.

Not eaten alive. Emiel's heart pounded in his chest. Out on the road when he traveled from city to city selling and trading his spices, he'd seen on more than one occasion, a predator bring down its prey. He remembered the first time he'd seen an eagle drop out of the sky to grab a rabbit. The terrified cries of the rabbit, clasped in the powerful claws of the bird, rang loudly in his mind. There were larger animals as well, and he'd seen them struggle and squirm to free themselves from the jaws of their hunter even as the life drained from them.

The ground vibrated under the thudding footfalls of the big animal as it closed the distance. The hairs on the back of his neck stood on end, and Emiel heeded his instincts and dove aside. Spittle hit his neck when the long glistening teeth snapped mere inches from his head.

He rolled to his feet and kept running, no idea in what direction he fled. A paw slapped his feet from under him and he crashed onto his side. The wind blasted from Emiel's lungs in a heavy gasp. He squinted his eyes shut against the pain in his ribs.

The predator fell over him, snarling, spitting, and biting. Emiel hollered as he tried to fight it off. He clamped his hand under the snapping teeth where he thought the neck would be and tried to hold it back. Claws sliced into his arms, his chest, and legs. The sound of ripping clothes filled his ears. This was how he would die. All his life Emiel had been careful not to place himself in a vulnerable position while on the road. He'd always drilled into the girls to be careful where they were, and always heed their instincts if they ever found themselves out in the wild.

The stray thought of his girls gave Emiel a flicker of strength, and he grasped onto it like a lifeline. He dealt the animal a left hook in the side of the neck and nearly broke his hand. It felt like he'd hit a block of solid muscle. The thing swung its head and batted his hand away. Sharp teeth bit into his arm, and Emiel screamed as the bones broke.

He tried to pull free, but it held on and began to shake him. It would tear his arm off if he didn't get the thing off him. "Amoura!" he shouted. "Lief! Bone!"

Nothing.

Emiel tried to drive his knee up into a leg, abdomen, anything. His efforts had no effect. "No," he gasped. Pain exploded in his arm at the same time he heard his bones cracking. "Nnnnurgh." He grabbed a handful of fur and tried to move with it as it shook him left to right, trying to tear his arm off. An electric current shot through his arm and the teeth and pressure was suddenly gone. Emiel's chest rose and fell with each ragged breath.

He rolled onto his side and used his functional arm to push himself up to a kneeling position. Once again the ground vibrated under the thud of circling footfalls. It was still there, and still very much intending to eat him.

A trickle of the essences *air* and *water* flowed in the space just outside his body. Emiel started to sweat from the humidity, and his body trembled from the faintly charged power. He thought of his travels, and what the air felt like just before an electrical storm happened. He forced himself to ignore the padding paws thudding closer toward his back, and concentrated on the feeling.

Another electric current went through his body and he trembled in surprise. The thuds came quicker and louder as it charged. Emiel closed his eyes, thought of a lightning storm inside him, and visualized it leaving his body.

A heavy fur-covered body collided with him just as the electricity exploded out of him. The jolt and the animal hit at exactly the same time, blasting both in opposite directions. Emiel rolled several times before he finally stopped on his back, trying to breathe through the throbbing pain in his arm. Somewhere in the darkness, he heard the animal shake its body and snap its jaws, followed by a long and—seemingly—pained moan.

Emiel forced himself to stand. He used the same method as with the lightning and intense heat filled his body. When the bear went silent, he pushed the fire outward. It felt as though flames spouted from every pore in his body. A cloud of fire spat in every direction into the darkness. He turned at the sound of the bear's agonized howl from behind. An animal easily twice his size writhed in flames, swinging burning limbs at the open air.

The fire started to build inside him again. Emiel held his hand out towards the animal and focused. Nothing happened at first, but he kept trying. Eventually he could contain the heat no longer. He focused the fire into a single point, his hand, and released it into the already burning animal. It roared and stood up on two legs. The walking pillar of flame shambled toward him, and Emiel nearly retched when the stench of burning fur and flesh found his nostrils.

Emiel backed away and threw his concentration into the essences again. He thought of *earth*, and this time the essence leaped to his call. He formed several stalagmites in his mind and visualized them racing at the beast. The sound of crumbling ground erupted from behind, and a heartbeat later, whooshed past him in the darkness. The sickening sound of sharp objects punching into the fiery body made him want to vomit again.

The beast thrashed and howled until it finally fell over into a lifeless lump, flames dancing in triumph over the still form. Emiel's shoulders rose and fell with a sigh of relief that turned into a gasp of astonishment. The predator growled and rose again. With the flames having spread all over its body, now, Emiel could finally see it more clearly.

On all fours, it still stood as tall as him, and twice as wide. The beast rose up on its hind legs and bellowed, affording Emiel a clear view of fangs as long as any of his fingers. Emiel forced his stomach to keep from lurching at the sound of cracking and popping bones. The animal's legs jerked and twitched, its head tilting to one side. It took a clumsy step toward Emiel, and as it did, it grew a bit taller.

"What in the name of the blasted underworld is this thing?" Emiel continued to retreat step by step as the beast struggled toward him. Emiel's nostrils flared as he concentrated on accessing the essences again. When the beast opened its maw, instead of a roar, it growled as four fangs in its upper and lower mouth extended until they were as long as Emiel's head.

"How is this thing still alive?" Emiel murmured as he watched the thing's ears lengthen, its body thicken with even more muscle all the while flames licked up and down its torso. It held its paws out, pads facing upward as each claw elongated with nails as long as Emiel's forearm.

"No." Emiel started to back away faster. "Oh, no. No no no. A bear wasn't bad enough. This had to be a bearverin. A Fallen-cursed bearverin." Emiel almost let slip the thought of what could possibly be worse? He killed that thought before it could fully sound off in his mind, lest this cursed place offer just that.

It rose to its full fifteen feet and let out a bellow that made Emiel's chest vibrate. The fearsome beast looked at him with large predatory eyes that made his legs buckle.

The bearverin stalked toward him as if the flames covering its body were little more than another layer of fur. Emiel's legs continued to wobble as he backed away. The icy claw of fear gripping his heart gave way to terror, and threatened to strangle his last bit of courage. Part of him wanted to find the edge of the platform —if he was still on it—and jump off. A fall to his death would be better than being ripped apart and devoured by this horror.

Amiya. Nandi. As repulsive as the idea was, Emiel forced himself to imagine that it was his daughters standing before this thing. He visualized them as the focus of the bearverin's enraged gaze.

His lips wrinkled in anger, his hands balled into fists, and the essences leaped to his call and filled him. He sprinted toward the bearverin, and the animal dropped to all fours and charged. The two closed the distance between them quickly, and the bearverin swiped a huge claw that would have sliced cleanly through a tree.

Without a thought about what he was doing, Emiel brought his left arm up as a layer of solid stone grew up its length. Sparks flashed as the claws skipped off the stone, and even then, they scored the surface. The force of the swipe rattled Emiel's teeth and sent him into a sideways flip.

Whether through force of will or simple desperation, Emiel held the presence of mind to chop his right hand outward while still airborne.

A thin sheet of ice extended from his flat hand. The edge of the frozen sheet might have been honed on a blacksmith's anvil, for it sheered easily through the tops of the bearverin's ears.

Emiel hit the ground as the monster threw its head back in an angry howl. "Urgh," he grunted when he landed on his sore ribs again. He curled his right arm back and thrust his still flat hand forward. The flat ice that had extended from his hand, stretched and narrowed into a spear tip. The bearverin's roar choked off into a gurgle when the ice spear took it in the mouth. The monster bit down on the weapon and shattered it in a spray of shards and blood.

Emiel briefly forgot about his broken arm and started to prop himself up, only to hiss in pain and fall onto his back. He forced himself up into a sitting position and felt the ground beneath him start to creep up his body. Rational thought had long fled, so before he could think of what was happening, he pointed at the monster with his good arm. Rock slid over his body and shot from his arm in a geyser. Emiel aimed for the bearverin's face and willed the assault to intensify.

The bearverin lowered its head and powered through the bombardment, making its way steadily closer. Emiel delved *water*, and combined it with *earth*. The rocky stream turned into mud, which quickly filled the monster's eyes, nose, and mouth. It slipped and toppled over as the mud fell around it.

Emiel delved *air* and *water* while the bearverin coughed and blew mud out of its nose. Water collected in front of him, and Emiel envisioned the floating water as a thin trickle. He then envisioned air as cold as the coldest winter night and surrounded the thin stream of water with it. The water froze into a spear twice as long as Emiel's body.

He made a throwing motion. The spear of ice shot into the monster's face with such force it fell backwards into the darkness. Many nervous heartbeats passed before Emiel allowed himself to breathe. He growled against the pulsing pain in his arm and ribs, and climbed back to his feet. For many nervous moments he stared at what he hoped was the lifeless lump of his vicious adversary.

The flames lighting the monster's body winked out and cast Emiel into complete darkness. Just as he thought to try delving fire to light the area, a circle of light shattered the darkness. Emiel shielded his eyes against the sudden brightness swirling like a whirlpool merely a dozen paces away. He sighed with relief at the realization that he'd defeated the bearverin werebeast. Now, maybe he could finally be gone from this horrible place.

Emiel shook his head. "Not without my friends—" he'd barely gotten the words out of his mouth when his feet swept out from under him and he flew toward the swirling light. He hollered as he entered the light in a blinding flash that ejected him into a meadow surrounded by mountains.

For a mercy, he hit the ground on his right side. He tried to roll with the fall as best he could to avoid hitting his broken arm and tender ribs. When he finally stopped, he just lay on his stomach, the left side of his face buried in wildflowers.

Exhausted, Emiel lay there for a time, smelling the sweet

aroma of the wildflowers in his face. He closed his eyes. The fight with the bearverin left him so spent, he barely felt the wave of pain that came from his left side with each weary breath. Now that his adrenaline ebbed and fatigue descended, Emiel thought his body must weigh ten times normal. He must have had the Creator's own luck with him, having managed to kill that thing before succumbing to his injuries and exertion. *Need rest. Just for a while.* Just as the bliss of sleepy oblivion claimed him, warm breath puffed next to his ear.

8

EMIEL

Baaa ah ah ah ah ah. Brrraaa ah ah ah ah ah. Whooomf. Whooomf.

Emiel scrunched his face and shrugged away from the loud hot wind in his ear. "Mmph. Uh mmmph."

Brrra ah ah ah ah. Baaaaa ah ah ah ah ah. Whooomf.

"Umph. What …" Emiel felt another whoosh of hot moist air on the side of his face. What was that sound? Whoosh. Something hard nudged his side. Brraaa ah ah ah. *Not air*, he realized. *Hot breath.* The smell of heavily masticated grass hit his nostrils as soon as the realization came.

Emiel cracked an eye open and was greeted by an up-close view of a narrow mouth with small teeth that seemed to grin at him while grinding a mouthful of grass. Braaa ah ah ah ah. Emiel let out a relieved sigh. Bighorn sheep.

He started to roll onto his right side and prop himself up, but winced and lay on his back. The sheep flinched away and lowered its head, brandishing the backward curling horns growing from its forehead. Emiel lay on his back and simultaneously laughed and winced in pain. "So, this is how I go? I kill a bearverin and end up being taken down by a sheep?"

Brraaa ah ah ah ah. The bighorn sheep raised its head again and watched him. Emiel carefully sat up, and he and the sheep remained where they were, staring at each other across the ten feet between them.

"Look, buddy," Emiel said. "I don't want trouble. I know you could butt me clean out of this meadow and I'd probably be dead before I hit the ground. I just want to sit here for a while and try not fall unconscious. After that, this place is yours again. He pulled free a handful of grass and offered it. The horned sheep continued to stare at him while it sideways chewed the same mouthful of grass since it had found him.

Emiel dropped his hand and looked around at the green and yellow grass splashed with pink, yellow, and orange wildflowers. He first thought he must be at the base of a mountain, for it was so close he could walk for only a few minutes to reach it. He looked around and saw that he was surrounded by mountains. "I'm *in* the mountains. How did I get up here? And where is here?"

Brraaa ah ah ah ah.

Emiel looked back to the sheep. "Oh, no thanks. I don't need a ride. Just keep eating."

A breeze passed through the little meadow. It wrapped around Emiel, informing him that he was, in fact, very high up, and that he was not, in fact, wearing any warm layers.

"Whew." He hugged himself against the cold and looked at the sheep again. "You're lucky you have a built-in wool coat. It's kinda cold up here." He looked around again. As beautiful as it was, he needed to get moving. He didn't know where everyone else was, and the last thing he wanted was to be caught up here at night with no shelter. He glanced up at the sun and saw that it was still morning. "What to do now?"

The bighorn sheep lowered its head and dug at the ground. Brrraaaa ah ah ah. Emiel slowly raised himself into a crouch. "Woah, woah, buddy. Something I said?" The sheep raised its head, looked past Emiel, then spun about and ran off.

Emiel sighed. He didn't want to look behind him but he had to. "What now?" He turned around and saw a figure walking toward him. Another gust of wind blew in his face, carrying the smell of death and rot. Emiel concentrated on the essences. He forced himself through the pain in his arm and left ribcage, and the scratches across his chest, arms, and legs.

The power came hesitantly and he grasped at it, drawing in as much as he could. *Earth* came the easiest, but a small bit of the other three trickled in as well. "Okay," he called out to the approaching figure. "I'm guessing you must live here and you're coming over to welcome me with cheese, ale, and hazelnuts." The figure said nothing, so Emiel climbed to his feet. *I must cut an intimidating figure on these wobbly legs.*

Emiel squinted at the approaching figure, trying to appear puzzled as he continued to build the essences. They grew inside him, little by little. He hoped this person wasn't an essence wielder, or at least wasn't a powerful one, but he had a suspected that wasn't the case. The terrible smell of death and rot, and the general feeling of uneasiness that intensified as it drew closer made him sure of that.

I'm in no condition to fight, he thought. But he had to. "You live up here?"

Before the figure got close enough for him to make out any distinct features, it started to circle around him. Emiel remained facing the other person until they finally stopped; right in front of the sun.

Emiel shielded his eyes with his hand. "Well, if you're not going to talk, I'll be moving on." He heard a loud intake of breath, then a blissful exhalation. The figure let its head fall back and spread its arms and inhaled again.

"Aaaah," it sighed.

A chill went down Emiel's spine. The loud, deep baritone of the voice barely sounded human. He took a step back.

The figure shielded its eyes as it looked at the sky. "How many years, centuries, millennia have passed since I've smelled the fresh, fragile air? How long since I've felt the fragile ground beneath my feet?"

Emiel frowned. *What* ... His frown fell away as the feeling of sickness spread. Even the air between them seemed to shrink away in terror. The ground beneath the figure's feet looked parched and dead. Emiel was sure there had been grass and flowers there a moment earlier, but now it was dead earth, starting at the cloaked figure's feet and winding away, back in the direction they'd come from.

Not knowing what else to do, Emiel tried to flood himself with as much of the essences as he could, as quickly as he could. The effort was agonizingly slow.

The figure's responding chuckle felt like death itself laughing. "Mmmm. The sweetness of pure essence, even if it is a pathetically small amount. I cannot recall the last time I've smelled it. What do you plan to do with that, little man?"

Little? Emiel said nothing, just continued to build up the power inside.

"Hm hm hm hm hm hm. You aren't planning to battle me with such a paltry command of the power, are you?" The figure took another step forward, giving Emiel an unwanted view of a face that looked like a burned map, charred-looking, and covered in deep creases.

A confident grin stretched across the lines and cracks on his leathery skin, a dry ravine splitting a sun-parched desert.

Emiel looked up into a pair of eyes as black as the darkness in the Maze he'd just escaped. *This isn't good at all.* Somehow he knew that even if he hadn't been injured he wouldn't be a match for whatever this thing was. "Look, I don't know who you are, and you don't know who I am. How about we just part ways. You can enjoy whatever it was you haven't experienced in a bunch of years, and I'm off to find my way down this mountain."

The man tilted his hairless head. "I confess I'm intrigued at your ability to conquer the Maze. There hasn't been a single record of such an instance. Countless bodies populate the space below the pathways."

Emiel's curiosity got the better of him. "The space below the pathways? Don't you mean the bottom?"

"If there is a bottom," he said in a voice like stone grinding against stone, "it is known to none." He tapped a leathery cracked finger to his cheek. Everything about this man looked like death. "I am curious how a man with such a minuscule knowledge and command of the essences survived the Maze, let alone conquer it. Such a feat I could not achieve in the endless time I've spent imprisoned within."

"Maybe talk that up with the ones who imprisoned you there?" Emiel suggested. He wanted to take another step back, maybe turn and run, but he couldn't make himself do it. Besides, how fast could he be with a broken arm and injured ribs? He tried to appear confident despite the fact that he was in trouble.

"I intend to do just that after I've dealt with you."

Those last words let Emiel know he had no hope of talking his way out of this. He struck with all the power he had in him. He blasted the man with a cone of fire, then struck with several spears of ice, and used his remaining energy to delve *earth*.

All around the cloaked man, stalagmites sprang from the ground. They angled at his back, front, and sides. All exploded as though they'd hit an invisible barrier.

The last bit of fiery ashes winked out, and the dust and debris settled to reveal the man standing at ease, an amused expression coloring his twisted features. "An admirable effort. I appreciate your lack of cowardice despite your inadequacy. In appreciation of that, and your freeing me from my endless incarceration, I will make your death quick and relatively painless."

Emiel's heart fluttered when he felt the massive amounts of power building and flowing into a shining ring on the finger of the man's left hand. He tried to reach for the essences and barely succeeded in grasping *earth.* He may as well be holding a butter knife against a swordsman.

"Such is my gratitude," the man said, his deep, grating voice sounding over the suddenly galeforce wind whipping about the meadow, "that I will even leave nothing of your corpse for the scavengers to feed upon. I will leave only a scar upon the earth to serve as your epitaph."

A swirling flash of light split the air to the side, and out rolled Lief. The tinfar woman rolled to a crouch, looked at the man across from Emiel, and hissed.

The sheer rage on the tiny woman's face took Emiel aback. He'd never seen her like this before. "Abomination," she shouted.

Stalagmites burst from the ground around the man. With a swipe of his hand, he blasted them apart, then swept his other hand in an arc behind him. A chunk of rock that Lief had sent speeding toward him split apart and landed on either side. Before they stopped sliding on the ground, they lifted in the air and crashed into him from both sides. Or would have—for they exploded before impact.

Emiel used the little strength remaining to him and struck with *earth* and *fire,* spreading the latter's namesake into a formless blast of fire that engulfed his enemy.

Laughter rolled over the cacophony. The ground rumbled and Emiel fell to his knees. He gritted his teeth against the waves of pain rippling his body and tried to stand. On the other side of the man, Lief knelt and touched the ground. The tremors settled.

"So, the secret is revealed," the man said. "You had the aid of an *e'ta* tinfar. Curious indeed." He struck at Lief with a wall of fire so quickly, Emiel knew he would have been incinerated if he'd been the target. How could he manipulate the essences so quickly?

Lief proved equally as fast. The tinfar raised a wall of stone between herself and the flames. The man continued to blast the wall just as Lief sent it speeding at him. For the first time, the man looked like he had to expend an effort. He broke off his attack and sidestepped the speeding slap of stone.

The enraged tinfar launched stalagmites and boulders at him. She raised a chunk of earth from the ground and dropped it on his head, then, when he burst the rock apart, she sent it arcing around and streaming into his back.

Another blinding swirl of light split the air several paces away from Lief. In the storm of dust and debris, Emiel was barely able to make out billowing robes. A powerful blast of the essences clued Emiel in to Amoura's presence.

Her magus robes flapping in the wind, Amoura Xanna threw gouts of flame, walls of rock, and sheets and spears of ice at the man. A cloud of dust parted, giving Emiel a glimpse of black braids whipping about in front of a baleful gray glare.

Amoura strode through the chaos and made another gesture. A storm of stalagmites rose from the ground and zipped past her toward their enemy.

The stone spears exploded before they got close. The man snarled and threw his hands out at his sides, then clapped them together. Emiel fell over and clamped his hands over his ears. The air itself sounded as though it exploded, and Emiel thought his ears would do the same.

Another swirl of light opened right beside the man, and an instant later, Bone fell through. The mercenary hit the ground and sprawled onto his stomach. With a groan, he looked up and saw the horrid face staring down at him in surprise. Bone barked out a cry of surprise and simultaneously snatched his sword from its sheath and swept it at the man's ankles.

The cloaked essence wielder hopped back just as a stalagmite burst out of the ground behind him. The sharp tip of the stone angled at his back and struck true. The man let out a booming cry of mingled pain and rage. The stone spear exploded and the fragments raced toward Lief.

Bone leapt to his feet and threw himself at the man. His sword was a blur that cut the air in every direction as the mercenary tried to use the surprise injury to his advantage.

The man's hands were equally swift. Every swipe of Bone's sword was met with a skinny column of stone that shot up from the ground. Emiel watched in pure amazement before he snapped out of it and tried to access the essences and help the mercenary.

Several more stalagmites burst up from the ground behind the man and drove through his back. His responding shout echoed across the meadow. The stalagmites burst apart and the stone piercing his torso crumbled away.

Little more than trickles of blood flowed from the puncture holes inflicted by the stone. *No time to worry about it now.* Emiel struck out with a stream of fire that wouldn't have burned more than the wildflowers in front of him. His energy was sapped, his body worn out.

The man dealt Bone a backhand to the side of the head. As Bone stumbled away, the man shoved him further, then sent a barrage of ice spears speeding into him. If he'd been wearing steel armor, those spears would have skewered him. But teliak bones were nearly indestructible.

Still, the force of the rapid-fire assault jerked Bone around like a cloth doll. All the staggered young warrior could do was shield his head from the bombardment until he finally tumbled over.

Amoura and Lief attacked in unison. The magus hurled balls of fire and ice at the man, while Lief hurled boulders and raised the ground around him and dropped it on his head.

Concentration replaced the smug grin on the man's wrinkled face. He picked off every one of their attacks, but barely.

Emiel tried to find the essences again. If he could do anything at all, it might tip the balance in their favor.

"We will continue this another day," the man's voice boomed through the thunderous exchange. "I promise this."

While still fending off Amoura and Lief, he rose into the air.

Lief cried out in rage. The ground lifted underneath the man and formed into a huge stalagmite. It shot straight up for him.

Emiel winced. If it struck true, the result would have been messy. The man waved a hand in the direction of the stalagmite and it shattered. He blew apart several more of Amoura's ice and fireballs, and rose higher into the air until finally disappearing in the sky.

For a long time, the four companions didn't move. Everyone stared at the sky in silence. With the battle ended, Emiel's injuries demanded his attention again. He groaned when the full weight of the pain in his arm returned. The scars from the claws of the bearverin burned as well. He lifted himself up on the elbow of his good arm and looked around.

Lief practically glared at the sky. Her teeth were bared, her disheveled clay-red hair sitting wildly about her head. Despite her height, she cut an intimidating figure just then.

Amoura's tense posture spoke volumes about their foe. She stood turned at the waist, looking over her right shoulder, her right arm crossed over her midsection. The essence ring on one of the curled fingers of her right hand pulsated. Though not on the edge of rage like Lief, the intensity in her steel-colored eyes made her both fearsome and beautiful.

A groan drew his attention to Bone. The mercenary rolled onto his back. His chest rose and fell as he tried to catch his breath. "That was brutal." He sounded as exhausted as Emiel felt. "Wouldn't mind never seeing him again."

"Couldn't agree more," Emiel replied. He hissed through his teeth as he pushed himself upright. His ribs and arm screamed at him. "I take it our escape opened the portal for one of the Fallen?" He shook his head. "That's all we need."

"That wasn't a Fallen," Amoura said. Her quiet voice cut through the air like dagger in the night. "That was a droughtlord."

"A *what*?" Emiel asked. "There's something more powerful than a Fallen?"

"If that's the case," Bone said, rolling onto his hands and knees. "I'd say they're not as tough as the legends suggest. Not that that guy was a pushover."

Amoura finally straightened and ran a hand through her braided hair. "Droughtlords serve the Fallen. If it had been his master we fought, we would be dead."

Emiel's mouth fell open. He glanced over at Bone to see the mercenary's mouth equally agape. "That guy was a servant?" the spicetrader exclaimed. "A *servant*?"

"An abomination," Lief growled. "An affront to the natural world, the essences, and life itself. They are an insult to creation."

"I don't think she likes them," Bone muttered, finally climbing to his feet.

"No," Lief snapped. "I don't. No living thing should be re-created into something else. It is wrong. The existence of *g'mor-shru* is an affront to existence itself."

Bone walked over to Emiel and helped him to his feet as Amoura and Lief approached. Lief finally pulled her baleful gaze from the sky to give Emiel a onceover. "Your Maze trial must have been really bad. You look awful."

"Much appreciated," Emiel said dryly.

Amoura inspected his arm without touching it. She pressed her lips together when she saw the torn away sleeve, puncture marks in his skin, and the crushed bone. She looked up at him with an unfamiliar expression of concern. "Do we have any food left?"

"Only some jerky and a few root vegetables," Bone answered.

Amoura looked from Emiel's arm to their surroundings. "We're in the mountains somewhere. We need to find shelter for the night," she looked into Emiel's eyes, "and for you to heal."

"Heal?" Emiel asked. "I think it's going to take longer than a night for this to heal." He refrained from looking at his arm, as the pain was nearly unbearable. Just thinking of it made his head spin.

"I will help with that." Amoura looked to Bone. "Would you hunt for food while I work on him?"

Bone glanced from Amoura to Emiel several times and a tiny grin spread across his face. "But of course."

Amoura narrowed her eyes. "Get out of here, mercenary."

The young warrior held his hands up defensively. "Now, now, no need to be so feisty. I'll give you two your time. Off I go."

The magus glared at Bone's back as he crossed the meadow and hiked over a rocky hill. Emiel stared after him, not in a glare, but hoping the mercenary wouldn't come across and slaughter the bighorn sheep he'd met earlier.

"It would be best if you lie down," Amoura said.

Emiel complied, gingerly easing himself down on his side while groaning the entire way. Amoura placed a hand on his back and helped him to the ground. The flowery bed of grass felt somewhat soft under his back.

While Amoura circled around to his left side, he watched a few puffy white clouds drift across the blue sky. This would have been a nice way to relax under better circumstances, like not having been chewed up by a werewood monster.

"What did this to you?" Amoura asked.

The soft tone of shock in her voice reminded Emiel that he hadn't had the chance to inspect his arm. He thought it best he didn't do so now, and continued staring up at the sky. "Bearverin." He heard Lief's intake of breath from his right, and the magus's sigh on his left.

"You're tougher than you let on, spicetrader," Amoura said.

Emiel turned his head to see her faintly smiling at him. "I really had the thing beat early on. I just had to make it look good so they wouldn't throw other challenges at me." She snorted at that, and he grinned.

"Humans are odd," Lief said. "You're all mangled up and you still make jokes?"

"Thanks for reminding me of my condition."

"What, you are pretty beaten up, Emiel? You're all slashed up and your arm—"

"I don't think he needs to hear about his injuries in detail," Amoura thankfully interrupted.

"He doesn't?" Lief asked. Her tone reflected pure innocence. "Why not?"

"It will increase his discomfort," the magus replied.

Emiel felt a warm sensation traveling up his arm. "Mmm. That feels good."

"Only for a moment," Amoura replied. "Then it will hurt."

Emiel couldn't imagine his arm hurting any more than it already did, and this small comfort was a relief. When the pain did hit, it hit hard. He sucked in a breath and nearly sat up on reflex.

Amoura placed a hand on his forehead and the other on his chest, and pressed him down. Warmth radiated from her hand and washed down his head, face, neck, and into his chest. It felt like bathing in warmth instead of a hot bath. The pain in his arm was still there, but more distant.

He turned his head just enough to see Amoura studying his arm. Her braids hung over her face, obscuring her features, but he saw her fatigue through the gaps. Just then, he wondered what trial she'd had to face to escape the Maze. If it was anything as trying as his had been, followed by dealing with the droughtlord, she must be ready to sleep for days.

She smelled of rose petals after a fresh rain, and perspiration. Whether it was the power she used in his healing, or just her closeness, Emiel felt himself relaxing further.

"I, um, think I should check on the Bone boy," Lief said.

Emiel frowned. Why did she sound so shy?

"I'll make sure he doesn't kill half the mountain's animals," she continued.

"You're not going to disappear for another few days, are you?" Emiel asked. Every time the tinfar woman left, he felt her absence deeply. He hadn't realized how much of a lifeline she'd been to him during the times in Carlayn and Altarra when she'd not been by his side.

Lief's face blocked out the sky when it suddenly appeared over his. Her dark brown eyes twinkled when she smiled at him. "I'll be back after you've eaten. I promise. She glanced past him at Amoura, he guessed, then looked back at him with an unreadable expression. "See you later."

Before Emiel could say anything more, she was gone. *Feels like everyone's in on a secret I don't know.*

"Your tinfar friend is a strange one," Amoura said. Oddly, her tone sounded softer, now. "She gives me strange looks from time to time, as though studying me." Emiel winced at a shooting pain up his arm. Amoura's warm palm on his forehead felt like bliss mingled with agony. "Try to relax. I'll be done soon."

Emiel closed his eyes. "You have any idea where we are?"

"If we're still in the region of Jietar," she replied, "we are either somewhere on the Sleeping Morghan, Mount Blood, or the Ridgeline. The lack of blood-red rock rules out Mount Blood, so it would be either of the latter."

Emiel listened and enjoyed the uncharacteristic softness to her voice. "Hopefully we're somewhere on the Ridgeline. It's close to the divide between Altarra and Vyne and we could cut across. If the girls aren't in Altarra yet, we might still intercept them."

"Have you thought about the possibility that your daughters aren't coming to Altarra?"

Emiel sensed hesitance in her voice despite her steady tone. He appreciated her strength while treading such a delicate subject.

"They might have fled to the closest town, or found passage to Carlayn," the magus explained.

Emiel was shaking his head before she finished. "You haven't met those two. Nandi would be determined to rescue me." He snorted. "And Amiya? Well, let's just say she'd be even more determined."

"She's the spirited one?" Amoura asked.

"Fiery is more the word I'd use."

"It's good that they have each other," Amoura said. "Traversing the wilds to distant places among strangers can be unnerving for an adult. Far worse for a child."

Emiel chuckled. "Those two together are quite a force. They've been a lot to keep up with even when they were very young. They're good girls, though. They've never given me any real problems aside from the normal child stuff. They look out for me as if I can't take care of myself, but more importantly, they look out for each other."

Amoura's hand relaxed on his head for an instant, then she reapplied the pressure. "They sound like lovely girls and good sisters to each other."

"You have any sisters?" Emiel asked.

"No. I … yes, but she died."

"Oh. I'm sorry, Amoura—"

"I never met her," she continued. "I only know of her through my parents, and a family portrait of them and my sister that was painted before I was born. We obviously aren't twins, as she was seven years old when the painting was created, but she looked very much like me at the same age. My parents said the painting captured her perfectly."

Emiel listened as the magus spoke. It was the most she'd talked to him at one time, and far more personal. Without the usual iron in her voice, she almost sounded like a different person.

"She died when my parents were caught in the middle of a skirmish between Marai soldiers and a band of Khatala. They never found her body."

Emiel didn't know what to say. "Do you think maybe they were just separated and never found each other?"

The hardness returned. "Then, she would likely have wished she had died on that battlefield. I don't pretend to know what the Khatala would have done with her, and men drunk on the bloodlust of battle …"

She left the rest of that thought hanging, and Emiel thought it best to as well. "I never did thank you for saving my life all the times you did on the road to Altarra." It sounded ridiculous, but he couldn't think of anything else to say."

"I was tasked to deliver you safe and whole to the magi master," came the stiff reply. "It was … my job."

Despite the truth of it, Emiel found he couldn't hold any anger toward the woman anymore. "I know."

"You were … a brave and easy charge to protect. I wish I hadn't been tasked to do that. I will do everything in my power to help you find your beautiful daughters, Emiel."

Her hand moved from his forehead to slide over his shaved head. For several fluttering heartbeats, she stroked his bare scalp. Emiel closed his eyes and tried not to breathe for fear of appearing to enjoy the caress too much. Her hands were soft and surprisingly gentle. Maybe in a few days he'd break his other arm.

"Emiel."

"Mmm."

"Ah, em. Emiel."

"Hmm?"

"If you grin any wider, you'll injure your face."

"Oh!" He popped his eyes open, expecting to see Amoura rolling her eyes at him. He saw instead, a furrowed brow above a tiny smile. Her hauntingly beautiful gray eyes looked down on him with a subtle mix of affection and sarcasm. "It just felt … comforting, that's all. I mean, the pain, and the warmth radiating … it just helps with the pain."

She rubbed his head again. Emiel fought not to let slip a blissful sigh and embarrass himself further.

"You're a kind man, Emiel Dharr. We will find your Amiya and Nandi."

"How do you know they're beautiful?"

"What?" Her hand stopped moving.

"You said my girls were beautiful. You've never seen them."

"All children are beautiful."

Emiel opened his eyes and stared at her, and to his surprise, she chuckled. "Their father isn't overly difficult to look at, and I imagine their mother must be striking."

"Ah," Emiel closed his eyes again. "Well, you're not wrong. Their mother was the most beautiful woman I'd ever seen. She stood barely taller than my shoulder and wore her hair in a black puff at the back of her head. She had a way of looking at you that let you know she could see everything she needed to know about you. One of the things you two have in common."

"She sounds like a lovely woman," Amoura replied.

"She was."

"Was?"

"Yeah. She left this world shortly after giving birth to our girls."

Amoura laid her other hand on his arm. To his surprise, he found her touch not painful, but comforting. Warmth passed into and through his arm, and he realized the bone had knit back together.

"I'm sorry, Emiel. That sounds heartbreaking. She never got to meet her own daughters."

"She did," Emiel replied. "Only for a few moments, but she did." Tears trickled out of the corners of his closed eyes and ran down the sides of his face.

Amoura's grip on his arm tightened. "What other things?"

She waited patiently while Emiel swallowed the lump in his throat. He finally spoke when he trusted his voice not to come out in a croak. "Other things?"

"You said her way of looking at someone was one of the things we have in common. What other things do we have in common?"

Emiel wasn't sure how he wanted to answer that question. He had said what he had before he'd been able to think and filter his words. "I—"

Her hands quickly moved away.

Emiel blinked through the tears as he forced his eyes open and looked for Amoura. The magus was standing over him, looking down at his arm with satisfaction. The warmth she'd shown earlier had fled as quickly as the sun's warmth would in these mountains come nightfall. He looked past her and saw Bone returning with several rabbits and what looked like a few large lizards strung over his shoulder.

"Aw, ain't that quaint," the mercenary called from across the meadow. "The spicetrader and the magus sharing a tender moment. You two manage to sneak in a little cuddle time while I was gone?"

"Thank you for hunting food," Amoura replied. "Now that I'm finished with the healing, I'll find wood for a fire."

"Actually, I can go." Emiel flexed the fingers of his healed arm. It was still sore, but amazingly no longer broken.

"I will go," Amoura insisted. Her tone brooked no room for argument. "Get the meat prepared. I won't be long."

Emiel nodded. "Amoura," he said when the magus turned to go. She looked over her shoulder, affection gone, steel returned. "Thank you for healing me."

She stared at him for several moments. As with the first time he'd met her, the woman's eyes, in striking contrast to her dark complexion, made it difficult to hold her gaze. He forced himself to do it, though.

A tiny flicker of affection came and went. It happened so fast, he almost missed it. "You are welcome, Emiel Dharr."

9

EMIEL

Nighttime in the mountains turned out to be the exact opposite of the warm crisp day that had long fled the meadow. Emiel pulled his travel cloak in close and tried to stop shivering. It might have helped if it wasn't riddled with slashes and the right sleeve wasn't torn off.

"There's a crook in the mountain just there," Lief said, pointing ahead.

Emiel tried to shrink further into his cloak. The wind blew nonstop, slithering through every hole in his tattered garment. He tried to remember what it was like to be warm, but the memory proved more fleeting than any comfort his cloak provided under these conditions.

Bone's teliak armor seemed to offer the mercenary some protection from the cold, and his travel cloak was in better condition than Emiel's. Of the four of them, Bone and Lief came out of their trials with no physical signs of struggle. Emiel managed to forget the cold long enough to wonder what trials the mercenary and tinfar woman had faced. Perhaps more psychological?

He glanced at Amoura. She had her robes wrapped around her similarly to Emiel, and wore the cowl on her head as well. Despite the exhaustion he'd seen in her face after their battle with the droughtlord, and the crisscrossing winds pounding at them from either side, the magus walked with the gait of a queen. He couldn't imagine anything that could break Amoura Xanna, which made her all the more intriguing. What adversity had she faced in her younger years to hone the unbreakable will of the woman now walking beside him?

They reached the crook in the mountain wall and settled in for the night. It provided good protection from the wind until it shifted direction, which was constantly.

"Good thing about this shelter," Bone said, "is that it blocks the wind. Bad thing about it is that it doesn't block the wind."

"Feels like a tease," Emiel agreed. He looked at the base of the mountain for a while, and an idea struck him. If he could use *earth* to pull huge chunks of stone from the ground and shape it into walls or stalagmites, maybe he could form a dome around them to block out the cold.

Moments passed as he concentrated on finding the essence. He did little more than just that, for every time he tried to grab hold, it slipped away.

"You look like you're trying to do something that requires you leaving camp and digging a hole, spicetrader."

Emiel opened his eyes and glared at the mercenary, who grinned back at him. "Well, I'm trying to build us a shelter from the wind."

"Oh, is *that* what you were doing?"

Emiel ignored him and turned to Amoura. "I can't find the essences. Think you can?"

The magus shook her head. "We were extremely lucky the droughtlord fled when he did. My ring and my strength is depleted. I must replenish it first."

"Oh, is that what you need?" Lief's tiny voice reflected not a bit of discomfort. "I'm sorry. I forget that humans aren't connected to the earth in the same way."

Lief never moved from her cross-legged seat as the ground rumbled, then rose in a semicircular wall to enclose them against the crook of the mountain. The wall continued to rise, then arced overhead to form a dome. The stone stopped with a two-foot circular opening in the ceiling, allowing fresh air to flow in.

"Cozy," Bone said, inspecting the stone dome with a carpenter's appreciation. "Thanks, little lady."

Amoura gave a smiling nod of thanks and sat cross-legged with her back against the mountain. After a few measured breaths, she closed her eyes.

"Thanks, Lief," Emiel murmured.

"What's wrong?" the tinfar asked.

"Frustrated," he replied. "The only time I seem able to use the essences is when my life is in danger. And even then, sometimes I can't grab hold of them."

Lief responded almost before he finished talking. "Yup. You just told me the cause of your problem."

Emiel ran through what he'd said again, but found nothing unusual. "I don't understand."

"You're trying to find, or grab hold of the essences," Lief said. "That's where your problems are coming from."

"How else am I supposed to use them?"

"By not *using* them at all," the tiny woman said, a bit of impatience in her tone. "The power isn't something you just grab and wield like a tool, even though that's what a lot of you humans do." She stole a disapproving glance at Amoura. "The power is an elemental thing, Emiel. It's part of this world in much the same way that the blood in your veins and the spirit energy in your body is part of you.

"Do you grab hold of water when you drink? You might get a little collected in your hand, but not enough to quench your thirst. You cup your hands in it, or if it's a running stream, you sip from it or use something to guide it to your mouth. The essences are just as insubstantial."

"Which is why I rely on good solid steel," Bone said. He patted the sword lying across his lap.

Lief pointed at the boy as if he'd made her point for her. "Weapon. That's my meaning. Humans only see things …" she shook her head. "You have to think of the essences as a part of life, not a tool or weapon. That's why the Khatala humans are able to delve without the use of the stone rings you use."

Emiel glanced at Amoura. The magus still sat cross-legged and erect with her eyes closed.

"Those rings," Lief continued. "I can feel what they do because they're made of the earth. That kind of stone is the only thing in the world that's so charged with the essences that they can be used to attract them."

Emiel thought on that. "So, the stones attract the essences?"

Lief nodded. "When humans discovered that, they learned how to use the rock to channel the power and *mold* it."

Emiel was taken aback by Lief's obvious disdain. He tried to see it from her point of view and understand why it was a bad thing to use anything as a tool, so long as it was used for good purposes. It might be bad to use the tool to destroy, but not everyone used it that way. "Sounds like you don't approve."

"It's why my people stay away," Lief said in a regretful voice. "We used to be open with humans, but not for a long time."

"Why not?" Bone asked. "What changed?"

Lief stared at her hands folded in her lap. Her voice went quiet, and Emiel had to strain to hear.

"When you discovered a way to use trees, what did you do?"

"Build homes to protect us from the elements and fires to keep us warm and cook our food," Bone answered without hesitation.

"And spears," Lief added. "And those things you build to hurl huge pieces of rock and balls of fire at each other." She sighed. "What did you do when you learned how to make steel, or fire?"

The mercenary patted his hand in the air. "We get it, tinfar. Humans are terrible and evil and exploitative."

"If that were completely true, I wouldn't be here, young human."

Bone frowned and grumbled under his breath.

Lief sighed. "I don't mean to talk down on you or your species. I'm telling you what the others you share this world with think of you."

"Other tinfar?" Emiel asked.

"More than tinfar."

Emiel's eyes widened. "There's more than just you?"

She laughed. "If you want to defend yourself with the essences, my friend, you'll need to build a relationship with them beyond wrestling them into submission. They're too powerful for that. Or you could just use a stone," she waved a hand in Amoura's direction. The magus's left eyebrow twitched. "Honestly, you don't need one, though. You share the same connection with the earth as the Khatala humans."

Emiel thought about the tinfar's words long into the night while the others slept. He had no reason to disbelieve his friend's words, which ultimately led to more questions. How did one have a relationship with an insubstantial force? Apparently the Khatala had done such a thing, but weren't they born that way? And even if they were, through effort, could a Marailander use the power at least to some degree?

Few answers and more questions. Emiel lay on his back and stared through the opening in the stone dome. At this altitude, the stars looked close enough that he could reach up and grab them. The girls would love this, having never been in the mountains before. He could see them in his mind's eye, sitting with their legs out in front of them, propped up on their elbows and staring at the stars so close in front of their faces for hours. Nandi would verbalize her awe, while the equally amazed Amiya would have teased her for it.

He shuffled to get comfortable on his back, and closed his eyes. "Watch out for each other, ladygirls," he whispered. "Keep each other safe until I find you."

*a.

EMIEL AWOKE to warm sunlight on his face mingled with the chilly breeze of early morning. He cracked his eyes open to see everyone else already up and about. Bone had apparently gone hunting again. He crouched over a cookfire a short distance away, roasting some sort of meat.

He looked around until he spotted Amoura. She stood at the far end of the meadow, a small figure in the distance with her arms open at her side, palms facing the sky. Her posture suggested she might be in some kind of standing meditation, so Emiel decided to leave her alone.

"Hi, Emiel," Lief chirped from behind.

Still sitting on the ground, Emiel twisted around to see her leaning against the mountain. His mouth nearly hit the ground when he saw that she wasn't exactly leaning on the wall, but stuck to it. Her crossed legs hung suspended five feet from the ground. She crossed her arms over her chest and grinned at him with a little wink.

"I didn't know you could do that," Emiel mumbled.

"You seem to have slept well," Lief said.

Emiel looked back and forth to their two companions on either side of the meadow. "Maybe too well."

"Your body needed it and you listened. There will be plenty of time to not get enough sleep. You need your strength for what comes ahead."

"What would that be?" Lief shrugged, so he changed the subject. "I thought a lot about our conversation last night. I'm going to be better. I don't want to be the kind of human your people don't trust, and I don't want to exploit the power for my own gain, either. Honestly, I'd rather not use it at all."

"Stay that way and the power will never intoxicate you. You don't take it lightly. That's good."

Emiel tried to think of a careful way to ask his next question but couldn't, so he just threw it out there. "Think you would mind teaching me?"

Lief laughed. Coming from the tiny woman, it sounded more like a little girl's giggle. "I was wondering how long it would take you to ask. Of course I'll help you. We're friends! You'd help me if I asked, wouldn't you?"

"Of course," Emiel said.

"Well, remember that," Lief warned. "One day I might need your help."

"When that day comes, you'll have it," Emiel promised. The tinfar's responding smile was like a warm sunrise; warm, innocent, and genuine.

"I'll only be able to help you so far, though. There are certain things about humans I can't relate to. You'll need her help for a human perspective." She nodded in Amoura's direction.

"But, if I'm some sort of hybrid," Emiel said, "how could she help me in matters where the ring isn't used."

Lief looked across the distance at the magus with a knowing expression. "She's more than you or even she herself realizes. The way she fills her essence ring and channels them makes it so obvious."

Emiel followed Lief's gaze to where Amoura sat, wrapped in her own thoughts. "I don't understand."

Lief opened her mouth to respond when Bone's muffled footsteps interrupted her. The mercenary had several skewers of meat in hand and leaned them against a rocky part of the mountain. "Shouldn't take long for them to cool. Then I'll wrap and pack 'em up."

"Thanks, Bone," Emiel said.

"Thanks for what?" came the typical sarcastic reply. "I leave it to you, I'll starve in a short order."

"Right." Emiel said. "Well, I'm going to *hunt* for some herbs to spice up the food. Since you're such a survivalist, I'm sure you won't want any flavor for that."

"Yeah, yeah," Bone waved him away and turned back to the skewers. "Go hunt down and kill your spices, wild man. We'll be here awaiting the fruits of your spicy prowess."

Emiel felt betrayed at Lief's rather loud laughter. He quickly turned away and stalked out of the camp and past the mercenary's dead cookfire.

By midday the party had begun their hike down from the meadow, navigating around the steep slopes in favor of the more gradual ones. Once they'd gotten a clear view of the land below, Amoura determined that they were in fact in the Ridgeline mountains, west of the kingdom of Jietar, and even Altarra.

The descent was mostly easygoing, as well as the conversation along the way. Bone spoke of his highland homeland, particularly what the food and drink was like. Lief shared tidbits about her homeland and people as well, though not in any great detail. Emiel wondered if her trust in him didn't extend quite as far to the others.

As normal, Amoura rarely spoke. With a bit of nudging, she grudgingly shared parts of her past. Even that, however, was vague at best. She remained almost exclusively to the periods in her life before or after her training to become, and her life as, a magus.

Emiel tried not to glance at her as often as he felt inclined. She was easily the most aloof and mysterious person he'd ever met. She seemed to have more walls about her than a fortress.

He didn't push it, though. Not only would it do no good, but it would probably damage what progress he'd made with her so far. He wondered what the girls would think of her. If what Amoura and Vladrick had said was true, then his ladygirls would have the same use of the essences as he did. They'd need a teacher; someone all of them could trust.

Emiel liked the idea of Amoura teaching his girls how to access the essences. She might come off as cold and hard, but she'd also shown him a different side to herself. The girls would like her, and Emiel felt confident she'd like them as well.

His heart grew heavy again. He needed to find the girls before he could think about anything else. They were out there somewhere. They had to be. If something had happened, he'd have known. He'd have felt … he shook his head. Best not to let his mind travel that road. Especially considering the horror he would bring on Decius's head if something *did* happen.

No. No need to think about it, because nothing had happened to his girls and nothing *would* happen. Amoura told him they'd fled Vyne. He'd told them where he was going before he left, so they'd be on their way. And now that Emiel and the others knew they were in the Ridgeline, they would continue south, then cut across Jietar until they reached the road leading to Altarra. Once he had his ladygirls again, he could think about other things.

"You over there arguing with yourself, spicetrader?"

Emiel looked up to see Bone staring at him, a crinkled grin plastered to his freckled face. Emiel wondered if he'd ever seen anything other than sarcasm reflected in the boy's sparkling green eyes. "I am," he answered. "Trying to decide if that smell is you or not."

"Oh? What'd you end up with?"

"Probably not you. Smell isn't that strong."

The red-headed mercenary shrugged. "Must be you, then, since it's not strong enough to be a man smell."

"Do all human males spar like this?" Lief asked Amoura.

"Unfortunately, yes, in some way or another. It's how they make themselves and their companions believe they're clever."

"Nah," Bone replied. "We're just forced to find any way we can to lighten the mood in the presence of you, the Queen Solemn Grim."

"That was a witty use of so many syllables," Amoura replied. "That must have fulfilled your daily quota. Now you can be silent."

Bone shrugged. "I'll be silent when I'm done talking."

"You need air to talk."

Bone cut a narrow-eyed look at her. "You planning on cutting off my air supply?"

"It can be done easily enough."

"Well, that turned dark quickly," Emiel said. "In case you two forgot, we're kinda like friends now, remember?"

"Says you," Bone grumbled.

"No one's forcing you to be here with us, Bone," Emiel replied.

"Where in the name of the curse blasted Fallen would I go, spicetrader? In case you forgot, I got dumped in that Maze same as you."

"You could have left us to fight that droughtlord, or even after."

"Ya. Great. So I'm a coward and a monster all at once. Leave you to get killed by a droughtlord, *or* leave you to starve." Bone quickened his step down the hill and threw a hand up as he continued to fuss. "Good to know what you *think* about me."

"You know," Lief said as she watched Bone slip around a boulder a little too fast. He slid on his backside for a good dozen feet before recovering. "I've studied a good number of humans, hidden from them, mind you. I don't think I've ever seen a group who argue as much as you three."

"Practically family already," Emiel muttered.

"Human families argue like this?" The incredulous tinfar looked up at him. "Truly?"

Emiel chuckled. "Some do, and some are worse. But not all. My wife and I argued on rare occasions, but in the end, there was always love. My girls sometimes disagreed with my decisions or rules, but they obeyed. Mostly." He mumbled that last part under his breath, but Amoura's quiet snort said that she'd heard.

When grass, small trees and shrubs gave way to dusty, gravelly terrain, Emiel found himself missing the little meadow. He thought about it frequently. If not for the circumstances he'd probably have become a hermit and built a cabin up there. If he knew how to build a cabin, that is. The girls would have liked it up there, especially Amiya. Her love of flowers and pretty things belied her rather brisk personality.

Emiel smiled to himself. They were … fine. He couldn't bring himself to use the word "alive", even in his mind. Just the thought of that word in relation to his girls in this situation would crush his heart. They were all right. He didn't just need to believe it, he did. He could feel it deep inside.

"Hey, Lief," Bone called from further down. "It gets pretty rough from this point. Can you whip up some kind of plateau we could stand on and slide down?"

"You really are a cotton-headed boy, aren't you?" Lief yelled down.

Bone leaned into the gravelly slope, frowning at the tinfar in confusion as she indignantly shuffled her way past him, walking down the loose rocky terrain as though it were solid ground.

Amoura's expression remained unreadable as usual, though the tiniest flicker of amusement touched her features. Emiel figured the only reason he recognized it was because he'd spent so much time with her. Anyone else would struggle to read anything off the magus's ever-neutral features.

Bone's warning hadn't been an exaggeration. The descent from that point grew more steep, and every step saw their feet sinking into the gravel down to the ankles, and in some spots, down to their shins. Bone grumbled about this being a lot easier if *some*one could help out and maybe solidify the ground. Lief continued her leisurely walk down the slope as if she never heard a word, and Amoura picked every step carefully, her eyes darting left to right as she inspected the terrain before taking each step.

It was several hours of a slow-going hike; high stepping, stumbling, and sliding. Emiel glanced at the sky. The sun continued its smooth and lazy descent toward the western horizon as if to mock their struggle down the mountain. "I'm gonna be honest. I feel vulnerable out here. If that droughtlord decides to swing around the mountain and float over us, there wouldn't be much we could do."

"It takes a lot of effort to hold oneself aloft while wielding the other essences offensively," Amoura replied. "Even for a droughtlord."

"Guy seemed plenty powerful to me," Bone muttered.

"Even still," Amoura replied. "And he wouldn't try it now, in any case. We dealt him severe enough injuries that he's going to take a while to heal."

"Impaled and burned." Emiel shook his head. "How could anyone survive that? He should have died several times over."

"Droughtlords are created by the Fallen," Amoura explained. "They are more difficult to kill than a normal essence wielder."

"These guys more powerful than magi?" Bone asked. He stumbled when his foot sank in a deep pocket of gravel, then sneezed when a cloud of dust puffed in his face.

"There are only a handful of magi who could defeat a droughtlord alone," Amoura answered.

"You one of those few?" Bone looked at her with sincerity. "Think you could have taken that guy down if we weren't there?"

"No."

That single word sat heavily on Emiel's shoulders. Judging by the resulting quiet, he guessed the others felt the same.

"I dunno," the mercenary said. "I know you know your stuff and all and have a good gauge of what you can do, but I think you could take him. You might come out messed up and not so pretty, but I think you could have taken him."

"The most backhanded compliment I've ever heard," Emiel said. "You're getting soft."

"Ah, shut up, spicetrader," Bone shot back. "You looked like you were about to cry when he thumped you across the meadow."

"That's because I had to singlehandedly kill a bearverin first, *and* I managed to survive long enough until you all showed up. I think I did pretty good."

"That bearverin was probably about to slaughter you," Bone

countered. "But probably stopped and ran off when you started whimpering." He laughed at his own joke, by himself.

"Thank you for your confidence, mercenary," Amoura finally said. "Perhaps I'll point out that even with us there, an essence wielder of that power could have easily skewered three competent swordsmen in short order. You did well, before he curled you up into a little ball on the ground."

Emiel and Bone raised their eyebrows and looked at her. A conservative grin crept across her face. Bone must have felt as astonished as Emiel had at the joke. Lief burst into laughter, her tiny voice cackling from further down the hill.

They reached the base of the mountain as the sun reached the western horizon. Having spotted a farm not too far away, they decided to push on a little further. As usual, Lief departed before they came upon the farm.

Early into nightfall the party arrived to a wary, pitchfork-held reception. Once the farmer saw Amoura's dusty but still splendid blue-black robes, and spotted the essence ring on her finger, he nearly threw the pitchfork aside as he welcomed them into his home.

Despite Emiel's insistence on doing chores to compensate for a night and meal, the man refused. "Don't get many visitors out this way," Farmer Garlan said. "Aside from Altarra or Jietar Kingdom wantin' extra food to store over the lean season for their insatiable troops. But then, I guess they are keepin' us safe 'n' all."

"That they do," his wife, Maralyn said from the kitchen. She wiped her hands on her apron and brought a large platter to the table. She smacked her husband on the shoulder. "So maybe we shouldn't go about badtalkin' the ones's protectin' us."

"Ain't no one badtalkin' nobody," Garlan said. Hands stuffed into the sides of his overalls, the big man leaned away from the slap and looked up at his wife. "I'm just statin' what's true. Them troops eat their weight in food." He looked at his visitors. "Not to mention how they come lookin' down their nose at us even though they'd starve real good without ole Garlan and Maralyn to feed 'em full. Can't raise no sword without food in your belly."

The meal consisted of root vegetables, dark green plant leaves, and wild mountain goat. Emiel mostly went for the roots and vegetables, as the goat reminded him of the bighorn sheep that had woken him back at the meadow. "This is really good, ma'am," he commented between bites. "We don't get tender cooked green leaf plants quite like this further south. It's mostly boiled roots and the small greens."

"It's the soil," Maralyn replied. "You'll have a hard time growin' these type of big leaves in southern Marai soil. Too sandy."

"Mmm." Emiel nodded. "I'm picking up a tiny bit of cinnamon, as well as taryan red spice. Has that distinct kick to it."

"You really have the buds for seasoning," Maralyn said. "I'm impressed. Most of the soldier men we get comin' through here eat like him." She nodded at Bone, who chomped and swallowed his food like a shark.

"It's my profession," Emiel replied. "I'm a spicetrader."

"Oh really?" Maralyn replied, fully interested now.

After a while, Bone gave up and retired to his guest room, while Emiel and the lady of the house talked well into the night about food, spices, and various little-known combinations.

Garlan had tucked his hands into his overalls again and fallen back into his chair, fast asleep, while Amoura listened to Emiel and Maralyn.

"By any chance," Emiel asked, his eyelids growing heavy. "Have you seen two twin girls pass through the area? They may have been with an adult or a wagon. Perhaps a caravan."

Maralyn thought about it, then shook her head. "No, I'm afraid not. Haven't seen any passersby since the attacks and the wilders. Seems like the whole world has gone to chaos."

From the periphery, Amoura looked at the woman. Coming from her, it might have been a gasp from anyone else.

"Attacks?" Emiel asked. "You've had attacks all the way out here?"

"Not here, blessed we be by the Creator." She held her hand to her heart, kissed her fingers, and held it raised it above her head. "But not far enough away. We seen wilders marchin' through the area, and scary creatures stalking around. You ask me, I think they brought the things here. Ain't seen a one before they start comin' through."

"Ma'am, do you know where the attacks have happened?" Amoura asked.

Maralyn looked over at the magus in surprise. Probably the woman had forgotten Amoura was even there. "Several places, Magus," she said formally. "Mostly along the Ridgeline mountains, but further north. Word has it the Sleeping Morghan must've woke up. Heard word they come outta there as well." She glanced at her snoring husband. "Not sure whether I'm glad we sent three of our sons to be soldiers in Jietar, or not. And I'm not sure it's good we let the other two stay here."

"Where are your other two sons?" Emiel asked.

"Few hours from here, huntin'. They like to spend the night huntin' elk even though they know I can't stand them out in the wild like that."

An uncomfortable silence settled around the table. Maralyn wiped her hands on her apron. "There's always been tensions with them wilders, so we didn't think there'd be no harm in letting them go to Jietar like they wanted to. Wasn't no wars going on. Now we get this luck, and the wilders start actin' up." She pressed her lips together and sighed. "Now they bring monsters prowlin' around. Least we got two sons and Garlan to protect the farm if they come wantin' to steal our food. But what if they bring them monsters with 'em? Out here, we don't stand a chance."

Emiel didn't know much about the conflict between Marai and Khatal, but he'd met enough different types of people in his life to know that there were two sides to every story. He wondered if the

Khatala thought the same about Marailanders as they did about them.

Maralyn stood and wiped her hands on her apron again. "Well, I'm sure our king will get it under control; drive them wild folk back to where they come from. I'm sorry." She offered an awkward bow to Amoura. "Ole farm woman ramblin' when you probably need your sleep. We got a spare room for you, Magus." She looked to Emiel. "If you don't want to share our other guest room with the young man, we got the floor in the family room."

"The room will be great, ma'am," Emiel said. "You're very kind."

She waved him off. "That's what good folks do."

They left the farm the next morning rested and provisioned. The farmer couple had been generous to the point that Emiel felt guilty. But they had insisted that Amoura's order was doing good work, and it was the least they could do.

For what must have been the fourth time, Bone yawned and stretched his arms over his head as they walked. "We need to take you with us everywhere," he said to Amoura. "The way those people practically worshipped you, we'd be treated like royalty everywhere we go."

"They weren't worshiping anyone, mercenary," Amoura replied. "And you'd find my presence more a hinderance than a boon in more places than not." Bone flinched at the sharpness of her tone, but let it go at that.

"Is your head stuffed with mud, bone boy?" Lief asked. As usual, the tinfar had found them as soon as they were out of sight of the farm. "You sure know how to say the wrong thing the wrong way?"

Emiel understood what she said. Even though he'd grown comfortable in her presence, he had no desire to spend any amount of time around any other magus. There was something about them that made him uneasy. Perhaps it was the power they wielded, or the overbearing air of authority the ones he'd met exuded. While he hadn't met many, Emiel found the few magi he had met intimidating."

He thought of Amoura Xanna walking beside him. If ever an intimidating presence could be found, this magus fit the description. She wasn't rude, or sharp of tongue, or threatening. She carried herself with poise, and spoke respectfully to everyone they encountered, but her aura could fill a room while being subtle at the same time.

"What'd you think about the bands of Khatala passing through?" Bone asked.

"Honestly," Emiel replied, "if it doesn't lead to finding my girls, I really don't care."

"You should," Amoura said. "It's possible they might have come across a band of Khatala if they've been seen in numbers in the area."

Emiel felt his stomach go cold. "You don't think they'd harm young girls, do you?"

Amoura looked on him with sympathy. "Who can know for certain? They are people just like us and anyone else. From my limited experience with the easterners, they seem an honorable people."

Emiel took a deep breath and nodded. There was no way to know what would happen if the girls ran across a band of Khatala. His experiences had been the same as Amoura's, so he held onto to that like a lifeline.

They passed another small town and stopped long enough to ask questions. No one had seen two twin girls traveling through the area. People were more than willing to talk about other things, however. More than a few people spoke of hulking silhouettes in the middle of the night, areas of land that looked parched and dead, and a general uneasiness in the air.

Suddenly, Amiya and Nandi coming across a band of easterners seemed like the least troubling thing to happen. Emiel said a silent prayer to the Creator that they were safe. That they had survived what was rumored to have been a terrible attack on Vyne gave him hope. They were tough little girls, young or not. They'd find a way to stay safe.

"We should talk about how we're to progress from here," Amoura Xanna said when they stopped for lunch.

"You mean like where to find horses?" Bone said.

"And buy them with what?" Emiel asked.

Bone responded with a downturned smile and a shrug. "I've got money, spicetrader. I'm sure our magus, here, has some good hard Altarra crowns in a pouch somewhere as well. Magus money stretches far."

"So you'd buy a horse and leave me walking?" Emiel asked.

"Not my fault you're broke."

"Actually, it *is* your fault he's broke," Lief interjected.

"I think no one would argue against the desire to avoid Altarra," Amoura continued, as if no one had spoken. "Everything that's happened these past weeks is starting to look like a sign."

"A sign of what?" Emiel asked.

"I don't know," Amoura admitted. "I might have been able to find out, but my books are in Altarra." She stared out at the distant Ridgeline mountains from where they'd come, then turned to face north.

"Oh, no." Bone shook his head. "You can't tell me you want to go back there." He looked to Emiel. "Look, I appreciate that you want to find your daughters, and to be honest, this whole mess has felt a little more greasy as the days went on, which is why I helped you get out of there. But if we step foot back in that city, we're done. Vladrick would probably die of laughter even as he pulled the lever to the gallows."

"Your death would be swifter than that, most likely," Amoura said. "And you stand a half and half chance of survival as well, since they want to mold you and your daughters into something they can use. Myself, on the other hand." She smirked. "Magi Master Vladrick would find some creative way to end my life after my public dishonoring, being stripped of my essence ring, and subsequent removal from the Order of Magi."

"Yeesh," Bone replied. "You magi are serious business."

Amoura actually smiled and ran a hand through her thin braids. "I attacked and injured three fellow magi, as well as the magi master himself. My actions have leapt me over disciplinary action and straight to capital punishment. To attack a fellow magus is serious in itself. To attack the magi master …" She left the rest hanging.

Emiel stared at the woman through it all. "With one danger after another coming for them following their escape from Altarra, and his daughters occupying nearly all his remaining thoughts, Emiel hadn't considered what this had cost his companions.

Now that he thought it over, he realized that Bone may well have sacrificed his reputation, mercenary or not. If word of his actions spread, who would hire him? Lief hadn't sacrificed any social standing that Emiel was aware of, but she had risked her life to have a hand in his escape as well. And Amoura. She'd risked her life, most certainly thrown away her rank as apprentice, severely damaged her reputation in the order, and placed a bounty on her head.

He looked his companions over as they talked about where to go from here. Could he find any truer friends?

"Ah, knock it off, spicetrader," Bone said. He looked pleadingly to Amoura and Lief. "Will one of you stop him before he starts blubbering about loyalty and friendship. I can see it in his Fallen blasted eyes. He's about to get all mush-mouthed about how we "helped him out at great cost to ourselves." I'm telling you," he said, looking over at Emiel. "You start on me with that jarku dung and I'll knock you upside your head with this."

The mercenary unsheathed his sword, but left the latch in place, drawing the sword with the bone lining that covered the cutting edge for sparring.

Emiel pasted a grim look on his face and walked up to stand in front of the young warrior. They stared into each other's eyes for several heartbeats before Emiel started to turn away. He spun back and wrapped Bone in a hug and lifted him off the ground.

"Ugh, let go, fool!" Bone looked disgusted as he tried to extricate himself from the taller Emiel.

Lief's high-pitched laughter choked off when Emiel knelt and wrapped an arm around her as well. "All right, all right," she said, forcefully smoothing her little brown dress and glaring up at him. Her angry expression failed to hide the fact that her nearly translucent sand-colored skin had flushed a considerable red. "Never thought I'd agree with bone boy over there!" She shifted awkwardly from foot to foot, then kicked Emiel's foot. "You're … you're welcome, Emiel. Just don't go crushing me like that again. It's not proper."

When Emiel turned to Amoura, the magus was looking at him with a very direct "don't even consider it" expression. He took a half step toward her.

"I will wrap you in a glob of air and send you halfway across Marai before you land."

Emiel's mouth crinkled in a repressed smile as he tried to weigh the sincerity of the threat.

"C'mon, man," Bone taunted. "You just grabbed me and almost got impaled for your trouble. You not going to show your gratitude to Magus Grim? Not scared, are you?"

"There is a library in Shiedra comparable to that of Altarra," Amoura stated. She pointed in the direction they'd been traveling, which was east, across the general area Nandi and Amiya would have been traveling if they were coming to the Jietar region. "There's a lot we don't know, Emiel. Carlayn sits between Vyne and Jietar. There are a sprinkling of farms and small towns along the way as well. We don't know how swift their travel has or hasn't been, or if they've come in this direction at all."

"They're coming this way," Emiel said. He couldn't explain

how he knew, but he could feel it. "I'm not leaving my girls to chance, Amoura."

"I'm not suggesting you do, but we must find out what's happening with these attacks. It could help us protect them."

"By turning north?" Emiel asked. "That's putting my back to my girls. How could you ask me that?"

"She might have a point," Bone said. "If there are bands of wilders roaming west of the border, they might give Castle Jietar and Altarra a wide berth."

"Which would send them closer to the Marai Khatal border," Emiel said. "I can't imagine them doing that."

"Khatala will not attack simple travelers," Amoura said. "They see this conflict as one between the king and Terratoma chief. And don't forget, they travel beside a Khatala man."

Emiel frowned as he considered that. "I really don't understand how turning away from my girls is going to help them. If they make it to Altarra and your magi master intercepts them, he'll do to them what he tried to do to me. I will never let that happen."

"The Khatala man they travel with would not set foot inside Altarra," Amoura said. "They'd try to figure out a way to find out if you were there."

Lief stepped between them all. "I might be able to help." Everyone looked down at her. "There are tinfar cities between your human ones." She looked up at Amoura. "You mentioned that they had escaped with a Khatala man into the wild. If that's true, they would have passed close enough to any one of our cities and been seen."

Emiel's heart lept. "What can you do?"

"Stay here and give me the rest of today," Lief replied. "I'll travel back and see if anyone saw anything."

Bone laughed. "Um, that's a week of travel at least."

"For you," Lief said.

Amoura pointed to a patch of woods east of their position. "We will camp there and wait for your return."

"I'll see you tomorrow." Lief knelt and seemed to just fall into the ground. The three humans blinked at the spot.

"That's interesting," Bone said. "Didn't know she could do that, but it explains how she just disappears when we enter human civilization."

The woods Amoura pointed out had looked a lot closer to Emiel than they were. The trio reached their destination at the height of the day.

Leaves had begun to sprout on the limbs of the trees and plant life coming out of dormancy. Soon, the brown woods that they could see through for hundreds of yards would be filled with lush green vegetation. Spring was near.

Bone rationed out some of the meat he'd already roasted, and Emiel seasoned it with spices from the little pouch in his bag. Conversation remained sparse as the trio ate, everyone no doubt wrapped in their thoughts about the days to come.

After stating that she would take first watch, Amoura moved to the edge of camp and stared into the surrounding trees. The moon's pale light gave the woods a majestic and eerie quality that Emiel found, oddly enough, comforting.

Emiel moved beside her and they stood in silence for a time, the only conversation being that of nocturnal insects who buzzed at each other across the huge world of trees and leaves. Every so often, the whoosh of an occasional night bird taking wing interrupted the song of the nighttime forest.

"We'll find them," she said, never taking her eyes off the surroundings. "I don't pretend to understand how much it tears at your heart to be away from your daughters, but I will do everything in my power to help you find and protect them."

"Thank you." Emiel couldn't think of anything to say, so he just stared out at the woods, the magus content to do the same. "I need to be able to protect them, myself," he finally said. "As much as I hate to admit it, that's one thing Vladrick was right about."

"He presented a logical argument that suited his own desires,"

Amoura said. She looked into his eyes. "If you wish it, I can teach you. I don't understand how you access the essences without a ring, but I'll teach you as best I can."

Emiel smiled and nodded in appreciation. "Thanks." She surprised him by wrapping him in a tight embrace. Emiel hugged her back without hesitation, feeling her body pressed to his. He lived in the moment as though time itself had stopped. He tried to calm his pounding heart, but it was impossible with his breath coming in short bursts.

Finally, she pulled away. "You're welcome, Emiel Dharr."

10

THE TWINS

Nandi sat next to her sister inside the wagon as it bumped and sloshed along the rutty, wet road. Things had gone well for most of the morning until the rain arrived. The deluge came swift and hard, and flooded a patch of lowland through which the very trail they followed passed.

"I ever mention how much I hate the rain?" Amiya asked.

"Yes," Nandi replied. "You know it could be worse, right? They let us sit in this wagon. Most everyone else is out slogging in it."

"Ugh," came the reply.

The wagon hit a bump and tossed Nandi into her sister. Amiya pushed her off but huddled closer. "I've made up my mind."

"On what?" Nandi asked.

"When this is all done, I'm paying Bigbelly a visit. I haven't figured out how, yet, but when we get back to Vyne, he's going to have a really bad time."

As much as Nandi wanted to chastise her sister for harboring such vengeful feelings, she couldn't. Huddled together for warmth with their backs against the wall while being jounced about, with a storm outside, she found herself agreeing. Decius was the reason they were out here in the first place. She thought about Dad, and wondered if he was caught out in this mess as well.

The back flap of the wagon opened, and a green-haired head peeked inside.

"Hi, Sama," Amiya said.

The tatamble girl climbed in and cast a wary glance back at the flap. "Girls squat inside smelly, stuffy place when fresh clean water falls from the sky. Beautiful night outside. You hide in here, Sama not know why."

"We don't want to catch a cold, Sama," Nandi said.

Sama tilted her head at that. "How girl catch the cold? Not something you can hold. Must be that thing you do. Steal the Mother's power for you."

Amiya sighed. "We've told you so many times, Sama. We're not stealing anything."

The wagon hit another bump. This time Amiya fell over on Nandi. Despite having never ridden in a wagon, Sama easily kept her balance. She crouched on all fours, her spindly arms and legs that seemed too long for her body, held her steady as though the wagon hardly moved.

"Anything interesting happening outside, Sama?" Amiya asked.

Sama lowered her head in thought. "Humans splash and stomp as though they try to flatten the ground. Make so much noise, animals hear from all around. Yell and bark at each other, hunched forward like the air is cold." She looked on them with curious black eyes. "Sama think she never understand how humans survive out in the world. Big man that is your friend is only one not act like he will die."

"He's your friend too, Sama," Nandi said.

Sama turned away. "Must go. The smell of wet adult human gets closer.

Before Nandi or Amiya could say anything more, the tatamble disappeared back out of the rear animal-hide patch. A moment later Darry ducked into the flap. "Hey, girls. Just lettin' you know we're close to the next town. We'll stop, provision up, and keep going."

"Why don't we just stay the night?" Nandi asked.

The man gave her a patronizing look. "Well, little lady, that costs money. Sometimes when you're out on the road, you don't always have the money to stay in every town you pass—"

"Thank you, Mister Darry," Nandi said, making her best effort not to roll her eyes while her sister did just that. "I get your meaning."

After he left, Amiya raised her hands to her shoulders and started flapping them. "You see, little lady. That costs money. Sometimes when adults are too stupid to plan ahead for when bad stuff happens, they have to sit in the rain."

Nandi giggled, but elbowed he sister. "They're giving us a ride, you know."

"Yeah, yeah, I guess so." Amiya grabbed a handful of straw and let it fall through her fingers. "I just can't believe we passed Altarra, and maybe even Dad. Now we start to make our way back, and this happens. What do you think we're going to do once we find him? I'm pretty sure he won't want to go back to Vyne."

"No," Nandi agreed. "We'd probably head straight for Barbaros Island. That's where we were going to move before this whole mess, anyway."

"Ya," Amiya agreed. "Before that giant stubble-necked dung beetle had us kidnapped and sent Dad all the way out here." She clenched her hands into fists. "Ooooh how I'd love to get hold of Bigbelly now. If we could have done, then, what we can do now—"

"We'd probably be in bigger trouble," Nandi interrupted. If Amiya got a full head of steam, she'd just keep going. "And Dad, too."

"I wonder if one of those four-armed things got Bigbelly," Amiya remarked.

"Amiya!" Nandi looked at her twin in shock. "How could you say such a thing?"

"I'm not saying I *want* one of those things to pound him into a giant bowl of pudding," Amiya said. "I'm just *wondering* if they did. That's all."

Nandi blinked. "A bowl of pudding?"

Amiya shrugged. "I hope Dad didn't already finish his business in Altarra and start back for home. That would be the luck of the Fallen if so."

"Watch your mouth, girl," Nandi said.

"Oh, be quiet, prude," her sister shot back.

"Pssh!" Nandi hissed.

"PSSSSSHH!" Amiya hissed back.

They had a quiet chuckle and sat in silence Amiya spoke again. "What about mountain man?"

"What about him?"

"You think he's going to leave once he's helped us find Dad?"

Nandi frowned. "Um, why wouldn't he? Joga's got his own family to get back to, I'm sure."

"Yeah I know," Amiya said. "It's just, it'd be nice if …"

Nandi leaned away and looked at her sister. "Oh, don't tell me you've got a *crush* on him."

Amiya shoved Nandi over, but it was too late. She was already laughing so hard her stomach hurt. "You, Amiya?"

"Shut up!" Amiya growled. "I don't have a crush on him. I just think he's … nice. He's helping us find Dad, and all. And he's kinda strong."

"And he's kinda old enough to be our big brother," Nandi added.

"Yeah, he is," Amiya agreed. "And I don't care, because I said I didn't have a *crush* on him."

Nandi bobbed her head in exaggerated agreement. "Right, sure. Well, maybe Dad'll agree to the wedding. Joga is a nice enough guy … hey!" she said when Amiya punched her in the shoulder. "Fine, it can be a small wedding." Nandi giggled.

Her sister fell over her, and the two wrestled back and forth until the wagon rumbled to a stop. Still lying in a tangled heap, the twins shared a questioning look, then disengaged.

The girls wrapped their warm cloaks tightly about themselves and peeked out the flap. They saw no one from their rear-facing view, so they hopped out and were immediately soaked. Nandi felt her cloak and clothes underneath growing soggy and heavy. Rivulets of water ran down her scalp between each of her cornrows to spill down her back.

Nandi and Amiya peeked around the wagon. The entire group of travelers stood clustered together facing another group of unarmed and much taller people from a dozen feet away. One of the tall people walked forward and spoke in a language Nandi didn't understand.

While she and her sister, and everyone else in their party stood holding their cloaks tight against the rain and wind, the people before them stood with cloaks hanging loose and billowing in the wind. They were soaked, but neither the wetness nor the wind seemed to bother them.

Nandi leaned forward and peered between the bodies and lit torches. The torchlight illuminated the smooth, reddish brown face of a woman. Rain streaked around her thick eyebrows, around the inside of her eyes along the bridge of her broad nose, and down her full dark lips. Her thick black hair was pulled back her face, and the rain seemed to simply bead up and slide off. She spoke again in a tone not aggressive, but direct and powerful.

"She kinda makes me want to bow, or something," Amiya said.

Nandi agreed. The woman—head and shoulders taller than anyone in their party—radiated power and grace.

Amiya pointed past Nandi, to the right. "Is that Joga?"

She looked in the direction her sister indicated. Easily the tallest and largest man from their side of the two groups , Joga stepped forward. He, too, allowed his warm cloak to billow in the rain, leaving him exposed to the cold.

Joga slapped his right palm over his heart, then pressed his hands together and bowed. He straightened and spoke loudly over the downpour in what sounded like the same language.

Nandi jerked her chin in the direction of the foreign group. "Khatala."

"You should become a ranger or a tracker with those superior observation skills," Amiya remarked. Nandi threw a mock glare at her sister, who chuckled. "I wish they'd hurry up," Amiya complained. "It's cold and being soaking wet is making me colder."

"You could crawl back inside and huddle up if you want," Nandi replied.

"Wow," Amiya said, ignoring her. "I know Khatala people are supposed to be tall and big, but that woman is a good bit taller than Joga."

The two went through another exchange, Joga and the other Khatala seemingly unaware of the weather conditions. Some of the younger Marailanders tried to stand tall and look as stoic as the Khatala opposite them, but their involuntary shivering spasms betrayed them.

Joga turned back and stood beside the woman who Nandi guessed was the leader, or at least, spokesperson. "They are Nassak Nation," Joga announced. "They greet us in kindness and offer trade if you wish."

"Maybe we can erect a tent or something," Anne yelled back. "Kinda wet."

Joga translated, to which the towering woman nodded her assent.

"Billy!" Anne called out. "Moira, Jakland! Get some help and get the tarp out and get it up. We got trading to do!"

Amiya slapped Nandi on the arm with the back of her hand. "C'mon, let's go!"

Nandi shared her twin's enthusiasm. Other than Joga, they'd never met Khatala people before. Would they be of the same temperament as Joga? Did they have the same beliefs and customs? Did they use the essences in the same way?"

When they trotted up to Joga and the tall woman, he turned and smiled at them, opening a hand to invite them over as if he'd expected they would come. "Introduce you," he said, hurriedly waving them closer. "Is, in your language you would call, chief. Is chief of Nassak Khatala. Honorable Chief Oguye Nunuata of nation of Nassak."

"Honored to meet you, Chief Og … guye Noonooata of the nation of Nassak, the twins stumbled in unison."

The corner of the chief's mouth twitched as Joga translated. She reached down and offered each hand to Nandi and Amiya, palms facing up. Not knowing what to do, Nandi and Amiya repeated the gesture. The woman responded with a slanted smile while Joga explained.

"Offers hand in greeting and friendship. This gesture means she sees heart, and that good soul is there. Take her hands."

"Oh," Amiya said beside Nandi, who was thinking the same. They took Chief Oguye's hands, and the woman squatted in front of them. Even this low, they still had to crane their necks to look up at her. She smiled, gently squeezed their hands, and placed them together between her palms. Then she lifted them to her heart, and spoke.

Through the whole greeting, she looked down at them with a kind, but unblinking gaze that Nandi found hard to hold.

"Twin flames like eyes of Creator *Amyadali*," Joga translated. "Know the Nassak as friends."

Nandi was about to say something when she heard a commotion in the distance, followed by surprised shouts and more than a little cursing.

Chief Oguye released their hands and stood. She took two long strides back to her band, and they turned as one to face the commotion. The warriors behind her stood erect. Again, they took no hostile posture, but their movements were quick and precise.

The group Anne had tasked with erecting a trade tent had just gotten the poles secured and were fastening the tarp when a group of armored soldiers on horseback galloped into their midst. The soldier at their head held up a fist while pulling up a heavily-muscled horse. The mount snorted as it skidded to a stop, then stood stock-still. The soldier raised his visor to reveal a man with a clean-shaved face and tight mouth underneath unfriendly eyes that could have been green or blue in the dim torchlight.

The mounted soldiers fanned out and surrounded the Marailanders as well as the Nassak. Silver armor gleamed in and out of the wavering torchlight, as did the dark blue capes attached at shoulders.

Joga grabbed Nandi's shoulder and shove her behind him. "Oof." She collided with Amiya and almost fell, but her sister helped her stay upright. The sudden move startled her. Adults were obviously stronger, and the larger stature of Khatala was well known in Marai. Being so easily yanked around like that, though, made it all the more real and frightening. If he'd wanted to kidnap them, he could have easily done it.

She looked up at their Frostland guardian. He stood squared in front of them in a protective stance. Nandi didn't doubt for a moment that the man was a friend who would give his life to protect them, but the ease at which he threw them behind himself planted a warning in her mind that there were other adults who were just as strong, and not so honorable.

Travelers shouted in complaint, soldiers barked orders, horses snorted, mud and rock spat from under trampling hooves. Through the dizzying chaos of movement and incoherent voices all mixed together, the Nassak silently took it all in.

Nandi watched the towering band of Khatala in admiration. They might have been tightly formed statues, for even the wind did not move them, and only their eyes shifted as they analyzed the mayhem. They didn't even move when the soldiers formed up behind them.

Anne walked up to the mounted soldier who had led the charge in. "What's the meaning of this? We've done nothing wrong to warrant such treatment!" When the soldier turned his icy gaze on her, Anne visibly shrank away. The caravan leader straightened her back in attempt to project some form of strength.

"This is Shetar, of Marai, ruled by King Alyn Menegard." The soldier nodded at the Nassak band. "Do you realize we are at war with Khatal?" His every word sprayed a mist of water from his mouth. Like the Nassak band, he paid no heed to the rain blowing in his face.

"We're *barely* inside the Shetar boarder," Anne shouted back. "And these people showed us more good will than you have, charging in here and almost killing us." The rain seemed to intensify as if accentuating her anger. "They were passing through, just like us. We decided to trade, then you come storming in."

The soldier's light eyes hardened. "You admit to trading with the enemy."

"They're not the enemy," Darry argued, moving to stand beside Anne.

"Step aside," the lead soldier ordered."

Anne placed her hands on her hips. "Or what? You gonna run us down? We're innocent travelers who stopped to have a friendly trade with passersby."

The lead soldier looked at Anne as if she were naive, then looked past her at the Nassak. He walked his horse past the indignant Anne and Darry—who were forced to shuffle aside—to stop several paces in front of the Nassak Chief. The two locked stares for several tense moments while every one of the watching travelers seemed to hold their breath.

"By traveling through Shetar territory," the soldier stated, "you are suspected of acting against Jietar Kingdom and by extension, King Alyn Menegard."

Chief Oguye continued to stare at the leader of the Shetaran soldiers while a woman to her left spoke. "Not act against Marai or its king."

The soldier looked to the speaker, then back to the chief. "Tell your leader that your people are in open war with the kingdom of Jietar, and by extension, all of Marai. Your presence here is seen as a threat." When the woman didn't translate, he looked at her. "Do you refuse to translate my words?"

"Honorable Chief Oguye Nunuata already understand words of easterner."

The soldier slid his gaze back to the chief. "Yet you refuse to speak with me?"

"Honorable Chief Oguye Nunuata," the speaker continued, "would speak with Marai soldier if Marai soldier acted with respect and honor toward herself and her people."

Nandi watched in rapt attention as the situation slowly deteriorated. The band of travelers remained frozen where they stood, wide-eyed and tense. The soldiers had them and the Nassak completely surrounded, while their leader spoke to Chief Oguye in a manner the Khatala band deemed not only improper, but disrespectful. Still, despite the men and women surrounding them with hands resting on swords at their hips, or bows in their laps, the Nassak remained unperturbed.

"This is probably going to get ugly," Amiya whispered.

"Yeah," Nandi whispered back. She looked at the surrounding face-off while noting that she, Amiya, and Joga were standing closer to the Nassak than the travelers, who had discretely backed away from the soldiers. She looked over her shoulder and saw several soldiers with their eyes on Joga's back. One caught her eye, then looked up at Joga. *That guy thinks Joga's trying to kidnap us,* she thought.

"By authority of King Alyn Menegard," the lead soldier stated, "I order you and your people to leave Shetar immediately."

Chief Oguye's eyes widened, and she barked a single word in their native tongue. As one, the band of Nassak \ turned to face every direction while dropping into a defensive stance. The Shetaran soldiers unsheathed their swords while archers nocked arrows and trained them on the Khatala band.

"Great," Amiya said.

Joga also settled in a defensive stance, and Nandi felt him delving. "Joga?" she asked.

"Evil from world below—" Joga yelled.

The ground underneath Anne and Darry erupted in a shower of earth and blood, and spear-like tentacles whipped in the air.

Nandi's eyes went wide and her mouth fell open. One moment Anne and Darry had been standing there, the next, they were gone in a splash of blood and soil.

The standoff fell into a frenzy. Travelers screamed and ran, while Shetaran soldiers wrestled rearing mounts and tried to form into a defensive position. Armored heads swiveled this way and that as they tried to pinpoint the threat.

An arm fell beside Amiya and blood splattered onto her leg. She shrieked and skittered backwards, then turned aside and emptied her stomach on the ground.

The ground exploded in a different area underneath several mounted soldiers and nearby travelers. Horses and men screamed, and many died.

Nandi felt massive amounts of essence building from the direction of the crouching Nassak. They were chanting some type of cadence in their tongue.

"Tunneler!" someone shouted.

"Must get away from here!" Joga yelled at the lead soldier.

Nandi hurried to Amiya just as her sister was wiping her mouth. "Ugh," I feel sick," she groaned.

"Feel sick later," Nandi said, forcing her own churning stomach to settle.

"Oh atama oooooah HA. Oh atama ooooah HAAA." The Nassak continued their chant, eyes furiously casting about as the carnage ensued.

They're trying to find a target, but there isn't a clear one, Nandi realized.

The ground burst again beside several soldiers while another eruption sent bodies whole and otherwise flying into the night. Torches fell to the ground and winked out, casting more of the area in darkness.

Nandi tried to focus through the horror. Dark silhouettes of waving appendages impaled bodies, dismembered them, and hurled them through the air. She tried to block out the terrible sounds, but it was hard. Beside her, Amiya had recovered some-what. She strained to delve, and Nandi sensed her find a trickle and build on it. Nandi opened herself to the essences and they came to her call.

She filled herself with as much of the power as she could bear while her mind raced through possibilities of what to do with it. A crackling sound drew her attention to the ground. She looked down and saw the earth beneath herself, Amiya, and Joga hardening.

"Great idea," Amiya said to the kneeling Joga.

Nandi and Amiya followed his lead and concentrated on hard-ening the ground. Several appendages burst out of the ground around the Nassak, while more burst out of the ground somewhere in the night. Screams rose and died in the distance.

With nothing between them and visible targets, the Nassak struck out. They struck with *fire* and lit the appendages with the essence's physical namesake. There was a responding shriek, and the ground exploded nearby. A large four-legged beast burst out of the ground in a flurry of slashing claws and snapping jaws.

Nandi didn't have a chance to see what happened next. The ground beneath them lifted, throwing the trio off balance. Several spear-like appendages shot out of the ground. Joga lit them on fire and kept burning them until the flesh began to melt.

The monster responding shriek rent the air like claws through fabric. The hard slab of rock they'd created dropped back to the ground hard, but held together. What was left of the appendages slid back into the ground.

Underneath the Nassak band, a solid patch of ground like the one Nandi and the others had created lifted off the ground with such force, it threw the Khatala warriors into the air. Less than a heartbeat later, the same happened underneath Nandi and the others. Joga flew toward three of the only surviving travelers, while a screaming Amiya disappeared into the night.

Nandi's world flipped end over end as she, too, was hurled into the dark night.

UP, down, in every direction, dark sky, ground, and smatterings of torchlight passed in a blur across Amiya's vision. An endless scream tore from her throat as she spun and twisted out of control in the air. Despite the good fortune of not landing on her head, the impact still blasted the wind from her lungs.

When she finally stopped rolling, Amiya forced herself to her hands and knees, wheezing as she tried to catch her breath. The screams of dying humans and animals sounded far away. How far had she been thrown? When she finally collected her thoughts, Amiya realized she was alone.

Her breath came in short, frantic pants. Where was Nandi? She started to call out to her sister, but that might attract one of those things Joga had called a tunneler. That thought brought her to the Khatala man. What had happened to him?

Amiya forced out of her mind any possibilities that didn't

involve Nandi and Joga's survival, and climbed to her feet. She didn't have to listen for the sounds of chaos, it lit the night like an audible beacon. While fear tried to wrap its claws around her heart, the need to get to her sister triumphed. She jogged in the direction of the conflict, then broke into a run, eyes darting left and right, scanning for threats hiding in the dark.

She'd nearly reached the meeting place when she heard a sound that froze the pit of her stomach; loud and angry cursing in an unintelligible language. Amiya skidded to a stop, her heart pounding in her chest She knew that language, even if she didn't understand it. Every single one of those soldiers were going to die. If the Nassak were powerful enough with the essences, they might survive. "Nandi. Joga. Sama." She didn't worry much about the latter, as the tatamble girl could hide better than anyone But her sister and Joga were in terrible danger.

"C'mon, Amiya," she said to herself. "Courage." She forced her fear-induced wobbling legs to steady and ran on. Every step she had to stop herself from calling out to Nandi. Best if she find her without being discovered by any of those horrible four-armed monsters.

When she neared the killing ground—for that's all it was—she swallowed the bile building in her throat and ignored the body parts strewn about the ground. Unseeing eyes looked up at her, promising to visit her dreams when she next slept.

She heard the thudding footsteps, the swinging weapons, the piercing of armor. Sharp weapons sank into flesh, the screams of men and women mixed with infernal curses. Then she saw them. Four-armed horrors like the ones that had attacked Vyne. They dashed forward and stabbed, spun and chopped. The monsters were a whirlwind of death that engulfed any surviving traveler or soldier.

Amiya turned aside and skirted the area. She wouldn't allow herself to hope her sister was alive. She *knew* Nandi lived. And Joga, too. She noted as she scanned the carnage that the Nassak were nowhere to be seen, and none of their number lay with the Marailanders in death. That gave her hope. Maybe Nandi, Joga, and Sama had fought alongside the other Khatala and escaped.

The ground burst beside her. A slender appendage shot out of the ground and whipped toward her head. Amiya dropped to her stomach to avoid being decapitated. She felt the whoosh of air as the thing zipped inches above her back. She rolled away and rose to a kneeling position. Unlike her struggles before, the essences rushed to her call. She drew in as much as she could bear, reveling in the power that coursed through her body.

The tunneler clawed its way out of the ground and glared at her with red slits for eyes. Amiya wiped her sweating palms on her hips and struggled to steady her nerves. She thought of how this thing had separated her from her sister and tried to kill her. Amiya used the thought as a focus to light her heart afire and incinerate the icy daggers of fear piercing her chest. "I am going to melt you into a puddle."

The tunneler lowered its arrow-shaped head and screeched. Flames surrounded Amiya's body. Twice the size of a brown bear, and even more deadly, the four-legged monster tore up the ground and knocked over trees as it charged toward her.

Amiya screamed. The fire encircling her body funneled toward the charging monster. It skidded and dodged to the side, then kept coming. Amiya's breath caught in her throat, and for a terrible moment, the flames diminished. She grabbed hold of *fire* again and sent it streaming at the monster, all the while feeling the ground vibrate with each thudding stomp bringing it closer.

The beast tried to dodge again, but on pure instinct, Amiya spread the flames out like a small ocean wave. The tunneler screeched in agony when the flames washed over it. Amiya narrowed the flames and focused them on the tunneler. She sent a single, thick funnel of fire blasting into the monster. The flames roared as they grew, engulfing the tunneler in an inferno.

The ground vibrated under the weight of heavy footfalls behind her. Amiya turned and gasped when three four-armed monsters bore down on her, rocky swords and clubs raised high. She cried out and dove aside. Mud and dirt splashed over her from the impact of a lava rock club. She kept rolling and came to her feet, then had to dive aside again when a sword stabbed straight for her face.

Amiya's short height saved her, for three of the monsters meant twelve arms, each holding a weapon that would skewer or bludgeon her to death. She dove to the side of a pounding club, rolled past a stomping foot, hopped just out of reach of a swinging lava rock sword. She tried to block out the terrifying voices spitting endless curses at her.

Her knees threatened to buckle under the glow of those hateful red eyes, but Amiya was in survival mode. She couldn't think, couldn't plan any strategy, and certainly hadn't enough time to think long enough to reach for the essences.

She squinted her eyes against the splashing water and mud, and kept moving. Somewhere in the distance, the sounds of more fighting found her ears. "Must be the Nassak," she thought aloud, for it looked like every one of the travelers and soldiers had been killed.

Again Amiya rolled out of reach of a swinging blade and came up sprinting. If she could outrun these things and get to the other side of camp, she might find the others. Together, she, Nandi, Joga, and Sama could beat these things.

The rapidly nearing thuds told her she wasn't fast enough, her legs not long enough. Amiya reached for the essences, but they didn't heed her call. She strained to grab hold of the power, but still it eluded her. With her anger diminished in simply trying not to be cut apart Amiya struggled to even feel the essences, much less wield them.

The ground burst in front of her and she skidded to a stop. Another tunneler slashed its way out of the ground. Amiya turned just in time to see the swing of a rocky sword toward her face. She cried out and threw herself to the ground. The sword passed harmlessly overhead, but when she looked up, she saw the sword in one of its lower arms stabbing straight for her belly.

Instinct took over again. Amiya slashed her hand across the air between herself and the sword. The rocky weapon descended into a ripple in the air and disappeared along with the monster. The ripple grew until it swallowed her, the monsters, and seemingly the entire world in its depths.

11

JOGA

The Nassak never broke their box formation despite having run for miles. They had remained and tried to help the outlander soldiers fight off the creatures from the world below, but the foolish outlanders had turned on them.

The sun peeked above the eastern mountains to cast light on a clear sky. The damp smell of rain-soaked earth lingered in the crisp morning air, which carried the soothing sound of bird chatter. The birth of a new day.

Jogging at the front of the band with chief Oguye, Joga punched himself in the chest in frustration. What was wrong with these outlanders? They turned greetings into hostility, interrupted friendly trade, and accused their western neighbors of being so evil that they could somehow raise the minions of the world below. Madness.

On top of it all, he'd lost the twin girls. His friends. Guilt wracked the Frostlander. He'd almost fought his way back to Nandi, but a tunneler had smacked him hard in the side and sent him flying into a tree. If not for the presence of the Nassak, Joga was certain he would now be among the ancestors in the True

Home. They had not only saved him, but carried him for miles until he'd woken.

The Nassak chief called for a halt. "You are troubled," Oguye said to him. "There is no need to be frustrated at the easterners. They blame us for what they cannot understand. They think we bring the return of mgomu and its faithless."

Joga frowned. "Mgomu?" he asked, using the Khatala word for the void aspect Marailanders called Shurza. "Mgomu and the faithless?"

Oguye nodded. "Dazra have been seen. Their masters, the faithless must be awake, or will be soon."

"Dazra," Joga echoed, his mind racing north to a volcano many miles away. Marailanders had a name for dazra as well; droughtlord.

Oguye studied his face. "You have seen one."

Joga nodded. "When I went to fulfill my bloodmark, one of the dazra attacked us."

"Us?" Oguye asked.

Joga's shoulders slumped. "My bloodmark was to battle a mulgin that lived in the volcano over New Dama."

The band of Nassak sucked air through their teeth at that, with murmurings of "mulgin" traveling around the group.

Chief Oguye's eyebrows rose. "Creator *Amyadali* gave you the bloodmark to battle a mulgin?" She made a gesture of respect. "Truly the Creator uses Her charges hard, but there must be great power in you for Her to task you such."

"I would have died," Joga admitted, "but the two girls I introduced you to saved me. And when the mulgin was dead, a man with skin like molten rock rose to challenge us. The space around him felt like hot death."

The band of Nassak warriors had gathered around and sat cross-legged, listening as Joga recounted the battle with the dazra. Gasps and mutterings complimented his story, and when he finished, the band made gestures of great respect.

"I regret that we left your companions," Oguye said. She placed a hand on Joga's shoulder. "We circled the battle and tried to find survivors, but when the cursing trogk attacked with the tunnelers, we were forced back." She shook her head in bewilderment. "They think we summoned the monsters. I will never understand these people."

"There are some that are reasonable," Joga said. "The borderland city, New Dama, shows that our two peoples can coexist."

Oguye nodded. "It is their ruler that builds the barrier between us. If he would stop hiding behind his soldiers and face the Chief of the Terratoma, this could be settled as it should have been."

Joga bowed with respect. "Despite the wisdom of your words, that is our way, not theirs."

They remained in the open fields of Shetar to break their fast, while lookouts ensured they weren't ambushed by the mistrustful outlanders. When Joga considered their location, however, it was in fact, himself and this Khatala band who were the outlanders.

"The Terratoma and Dokayuk battle the Marai king's forces," Oguye continued. "My scouts speak of Marailander sightless' wielding of Mother *Illyu's* aspects like a wicked weapon. And they are different. Some are more ruthless than others. Some wield certain aspects more effectively than others."

"That could be something to use as an advantage," Joga replied. A part of him felt guilty, for the two girls who'd become like little sisters to him were Marailanders. Whether or not they were Barbarosian islanders mattered little, it was still in the territory of Marai.

Chief Oguye read his eyes. "You are conflicted, young Frostlander. About your Marailander friends."

"I promised to help them find their father. They helped me fulfil my bloodmark and saved my life. They might have returned to the True Life now, and if not, they're lost to me all the same. I've failed them." Saying it made Joga feel heavy with guilt. He felt his spirit dim with each word.

"They might have awakened to the True Life," Oguye said. "You do not know. They are lost to you, yes. But while you do not know their fate, you have not yet failed them. None can know the path Creator *Amyadali* has placed before any of us."

Joga thought on her words while they finished their meal. The Nassak spoke of the mood of the conflict, and how the Marailanders refused to enter into any peace talks until the people of Khatal ceased their "reckless" use of Mother *Illyu's* aspects; the power they called essences. Joga heard the underlying anger in the conversations and couldn't blame them. Ever since first contact, Marai had not only misunderstood, but disrespected Khatala culture in a number of ways. That in itself wasn't grounds for war, but the Marai king drew first blood.

Their meal finished, the band gathered themselves to continue on. Joga admired the tall, lean warriors with their radiant reddish-brown skin and kind smiles. "You travel to join the war?"

"We go to speak with the Terratoma and the Dokayuk," Chief Oguye corrected. "They have been leaning on the Sandland and Dryland nations to join them. Relations have been tense, as the two nations have been reluctant to get involved."

"Because conflict is only between those initially involved," Joga said.

Oguye nodded. "But this is different. Marailanders don't think as we do. The Terratoma and Dokayuk are learning this. It's only a matter of time before the embattled nations turn their sights to the Nassak."

Seeing the chief's resolve in the face of inevitability made Joga resent the Marai king even more. Of all the nations of Khatal, the Nassak were the most easygoing, the most gentle and eager to give of themselves. He then thought of his own homeland.

If the Sandland, Dryland, and Nassak nations were pulled into the escalating conflict, surely eyes would turn further south —to the Frostland nations. He needed to warn his people. Even now they were likely awaiting his return, but he couldn't abandon Nandi and Amiya, and if he was truly honest with himself, Sama.

Joga couldn't help a little smile at the thought of the tatamble girl that had become his friend. Of the things to happen to him since the misadventure that landed him in Vyne, and everything hence, never would he have thought to have become friends with a tatamble.

Oguye stared into his eyes with approval. "You have an obligation to your family that you will fulfill."

"Yes," Joga agreed. "The Frostland nation needs me, but so do Amiya, Nandi, and Sama. They are my family, too."

"Sama?" Oguye asked.

Joga chuckled. "You did not see her because she is tatamble."

Oguye's brows raised in surprise. "A tatamble? This is a story I would hear, one day."

"It's a story I look forward to telling you."

"Change swirls around you like the air we breathe, Joga of the Frostland nation," Oguye said. "To become family with Marailanders and a tatamble." She shook her head. "Fascinating times are upon us. Go and find your tatamble and Marailander sisters, friend. Bring them with you that I may hear their view of your grand tale."

THOUGH HIS HEART ached with each step, Joga turned toward the last place he'd seen the girls. He didn't want to think about the possibility of what he'd find at the killing ground, but he had to know.

He jogged through the day, stopping only long enough for the occasional snack and water. He removed his outer layer of furs and tied them to his pack once the sun rose overhead. Being from the Frostlands, what some considered chilly felt warm to him.

He reached the place by dusk and stopped less than a mile away. Carrion crows crowded the area, as well as a few four-legged scavengers. Joga offered a silent prayer to Creator *Amyadali* for the souls of the slain, and for the regretful fate of their shed bodies.

The scavenger birds shuffled aside and squawked in irritation at him as he drew near. Joga concentrated on the task at hand and tried not to let his mind linger on the stench of death and the tearing and crunching sounds as the scavengers did their work.

He offered prayer after prayer as he gingerly stepped through the carnage. These poor travelers hadn't deserved this fate, nor had the soldiers. Despite Joga's anger at their king and this war, he couldn't deny that if the soldiers had truly been evil, they would have attacked immediately. Instead of attacking them outright, the leader had given the khatala a chance to leave. He found the man— or rather, part of him—in the middle of it all. He'd died beside his men.

The crumbled remains of what looked to be one or two trogk lay in piles, surrounded by the bodies of more soldiers. Before Joga had been knocked unconscious, he's seen at least four of the creatures and two tunnelers. The terrible monsters had slaughtered an entire contingent of soldiers and a group of travelers, and only lost two of their number.

He moved on, needing to be done with this quickly. He searched for over an hour, forcing himself to cover every inch of the area as well as the area outside the place of death. There were no signs of bodies being dragged off, and no blood or remains anywhere outside the immediate area.

Joga couldn't exactly feel happy that he found no signs of the girls, but rather, overwhelming relief. Though he couldn't be completely sure, somehow, he knew they'd survived. The resourceful twins along with the crafty tatamble girl would have found a way to escape.

He stood upwind from the killing ground and looked upon it from a distance. He forced himself to remember the slain, to hold the image and the memory of this event as a reminder that the hostilities between Marai and Khatal were petty under the shadow of what was coming.

Mgomu, the void aspect. The thought of it gave Joga a chill. With one last regretful sigh, he turned to the south. The girls could have fled anywhere, and the only thing he had to go on was the last place they knew their father to be. Joga wasn't sure how far away Altarra was, but he could think of no other place they would go.

He started jogging. Hopefully he could overtake them, given his longer strides. He hoped the girls knew which direction Altarra lay and that they had found Sama. The tatamble might not know where the Marailander city lay, but all tatamble knew the land.

Joga jogged through the rest of the day and into the night. He used his limited knowledge in tracking to search for signs of passage, but found nothing. In the fading daylight, Joga came to a copse and climbed the tallest tree he could find. Perched above most of the woods, he looked into the distance and saw the faint outline of a civilization with a huge structure towering above. That must be Altarra.

The sight of the great Marai city waiting in the distance threatened Joga's resolve. He climbed down from the tree and searched for another with larger, sturdier branches. He moved quickly to find his perch for the night as the last rays of daylight fled behind the western horizon.

He found a suitable tree and climbed to the highest branch that would support him. Predators roamed every land, and with only himself out here, a campfire would be little more than a beacon to unwelcome visitors both two-legged and four.

Joga untied his bedroll and tied it across the crook of three branches close together. Once secured tight, he positioned himself against the trunk of the tree. It might not be as comfortable as stretching out, but he needn't worry about anything finding him out in the open on the ground.

He closed his eyes and listened to the songs of the nocturnal insects until he drifted to sleep. Amiya, Nandi, and Sama were out here somewhere. The tatamble girl's instincts would lend them an edge to survive out in the wild. He just hoped he could move quick enough to catch them …

Joga slowly, carefully cracked his eyes open. He lay still, not daring to make a sound or a move. Hot breath puffed in his hair, and a long, deep growl rumbled in his ear.

12

NANDI

The campfire had died a long time ago, yet Nandi gazed into the faintly glowing embers. Her mind raced through the events of that terrible night over and over again. She saw clearly with her waking eyes the blood and evisceration, the lifeless stares of those who'd been cut down by the underworld monsters.

Nandi stared at the chalky gray and black remnants of the wood Sama had gathered for the campfire. The tatamble girl didn't need it, but she'd seen Nandi sitting in the same place she was now, shivering but unmoving. Nandi had barely registered her companion's compassion, having gathered wood and created a campfire right in front her.

Sama had poked her, shaken her, gotten to within a finger's width of Nandi's face to look into her eyes with her own deep black pools. The tatamble girl had been nervous for her and still was. Somewhere deep in the back of her mind sat the realization that Sama had become like a sister.

Nandi closed her eyes and was again dragged through that awful night. The tunneler had blasted the ground apart beneath them. The last she'd seen of Amiya and Joga was them tumbling through the air to be swallowed in the darkness. Much like herself.

"Girl not sleep after all this time," Sama said from the other side of the campfire.

Nandi didn't respond. In the deep recesses of her mind, she appreciated that Sama had cared for her. She'd forced Nandi to run away despite her protests that she had to go back for her sister.

That couldn't have happened, of course. They'd both seen her sister do something to the air around herself and disappear, taking two of the four-armed monsters and a tunneler with her.

No, she hadn't slept. How could she? How could sleep navigate the gruesome death that had surrounded her, and the many shards of her broken heart at being separated from her twin sister?

The green-haired girl huffed impatiently. She didn't understand. Only a twin could. It would have been devastating enough to have lost Amiya even if she'd just been her sister, but she was Nandi's twin; the other half of herself. They were two sides of the same coin.

"Sama see girl's sister do unnatural thing with Mother's power. Sama see her escape death. Sister is tough for human. Sama think she survived."

Nandi appreciated Sama's efforts to make her feel better. After all they'd come through together, the tatamble had become like a sister, as well.

Sama leapt to her feet in a spray of dirt, and glared at Nandi, her hands balled into fists. "Nandi girl not care about Sama. Sama not even exist to Nandi." Confused, Nandi looked up at the angry girl. Not angry, hurt. Sama's deep black eyes looked genuinely wounded. "Sama drag Nandi out of death and keep her safe even when she refuses to talk. Just sit there and ignore Sama, and still Sama care for her. Nandi girl only has *one* sister. Sama means nothing—"

"No, Sama." Tears blurred Nandi's vision of the pale, green-haired girl. Sama cut off her rant, likely surprised at hearing Nandi's voice after so long. "I do not feel that you're nothing."

"Amya is sister, but Sama is nothing."

"No."

"If Sama disappear and not Amya girl, maybe Nandi not be so hurt—"

"No!" Nandi was on her feet before she knew it. The sudden move surprised Sama, but she didn't flinch; didn't shrink away or take a step back. She glared at Nandi, her face a mask of anger, pain, betrayal. "Sama is more than my friend," Nandi said in a quiet voice. "Sama is my sister."

"Nandi girl say those words, but Sama see different."

"You don't understand, Sama." Nandi wiped the tears from her eyes and her wet cheeks. "Losing Amiya is different even than losing our father. She is my twin, Sama. She's my other half. We've been together since before we were born and have never been apart."

Sama's face softened in confusion. "Nandi girl is not half herself? She stands here whole in front of Sama."

"I don't know how to say it to make you understand," Nandi replied. "She is my twin, part of me in a way no one but another twin could understand. It hurts, Sama. It hurts me inside like nothing I could imagine. I don't know what to do."

"If what Nandi girl says is true, Amya girl's life is connected to you. If Amya girl no longer lives, Nandi girl would know."

Nandi searched deep in her heart and found through the pain that she was not broken in the way she knew she would be if Amiya had …" she couldn't even think to finish that thought, but she knew Amiya was alive, and that lifted her spirit. She smiled. "Sama is right."

Sama looked into Nandi's eyes, the hurt still there. "Then Nandi girl will find her sister and be well again and whole again?"

"No," Nandi said. The tatamble tilted her head and gave Nandi a curious look. "Nandi and Sama will find *our* sister," she continued. "Amiya looks for me *and* Sama, just like I would look for her *and* you, if it were you and her together."

She crossed around the smoldering embers and stopped in front of the tatamble girl. Sama's face was a map of scratches and scars detailing a lifetime of survival in a brutal, wild world. She watched Nandi with big black orbs that reflected a desire to be loved yet a hesitance to open herself up to it.

Sama still didn't back away as Nandi moved closer and wrapped her in a tight embrace. "What is Nandi girl doing to Sama?" she heard the tatamble ask, her voice muffled in Nandi's shoulder.

"I'm giving Sama, my sister, a hug. If not for my sister Sama, I would be dead, and Amiya would be somewhere broken; just like we would be broken if something happened to Sama."

"Nandi girl just says the words? Nandi girl wants Sama's help to find her sister?"

"Nandi girl says words that are true," Nandi said. "Nandi girl needs her other sister to find Amiya." Sama stiffened when Nandi hugged her tighter. "This is how humans show love."

"By squeezing air out of others and making it harder to breathe?" came the muffled reply.

Nandi chuckled and sniffed. She started to let go, when Sama's arms suddenly sprang up and slammed into her back in a crushing hug. The tears she was about to wipe from her eyes were instead jarred out of them by the sudden impact. "Uuh!" Nandi wheezed, while trying to recover her breath. She'd forgotten how strong the girl was. She was probably as strong as an adult. "Sama," she groaned, "please."

"Nandi and Amya girls are Sama's family. Girls with same face always Sama's family."

"Mmmmyus," Nandi gasped. She could feel her ribs shifting. "Sama must let go or she will crush her sister … UUH!" The arms were gone so quickly Nandi fell onto her backside with a bounce. She sat there gasping for sweet air and rubbing her ribcage. *That's the kind of love that'll kill you*, she thought.

"Now that Nandi girl, Sama's sister, has her mind again, we go and find Amya girl, our other sister."

Nandi sniffed again and wiped the last tears from her face. "Yes." A wave of love and gratitude washed over her for the tatamble girl. Sama had reunited them once already, when Nandi had been taken by the horrible ghuza creatures and used as a conduit to feed on the essences. She had continued on with them, saving herself, Amiya, and Joga from a terrible death by the claws of a pack of darkwood cats. She'd even gone into the belly of an active volcano, battled a lavakan, and that molten man with the lava rock skin.

Sama frowned at her. "Why Nandi girl look at Sama that way?"

"Because I'm glad for the day I met Sama. Because I'm glad Sama is here, and that she is my sister."

They stared at each other for a long time before Sama turned away and began awkwardly stomping out the smoldering embers and covering them with dirt. "Must go now and find sister."

Nandi nodded and sniffed again. "Yeah." She stood and looked around at the endless wild landscape. Her backpack was gone, likely still sitting in the wagon where the attack had happened. She had no intension of going back there. She couldn't bear the sight of all that butchery again. "Amiya knows that Dad had been taken to Altarra. Since that's where we had planned to go, she'd guess that's where we would go, too."

She thought of Joga, and Nandi felt a stab of guilt. If Sama had become like a sister to her, then surely the Khatala man had become like a big brother. In all her grief at being separated from Amiya, she had mentally pushed out Sama and Joga. "Do you think they might have found each other?" she asked the other girl. "Amiya and Joga?"

Sama responded with a disgusted look that was far too dramatic to be sincere. "Hope not, for sister Amya girl's sake. Khatala boy is crude and smelly."

Nandi kept her laughter internal. The irony of that statement was staggering, considering that she could smell the tatamble from ten feet away. "Maybe we'll find a river or creek to bathe in."

"Bathe?" Sama looked over her shoulder. "Is bathe human word for drink? What else is there to do with water?"

"Oh, you'll see," Nandi replied. "And it will be lovely." Sama gave her a dubious look. "Um, Altarra is south," Nandi said. "Which way is south?" Sama pointed past her. Nandi turned to look in the direction the tatamble girl pointed and saw nothing but endless land spread out before them. She sighed. "Let's go."

They walked all day, stopping occasionally for food and to find water. Nandi tried to hunt for their meal, but she had no skill at it, and found she didn't have the heart for it either. Sama had looked at her in genuine confusion and had even asked her how she'd survived this long without being able to hunt and kill her food. She'd asked the tatamble if there were many plants and roots they could eat that she might forage. Sama had responded to that with an unreadable expression that made Nandi think the girl had been trying not to laugh at her.

At her request, Sama had led her to a running stream that hadn't been too far off their path. She wondered if all tatamble were as adept at finding anything in nature as Sama was.

When they'd reached the stream, Nandi stripped down and hopped into the water. It would have been nice to have soap, but it was better than nothing. After some coaxing, she got Sama to wade waist deep.

Sama had looked about her as though afraid the river itself would rise up and snatch her into its depths. It had taken some time, but she'd finally gotten the girl to relax and even taught her how to hold her breath underwater. That had nearly resulted in the stronger girl drowning Nandi in a panic, but she'd eventually gotten her to relax, somewhat.

"Doesn't your skin feel good, now?" Nandi asked. Even without soap to scrub away the grime, she still felt much better.

"Sama's skin looks different," she said, looking at her pale hands and arms.

"That's because the dirt is gone," Nandi said. "Well, most of it. It's called being clean."

Sama wrinkled her nose.

"Don't look like that, Sama," Nandi said. "You know it feels good to be clean." She lifted her arms over her head. "You can feel the air blowing over your skin now!"

Sama lifted her arms over her head in the most awkward gesture Nandi had ever seen. She tried to stifle her laughter, but it exploded straight from her belly. Sama slapped her arms back to her sides and scowled at Nandi.

"Oh, Sama." Nandi walked over and grabbed the tatamble girl's hands. "I'm not laughing at you."

"Looks that way to Sama."

"I'm laughing because I'm happy to see you experiencing new things." It was only a partial lie, for it was indeed a hilarious sight, but no need to hurt the other girl's feelings. "We should get moving."

They trekked through the rest of the day and into the night until Sama recommended they stop and make camp.

Nandi hugged her furs around herself against the increasing chill as the day waned. "Wouldn't it be better to sleep up in a tree?" She pointed at the wall of trees less than half a mile away. "We'd be off the ground and away from hunting animals."

Sama shook her head vigorously. "No. Too close to darkwood, that is. Things that live in darkwood roam near. Can climb trees as quiet as a snake. Snatch you out of tree before you wake."

Nandi shuddered at that. "Okay, the ground sounds fine."

Sama nodded. "Sama will keep watch. Keep sister Nandi girl safe."

Nandi appreciated the sentiment, but it made her feel helpless. "I can keep watch while you rest, Sama."

Sama blinked at her a few times. "Nandi girl will sleep and Sama will watch."

Nandi started to argue, but Sama turned away as if the conversation was ended. She pulled her furs close and curled up on the ground. Thoughts of Amiya, Joga, and Dad made sleep elusive. She wondered if they were all okay. Dad was likely fine, since he was in a big city. Hopefully he would still be there by the time she found Amiya and Joga and made it to Altarra.

Amiya would be okay. She had to be. She was the tougher of the two of them, so if Nandi was still breathing, Amiya was surely fine. Nandi said the words in her mind over and over again, willing it to be true. She'd put on a strong face for Sama but the fear that tore at her heart about the possibility that Amiya had fallen was near crippling. From the moment they'd left camp earlier and made it here, Nandi had been functioning on sheer will.

She had to keep going, though. She owed it to Amiya, Dad, Joga, and Sama. Nandi cracked an eye open to look at her tatamble friend; her sister. She'd meant every word she said to Sama. She and Joga had indeed become like family to Nandi and Amiya. But she'd also spoken truthfully that it was different being separated from her twin. It wasn't something she could explain, but she hoped Sama would one day come to understand.

Grief overtook her again. She closed her eye and endured the tiny convulsions of sobbing. Dad was gone, Amiya was gone, Joga was gone. Even though Sama's presence helped, Nandi felt so alone, and she felt guilty for feeling alone despite having Sama with her. The world suddenly seemed so big and overwhelming. When she and Amiya were together, there was nothing they couldn't handle. Even after been kidnapped and separated from Dad, avoiding being butchered during the attack on Vyne, traveling out in the wild with a strange man from a distant land, and attacked by every manner of monster she could have imagined, Nandi and Amiya could handle it all together.

Now, Amiya was lost to her, out there somewhere alone, just like Nandi. She wondered if her sister was lying down to sleep in much the same manner, thinking about Nandi and how to get back to her. Amiya would likely try to put on a strong face to it all, even if only to herself. Nandi choked out a little huff of laugher through the sobs. She knew her twin sister as well as Amiya knew herself. She would be just as overwhelmed as Nandi, and trying to run from it through aggression or anger.

Nandi lay there for a long while, sobbing quietly into her furs so Sama couldn't hear. With Sama finding no signs of Amiya's passage on the way to Altarra, Nandi figured she must have transported herself to a location that would have her moving toward Altarra from a different direction.

She felt eyes on her and opened her own to see Sama kneeling right in front of her. The sight of the black-eyed girl with—now—skin that had gone from pale to dark would have been frightening if she hadn't known the her. Sama wore a curious but sad expression. "Why Nandi girl cry? Already going to find sister Amya? Even agree to find brother Joga."

Nandi hiccupped. "Did … you just call Joga your brother, Sama?"

Sama snarled. "Not call smelly boy that. Nandi girl call him that, so Sama call him that to you."

Nandi started to raise up on her elbow to tease the girl when a cold breeze passed under her side. "Whoa." She settled back down.

Sama watched her for a heartbeat, then stood and moved out of sight. Nandi felt thin strong arms settle around her. "Sister Nandi is cold and Sama is warm," the tatamble said into her ear in that husky loud whisper of her voice. Sama share warmth with sister Nandi."

"Thank you," Nandi replied. After a few quiet moments passed, Nandi found herself curious. "Sama?" When no answer came, she figured the girl had fallen asleep.

"Why Nandi girl call Sama's name but say nothing?"

Nandi blinked her eyes open again. "Oh. When you didn't answer, I thought you'd gone to sleep."

"How would Sama answer a question not yet asked?" Sama replied.

"I … never mind. Let's start again. Why are you alone, Sama?"

"Sama is not alone. Sama has sisters, now."

"Of course," Nandi agreed, approaching this as delicately as she could. "What I mean is, where is the family you were born to? Where is Sama's mother and father?"

Her answer came in the form of silence that stretched for so long, Nandi thought Sama had decided not to answer. But she did.

"Had family, once. When Sama was little girl, she have family. Mother, father, and brother."

"Where did you live?" Nandi asked, intrigued.

"Everywhere," came the answer. "Sama family live in the cold lands south, the hot sandy places where live the big people like brother Joga. We live in the forests, the snow, the mountains."

Nomads? Nandi frowned in thought. *That's a lot of moving around for her to have been so young.* "Why do your family move around so much?"

She felt Sama's arm shift as she got comfortable. "Why wouldn't Sama's family live in many places? World is big and beautiful and different everywhere. Much to see and learn and do. Would love world more if Sister Nandi see it, too."

"You're probably right," Nandi agreed. "Did … did you lose them?"

A tiny growl rumbled up the girl's throat. Nandi felt the power of it creeping up her back. She lay with her eyes wide open, staring straight ahead, wondering if she'd said something to trigger the dangerous girl's emotions.

"Sama did not lose her family. Sama's family taken from this world."

Nandi picked her words carefully. "If you don't want to talk about it—"

"Sama's family roam the world until one day, find tall men fighting. Tall men fighting with flat silver shining sticks and long tree branches, but very straight."

Swords and pikes, Nandi realized. *They wandered into a battle of some kind. Between Khatala and Marai soldiers?*

"Normally, my people stay away. Normally we never seen by tall people that look like brother Joga, or smaller people like men in hard metal furs that die back there." She lifted her arm off Nandi to point back in the direction they'd come. "But some of them steal power of Mother. They take from Mother that we all eat and sleep and live on, and use as weapon. They use life to kill."

The girl growled out those last words. "Family had been asleep in the trees when tall people come with ice and stone and fire death. Trees burn and smoke choke us. Try to run, but smoke get thick. Long sticks of ice with sharp tips shoot past as we run."

Nandi heard Sama's husky voice crack. It was the first time she'd ever heard any kind of emotion or vulnerability from her. Nandi felt her heart break bit by bit with every painful word she knew would follow.

"Sama's moth … mother fall when sharp ice cut through her. Try to go back, but could not. Sharp ice flying everywhere. One hit father and pin him to tree. Sama and brother try to … try to free father but cannot. Tell us to go. We go."

Nandi heard the girl gasping behind her as Sama tried to martial her nerves. "Come to end of the smoke when brother leap far past me and disappear out of cloud. When Sama come clear and look around, she saw brother. He … hhh … hhh, he lay on ground with sharp ice sticking out his back. Sama try … Sama try to help brother. Try to make him get up and run, but he lay there. Look at nothing. Gone."

Nandi rolled over to see agony twisting the other girl's features, but no tears fell. She wrapped her arms around Sama, who breathed heavily into her shoulder. She felt no wetness against her arm, no moaning or sobbing, just gasping. Maybe this was how tatamble wept. "I'm so sorry, Sama," she said into her adoptive sister's hair. "I'm so, so sorry."

She held the girl until Sama pushed her away and stood. "Only family know Sama's story, and I am only one left. Now sister Nandi know Sama's story because Nandi is Sama's family." The tatamble girl looked down at Nandi. Though she couldn't see the other girl's eyes in the dark, she felt the hard determination radiating from the other girl. "Sister Nandi never leave Sama like other family," she said. "Sister Nandi must promise."

"I can't control what happens, Sama," Nandi tried to explain, but Sama would have none of it.

"Sister Nandi *promise*."

The demand was so strong, Nandi found herself bobbing her head like a fool. "Nandi promises," she said. "Nandi promises sister Sama that she will never leave her."

The girl nodded. "When find sister Amya, she promise, too." Nandi lay there watching the tatamble girl who stared back at her with a sour expression for several heartbeats before she added, "and … make stupid brother boy promise, too."

Nandi laughed. "We'll make them promise."

Sama stared at her again for an uncomfortable period of time. "Sister Nandi sleep. Sama keep watch." The girl leaped clean over Nandi and landed several paces away. She sat down cross-legged and stared off into the distance. Nandi stared at the other girl's back, figuring Sama had wrapped herself in the memories of her lost family. She couldn't imagine enduring such a thing.

Watching the girl as she did, Nandi realized Sama's physical strength was only part of her true power. The girl had survived the death of her entire family and lived on her own ever since. Only sharp cunning and a strong will could endure such horrible trauma and carry on.

Nandi closed her eyes. There was something to learn from the strange girl named Sama; a young girl not even human, but of a race of beings illusive to humans. She wondered if anyone other than the Khatala even knew what a tatamble was. She'd never heard of one and never heard any stories from adults about them.

Joga had known, though. Perhaps Khatala people knew more about the world than Marailanders.

She settled quickly into a deep slumber, her body drained from grief. She hoped they'd find Amiya and Joga along the way. The thought of entering Altarra on her own—for Sama would not enter a human civilization—was undesirable at best. In the end, it didn't matter. She had to find Amiya, Dad, and Joga. If she had to go through every magus in Altarra to get to them, so be it.

13

AMIYA

One moment Amiya was lying on the ground about to be pounded to a pulp by a four-armed monster, the next, she was someplace else.

She hit the ground with a grunt, but had no time to catch her breath. Whatever she'd done to get herself from where she'd been to where she was now, Amiya had inadvertently brought the monster with her. No, not monster, she realized. Monsters.

A second four-armed horror dropped out of nowhere behind the first. Amiya scrambled away as she reached for the essences. She found *fire* and grabbed hold of it with desperation. She was just gaining a grasp on air when the tunneler appeared.

"Oh, for the luck of the blasted Fallen," she cursed.

The two four-armed monsters spat their infernal curses at her while banging the weapons gripped in the hands of their lower limbs on the ground. They looked at her with pure malice while the tunneler stalked around from behind them. Its slitted red eyes bore into her as well, as it stalked around the other two creatures.

"This is discouraging," Amiya said. She strained to find the other essences. If she didn't find them soon, these things would have a harder time fighting over what was left of her, than any threat she might pose.

The tunneler twitched the stubs of the severed appendages on its back. Amiya started backing away, while the three monsters stalked forward.

Amiya clenched her jaw. She couldn't outrun them, and the thought of fighting just one of the things was laughable, given what she'd seen a single drauk do to a team of soldiers. She would either fight with the essences or die right here, right now. A cold line of fear ran down her spine at the thought of what these things would do to her. The gruesome aftermath of what they'd done to the travelers and Shetaran soldiers would be forever burned into her memory.

She stopped backing away and stood her ground, straining with every ounce of her will to find and grab hold of the other essences. She *would* survive this. Nandi was somewhere—

The two four-armed monsters lunged toward her, weapons raised high and out at their sides. They covered so much ground with their outstretched limbs that Amiya had no hope of getting around them. Thoughts of her twin sister flashed through Amiya's mind. She'd been separated from her other half, all because of these things.

The icy layer of fear freezing her spine melted under an inferno of rage. Amiya curled her fingers at her sides, her teeth bared in a furious snarl. *Fire* sprang to her call. No, not her call, her demand. The essence lit around her body, shining like a torch that could surely be seen from the stars twinkling in the night sky.

At the last moment, she truly looked at the monsters for the first time as they tore across the distance between them. Their skin was like cooled lava rock with tiny lines of red flowing lava coursing over and through their bodies. If she launched the flames into them, it might well invigorate the things.

Fire winked out of her left hand to be replaced with *air*. She struggled to find *water* even as she heard the thudthud thud, thudthud thud of the tunneler's heavy footfalls as it charged behind the four-armed monsters. She thought of Nandi, Dad, Joga, and Sama. She'd been separated from them because of Archminister Bigbelly. Whether his hand in it was direct or indirect, or how absurd it might be to blame him for the monsters bearing down on her, Amiya used him as a focal point of her ire and magnified it many times over.

The closest four-armed monster leaped into the air. Amiya launched ice spears at it. The spears were wider around than her body, far more power than necessary. The ice punched through the rocky monster with such force, its body jerked wildly before it crashed to the ground in a splash of earth and debris.

Amiya dove aside, barely avoiding the chop of a rocky sword. She rolled onto her side and opened her palm. Freezing wind swirled in front of her until it looked like a tiny hurricane that could fit in the palm of both her hands. She released it at the same time the second monster turned and struck down with the club of the nearest lower limb.

The wind froze the club as well as the arm. She saw the tunneler leap into the air and ram its narrow head into the ground while slashing its paws. It disappeared into the ground, leaving a huge hole in its wake.

Amiya didn't have more than a heartbeat or two before that thing would come up from under her. The tiny hurricane enlarged the moment she released it. The power of the tempest threw the drauk off balance long enough for Amiya to freeze the air in front of her while grasping for *earth*.

The ground rippled as the tunneler made its way toward her. Amiya finally found *earth* and hardened the ground beneath her like Joga had done. At the same time, she released a storm of freezing wind into the lava rock monster.

Laboring grunts mingled with the monster's growling curses. It dropped to its knees, lower hands balled into fists that pounded the ground. It leaned forward to resist the assault, but the frigid air stole the heat from its rocky skin.

The slab of hard ground beneath Amiya burst up, as she knew it would. She knelt and touched the ground. When the tunneler burst up underneath her and hit the hard slab, Amiya used *earth* to create dozens of small stalactites punching down from the underside of the slab and into the tunneler's flat, plated head. At the same time, she sent larger stalagmites growing out of the ground, angling toward the beast.

Her timing was perfect. The tunneler died impaled between the stalactites under her platform, and the stalagmites risen from the ground.

Amiya had nearly tumbled off the slab, but somehow remained on her perch. She looked down to see the kneeling lava rock monster, red, black, and brown rocky skin turning blue as it crumbled apart.

Amiya plopped back onto her backside and panted. *How in the name of the Creator did I do all that?* She looked at the remains of the skewered and frozen rock monsters, then at the slab beneath her. Normally she struggled to grasp even one essence, yet when her need was desperate, they readily heeded her call.

Amiya leaned back on her hands and looked around while she caught her breath. Endless hills of stoutgreens carpeted the mountains as far as she could see in any direction. A snowcapped mountain stood nearby as if having born witness to her narrow survival under the pale light of the moon. It wasn't until the crickets began to chirp that she realized everything had been deathly quiet. No doubt every living thing for miles had heard what happened here.

She shimmied to the edge of the slab and swung a leg over to climb down when she heard a rustling in the trees nearby. Eyes fixed in the direction of the noise, Amiya silently brought her leg back up and moved away from the edge until she was crouched in the center of the platform.

A set of yellow eyes appeared in the dark brush. Another

appeared several feet to the right. Amiya's eyes moved left to right as she silently watched pair after pair of yellow eyes appear in the woods less than fifty feet away.

Great. Without thinking, she crouched lower and placed her hands on the stone. She felt its composition, all of the large and small bits that came together to form the solid block of stone that held her aloft. She sensed the tiny forms of life moving through the stone.

Amiya frowned. What did that mean? The bushes rustled again when the eyes started moving closer. Amiya tried to ignore her heart hammering in her chest while she tried to figure out what to do about this new problem.

Tiny mites, flees, worms, and many forms of living rock all became apparent to Amiya through the stone platform she touched. She might have enjoyed the sensation if she wasn't near panic. Could she do anything with this? The silhouettes of bodies attached to the yellow eyes materialized out of the darkness and into the light of the moon.

When the mischievous mewling started, Amiya felt her heart sink into her stomach. The mewling continued, playful, taunting, a promise of death. Darkwood cats.

Amiya glanced down at her stone perch. If it were another fifty feet higher, she might be out of reach. As things were, she was little more than a snack for one of those things. Another pair of eyes appeared in the brush, these hovering much higher than the others.

The sight of the thing tore a curse from Amiya's mouth that would have had her in trouble with Dad in spite of the pack of lethal predators. She frantically reached for the essences, but barely found a trickle. "Not now!" she growled. She strained harder. The Fallen blasted power *would* come to her. She would not die here. The thick, musty odor of furry predators crept into Amiya's nose. Just the smell of the things nearly undid her.

Amiya looked around. Maybe a random weapon somewhere? A

fallen branch with a sharp tip? Maybe they wouldn't try to jump her up here with that dead tunneler skewered below.

The darkwood cats converged in an arc, mewling like kittens. Humongous kittens. Their angular feline faces showed no murderous intent, just an intense interest. Amiya tried not to focus on the tips of many pairs of teeth protruding from the top of their whiskered muzzles.

In the moonlight, she saw that these weren't the black cats with wavy white stripes she and the others had encountered before. These had green coats, with wavy brown stripes. Was there any difference between the two types other than the color of the cat eating you? Maybe a difference in temperament? Looking at the many yellow eyes focused on her, she had no intention to climb down and find out.

The largest darkwood cat that Amiya figured to be the alpha, moved closest until it was only a few feet away. Sweat trickled down the side of her face. That thing could easily bound up on the stone platform and snatch her up in one bite. At least it would be quick. Maybe it would take her in the neck. Hopefully she wouldn't feel much.

Amiya started to close her eyes, but no, never. If death had found her this day, she wouldn't cry or be afraid. The essences ignored her call and she couldn't fight these things. There was nothing she could do. She stood tall and stared down at the alpha darkwood cat.

The giant cat watched her for several tense heartbeats and seemed to acknowledge her challenge. It reared back and stood up on its hind legs. The thing already stood taller than Amiya on four legs. On two, it stood almost tall enough to look over the top of the stone slab, which sat over ten feet high.

Amiya felt the blood in her veins run cold and settle into the pit of her stomach. This thing would shred her without a thought. She stood transfixed by its unblinking yellow stare and didn't react when it placed one big paw on the side of the platform.

Not like this. She couldn't die like this. Amiya's face tightened in concentration. Once again, she willed the essences to come, demanded it of them. She screamed in her mind until it burst free in a shriek that quieted the chirping insects and shattered the resulting silence at the same time.

The alpha continued to stare into her eyes as if it had heard nothing. She wondered if it was somehow trying to comfort her; maybe tell her it was okay, and that it would all be over soon. Maybe it was curious that she didn't run like prey normally would.

Its paw compressed against the stone as it prepared to hop onto it, but then it stopped. One long pointed ear swiveled in the direction of the woods to Amiya's right. Other sets of ears swiveled in the same direction as yellow eyes turned their focus from Amiya to the trees.

"What mark on this day is it that I find such an impressive pack of cats, led by such an even more impressive alpha, focused on a single, unimpressive prey?"

The voice came from the woods. Amiya knew sound couldn't have weight, but the voice, a woman's voice, drifted heavily through the air.

"What brings cats of the werewood so far from home, to hunt such a small morsel?" the voice continued. "Is food so scarce?"

The giant cat in front of Amiya released the platform and dropped down to four legs. It turned in the direction of the voice, as did every other of the feline predators.

Amiya's eyes darted from the predatory cats to the trees and back. The voice brought her no comfort at all. She wondered which she'd prefer dealing with.

A person finally stepped into view, the moonlight barely illuminating her enough to be little more than a shadow.

Amiya stared in openmouthed disbelief. The woman, while tall, looked to be no more a physical threat to this pack of darkwood cats than she. Maybe she was some kind of insane woman who'd lived out in the woods for too long, away from people, and had lost her mind. She didn't know what to expect from this, but if that woman was indeed crazy and threw herself at a pack of darkwood cats, Amiya prepared herself to take off the instant she did.

Despite those thoughts, however, Amiya found herself instead continuing her struggle to grab hold of the essences. She didn't intend to die if she could help it, but she wouldn't leave someone else to die, either, crazy or not. Plus, the woman had bought Amiya some time.

Round eyes the color of violet focused solely on Amiya, as if the presence of the giant cats were of no consequence. When she met that gaze, what little grasp she had of the essences fell away.

The cats started mewling again. Amiya's terror bubbled to the surface again, and she tried to crush it. The cats had forgotten her, however. Every set of eyes had focused on the woman who'd stepped into their midst.

Amiya watched as the big alpha moved toward the woman. Its smooth coat slid like silk over bulging muscles that could probably spring the thing a dozen feet into the air. Maybe higher.

The more Amiya saw of the animal, the more she wanted to be as far away as possible from where she stood. These things were killing machines. The sheer power she saw in it, just casually walking toward the unafraid woman told Amiya that nothing short of wielding the essences themselves gave her any chance of surviving an attack by one, let alone a pack.

She realized that the cats knew it, too. She saw a natural confidence in all those yellow eyes that spoke of life at the top of the food chain.

It strode toward the woman as if in amusement, and stopped right before her. It let out a deep mewling sound that revealed a set of upper fangs half the length of a man's hand.

Amiya fought not to shiver at the sight of those very large teeth, only a few feet away from the woman who seemed not at all concerned. She wanted nothing more than to quietly slip away and run away as fast as she could.

The impossibility of that thought led her to another. What was that thing Nandi had done back in Vyne? The moment before being discovered by one of the four-armed monsters attacking Vyne, Nandi had done something to make them invisible. How did she do it? The answer eluded Amiya as easily as did the essences she so desperately sought.

With another deep mewl, the darkwood cat licked its chops as it moved just a little closer. Amiya could see it was preparing to spring. It didn't. The alpha cat tilted its head at the woman, as if it was as surprised as Amiya that it hadn't pounced on the woman and began devouring her.

A strange sensation settled over Amiya. Subtle at first, but building, she felt the woman's presence grow, as if she had a non-physical body that began to grow inch by inch. Amiya shrank away to the edge of the stone platform. She wasn't the only one. The other darkwood cats backed away, mewling in what clearly sounded like hesitance.

The alpha snarled, even snapped its jaws. It rose up to its full height to tower over the woman. She tilted her head to look up at it. In the pale moonlight, Amiya thought she saw a grin on the woman's face before a cloud passed and cast her in shadow.

"You are magnificent," the woman said. She gave a casual wave of her hand as if dismissing the beast.

Amiya's mouth fell open again. Apparently the gesture was just that, for the alpha dropped back on all-fours, made a rumbling sound deep in its belly, and turned aside.

The woman looked back to Amiya as she gave the feline a single pat on its side, letting her hand drag along its flank as it moved away.

At some point, Amiya must have sat down, for that's where she remained, on her backside, frozen in fear like a cornered mouse as the woman approached. She thought she caught the scent of roses and fresh rain as the woman drew near.

"Who is this little creature that has wandered so far from everything?" Her dark blue cloak hung over her shoulders, partially concealing the rest of her body. With each step that brought the woman closer, Amiya felt her heart thumping heavier in her chest. The corner of the woman's lips were stretched into a half smile. She was as beautiful as the long gone darkwood cats, but Amiya got the feeling she was far more deadly.

Amiya didn't realize she'd been backing away until she reached the opposite edge of the stone slab. With no more space to retreat, she watched as the woman stopped to within several paces of the raised platform and inspected it. She arched an eyebrow. "Impressive. In fact, I'd say this work of art is rather creative."

Strands of her smooth and thick black hair fell over her face when she tilted her head to look over the impaled monster. She nodded in appreciation, then looked back at Amiya. "Would you tell me, girl, how it is that you destroyed two drauk and did this," she waved a hand at the dead monster, "to a tunneler, yet nearly became the meal of a pack of werewood cats?"

"Dumb luck," Amiya said. She meant it, too. How could she have killed three monsters by herself yet freeze up, now? She was so angry with herself she could have spat.

The woman studied her face for a long time. Normally, Amiya would have asked what she was looking at and why, but not this woman.

"You have power you've yet to master," she said. "Quite a bit of it, actually. Intriguing."

Amiya didn't know if the woman was talking to her, or herself. Not knowing what else to do, she sat down at the edge of the stone platform and sized the woman up. Medium build, tall, but not a runner's body. Even with her shorter legs, Amiya might still be able to outrun the woman. She remembered the little encounter a few minutes ago and cast that notion out.

"You want to run," the woman observed. The half-smile returned. "I suppose that instinct is correct, but so is your hesitation. You'd be caught before your feet touched the ground."

Amiya marshaled whatever courage she had and stood up. She walked to the other edge of the slab and looked down at the woman. "I'm not running anywhere."

The half-smile turned into a full one.

Amiya returned the violet stare even though her knees wanted to buckle and every instinct in her body screamed at her to flee. "Before you do whatever you're going to do, at least tell me your name."

"Are you sure, girl?"

Amiya frowned. "Why not?"

"Because you will be more afraid than you are, now."

"Try me."

The woman arched an eyebrow at that. "You're a strong one. Very well. I've been known by several names throughout the ages. Eycia, Belerada, Mariella. But you, my strong little girl. To you, I give my real name. It is Estrella."

Amiya frowned. Why did this woman have four names, and what was "throughout the ages" supposed to mean? Again Amiya suspected that living out here with no human contact must have gotten to this lady's wits.

The smile on Estrella's face remained, while her violet eyes narrowed. "Not very learned in history, are we? That may be for the good. Those who believe they know the truth of events long past often lack the finer details lost to time."

Amiya's mouth hung open until she found her voice again. "Miss Estrella. I haven't the slightest idea what you're talking about, but, um, thanks for saving me from those dark … I mean werewood cats."

Estrella stared at her for several heartbeats before responding. "You are welcome, girl. And you are lucky. Darkwood cats are fierce enough, but werewood cats are not only smarter, but have a tendency to play with their prey before the kill. Though both can transform, they are distinguishable by their color and size. Our departed friends," she waved toward the woods, "are larger than their darkwood cousins."

Maybe I'll survive this after all. "Thanks for the education,"
Amiya said. "I wasn't sure if that big one was planning to eat me
or play."

"Possibly both."

"That's pretty cruel," Amiya said. She needed to keep this
Estrella talking while she figured out what to do."

Estrella shrugged. "There are other animals that share the trait."

"Yeah," Amiya said. "I've seen regular small cats do it, too."

"Now then," Estrella said. "Please sate my curiosity by telling
me how a girl of your age managed to *bridge* herself and three
others all the way up here. When last I was awake, there wasn't a
human civilization nearby for many, many leagues."

"When you were awake." Amiya frowned. "Are you not
human?"

Estrella responded with a slow blink, that lazy smile just
beneath the surface.

"Um, okay." Amiya ran a hand over her head. She'd need to re-
braid her cornrows, but Nandi wasn't here. Thinking of her sister
threatened to break her heart. She pushed it away. No time to fall
apart now. "I don't know where "here" is, and I don't know what
you're talking about when you say *"bridge"* either. One minute I
was in the middle of a camp that was attacked by a bunch of four-
armed monsters and three tunnelers, the next minute I'm here."

"Somehow you are here," Estrella replied. "Having dispatched
two drauk and a tsorek, or tunneler, as you've called it."

"Whatever they're called," Amiya said, "they're terrible; cut
down a bunch of innocent travelers and some Shetaran soldiers,
too."

Estrella's lips parted at that. "Shetaran soldiers. Impressive
indeed."

Amiya scrunched up her face at that. "How so? I mean ..." she
waved a hand to indicate the pile of rubble that remained of the
two drauk, and the impaled tunneler under the platform, "yeah, I

won't be stupid and say this was nothing, but I doubt that's what you're talking about."

"Dispatching two creatures of the underworld and one that surfaces only during the darkest of times is indeed an impressive feat," Estrella agreed. "But to have used a technique forgotten to time by all but the most studied magi … that is most impressive."

"You mean that *bridging* thing?" Amiya asked.

"I mean that *bridging* thing," Estrella answered.

"Um, how far am I from Shetar?" Amiya asked. In truth, she couldn't point out Shetar on a map unless the name was written on it."

"A day or two on a swift bird's wings," came the answer.

Amiya's eyes widened. "What?"

"Would you like to continue our conversation down here, girl?" Estrella asked. "I'm not of a mind to continue looking up at you, nor standing in front of a deceased tsorek draining lifeblood."

Amiya tried to figure out something to say to that, but no words came. She didn't want to get down, but she also knew that if the woman wanted to come up there, or bring Amiya down, herself, she could probably do just that. "Okay."

Estrella smiled at her. "There's a good girl."

Amiya growled at that, to which the woman responded with a heavy and haunting chuckle. Once again Amiya felt the weight in Estrella's voice and wondered who or what she was?

"You have a way of pushing past your fear," Estrella remarked. "That is good, but you use anger to do it. Anger is an unreliable conduit."

Amiya tried to appear casual about it. "Eh. It's served me this far."

"Until it didn't," Estrella countered.

Her bluster dissolved, Amiya could do nothing more than shrug.

"Walk with me," Estrella said. She didn't wait for a reply, but started toward the trees from where she'd come."

Amiya stood and watched the departing woman until she was nearly to the tree line, then bolted in the other direction. She ran as quietly as she could, trying not even to breath heavily. She didn't look back until she was well into the woods. She hid behind a tree and peeked around the side. It didn't look like Estrella had pursued her.

She turned back and kept running. There might be darkwood cats or werewood cats or whatever the Fallen blasted things were called, but she'd deal with the situation if it came. But that woman? No. Something felt decidedly off about Estrella, which made Amiya uneasy. Not to mention her eyes. Nobody had violet eyes.

The terrain started to decline, but with the thickness of the forest, Amiya doubted that Estrella woman could find her in here. She'd figure out how far she was from Altarra later, then work her way there. Nandi, Sama, and Joga would be moving in that direction, she was sure.

So wrapped up in her thoughts was she, that Amiya didn't notice the drop-off until it was nearly under her feet. She choked off her cry of surprise in desperation when she stepped into open air.

There were no roots or vines or tree branches to grab hold of, no sloping ground to ease her fall. Amiya plummeted swiftly toward a beautifully vegetated, and rocky death complimented by several waterfalls all escorting her to oblivion.

Despite the futility of it, she kept reaching out even as her body turned end over end, desperately reaching for a handhold that wasn't there. She was dozens of feet away from the sheer cliff wall, and there was nothing but solid mountain there anyway. The world suddenly slowed and wavered, like rippling water after a stone had been cast in.

"Ugh." Amiya hit the ground on her side. She blinked several times, then looked herself over. She ran her hands over her arms and legs, her head. How? "Did I do it again?" she thought aloud.

"I could have provided better directions, had you asked."

Amiya scrambled to her feet and spun to see Estrella standing with a hand on her hip, some of her thick and wavy black hair draped over her shoulder. Her smile was terrifying. "Careful what directions you take in life, girl. Or you'll find, too late, that you have fallen."

14

THE FALLEN

Devrin waited in silent darkness as one after another of the Myrtolus arrived. The weak-minded of every age referred to them as the Fallen, but nothing could be further from the truth.

The Fallen.

Devrin let his eyelids droop in boredom at the stupidity of the term. He had to give the Order of Magi credit, though. They'd managed to attach to Devrin and the others a term that had an intuitively negative connotation to it. That Devrin and the other Myrtolus had attained such a high level of knowledge and mastery of the essences had only made it easier to make them out as monsters to the uneducated and weak-willed. No, they were not the Fallen, but the Myrtolus; the power, the ascended.

As expected, Revdrak entered the meeting chamber first. As soon as the brute's silhouette filled the entryway, Devrin commanded *fire*. One by one, the torches lining the walls flared to life.

Revdrak let out a quiet snort. The man had taken on many a different look over the ages. Defeat after defeat at the hands of the Illuminarians had driven Revdrak to alter his appearance to match his mood. Now, several red rings held up a long ponytail sitting at the top back corner of his otherwise shaved head. His bushy eyebrows arched up at the corners, and angled down toward the bridge of his nose in a perpetual scowl. He took a seat in the circular chamber directly across from Devrin, as was his typical choice. They locked stares as Revdrak stroked his thick chin goatee.

Next came Sebanavick. The man practically stormed into the meeting chamber, stopped just inside, and favored Devrin with a devious grin. Average height, somewhat thin build, and overall unremarkable presence, one of the man's best weapons was his ability to be underestimated. Devrin returned the grin with a more conservative one, and a nod of acknowledgement. While he wanted to serve as Devrin's right hand—his sword, as the man referred to himself—in the inevitable battle against the Order of Magi, Devrin understood well, the nature of that one. Sebanavick loved violence and destruction. So long as there was conflict, Devrin could control him. But once the master of the Order of Magi was removed and Devrin took his place, Sebanavick would have to be … met with.

Lenara practically glided into the room. Her blonde curls bounced as she made a show of dusting off her already pristine blue shirt, breeches and styled overcoat. Devrin watched it all in minor irritation. It was worse than if the woman had simply stated that she didn't like meeting in a chamber carved inside of a mountain. Not that it would have mattered, for this was exactly where they'd met for ages past, and Devrin wasn't about to hunt for a new location just to suit the high maintenance woman.

As with every other meeting of the Myrtolus, she took the seat that placed her exactly to the side of Devrin, where she could easily see everyone. She was smart and quick of wit, but Devrin found her scheming an annoyance at best, and dangerous at worst. There was, however, the fact that she'd been smart enough to see the potential pitfalls of creating Shurza. That she'd seen it as a bad idea while Devrin himself had not was a mark in her favor. If he could harness her conniving to serve his own needs, it could make things easier.

The short and powerful form of Mordayne appeared next. Her auburn hair practically glowed in the warm light of the crackling torches. Of all the Myrtolus, she was the one Devrin hoped to sway to his ambitions. While she might not care much for anything that didn't serve her own purposes, if he could find the proper carrot to dangle in front of her nose, there might be something there to work with.

As the moments passed, private conversations ensued. Devrin looked at the two empty seats on either side of the circle and mentally sighed. One, fashionably late, the other, unpredictable.

On of the stragglers arrived as if called by Devrin's thoughts. Udorian sauntered into the chamber as though all had been waiting in anticipation of his arrival. From his waist-length flowing white hair to his perfectly fitted silver shirt, pants, and black boots with matching silver overcoat, Udorian looked as though he'd just arrived from a meeting with royalty.

"I see I'm not the last to arrive, after all," Udorian said, looking at the empty seat across from him.

"Not for lack of trying," Mordayne quipped.

"Let's be on with it, shall we?" Revdrak said. His booming voice quieted the chamber. "The Shurza is free, we are returned to the world … once *again*, and time moves."

"You speak as someone not living outside the confines of mortality, Rev," Lenara said. "Have you someplace urgent you must be?"

Revdrak's face tightened, his hands resting on his knees balled into fists. "If we are free, who else might be, Lenara? Even now, Malkiem is likely brainstorming against us, and it."

It. Devrin watched the man as he spoke. He didn't know which Revdrak hated more, Shurza, for bending them to its will, or every other Myrtolus for agreeing to create it. The man wasn't stupid, but rather, straightforward. The typical warrior. Devrin could practically hear the man's personal philosophy in his mind. "Defeat your foe yourself, and not with underhanded advantages to compensate for personal weaknesses."

Devrin wondered if the man's sense of honor would be his undoing, one day. And he wondered if it would be one of those seated here that would bring it about.

"Malkiem is probably smelling flowers and collecting himself again before he thinks of doing anything aggressive," Sebanavick replied. "He's probably founding some church of morality, preaching of the responsibilities of wielding power while people throw themselves from nearby cliffs to get his pontificating out of their ears."

Mordayne partially turned her head toward Devrin and scratched her eyebrow to hide her eye-rolling. Lenara, sitting perfectly erect in her seat, legs crossed at the knee, blinked slowly at the dramatic statement.

"Well," Udorian said. "Now that we've gotten the day's irony out of the way, I'm interested to know what the world looks like, now, and how we've come to be here."

The assembled fell into silence while Devrin studied them all. Directly across from him, Revdrak never took his eyes off Devrin. He wanted a plan and he wanted to take action. Several defeats resulting in their being imprisoned with Shurza had made him progressively more angry. Devrin couldn't blame the man. He also had no intention of returning to their imprisonment, especially with Shurza in the bargain. Just thinking about the timeless space they'd occupied with the blight essence's ever-present malevolence gave him chills.

"Unlike us, Malkiem has complications to deal with," Devrin began. "Unlike previous times," he pointedly didn't look at Revdrak, "three of them were yanked into the void by Shurza. Without the connection to it that we possess, can you imagine what that would do to someone? Assuming it didn't rip their souls asunder and devour them, they would doubtlessly awaken quite damaged."

All around the circle were nods of agreement at that. Shurza's mere presence was overwhelming to the point of being maddening. Devrin had struggled not to flee its presence despite being the leader in its creation. It was pure evil, the absence of all light, and devourer of life.

"I have a hard time believing all three of them survived their time in the void, but if by some slim margin they have, they will be damaged, Malkiem included."

"The easier to pick them off one at a time or all at once," Sebanavick said.

"I'm sure it'll be exactly that easy," Mordayne replied.

Sebanavick snarled at her. "Would you have us weave blankets and swaddle them instead?"

Udorian laughed.

"Perhaps it's time for a different approach." Lenara looked at Devrin, and he nodded for her to continue. "Ever has our conflict with the Illuminarians been as one unit. It has always been a battle between our two factions. Perhaps this time we should each appeal to one of them on our own? It could be that without the collective energy of conflict fueling the endless hostilities between us, we might have a breakthrough."

Revdrak and Sebanavick looked at her as though she were insane, Udorian favored her with an openmouthed grin, while Mordayne stared at her with an unreadable expression.

Devrin, too, kept his expression neutral. Of everyone in this room, he trusted Lenara the least.

"Do you truly believe that?" Sebanavick asked. "They've been our mortal enemies for thousands of years. They've pushed us into imprisonment in the void ... over and over again ... for *thousands* of years. You want to approach one of them and trade baking tips, go right ahead, Lenara. The only thing I'm planning to do when I see one is obliterate them on the spot."

"As with every other meeting," Lenara countered, "you lay out a detailed plan of defeating the Illuminarians by way of obliteration. Your plans have been fruitful, I'm sure?"

Sebanavick waved a hand from her to Devrin. "What is this nonsense? Can we get on with the real meeting, or shall we continue to entertain this idiocy?"

"Amusing that one who specializes in nothing more than destruction, finds himself repeatedly beaten upon encountering a competent foe." Lenara favored him with a sweet grin. "Yet, you label my words idiocy."

"Take care, Lenara," Sebanavick warned, his tone low and even.

For the first time since his arrival, Revdrak looked to be enjoying himself. He looked from one to the other with amusement.

"I merely point out the obvious, Sebanavick," Lenara continued. "You are obviously good at what you do, yet if an Illuminarian is good at one thing, it's teaming up against one of superior might. You could easily crush any one of them on your own, perhaps even Malkiem himself. They know this. Why else do you find yourself battling more than one of them every time we've clashed."

Lenara's thin red lips stretched into a smile. "My suggestion places you face to face, one on one, with one of them. Not two, not three. Just one. I wonder then, how different the outcome might be."

Sebanavick leaned back in his chair and rubbed his chin. "There is truth to your words. Though I wish you'd just come out with it in the first place instead of taking the winding road to your point."

The corner of Mordayne's mouth twitched in a flicker of a smile, and she dropped her gaze to the floor then back to the speakers. It happened so quickly, no one noticed. No one except Devrin, that is. With Revdrak focused on the conversation and not staring at him, Devrin looked directly at the woman. Mordayne returned his look from the corner of her eye for nearly a heartbeat.

There might be something there. While he had no doubts on Sebanavick's loyalty to him, Devrin also had no doubt that such loyalty would only last as long as there was a foe to fight. He needed an ally for the endgame, once the Illuminarians were finished.

The Order of Magi had turned its back on Devrin out of irrational fear. Why study and pursue power, then stop short of greatness? That they had first commanded Devrin to cease his ambitions to further push the limits to what could be done with the essences was bad enough. But the hypocrisy of allowing Malkiem and his ilk to purse that same power in order to stop Devrin was unforgivable. The Order had remained stagnant from that very moment.

The irony was as amazing as it was enraging. The Order thought it knew best, yet any one of the individuals seated here could decimate a good portion of the fortress of their little organization singlehandedly. Devrin had tried appealing to the then magi master, centuries ago, but the man had been weak, intimidated by the power Devrin had shown him. Jorn might be long dead, but his cowardice lived on in every magi master that had succeeded him.

And here they were again. Devrin watched as Lenara weaved Sebanavick into her web like a spider wrapping up a fly. Revdrak watched it all with suspicion, not entirely sure of the woman's sincerity, while Mordayne and Udorian looked as though they were trying to keep from laughing. And through it all, Devrin wondered where in the world might be the one person he felt he may be able to trust.

Where was Estrella?

"… simply saying, once again, that Malkiem and his sheep will be expecting the same from us. We must go to them, one to one. It could prove advantageous and reduce the risk of them banding together against any one of us who might normally best them."

Revdrak actually nodded at that. "There may be something to what you say."

Lenara smiled and nodded.

"Your example may well work out," the big man went on. "I know you have a personal feud with Amadon. Maybe you could reach out and sway her to a personal meeting? Or perhaps Zeraphal?"

Lenara's smile evaporated while Revdrak's grew. Not a single person in here thought for an instant that Amadon and Lenara could be in each other's presence for longer than an instant before it came to blows. The suggestion that she meet with Zeraphal said quite clearly that Revdrak hadn't taken the bait as Sebanavick had.

The latter snorted. "Zeraphal?" Sebanavick leaned forward and rested his elbows on his knees. "Best leave that one to me, Lenara."

Mordayne lowered her head and cleared her throat to hide her laughter. Lenara glared at Revdrak, then Sebanavick. "Not a bad idea, since you both cut like a sword, but possess the wit of its scabbard."

"The wit of its scabbard?" Sebanavick echoed.

"Scabbards are blunt-edged," Udorian explained. "She's saying your dumb, Seb."

"Not dumb," Lenara said, her voice as smooth as the web of a black widow. "Merely straightforward and hard of exterior to—"

"That will be enough," Devrin said. "The Illuminarians are either awake and returned, as we are, or will be soon. The souls of three of them will have been returned to their bodies. This will be a jarring experience, considering where they were and the endless time they spent trying not to be devoured. If they perished, all the better, but we will act as if that is not the case.

"Those who have seen the true potential of the existence we lead will have continued their work and continued to nurture the factions we created within the order. Our droughtlords will have awakened from their dormancy. While only one of them can move about undetected, their underlords carry no markings to distinguish them. We must learn the mood of the world and what happens. It could be the Order has already been taken over, and simply awaits our return. Or it may yet remain hobbled by the superstitious and feeble beliefs that have held it back, age after age. We must find out."

"Says our leader?" Revdrak asked, his tone thick with challenge. "The same leader who has led us to ruin time and again?"

"If you've a better way to begin, let us hear it, Revdrak. I've not covered everything yet, but if you have something to offer …" Devrin spread his hands.

"It is awake and loose upon the world," Revdrak stated, still refusing to call Shurza by its name. "Anyone with a pedestrian knowledge of history will see it as the coming of the ruination, and rightly so. The thing will have left desolation in its wake wherever it's gone. The Illuminarians won't be the only ones looking to find and destroy it." He shrugged his massive shoulders. "Leave them to it."

Udorian looked as if he wanted to move as far away from the man as possible. Everyone else did as well. Even Devrin found himself fighting the urge to move away. He didn't know how the others felt about their servitude to Shurza, but Devrin hated it. Still, to speak in such a way was the worst kind of suicide, should the blight essence hear his words.

"I'm not saying leave them to destroy it," Revdrak clarified. "Could they do it, anyway? I doubt so. I merely suggest we let these children who call themselves magi find it. They will die to a person, while the Illuminarians are collecting themselves. With the order of children sacrificing themselves, there will be nothing to interfere with us. We can finally deal with our enemies decisively."

Udorian chuckled. "There would be a pursuit, all right."

Devrin caught the other man's meaning. Revdrak's plan wasn't the worst, aside from the fact that if there was a single magi in the Order with even a smattering of historical knowledge, it wouldn't happen that way. There would be a hunt, but it wouldn't be for Shurza or themselves. It would be to find the Illuminarians.

"You sound like you have something better in mind," Revdrak said.

"I do?" Udorian replied. "Allow me to set things straight, then. I don't have anything to suggest other than having no desire to return to that cursed void again. Even if it means finding a quiet corner of the world and settling in."

"Ha!" Mordayne finally broke her silence. "An endless existence of picking weeds and flowers on some mountain or in some meadow, Udorian? You would break the world through boredom-induced insanity."

"Have you spent your time in the void nursing your desires to take over the Order?" Revdrak asked.

Devrin met the man's fierce gaze without blinking. "I have."

The brute made a disgusted sound and looked away.

"Feel free to do whatever it is that pleases you, Revdrak," Devrin said. "I will pursue my ends, which I believe to be in alignment with Shurza. You are obviously welcome to leave, if that is not the case for you."

"I know that," came the reply. "I would have left if I wished. I would not have come here if I did not wish to. I do not come here at Devrin's command."

"Of course not," Devrin said. The room had gone quiet and still while the two men locked horns.

For a moment, Devrin thought the situation would further deteriorate until Udorian cleared his throat. "Well, as energetic as this all is, we have a lot of work to do. I'm sure I don't have to tell anyone that we'll need to be the ones finding Shurza as quickly as possible."

That brought a round of rumbling agreement. Only once had they tried to ignore Shurza's subtle call while pursuing their own conquests. The result had been a rather undesirable visit from the blight essence, resulting in being drained to within inches of their lives. It was one thing to be beaten nearly to death with a weapon. It was another thing to be used as a conduit to drain essence at such an accelerated rate that it left you almost a dried-out husk, simultaneously clinging to the flicker of life left to you while wishing for the release of death.

Their relationship with Shurza resembled a symbiotic relationship more heavily leaning to one side, yet no one had a choice in it. They would find Shurza and collectively feed it so that it could sustain itself long enough to build the strength to move on its own. Then, it would find and eliminate the Illuminarians. If they didn't do as expected, it would find them, and inflict that terrible torture.

"I suppose our *master* will be all settled in wherever it is, shortly," Lenara said. "Then we'll get our *summons*."

"Don't call it that," Revdrak said. When Lenara looked questioningly at him, he said in a much quieter voice, "master. Don't … call it our master. We created it and fight alongside it to achieve our goals."

Lenara favored him with a dubious look. "Speak as you wish."

Revdrak glared at his fists. Devrin understood the man's frustration. The surrounding sour expressions spoke of mutual feelings by all. Well, there was no way to know for sure, because no one dared speak ill of it. The only reason Revdrak dared speak as he had was because, despite their connection with the blight essence, Shurza would not have full cognizance yet. At the moment, it would have found someplace remote to gather itself to call to them and await their arrival.

"It is as it is," Mordayne replied. "Devrin is correct. Until Shurza calls on us, it's best we learn what happens in the world and plan accordingly. If anyone is aware of Shurza's release, word will spread quickly."

"And denial will chirp just as loudly or more so," Udorian said. "People will not want to believe our return. That will buy us time."

"Not a lot," Mordayne warned. "Some of the general populous would deny our return even if Shurza were to hover over their very homes. But those who matter, those who will actively stand against us will believe. And they *will* act swiftly."

"Mordayne speaks with wisdom," Lenara said. She opened her hands on her lap when Mordayne cast her a suspicious look. "Tis true, sister. Your words hold wisdom. There is a reason the strong of mind lead their opposites. While most of the world denies, the strong will prepare for us." She shrugged. "It will matter not, but they will prepare nonetheless."

"And what we do not need," Devrin added, "is anything detracting from our immediate goal, which is to find the Illuminarians and dispose of them before they've collected themselves and begin looking for us."

"In that case," Udorian said, "we'd best get our eyes and ears looking. Once I know their condition, perhaps I'll send a droughtlord or four to pay one a visit."

Lenara tittered while Revdrak let out a thunderous laugh. "Unless your chosen target is lying on death's door, you'd best be looking to create a new "droughtlord or four" with that plan."

Udorian shrugged as if it didn't matter. "There are always others vying for the job."

"And there's plenty of time to train and strengthen one, *surely*," Mordayne remarked. Again, Udorian shrugged. This time Mordayne didn't hide her eye-roll.

Devrin narrowed his eyes at Udorian's nonsense. No one would believe him that much of a fool. "You must be growing bored, Udorian, for why else would you make such a ridiculous suggestion. If you find this bothersome, feel free to be gone."

"That's harsh," Udorian said, feigning hurt feelings. "I'm merely verbalizing possibilities."

"Now *I'm* growing bored," Devrin replied. "We will keep this simple and to the point, before I grow tired of all of you." That brought a round of surprised expressions, some laced with curiosity, some unconcerned, and one in particular, outright challenge.

"We might have days before Shurza summons us," Devrin

continued, "or we might have weeks or months. Or maybe even hours. There is no way to know."

"The thing is unpredictable at best," Revdrak spat.

"Not so," Mordayne replied. "We know it will do exactly what it was *created* to do."

She didn't elaborate, for she didn't need to. They created Shurza to suck the power and life out of the Illuminarians and feed it back into each of them. This was supposed to have supplied each of the Myrtolus with the ability to wield massive amounts of essence like nothing any essence-wielder dared dream of. Things hadn't gone according to plan, of course.

Devrin studied the tight faces in the circle and knew they were each remembering that fateful day. Their biggest accomplishment, and their biggest mistake.

AMOURA

Amoura stole yet another glance at Emiel Dharr, who studyed the ground in front of him as they neared the distant town. He hadn't taken the news from Lief well. Of all the *et'a* tinfar cities she'd visited, only two had "possibly" seen his daughters. One had indeed seen them traveling north toward Altarra, while the other had seen only one of them traveling with a tatamble.

That had been an odd twist. Amoura had only heard of the illusive people—if they were in fact people—through some of the many books she'd read. Practically nothing was known about them, and the only recorded interactions had been so long ago, little remained beyond scant details and rumor.

Oddly enough, that bit of news had nearly broken the man and given him hope almost at the same time. That only one of his daughters had been seen had nearly crushed him, but then he'd started asking questions. "How did she look? Did she look heartbroken? Crushed? Did she look sad, but strong?" He'd asked a number of questions to which Lief had no answer. But the tinfar had seen the desperation in the man's face and had decided to return to the city that had spotted the girl.

It had been a quiet walk for the hours hence. Even Bone let the spicetrader be. Then, Lief had returned. Emiel had nearly fallen over her demanding answers. For a mercy, the answer had been somewhat positive. The girl hadn't been in the best of spirits, which was to be expected, but she'd not looked to be broken or crushed, or any other such thing. She and the tatamble girl had been moving along quite well while passing through the area.

"They're both alive," Emiel insisted. "I can't explain it because I can't relate, but I know them. Ever since they were born, they could sense anything going on with the other, even if they weren't together. If something had happened to one of them, Nandi or Amiya, whichever they saw, would have looked noticeably distraught. Worse than distraught. Something separated them, but they're okay. I'd bet my life on it."

Bone had looked doubtful, but offered not rebuttal. Having been born after her sister's death, Amoura couldn't relate to what it was like to have a sibling, much less one so connected to her as a twin. If the man thought what he did, that would have to be enough.

"How are you?" she asked him, surprised at the softness in her own voice.

Emiel's dark brown lips pursed into a polite smile. "As well as I can be, I suppose."

"Of course," was all Amoura could think of as a response. *Quite the smart question, Amoura,* she chastised herself. She tried to think of something else to say, but nothing came to mind. Perhaps all those years at the Tower of Magi buried in her books and training weren't the best preparation for social skills. Then again, she hadn't gone to Altarra for that.

"We will find them, Emiel. I don't pretend to know how, but you have my best efforts at your disposal." Amoura wished she weren't so formal, but hopefully the point got across.

The spicetrader looked over at her with genuine gratitude and something more. A smile flickered across her face, and she gave him a sharp nod of encouragement. He responded with a wrinkled smile that seemed to border on amused.

Amoura resisted the urge to sigh. What was she going to do about him? That he had developed feelings for her was undoubtable, but she didn't have room in her life for that. Her training and studies didn't allow for opening herself to feelings.

What training? A simple question she asked herself that had a list of answers. Other than the training she put herself through, there *was* no training. She could never return to the Altarra branch of the Order. For that matter, she couldn't go to any branch. Vladrick would have had word spread across every branch of the Order that his former apprentice had turned against him and the Order of Magi and gone rogue.

A breeze passed between the trees dotting the flat landscape, rustling her thin braids. Patches of green were just starting to show up as spring got a stronger foothold.

"Emiel!" Lief exclaimed. "Look!" She pointed into the distance where a long line of deer galloped across the open land from the woods far off to the right and into the distance to the left as far as they could see. A large buck with the beginnings of new antlers stopped in the middle of the procession. It raised its square black nose to the sky and sniffed the air, then looked in their direction.

"That's amazing," Emiel said. "I've seen a deer here and there, but living in a city, you don't see that many all at once. The girls would have loved this."

Amoura's heart ached for him, an unfamiliar feeling. The only friend she truly had was Hashma, back at the magi fortress. The woman was like a grandmother, and the only person Amoura had felt inclined to keep company with.

The last of the herd diminished into the distance while Lief excitedly related how deer were frequent friends who visited the many earth tinfar cities around the world. "They're such amazing and curious and fun animals," Lief said. "There was one in particular who would lie on her side with her legs curled around me while I sat against her warm stomach and made pottery."

"You made pottery?" Bone asked. "Sitting on the ground? What were you doing, sitting in a pool of mud? And how did you spin it?"

"I'm *et'a* earth tinfar, bone boy. Surely you can't have forgotten."

"In fact," Emiel added, "you don't even need to be an earth tinfar. You just need to be able to use essence."

"What're you, an expert now?" Bone replied.

"Only at using my brain, kid."

Bone looked like he was going to say something more, but rolled his eyes and looked away.

Amoura wondered what the story was with the mercenary. He could have long ago gone on his way and found another job. With his skills, he could likely have done several by now and been paid handsomely for them. Underneath all that sarcasm and seemingly indifferent attitude lay something deeper that would reveal itself in time. That would be an interesting day.

They finally reached the town and stopped long enough to replenish supplies and procure a couple of horses. Once again, Amoura found her status as a magus to be a boon. People might generally mistrust the Order, but at the same time they were intensely polite and eager to please.

Bone gave his horse a pat on the neck. "I made sure we bought geldings bred for endurance. Now that we're riding, Nashma is only a several hours away, and Shiedra only another hour or so within its borders. He unfolded the map he'd bought and held it against the saddle. "We're here." He pointed at a spot several inches from the dotted line indicating Nashma's border. "If we keep them at a steady canter, we'll be in Shiedra well before dusk."

"Then let's get going," Emiel said.

"I will ride with you," Amoura said to Emiel. When the spicetrader smiled, she added, "the mercenary is armored. It would add extra weight."

Emiel's smile faded. "Oh. Of course, that makes sense." He indicated the horse. "I can take the reins unless you prefer to, magus."

The formality stung, but Amoura couldn't blame him. She couldn't deny even to herself that she'd been sending the man mixed signals. One moment she was more personable, the next, reserved. Emiel had a great heart. He deserved better than what she could give him. "I will ride behind you."

Emiel inclined his head. "Very well." He placed a foot in the stirrup and lifted himself astride the horse, then offered his hand. Amoura started to refuse, as she could climb up herself, but she accepted his hand instead. Once astride, her hands lifted of their own accord toward his waist, but she stopped and instead placed her hands on the back of the saddle.

"I'm riding with you two," Lief said. A section of the ground beneath her suddenly sprang upward, launching her into the air. She grabbed hold of the gelding's mane and swung herself astride his neck.

"Ready?" Emiel asked over his shoulder after Bone had mounted.

"I'm ready," Amoura replied.

They kicked off into a trot for the first little while, then once the horses were warmed up, they picked up the pace.

"Is this not a gallop?" Amoura asked. The mercenary called it something else."

"Not exactly a gallop," Emiel replied. The hard edge to his voice had softened a bit. "A canter is slower than a gallop, but the action of the horse is the same. Think jogging instead of running."

Amoura nodded, though Emiel obviously didn't see. Once again, without thinking, her hands left the saddle and moved toward his waist. After a moment of hesitation, she slipped her hands under his arms and wrapped her arms around his waist. She felt him tense up at the sudden contact, and she stared at his back, trying to decide if she should let go. He finally relaxed, and she did as well.

She watched the trees come and go, the hills and mounds move by. Dark clouds rolled in and the smell of rain dampened the air. Luck remained with them, however, for the clouds only sprinkled down on them before moving on.

Bone wrapped his reins on the horn of his saddle and reached into a pouch to retrieve his map. "Just as I thought. We've crossed into Nashma. Not long to go. We've got plenty of time to give the horses a break."

They slowed their mounts to a trot, then a walk to let them cool down. Finally they stopped, and Lief hopped off and touched the ground. "Save your water," she said to Bone, who was about to offer it to his sweaty and lathering horse. She pointed straight ahead north. There is a small lake nearby. You could walk and be there in little time."

They heeded the tinfar's advice and found the lake a short time later. Bone and Emiel shared some dried meat while the horses drank from the lake. Amoura declined, preferring a handful of dried fruit instead, which she shared with Lief.

"I judge us to be an hour or less from Shiedra," Bone said. "I've got money enough to share a room with you, spicetrader." He jerked his chin at Amoura. "I'm guessing she'd probably want her own room."

"You're guessing correctly, mercenary," Amoura replied. "And you've also guessed correctly that we're less than an hour from Shiedra."

Bone's eyebrows rose. "How do you know?"

Amoura didn't respond. She continued to stare to the east at the small figures steadily growing larger as they approached.

"THEY'RE RIDING IN FAST," Emiel observed.

"Border patrol," Bone said, his voice muffled around the last bite of food. "No big deal. Might even escort us in."

Amoura heard Lief quietly tell Emiel that she wouldn't be far away. What was it about the man that the tinfar found so fascinating that she watched over him like a mother hen?

They retrieved the grazing horses and waited for the patrol to arrive. Soon enough, soldiers in green plated armor with red capes arrived. Bone spread his hands in greeting as the contingent pulled up in front of them. The lead soldier bearing a more elaborate helm adorned with scale-like ridges growing away from the faceplate silently scrutinized the mercenary.

"Greetings, soldiers of Shiedra," Bone began. "We've come a long way to arrive ..." he trailed off when he noticed the captain's attention not on him, but Amoura.

The captain lifted the faceplate of his helm and stared directly at Amoura. She returned his gaze, not liking what she saw in the man's face. She'd never been to Shiedra, only heard of the place in conversation about its formidable library. Did they mistrust magi, here? She couldn't imagine a major city such as Shiedra not having some sort of relationship with magi, if not its own branch.

She watched as his round hazel eyes grew rounder and his nostrils flared. He made a forceful gesture with an upraised hand, and the soldiers kicked their mounts into motion and surrounded the trio.

The sound of swords being drawn from sheaths filled their ears while the horses drew in closer. Emiel and Bone held their hands up at their sides.

"Woah, woah, hey," Bone said with a nervous chuckle. "I promise you that's unnecessary."

The horses had moved in so close by then that the trio were forced tight in together. The captain barely spared Bone a glance. His attention remained square on Amoura. The man's jaw was clenched so tight he looked like he might break his teeth.

Amoura's gaze darted from the captain's face to the very tight grip he had on his still sheathed sword. "Have we met before, Captain?" she ventured.

"By order of Her Excellency Royana Lindra, I place you under arrest for the assassination of Royain Dimitri."

"Under arrest for the what?" Bone asked.

Amoura frowned. Assassination? "I assure you, captain, there is a mistake. I have never set foot inside Shiedra nor the land of Nashma."

The captain snatched his sword from its sheath. Before the steel was fully free, Amoura had already accessed *air* stored in her essence ring. She didn't want to hurt any of these men over a misunderstanding, but she had no intention of dying here, either.

"If you speak another word, murderer," the captain growled, "it will be your last."

He meant every word. The man was at the edge of restraint. Amoura glanced about the other soldiers. Every one of them looked just as tense.

Beside her with his hands still up, Emiel stole a glance at her, his mouth open as though he wanted to say something but thought better of it.

The ride to Shiedra was far different than what the small party had expected. They entered the city of Shiedra surrounded by men ready to cut them down at the slightest provocation.

The horses clip-clopped along the hard-stone streets, passing by buildings with colored awnings extended over ornately woven carpets on which sat a variety of items for sale. Other buildings had carved and roasted meats for sale, while others still, had downward sloping shelves displaying diverse types of fruit and vegetables. A vendor district.

Hard clay buildings ranged in color from sandy brown, to red, to dark brown with semicircular red tiled roofs. Adobe, Amoura realized.

Both the men and women of Nashma were of a similar height

to the Khatala, though unlike the westerners, these people were not as largely built. As with the Nashmarese magi in Altarra, everyone wore a nose ring, had the same round hazel eyes, and radiant brown or olive-colored skin.

Amoura found them to be a beautiful people, the women with their long eyelashes and thick wavy locks falling to their waists, and the men with shoulder-length black hair, just as wavy, and their sparkling green eyes.

Despite the beauty of Shiedra and its people, a subdued pall hung over the city. Conversation was sparse and quiet, faces were solemn. Some that were near the path the soldiers took looked up at Amoura and the others with expressions ranging from mild interest to suspicion. What had happened here?

The soldiers led them straight to a structure made of nothing more than shin-high steps. At the captain's orders, the captives dismounted, followed by the soldiers.

"Please don't lose that," Bone said to the soldier holding his sword. "It's extremely valuable to me."

"I doubt you'll be seeing it for a long time, boy," the soldier replied.

Bone's face darkened. "Don't call me a boy."

The soldier, a full head and a half taller than the mercenary, lifted his face shield to reveal a hard, scarred face that had seen many battles. "Or what, boy?"

"That's enough, both of you," the captain said. "Baltazar, I expect better."

Baltazar faced the captain without a word and placed a right fist to his left breast. He bowed his head, then stepped back, Bone's sword firmly in his grip.

Bone glowered at the soldier until Emiel elbowed the young warrior in the side. "Let's not make a bad situation worse, all right?" the spicetrader whispered. Amoura couldn't have agreed more.

As it turned out, the steps—though high enough to look over a good portion of the city—ended on a flat plateau. Amoura tried to look out over the vast city to get her bearings, but being surrounded by soldiers who towered over her made it impossible.

A single soldier stood in the middle of the empty adobe plateau, and immediately offered the same salute to the captain that Baltazar had done. Once Amoura got a good look at the soldier, she saw that it was the woman that had ridden ahead of them back to Shiedra. To alert this Royana Lindra, no doubt. The captain nodded, and the solider stepped into a square opening in the plateau and disappeared. Several other soldiers followed until it was Emiel's, Bone's, and finally Amoura's turn, followed by the remainder of their guard escort.

They descended stone steps that took them down torchlit path-ways. Amoura looked about the immaculate halls in admiration. No filth or piles of dust and rock. No scurrying rodents.

Artwork carved into the walls gave the otherwise ominous passageways a cultural accent that Amoura might have appreciated under better circumstances. She smelled fresh air just before they rounded a corner where natural light filtered through.

Amoura wasn't tall by any measure, even for a woman, so she was all but blind while walking behind the clustered soldiers. Once they reached the end of the corridor, the armored backs parted to reveal an open patio of stone floors so well polished they reflected her image. Five-foot-tall clay oval pots with ornate carvings sat at each corner and side of the square patio, while towering palm trees swayed contentedly in the gentle breeze.

Beyond their stylish surroundings, Amoura spotted a single woman with her back to them at the far end of the patio. She wore a long flowing brown dress made of an unfamiliar material so light it drifted in the breeze. Her thick, wavy raven hair must have been styled by expert hands, for it was pulled back from her face and tied together by a band with flowers woven into it. Even pulled back as it was, her hair hung to her waist. Her thinly muscled arms were behind her back, one hand clasped in the other.

The captain removed his helm and tucked it in the crook of his elbow, followed by his soldiers. They bowed at the waist. "Your Excellency," the captain said. "We've found her."

Amoura also bowed. When Emiel saw her, he did as well, followed grudgingly by Bone. She could practically hear the mercenary grinding his teeth.

They remained bowed for several moments until the woman finally spoke. "Rise."

Amoura looked at the face of a woman perhaps a decade or more her senior. Her smooth olive skin carried the same glow as the other citizens of Shiedra. A tiny black mole dotted her right cheek, which only added to her striking beauty. And her eyes. Amoura could only appreciate the fierceness in her hazel eyes. She saw justness in those eyes. Hard, but just.

She had the look of one who felt the heaviness of the world on her shoulders, and had to grow stronger to support it. Amoura knew that look. Her mother had had the same, since she was old enough to remember. A look one developed after experiencing the many hardships life could throw at her, including loss.

"My Captain," Royana Lindra said. "Is it true?" She turned her head to look directly into Amoura's eyes and her voice hardened. "Is this the woman who murdered my husband?"

"She is, Excellency."

Amoura met the woman's gaze with unblinking resolve. Several tense moments passed as the two of them stared hard at each other. The Royana was a strong woman; very strong. Amoura found herself respecting that strength and wishing she could help find the one who murdered her husband.

"Nothing to say?" Royana Lindra asked.

"I was waiting for permission to speak, your Excellency," Amoura replied.

A tiny frown creased Lindra's brow at that. She looked back to the captain. "Adolphus, are you sure?"

Amoura stole a glance at the man. His head was shaved on the sides and cut short on top, which had been combed to stand erect. Bits of gray mingled with the black. He, too, turned and stared into Amoura's eyes, and again, she saw the barely restrained rage. "I am, Excellency. This is the woman who murdered our beloved Royain Dimitri." His chest heaved with each breath passing in and out of his flaring nostrils. "If you wish it, Excellency, I will cut her down where she stands."

"I do not wish it, Captain." Lindra's voice was compassionate, but firm. "We must know for certain. I'll not have the blood of an innocent woman spilled on a mistaken identity."

Captain Adolphus's head snapped back to the woman, and he bowed respectfully. "Excellency. My Royana. The memory is forever burned into my mind." He glowered at Amoura as he spoke. "The braided hair, the face, those eyes. I will never forget it. Never have I met someone with eyes like that."

"Perhaps it is common where she is from," Lindra offered.

The captain never took his eyes off Amoura as he shook his head. "I've traveled all of Marai and beyond. Not once have I seen eyes like hers."

Lindra looked Amoura over. "You spoke of an assassin in black, wielding blunt weapons and her body against your soldiers. She is dressed as a magus, which I find even more odd, given she could have easily refused being brought before me."

"A disguise, Excellency."

"Yet she doesn't plead her innocence," Lindra said.

"Because she knows she is guilty and has been caught," Adolphus replied.

Lindra looked back to Amoura. "What do you have to say?"

Amoura inclined her head, ignoring the puzzled look on Bone's face and the concerned look on Emiel's. "Your Excellency Royana Lindra," she began. "I am not the person you seek—"

The captain's hands tightened into fists at that. Lindra stilled him with an upraised hand and indicated that the magus continue.

"I have only entered the city of Shiedra once, and that day is today. I am indeed of the Order of Magi." Amoura said a silent prayer to the Creator that she wouldn't be asked of what branch she resided, and that word hadn't spread this far yet about her actions in Altarra. "I can also assure you that my studies do not include physical combat with my body, blades, or blunt weapons. Whomever brought this tragedy upon your great city, I assure you it was not I."

"Assurance from an assassin," Lieutenant Baltazar rumbled.

"Would we have been standing by a lake in this land, watering our horses if we were assassins?" Bone asked. "Is there an assassin anywhere in the world that stupid?"

"Would you like that sharp tongue of yours removed, boy?" Baltazar asked, his voice low and deadly. "Speak with respect in the presence of the Royana, and only when bidden."

Bone pursed his lips and stared straight ahead into the distance. Amoura hoped the boy would hold his tongue. However much danger they might be in, Amoura's life was at stake. In spite of that, she couldn't help wondering who else had eyes like hers. She agreed with the captain in that she also had never seen anyone in her travels with eyes like hers.

Royana Lindra looked at Emiel. "You seem the most out of your element, here. What is your part in all of this?"

Emiel made an awkward but respectful bow. "I'd first like to say that I am sorry for the loss of your husband, your Excellency. As for my part?" He indicated Bone and Amoura. "I've been traveling with these two for weeks. Our path began in Vyne and took us to Carlayn. We've been attacked by four-armed monsters as well as things larger than several buildings combined. I've seen more horrors out in the world these past weeks than I care to think about. But I can assure you neither I, nor this man or woman have set foot in this city since we've been together."

Amoura realized she'd been holding her breath, and released it. Emiel had purposely omitted Altarra from his account, correctly guessing that if he mentioned the place, and the Royana chose to confirm their story, it would be disastrous not only for Amoura, but all of them.

Royana Lindra listened without interrupting. Whatever she thought of the spicetrader's story, her features gave nothing away. "Their story can be confirmed or proven false by contacting Carlayn and the more distant Vyne."

"Need we go to the trouble, Excellency?" Captain Adolphus said. "They will say anything to delay their fate while planning a way out of this situation."

"That may be true," Royana Lindra agreed. "For now, see them to the prisoner accommodations."

The words had barely left Lindra's mouth when the surrounding soldiers grabbed the two men by the shoulders and shoved them away. Amoura was treated somewhat less forcefully, but a large hand still found the center of her back and prodded her forward.

She rubbed her thumb against her essence ring finger, feeling the naked skin where the ring should be. They'd taken it off her before the ride into Shiedra, mistakenly thinking she couldn't access the power within while not wearing it.

Not that she would use it. If ever there was a way to ensure her guilt in the Royan's eyes, it would have been to use the power stored in her ring.

"Never heard of "prisoner accommodations" before," Emiel muttered.

"Means dungeon," Bone said.

"Thanks," Emiel replied. "Couldn't have figured it out without you."

"Your welcome," the mercenary said.

"Shut up," Lieutenant Baltazar growled.

They reached a spiraling staircase, but instead of going down, they were led up. The hard stone walls echoed Emiel Dharr's heavy breathing with every labored step up the seemingly endless climb.

"You really need to get in better shape, spicetrader," Bone said, his teliak armor creaking as he leaned forward into his own climb.

They finally reached the top floor and continued down a hall that opened to rows of cells with a single tiny barred window emitting and equally small square of light into each cell.

Emiel was shoved into the first cell, and Bone into the second. The final cell awaited Amoura, and this time a soldier rammed his hand into her back and slammed the door before Amoura hit the floor. Apparently the lack of rough treatment was for the Royana's sake.

Amoura rose and turned to face the barred door, determined not to acknowledge the pain between her shoulder blades. The soldier who'd shoved her in wasn't a man, but a woman. She held her helm under her arm, glaring murderously at the magus.

Knowing nothing else to do, Amoura met the other woman's gaze until the soldier spat on the ground and walked away. She watched the armored woman shoulder past one of her comrades and leave the jail without a word.

"Shiedra appears to have loved their ruler," she heard Bone say from the next cell.

"Of all the Fallen cursed luck," Emiel swore. "How in the name of the Creator could this have happened? Amoura. Are you sure you're not from some heritage where people have eyes like yours and they're simply uncommon in this land?"

When Amoura didn't respond, Bone said, "I've traveled a good bit across Marai, so I can answer that question. Nope."

"Well, there must be someone out there," Emiel said. "How else do you explain …"

Amoura stopped listening. She moved to the center of the cell where light shined through the solitary window and hit the floor. She sat cross-legged in the warm sunlight, closed her eyes, and let it wash over her face.

Who could this mysterious assassin be? Amoura had only seen one other person with eyes like hers, and that person existed only in her memory of a portrait from her childhood. Many a day, a young Amoura Xanna sat in front of the painting hanging on the wall of her home. A portrait of her parents and a seven-year-old girl who would have been about eight years older than Amoura.

Was there a relative Amoura didn't know about who had eyes the color of steel? Did she have distant family with traits she shared but her parents somehow did not? It seemed unlikely. Had her sister survived and her parents simply didn't know because they hadn't been able to find her all those years ago?

Amoura remembered her mother's cheeks, moist with tears. Was it good or bad that they hadn't found her sister's body, all those years ago? Might their daughter be alive still, or had she simply been blasted to nothing by an errant shot from an essence wielder?

For many days, the young Amoura would sit on the floor in front of the painting, gazing up at the portrait of her long dead sibling, wondering what it would be like to have a sister and wishing it could be so. She'd stared at Rayna Xanna's face for many, many hours. A face that looked so much like her own. A beautiful dark face with eyes the color of steel.

RAYNE

Rayna kept her gaze down as she moved through the busy streets of Carlayn; just another body in the numerous mass of citizens. Early into adolescence she learned that her eyes were unusual, and that her dark complexion only accentuated them. She preferred to navigate the streets at night when it was easier to move about no matter how thick or thin the crowds were. But the Khamra had called, and that call had been urgent.

She navigated various avenues, passing through shaded areas that reminded her of the pre-spring chill still present out of direct sunlight. This being her first visit to Carlayn, Rayna slowed her pace once she reached the residential district and looked for the signs.

She turned down another street and found a man giving meat-filled buns to a line of people dressed in little more than rags. The destitute folk waited patiently in line as the man handed over bun after bun from a cart beside him. Rayna slowed and watched until the man noticed her.

Arms hanging at her sides, Rayna pressed together the middle and ring fingers of her right hand while crossing the ring finger over her little finger. At the same time, she spread her index finger and thumb. Her posture nonchalant, she flashed the **K** gesture so quickly no one who didn't know what to look for would have seen it or thought it anything more than her stretching her fingers.

The man, however, did notice. Without missing a beat in handing out the buns, he smiled and nodded to a man who thanked him. With barely a flicker of movement, the man quickly glanced to the right.

Rayna continued on and turned right, her step slow and casual as she scanned the street. Two buildings down, she saw the telltale insignia of a watching eye nestled in the corner of where two walls of a house met overhead. The eye was half the size of a coin, and facing an inconspicuous direction to be found only by one who knew what they were looking for. And even if someone noticed it, they wouldn't know what it meant.

The location of the eye also indicated where Rayna should look next. She continued down the street, her attention now on the over-hanging roofs. She spotted another eye halfway down the street, and on the opposite side. She reached the end of the street and turned left. The occasional passerby moved along with a smile in greeting, which she returned while keeping eye contact as brief as possible, all the while scanning the roof overhangs.

Ranya could feel eyes on her, but she kept walking until she heard a chirp from above and behind on the left. Without stopping or looking, she turned left at the next doorway. It led to a courtyard with a statue of a water bearer in the center of a fountain. Potted plants occupied each of the four corners of the courtyard, as well as a black-striped brown cat.

She smiled at the feline as she continued past. Another chirp sounded from above and to the right, and so of the three paths she could have taken from the left, straight ahead, or to the right, she took the doorway to the right.

Rayna quickened her pace, knowing the one who had guided her would now be following behind. She took a short flight of steps down and entered a covered hallway. She continued on until finally she reached a circular disk enclosed by a waist-high rail.

When she heard steps from behind, she knew that the agent who'd followed her in had purposely made his presence known. A man turned the corner a moment later and approached the disk. He flashed the **K** to Rayna, who reciprocated, then moved onto the disk with her. He manipulated a series of switches and pulled a lever.

Rayna heard gears catch into place, and stone grinding as the disk began to rise. She looked up to see an opening in the ceiling the same exact size as the disk upon which she stood. It lifted them to the ceiling and through the circular opening.

At eye-level, the floor of the circular room was clean and well kempt, the curving walls bare and unpainted. At the far end of the room was a simple door through which Rayne and her silent escort entered.

They came to a set of stairs and another door that admitted her to the roof of the building and nothing above but the open sky. A group of men and women dressed in the typical clothes of any other resident of Carlayn looked out over the city below.

When they heard Rayna and her escort, they turned, crossed their arms, and made the symbol of the **K** with each hand, facing opposite directions. Rayna responded in kind. Opposite facing **K**s. The Khamra watched everywhere.

The group parted to admit the new arrivals, and Rayna came to stand beside a woman staring out at the city below. "This is your first visit?"

"It is," Rayna said.

"Carlayn is a good city. Its economy thrives, its poor are looked after and sheltered from the elements, and trade is healthy. Prime Minster Cravel is a smart man."

"Word outside of Carlayn speaks of him being somewhat isolationist and cowardly," Rayna replied.

"Nothing more than a front," the other woman said. "Cravel's peers are respectful but underestimate him. They see no threat in the man, and therefore do not see an opponent with which to spar. Cravel gets most of what he wants in trade because he's managed Carlayn's affairs well by not allowing it to descend into large debts to other cities. This is also the only city other than New Dama that will openly trade with the Khatala. Though as of late, he's had to keep trade relations with the westerners close to the hip. The scale of Carlayn is well balanced by the wisdom of its leader."

"Quite the accomplishment," Rayna said.

"Cravel is a smart man," the woman repeated again. She turned her icy green eyes to Rayna. "I am Alydria. I guide the eye of the Carlayn Khamra."

Rayna nodded in greeting. She didn't share her name because Alydria knew it already. The "Guiding Eye" as Alydria's rank was called, had been the one to summon her here.

"I admit looking forward to meeting the one who slipped inside Castle Jietar and eliminated the vipers whispering poison into the king's ears. While your accomplishment in Shiedra is admirable, your success in Jietar has created quite a reputation for yourself."

"I merely go where the eye of the Khamra is focused," Rayna said.

"The eye has focused on several who undermind Marai's efforts to return to balance with the Khatala," Alydria began. "Our agents across Marai have identified two women from Altarra who've just arrived in this very city to speak with the Prime Minister. They are in favor of the war, and seek to entice Cravel into lending his forces in exchange for a portion of a rich deposit of corlite found in a recently discovered cave in Dryland Khatal. Of course, the Drylanders have known about this deposit for generations, but share a different belief about the stones, which they consider sacred."

Rayna's steel-colored gazed flicked over the city below. Carlayn had done well for itself under the guidance of its prime minister. She'd seen the vibrant and healthy merchant district, the well-dressed citizens and the facilities designated for assisting the less fortunate. From up here, she also saw clusters of healthy trees and flowers scattered throughout the sprawling city.

The assassin couldn't help but appreciate the man's shrewdness and guile. To be perceived not only as a paranoid isolationist, but also securely under the king's thumb while using that reputation to the benefit of his city was quite the accomplishment.

And these two women came to throw all of that out of balance. Rayna narrowed her eyes as if to obscure her waking vision of the battle that had separated her from her parents, who probably died in the endless explosions. The foolish wars of men served only to create misery for those who unwillingly financed it.

"There is more."

Alydria's voice startled Rayna out of her daydream. "As always."

"The king has two new advisors who have not spoken against the war, but have not spoken in favor of it either. Our agents say that these men have been tasked by the king to follow up on rumors of yet another corlite deposit; this one several miles east of Mount Blood and near the border to the Shattered Lands."

Rayna glanced at Alydria. "How large a deposit?"

"Large enough to light the Jietari economy as if it were struck by a lightning bolt. If reports are even half true, every magus around the world could have an essence ring on each finger and still there would be plenty left over."

"King Alyn would have near endless resources to fuel his war," Rayna whispered.

"While pushing the Khatala back into their own lands and taking over their own corlite deposits," Alydria added. "There is still more. An agent in New Dama sent word of a strange-looking woman with skin like parched earth. She apparently seeks the mayor's ear regarding the war, and the possible financial benefit to allowing Marai troops to use the borderland city as a rest stop."

Rayna's lips parted in disbelief. "New Dama has been neutral since its founding. It is a hub that attracts people from every corner of the world. Its mayor would never agree to such a thing."

"Given the potential wealth Alyn seeks while embroiled in his war with the westerners," Alydria said, "it would be but a drop in the well to offer New Dama enough corlite wealth to see realized any ambitions its mayor might have."

Rayna digested the information through the lengthy pause that followed. She wondered about the state of things in Khatal. No people were infallible. Were any similar ambitions being spoken about in the nations west of the Marai border.

"Shetar is also being targeted."

Rayna tore her eyes from the view over the city to look at the Khamra guiding eye. "Shetar?" Where did it end? *Did* it have an end?

Alydria, nodded. "Two agents have sent reports that an emissary was dispatched from Jietar to meet with the Shetaran prime minister. Shetar has remained out of the war thus far but looks to be only a good shove away from leaping headfirst into it. If intelligence is accurate, the city is a volcano ready to blow. All it would take is one wrong move by the Khatala, one hostile action, and Shetar will leap to King Alyn's call."

"If this is true," Rayna said, "it might not even take that much if Alyn brings promises of corlite wealth."

"Correct," Alydria replied.

Rayna sighed. "All of Marai united against Khatal, while Alyn had an issue with only one nation."

"Marailanders are largely ignorant to the differences between Khatala tribes," Alydria said. "Alyn prods a sleeping teliak."

"The Khatala are far fewer," Rayna said. "He doesn't need to unite all of Marai against them."

"Yet if he does, he wages a war he is certain he will win, with every banner in Marai at his back. Any detractors of his will be silenced. Who would dare speak dissent at a time when all of Marai stands united?"

A sinking feeling crept into Rayna's stomach. "Where does the eye focus?" She fought to keep the weariness out of her voice despite feeling very much so.

"Everywhere," Guiding Eye Alydria replied. "But the eye of the Khamra settles first on a Eryn Tolen, advisor to the prime minister of Shetar. From there, the eye turns south to New Dama, then returns to the kingdom of Jietar."

"Jietar?" Rayna frowned. "Again?"

"The beast of war has grown several heads," Alydria replied. "Balance has never been so threatened. Poisonous tongues must be removed, as must be the heads that spew such poison upon the world. And so, too, must be removed those who might grow to replace each head."

Ranya clenched her teeth to keep her mouth from falling open. Surely the guiding eye of Carlayn wasn't saying what she thought the woman was saying.

"The Khamra will be in communication," Alydria continued. "For now, the eye looks upon Shetar."

Rayna took a deep breath and steeled herself for what she must do. For she was of the Khamra, the final barrier between balance and chaos. "And so in Shetar, shall it Rayne."

17

ROYANA LINDRA

Lindra Arella, Royana of Shiedra, seat of power of the land of Nashma, remained in the luxurious outdoor courtyard for a long time after the departure of her soldiers and their captives. She looked out over the personal gardens of her mansion, the Alcazar de Masarile.

Dimitri. So fresh, the wound, that it opened raw every time she thought of her husband. And with such thoughts, she saw his charming smile and genuine love for her and their sons.

The widowed Royana sighed. Marcos and Darien, only five and nine years old couldn't begin to understand why someone would have done such a thing. They thought the person who'd killed their father evil and should be punished.

The simple world of a child. Dimitri had been a man of complicated layers, no different than anyone else. Everyone had a shadow dogging their steps, watching them from behind, before, beside. Some cast darker shadows than others.

She walked down the expansive stone steps of the upper courtyard, gazing out at the landscape beyond that gradually sank away from her field of view. A parade of dark clouds glided across the sky, bringing with them, the sweet, damp smell of the promise of life-giving rain. Towering palm trees started to lean in the same direction of the traveling clouds, while the shorter stouter palms and rose bushes sat stoic in anticipation.

Sandals crunched the fine gravel path just behind her, followed by heavy boots. She sighed. There was a time she might have walked her beloved gardens by herself, with her sons, or with her attendant, Mariala. Ever since Dimitri's assassination, Captain Adolphus had been adamant to the point of obsession about her having an armed guard present having an armed guard present she walked.

It wasn't necessary, of course. Lindra knew that as certain as she knew she couldn't tell anyone, especially good and loyal Adolphus and his soldiers. She didn't have the heart to break theirs.

She passed a patch of glistening blue and yellow noon buds, their flowers all raised to the sky. The little shrubs could smell the rain, too. Further down the path the night blossoms had already closed and sealed up tight for the day. Lindra cupped one of the bulbous pods in her fingers. The only tree in the world to bloom glowing flowers at night, night blossoms were unique to Nashma alone.

The soldiers followed in silence, as always. So did Mariela. The woman was a master at discretion and had the ability to read what a person needed, and feel what they were feeling. Another thing Dimitri had done for the good of his wife, at the cost of someone else.

She felt a hand rest on her shoulder. Lindra reached across her chest and lay her hand on top of it. Tears welled up in her eyes and spilled over, trailing down her cheeks like an overflowing damn.

Lindra endured the moments of grief wracking her body as she tried to keep from convulsing in violent sobs. Mariela's hand remained on her shoulder, radiating warmth and love. Love that Lindra surely didn't deserve.

"You gave me a choice long ago to follow my heart," she heard her attendant's soft voice behind her. "So I have, my Royana."

Lindra fought to keep her back erect. She wiped away her tears with a finger and took a deep steadying breath. "I know."

"Your mind knows, but your heart does not. You won't let it."

Lindra gave the other woman's hand a final squeeze and let go. A single act of compassion from a happenstance encounter had forever altered Mariela's life.

"If I had not lain my hand on you that day, you would have died before giving birth, my Royana."

Lindra closed her eyes to fight off a second wave of tears. Darien, her second child, had long and difficult breech birth. At worst, she and her son would have died. At best, Dimitri would have had to choose one of them to live.

In the span of a moment, she relived that moment as she had many times since. The agony, the contractions, the realization that something was horribly wrong inside her body. The midwives had taken authority over everyone else and ordered Lindra to be rushed off the street and back to the mansion. She would have died on the way. Lindra had felt it as surely as the unearthly pain tearing her body.

Rows of concerned Shiedrans had made way for soldiers gingerly carrying Lindra to the carriage that would whisk her away to the mansion. That day had been a true miracle of the Creator, for under any other circumstance, emergency or not, the soldiers of Shiedra never allowed an opening for anyone or anything to make uninvited contact with the Royain and Royana.

A single arm had reached through the crowd, a woman stretching to the limit of her reach. Her gentle hand had grabbed hold of Lindra's, and for that brief moment, the suffering had lessened.

One of Adolphus's men had been about to punish the woman until Lindra screamed at the top of her lungs to let her through. Without a word, the beautiful soul named Mariela rushed to Lindra's side and placed her hands on the royana's swollen belly. The pain retreated, and Lindra relaxed.

The shocked expressions came and fled with Dimitri's orders to gather the woman into the carriage. Lindra had blacked out by then, and awoke to fresh pain, and again, Mariela and her healing hands were there. Time and again, the woman had soaked up Lindra's pain into her own body. Veins bulged from her trembling arms, her face a mask of pain and determination.

That one decision to save two lives instead of remain invisible had tethered Mariala to the royana's side for the rest of her life.

"I made my choice, Royana," Mariela said.

"He took your choice," Lindra replied.

"And you returned it. My family lives comfortably because of you."

Lindra could hardly stand it. The pain of the loss of her husband, the pain of having an empath attendant at her side by the order of Dimitri without regard to this woman's own family, and the full weight of responsibility of ruling Nasma sat heavily on Lindra's shoulders. Grief, guilt, responsibility. Life.

She took another deep breath. How much better it would have been to have had Mariela at her side when Adolphus had brought in the supposed assassin. Surely the empath would have had some insight into this strange situation. But the boys needed Mariela. Dimitri's death had been hard, especially for the older Marcos.

She opened her eyes and wiped them again. Mariela had become like a sister to Lindra, a gift Dimitri had had no right to give. But a gift nonetheless.

"I intend to speak with the woman and her companions again," she said once she trusted her voice to be steady. I want you with me."

"Of course," Royana.

Lindra disliked a woman she considered family to have to speak so formally, but this wasn't her private rooms.

"You doubt she is the one," Mariana said.

"Something isn't right. Based on the account of every soldier who'd engaged the assassin, the woman Adolphus brought before me matches the description. Yet I saw no lie in her eyes when she told me she'd never set foot in Shiedra, or Nashma. Adolphus found her with two companions and two horses at a lake. They'd made no effort to flee, and the boy in the strange bone armor stated they were coming here."

Lindra marveled at the strangeness of it all. None of it made sense. A supposed assassin eludes capture and disappears for months, only to return dressed as a magus and traveling beside a supposed mercenary and a spicetrader. Under different circumstances, it would have been humorous.

"Mariela. I don't want to believe her. I want her to be the woman who assassinated my husband, but I'm not sure she is."

"Magi are known for being composed," Mariela said.

"They're also known as protectors, not assassins. If this woman is impersonating a magus, she's done a perfect job down to the finer details, including owning an essence ring and a commanding presence in spite of being surrounded by soldiers and accused of such a heinous crime."

Lindra stopped in front of a wooden fence covered in beautiful blue ivy. She reached out and stroked a veiny leaf, staring at it without seeing it. "If all of that weren't apparent, I still would have my doubts. I just don't see it her eyes."

There was one other factor she didn't mention. She couldn't; not in front of her armed escort. The assassin had struck in the bedroom in spite of armed guards outside the door and the near impossible climb it would have taken to reach the window from the cliffs. Lindra pursed her lips at that. Perhaps it had been a magus who'd struck, for who else could have climbed over sixty feet up a sheer rock wall with no handholds? There was no way to enter the mansion from the front or sides. The only way to enter undetected would have been from the base of the plateau on which the mansion stood.

She doubted the assassin was a magus, though. There had never been an instance of this that she was aware of. Such a seemingly impossible feat was signature to the Khamra. Just thinking of the ancient assassin organization gave her a chill. There wasn't a political figure, ruling family, or monarch in all of Marai who didn't know about the Khamra, but ironically, most thought themselves above the reach of the assassins. In all of known history, ever had that been the lethal mistake of every man or woman who wielded power.

Lindra gave a subtle shake of her head. The Khamra rarely struck. Despite being an organization of assassins, they rarely appeared, preferring to allow provinces to work themselves out. Likely it was the fact that they rarely came calling, that rulers who began their descent into corruption thought themselves immune to a visit from the feared assassins.

Dimitri. Her beloved Dimitri. Lindra clasped her hands together. He was a good husband, a good father, and had managed the affairs of Shiedra well. But he hadn't been a good person; not like the man she'd married. These last several years he'd become overambitious to the point of running over anyone not in line with his designs. She should have seen the whisper of what he would become when Dimitri had "invited" Mariela to become part of their household. Sure, her parents had been taken care of, but any plans she might have had for finding a mate to share her life with had been taken away.

The sound of rapid footsteps crunching on the gravel pathway ahead interrupted Lindra's contemplations. She briefly closed her eyes and smiled for she knew the sound of that gait before the woman appeared around the bend. Her shin-length sandy brown dress swished at the bottom with each brisk step, the sparse red and white floral patterns swaying as if in a breeze. With a fat logbook nestled in one arm, the Royana Advisor stopped before Lindra, grabbed the side of her dress with her other hand, and spread it out as she dipped into a curtsy. "My Royana."

Lindra returned the gesture with a stately but friendly nod.

"Hello, Esperanza. I suppose your hurry isn't due to your fervent desire to be in my company?"

"Your company is always of great value, my Royana. Unfortunately, I bring news of the impending arrival," Esperanza wrinkled her nose, "or should I say incursion, of the Somallar Draygen Braga."

Lindra forced herself not to sigh. It seemed she did that a lot, lately. "Incursion seems a rather extreme description."

"Braga tries to dominate every environment he enters, my Royana," the older woman said.

"His projected presence is of no concern to me, Esperanza," Lindra replied. She started walking again, the two women and her personal guard falling in step.

"He knows this," Esperanza said. "Which is why he's taken a personal interest in leaning on you to take a more aggressive part in the war with the wilders."

"Hardly a war," Lindra said.

"The king thinks otherwise," Esperanza replied.

The easier to sell all of Marai on the notion of uniting to crush Khatal, she thought. Dimitri had been sold on the idea, though he'd remained quiet about it aside from their frequent disagreements about it behind closed doors. Lindra didn't like King Alyn, which made her more prone to sympathy toward the Khatala, though she was careful to keep that bit to herself.

"How long till Somallar Draygen arrives?" Lindra asked.

"He has sent a messenger requesting an audience at your earliest convenience, Royana," the advisor said. "Also," she looked down at the tome in her hands as if it might deliver the next bit of news instead. "The Domayana Mirtalis Semada, and the Manti de tableijar, Melren Spraza also request audiences."

"Of course," Lindra said, not at all surprised by the timing. "Doubtless they'll want an audience all at once."

"They do, Royana," Esperanza replied. "Shall I allot them individual sessions?"

"I'll see them together," Lindra said. Every one of those four words tasted bitter as she spoke them. The last thing she wanted right now was to spar with that opportunistic trio, but there was no choice in it. The only way she could keep those three in check was to show that she could handle them all at the same time.

Adviasar Esperanza Aiyela tipped her head as she dipped into another curtsy. "Of course, my Royana."

"I'll have you and Mariela in attendance," Lindra continued. Any ally she could surround herself with would be a boon. "I want Captain Adolphus in attendance as well."

"Of course, my Royana." In a swish of her dress, Esperanza whirled and sped away.

Her walk in the gardens at its end, Royana Lindra led her company toward the Alcazar de Masarile. Mariela went ahead of the party and met her at the mansion with a group of attendants that whisked her away.

Under Mariela's watchful eye, the attendants fitted Lindra into a sleeveless red dress with a single black swirl extending from her right shoulder across the front to her left knee, and around the back. Given the hint of muscle in her arms, Lindra agreed with her lead attendant that a sleeveless dress would display strength.

They combed her hair back, gathered it, and twisted it up from the nape of her neck to the crown of her head, then secured it with silver pins.

Lindra let the women fuss over every detail. Braga, Semada and Spraza had been nothing if not constant pains in her side since Dimitri's death. They'd liked her husband well enough because much of his ambitions had aligned with theirs. The only reason Shiedra hadn't gone headfirst into the conflict with Khatal was due to Lindra's constant battling against her husband on the subject.

The more she thought about that, the more Lindra found it a mystery why the Khamra hadn't come for the three she was about to meet. Maybe the assassin was biding her time. Maybe she *did* return in the guise of a magus, waiting to eliminate Braga and the others.

Despite that very real possibility, Lindra felt no fear for her own life. That she and the Nashma ambassador, Lyle Tobain still drew breath served as testimony enough of the Khamra's knowledge of both their stances on the war. What little comfort that brought evaporated with the thought of *how* the Khamra knew about her and Lyle. The ambassador had come to her that fateful night, shaken but alive. Not many survived a visit from one of the legendary assassins, but the woman had stayed her hand and questioned him first, before leaving him among the living.

The attendants finished their work and Lindra swept from her private rooms, Mariela in tow. Her lead attendant and dearest friend had to occasionally trot to keep up with Lindra's swift pace. "Remember, my Royana, that they must all unite their strength to stand before you."

Lindra reached her hand out at her side, a subtle gesture, but one Mariela had grown accustomed to over the years. The lead attendant took her hand, and the Royana gave it a squeeze before letting go.

As they neared the audience chamber, Lindra wrestled her thoughts to the task at hand. The time for considering the implications of the assassin's sparing of Tobain and herself would have to wait. It seemed like every matter even resembling personal in nature had to wait, these days. Together, she and Dimitri had led Shiedra well, even considering some of her husband's more questionable ambitions. Now, everything fell to Lindra, and truly did she feel the weight of burden on her solitary shoulders.

They came to the meeting room where Esperanza waited, voluminous tome cradled in her right arm. The advisor offered a conservative curtsy. "My Royana, your *guests* await."

The corner of Lindra's mouth twitched. "Then, let's not keep them waiting any longer."

"Why not?" Esperanza quietly asked, to which Lindra shushed her to hide her chuckling.

The advisor stifled her smirk as she opened the door. Three predatory gazes fixed on Lindra the moment she entered. They rose and offered bows and curtsies, while the royana met their eyes with an expression she hoped projected unwavering confidence.

She sat in her high-backed chair across from the other three, whose seats were comfortable, but humble. Though she disliked such optic posturing, it was sometimes necessary; especially with these three.

The room was far more intimate than the normal audience hall. While Dimitri preferred the formal, larger chamber where he could dominate the room, Lindra preferred the intimacy of the smaller chamber. Bookshelves lined two of the walls, and behind Lindra's seat hung a larger than life painting of the legendary Royana Aelina Velazcia.

Lindra sat erect with her legs crossed at the knees, hands resting on the armrests and made quiet eye contact with each of her three adversaries. Esperanza, to her left, complimented her knowledge, while Mariela, to her right, complimented her empathy. At her back, the noble Royana Aelina Velazcia lent her strength.

Melren Spraza cupped a fist to his mouth and cleared his throat. He opened his mouth, but Draygen spoke first. "Greetings and gratitude for granting us an audience on such short notice, Royana." On the other side of Mirtalis, Melren glared at the wall on the far side of the chamber.

"My responsibilities were light today," Lindra responded. "Your lucky day."

"You've my admiration for bearing such responsibilities alone, Royana," Melren predictably commented. "Surely it must be diffi-cult on the best of days. Far more so given Nashma's current tragedy."

"You remind me of my appreciation of your expressed condo-lences of Nashma's loss when first it happened, Manti de Tableijar," Lindra responded. The board of councilors bristled at Lindra's formal use of his title. Good. "As with before the loss of our esteemed Royain, the welfare of Shiedra, and by extension, Nashma, sits at the front of my every action, as I'm sure it does for all present."

"It does, of course," Mirtalis replied cooly.

"And now, I ask. How heavy is this matter that requires your combined presence to carry it to me, today?"

The trio blinked.

"I fear our trade affairs must be addressed, Royana," Mirtalis Semada began. Word of Excellency Royain's assassination has spread across Marai. Trade negotiations with Shetar have become less smooth, and the ever-paranoid prime minister of Carlayn balks at the idea of strengthening trade with regard to corlite currency. Given our positive relations with Khatal, Cravel likely sees it as a potential black eye in his relationship with King Alyn. The little man is nothing if not cravenly."

Or smart, Lindra thought. "Give the man time to calm down as the situation cools. Cravel will come around, and with him, his minister of trade."

"You give him a lot of credit," Draygen Braga remarked in his rumbling baritone voice. "The man is suspicious of his own shadow."

"As to your concerns regarding Shetar," Lindra continued. "I would imagine they number among all other provinces of Marai at the moment. The battle with the Terratoma and Dokayuk nations grows hotter. As Alyn casts his gaze over more provinces to join with him, the nations of Khatal are likely to do the same."

Draygen leaned back in his chair and frowned. No doubt he prepared to state that very argument. Now he studied her with suspicion. Lindra allowed herself a mental smile. She'd guessed his reason for being here correctly and taken his argument right out of his mouth.

"We have many options," Lindra pressed on. "New Dama

remains a firm trade partner for their precious naguave syrup. Given the general adoration the diverse population of the borderland town has for our fruit and non corlite precious stone productions, I'm confident should Shetar distance themselves, New Dama would happily increase trade activity."

Mirtalis grinned. "You suggest we call their bluff? Perhaps even renegotiate trade terms and raise our prices? No other province in Marai grows serrafruit and greenskin vines. Our diamond, belicythist, and amirik precious stones are sought after across Marai." The woman steepled her fingers beneath the greedy hazel glint in her eyes. "This could actually work to our favor, Royana. They've tried to exploit what they think is our weakness. We can clap back with increased prices and harder trade terms. I would especially enjoy presenting such terms to the archminister of Vyne. I would even be willing to present such terms personally."

That last bit drew a round of chuckling. Few Marailander leaders were as disliked as Archminister Decius. As much as Lindra disliked admitting it, Mirtalis had a point. The trade and negotiations branches in other provinces saw blood. Lindra may well have to deliver that clap back with a pair of iron hands.

"Those provinces who wish to renegotiate are of course free to do so," the royana said. "They are welcome to send representatives here. Beyond that, we will see. Nashma has been generous with her prices and trade terms, but if they wish to revisit their agreements, that will happen."

Domayana Mirtalis lifted her wrinkled chin, her jaw-length brown hair sweeping back from her face to reveal naturally blushy cheeks. "Out of curiosity, Royana. Should they call *our* bluff, what then?"

"We have many options," Lindra repeated.

Melren had been squinting at the floor over the top of his narrow spectacles. Now he looked up at Lindra, face brightened with realization. "You would trade with the wilders."

Draygen's broad shoulders bounced as he chuckled at the question. "Would that not be ill advised? Trading with the enemy?"

"I never suggested trading with the enemy," Lindra replied.

"What would be these "many options" you speak of, then, Royana?" Melren asked.

"Terratoma and Dokayuk are two of many Khatala nations," Lindra said.

"They are the enemy," Draygen said, his voice going dangerously even. "What you suggest is treason."

Lindra's expression never changed, but she let her tone dip low and icy at the challenge. "Do not presume to understand my actions if you fail to understand Khatal, Somallar."

The commander chief of the Shiedran military stiffened. "I assure you, Royana, that my knowledge of Khatal is more than adequate."

"Then you are fully aware that every nation is individual."

"I appreciate the reminder, Royana," Draygen replied. The man's face grew tight as dried parchment. "I am very aware that each nation by shared Khatala culture considers a disagreement isolated to the involved individuals. I am also aware that they believe our king to be cowardly for not engaging the chief of the Terratoma directly. That hardly changes how our king feels about them."

"Yes," Mirtalis chimed it. "But surely King Alyn would not be angered by our relations with uninvolved nations. That could actually be a catalyst for cooling the situation."

Melren snorted at that. "You don't believe that any more than we do."

Mirtalis looked squarely at the manti de tableijar. "Why not? With a new and firm trade relationship with the east, the western nations not embroiled in this conflict may be less likely to get involved."

"I hadn't realized the Domayana had such military knowledge," Draygen remarked.

"Am I wrong, Somallar?" Mirtalis replied.

"Not completely, but the possibility of you being wrong comes with undesirable consequences," Braga said. "If we foolishly set aside King Alyn's nearly guaranteed ire, imagine if the nations trading with us *do* decide to enter the conflict." He looked to Lindra. "What you suggest may not be treason at this moment, but if the latter possibility comes to pass, that will change overnight."

"As would our actions, Somallar," Lindra replied. "The coin could land on either side. It would be hard to argue against our intentions for sowing peace with the uninvolved nations, should we make our intentions to do so clear."

The somallar tapped his fingers on his lap at that, while Melren Spraza glanced from the commander chief to Mirtalis and back. "What you suggest, Royana, is as dangerous as it is ambitious. I am unsure the council will see this through the same lens."

"Fortunately, I am excellent at my job to present the situation clearly," Lindra replied. "What of you, Manti de Tableijar? What does the Head of the Board of Councilors think?"

Melren Spraza pushed his spectacles up from the tip of his nose, then replaced them to their original position a moment later. A nervous tick that surfaced only when he was about to say something Lindra wouldn't like. "Speaking as the voice of the council, I do not like the idea for reasons the Somallar has already stated. The negative potential outweighs the positive."

Spraza plastered an expression on his face that he no doubt thought was compassionate, but only served to set Lindra's blood boiling. "Please, consider the possibility that you suggest such a risky endeavor at least partially influenced by your grief and the no-doubt taxing situation of suddenly leading a province alone?" Beside him, Domayana Mirtalis Semada narrowed her eyes.

Lindra focused her gaze on the man. "I'm afraid I don't grasp your meaning, Manti de Tableijar." She lifted a hand toward him. "Please elaborate."

Melren Spraza cleared his throat and opened his mouth, then

closed it. He stole a glance at Mirtalis, who slowly blinked, and slowly turned her head to regard him with the most venomous glare Lindra had ever seen from the woman. Even Draygen surprised the royana with the frosty look he gave Melren.

Spraza took a few tense heartbeats to consider his words. "I mean not to insinuate that her Excellency is incapable of leading the province—"

"Good," Mirtalis interrupted. "Then what did you mean?"

Given the circumstance, Lindra allowed the other woman's breech of etiquette and continued to look expectantly at the Head of Councilors. After a few moments more, she arched an eyebrow at him.

"I'm … ahem. I'm merely suggesting we allow a little time to consider placing ourselves in such a potentially precarious situation," Melren amended.

Lindra lifted her chin, nodded, and laced her tone with iron. "Your concern is duly noted, Manti de Tableijar. I place the well-being of our great province above all else."

"As every previous matriarch of Nashma has, throughout history," Domayana Mirtalis Semada added. She and Lindra shared a quick glance, and in that flicker of a moment, Lindra saw an ally. Whether such an alliance would be as brief as this no doubt tense moment for Melren remained to be seen. Still, Lindra wouldn't forget the Domayana's show of solidarity.

"I do not always agree with the Royana," Draygen rumbled. "But she leads with a strong hand. You would agree, would you not, Spraza?"

"I … of course," Melren sputtered. The stubborn wisps of hair remaining on his mostly bald pate drifted across his head as he looked to either side of himself at allies that had possibly become adversaries. He pushed his spectacles back up his nose and looked to Lindra. "Apologies, Excellency. I meant not to insinuate any inability by you to lead. My words came across badly."

"Of course, Manti de Tableijar," Lindra replied formally. "I'm sure you will find the correct words when next we convene with the council."

"Of course, Excellency," Melren replied with a dip of his head.

Lindra turned her focus to Mirtalis. "The fact that Nashma is in mourning bears no effect on her value to Marai, nor her strength and stability. We will politely but firmly remind the rest of the country of this fact, if need be."

Mirtalis inclined her head. "Of course, Excellency."

Lindra looked to Draygen. "Nashma will not engage in any action against her own and by extension, Marai's best interests, Somallar. But she will also not stoke the flames of a conflict into an outright war if it can be avoided. Nashma will, in fact, do her best to bring about the opposite effect."

"King Alyn—" Draygen began.

"Views Khatal as he does," Lindra cut in. "Nashma will of course cooperate with the rule of Jietar, but not without presenting a case for alternative actions that could diffuse the situation. If the rest of Marai can refrain from this conflict as the rest of Khatal does, and trade between uninvolved provinces and nations were to flourish, might that it would encourage Jietar and the Terratoma and Dokayuk nations to sit down and have talks."

"A rather optimistic view, Excellency," Braga replied.

Lindra favored him with an icy smile. "Quite diplomatic for a military commander chief. There may yet be a career in court for you, upon your retirement from your post."

Braga huffed a bit of quiet laughter at that. "You'd not want this old dog of war in your court, Royana."

The royana turned her attention to the head of councilors. "Even the King of Marai must consult with his cabinet before making decisions whose implications spread across Marai. So too does the Royana of Nashma consult with hers. As I am aware of this, I also have the utmost confidence that Shiedra's manti de tableijar is aware of my unwavering commitment to the good of the province, and that of Marai. The very title I occupy and the legacy behind it demands no less."

"Of course, Excellency," Melren Spraza replied.

Lindra spread her hands. "Good. I continue to lay my faith in each of your abilities to perform your duties with the good of Nashma foremost in your minds."

"First and foremost, Excellency," the three responded.

"I think that went well," Lindra said once the trio had left.

Esperanza had been thumbing through her huge book. Lindra thought the woman must be as strong as a bear to be able to hold that thing for so long. "Hmm. The Domayana spoke partial truth about trade relations between Nashma and our neighboring provinces. Things are only a bit strained, but not to the degree she insinuates. My contacts inform that while Shetar is watching us to see how we surface from," she cleared her throat, "recent events, Carlayn, New Dama, and Altarra have shown no indication of trying to take advantage of our situation. And Cravel is careful, but unlikely to turn his back on healthy trade."

The trio moved about the open-air hallways of Alcazar de Masarile while Lindra listened without interruption as her advisor corroborated and refuted the accounts of the meeting. It was a blessing from the Creator that she had such women in her life. Esperanza had traveled extensively across Marai before coming to be Lindra's trusted advisor. As a result, the woman had contacts everywhere, and was able to see the truth of the situation outside Nashma's borders.

"If it pleases you, my Royana," Esperanza said once they reached the door to Lindra's private rooms. "I will send for up-to-date information in Shetar and Carlayn. Vyne won't be necessary, as anyone having spent a paltry of time in the archminister's presence knows what he is about."

"Correct as usual," Lindra said. "However, I would like information from Vyne as well. However predictable the archminister might be, I would still know his actions. Thank you, Adviasar."

Esperanza responded with a curtsy and departed the way they'd come.

Mariela followed Lindra into her rooms and closed the door. Lindra inhaled the soothing aroma wafting from a pitcher across the room. Every one of the attendants of Alcazar de Masarile were attuned to the needs of their Royana. Lindra might be the leader of an entire province, but she couldn't do it without her most capable staff. Even the small things, like moving ahead of her to have hot tea available for her arrival, helped Lindra get through every tiresome day. "Tea?" she asked her attendant and friend.

"Oh, please let me, Royana," Mariela said, starting to reach for the pitcher.

"We're in my private rooms, Mari," Lindra said. "You know better than that."

Mariala chuckled in defeat. "Of course. You must forgive my force of habit, Lindra."

"Only if you stop calling me "my Royana" in private. It's tiring enough in public."

Lindra took the pitcher from the table and poured two steaming mugs of citrus tea, handing one to Mariela. "Do you know who brought this?" She held up the pitcher.

"For today, Arianna," the lead attendant replied.

Lindra nodded in thought. "What would be a proper gift of appreciation? A bouquet? Monetary bonus?"

"Every one of your staff serve you with love," Mariela said. "It truly is our pleasure to be of service to you, who so graciously are in service to all of Nashma."

"Words as sweet as naguave nectar," Lindra chuckled. "Send an invitation to her for her entire family to join us and the boys for dinner."

Mariela smiled deeply at that. "She will be overjoyed."

Lindra returned that smile, but the bright mood passed quickly.

Mariela watched her over the rim of her warm mug. "You're

worried about your sons, and your second meeting with the detained woman."

The royana closed her eyes and smiled. "Are you sure you don't read minds?"

"Read? No. Feel, yes." Mariela took another sip of tea. "You're right. The meeting did go well. By stepping ahead of Draygen Braga's argument about the conflict to the south, you threw him off balance just long enough to get him to listen. You don't need me to tell you that, of course. But he is conflicted. He wanted to join in the battle with Khatal, and thought to walk right over you to do it. These past weeks, he doesn't know what to make of you."

Lindra cupped the warm mug in her hands and held it under her face. She inhaled the warm scent of rosebuds and citrusy serrafruit. "Mmm." She sipped the hot, sweet liquid and enjoyed the warmth traveling down to her stomach. "He's from a village in southern Nashma. Delain, its name is. It is a patriarchal society there. I've dealt with his struggle to see me as a strong leader since the day of Dimitri's death, but he will learn."

"I feel that the manti de tableijar may not," Mariela said. "Despite Braga's upbringing, he tries to see you for who you are through the filter of the prejudices of his upbringing. Melren Spraza does not care about your ability to lead, but rather the possibility of manipulating you."

The other woman's face tightened with repressed anger. Mariela was genuinely more upset at Melren than Lindra herself.

"The moment he came before you after the Royain's death, I saw hunger in his eyes. He thought to be quick in exploiting your nonexistent vulnerability. He wishes more influence in the governing of Shiedra, and eventually all of Nashma."

"Do you think he had a hand in the assassination?" Lindra asked, forcing down the lump in her throat." *Not now. Hold it together. Dimitri. My dear overambitious Dimitri.*

"He didn't," Mariela replied. "But his intentions to capitalize on your grief are without doubt. He hadn't expected you to be so strong." The lead attendant glowered. "Perhaps he is from the same village as the somallar?"

Lindra laughed. As with Braga, it hadn't taken an empath's ability to see Melren's intent. "Born and bred Shiedran stock, I fear. And what of the domayana? I'm curious of your thoughts there."

"Melren's blunder toward the end of the meeting may have gained you a temporary ally who could become a permanent one," Mariela said. "She didn't like his final remarks any more than we. You saw this, surely, for it played brightly on her face. It could be that the legacy of Shiedra burned through some of her greed. There is more underneath her reaction to the manti de tableijar's misstep. Her reaction felt personal, as if he had insulted her, instead of yourself."

"Interesting," Lindra said. Lindra took one final sip and placed the mug back on the little table. She moved to sit in a plush chair by the unlit hearth. Mariela took the seat opposite the royana, and both women sat in silence for a while.

"You plan to meet with the prisoners soon," Mariela said.

Lindra nodded absently as she stared into the recess of the blackened fireplace. "That needs to be addressed as quickly as possible. For my own piece of mind, Captain Adolphus, and all of Nashma. If she is the assassin, it will hearten the people to know the culprit has been caught. If she's not, best to keep this quiet." She nodded at Mariela's dubious expression. "Unlikely, I know. Tongues flap, especially if there is drink involved."

The door opened, and Lindra and Mariela turned to see Marcos and Darien spring into the room and make straight for them. They tackled Lindra with crushing hugs, then climbed into the seat with Mariela where they settled in.

"I think they like you more than me, Mari," Lindra said.

"It's the stories," Mariela said. "Without my stories, I'm useless." She put on a mock sad faced.

"That's not true, Essa," Marcos said. "We love you! But can we have a story?"

Mariala laughed. "Of course. If it's okay with mama."

Lindra held up her hands to ward off the expected pleading. "Dinner first, then wash up, then stories." She made a shoeing gesture. "Go to the kitchens and eat."

"Aren't you going to eat with us, mama?" Darien asked.

"I will be there shortly," Lindra replied.

"Are you coming, Essa?" Marcos and Darien asked. "You're going to eat with us?"

"Aaaw. Of *course* I am!" Mariela said with a long groan as she hugged the boys tight. She looked to Lindra, who made another shoeing gesture. "I'll be there shortly."

Mariela gathered the boys and herded them out the door, speaking excitedly of the stories to come. Lindra stared at the closed door, feeling a mixture of joy and melancholy. Dimitri had taken Mariela's future at having a family away from her, yet the woman insisted that Lindra and the boys were her family. She couldn't think of a time when they'd all needed each other more.

Lindra rested her chin on the top of her fingers and looked out the window at the darkening sky. She wouldn't go up to the prisons today. That would wait till tomorrow. The shock of even the possibility of her husband's killer being apprehended was a lot to digest. She needed rest before the second confrontation. Whether the woman proved to be innocent or guilty, Lindra's heart would be broken all over again.

NANDI

One foot in front of the other. After days of travel on foot, those words had become a mantra. Nandi looked at the afternoon sky, wishing the sun could stay up longer. She didn't know what she dreaded more, the mosquitoes, constant rattle of the cicadas and bugs she'd never seen before buzzing in her ears, or the cold and sometimes breezy nights that rushed in on the heels of dusk.

She closed her eyes and leaned her head back to let the sun warm her face. Direct sunlight kept her warm enough during the day, as long as she avoided shade and wooded areas. She opened her sack and fished out a snack. Sama had hunted for them for the first day, but the tatamble had insisted Nandi learn as well. As much as she hated the idea, she knew Sama was right. She needed to know how to survive out in the wild.

Nandi stumbled over a bump in the ground and nearly fell face first to the grassy earth. After several exaggerated steps with her arms flailing out in front of her, she caught her balance.

Several paces away Sama stared at her with a puzzled frown. "Sister Nandi should walk with eyes open. If not, maybe trip on something, or walk into tree, or fall off cliff."

"I know, I know," Nandi said.

"If know, then why eyes closed?" Sama asked.

Nandi sighed at what she knew was a genuinely sincere question. "I was just enjoying the sun, is all."

Now Sama looked even more confused. "Cannot enjoy sun with eyes open?"

There was no point in trying to explain. "Yes, I suppose I could. I just … wanted to feel the sun on my eyelids. How far do you think we are from Altarra?"

Sama sniffed the air. "If Nandi girl could run faster, maybe one day. But she can't, so two or three."

"I already told you, Sama," Nandi said, trying hard to keep the exasperation out of her voice. "I can't run like you do for that long."

Sama grunted in that husky voice of hers that told Nandi that the tatamble girl thought she was making excuses for being out of shape. Whatever.

"Two to three more days." She sighed. Ridiculous as it was, she'd spared a flicker of hope that they might come across Joga or Amiya, or at least someone who'd seen them. It turned out the luck of the Fallen must be hanging over them, for not only did they not find Joga or Amiya, but they'd encountered no one for the past few days. Not a single person.

I hope they aren't being held in Altarra. Nandi didn't know how she'd get them out if that were the case. She didn't even know what Altarra looked like, let alone where to find them. A great big city. That's all she knew about the place.

A chill crept into the air, signifying impending dusk, and with it, another cold night. More dried jerky meat. She wished they could make a fire so she could cook a hot meal, but Sama would have none of it. Nandi couldn't fault her. A campfire in the middle of the night would be a beacon for anything to find them.

Nandi had tried to use *fire* to cook something on the second night, to disastrous effect. Between charring the meal into a blackened lump of coal and Sama's constant lamenting about the wasted food and use of Mother's power, she thought it best not to try again until she learned better control. It sapped her energy as well, and she needed every bit of it for this endless journey.

She was so wrapped up in her thoughts that she almost stumbled over Sama, who had dropped into a crouch so low she nearly disappeared into the high grass. "Sama?"

"*Hssss!*" The girl stared straight ahead.

Nandi dropped to the ground beside her and followed her gaze. Tiny pinpricks of light glowed in the encroaching darkness far ahead. Nandi's heart leapt. Civilization. Food. *Hot* food! She started to say as much, but the tatamble girl was staring intently at the lights, as though watching a dangerous animal.

She stayed low to the ground beside Sama and looked around, straining to see what had made the girl so nervous. Those lights up ahead weren't the first time Sama had encountered human civilization with Nandi and the others. Usually the tatamble would accompany them up until they were within eye-range of a bowman, then flee into woods or any other place to avoid a human patrol while she waited for the others to leave.

Watching Sama now, Nandi felt something else was going on. The other girl was on alert. "What's wrong, Sama?" she whispered.

"Men come on backs of animal slaves," Sama hissed. "Must flee, you and me."

"Sama they're just riders ..." Nandi trailed off when Sama slinked toward the nearby woods. Though not nearly as graceful as the tatamble girl, Nandi did her best to stay low to the ground and followed after her. Soon enough Nandi felt the vibration of hoofbeats followed shortly after by the rumbling of the riders' approach.

Nandi lifted her head to see a cluster of riders making straight for them. Wide-eyed, she dropped down and looked to tell Sama, but the tatamble had blended in with the high grass. *Me*, she thought. *They spotted me.* "They see me, Sama," she whispered. "I have to run."

"Nandi girl can't outrun horse," Sama said.

"Maybe they're coming to help," Nandi suggested, yet she felt a chill in the pit of her stomach that suggested otherwise."

"Flatten to the grown and crawl," Sama said.

Nandi did her best, scurrying along the like a lizard, though she doubted lizards scraped their bellies on the ground.

The hoofbeats drew closer, and she lifted her head. The riders had veered slightly away, but their eyes were sharp. As soon as Nandi saw them, someone spotted her and cried out.

No more hiding for me. She ignored Sama's hiss in protest and hopped to her feet and ran. The woods weren't far. With any luck they'd be too thick for the horses. They'd never find her if forced to pursue on foot.

Sama flew past her but slowed and reached back her hand. Nandi grabbed it and the tatamble nearly yanked her off her feet. Nandi must have taken one long floating stride to Sama's two, so fast did the other girl drag her along. She had to bend her arm just to keep it from being dislocated. She wondered what this girl would be like once she was an adult, if she was this strong now.

As soon as they reached the woods, Sama let her go so that they could navigate the foliage. Nandi figured that was more for her benefit than Sama's.

They leaped over and slid under fallen trees, darted around patches of shrubs and bushes, zigzagged around huge dormant trees as well as the occasional out of place stoutgreen. Nandi looked over her shoulder and her heart fluttered with fear. These woods were mostly dormant, which meant she had a clear view of the pursuing riders, who also had a clear view of her.

Nandi heard hoofbeats from the side. They were flanking her. The horses powered through the debris and leapt over low-lying trunks. She heard men shouting, now. When she looked ahead again, she saw barely a flicker of Sama's green hair as the swift girl practically snaked around, over, and under every obstacle in her path.

"Sama!" Nandi called. "Keep going." She saw Sama stop and look back in alarm. "Don't stop," she implored.

"Sister Nandi promise not leave Sama."

The pain in the girl's voice was enough to break Nandi's heart. "Nandi isn't leaving sister Sama. But Sama must get away, so that Nandi can find her later."

"They catch you," Sama said. They were still running, but the tatamble had slowed her pace so that Nandi could keep up. "Will catch Nandi."

"Yes, but not you," Nandi said. "They just not catch sister Sama." She was starting to tire. Her breath grew labored and her legs were starting to burn. "Please, Sama. Escape. Nandi will be fine with humans, and will leave and we find each other when she does." She tripped over an exposed root and flailed but managed not to fall.

Now she heard the voices calling out to her. "Girls! Little girls! Why do you run! We will not harm you. Stop!"

Nandi ignored them and kept running. "Sama, please. They will never find you, but you can find them. You know where they'll take me. Just wait for me."

"Hhh, hhh, hhh, hhrraaagh!" Sama's emotional wail further broke Nandi's heart. The tatamble dropped to the ground several paces ahead.

At first Nandi thought Sama had been shot by an arrow, but when she reached the spot where Sama had gone down, nothing was there. She lowered her head and kept running. Maybe she could lose them. The last rays of sunlight were rapidly fading. If she could elude them till nightfall, maybe they'd lose her and give up.

A hand grabbed the back of her shirt and lifted her off the ground. Nandi kicked and screamed, but an iron-like arm wrapped around her torso and held her fast while the horse trotted to a stop.

"Where's the other one?" she heard a man's voice call out.

"They're searching, sir," another voice answered. "It's like she just disappeared."

Nandi felt a bit of satisfaction that Sama had gotten away. She held onto that to keep the terror down as a group of armed and armored men surrounded her. Horses snorted and shuffled underneath their riders, who stared at Nandi with a range of expressions from curious to annoyed, and anything in between.

A man wearing boiled leather armor and a sword strapped to his hip wove his mount through the crowd and looked down on her with hard eyes. "Where did she go, girl? Where did the other one go?"

Nandi looked into his unfriendly eyes and thought to reach for the essences right then. Whether it was her fear, or the fact that she couldn't bring herself to use the power as a weapon against another person, she didn't.

"Speak!" the man demanded.

"She may be too afraid to speak, sir," another rider said.

"Or a mute," said a third, to a round of chuckling.

The rider the other man had called "sir" stared hard at Nandi for several heartbeats. "We know these woods and this land, girl. We will find her. Best if you tell her to come out. We have no intention of harming either of you." When Nandi didn't respond, he took a deep breath, visibly marshaling his patience. He waved a hand to encompass the darkening woods. "Look around you, girl. Where can your friend go?" He moved toward her, and Nandi reflexively leaned away. "Is she your friend? Your sister?"

Nandi looked at the scar on his left cheek, the large pores dotting his face. His thin lips wrinkled when he spoke, and his bushy eyebrows collected together above his hard hazel eyes. Nandi felt no trust for this man. She started to reach for the essences when two riders approached.

The man straightened away from Nandi to acknowledge the new arrivals. "Nowhere, sir. It's like she disappeared. There's no way she could have outrun the horses, but there is no sign of her anywhere."

With a deep exhale through his nostrils, the man nodded. "Very well." He looked down at Nandi again. "Have it your way, girl. But these woods are rather inhospitable to small animals. And human or not, the predators that roam here will see her as a small animal. Last chance. Call out to her, that we may take her with you back for a warm meal and bed. Then we might find out where you're from and see you returned."

Nandi wanted to believe it, and she certainly wanted that warm meal and bed, but something about this didn't seem right. She remained silent.

"As you wish," the man said.

The ride back through the woods was filled with chatter about whether the rumors of distant monster attacks were true, to what each were having for dinner that night.

Nandi kept her eyes focused ahead while she listened. Mostly they sounded like everyday normal people, only with an accent she'd never heard before. Were these people Nashmarese, or had she and Sama crossed into Jietar. How far of a walk was three days, as Sama had said they were from Altarra?

"What do you make of that one?" one of the soldiers asked.

Nandi didn't have to guess that the man had referred to her. It was a fair enough question, since she didn't know what to make of them.

"Who knows? The closest place to the border is Delaine Village, and she ain't no Nashmarese, that's for sure."

"You forgot New Dama," the other man said. "It touches the border, too. It's the only place I can think of where she could come from."

"What about Zal'eshma?" yet another rider suggested. "Other side of the woods east."

"Not from the direction she came from," the other soldier said.

In the brief silence that followed, Nandi felt eyes studying her. She forced herself not to look at them.

"I give a good care how in the Fallen-cursed underworld two young girls survive out in the wild as long as they did. Ain't nothin' safe about anything out here. Wolves, bears … even seen a couple'a darkwood cats draggin' off a little girl about her size—"

"Will you shut up tryin' to scare her," another man said. "She ain't payin' you no mind."

"Oh, she's listening." Nandi recognized the voice as belonging to the man with the scar. "She's listenin' to everything you're saying."

Another pause. "I guess if you're a mute, listenin's all you got."

"Ain't no mute, either," the scarred man said. "She's just smart. Smarter than you, whose doin' all the talkin'."

If she wasn't being held against her will, Nandi would have enjoyed the ride across the high grass fields despite the cold air rushing in her face. She and Amiya rarely got to ride horseback, but she loved it.

All too soon, the distant lights she and Sama had seen grew closer. She started to make out the outline of houses and small buildings as they drew closer. The candlelit poles and burning torches in sconces lit the nighttime pathways along the town.

They rode through the entrance to the wooden fence surrounding the little town and onto the dirt road. Apparently these men were soldiers, or town guards, for they were greeted with warmth and occasional inquiry about Nandi. The men mostly responded with noncommittal sarcasm.

Nandi tried to keep track of the various avenues they turned, and which direction they traveled with each turn, but it was too dark, and the horses moved just a little too fast. She didn't give up, though. Even if she could keep a vague idea of what direction they were headed, it might help when it was time to get out of here. Part of her hoped these people were simply trying to help her. She could imagine what it must look like to an adult to see a child her age roaming the land.

The ride ended at a four-foot fence surrounding the yard of a large house, easily the size of Decius's mansion back in Vyne. The scarred man walked up to the left side of the horse carrying Nandi and her captor, and he lifted his hands toward her, expectantly.

Nandi stared at his hands, then him. The situation was impossibly against her, but she had no intention of willingly diving into the arms of that man.

"I think she likes riding with me," the man sitting behind her said. She felt his hot breath in her right ear. "This mean you wanna stay with me instead, girl?"

Nandi had shoved her hands down on the saddle horn and vaulted clean out of the saddle.

Surprised laughter ensued as the scarred man scrambled to the side and caught her. As soon as his hands touched her underarms to stop her descent, Nandi twisted her body and slipped out of his grip.

"Woah, hey now!" someone called out. She kept moving, trying to zigzag her way free. But she was only one, with legs too short against many long arms.

One of the few remaining soldiers that hadn't broken away from the group caught her by the arm, and an instant later she felt the ungentle grip of the scarred man's grasp around her elbow.

The rough manner in which the man yanked her around and dragged her back to the house made Nandi second guess her decision not to use essence against him.

"You got spirit, girl. I'll give you that." The scarred man effortlessly dragged her by the arm toward the fenced house, despite her silent struggles. "Will you quit fighting me? We ain't gonna do anything bad to you, but you are makin' me wanna throw you in a patch of mud if I can find one."

Nandi saw three women standing at the open fence door, all

wearing some manner of dress, with their hands clasped in front of them. They watched passively as the man dragged her to them.

When they stopped, the scarred man looked down at her. "I got a deal for you, girl. I let you go and you talk to the nice ladies here," he jerked his chin at the three women. "Or, I let you go, you bolt, we catch you again, and I tie your wrists and ankles together, then I tie your wrists to your ankles and carry you in the house and lay you on the floor on your belly. "Your choice."

Nandi clenched her teeth and stared at the ground. She'd had just enough practice to, what? Set him on fire? Impale him with stone or ice? Shoot him with water with enough force to tear his skin? She didn't have enough control to use the essences just enough to afford her escape, and if she truly let go, she might kill someone. Maybe a lot of someones.

"She's an angry one," one of the women said. "Look at her fists, her tense arms and jaw." A finger gently touched Nandi's chin and pressed upward.

As much as Nandi wanted to break that finger, she lifted her head to look into the woman's brown eyes. The torchlight dancing across her face gave the woman's smile an unnerving quality.

"She's afraid," one of the other women said. "Look at her."

The woman holding Nandi's chin squatted down to her height. "You are safe here, child. No one will harm you. Do you believe me?"

Her smile looked genuine, but genuinely what, Nandi couldn't be sure. At that moment she realized any resistance was pointless. Best to cooperate and get out of here.

"No tricks, or you're hogtied for sure," the scarred man said when he felt her arm relax.

"I don't think she's going to run, Patrem."

Nandi refrained from snatching her arm away when Patrem released her. She continued to look into the woman's face, trying not to let her boiling anger and fear play on her face.

The woman studied her for a moment, then looked up. "Why

don't you old dogs head to the tavern? You've done a good thing in finding this lost girl, but you're making her nervous."

Patrem laughed. "You wasn't out there, Jasindi. This girl might or might not be a bunch of things. But I got a feeling scared ain't one of 'em."

"Whatever the case, your presence isn't helping," the woman calmly responded. "Go have a drink, shall you?"

"Eh, fair enough." Patrem turned away and started walking. "You heard her, get goin'. Hey Trass, drinks'r on you."

"I know they can be unpleasant," the woman whispered conspiratorially. "With their mouths and their smell." Nandi forced herself not to laugh, but the woman studied her reaction and smiled. The smile faded when she noted Nandi holding her cloak tightly about her body. "Dear me, how inconsiderate of us. You're cold." She stood and walked toward the fence, then stopped and turned back. "Come, child. You will be safe from the cold and your hunger."

As if it had heard that pronouncement, Nandi's stomach growled. With great trepidation, she followed the woman through the entrance. The other two women fell in on either side of her. It felt like a procession leading her to a dungeon. She suddenly had flashbacks of when Decius's armed soldiers had come to their home and taken her and Amiya away. She and her sister had been "guests" then, too.

Nandi tried not to let those memories throw her into a panic. These people were doing what they thought was right. Who would think for even a moment that a girl her age out in the wild wasn't lost or in danger? She told herself they weren't bad people, but just wanted to help.

She followed the woman named Jasindi into the house to be greeted by the curious stares of girls ranging from her age to younger and older. They swept the floors and cleaned the walls, mostly watching her in silence, their whispers following her as they passed.

They climbed a spiraling set of stairs and took several hallways until the women stopped her at single door. Jasindi turned and smiled. "We have many questions for you, as I'm sure you have for us. For now, let's have you rest. Tomorrow is a *new* day, and we are excited to have you."

She reached out her hand. "My name is Jasindi."

Several moments passed while Nandi stared at the proffered hand until it became clear it wasn't going away until she shook it.

"Very good," Jasindi said. "This is Laryn," she indicated the woman to Nandi's right, then the one to her left. "And Myleshia. What's your name?"

Nandi didn't want to answer, but she didn't want to be impolite, either. These women were trying to welcome her into their home and she was being difficult. Didn't she owe them at least the courtesy of a name? "T … Tyshia."

Jasindi clapped her hands together and held them in front of her chest. "Very good!" She looked at the other two women. "I do believe we've made progress." She looked back to Nandi. "Fortune has shined on you, this day. Be welcome to the House of Valragan Arts."

Since she'd already spoken, Nandi figured she might as well try to figure out her situation. "What are Valragan Arts?"

"Tomorrow," Jasindi said. "I can't imagine the trauma of being picked up by a group of men after wandering in the wild for however long you were." She opened the creaking door and gestured inside. "Take a bed of your choosing. It is normally required that you get cleaned up before climbing into fresh bedding, but you've been through enough tonight. We'll get off to a fresh, clean start tomorrow."

The woman held the door open so the light from the hallway illuminated her path between the beds. There must have been two dozen of them lined up in neat rows; only a few were occupied. Though most of the girls slept, several watched her as she passed. Aware that everyone waited on her, Nandi quickly scanned the room, passing by empty beds in the middle room for a solitary bed in the farthest corner from the door.

She hurried over to the bed and sat on the edge. Jasindi remained in the doorway and watched her for several moments. Across the room with barely more than a column of light splitting the darkness, the woman's face was shrouded in shadow. Nandi hesitantly raised a hand to wave. The woman offered a courteous nod and closed the door.

The silent faces staring at her faded away in the dark. Nandi heard tiny whispers drifting about the room, but she paid them no mind.

She slipped under the covers and lay on her side, staring into the nothingness. Where was Amiya? Her sister was alive, she knew. But what was happening to her? Was she well? How was Dad? Was he still in Altarra or headed back to Vyne? Had he already gotten back and seen the destruction wrought by those monsters. Was he searching for her and Amiya right now? What of Joga? Sama?

Nandi rolled onto her other side and put her back to the whispering. As much as she hoped these people would give her some provisions and let her walk out of here, the feeling deep in her gut told her that would not be the case. If it had been, those men would have simply invited her into Valraga and offered her a place to stay, and food. Thinking about that, they hadn't even offered her food, despite their kind words. She thought about what Amiya would say in this situation. Her sister would certainly be suspicious. "Nobody gives you anything for free for no reason," her sister would have said. "They want something." She could practically hear Amiya's voice in her mind. Nandi found herself agreeing. These people wanted something.

As exhaustion dragged her into oblivion, she vowed to leave Valraga tomorrow. They'd given her a bed, and hopefully food tomorrow. That shouldn't take longer than a day to work off. She'd do whatever labors they assigned for the day, find Sama—or more likely, Sama would find her—and move on.

Nandi closed her eyes and listened to her own breathing as she drifted to sleep, surrounded by a room full of kids, and feeling very alone.

NANDI

Nandi woke from a fitful sleep infected with nightmares of grisly death and dismemberment. She opened her eyes and tried to move, but couldn't. Panic set in and she squirmed in her restraints until she realized she'd wrapped herself up in her covers while she slept.

She set about extricating herself. Her smallclothes were damp from the cold sweat induced by the horrors of her sleep. Nandi pushed it all away. Likely, she'd be having nightmares about the massacre of those travelers for a while. She yawned and stretched her arms and legs. Amiya, Dad, and the others came immediately to mind, so Nandi rolled over.

Several girls stood around her bed, staring down at her. Nandi scooted away to the other side of the bed and stood with it between them. For a while they stared at each other in silence, Nandi alternating eye contact with each of the four girls looking at her.

"You were having a nightmare," one girl said. She was about Nandi's height, with long curly red hair and freckles on her cheeks. Her green eyes practically sparkled as she reached across the bed and offered her hand. For some reason Nandi instantly liked the girl. She grabbed her hand and gave it a squeeze.

"Dreaming about being lost out in the woods?" one of the other girls asked. "I remember when my parents were killed by a pack of jarku. I'd been out in the woods for over a day and a half before they found me half-starved and dehydrated. You're lucky." This girl stood about a head taller and looked to be a bit older than she and the girl with the red hair. She slid a stray brown lock behind her ear and folded her arms across her chest. "It's good they found you. You'd have been dead soon if they hadn't."

If Nandi hadn't been with Sama, the girl would probably be right, but Nandi still bristled at the comment.

"Time for cleanup and food, ladies!" a girl called out from the front of the room.

Nandi's audience scattered and went about making their beds and cleaning up personal clutter. The red-haired girl stayed long enough to offer a hesitant smile. "Don't take Ingris to heart. She's actually not a bad person, just doesn't know how to talk to people right."

"Ailith!" the girl at the front of the room called. "Is your hearing impaired?"

"Is your hearing im*paired*," the girl named Ailith mocked under her breath. "Better get to making up your bed, or Nimi will get after you."

Nandi struggled to contain a chuckle at that comment, which came with an eye-roll. She watched the girl trot away, her wavy red curls bouncing down her back with each step. She didn't bother to look at who she guessed to be the girl in charge, but went about making up her bed like everyone else.

She smiled as she went about her task. Nandi had only known Ailith for a few moments, but her temperament reminded her of Amiya. She pushed the thought away before the ache in her heart reduced her to a sobbing blob on the floor in front of all these strangers.

"Work makes you smile. That's a good sign."

Nandi nearly jumped when she heard the voice directly behind her. She whirled to face the girl Ailith had called Nimi. She had hair the color of a sandy beach, combed away from her face into a perfect bun at the back of her head. Not a single hair strayed out of place, and even her plain brown dress looked too afraid to have a single wrinkle on its surface.

She stood head and shoulders taller than Nandi, and looked down on her with an air of authority. "Your bed looks decent for now. You'll learn the proper way to make it before the day is over."

Nandi just looked at her, wondering how strongly her instant dislike played on her face.

A tiny frown flickered across the taller girl's brow; there and gone in an instant. "You don't like me much, do you? Does authority put you off, girl?"

"Not at all, girl," Nandi replied.

Nimi's frown returned. "Not at all to *what*, exactly?"

The tiniest of smiles stretched the corner of Nandi's mouth. This one wasn't used to challenge. She thought of Amiya. Her sister would have already provoked the girl enough to make a mistake, then put her to sleep right in front of everyone. She had to concentrate not to laugh.

"You find something funny, I see." Nimi raised her chin perfectly in line for a well-placed uppercut. "Well, I'll be sure to inform the head mistress of your mirthful attitude."

Nandi didn't say anything. She stared at the girl until she grew exasperated and glided away. *What have I fallen into?* Nandi watched as Nimi patrolled the room, stopping from bed to bed. She inspected the tightness of the covers and neatness of the little chests at the foot of each bed. The whole thing gave Nandi the impression of what a military training for children might be like.

"Beds are sufficient," Nimi declared. "However, due to the lack of gratitude displayed by our newest arrival, we will be forced to do extra chores *after* an *extended* run." She clapped her hands together twice. "Let's go. *Now*."

More than a few glares found their way to Nandi as the girls filed out. *Off to a great start*, she thought, moving toward the door.

Nimi stepped in front of the door just as Nandi reached it. "Not you. First, you will be seen by the house mistresses, *then* you will have your run, *then* you will have your chores."

Her eyes seemed to flare like blue flames of gratification with each pronouncement. Despite the sinking feeling in her stomach, Nandi narrowed her eyes at the taller, older girl without blinking. She'd been separated from her sister and her father. She'd nearly been killed more times than she could count, traveled across a good bit of Marai, fought all manner of monsters including a lavakhan. There was nothing this *Nimi* could think of doing that would break her.

The flames of superiority in Nimi's eyes seemed to waver at Nandi's lack of reaction. Nandi continued to stare at the older girl until Nimi finally cleared her throat. "Follow me, she said. Nandi thought she heard the girl's voice crack despite her crisp tone.

Nandi almost had to trot to keep up with Nimi's long-legged stride, all the while hoping she wasn't digging herself into a terrible hole.

They exited the house and stepped onto the front porch, where two of the three women Nandi had seen yesterday stood with their hands clasped behind their backs. They watched over several girls tending a garden she hadn't seen in the dark, the night before.

Nimi thrust her palm at Nandi, indicating she stop. With a swish of her nearly shin-length dress, the girl swept herself to the side of the two women and waited silently until they acknowledged her. They spoke too quietly for Nandi to hear, but she was sure she could guess what was being said.

Nimi finished her inaudible report, and with a rather dramatic curtsy, took her leave.

Nandi figured etiquette dictated she remain where she was until called. The irony of her making an effort to guess the rules after what had just transpired wasn't lost on her.

Finally Laryn waved her over. Nandi held a hand to her growling stomach as she approached. She stopped next to them and waited.

"Nimi tells us that you have a good eye for detail and cleanliness," Laryn stated. "She says you have potential."

Not knowing what to say to that, Nandi blinked.

"She also said that you have a defiant streak and are too willful for your own good."

That's more like it, Nandi thought dryly.

When Laryn turned her head toward Nandi, she got a better look at the woman than in the dim light of last night. She had light brown hair and round, earnest eyes that bore into Nandi. "Do you have anything to say to that, Tyshia? Are you not happy to have been rescued and given a place to lay your head?"

Nandi picked her words carefully. "I apologize, House Mistress," she began, remembering Nimi's use of the title. "I'd awoken from nightmares and been challenged by someone I didn't know." She clamped her fingers over her growling stomach.

Laryn responded with a slow, deliberate nod of her head. "You are forgiven, child. But if you're to grow into a woman of proper use, you'll need to learn your place in the world. Do you understand?"

Grow into a woman of proper use? My place? At that moment the need to get out of here became a sense of urgency. Nandi had never met a laborwife before, but she'd heard stories. The way this woman spoke practically screamed it at her. Before she could stop herself, her eyes darted in every direction, looking for a place to run—"

She suddenly found herself on the ground, stars dancing in her vision as she held her hand to the side of her throbbing face. She shook off the pain and climbed to her feet, trying to think through her dazed confusion. What just happened? She looked up at Laryn. The woman was facing her, now, and wore a surprised expression.

The other woman, Myleshia, moved to stand beside Laryn. Her expression seemed more curious than surprised.

Nandi felt her pulse in the side of her face. She gave her head a little shake, then stood straight, a confused frown creasing her brow.

"Not a single tear," Myleshia observed, her voice soft and appreciative. "Impressive."

"Self-destructive," Laryn disagreed. "Nimi is right. This one is far too willful."

Now that Nandi had cleared away her befuddlement, she realized the woman had struck her. Struck her so hard and so fast that Nandi had been on the ground before she knew what had happened. But why? Her frown deepened as anger replaced her confusion.

Laryn responded with an openmouthed frown and swung her open hand for Nandi's face. This time, Nandi saw it coming. She barely ducked the incoming hand, but not the backhand that caught her as soon as she straightened. On the ground once again, the other side of her face throbbing, Nandi rolled over and climbed to her hands and knees, the essences flooding into her in a raging inferno. At that moment, she could burn that woman into a giant lump of coal and set her entire house ablaze.

That horrible thought not only brought back the horrors of the traveler massacre, but the shock of having such dark feelings. She struggled to contain the essences as well as her temper, lest she lose control and murder this woman by accident. *This is unlike me*, she thought. Ever since their captivity by Decius and everything that followed, she'd noticed occasional yet uncharacteristic anger in herself; especially after her torture by the ghuza.

"It's okay to cry, child," she heard Myleshia say. The blonde woman knelt in front of her and placed a hand on Nandi's shoulder. "You don't have to hold it in. Let it go. It's good and cleansing."

This lady had no idea how close to a terrible death she was.

Nandi didn't want to hurt anyone, but she also had no intention of taking a beating from anyone.

Once she felt confident she wouldn't lose control and incinerate these women, she climbed back to her feet again and gave her head another little shake. She took a deep puffing breath, and looked back up at Laryn. The woman looked as if she didn't know what to make of her.

"I apologize if I seemed unappreciative of your help," Nandi said. "I can work off the debt of my night's lodging and be on my way, of no further burden to you."

Laryn's eyebrows rose. "Work off your lodging debt? Whatever for?"

The sense of dread she felt overpowered the pulsing pain on both sides of Nandi's face. "I would like to be on my way as soon as possible."

"On your way," Myleshia echoed. "To where, child? You are a long way from the next city. You would die out in the wild."

"I've come a long way already, House Mistress," Nandi said. "I can make it just fine."

"Like you did when Patrem and his men found you?" Myleshia countered.

Nandi ground her teeth. The woman had a point, but she'd rather die and be food to a pack of jarku than stay here and be brainwashed by these women.

"Assist with the gardening," Laryn ordered. She snapped her hand in the direction of the girls working the rows of vegetables beyond the porch. After you've completed that task and the disciplinary run, you will eat."

Just the word "eat" set Nandi's stomach to complaining again. She was so hungry she could barely stand. She had to do yardwork and run before a meal? She started toward the garden.

"Have you forgotten something, little girl?" she heard Laryn say from behind. The woman's whip-like tone suggested a transgression, likely manners.

Nandi turned back. "Yes, House Mistress," she said with a curtsy, every bone in her body screaming in rage as she made the gesture.

"Very good." She lifted her hand, palm facing down, and flicked her fingers away. "Go. The sooner you complete your work and punishment, the sooner you may eat."

As she descended the porch steps, Nandi heard Myleshia quietly remark, "fascinating, that one."

"A danger to herself," Laryn replied. "If she doesn't learn her place, she will not survive."

"She may take a while," Myleshia said.

Laryn's response sent a chill down Nandi's spine. "She has many years ahead of her to learn."

⚶

THE CLIMATE here was warmer than Vyne, but spring hadn't fully left yet. If it had been hotter, Nandi would likely have passed out. With no food in her belly since the previous day, and the exertion of working the soil, she found her movements labored and slow. The run was especially brutal. Had she been fed and strong, Nandi could have likely outrun all these girls. As it was, she dragged on, dead last and equally dead on her feet.

Ailith, the girl with the curly red hair, dropped back to run beside her. "You okay?" she asked. "You look pale."

Nandi could only nod. She felt like she'd fall over if she spoke even a single word.

"It's the same for everyone in the beginning," Ailith went on. Nandi thought she caught a whiff of Border Highland in her voice. Was that where this girl was from? If so, how did she end up here? "They bring you in for the night and put you to work the next day. You don't eat until you've worked, and since you don't know the rules, it's usually easy to transgress and cause some kind of punishment for everyone else. It keeps you off guard and too weak to even think of running away. And they'll not give you enough to eat to fully regain your strength until they feel you're sufficiently cowed."

They slowly jogged the snaking pathways between houses and shops, taking a little arching bridge over a pond with red and white fish as long as Nandi's arm. She tried to ignore the smell of fresh baking bread as they passed what must be a baker's shop. Birds chirped from the rooftops as if mocking her with their freedom. They could fly away at will. Nandi wondered if it was possible to do that with the essences. Once she got her strength back, maybe she'd try that.

Ailith led her to the right, taking a path that went toward the perimeter of the town. Nandi noted this, thinking her chance might have come. The thought had barely entered her mind when she spotted a man astride a long-legged horse, a bow slung across his back. She heard giggling and looked at Ailith to her side.

"That's the same for everyone, too," the redheaded girl whispered. "You think you can make a run for it until you spot one of those sons of a jarku. There's at least one for every corner of the town perimeter. All on horseback. They double the guard at night."

Nandi wanted to ask why, but she couldn't. It was all she could do to keep her heavy legs pumping.

"I can see it in your face," Ailith said. "The outlander market. You know what that is?" Nandi shook her head, so Ailith continued. "The laborwife market isn't a great deal profitable in Marai, but in the more distant land of Nogth, they pay a premium for a well-trained woman."

Ailith huffed another bit of laughter at Nandi's resulting frown. "Trust me, friend. I went through what you're going through right now. It was two years ago. They have control over me until the day comes to sell me off, if I haven't found a way to escape. If that happens, I'll let some Nogatha ape pay a premium for me, then I'll slit my own throat. Let him come back and drop his ire in their laps. I'll be free and this place's reputation will be tarnished."

She glanced at Nandi and noted her horrified expression. "Not the outcome I hope for, but preferable to being sold off as a labor-wife to some man thirty or forty years or more my senior, and performing any task he has for me. Never that. I'll take my life back into my own hands before that happens; even if it means ending it."

Nandi found she couldn't disagree, though she had no intention of letting it get to that. If she was forced to use the essences for her escape, she'd do what she had to do.

"You're strong," Ailith said. "As much as I hate to admit it, my bottom lip kinda trembled the first time I got the slap." There was a moment's pause before the girl snorted. "Okay, that's a lie, I cried. But it was only a little bit! My eyes kinda watered and my lip quivered. But I didn't break into a fit of bawling like Jessly did. That girl was inconsolable for hours. They didn't have to do much to break her. She got a full meal in her belly that same night and every night since. Performs every task with a hop in her step." Ailith made a disgusted sound.

By the time Nandi's jogging tour ended, her legs could barely hold her up. They felt like lead weights threatening to drag her to the ground.

They arrived back at the house where the rest of the girls waited. Nandi expected her late arrival to be normal, given what Ailith had told her. As soon as they arrived, however, Nimi stepped right up to Ailith, grabbed her by the crook of her elbow and stormed her up the patio to the waiting Laryn and Myleshia. Nandi strained to listen, but couldn't make out anything more than loud-talking.

Laryn's hand snapped across her torso in a blur, and Ailith's shock of red curls whipped through the air as she went down in a heap. She sat up on her side with her legs folded under her, hand pressed to the side of her face as she quietly sobbed.

Nimi pointed at the rest of the girls with a stiff finger, then whipped her arm toward the door. The girls silently filed into the big house. Nandi followed, keeping her gaze forward. She did steal a glance at Ailith as she passed. The girl's mass of wavy curls had spilled over her face. She lifted her head just barely enough to meet Nandi's eyes and give a quick wink, all while still sobbing. The girl even had tears in her eyes.

As Ailith had warned, lunch for Nandi had consisted of a roll, two slices of carrots, two wispy thin slices of some form of meat, and water. Nandi was determined to eat her meal as slowly and dignified as she could, but once the food was on her plate, she almost didn't make it to her solitary table before shoving everything into her mouth.

"Mind if I sit here?" Ailith asked. Nandi nodded her assent. She'd barely sat down before Nandi had finished her paltry meal. "I know what it's like," she said quietly, keeping her eyes on her plate. "Trust me, I do. I'd offer you some of mine but they'll take it away and feed it to the dogs, then you'll get nothing for the rest of the day and I'll get nothing while doing extra work. *And* they'll keep us separated. The one thing they allow is for us to have friends if we want them. But if they get a whiff of any kind of plotting or alliance, they keep you separated and working almost nonstop."

"Why do they allow friends?" Nandi asked. She imagined the women would want to keep them all as miserable as possible.

"Morale," Ailith answered. "They keep us just happy enough that we don't hang ourselves." She tittered darkly at that. When she brushed a few curly locks from the side of her face and took a few bites, Nandi saw her bruised eye. "Hope is interesting," the other girl went on. "The good thing is that it keeps you going. The bad thing is that it keeps you going. I've been here long enough now that I've seen a group of girls sold off to Nogth. They knew it was coming but held out hope they might escape their fate. They *hoped* all the way down the porch and into the wagon that carried them off."

Nandi thought on that for a while, trying to decide if she agreed or not. Ailith let her think in silence while she ate her meal. The lunchroom had two rows of three long tables each. All of the twenty-four girls could have occupied two tables, as they could seat twelve girls each. As it was, everyone had broken into factions. The girls looked to range in age from five years to about twelve or thirteen, and had sectioned off accordingly. Most engaged in quiet conversation over their meals, some stealing the occasional glance Nandi and Ailith's way.

The older girls sat together at a table at the far end of the dining hall. Even a few of them glanced across the room at Nandi and Ailith. Nandi didn't think the looks were adversarial, but rather a mixture of curious and hesitant. "Why do they look at me that way?" she asked as an attempt to distract her from her unquenched hunger.

Ailith casually waved her spoon in their general direction. "They don't know what to make of you. During my time here, the girls that show up are either sufficiently cowed or flat out broken by the first day."

"Really?" Despite the fact that Dad rarely even raised his voice at them when he was angry, Nandi couldn't imagine being broken down by a couple painful slaps. But then, she remembered some of her friends back home, and a few were rather sensitive, so maybe it made sense. She felt sorry for the ones who were already beaten. What life waited for them once they were taken away?"

"Yup," Ailith went on. "Not everyone grows up tough like us. Mah Da started teachin' me tae fight as soon as I cud walk."

Nandi's mouth slowly fell open as she tried to decipher that. "Your dad taught you to fight as soon as you could walk?"

"That's what I said, isn't it?" Ailith replied.

"I think so," Nandi said with a laugh.

"Ah, my Border Highlands tongue slipped out, didn't it?"

Ailith asked with an exaggerated guilty look. "You come to my homeland and you'll not understand us easily."

"Sounds fun," Nandi said.

Ailith nodded, her shock of puffy red curls bouncing. "The Border Highlands are great. All plateaus of bright green hills standing tall over the ocean. Green mountains with caves at the bottom. And huge trees with limbs that spread far out and reach high. You could build a house on some of them."

Nandi listened as her new friend wistfully described her homeland. She wondered how long Ailith had been away from her home, and how she came to be here.

"I swear by the Creator that I'm gettin' outta here," Ailith said, careful to keep her voice low. She looked at Nandi, giving her a full view of the black eye on her pale freckly face. "You'll get outta here, too. I can tell. Maybe you'll come see my homeland and I'll come see yours."

"That's going to happen," Nandi said. "And you'll get to meet my sister. You two would get along perfectly."

Ailith responded with a firm nod. "Well that's it then. Whether we get outta here together or separate, with the Creator as our witness, we're having some kind of adventure together." She crossed her arms and rested them on the table, covertly extending her pinkie finger from under her arm. Nandi did the same, and they hooked pinkie fingers and shook on it.

"Now to figure out how to do that," Ailith said. "They watch us like hawks. Always a patrol, always adults walkin' around. House mistresses lurking around the house and outside it, too."

Nandi thought about sharing her ability to use the essences. Maybe they could figure out a plan. She couldn't think of what, though. At the best of times her abilities were barely reliable. In her weakened condition, she couldn't access even a trickle. That episode on the porch had taken a considerable amount of her energy just holding that much. Now, just the thought of wielding any of the power made her feel faint. "We'll figure something out. I'd rather die than be a laborwife, and I'd rather live than die."

"We're in this together, then," Ailith said. "I don't leave without you, and you don't leave without me. Deal?"

Nandi looked into the other girl's fierce green eyes. "Deal."

The end of lunch came with more chores. They cleaned up after themselves and the lunchroom, then swept and polished the floors and tables. Potatoes were skinned, vegetables cut and packed, fruit was picked and either stored immediately or sliced first before storage.

With the arrival of early evening came the walking drills. "Every girl must know how to walk properly, that she may be attractive to her house patriarch," Nimi said after smacking Nandi on the side of the leg with a switch. "You don't stomp, you glide. Like this."

Nandi watched the older girl move about the room, chin up, but not too high. She had to admit, Nimi was graceful. If she hadn't been able to see her feet, Nandi would have thought the girl literally glided across the room.

No matter how much she tried, however, Nandi couldn't get her body to move like that. She felt stiff and awkward, which only added to her frustration.

The end of her day came with bruised legs, exhaustion, and a lot of anger. The latter only strengthened her resolve, however. Nandi didn't know how long Sama would wait around for her, and Amiya, Dad, and Joga were out somewhere as well, everyone trying to find the other. She would *not* spend years of her life training to be someone's slave. Laborwife or whatever they called it, it was nothing more than a fancy word for woman-slave.

Nandi rolled over on her side and faced the wall. Her body gave a little tremble to herald the sobs to come. She clamped her eyes shut and tensed her body. She would *not* lay in the dark and cry. She would be strong, and she would get out of here. They would not break her. She thought of how Amiya would react if she knew what had become of Nandi, and that drew a bit of laughter to mingle with the sobs. Her twin would be so enraged she'd likely burn the whole city down.

Once she got her emotions under control, Nandi sniffed and opened her eyes again. Not that there was any point. In the darkness, she could barely see the wall in front of her face, which was why she nearly screamed when she'd opened her eyes to see another pair staring back at her.

BROTHER AMERUS

Brother Amerus Layun looked over the kneeling monk who inspected some unidentifiable remains amidst a cluster of broken branches and split rocks. According to Brother Landon—who by the blessing of the Creator had survived his wounds—they'd been attacked in this area. As much as he needed answers, part of Amerus hoped this was all that was left of an animal after a predator's successful hunt.

Brother Stych looked over his shoulder at Amerus, and the expression on his face said enough. When the monk lifted a pendant in the shape of a blazing sun, there could be no question. These remains were a monk of the Brotherhood of the Source.

Amerus did his best to ignore the bits of flesh and blood staining the ground while looking at the pendant. He had no way of telling who it belonged to, as every brother wore the same one. Amerus absently reached to his chest and stroked his own pendant between his fingers. "Let us move on. Be ready for anything, brothers."

The party of seven solemn monks continued along the route the previous party had gone. Everyone held a corlite stone in hand.

Amerus could feel the tension in the group. They would likely burst into lethal action at the slightest provocation. "Control your fear, brothers," he said. "Remember who you are."

They hiked uphill, then climbed a series of rock formations and made their way across a creek. The random terrain ranging from easygoing to somewhat rough would have made it tricky for anyone fleeing pursuit. More than once Amerus had to take his steps with care, lest he twist an ankle or his foot slip through an opening between two boulders. It was slow going, so he couldn't imagine being in a situation where he'd have to fight or flee.

The senior brother placed a hand on his knee and pushed himself up a high step atop a mound and stepped over it. One thing that bugged him was the lack of any other distinguishable evidence. The remains of the unfortunate monk included only his pendant. No other personal effects, no robes, or other garments. Just blood, bits of torn flesh, and a pendant.

"Do you think our brother might have been injured but escaped?" a younger monk asked.

Amerus shook his head. "I do not believe so, young brother."

"I see," the crestfallen monk replied. "Might that the lack of any substantial remains be due to scavengers?"

"Possible," Amerus said, though he wasn't so sure. Scavengers would have left the robes and other clothing behind. There wasn't even a bone in sight. The misfortune of the slain monk aside, something about this didn't sit right with Amerus.

After Layun's account, he'd been sure they were attacked by a droughtlord. But why hadn't there been any other remains? Per his own account, Layun had been certain he was the only survivor, meaning he'd have witnessed each of his brothers die. But if they all perished, why had they only found signs of the attack in that one area? Had they been scattered and killed one by one? Or had they died together, except Layun and the monk whose remains they'd found?

Amerus again stroked the pendant around his neck and said a

silent prayer to the Creator for guidance. The more he thought about it, the more convinced he became that something was off.

"Senior Brother!" one of the monks called out.

Amerus turned to see the other of the two youngest monks waving him over. He moved beside the kneeling monk and peered over his shoulder. The young man was looking into a dark recess between two boulders. "What is it?"

"I'm not sure," the young monk said. "It looks like two shining red objects, but I can't make out what they are."

Amerus leaned down and squinted. Sure enough, saw two red orbs dimly glowing in the dark hole. Amerus squinted harder. *What is that?* The two orbs suddenly grew narrow, and the hairs on the back of Amerus's neck stood on end. "MOVE!"

In one motion he straightened, lifted his feet from the ground, and kicked the young monk in the side of the arm, propelling the boy and himself in opposite directions. The boy cried out as he fell aside, but the kick saved his life. The giant boulders burst apart and a large, four-armed monster slapped the ground as it lifted itself out of the hole.

"Drauk!" Amerus cried. "Fighting monks, form up!"

The ground burst in an explosion of dirt and rock and small trees as another drauk broke free from the ground. Then another, and another.

Ten fighting monks. Amerus had brought ten fighting monks with him, all proficient in the use of the essences, but also in physical combat. Five were numbered among the Vyne branch of the brotherhood's finest fighters, while the other five had shown the greatest potential but needed field experience. They were about to get that experience.

The monk that Amerus had saved scrambled to his feet and sprinted past the rising drauk. As he went by, he raised the corlite stone in his hand and summoned *air.* The monk sent a freezing blast into the drauk's face. The effort did nothing to injure the monster but that wasn't the intention. The freezing air stung the drauk and distracted it just long enough for the monk to get safely by.

The young monk skidded to a stop when he reached the others, and the brothers formed a circle, back to back around Amerus, who'd found a protruding boulder to stand upon.

One after another, drauk burst from the ground all around them, shouting and growling their infernal curses. The monks tightened their robes about their waists and took defensive stances, corlite stones gripped in their non-dominant hands.

The drauk charged. The monks met the charge with evasive maneuvers while Amerus shouted commands and warnings from his vantage point. Unlike most monks of the brotherhood who knew only how to manipulate *fire* and *air*, Amerus had at least some proficiency with all four essences. Corlite stone in hand, he sent forth blasts of *air* and *water* to aid his brothers.

Every one of these monks had encountered drauk monsters during the attack on Vyne, months ago. Some of the more experienced men had discovered the weaknesses of the beasts. Knowing that attack had been a prelude of what was to come, Amerus had set every monk in the Vyne branch, including himself, to training to combat these creatures.

The Vyne monks fought well. Endurance and dexterity had been heavily focused on, and today those efforts bore fruit. Brother Stych ducked a chop at his head and immediately dropped to his stomach at the follow-up downward chop by another arm. He pushed up and tucked his feet under himself, planted his feet, and leapt straight up.

Stych turned mid-air and delivered a spinning sideways kick into the monster's face. The blow did nothing more than snap the monster's head back, but that instant was all he needed. Still midair, Stych tucked his body in close, making himself as small a target as possible. Sure enough, the drauk had blindly swung one of its lava rock swords and missed the bottom of the monk's feet by inches. He thrust out the hand holding his corlite stone, and dealt a blast of freezing air in the face.

He landed as the drauk choked, and summoned *air* and *water* again. A spear of ice formed in front of the drauk and shot toward its neck. Ice punched through lava rock skin, melting but also cooling its neck and choking it. The sizzle of the rapidly cooling monster filled the air as the drauk dropped to its knees, upper hands weakly gripping the ice spear.

"Stych! Behind!" Amerus shouted. He hit the advancing drauk with a blast of freezing air. It stunned the monster just long enough for the young fighter to turn his attention to it. Behind Stych, the drauk he'd felled tried to rise. Amerus launched an ice spear into its back. Finally, the thing fell face-forward and started to break apart.

Two monks double-teamed another drauk off to the right. Despite swinging its clubs and swords with the same lethal reck-lessness that had killed Vyne soldiers five to one, they had the thing kneeling under the force of their onslaught. One of the monks summoned *air* and hit one of the monster's arms with a steady blast of freezing air.

The drauk tried to move away, but the monk kept on it while his partner blasted one of its legs. The creature stumbled and took an awkward lurch toward him. As soon as it turned away, the first monk formed a heavy gust of freezing wind and focused it on the creature's head. It tried to turn back to the first monk, but the second had nearly frozen one of its legs and now focused on the other.

With its head rapidly cooling, and legs frozen, the drauk dropped to its knees. The impact shattered its legs. Before it toppled over, the second monk ran and leapt into a backwards turn, delivering a reverse spinning kick. The monk's powerful blow shattered the frozen head, sending chunks raining to the ground.

Amerus's robes whipped about him as he turned in every direc-tion, supporting his brothers as best he could, stopping a killing blow from behind, freezing the ground under an approaching drauk's foot so that it slipped and gave an ally an opportunity to bring it down.

An agonized scream had Amerus spinning around to see Brother Rigan impaled by a rocky sword, tiny veins of lava flowing through it. The drauk lifted him high over its head and yanked its arm to the side.

Brother Amerus howled as his friend fell off the sword, nearly cut in half. He formed another ice spear and sent it speeding at the drauk. The infernal monster shattered it with a downward chop of a club, but Amerus had formed a second one and sent it speeding behind the other.

The drauk tried to hit that one too, but it had committed to the first blow. The huge ice spear drove through its chest with such force it passed through the hot rocky flesh and came out the other side, barely melted. Adrenaline pumping, Amerus grabbed *air* and reversed the spear's direction. He rotated it back toward the trembling beast and drove it through the back of its head. The drauk toppled over and fell apart.

Amerus forced down his grief and turned to see where his brothers needed assistance. The monks fared well in the mayhem. They stuck to their training, not getting greedy and going for the kill when they had a monster down, but instead, watching each other's backs and keeping on the move.

Each drauk was a whirlwind of chaos, swinging and stabbing swords, and pounding clubs. They turned circles, lunged, turned again, all the while spitting their indecipherable curses at their enemy. Amerus picked his targets wisely, supporting fighters who looked to be falling to the defensive, then lending advantage to those fighters who were on the verge of besting their adversary.

Twice the skirmish almost fell to disaster when the remaining drauk suddenly surged into a brutal offense. The warrior monks kept their wits and their training, however, and kept the monsters in check as they fought for an advantage.

On both instances, Amerus almost jumped down to fight, but he forced himself to hold his position. The monks may be fast and dexterous, but the drauk were just as fast, vicious and larger, while wielding four weapons.

The clash ended with every one of the drauk a steaming pile of rubble, while Amerus's team had suffered an unfortunate casualty and a host of injuries. He hopped down from his perch and motioned Stych to his side. The man was better at healing than Amerus, so together they moved from one brother to the next, healing injuries as best they could so that the men could at least make it back to Vyne.

The healing done, now came the grim task of gathering up the body of Brother Rigan. One of the younger and less experienced monks ran a few feet away to retch, while the others removed their robes and tied them together. They lay the body on the combined robes, and two monks lifted it. Amerus tied his robes together with another, and lay it over the body.

The tired procession started home. Amerus kept a watchful eye all about them. Now would be the worst time for another attack. "Brother Stych. Keep watch at the front."

"Of course, Senior Brother Amerus," Stych replied.

Amerus watched him go. The young man had been impressive in battle and proved to be an adept healer. He'd need to keep an eye on Stych. The boy showed potential, and the senior brother needed as many such men as possible for the times to come.

"Senior Brother!" a monk called.

The party turned to see Brother Joryn staring at something downhill to the side of the path. Amerus rushed to the man's side, and Joryn looked up at him with concerned blue eyes, then pointed at a man lying on his side. His disheveled gray robes marked him as a brother of the Source.

The others rushed to Amerus and Joryn's side, and several gasped. "We've got to get to him," said Brother Trisk. "He may yet be alive."

"Wait," Amerus ordered.

Trisk looked up at him in confusion. "But, Senior Brother, he may be a survivor—"

"Wait," Amerus repeated, this time with a note of finality. The other monk quieted. Amerus leaned forward and called out. "Brother. Can you hear me?" Beside him Trisk shifted in agitation but he knew the man would do as he was told. Downhill, the monk moaned but didn't move.

"We're going to help you," Amerus said. "Do you hear me? We will throw a rope to you."

"All … dead," the robed figure moaned. "All dead."

Several monks looked at each other and stole glances at Amerus, clearly not understanding why they didn't just go down and help the man. While a brother fished a length of rope out of a sack, the hairs on Amerus's arms stood on end. This whole situation felt wrong. He pointed to two brothers standing off to the side. "Watch the trail; both directions."

While the two men moved off, Amerus accepted a length of rope from another brother and tossed it down. It landed within a foot of the downed man, who didn't seem to register the object. "The rope is near you," Amerus called down. "You need but to grab hold." The man shifted and groaned, but little more.

Amerus peered down the slope and studied the figure. His cowl lay back away from his head, which hung to the side. He had sandy brown hair that grew past his ears, and Amerus thought he saw a light scar along the length of his cheekbone. "Brother Lazerae?"

The man groaned again and shifted just a little, but otherwise gave no indication he'd heard his name.

Amerus fought down the sinking feeling in his stomach and took the rope from another monk. He spread his feet, bent his legs, and lowered his center of gravity. "This is Senior Brother Amerus, and we are here to help. Grab the rope and I will pull you up to safety."

"Sen … ior brother … Ame … rus," the monk groaned.

Amerus waved the other men away as they moved to grab the rope. He gripped it tight in one hand and used the corlite stone in the other hand to summon *air*. "I've got the rope. Take hold—"

The words had barely left his mouth when the downed monk grabbed the rope and pulled with inhuman strength. Amerus, who had expected as much, leapt forward at the last moment to avoid having his arm pulled from its socket. Still, the sudden yank stung. It also sent him higher into the air than any jump possibly could have.

He barely heard the surprised shouts of the other monks as he let go of the rope and focused on the corlite. The other man had hopped to his feet, all pretense of injury gone. He looked up at Amerus with a predatory smile as he waited for the senior monk to land.

Amerus used *air* to slow his fall, which bought him just enough time to see that his adversary also had a stone. The "monk" moved right into the path of Amerus's descent, and held the corlite stone in front of him. Amerus did the same, and summoned *air* and *fire*. The other man did the same, and the power of both stones summoning the same essences rebounded from each other. The force of the impact hurled Amerus backward. The stone shattered in his hand and singed his palm.

The senior monk hit the ground in a backward roll and came up to his feet to see the robed man walking casually toward him. Several spears of ice zipped through the air from above and angled toward him. He waved his fist toward the descending missiles and they shattered into a rain of icy shards.

"Hmph." The man looked at the remains of the corlite stone in his hand and dropped the crumbles. He never stopped walking as he dusted his hands off each other and wiped them on his dirty robes.

Amerus looked up at the brothers uphill. They were summoning more power to hurl down the hill. The man glanced up at them with a grin and sprinted across the remaining distance between himself and Amerus. "No rescue for you today, *brother*."

With the man now right in front of him, there could be no doubt that this was indeed Lazerae. The ear-length sandy brown hair, scar along his cheekbone, and the downturned grin were all distinctive to the man.

"Brother Lazerae," Amerus managed to get out as the man punched for his face. The senior monk ducked the attack and brought both hands together to slap down the foot he knew would follow up. He straightened and blocked another kick that snapped up toward the side of his head. "Why do you attack me?"

Amerus defeated another series of snapping kicks toward his face and groin. He leaned away from an uppercut then countered with several jabs to the face and a foot sweep. The punches connected, but if they had any effect, Lazerae gave no indication. When Amerus struck Lazerae's leg, he merely moved with the impact to absorb the blow. He continued to bring his leg up and around in an inward to outward arc toward Amerus's right side.

He brought his arm up to block the incoming kick, and grabbed Lazerae's leg. Amerus ran forward, thinking to push the man off balance, but Lazerae leapt backward with him. The man landed, still on one leg, and reached forward. He clamped a powerful hand around Amerus's throat and squeezed.

Lazerae leaned forward, past his own leg which Amerus still held up, and smiled in the senior monk's face. In the center of those icy blue orbs was a pinprick of red. "You have no idea what you're dealing with, Amerus. There is power beyond your tiny understanding. Already, in this short time, I surpass you."

Amerus let go of Lazerae's leg before the other man could crush his throat. He snapped one hand up under Lazerae's elbow while slapping the other down on his wrist. He'd done it with all his strength behind it, which should have broken the elbow or at least severely hyperextended it. He barely succeeded in loosening the grip enough to get free and back away. Lazerae grinned.

Senior Brother Amerus continued to back away while the other man paced him step for step. Overhead, the other monks were shouting and starting to climb down. Coughing, Amerus waved them back and straightened. He had overseen the training of every monk in the Vyne branch of the brotherhood. He'd made it a point to learn the strengths and weaknesses of every monk in his charge not only to help them become better, but also for just such a possibility as this. No man or woman was infallible. Some would stay true in their devotion to the Source, the Creator. Others would bend to the temptation of power. It was an inescapable truth.

The former brother Lazerae had always been aggressive, preferring to overwhelm his adversary quickly. He was one of the stronger monks, and possessed of average speed. The weight behind his blows, however, could leave his opponent in pain or even with a broken bone after a block.

They circled each other, Lazerae with a predatory grin on his face, Amerus studying his movements. Lazerae tended to lean toward overconfidence, which grew if he thought himself better than his opponent. At forty years old, Amerus was twenty years his senior. The younger man thought him old and slow, he could see it in his face, a face with the beginnings of the deep creases that infected the flesh of a droughtlord.

An underlord, then. The texts he'd read recently spoke of two types of followers of the Fallen. The more powerful were the droughtlords, but they couldn't mingle about the normal populace due to their unsightly appearance. Underlords, however, were not yet droughtlords, and still appeared largely human. It wasn't until they'd started to become more powerful that the telltale signs would appear.

The red mote in Lazerae's eyes and the faint beginnings of the creases in his skin said that he was becoming more powerful. If Amerus didn't put an end to him here and now, the man would likely become a droughtlord. If that happened and he and Amerus met again, the senior monk had no doubt he would perish.

They clashed again, and it was an effort to keep from being slung around like a child. Lazerae was physically stronger than he'd ever been, and faster than Amerus remembered the last time he'd tested the man.

"Feeling slow and weak, old man?" Lazerae asked. He remained just close enough that the other monks couldn't shoot him without the risk of hitting Amerus.

"Still the same Lazerae," Amerus replied. "Strong, somewhat competent, over-confident, and not much likable."

Lazerae smirked. "Trying to goad me into anger to make a mistake?"

"I'm sure you're too smart for that."

Lazerae snarled at the resulting laughter from above. "You won't find this funny once—"

Amerus sprang forward with a flurry of kicks and punches, knee thrusts and sweeps. He'd caught Lazerae off guard and managed to land a couple of blows, but the former monk recovered quickly and went on the offensive. Amerus met the other man's attacks, parrying and evading, countering, and blocking.

Whatever change Lazerae had begun, much of his personality remained. Recognizing that, Amerus slowed his movements, which spurred Lazerae on. The younger man redoubled his efforts and threw the senior monk on the defensive.

"How long can you last?" Lazerae kicked for Amerus's face, and the senior brother grabbed his foot and pulled. When Lazerae hopped forward, Amerus twisted his leg. Lazerae whipped his other leg around Amerus's neck as he fell, and both went down.

Amerus shrugged off the stars in his vision and thanked the Creator that the blow to the side of his neck hadn't knocked him out. Lazerae snapped his other leg up and clamped them around Amerus's neck. Just as the former monk began to squeeze, Amerus drove two stiff fingers into the pressure point in his Lazerae's inner thigh.

They tumbled round and round, each man trying to gain advantage over the other. Lazerae rolled onto all fours and snapped his foot out at Amerus's face. He brought his arm up just in time to accept the blow and turned with it.

Amerus rolled backward and tumbled to a stop several feet away. Lazerae was right there, falling over him to wrap him in a chokehold. He wrestled Amerus around so that they were facing the other monks, who stood with corlite in hand, waiting for the other man to make a mistake.

"Are you good enough … to best … all of them after … killing me?" Amerus asked. Stars danced at the edges of his narrowing vision. "Has your new … ill-gotten power given … you such prowess?"

"In a moment that won't be your concern," Lazerae said into Amerus's right ear. "Perhaps without your irritating voice filling their heads, they'll come to see that there is power in the shadow that far eclipses this foolish light of the Source you and the other heads of the brotherhood chirp endlessly about. It's only a matter of time before our messengers in the brotherhood get enough of the non-brainwashed to see reason."

"A shame … you're not smart enough … to catch the irony … of your own words, Lazerae." Amerus thrust two stiff fingers a few inches above where he judged the sound of Lazerae's voice to be. His aim was true, and his fingers found the soft flesh of the other man's eye and drove through it with a sickening squish.

When the screaming man let go, Amerus fell onto his back and rolled away as fast as he could. The sound of speeding ice spears and gouts of flame filled the air and drowned out the man's agonized howls. Amerus coughed and winced at the tenderness in his bruised throat. He climbed to hands and knees and looked toward the cacophony.

The former monk stood propped up by several ice spears that had punched through his body and stabbed into the ground. Blood leaked down the length of the hard ice, while his charred flaky skin fell and drifted away. His now hairless blackened head fell sideways toward Amerus, one empty socket and one filled with the remains of a melted eye staring at the senior monk as if in disbelief.

Several brothers scrambled down the hill and gathered around Amerus to help him up. The senior brother allowed them to lift him to his feet and support him until he was able to stand on his own again.

"I can't believe it," one of the monks said. "How could one of our own turn against us?"

"I've sparred with that one," another answered. Amerus recognized the voice behind him to be Stych. "He had a dark streak in him, and he enjoyed hurting his opponents. If anyone were to tell me one of our brothers turned against the Brotherhood of the Source, his would be the first name to come to mind."

They climbed back up the hill, Stych remaining by Amerus's side to make sure he was strong enough. At Amerus's order, one of the monks had taken Lazerae's pendant from around his neck.

"I don't want to see this as a possible reason we haven't found any other remains, Senior Brother," Stych said.

"Neither do I," Amerus replied. Something nagged at the back of his mind; something Lazerae had said while he'd had Amerus in a headlock. When the realization hit him, his eyes went so wide, several other monks turned questioning looks on him. He pointed at a single monk. "You! Remain with them!" He pointed at the two who were carrying the body of Brother Rigan. "You three get him back to the monastery and see that he gets a proper last rights. Everyone else with me!"

Amerus ignored the pain in his throat and minor injuries and took off at a fast jog back for Vyne. The other monks silently fell in around him. They made swift time, the winding and hilly terrain not at all slowing the well-conditioned monks.

How could he not have known? The more Amerus thought about it, the more he chastised himself for not having a deeper conversation with Landon before leaving to look for survivors. He'd wanted to let the man rest, but now he felt much the fool.

When Vyne finally came in sight, Amerus quickened his pace. They passed through the gates without incident and slowed to a jog. Everyone milled about as usual, stopping to offer a bow of respect to the passing monks. When they reached the monastery, nothing seemed out of sorts. The brothers behind him must have picked up on his wariness, for they remained casual while fanning out in a defensive formation.

Monks passed by and offered greetings, while some with more advanced martial training casting a curious eye over the group's defensive arrangement. Everything seemed normal. Amerus wondered how many monks that passed by had given their souls over to the blight. His contingent in tow, Amerus made straight for the medical wing.

Nurses moved about, administering treatments to patients, offering consultations, everything normal to a medical facility. When they reached the room housing Brother Landon, Amerus stopped and stared at the door.

The nurse took in the grim look on Amerus's face and the disheveled state of his robes and injuries. "Is something amiss? We should get you treated for your wounds, Senior Brother."

Amerus barely heard the words. He opened the door and stepped in. Brother Landon was seated in a chair looking out the window. When he heard Amerus's entry, he looked over his shoulder and smiled. "Good day, Senior Brother."

21

AMIYA

The world fell away into a dark void that left nothing but Amiya and the woman standing several feet away. Amiya stared into Estrella's violet eyes. The woman returned her gaze, not smiling but not threatening, either. Every part of Amiya's being screamed at her to run as fast as she could, put as much distance between herself and this woman as possible.

What would be the point? That knee-jerk reaction had already sent her falling to her death, only for Estrella to rescue her. The woman hadn't issued a single threat, ultimatum, anything. She'd simply bade Amiya walk with her, and hadn't waited for her to follow. If Amiya hadn't run off that cliff, would the woman have intercepted her, or left her to go on her way?

"I can almost hear your thoughts, child," Estrella said. Her voice sounded like honey sliding down silk that had been stretched across iron. "They play so loudly across your face. Your answer is no."

Amiya waited for more, then frowned and leaned forward, still waiting. "Um. Okay. No, what?"

"No is the answer to your unspoken question."

"You never even told me what my unspoken question was," Amiya replied, on the verge of exasperation.

"Do you not know your own thoughts?" Estrella asked. "Is my answer inappropriate to the question swirling in your mind right now?"

"A one-word answer could be applied to any question." When Estrella arched an eyebrow, Amiya amended, "okay *most* questions."

Estrella started away again. "Walk with me or do not walk with me. You are free to do either, though I would advise you not to run off a cliff this time."

Amiya snarled at the woman's back, but fell in behind her. "Didn't do it on purpose," she grumbled.

Estrella half turned to smile over her shoulder. Her long, raven hair hid all but her eyes, which narrowed at Amiya in what looked like a playful manner. "That is a problem you need to fix, little one."

"Huh?" Amiya asked.

No response came, so Amiya let it go, though her mind lingered on it. She trailed behind Estrella for a time, like a mouse following a cat. Despite feeling content to keep just out of arm's-length, it felt stupid. The woman could have done any number of awful things to her if she'd chosen, but she couldn't bring herself to get too close. Not yet.

"Your proficiency with the power is impressive for someone your age," Estrella said, not bothering to look back. "Your reflexive use of it leads me to believe you are self-taught, yet there is a level of skill that suggests some manner instruction as well. An education that ended before it was complete?"

"You could definitely say that," Amiya muttered.

"Do tell," came the reply.

Amiya couldn't think of any harm in sharing her experiences up to this point, though she omitted her sister. Estrella listened in silence as Amiya started from the attack on Vyne. As the terrain started to decline, so too did the population of stoutgreen trees. Having never been in the middle of beautiful trees in such numbers, Amiya wished they could have remained longer.

The sweet earthy smell of the woods gradually faded away, as did the occasional bird chatter. A red fox trotted across their path and disappeared into the wall of stoutgreens that marked the end of the forest. If Amiya hadn't been finishing up her story by then, it surely would have died on her lips when her mouth fell open at the sight below.

A valley of dry, cracked earth littered with what Amiya could only have described as broken pillars and crumbled mountains lay before them. Not a single tree or plant grew in sight, nor did there seem to be any other signs of life. "What in the name of the Fallen is that place?"

"Do you know of the Shattered Lands?" Estrella asked.

Amiya shrugged, then realized the woman wasn't looking at her. "Um, no. Not really. I mean, I've heard stories, but not much. Adults act nervous when they talk about it for some reason."

Estrella responded with the faintest of nods. "It is the history, girl, though few know the truth of it."

They started down, and for a long time Estrella said nothing. It was just as well, for although the descent was mild, Amiya found most of her concentration went to avoiding a misstep that would result in a twisted ankle and a painful and embarrassing bounce downhill. Just ahead, Estrella descended the slope with the ease of familiarity.

If Amiya had thought the place looked broken from a distance, she stood in horror-stricken awe once they were up close. "It's terrible, but there is a sort of beauty in it, too."

Huge chunks of the ground looked like they'd been raised and dropped, like an enormous hand had lifted a pile of rocks and let them fall where they may. The brown, dry earth sat barren of any hint of life. Not even an insect buzzed in the weighty silence.

She followed Estrella into a crater and out the other side,

through the shadows of huge scattered chunks of earth. "This place makes me nervous." Amiya reached up to touch a wedge of earth the size of a house. It felt a bit cool to the touch, dry and flaky. A buzz of energy zipped through her hand. Amiya gasped and snatched her hand away.

"This is a place of power," Estrella said.

"Power?" Amiya trotted up to walk beside Estrella, her curiosity stronger than her wariness, although she did keep a side-eye on the woman. She would *not* be caught off guard.

"It sits in the ground beneath our feet and pulses through the broken earth all around."

"Do you mean that this place is the source of the essences?" Amiya asked.

"The Shattered Lands are not the source of the essences, but the site of a great battle where enormous amounts were wielded."

"Ugh." Amiya rolled her eyes. "More fighting between Marai magi and Khatala people, then."

Estrella smirked. "Hardly. It would take legions of magi and Khatala to inflict upon the land what happened here."

"I dunno." Amiya looked around at the tranquil remnants of destruction. "I've seen some pretty powerful wielders."

"I'm sure you believe so, but they are children playing at things of which they have only a pedestrian understanding."

Amiya thought about the magus who'd begun hers and Nandi's instruction. What was his name again. Sever-something? No, Selvetar! Amiya glanced at Estrella. The woman might think differently if she ever met that man. Even though she'd only seen a flicker of what he could do, she could somehow feel the level of power he could control, and it was substantial. "Okay. So, if it wasn't magi and Khatala that did this, who did? Are you saying this is the place where the immortals fought; the Illuminarians and the Fallen?"

"The Illuminarians and the Fallen." Estrella looked to the sky and closed her eyes, letting the sun warm her face. "Over the centuries, the ages between then and now, the battle had been referred to as the war of the immortals. Yes, this is where the final conflict of the previous age took place."

"The war of the immortals." Amiya hugged herself against a chilly breeze as they passed through the shadow of another uplifted wedge of earth. "I've only ever heard it called that, but nobody wants to talk about it. It's like they're afraid if they do, it'll happen again, or something."

"People can be superstitious. This land is indeed the final site of the war of the immortals. They battled in many places around the world, destroying that which they claimed to protect or improve. This place"—she opened a hand to indicate the blasted landscape—"is where the last battle occurred."

"When the Fallen created that thing?" Amiya reflected on when she and Nandi had snuck down the hallway and listened to when Dad had been talking to a neighbor. They'd talked about a lot of boring stuff, but just when she and her sister had given up and turned back, the conversation had turned to the war of the immortals. She remembered the shudder in their neighbor's voice when he'd talked about some evil force the Fallen had created. Dad hadn't seemed convinced.

"That thing," Estrella said. "That thing was the worst mistake in all of creation. It could be described as anti-creation, and was conceived in the womb of hubris."

"You talk like you were there." Amiya didn't know whether Estrella had heard the comment or not, for she didn't respond.

"There is a great deal more to the essences than simply wielding them to execute one's will," Estrella continued. "Magi think that corlite is the only reliable method to access the power. The people of Khatal are closer to the truth, but it takes centuries of knowledge and conditioning to be able to access the amount of power such as the, immortals, as you call them."

Amiya watched the woman as she spoke. How did she know so much about this? Was she some sort of scholar who'd decided to leave society and hole up in a cabin in the mountains? When she asked as much, she received a cryptic response.

"Knowledge remains once it is gained, even if forgotten."

"Am I supposed to know what that means?" Amiya touched another giant piece of broken ground and felt the same electric zip of energy. "Ah! What is that?"

Estrella looked at her in surprise. It was the most expressive Amiya had seen her since they'd met. "What did you feel, little one?"

Amiya slapped her hands together. "It felt like a static shock. Not painful, but more of a surprise. Like a jolt of energy. I can't really explain it."

"Interesting." Estrella looked at Amiya without seeing her. "Could it be possible? After all these centuries and ages long past?"

"What are you talking about? And why are you looking at me that way?"

"Give me your hand." Estrella reached for her, but Amiya recoiled.

"Woah, you're acting weird, lady. What do you want with my hand?"

Estrella lowered her hand back to her side. "Do you want to know what it is you felt just now?"

"As long as it doesn't mean something crazy is going to happen," Amiya said, taking a half step back.

Estrella held her hands out at her sides and closed her eyes. Amiya felt a tingle of energy that alerted her to whenever someone was accessing essence.

"What do you feel, little one? Do you feel anything at all?"

Amiya shook her head. "What are you talking about? I don't feel anything."

Estrella opened her eyes and locked gazes with Amiya. The intensity of her violet eyes bore into Amiya and held her fixed where she stood. "What do you *feel*, little girl?"

"I feel you accessing the power," Amiya answered without thinking. In that moment it didn't even cross her mind to lie. Something about this woman felt powerful beyond anything she could imagine. At that moment she didn't dare speak anything but the truth. "It feels like your grabbing hold of essences."

Still staring into her eyes, Estrella nodded. "Very good. Interesting." She released the essences. "How about now?"

"You let it go."

"Fascinating."

Amiya frowned. "Think you could tell me what you're talking about?"

"Firstly, the proper term is delving. Only magi children refer to it as "grabbing hold of" or "manipulating" the power, because that is the only way they know how to do it with their little rock toys. For those who truly understand the power, it is more than that.

"Marailanders do not have an innate connection with essence, so they use the stone they discovered as a natural conduit capable of storing essence energy. Khatala have an innate connection with the earth that allows them to delve into and guide the essence to their purposes, yet they have no use for the stone." She paused long enough to give Amiya a rather studious look. "You possess the capability of delving without the use of corlite, while with it you can amplify your abilities. You number among a small few, throughout all of human history, capable of this."

Amiya looked at her hands as if they held the answers to the questions swirling in her mind. "The power comes easier to me if I have a piece of corlite. When I don't, sometimes it's like trying to grab a squirming fish, other times it's like trying to wrestle a bear into doing what I want. The bear thing is usually when I can't do anything."

Estrella's resulting laughter was both even and ominous. Amiya felt like the woman was naturally intimidating without even trying. *Years of practice, must be. I need to learn that.* "Accessing the earth's power is not unlike anything else in life." She continued walking. This time Amiya fell in step beside her. No point in playing the skittish mouse any longer.

"When you force anything, it will resist," Estrella explained. "Forced fealty is only so strong as the lord's hold on the vassal's fear. Forced labor yields results from a resentful hand. And there are some things, such as love, that cannot be forced."

Amiya looked up at her. She thought she heard a flicker of regret in the woman's voice. For what? Was she some disgraced lord whose servants turned on her? Amiya doubted that. So, what? Love? Amiya looked out ahead again. She had too much to worry about without trying to understand adults and love.

"The essences will not be bent to anyone's will," Estrella said, interrupting Amiya's drifting thoughts. "That's why Marailanders use corlite to manipulate them. The stone is a conduit that can be tapped. It is a powerful tool, but only a part of the whole."

"You seem to know a lot about all of this," Amiya remarked.

"I've some knowledge, yes."

Amiya's mouth twitched. "Some knowledge."

"This place," Estrella said as they neared the end of the barren landscape, "was once a beautiful canyon filled with towering stone formations, sloping mountains, and plateaus. The conclusion to the war of the immortals destroyed it."

"I can't imagine this place as a beautiful stone canyon." Amiya looked out at the landscape, baren except for the gigantic chunks of earth strewn about the place as far as she could see. Even the silence, here, seemed so thick she felt like they were wading through it. "It's just so broken and desolate."

"Yet buzzing with power. The irony of the Shattered Lands is that it was once beautiful, but was destroyed by the very power that made it one of the most potent sources of the essences in the world."

"I can't imagine a bunch of people throwing that much power around that it absorbed into the land like that," Amiya said, her voice almost a whisper. "How can that be possible?"

"You know not the half of it, girl. The immortals had a knowledge of the essences that has been lost to time."

"Too bad," Amiya said.

"Not necessarily. Power is beautiful or terrible, depending on the heart of the wielder."

"Sounds to me like both sides were terrible," Amiya said.

Estrella shrugged. "Some were."

When they neared the edge of the Shattered Lands, tall swaying grass came into view as if it were a living border. Plant life large and small dotted the landscape leading to the base of a rocky mountain range extending as far as the eye could see.

"That is one big mountain," Amiya said.

"The Sleeping Morgan."

Amiya squinted at the distant mountain in an effort to see the telltale signs of ancient wind and water erosion that gave it its name. She thought she could see what looked like an enormous leg curled under a long body. If she strained hard enough, she thought she could make out a long neck curled to the side. "People say it looks like a sleeping animal. That thing is like the stars at night. People say they see things in it, but I can't make out much of anything."

"It's our angle," Estella said. "Given the right perspective, you can see a great many things that others may not."

"Where are you from?" Amiya asked. "You talk in this worldly wisdom kind of way. You're taller than most women who aren't Khatala, and you look like the few Nashmarese I've seen passing through Vyne. But you don't talk like them or anyone else I've ever heard."

"I've not called any one place home for a great many years, girl."

A sarcastic response popped up in her mind, but Amiya repressed it. *No. Not with this woman.* "Sooo, where are we going? If I remember, the Shattered Lands are the farthest north of Marai that you can go. If that's the Sleeping Morgan," she pointed at the endless mountain range before them, "shouldn't we head south-west? That's Altarra is, and probably my dad."

"When did I mention going to Altarra?" Estrella looked down at Amiya with an unreadable expression. "What reason have I to visit Jietar's den of magi?"

"I … well, I mean …" Amiya struggled for words. Why all this conversation and wanting to know her situation if Estrella had no intention of helping her? Why were they even walking together? If she hadn't intended to help Amiya, why did she save her life? Twice?

She balled her fists as bewilderment gave way to irritation. "Okay. Well, fine. You go ahead and have fun walking nowhere, or somewhere, or wherever it is you're going. I'm off *that* way," she stabbed her finger in the direction she figured to be Altarra, "to find my father and sister."

Estrella arched an eyebrow. "You should never expect someone to help you on a lie or half-truth, girl."

Amiya frowned at her. "What, lie? What are you talking about? And my name is *Amiya*. You've been calling me 'girl'"—she did her best to make her voice sound husky at that word—"since we marched out of your mountain home, or retreat, or wherever it was you came from." She knew she probably should rein in her temper, but, was this woman toying with her? She needed to find Dad and Nandi. Sama and Joga, too. She didn't have time to play around with some woman who may or may not be completely insane.

"You've quite the tongue on you, little viper," Estrella replied, her calm demeanor not the slightest disturbed.

"It gets that way when people play around with me," Amiya snapped. Dad would have had her by the back of the neck for speaking to her elders in such a way, but he wasn't here. He was far away, and this lady was wasting her time, which was *exactly* why she spoke this way. "If you weren't going to help me, you could have—"

"Allowed you to die? Yes. Allowed you to die a second time?

Yes. Saved you and allowed you to wander the woods of the mountain for the rest of your shortened life, yes. All of those things, I could have and still can do."

"Then, why don't you?" Amiya yelled. "Why'd you string me along all this way, spewing a bunch of history that has nothing to do with me or where I'm going—"

"It has more to do with you than you think."

"I don't see any Fallen-blasted way—"

A powerful gust of wind knocked her on her backside. Amiya hit the ground with a stinging bounce, but jumped to her feet, fists balled, teeth bared. "I've really had about enough of you, lady. You want a fight? I'll give you one." Estrella responded with an amused grin, which infuriated Amiya all the more. A tiny voice in the back of her mind warned her to calm down, but it drowned in her anger.

Fire sprang to her call, but she couldn't kill someone for making her mad. She instead called upon *air* and sent the same gust of wind back at the woman, only freezing cold. Estrella dismissed the cold air with a lazy wave of her hand.

What? Amiya combined *air* and *water*, sending a blast of moist cold air at the woman, who again defeated her with little more than an absentminded gesture. Estrella stood at ease, her weight shifted to one leg, hand on her hip with that grin still on her face. Amiya tried *earth*. She sent a small tremor rippling through the ground, which parted when it reached Estrella.

"Not bad," Estrella said.

Amiya growled. She combined *air* and *fire* and sent a blast of sweltering hot air at Estrella. Same result.

"You're holding back, girl. Try harder. Let loose. Draw upon every ounce of the power you can and unleash it!"

Amiya screamed. She drew upon *fire*, which came the easiest to her call. She created a huge ball of fire several times larger than her target and dropped it on top of her. The resulting explosion was deafening, the space around where Estrella had been standing, bathed in a swirling ball of flame.

In one shocked gasp, the essences fell away. Amiya stared in horror at what she'd wrought. How could she have lost control like that? She'd killed someone! She'd—

Estrella's deep, husky laughter escaped the fiery destruction. She stood in the middle of the inferno, arms outstretched and seeming to revel in the blaze.

Thunderstruck, Amiya experienced a fear like nothing she'd felt before. Not the four-armed monsters, nor the tunneler, or even the lavakhan had invoked such fear in her as the figure who seemed to delight in the flames engulfing her. Estrella's violet eyes fixed on her like some exotic creature of the underworld.

Amiya struck with everything she had. All the essences leapt to her call, now, and she wielded them to deadly effect. Stalagmites burst out of the ground toward the woman and shattered. Ice shards sped for her and broke apart.

Amidst the swirling sphere of flame, Estrella let her head fall back in ecstasy. Bits of earth lifted from the ground and began to orbit the sphere of fire. Ice formed outside the rock and did the same, then water.

Amiya took a step back, caught up in a mix of awe and terror. Fire, water, air, and rock—or rather, earth—deadly physical expressions of their essence namesakes, all flowing around the laughing woman.

The fiery sphere and its many satellites burst apart. The debris flew away from Estrella's left and right sides, arcing their way around toward Amiya.

She screamed and curled into a ball on the ground and clamped her eyes shut. When she realized she wasn't dead, Amiya opened her eyes and looked up. The raging maelstrom had hit an invisible barrier and flowed around it.

Amiya started to rise, but the inferno pushed against the barrier. Amiya realized that she'd unconsciously created the protection. She searched inside herself to find what she was doing and focused on maintaining the invisible dome.

Estrella walked toward her. She had her hand back on her hip again.

Amiya tried to find her anger, her rage, but it fled in the face of her fear. Her hold of the essences started to buckle. The storm of fire, rock, wind, and ice pressed in and relented, then pressed in and relented again. Amiya gasped with each pulse. It felt like her body was being squeezed, and she weakened each time.

She was going to die, here, and all because she'd lost her temper. Nandi would know. The instant Amiya's life winked out, her twin sister would know, and she would be broken, maybe driven mad. Dad would be devastated as well. Joga and Sama, her new friends, her new family. They would be hurt when they found out, too. But Nandi, her other half…

No. Amiya marshaled everything inside her and pushed against the enclosing ball of flame. A guttural scream crept up her throat and burst free. With it, the ball of power exploded. Fire and debris flew in every direction, stopped, then sped back in.

Amiya focused on the barrier. The blazing projectiles and winds of fire crashed against her dome and shattered it. She screamed in dismay and wrapped her arms over her head, though it would do nothing to stop her coming immolation.

Freezing air and water combined to form a small sphere around her. Bits of earth flowed outside the water, and the roaring flames circled outside of it all. Amiya straightened and looked around. Her mouth hung open as she looked at her death from every direction, simply hovering just out of reach.

A pathway opened. Amiya gaped as Estrella strode through the tunnel and stopped in front of her. The pathway closed and the sphere was whole again.

Several strands of long black locks fell away from Estrella's face when she looked up at the freezing air and water, earth and fire flowing overhead. "It is beautiful, isn't it? A perfect expression of the one who summons it. To delve is to touch an intimate connection between one's self and the essences. It is the true way to know the power, and the purest way to call upon it."

Estrella looked down at Amiya, who forced herself not to shrink under that frightening violet gaze. She reached out and grabbed Amiya's hand, and this time, she didn't pull away. What was the point? "Feel it," the woman breathed. "See it, swim in it, drink it, *be* it."

With Amiya's hand in a firm grip, Estrella closed her eyes. Amiya felt a rush of power like nothing she'd ever experienced. It was huge and alive, great and terrible. It was a raging river of primal energy as alive as she was, but infinitely bigger. Amiya felt as if she were swimming in an endless current of power larger than anything her imagination could conjure. The possibilities of essence were limited only by her mind, and her capacity to comprehend their nature.

It was all too much, yet at the same time exhilarating. Amiya had thought she had a grasp on what the essences were, but she didn't. They were infinitely more, and no one lifetime was enough to learn even a fraction of what they were.

She felt like a tiny grain of sand sitting before an ocean of power so immense, her mere existence felt less than inconsequential. If the ocean of power swallowed her up, it wouldn't make the slightest difference.

Just as the experience grew overwhelming, Amiya felt Estrella's presence. In the raging river of power, the woman was an anchor that kept Amiya from being swept away. Estrella's voice penetrated the torrent and found her mind. "Embrace the power, Amiya. Become one with it. Do not just understand its nature, *be* its nature. Live it."

Rationally, Amiya didn't understand what that meant, but her body, her very existence understood it on an intuitive level. She breathed in the power through her mouth and let it fill her until she could hold no more, then exhaled it through her nostrils. The essences could create or destroy, build or dismantle, heal or injure, save a life or end it.

Amiya felt herself being pulled away. She scrambled desperately for the essences, clawed and scratched and reached for them. Estrella was too strong. She pulled Amiya back from the ocean of power and the bliss in which she swam.

When Amiya opened her eyes, she realized she lay on her back. When she lifted herself up onto her elbows, she saw Estrella a few feet away, looking to the northwest.

Amiya placed a hand on the ground to steady herself. It felt like the ground underneath her was shifting. After a while when she felt confident her legs would support her, she carefully stood up.

"Welcome back," Estrella said, still staring off into the distance.

Amiya pressed a hand to her head. She had a splitting headache. "How long was …" She winced at her dry throat. "How long was I asleep?" She looked in the direction Estrella gazed, then noticed her shadow leaned west. "Is it morning?"

"It is, little one." Estrella replied. "Once again you impress me."

Amiya clamped both hands to her head against the throbbing pain. "Yeah? How so?"

"The experience usually takes days to recover. You took less than a single day."

Amiya frowned. "Recover?"

"Tell me," Estrella asked. "Are they the same as you? Your father and your sister?"

22

NANDI

Nandi's blood curdled until she realized it was Sama. How had she snuck into the room? The entire house swarmed with girls throughout the day, not to mention the house mistresses patrolling the halls at any given time. She stole a glance over her shoulder to make sure no one was awake. "Sama," she said, barely a whisper. "What are you doing in here?"

"Nandi girl who say she Sama's sister, abandon Sama." There was an edge to the tatamble girl's tone that Nandi didn't miss. "Nandi girl find new family. No more care about Sama."

Nandi patted the air between then. "No, Sama. Nandi girl loves Sama and will always be Sama's sister."

"Then why leave Sama?"

"Because ..." Nandi glanced over her shoulder again. The dark room lay quiet aside from the scattered soft snoring that drifted in the air. Underneath the door, candlelight peeked in from the office of one of the house mistresses. "Because I was captured. They took me on their horses and brought me here."

"But Nandi girl not come back," Sama replied, a little too loudly.

Nandi patted her hand toward Sama and pressed a finger to her lips. "Please, quietly, Sama. If they hear, they will capture you too."

"Will never keep Sama," came the reply, though she did lower her voice. "Nandi can leave with Sama. Sama help Sister Nandi leave."

Well, at least they were back on good terms. "Not yet. I have to help someone."

In the dull candlelight Nandi saw Sama's dark eyes narrow. "Sister Sama must understand what happens here," she hurriedly whispered. "Girls captured just like Nandi. Girls not allowed to leave."

"What do girls have to do with sister Nandi or Sama?"

"If they capture Sama, wouldn't Sama want someone to help her?"

The tatamble seemed to think on that before giving a rather animated nod of her head. "Yes. Sama would want."

Nandi returned the other girl's nod. "That is why Nandi must stay a little longer. Must help."

"Sister Nandi cannot help every girl here. Too many."

She was right, of course. Even if Nandi used the essences to help every one of the girls to escape, she had a feeling not all of them would want to. She remembered hearing snippets of gossip between women in Vyne about girls who'd been kidnapped and raised as laborwives to be carted off to distant lands. After years of training and mental and emotional conditioning, it was all the girls knew. Nandi had even heard one woman say that if someone tried to escape, the others would inform their captors.

Nandi hadn't believed what she'd heard those few years ago, but thinking on it now, she had no doubt that if she found a way to rescue every girl in this room, including that awful Nimi who ordered them around, Nimi would surely report straight to the head house mistress. As much as she wanted to help everyone, Nandi had her own freedom to think about. She had to get out of here with Sama and find Amiya, Dad, and Joga.

But she wouldn't leave Ailith. The girl had vowed to help Nandi escape once she'd found a way. Plus, the girl was strong. She had a fire in her that wasn't unlike her sister. But how would the border highlander girl and Sama take to each other? Questions for later.

"Why Nandi girl sit there and say nothing?"

"Nandi is thinking," Nandi replied.

Sama clamped her vice-like grip around Nandi's wrist. "Must go now, while humans sleep."

Nandi winced at the hard grip and placed her hand gently over Sama's. "We can't go yet, Sama. I have a friend we must save."

When Sama's face darkened, Nandi would have giggled if not for the circumstances. Was the tatamble girl actually jealous? "Look, Sama. You are always Nandi's sister, but that doesn't mean we have no friends."

"Sama has no friends but Nandi and Amya. Now Sama has sisters Nandi and Amya, and sister Nandi want to stay and make friends."

Nandi took a deep breath. "Sister Nandi make friend that can help us."

"Sama and Nandi not need any help."

Nandi put on a hurt expression and rubbed at her eyes. She sniffed.

Sama tilted her head. "Why sister Nandi sad?"

Nandi sniffed again. "Because Sister Sama not trust Nandi. Nandi tries to do what is best, but Sister Sama doesn't trust."

Sama stared at her for so long, Nandi started to wonder if the girl wasn't buying it. In the end, though, the girl nodded in resignation. "Sama does not like this. Sama does not like other girl, and Sama not want to wait when could leave now." She let out a loud huff, and again Nandi silently shushed her. "But Sama will trust sister Nandi. If sister Nandi say girl is friend, then Sama will help."

Nandi sat up on the bed and wrapped the tatamble girl in a

crushing hug, then let go before Sama could return the gesture and crush the life out of her.

"What does sister Nandi want Sama to do?"

"I need a little more time. It will have to be at night. Can Sama help me? Help us?"

Sama thought on that, then nodded her head again. "Sama will help."

"Good," Nandi said in a loud whisper, and this time Sama smacked her finger to her lips. Nandi thought if the girl had done that to her, she'd likely have knocked out a few teeth. "Give Nandi time to talk to my friend. We must make a plan. Does Sama think she can come in here to meet with me again?"

The tatamble nodded. "Sama can do. Humans not very aware. Sama could stop every one of them from breathing before reaching sister Nandi, if she wanted."

Nandi shivered. *Good thing she's on my side.* "Come back tomorrow night if you can."

Sama nodded once more. "Sama will come."

"Please be patient for Nandi, Sama. We will get out and be on our way."

"Sama will come." She moved back, becoming less visible with each step until Nandi could see her no longer.

Nandi watched the door open ever so slightly. A sliver of candlelight seeped into the room, but the door silently closed before it could disturb anyone. Nandi thanked the Creator that the door wasn't squeaky.

She lay back down and stared at the wall for a long time. She had to think fast. No matter how much she implored Sama to be patient, the tatamble would only wait so long. She felt confident the girl wouldn't leave her, but if Nandi didn't move fast, Sama would likely take the matter into her own hands and do something drastic.

Nandi wouldn't have feared that outcome under normal circumstances, given her reasonable confidence that she could call upon the power at will, especially if threatened. But she was too weak. She ground her teeth at the irony of it. The house mistresses fed her just enough to keep going but not enough to have the energy to try to escape. They'd also unwittingly cut her off from the essences. To be able to wield the power, she needed food and sleep. If she could get her strength, she'd be ready to defend them all if it came to it.

No sooner had she closed her eyes than Nimi's annoying voice stabbed into Nandi's blissful sleep. She sat up and rubbed her eyes. At the front of the room, Nimi continued her needless litany of statements about discipline, doing the job right the first time, and ensuing every inch of the place was properly tidied. Beds must be well made, the covers tightly tucked. Breakfast after first chores.

Nandi found she would like very much to do something damaging to the older girl. The way she held her head up in an air of superiority was as annoying as the shorter Nandi receiving a clear view of the girl's nostrils. Deep down where she didn't want to acknowledge her own vindictiveness, Nandi wished she could see the day Nimi got carted off by a Nogthi. Though, considering the near zealotry at which the girl went about her tasks, here, Nandi wondered if Nimi actually looked forward to the day.

Beds and personal spaces were made quickly and quietly, after-which the girls lined up in the walkway in the center of the room. Hands clasped behind her back, Nimi walked between the lines, surveying each girl for tidiness of their brown, stout wool dresses. She commented on the importance of hair combed neatly back away from the face, and how one must always keep their gaze slightly down from the eyes of a superior, which meant someone older, or a man. That last bit set Nandi's blood at a steady boil.

"For those of you who are newer," Nimi said in a raised voice, "observe the proper curtsy. Ingris."

The girl Nandi remembered to be not unkind, but lacking in social skills trotted up to the front. At Nimi's bidding, she swept her right foot around behind her left. Toes of her right foot touching the floor, Ingris grabbed the sides of her dress and dipped into a low curtsy. She tilted her head as she lowered it, spreading her dress out wide at each side.

"This," Nimi said, "is a girl's curtsy. When you've reached your majority, you will learn the woman's curtsy." She waved Ingris back to her spot in line and took her place.

Like Ingris had done, Nimi grabbed both sides of her dress with delicate, practiced hands and dipped into a curtsy. She pulled the sides of her dress out only half as far as Ingris, and instead of sweeping her right foot around to the other side of her left, she placed it behind her left foot, toes to the floor. Her legs bent less than half of Ingris's very deep curtsy, and she only tilted and dipped her head a fraction as much.

Despite loathing everything about the intent of those curtsies, Nandi had to admit that Nimi's gesture was elegant; graceful, even. *Still want to lay her to sleep with a good punch*, Nandi mentally grumbled. She snickered when she realized the thought was something Amiya would have said; likely aloud.

"You find something funny, Tyshia?" Nimi's frosty glare settled over her. She had her hands on her hips, looking every bit like she wanted to throttle Nandi.

"Um, no, not about this." Nandi waved a hand to encompass the room. "I just had a thought."

"A thought," Nimi replied, her tone dripping with acid. "I see. So, my instruction and your future here, and beyond, doesn't interest you enough to pay attention?" She made a sharp gesture toward the door. "If all of this is beneath you, the wild woods where you came from is a better option?"

"Maybe it is," Nandi said. "I was eating better than before I got here. Happier, too. I'll gladly leave you to—"

"Shut up!"

"—your instructions on how to be a proper slave woman," Nandi continued.

"You are a disgrace and unworthy of this school!" Nimi shouted, but Nandi just plowed right on through.

"So, if you want to step aside," Nandi calmly said, "I'll happily return to the "wild woods" whence I came."

"You're going nowhere, you heathen," Nimi practically wailed.

Nandi rocked back on her heels, her face scrunched in a mixture of disbelief and repressed laughter. "Did you really just call me a heathen?" Now she did laugh. "A *heathen*?"

Nimi stomped up to tower over Nandi, her fists balled so tight her knuckles were white. Nandi looked up into the seething blue fires in the taller girl's eyes. Blood had rushed to her face to produce a bright red that contrasted starkly to the white of her bared teeth. "You, youuu, ooooh!" She bent her arms and thrust her fists down at her sides.

"Think real hard about what you're about to do," Nandi said in a low, even tone. Weak as she was from lack of nutrition, she was sure she had enough energy to properly dismantle this girl.

Nimi must have seen it in her eyes as well, for the girl visibly unruffled herself and took a step back. She eyed Nandi for several tense heartbeats before turning in a flourish of spinning dress, and stormed out of the room.

Tiny pockets of tittering erupted up and down the two lines after the head girl disappeared out the door. Nandi barely heard it. She sighed, knowing this would only make her situation worse. Nimi's threat of having her kicked out had been no more than that, a threat, to get her in line. The headmistresses had no intention of letting her go.

Nandi didn't know what was wrong with herself. Between herself and Amiya, she was usually the more levelheaded. Right now, however, she behaved exactly as Amiya would have. How much would this little interaction complicate her plans?

She felt the stares of the other girls and looked over her shoulder to see Ailith a few rows back. The girl had her hand clamped over her mouth, shoulders bouncing in repressed laughter. She gave Nandi a thumbs up.

The quiet laughter choked off at the sound of soft footsteps approaching. Head Housemistress Jasindi stepped into the room, followed by Nimi. The woman stood silently, hands clasped behind her back while she looked over the two parallel lines of girls, her expression calm and smooth.

"Twenty laps," the woman said in a voice like iron. "Run hard or forfeit lunch in addition to breakfast."

As the two lines of groaning girls filed out the door, the head housemistress stopped Nandi. "Not you, Tyshia. Such a mouth and spirit should be well-nourished. You will have breakfast and lunch instead of your run. Get to the kitchens and enjoy your meal."

Nandi received more than a few glares at that pronouncement. She moved past Jasindi where a smug-looking Nimi watched her pass. Nandi winked at her, and the girl's face flushed with stifled rage.

While the rest of the girls turned left toward the front door, Nandi turned right, toward the kitchen. She focused on not smiling. This might have turned out better than she could have hoped. With a couple of decent meals, she'd be strong enough tap the essences again. Maybe she could free the other girls as well. Nimi could stay here if she wanted, but the other girls needn't go down the route of servitude.

She walked down the hall with a brisk step, turning a few corners until she finally reached the kitchen. A woman with a kind face and gray hair pulled back into a frizzy bun greeted her with a sad smile. "Time for breakfast, I see." She waved at a pot on the stove. "Go on and dish your bowl and sit down. I've seen enough girls come in here alone to know that you've done something naughty. Go on. You're to eat as much as you like, though you're not likely to be happy about it."

Nandi couldn't imagine why not, until she reached the pot. When she raised up on her tiptoes and looked inside, she saw it was filled with some gray concoction that looked like porridge. Nandi swallowed and grabbed a nearby ladle. She had to apply a little pressure to penetrate the surface, and even more to stir it.

"As with every other girl sent here by herself," the woman said from the side, "I'm told you like it unheated, which makes it firm, I'm afraid. Try to stir it a little more. Loosens it up and makes it easier to get down."

Nandi did as instructed, then filled her bowl. The congealed gloop dropped into her bowl with an unappetizing plop. Nandi scooped up a second, then third helping and filled the bowl completely, then went to a table.

The woman smoothed her apron. "You gotta eat it all, you know? No wasting, around here." She leaned in and whispered, "you haven't taken a bite yet, so there's none of your germs. You can scoop a bit back into the pot and I won't say a thing."

"Thank you, ma'am," Nandi replied. "But I'll have it all." She forced herself to smile.

The woman's eyebrows rose and met at the center of her forehead. She nodded with a crinkled smile and indicated Nandi have at it. "And spare me the "ma'am" talk. My name's Mrs. Cindry, but the girls around here call me Mrs. C."

If it had been hot, the porridge might have tasted all right. Might. As it was, cold and thick, Nandi had to practically chew it to get it down. She took a sip of something she didn't recognize and tasted as foul as the porridge. She leaned her head back with a frown and looked up from her mug at Mrs. Cindry.

"You must be from someplace far away, girl," Mrs. Cindry remarked. "It's watered down ale. What would you be drinking with a meal where you're from?"

"That would be water, ma'am, er, Mrs. C," Nandi replied.

"You got that much water to drink with a meal?" Mrs. C asked in amazement. "I can't imagine where you could live that there'd be enough for everyone to drink it with every meal."

Nandi took bite after disgusting bite, forcing it down while fighting back her gag reflex. She tried her best not to let her revulsion show, out of respect for Mrs. C, but it was difficult. Still, she'd been through worse, and it *was* food.

It didn't take long before her body responded to the horrid-tasting nourishment. She felt herself growing stronger as time passed. After her last bite, she sat back and stared at the bowl without seeing at it. She gingerly reached out to the essences, a fingertip dipping into a pool of water. The power was there, waiting and willing.

"You must've been terribly hungry, girl," Mrs. Cindry said. "Three helpings of cold porridge?" She leaned over the table and looked into Nandi's empty bowl. "Incredible."

"It was good even if it was cold," Nandi lied.

Mrs. Cindry snarled at her. "Oh, go someplace else with that terrible fib, girl. It's disgusting and I'd rather graze out there with the cows than eat a spoonful of it, much less three bowls."

Nandi barely heard the woman. Her body—and thus the essences—grew stronger by the moment. It was time to leave. A smile crept across her face.

23

JOGA

Joga didn't dare breathe. He lay perfectly still and delved *naara*. As soon as he touched the aspect, a low growl rumbled in his ear. His eyes slowly turned to see a long muzzle quiver as it opened to give him a full view gleaming fangs that promised his death. Joga released the aspect and the teeth snapped once, then moved away from the side of his face to hover over his head.

He carefully let out the breath he'd been holding, his mind racing for a way out of this. He was almost certain it was a were-wood cat, which meant his chances of making peace with the animal were slim. The fact that he was still alive was a surprise. How long that would last depended on how creative he could be in the next few moments.

When he heard a voice from below, Joga didn't know whether to feel relieved or more wary.

"Looks like you have bad luck, up there."

Joga's eyes moved left to right as he tried to understand his situation. It was a woman's voice, and she sounded quite relaxed.

"Am no enemy," Joga ventured. "Please, can you call off friend?"

"Who says he's my friend?"

"Nobody talk around predator, especially werewood cat," Joga said. "And you know it is "he". Maybe companion?"

After a moment's pause, the woman replied, "True enough. You pay attention."

"Nothing to do but pay attention when about to die," Joga remarked. The resulting laughter gave him a sliver of hope that he might yet survive this.

"You talk like a Khatala. Surprising. You do know your people are fighting with Marai?"

"I know," Joga said. The werewood cat's hot breath continued to blow in his hair. "Have no fight with any Marailander. Between your king and those he have conflict with."

"He's not my king," the woman said. Joga noted a bite to her tone at that. "And I don't think he sees you as different from any other Khatala, no matter how different you are to any who have eyes to see."

Joga swallowed. "Maybe can talk on the ground?"

"I am on the ground."

"Maybe can *both* talk on the ground."

The responding silence had Joga's heart pounding, which he was certain the werewood cat could hear. Finally, the woman spoke. "Kokunde! To me."

The hot breath huffing on his head ceased. The animal moved so smoothly, Joga felt nothing from his branch when it retreated. It was like the thing just disappeared.

"You don't have to lie in the tree anymore, Khatala man. Why don't you come down."

Joga sat up and peered over the side. A woman with a clean-shaven head, holding a spear as tall as herself, smiled up at him. The werewood cat apparently named Kokunde sniffed the ground several feet away. Joga watched the huge feline. Even though it walked about with ease, he could see the muscles gliding under its coarse green, brown-striped coat. He didn't want to be anywhere near it. Then he reminded himself that the thing could have had him dead and eaten long ago.

She glanced at the huge cat and her smile slanted. "Don't do anything dumb, and he won't kill you." As if to drive the point home, Kokunde looked up, directly into Joga's eyes. It held him fixed in its yellow gaze for several heartbeats, and he had no illusions it was silently telling him exactly what the woman had said. It offered a lazy blink and went back to sniffing the area.

Joga thought about delving *naara* and surrounding himself with it as a protection, but dismissed the idea. First, he was in a tree, and second, if the move made the werewood cat angry enough, it might just transform into its tougher form. If that happened, a globe of *naara* wouldn't stop it from getting to him.

With a resigned sigh, he made his way down, all the while keeping an eye on the werewood cat. It seemed to have no interest in him at the moment, but that gave him no comfort.

Once he was on the ground, Joga saw that the woman stood barely up above his elbow; rather short, even for a Marailander. Whatever she lacked in height, however, she made up for with a considerably muscular physique. The furs she wore had the same coarse texture as her companion's, as well as the coloring.

She looked down at herself, then up at Joga. "If you're admiring my furs, Kokunde is protective of me, even against his own kind. If you're admiring something else—"

Joga waved his hands defensively. "No, no! Don't mean to stare. Just noticing how strong you look."

The woman's face tightened at that. "Then, you're saying you don't find me good to look at."

Joga's mouth hung open while his panicked mind raced for the proper response. All he managed to get out of his bobbing mouth was, "no. Not that either."

She stared into his eyes for several uncomfortable heartbeats before bursting into laughter. She even slapped her hip.

Joga didn't think what he'd said was funny, but different people found different things amusing, he supposed. He waited patiently until her laughter subsided.

"You're not bad to look at, either, Khatala man." The woman looked him up and down. "I see maybe a few Khatala men in my time." She gave him yet another once-over, her resulting grin worthy of her feline companion. "Maybe I want to move to Khatal."

The tension melt away and Joga stood a little straighter and gave a curt nod. "You would like Khatal, and Khatal would like you. Men or women, we are strong of body and spirit. Warrior like you would fit."

She tilted her head. "You flirt with me, Khatala man?"

Joga smirked. "Yes, if you like it. No, if you don't."

"Now you talk like a Marai man."

"Try to fit in."

"Don't," the woman said, her voice flat and unimpressed. She turned away and started through the woods. Kokunde didn't spare him a glance, but kept sniffing the ground, then bounded away in another direction.

Joga went after the woman. In a few of his much longer strides, he caught up and walked beside her.

She looked up at him, then back in the direction they walked. "Why are you in these woods?" she asked. "Marai is not friendly to you right now."

"Is a story long in telling."

"I have time. My camp isn't far from here."

Joga looked at her with raised eyebrows. "You would bring me to your camp and don't know me? Why?"

She shrugged. "I read a person good enough. Khatala people are good people, and if I leave you alone, you'll make another foolish mistake like your first one."

"What first one," Joga demanded.

"Sleeping in these woods and thinking the trees would keep you safe."

Joga wanted to argue, but he thought about how easily her companion—likely out hunting somewhere— had proven her point.

"My name is Nyimbe. So call me Nyimbe."

"My name Joga," he replied. "So … call me Joga."

She looked up at him with genuine curiosity. "What else would I call you?"

Joga frowned. "I … what?" When he saw her ample lips pressing together in repressed laughter, he threw up his arms and rolled his eyes.

The music of night insects filled the woods, choking off when they drew close, then picking up after they passed. The brilliance of the waning Sister Salah shed just enough of Her pale light for Joga to see in the darkness.

The deeper they went into the woods, the more diverse the foliage became. Old trees covered in moss grew straight, or at various angles, their twisting limbs reaching toward the sky like curled fingers. Vines snaked around the trunks of some and hung from the limbs like rope.

Joga looked around in wonder. The Frostlands had some plant life, but nothing as lush and green as this. The forests he'd passed through with the twins hadn't been this green. That stray thought about the girls dampened his awe. He hoped they were safe. They'd parted ways under the worst of conditions, and the fact that he'd found no sign of them anywhere …

He pushed that thought away. Nandi and Amiya were too stubborn not to have survived. For all Joga knew, they were in a better situation than himself. Maybe they'd already made it to Altarra and were waiting for him. He hoped so. He could never live with himself if something had happened to them.

Nyimbe's camp turned out to be a series of trees grown close together with interlocking limbs. With the familiarity of someone who'd spent a great deal of time here, she wove between the trees and found a low branch. With barely an effort, she jumped and grabbed hold with one hand, hoisting herself up.

By the time Joga had pulled himself up, she'd climbed several more branches overhead. He looked down, nervous at the drop twice his height and more.

He took a few deep breaths to steady his shaky legs, and continued. He grabbed each handhold in a white-knuckled grip as he forced himself not to look down again. After a while, he looked around but didn't see his new companion.

"Hey, Joga," he heard from behind and overhead.

Joga strained to look over his shoulder. Nyimbe lounged across several branches that had grown side by side as if for the sole purpose of creating a space for her to lie. He pulled himself up and grabbed hold of the next branch before taking another look around. "Is amazing," he said. Many branches grew together like the ones Nyimbe lay on.

"This is where you sleep if you don't want to be food, Khatala man," Nyimbe said. "Nothing climbs this far up."

Joga gingerly moved onto a pathway of branches and looked around. Sure enough, they were alone, but for the buzzing insects. "Never see anything like this," he said.

"They don't have forests in the west?" Nyimbe asked.

"Not traveled across all of Khatal, but in Frostlands, woods are not big and trees are not so tall."

"Frostlands?" Nyimbe wrinkled her nose. "That sounds cold."

"To Marailander, is cold."

Nyimbe sat up and leaned on her elbow. "You think I'm soft because I'm a Marailander?"

"No. Just not used to it."

"Where were you going, that you were so desperate to pass through these woods?" Nyimbe asked.

"Did not know it was so dangerous," Joga said. "Thought werewood cats only live in werewood."

"That is a common mistake that kills people," Nyimbe said.

"There are two types of shifter cats; darkwood, and werewood. Only werewood cats live in the werewood, and are a little bigger than my friend, here."

A darkwood cat, then. "Good to know." Joga couldn't help scanning the woods around them with all this talk about shifter cats. "I go to Altarra. Look for friends."

Nyimbe laughed. "You walk into Altarra, it will be straight into a dungeon, Khatala man."

"I know," Joga said, his voice falling quiet. "But must. Made promise to friends to help find father."

"Even if it puts your head on a block?"

"Save my life and like family," Joga said without hesitation. "Would die to help."

"Fool," Nyimbe said. "But an honorable fool. You will have the love and respect of all who mourn your death."

Having no answer to that, Joga shrugged.

Nyimbe put her hands behind her head and lay on her back. She wiggled one of her crossed feet while staring up at the *Salah*-lit sky.

Joga started to do the same when he noticed something glowing below. He crawled to the edge of the interwoven branches and looked over the side. His eyes widened. Thousands of tiny glowing lights dotted the darkness.

"The most beautiful things in nature are often the most deadly," Nyimbe said. She rolled onto her side and looked down as well. "These woods are no different. They're deadly if you don't know them, but they're beautiful, too. This is the only woods I've ever been to where the fireflies are so many, they look like glowing mist."

"Is beautiful. You call fireflies?"

Nyimbe nodded. "You don't have them in Khatal?"

"Not in Frostlands." He looked down again and saw the lights growing closer. "Are rising!"

Nyimbe chuckled. "Calm down, Khatala man. Yes, they rise. Soon they will be all around us.

She was right. In a short time, thousands of fireflies had risen to the highest point in the trees where they lay. The glowing insects flowed through large and small gaps between the tree limbs, just like mist.

Joga watched in amazement as they engulfed everything. He could barely make out Nyimbe a dozen feet away, lying on her back with her head resting on her hands.

He reached out and gently cupped several fireflies in his hands. When he felt them crawling around in his palms, he slowly opened them. The insects were small, and the light glowed from their rear ends. The light flickered in their bottoms a few times, then the bugs flapped their tiny wings with blinding speed and took off again.

Joga lay on his back and basked in the wondrous glow all around him. Many thoughts weighed heavily on his mind, from the fate of the twins and Sama, to the fate of his people. But tonight he would rest his mind. Surrounded by the beauty of this great green forest aglow in firefly light, he let out a content sigh, and drifted asleep.

THE PREDAWN LIGHT of Father *Alyu* coaxed Joga from a dreamless slumber. He yawned and stretched his arms and legs. When he felt the hard rounded surface beneath him, he opened his eyes and remembered that he lay high above the forest floor north of Altarra. He sat up and looked around. "Nyimbe, my friend?" he called out when he failed to spot his new companion. "Are you here?"

"I am here, Joga," came the answer from above.

Joga looked up and saw Nyimbe perched at the top of one of the tallest trees. He shook his head. How she felt so comfortable swaying back and forth so high in the air on so small a piece of a tree, he couldn't fathom. She hung on with one hand and one leg wrapped around the tree, her other foot pressed against the side of the trunk.

She looked down at Joga with a devious grin, the light of Father *Alyu* amplifying her inner radiance. "You climb up here with me, Khatala man?"

Joga shook his head. "Am high enough already. What do you see, so far up there?"

Nyimbe gazed to the south. "People. Don't know what kind, but they are a small group. They're too far away to tell if they're armed."

Joga sat up straighter. "No weapons?"

She nodded. "Not sure from this distance, but doesn't look like it."

"Khatala," Joga said. "Carry no weapons."

"Because you use the earth power," Nyimbe said. "That makes sense."

"Your people not like it."

"Not my people," Nyimbe snapped. She seemed to catch herself and softened. "I haven't lived among people for a long time. I prefer to roam the land and live in peace where I may, away from the rumors and gossip, fighting and conflicts that come when so many people clump together."

Joga nodded with a downturned smile. "Think like a Khatala. You get along with my people just fine."

"Too cold." With nimble grace, she made her way down. "Come. Let's go meet your people. If they *are* your people."

Their descent was slow-going because of Joga. It seemed every third branch he could hear Nyimbe's impatient sigh as he placed a shaky foot down. He ignored her and took his time. At least he'd be alive when they got down.

"They're probably back to Khatal by now," Nyimbe teased once they reached the forest floor. "Better hurry."

Joga barely got to enjoy being on solid ground again before

they took off in a fast jog. He felt something nearby, then caught sight of a four-legged silhouette further off to the side. He guessed —or rather hoped—it to be Kokunde shadowing them.

When they finally broke free of the woods, the giant city of Altarra was almost distinguishable in the distance. "Your people," Nyimbe said.

Joga followed her gaze to see a group of seven lightly clad people hiking indirectly toward them. They were close enough for him to see that they were indeed Khatala. "Must meet them," Joga said.

"Go ahead," Nyimbe replied. "We will wait for you here. Unless you wish to travel on with them, or alone. In that case, Kokunde and I will leave."

To his surprise, Joga found he didn't want Nyimbe to leave. "Why not come with me? Meet people with me."

Nyimbe looked as if she wanted to take him up on the offer, but shook her head. "I don't like people, Khatala man."

"You walk with me through the forest," Joga countered.

"You're not people," she replied. "You're a person." She pointed at the group of Khatala traversing the open land in the distance. "They are people."

Joga didn't want to press the issue, but he gave it one last try. "They go in opposite direction from us. You and I go south. You only meet them once. If you don't like, will leave anyway."

She looked up at him with suspicious dark brown eyes. "Why do you want me to meet these people after I already told you it is not my wish, Joga? What do you gain?"

Joga noticed the subtle shift in her body language from relaxed to defensive. She slipped her spear off her back with slow but practiced smoothness. Kokunde noticed it, too. He sat up, his pointed ears swiveling forward. He looked first at Nyimbe, then turned his big yellow eyes on Joga.

"No trouble." Joga held up his hands. "Just wish to welcome you to meet people you say you might get along with, remember? Besides…" He grinned. "What would I gain? Not a cannibal."

The joke fell flat, but Nyimbe loosened the grip on her spear. Kokunde, who had been staring intently at Joga, put his saber-like teeth on full display with a lazy yawn. He licked his chops and looked in another direction.

Nyimbe moved to the edge of the forest where her companion sat and pointed to the forest. "Wait for me, Kokunde."

The darkwood cat swished his bristly tail from side to side and huffed a deep breath at her. "Kokunde!" Nyimbe futilely shoved at the eight-hundred-pound feline when he brushed past and almost knocked her over.

Joga had never seen a more unlikely thing. A woman who stood a little above his elbow somehow made friends with one of the most fearsome animals in the world. Darkwood cats were said to be fearless. Joga figured if he was already naturally lethal, and could transform into something even more lethal, there wouldn't be much he'd fear, either.

"Let's go meet these people of yours, Khatala man," Nyimbe said.

They hadn't gotten far before the band spotted them and stopped to await their approach. Joga recognized their defensive pattern as that of the Frostlands. These were indeed his people, led by a woman who stood at their front. The closer he came, the harder Joga's heart pounded. "Mikuna?"

Nyimbe looked up at him. "A word of greeting or a name?"

"Mikuna!" Joga called out.

"Joga?" came the distant reply. She sprinted for him, and Joga did the same. They collided in a crushing hug that lasted a lifetime.

Joga closed his eyes and inhaled her scent. A small part of him hadn't been sure he'd ever see Mikuna again, but it really was her.

They hesitantly let go, but Mikuna held onto his arms. "You have grown stronger, yosha," she said in Khatalese. She leaned back and made a show of looking him over. "Leaner, too. Your travels have made you better." She looked past him and Joga turned to see Nyimbe's approach. "You've found a companion, brother."

Joga didn't miss the inflection in her voice. "A friend," he said, switching to his native tongue. "We met last night while I was sleeping in a tree. She might have saved my life." He pointed toward the forest.

"Oh, so you met in the forest, did you?" Mikuna said just as Nyimbe reached them.

Joga cleared his throat and stepped aside. "This is Nyimbe. Nyimbe, this is Mikuna." The two women assessed each other, and Joga wisely kept silent.

"Short," Mikuna said in her accented Marai. "Even for scrawny Marailander."

"Big and lumbering," Nyimbe said, giving the Khatala woman a onceover. "Slow, too."

Mikuna's eyebrows rose. Joga clamped his mouth shut. His sister's words were a good-natured jab, but he didn't know Nyimbe well enough to be sure of her reaction. As the silence lengthened, Joga felt he might step between them, but Mikuna spoke again.

"He thinks to come between us in case we fight." She jerked her chin at Joga. "The way he leans forward trying not to take step? If we not make friends, maybe he fall on his face."

Nyimbe gave him a sidelong glance. "He's a man. What else would he do, if not misjudge women?"

They snickered, while Joga's spine went rigid in indignation. "Not stepping between anybody."

Mikuna extended her hand. Nyimbe looked at it, then whirled her double-tipped spear over her head and drove one end into the ground. The two women clasped hands, and Nyimbe placed her left hand over the crook in her elbow. Mikuna imitated the gesture, drawing a smile from Nyimbe. When they released each other, Mikuna pressed her palms together in front of her and gave a sharp nod, which Nyimbe mimicked.

"Look like your first time seeing Khatala handshake," Mikuna said to Nyimbe while eyeing Joga. "Your manners are slipping, yosha."

"Did not have chance to shake hands," Joga replied more defensively than he'd intended. "How have you come so far from home, yisha? What happens?"

The rest of the Khatala band caught up by then. Joga had been so excited to see Mikuna again, he'd forgotten the others. To his elation, even Jista, Akrim, and Bayaku were there. Hearty greetings ensued, with Joga animatedly answering inquiries about how he'd completed his bloodmark. Everyone took a quick liking to Nyimbe. While she remained reserved and spoke little, Joga figured that was probably friendly, for her personality.

"Conflict grows hotter," Mikuna said, continuing her accented use of Marai for Nyimbe's benefit. "Their king grows more aggressive, and the two nations of Khatal have fewer numbers. Is fear that Mari king will try to unite Marai against them. Completely destroy."

Everyone's face darkened at that, including Nyimbe's, to Joga's confusion. The woman was a Marailander, after all, though unlike any he'd ever seen. This eastern land seemed to host a population possibly more diverse than Khatal, so maybe the dark-skinned woman hailed from some distant region he'd never heard of. He knew that not all Marailanders approved of the conflict, but Nyimbe's reaction was just as angry as theirs. Maybe more so.

"Ancients send me to assess conflict," Mikuna continued. "They feel the two tribes will look to the south for aid."

Joga nodded. "Already leaning on Nassak. I meet band of them on the way to Jietar. They say same as you."

"Then already has begun," Mikuna said. "Must hurry, Joga. If Marai king unites his land and forces Khatal to unite against him, will be very bad. Worse than Marai king believes, for he force us to into the calamity."

"No." Joga felt the pit of his stomach go cold. With great hesitance, the Ancients educated every Khatala about the second jahaka, which led to the fury. He shook his head, remembering the day he'd been taught the way of calamity once and only once, that he'd know how not to ever touch that side of the power. It had been glorious and terrible all at once. Like riding the back of a vicious beast that was one instant away from turning and devouring him.

Joga thought of the potential destruction it would lead to, and not just of the land and cities. Of both peoples. Somehow, that thought reminded him of something possibly worse. "Is more." He looked from Mikuna to Bayaku. The weathered veteran stared at him with stoney eyes and nodded. Joga took a deep breath. "When I first leave to fullfil bloodmark, was first attacked by a pack of jarku. Killed my horse and almost me. Then attacked by monsters with four arms and skin like cooled lava rock, with veins of lava flowing all over. They spit and curse in language I don't know."

Bayaku swore an oath under his breath. He turned away and put his hands on his hips, staring out at the distant lands.

Joga watched him with growing dread. He'd grown up with Bayaku's son, Bazara. Only one other person in all the northern Frostland tribe was more hardened and fierce than Bazara, and that was the man standing with his back to Joga. Not once had he seen Bayaku react in this way, no matter how grave a situation.

"Well," Akrim said with a nervous laugh, waving at Bayaku. "That's good sign."

Mikuna looked at the old warrior's back with concern. "Ushay. What is it?"

Bayaku turned back around and in two long strides stood in front of Joga, who craned his neck to look up at the taller man. Bayaku was near to triple Joga's age, but the lean hard muscle covering his body, the strength of his steps, and his vast knowledge of battle made him ten times more formidable than the youngest and fiercest of them. "Tell me with certainty, young warrior," he rumbled in Khatalese. "Are you absolutely certain of what you saw. There can be no mistake?"

"No mistake," Joga said, reverting to Khatalese out of respect. "I was attacked by them. I was also attacked by a tunneler. He described the events that separated him from the twins, as well as the monster that had attacked Vyne, though he left out where that had actually happened. The last thing he wanted was for anyone to know he'd used essences to *bridge*.

"Trogk," Bayaku growled. "The four-armed heralds."

Everyone looked around in confusion while Joga translated for Nyimbe. The Marailander also wore a look of shock. "Four-armed heralds?"

Joga stared at her and nodded.

Nyimbe growled a curse. "If what you say is what I think, your little fight with King Fool is a distraction that will kill us all."

Mikuna looked from one to the other with a look that Joga was sure reflected his own growing anxiety. "What do you speak of?" she asked. "What is trogk?"

Bayaku took on a faraway look as he stared off into the distance. "Our people call them trogk, of the World Below, and the heralds of the Mgomu." He looked from one person to the next to let the unfamiliar word sink in. "Mgomu, the blight aspect."

That drew curses and intakes of breath all around. Everyone looked around as if seeking answers from each other. Joga's heart hammered in his chest. The blight aspect? That meant the end of everything.

"How can this be, ushay?" Mikuna asked the old warrior. "The battles between the faithless and the Ishra are only stories passed around nighttime campfires."

"The passage of each year, each decade, each millennia, and each age, dulls the collective memory," Bayaku stated. "The survivors of disaster swear never to forget. They pass the knowledge to their children with fervor. Those children, who were born during or close to the events, pass knowledge to their children. But with each telling, the fervor fades, the fires of desperation to never forget what befell us begin to die, and events fade into history, and history fades into legend."

Joga translated for Nyimbe, who nodded sagely with each word. "I don't know what they call them in Marai, but some of us know the stories, too. What you call the faithless, we call the Fallen. I assume this Ishra are the Illuminarians?"

Joga nodded. "Ishra; the terrible mighty. Because power they wield was so great and destructive."

"If the stories are only half true," Nyimbe said, "it means the Fallen might have returned, and maybe the Illuminarians."

Joga looked to Mikuna. He saw the urgency in her eyes and knew what she was about to say.

Indeed, Mikuna opened her mouth, then closed it as she scrutinized him. "You don't come with us." It wasn't a question.

Joga slowly shook his head. "Cannot."

"Why not?" Mikuna asked. The sincerity of her confusion hurt. "Why not come with us, yosha? We need you. Your tribe needs you."

"I know," Joga said. "Will come, but not yet. Cannot. There are others who need me, now."

Mikuna looked past Joga to Nyimbe, who stood at ease with her hand on her hip. When she noticed the Khatala woman's look, she rolled her eyes. "I can take care of myself, big woman," she said.

"Two young girls," Joga clarified. "Saved my life when I battled the Mulgin."

That got a reaction from everyone in the party. Talk of the end of the world had trumped his near suicidal bloodmark. "Help me kill it, but also man with skin like four-armed trogk. Was too powerful. Might have died—"

Mikuna held up a hand, her face filled with wonder. "The twin balls of fire." When Joga looked questioningly at her, she explained. "I told you about my dream before you leave, Joga. Twin balls of fire that I think would somehow help you."

As the memory of Mikuna's dream returned, it started to make sense. The girls were certainly fiery enough, especially Amiya. They had to have been the twin fireballs Mikuna had seen in her dream. "I think maybe you right," he said.

"They are the ones you were separated from during attack," Mikuna continued. "Attack on travelers, yes?"

"Must find them," Joga said. "They save my life and I fail them. Must try."

He and his adoptive sister stared at each other for a long time, neither wanting to part ways, yet knowing they must. Finally, Mikuna sighed in resignation. "Go, yosha. Find them, then find me."

Joga stepped forward and wrapped her in another crushing hug. "I must fulfill my debt," he said, reverting to Khatalese, "then I'll find you, yisha. I promise. Be safe."

"We will see each other again," Mikuna said into his ear. "We don't go to fight, but if the fight finds us, we will be ready."

They released each other and Mikuna wiped tears from her eyes and sniffed. Joga found a bit of moisture collecting in his eyes as well. He wanted more than anything to go with them. He knew his sister and his people needed him, but he couldn't abandon Amiya and Nandi, or even Sama. The tatamble girl had helped save him as much as the other two.

Mikuna moved in front of Nyimbe. "Will travel by his side?"

"No," Nyimbe said, drawing surprised looks from Mikuna and Joga. "He travels by mine, for a time, at least. Who knows where life will lead, eh?"

"Is true," Mikuna said. "Hope to see you again, Marailander Nyimbe.

"Just Nyimbe," came the reply. "I'm barely a Marailander."

Joga thought that an odd response, but Nyimbe said nothing more.

"Go with my blessing," Mikuna said, "the blessing of the Ancients, and Creator *Amyadali*."

Joga repeated the blessing to her, then exchanged goodbyes with the others, sharing a few words with Bayaku.

"You've grown in more than size, boy," the veteran said. "I've seen great potential in you. You will rise high."

Joga slapped his hand to his heart and bowed in respect. The fiercest warrior in the Frostlands rarely issued such high praise.

The two parties split with no small amount of hesitance, especially between Joga and Mikuna. He wondered if she'd dreamed about him since their last parting. Had she foreseen anything of his adventures with the twins, or what lay ahead? Probably not, or she would have mentioned it.

"What's a yosha?" Nyimbe asked.

Joga's thoughts scattered at the sound of her voice. "Yosha is brother. Yisha is sister."

Nyimbe looked up into his face. "You don't resemble."

"Is my adoptive sister, and me, her adoptive brother. She is born of different tribe, but bloodmark sent her to my tribe. Sometimes she has dreams about things before happen."

"Bloodmark," Nyimbe said. "That tattoo?" She pointed at the markings flowing from under his furs, partially showing on his bare shoulder.

"Is not tattoo," Joga explained. "Is bloodmark. Ritual of the Ancients to reveal life task of its bearer."

They retraced their path back to the edge of the woods where Kokunde patiently waited. Well, mostly waited. The darkwood cat sat curled over some sort of meal he'd slaughtered. He sat up and looked in their direction, bloody muzzle shining in the sunlight.

They continued on through most of the day, but Nyimbe stopped when Altarra came fully into view. "I don't know how you plan to search that place, Khatala man, but I'll go no closer while the sun shines. You would be wise to do the same."

She was right, of course. Joga didn't understand Nyimbe's hesitance to enter the formidable city. She was a Marailander, even if "barely". Joga, on the other hand, would stand out no matter how he dressed. Shorter for a Khatala he might be, but he was still noticeably larger than the average Marailander. "Maybe can slip in at night. Look around."

"Maybe. I wish you had something to go on, Joga. Your search is too wide."

"Know only that they must find father," Joga replied, "and that father taken here."

"Do you know what their father looks like?" Nyimbe asked. When Joga shook his head, she grunted. "You have an *easy* task ahead of you, Khatala." She opened a hand toward the sprawling city. "How do you expect ..." she trailed off when Kokunde growled deep in his throat.

Joga looked at the darkwood cat, who stared off in another direction. He was glad that unnerving sound wasn't directed at him.

Nyimbe moved beside the cat. "What is it, Kokunde?" She placed a hand on his back. "What do you smell?" Kokunde continued to growl, then snapped his jaws at the air, lowering himself in an aggressive posture. The raised hackles on his back quivered.

Joga and Nyimbe stared in the direction the darkwood cat faced for a long time. Joga pointed. "There."

Something moved from a long way off, but even from this distance, it looked big. Nyimbe swore and took a step back. "That's a problem. A big one."

"What is it?" Joga asked.

Nyimbe took another step back and tried to pull at Kokunde, but he stood his ground. "That," she said, "is a teliak."

2 4

RAYNE

In the third-floor room of one of the most expensive inns in Carlayn, Rayna closed her eyes and slid lower into her steaming hot bath. Though she took no joy in her occupation, it did come with its perks. Healthy pay numbered among them.

She sank all the way down, past the suds and fully submerged herself. The hot mineral-infused water made her skin tingle from head to toe. She surfaced and wiped her face, then slid her fingers through her thin wet braids, massaging the oils into her scalp. The sweet heavy scent of incense drifted in the air and relaxed her mind, making it easier to think. Something didn't feel right about all this.

It wasn't so much the target in New Dama, or those in Shetar or even here in Carlayn. She would go where she was sent and do what she must. It was the end of the conversation that troubled Rayna. Guiding Eye Alydria hadn't come out and said it, of course, but she'd made her point clear. The khamra considered King Alyn to be enough of a threat to the balance to be eliminated.

She sank back down in the water to her chin. King Alyn. She inhaled deeply the soft sweet incense and let it out with a long hum. Taking any life was a last resort, and the assassin valued no life above another. But a king?

Rayna ran a hand over her face. Surely the khamra had considered the implications of such an action? The potential blame to the Khatala, regardless of the lack of evidence any khamra agent would leave. Those few who knew of the assassin organization would most likely say nothing, for fear of their own lives. With no other explanation, the remainder of the population would most certainly blame the Khatala. The uprising against the westerners would be terrible.

On the other hand, if what Guiding Eye Alydria had said was true, then the king already sought to unite Marai against the people of Khatal. If that happened the result would be the same. She sighed. From the look of things, a monarch could die, then many more, or a monarch could live, and an entire people could be decimated. The logic made sense, but it didn't make it right.

Rayna stood up and sponged the soap off her body, then toweled off. The minerals and oils from her bath made her skin feel rich and supple. She slid the back of her calloused hands along her muscled arm. She didn't get to bathe in this manner often. It felt nice to relax her muscles.

She wrapped a large towel around her body and used a smaller one to dry off her braided hair. Eryn Tolen of Shetar, a woman with skin like parched earth in New Dama, and the king of Marai himself.

Rayna narrowed her eyes. Before she made such a drastic move, she would study the situation with her own eyes. Rayna presumed these new advisors were the replacements of the ones she'd eliminated. She needed to find out where they stood with regard to the war. And what of the woman she'd spared? Rayna hoped the lady continued to speak to the king against further aggression, and advocate for peace talks. Could Rayna possibly visit the two new advisors and "nudge" them in the right direction?

With plenty of day left to explore Carlayn, she dressed and

headed for the door, her thoughts following her out. Too many questions, too many moving parts, Rayna could only be in one place at a time, and it took time to get to each place.

Rumors floated about the streets concerning some sort of attack. From the snippets of conversation Rayna had heard, some sort of four-armed monsters fell from the sky and charged the city. Word had arrived with just enough time for Carlayn's military to dispatch and battle the monsters with the help of a powerful magus.

It all sounded like fantasy to her. Likely it was a handful of werewood or darkwood cats that ventured too far from their habitat. It wasn't a usual occurrence, but it wasn't unheard of either. Rayna could easily see a small number of fully trans-formed shifter cats giving the city guard more than enough chal-lenge. The civilians likely embellished the tale more with each telling.

She stopped at a shop with a delightful patio for a mug of warm spiced tea. The cold of winter might be gone, but spring still carried a chill in the air. The tea felt good going down. She sat at a small round table and watched the people milling about. The more she took in the sights, the more Rayna found that she liked Carlayn. She hardly saw any poor or street urchins in the many avenues she'd walked; daytime or the night before.

The people here seemed relaxed. Rayna heard the occasional sarcastic remark about Cravel's personality, but they seemed to benefit from his governance.

A man with golden hair and eyes like the ocean appeared beside her table. She looked up into his broad smile and didn't return it. His smile faltered. "I hope I'm not intruding, my lady. I just hoped I might share your company." He waved a hand holding his mug to encompass the busy patio. "All of the tables are occupied."

Rayna put on her best smile. "And out of all those tables, you chose to keep me company? I'm honored."

Another fault line appeared in his smile as he puzzled out the genuineness of her remark.

Rayna leaned across the table and patted her hand toward the empty chair. "Please sit, and talk with me."

His smile reasserted itself, and he took the seat. "Thank you for your kindness, my lady." He extended his hand. "My name is Petri."

Rayna took his hand. "Aycella. A pleasure to meet you, Petri."

"The pleasure is mine," Petri replied. His chest rose and fell as he let out a contented sigh. "A beautiful day, today. I must wonder how many more of them we've left."

Rayna tilted her head. "How many left? The warm season has barely arrived."

Petri continued to people-watch. "Indeed. Yet dark things are happening across Marai."

"I'm sure King Alyn will find a way to bring about peace," Rayna ventured.

Petri waved a hand at that. "Perhaps, perhaps not. In the end, I wonder how much it will matter."

"I don't catch your meaning," Rayna said.

He turned his attention back to her. "You must not have been here during the attack."

"Ah," Rayna said indifferently. "I've heard. Lots of rumors about *monsters*."

Petri's blue eyes grew serious. "No rumors, my lady. I saw them with my own eyes. I was out riding my chestnut mare. I own a stable, you see." When Rayna failed to react to that, he cleared his throat and continued. "I was out for a ride in the woods, as I often do, when I heard a commotion. I rode hard until I rounded a part of the city to see a contingent of soldiers waiting in formation. Further afield were these horrendous monsters tearing down fields toward them."

He took a sip from his mug and Rayna did the same. "Awful things," Petri continued. "They looked like they'd climbed out of a volcano with cooled magma stuck to their bodies. They were huge, all with four arms. And that foul tongue they shouted in. Absolutely dreadful."

Intrigued, Rayna leaned forward. "What tongue did they speak?"

Petri looked around, then leaned in closer as well. "No one knows, but I'm a student of history. It was an infernal tongue, and the monsters are called drauk. They are from the underworld."

Rayna smirked. "You tease me, Petri." She lifted her hand and let it fall at the wrist in a dainty wave.

Petri remained serious, however. "Surely not, my lady. I know it sounds fanciful, but I know what I saw. And those weren't the only beasts of evil. There were other monsters shaped like upside down nautilus shells from the ocean. They were huge, my lady Aycella. We lost a good number of soldiers, that day." He rested back in his chair and took another sip. "Some like to whisper about our prime minister, but we're not dead because he acted quickly." He frowned, then peered into Rayna's eyes.

The contact made her uncomfortable. Was he here from Shiedra and recognized her? Several city guards had gotten an up-close look at her during their melee. Perhaps they'd put out a description?

"You know," Petri said while Rayna held her breath. "Come to think of it, I remember seeing a woman in the robes of a magus, wielding the power of the essences to deadly effect."

Rayna relaxed. The tiny polished corlite beads attached to each braid clicked when she tilted her head. "I'm not sure why that is reason for you to scrutinize me so."

Petri flushed from the base of his neckline, and Rayna watched in amazement as it crept up his neck to cover his face. He placed a fist over his mouth and cleared his throat. "Er, what I mean to say, my lady Aycella, is that the woman, the magus … well, I was at a distance, but I could swear she resembled you. Especially her eyes. I only got a quick glance, but I'll never forget the striking contrast of those gray eyes against her dark skin. Just like yours, if you'll pardon me for saying so."

"I can assure you," Rayna replied with more casualness than she felt, "I've encountered no other person with eyes like mine no matter their complexion, my good Petri. It must have been the heat of the action and your adrenaline."

Petri shook his head through it all. "The memory of that event is burned into my mind. Do you mean to tell me you've not a sister?"

Of course, Rayna did not have a sister, but the question took her back many years to when she was a child, separated from her parents. They'd died along with everyone else on that fateful day she became an orphan.

The flash of memory sparked a flicker of anger. Maybe the world being rid of Alyn might be a good thing after all. She forced the thought away. Vengefulness was *never* the answer to a problem.

Across the table from her, Petri had gone from flush to pale. "I apologize if I've upset you, my lady Aycella. I meant no offense."

Rayna forced a smile. "You've given none, Petri. Your words sparked an unwelcome memory. Nothing more …" she trailed off when she spotted two elegantly dressed women pass by.

Their dresses were of the Jietari style, with the multicolored swash of blue, green, silver, and red starting at the left hip and flowing across the front down to the right ankle. The four colors of the essences. It was a style unique to Altarra, a show of pride by the wearer for residing in not only such a wealthy city, but one that housed the magi seat of power. She found that ironic, given most people's discomfort around the essence wielders.

"Is something amiss?" Petri asked. He followed her gaze to the women just as they turned down another street. "Ah, Altarra *royalty*. At least, Altarrans believe themselves to be. I hear the city is beautiful, but I fear I'd likely smother in the arrogance, should I visit."

"I apologize, Petri," Rayna said, not taking her eyes off the women. "Those women remind me that I have a meeting to attend." She looked back to him and fluttered her eyelashes. "A lady must get prettied up, you see."

"You've already accomplished that, my lady Aycella. But if you must go, then you must go." He raised his mug. "It's been a pleasure I'd be honored to repeat."

"Then let us hope to cross paths again."

"I shall make a habit of this establishment until we do," Petri called after her.

Rayna barely heard him. She took an adjacent street and held the sides of her dress up and she broke into a trot. She made a right turn at the next cross street and slowed to a walk near the corner. Rayna kept her pace and demeanor casual as she stepped out onto the street. The elegantly dressed women had already passed, and were just climbing into a carriage when she spotted them.

There was no need to follow the carriage; Rayna knew where it was bound. She walkedacross the street toward the next one. She'd gotten a good look at the layout of the city during her conversation with the guiding eye.

Unfortunately, every street she took was occupied, so Rayna had to keep an unhurried appearance lest she raise eyebrows. As expected, the carriage had already reached Cravel's mansion by the time Rayna arrived. She noted the armed guards stationed in pairs at both front corners of the mansion as she walked by and turned left. She passed a roving patrol along the side of the mansion and figured the other side to have the same. The back of the mansion was guarded the same as the front.

Rayna turned down a mostly empty backstreet and moved away from the mansion. She made a show of gazing up at the architecture and potted plants. It was only half an act, for she found Carlayn to rival Shiedra in beauty.

When the moment finally came when she was alone, Rayna summoned *air* through her corlite beads and leapt straight up. The corded muscles in her arms bunched when she grabbed hold of a windowsill and pulled. She launched herself further upward and vaulted over the side of the roof.

She continued to draw *air*, the corlite beads in her hair glowing silver. Rayna sprinted toward the edge of the building and jumped. She glided across the twenty-foot distance and landed in a roll on the next rooftop.

Ranya ran from rooftop to rooftop, glad she'd been steadfast in her refusal of the local tailor to create for her a long dress in the typical Carlayn fashion. When she finally made it to the roof of the prime minister's mansion, she moved toward the back and peeked over the side.

The guards stationed at either corner of the house had no reason to look up over their shoulders at the roof. Rayna looked down the side of the building. The window below her was closed, but two more were open further down the side. She backed away from the edge and assessed herself. Her new dress was infected by several black stains that could never be removed. The tailor would likely die on the spot if he saw them.

With a regretful sigh, Rayna ensured her hidden weapons were secure. She reached under her dress, unstrapped her spring-loaded forearm blade from her left thigh and secured it to her forearm. No point in trying to blend in wearing a stained dress. She'd rely on stealth.

After only a few steps, she thought about the potential for running into house staff and had second thoughts. She used a dagger to cut a piece of her dress free and wrapped it around her arm, then gave her forearm a little nick to draw blood. She wrapped the strip of dress around her forearm to conceal the hidden dagger and pressed it against the little trickle of blood.

Satisfied at her handy work, her weapons secured, Rayna took a few deep breaths and prepared her mind for the possibility she would have to end a life today. She closed her eyes, centered herself, and lay Rayna to sleep. Her eyes popped open; even that move was sharp and precise.

As silent as a hunting cat, Rayne padded to the middle of the roof and leaned over the edge. After assessing the guards below once more, she summoned *air* and lightened her body. She remained crouched at the edge of the mansion, waiting for a gap in passersby down below. When the opportunity finally came, she slipped over the side, dropped down, and grabbed the windowsill as she fell past.

With strength honed from a lifetime of training, Rayne grabbled the ledge and stopped her descent. She hoisted herself up and into the window. She flipped through the window and landed in a crouch; right behind a rotund man in a pair of white pants and black shirt and waistcoat that marked him as a house servant.

With little more than a flick of her gaze around the room, Rayne made for the nearest hiding spot without a sound. The servant whistled to himself as he went about tidying the room. The assassin silently moved from place to place every time the servant turned, gradually making her way toward the door.

It stood ajar, just enough for her to slip through. Rayne silently moved down the halls, hoping she wouldn't encounter anyone, but preparing for the possibility. The sound of conversation seeped out from under a closed door just ahead. She stopped and listened, then moved on.

Another staff member appeared from a hallway intersection but kept moving. Rayne heard soft footsteps behind her, but kept moving as if she belonged. The footsteps died away when the person behind her turned down another hallway.

She finally reached the stairs and started down. She figured Cravel would have chosen a more intimate chamber to meet with his visitors, since it wasn't an official gathering.

A woman appeared at the bottom of the stairs and started up. As they neared each other, Rayne bent her arms and covered the stains on her dress. She planted an embarrassed expression on her face that deepened as the distance closed between them.

"Are you all right, my lady?" the staff member asked. She

stopped next to Rayne and looked her over, her eye lingering on the bloodstained wrapping on her arm.

Rayne hesitantly opened her arms. "I had an unfortunate misplacement of the foot, and my dress is ruined. I am so embarrassed."

"You're priorities are misplaced, my lady," the woman said. "Look at your arm."

"A minior cut that barely stings, ma'am. The damage to my dress is far more lasting."

"My, that *is* dreadful," the lady said, giving the dress another look over. She slid a brown lock of hair behind her ear as she leaned forward to look at the stains. She looked back up at Rayne with pity. "I fear these may be permanent, my dear."

Rayna's shoulders rose and fell with an exaggerated sigh. "I feared as much. I should be along back to my room to change."

The attendant was still looking her over. "Where in the world did you do this to yourself? Surely there is no such filth in the house."

Her beads clicked as she shook her head. "No. I was outside and fell. I came back inside to see if I could clean it, but, well..." She indicated the dress.

The servant tilted her head and clucked her tongue. "Oh, that is such a shame, my dear. It's a beautiful dress, if a touch short."

Rayne pointed toward the stairs. "I should be going. Thank you for your concern."

"Of course, young lady." The woman inclined her head and continued on her way.

Rayne reached the bottom of the stairs and scanned the wide hall for doorways. Unlike some of the other homes of the wealthy she'd "visited", Cravel's mansion was rather humble by comparison. She saw no overhead beams where she might perch to drop down on her prey from above. There were no overhangs or large flowing drapes or nooks to conceal herself in.

She moved to the nearest door, all the while checking left to right as she analyzed the room. She'd expected to pass several doors before reaching the room with Cravel and his guests, but when she pressed her ear against the door under the staircase, she heard the prime minister's.

While she strained to hear the muffled voices beyond the door, Rayne wondered if it were possible to use *air* to enhance her hearing. Something to try at another time.

Conversation started out calm, and she caught snippets here and there concerning the king's desire to unite, and the potential spoils. She heard something about corlite and the Drylands, and about the conflict with two tribes, though she couldn't make out the names spoken.

"Excuse me, ma'am," a stern voice said from several paces away.

Rayne sighed and turned to see the large staff member she'd slipped past when she'd first entered the building. He glared at her with meaty fists on his hips.

"Ma'am. I must ask what you think you're doing. That is Master Cravel's private meeting room."

"I … I wasn't sure what room it was or if it was occupied," Rayne stammered while still keeping an ear focused on the conversation inside. The voices were getting louder. She spread her dress. "I was looking for a place to try to clean this off. I wasn't sure if this was a room I could enter, so I was listening to make sure no one was in there. It's so ghastly." She gave the dress a little tug.

The servant pooched his lips out as he took in the stains. "Oh dear, that is quite terrible, but still not a reason to go snooping about the doors. You need only have informed a staff member…"

Rayne stared at the floor. She was sure she heard raised voices, then a moment later, shouting. What was going on in there?

"… at all listening to me, ma'am?"

She looked up. "My pardon?"

"I said that your dress is likely unsalvageable, and you will need…"

The shouting grew louder, and she thought she heard something hit the ground. Cravel's voice hollered in alarm, ending Rayne's need for subtlety.

She shouldered the door open and came face to face with a man head and shoulders taller than her. The moment she registered the man's presence, she knelt and punched him in the groin. Before he fully doubled over, she launched herself straight up. The top of her head flattened his nose in a crimson explosion.

The assassin shoved the choking man aside and sprinted for the two women squaring off against a single man in a fancy servant's uniform.

"What now?" Cravel wailed. "This is insanity!"

"Prime Minister?" The servant who'd confronted Rayne hesitantly peeked his head inside.

"Get word to the city guard!" Cravel shouted. "Now!" The servant disappeared out the door.

The women dove into a series of well-coordinated attacks against the servant, and Rayne thought him surely doomed. The man held them off, however, and picked off each attack without countering. He was measuring their abilities.

She sprinted toward them and heard Cravel call from behind. "Simion! Another is coming!"

His servant, Simion, maneuvered the assailants so their backs were to Rayne, likely thinking to force her to move around them. He unwittingly helped her.

Rayne drew her hidden daggers and attacked the woman on her right. The assailant leaned out of the way of the initial stab, then counterattacked with a dagger of her own. Rayne threw herself into a combination of stabs and counters, retreating then shifting to the offensive.

Normally, her sudden shifts from defense to aggression threw her adversaries off balance. The woman she fought flowed with her in the most unnatural way Rayne had ever seen, as if predicting her movements.

Not far away, Simion struggled with a similar situation. The man was formidable to say the least, but the woman he fought kept one step ahead of him. He took a cut just under the chest, then another on the shoulder. The servant narrowed his eyes, showing no indication he'd felt the injuries.

Rayne ducked a stab, at the same time sweeping her blade across her adversary's torso. She heard the rip of fabric and the resulting grunt as she followed through and dove into a roll.

Cravel cried out in dismay. She spared a quick glance to see three men clad like the one she'd dropped converging on the Prime Minister. The fourth man was still kneeling and doubled over, one hand holding his nose, the other his groin.

That quick glance almost cost her. A blade flashed for Rayne's face, and she barely leaned away in time. She countered with an upward swipe of her dagger and scored another cut to the woman's arm.

Behind her, Simion managed to grab hold of his opponent's wrist when she stabbed at him. As soon as the servant's hand toucher her wrist, he flipped the hand in the wrong direction, drawing a pained grunt. The dagger fell from her hand, which he caught and delivered a backward stab for her ribcage.

The assailant twisted her body out of the way, the blade just missing the mark, then leaped into a handless cartwheel to place her arm in a more favorable position. It was an acrobatic move that would have left a lesser fighter dead for such foolishness. This woman was quick and skilled, and the bold maneuver saved her life.

Simion still had hold of her wrist, and as soon as she landed, he thrust his elbow out. The blow connected with the side of her head, but she shrugged it off and drove into his solar plexus.

The master servant tensed his midsection and accepted the knee. Before she could retract, he looped his free hand under her leg and lifted her up.

Rayne caught most of the exchange from the corner of her eye.

She'd already worked her adversary around so her right side—and thus, the blade on her right arm—was in line with the other combatants. When Simion lifted the woman over his head, Rayne flicked her wrist in the direction of the aloft assailant. The instant the dagger left her hand, she flicked her wrist. The motion activated the spring holding the strapped dagger in place under her forearm. The faster projectile shot past the thrown missile toward its target.

The assailant raised her arms to balance against falling over, leaving her ribcage exposed. The spring-projected dagger found its mark between her ribs an instant before the other.

Rayne never saw the daggers hit their mark, but she didn't have to. Her instincts were every bit the honed weapon her body and blades were. She went into a series of attacks with her remaining blade, following up with low leg sweeps and punches. She kept her opponent on her heels long enough to retrieve another dagger strapped to her thigh, and continued to work her opponent back.

The woman snarled at her, trying to keep up with Rayne's endless barrage. Her light brown eyes dimmed, then darkened until they were the color of coal. Her movements became faster. Rayne felt the wind of each missed swipe, as the assailant put more power behind her attacks.

Impossible, she thought, but it wasn't; not for this person, this *thing*. The change in her eyes, the effortless way this woman adjusted to everything she threw at her; Rayne had never seen a droughtlord before, but they were part of the many studies of the khamra. She had no doubt this woman had given herself over to the Fallen.

"I will never grow tired," the woman said, creases becoming visible in her face with each word. "How about you?" The creases deepened until her face looked like a sun-baked desert.

The droughtlord grinned and winked. She met Rayne's attacks move for move, her wicked smile broadening.

Rayne noted the ease with which her enemy matched her

efforts where before she barely kept up. The woman's confidence increased with each moment that passed, gradually morphing into arrogance. She believed the assassin had been fighting to the best of her ability. Never fully revealing her hand, Rayne engaged her enemy long enough to get a sense of the limits of her skill. When the time came, she would push past it.

Rayne worked her enemy around while allowing the droughtlord to keep up. When Simion finally came into view, she saw that he nearly had his opponent down. Rayne's daggers were still embedded in the woman's side, though not nearly enough blood flowed from the wounds.

"So endearing that you think to protect your cravenly Prime Minister," the woman said. "Even if you were to best me today instead of dying here, which you will." She ducked a swipe at her head, then rushed in with a reverse stab of her own dagger, followed by a descending elbow when Rayne ducked. "You only delay the inevitable. Whether now or in the days to come, your cowardly leader will die; all who align with him will die." With a burst of speed, she darted toward Rayne, who dove aside. When the assassin came to her feet, the woman was there, daggers flashing in her face.

"All who have not learned to thrive in the shadow will live in ruin. The blight will spread until it covers the world over. Only those who embrace it will survive. Your efforts here are tiny and meaningless."

"Indeed," Rayne agreed, which drew a puzzled reaction from, the droughtlord. "All must die. As will you." She increased the speed and strength of her offense, easily matching and surpassing the efforts of the droughtlord. In three exchanges, she left the woman bleeding in a dozen places and had her back on her heels.

The smug grin disappeared and the snarl returned. Suddenly the woman's eyes glowed silver, and she spoke a series of guttural phrases that made the hairs on Rayne's neck stand on end.

Cravel passed her line of vision, the prime minister throwing down pieces of furniture between himself and his pursuers. He screamed and threw utensils, dumped food off platters and hurled them at the three men stalking after him.

From the corner of her eye, Rayne saw five more figures calmly enter the room. Where were the guards? Even if there weren't any in the mansion, surely at least one outside heard the commotion. And what of the servants? Wouldn't they have gone to get help?

Rayne figured she knew the answer, so she let thoughts of help fall away. The three men after Cravel were closing in, and there were five more enemies to worry about.

With no more time to fish out any more surprises from her adversary, Rayne stepped up her offense. She beat aside a stabbing dagger and sliced the same wrist. As the blade fell from the droughtlord's hand, Rayne moved in close. In the span of a heartbeat she spun left and planted her elbow into the other woman's mouth. As her head snapped back, Rayne spun right and delivered a right hook toward her jaw, butt of her dagger leading.

In that instant the droughtlord's eyes flashed silver. A burst of wind opposed Rayne's incoming fist. It didn't turn the incoming blow aside, for Rayne had put too much power into it, but it slowed her.

The butt of Rayne's dagger found its mark. While the blow didn't knock her unconscious, it sent the droughtlord stumbling back. Rayne's instincts screamed at her to drop to the floor. She heeded the warning and narrowly missed being decapitated by a sword speeding for her neck.

Rayne turned onto her back while scissoring her feet with the motion. She tangled her feet with the the new attacker and sent him stumbling to the floor. Rayne kicked her feet upward, the momentum lifting her off her back and onto her feet. She landed in a crouch, at the same time driving her dagger into the sprawled man's back. Two of the new arrivals were assisting in cornering Cravel while one converged on Simion, the other on Rayne.

They'd pegged her as the more dangerous of the two fighters. Rayne kept in a crouch and circled left. The new enemy did the same, while the droughtlord shook her head and rose. The man she'd dropped near the door struggled to his feet and lumbering her way as well.

Rayne's mind raced. If she didn't figure something out, Cravel was as good as dead. She needed—

A man and a woman darted through the door and parted, one banking left, one right. The woman held two weapons shaped similar to an **L**, but with the short side serving as the grip and positioned three quarters of the way down the long shaft. She held the grips so the long shafts were pressed against her forearms; the weapons became extensions of her fists, and protection for her arms.

The man produced a chain whip with a tip shaped like an arrowhead, but instead of striking down the bloody-nosed adversary, he sprinted past the man.

The woman sprinted behind her partner and jumped at Bloody Nose's back. Her baton flashed in an arc at the back of his head to a resounding crack. One less enemy to worry about.

Rayne released her concern for the prime minister. The khamra had come. She darted left and stabbed at the lesser enemy, then rolled right and came to her feet with a spinning kick for the lunging droughtlord's head. The woman leaned away, but Rayne managed to connect with her shoulder.

The droughtlord stumbled under the force of the kick, giving Rayne the instant she needed to launch herself fully at her second adversary. She beat aside his moderately efforts and forced his lead arm up across his body.

Behind her, the droughtlord had recovered and was moving in. Rayne stabbed the man under the armpit and retracted. The grunt barely left his lips as she slipped her arm under his and pivoted her body. She pulled down with her hip and arm, and spilled the man over her shoulder, forcing the droughtlord back.

As soon as he hit the floor, Rayne already had a dagger in his throat, retracted, and was on the move. She threw herself at the droughtlord. No holding back, no measuring her opponent. The woman had use of the essences, so Rayne couldn't afford to give her a chance to summon them.

The droughtlord fought with more skill than the man Rayne had just eliminated, but she could hold the assassin for only so long. The look in the other woman's eyes told Rayne that she knew it, too. She kept her movements fast and smooth, but remained alert. If this were a normal adversary, the realization that they were about to die typically hastened their demise, as their movements became desperate and sloppy. But this was an essence wielder.

Rayne's caution saved her life. The droughtlord's black eyes changed color again. Though not as skilled as a magus, Rayne had studied the essences and gained enough proficiency to augment her own abilities. She knew that when she summoned the power with her corlite beads, they glowed the color of the essence used. In the same manner, if a wielder used an essence bodily, their eyes glowed that color. Magi called it the *arah*.

The *arah* in the droughtlord's eyes glowed red. Rayne had been waiting for just that moment. With reflexes honed from a lifetime of training, she acted the instant she saw the change. She called upon *air* through her corlite beads as she leaped backwards. Her beads barely flashed silver. Rayne used only a quick flash of the power, a burst of air to assist her backwards jump and not send her gliding too far away.

The burst of wind carried her but several feet farther up and away than she could naturally jump, but it was enough. A sudden globe of fire appeared around the droughtlord and expanded in a mini explosion.

The flames obscured the woman from view, but it didn't matter. As soon as she'd leapt backwards, Rayne had launched one of her daggers at the droughtlord. Trusting in her aim and timing, Rayne charged back toward her enemy as soon as her feet touched the ground.

She heard a choking sound as she charged toward the flames. The fire died away just as she reached the droughtlord, grasping at the dagger in her throat. Rayne stole a quick glance toward Cravel, then at Simion. The former stood with his back pressed to the corner while the khamra agent easily took his would-be murderers apart.

The second agent had helped Simion dispatch the other droughtlord, and the two sprinted toward the second khamra agent, wisps of smoke rising from their singed clothes.

Rayne took it all in with the blink of an eye as she reached her dying adversary. The woman raised a bloody hand in a feeble attempt to ward her off. Rayne reached right past the clutching hands, and rammed the butt of her hand into the hilt of the dagger. She yanked the blade free as the droughtlord fell backwards, chocking on her own blood.

Rayne drove her dagger into the woman's midsection before she hit the ground, cut across her abdomen, and kept moving. Simion and the khamra agent had fallen upon the remaining assailants by then and were turning the tide. Rayne came up behind one of the taller men and dropped into a slide between his legs. She sliced his inner thigh as she passed then hopped to her feet.

Another enemy noticed her while the man she'd cut clasped at the grievous wound in his thigh. Rayne leaped straight up and turned her body. In one move, she kicked backwards while stabbing her dagger forward. Her foot connected with the top of the bleeding man's head, while she drove her dagger into the eye of the enemy in front.

Both men dropped, one dead, one soon to be. In a few moments, every attacker lay dead. For a few heartbeats, everyone stood where they were. Rayne looked from the khamra agents to the servant, to Cravel. Simion looked at her, then the other khamra before he seemed to remember who he'd been defending.

The khamra agents paid no mind to the man rushing to the prime minister's side. The three statuesque agents remained in their silent standoff until the male khamra agent finally broke eye contact. He started toward the assailant Rayne had left on the ground, still clutching at his rapidly bleeding leg. He produced a knife and quickened his step.

"We need to question him," Rayne said.

Without looking back, he pointed toward the downed droughtlord he and Simion had fought. "She lives." He slit the struggling man's throat and wiped the blade clean on his victim's shirt.

The female khamra started toward the droughtlord, Rayne falling in step. She moved aside as the other assassin slapped the unconscious woman across the face. The droughtlord grunted and the assassin slapped her twice more until she spat several curses and finally opened her eyes.

The khamra assassin held one of her batons sideways over the droughtlord's face. "Who sent you?" The other woman narrowed her eyes but said nothing. With a twitch of her arm, the assassin rapped the woman across the bridge of the nose. The strike had been just high enough and light enough not to break the woman's nose. Rayne understood why. It would be more difficult to talk with a broken nose.

"This will slowly become more painful," the khamra agent said. Her voice was as even and emotionless as a blade slowly piercing a target.

"As if you won't kill me the instant I tell you," the woman rasped. "Do your worst—"

The agent rapped her baton across the woman's nose again. This time, it erupted in a spray of blood down her face. Next, she smacked the woman in the left eye, then the right. "Do you know who we are?"

"Gurgh." The droughtlord coughed blood, her eyes beginning to swell. "Nrgh, no."

"If you did, you would have already told me what I want to

know. If you wish to continue with the option of pain, you will endure it in blindness."

The droughtlord's eyes had swollen shut by now, but she still said nothing. The agent looked to her partner. "Cover her mouth."

The male assassin knelt beside the droughtlord, whose breathing grew rapid, now. He tore a piece of fabric from the woman's coat, balled it up, and pressed it over her mouth.

Rayne closed herself off to the woman's suffering as the khamra agents inflicted gradual pain on the droughtlord. To the woman's credit, she endured the blunt force trauma to her body without giving up a thing. Of course, she screamed into the fabric when the khamra agent broke her left shin, then her right. She screamed again when the agent inflicted terrible damage to her joints.

"Impressive," the agent said. She looked up to her partner. "We'll get nothing from this one. Just saw off her head and be done with it. We'll discard the corpse out of the city limits."

"You're not going to do that in here, are you?" Rayne heard Cravel ask. Having finally recovered from the shock, he tentatively approached the trio, his formidable master servant at his side. "The cleanup will be terrible."

The male assassin had already placed a blade to the droughtlord's neck. The female assassin held up a hand. "Of course, Prime Minister." She nodded to her partner. "We'll dispose of the carcass outside the city limits, or just tie her down and let the scavengers do their work."

Simion approached Rayne while the other agents tied the droughtlord's wrists and ankles together and lifted her up to leave. The master servant had hard eyes, like he'd seen more than any normal house servant could in a hundred lifetimes. He offered his hand, and Rayne took it in hers. "Thank you for seeing that the prime minister walks the right path."

Rayne looked into his eyes with her own unblinking stare. She nodded, then released his hand and turned away. She followed the other agents out the door and into the empty hallways.

As they passed through the mansion, Rayne saw the answer to Cravel's question about his house guards. They were dead.

The assassins went out the front door uncontested. Rayne followed the two agents down the side streets where she recognized the path back to the hidden lair of the Carlayn branch of the khamra.

After some time walking in silence, the female assassin called a halt. "This is where we part ways, Journeyer," she said, using the khamra term for an agent with no home base.

"A quick word?" Rayne asked, indicating the battered woman hanging over the male assassin's shoulder.

The other woman nodded and Rayne grabbed the droughtlord's hair and lifted up her head. She spoke softly into her ear. "Your masters are dead, and you're going to die. Would your masters weep for you? Would they sing your praise for taking your secret to the grave?"

No answer. Rayne tried a different angle. "How powerful are your masters when two droughtlords have fallen to us?"

This time, the woman's face twitched and she forced open one of her swollen eyes. She opened her mouth and croaked in barely a whisper, "you … will know …"

Rayne mulled that over as the male assassin started walking again. The female agent moved in front of Rayne and the two locked gazes for several moments. "Your presence here is noted, as are your efforts today."

The assassin turned on her heel and walked after her partner. Rayne watched her go. That had been a clear warning, and one that left her with questions as potent as the attack she'd helped to thwart.

"A SEAT, SIR?"

Cravel nearly jumped out of his skin at the sound of Simion's voice. He looked down at the chair, then back at his bodyguard. "Oh, yes. I supposed I could use a sit down. Thank you, Simion."

"Of course, sir," Simion replied.

Prime Minster Cravel had to hold onto the arms of the chair to lower himself onto the plush cushions. His legs barely supported him while he'd been standing and gave out as he bent to sit down.

Simion ducked out the door and ordered another of the house staff to alert the city guard, then another still to bring some hot cider. He came back and knelt in front of Cravel. "Have you any idea who those people were that attacked you, sir?"

Cravel shook his head. He had no enemies that he was aware of. Many believed him to be a cravenly leader, but not a threat. If anything, most of his political opponents didn't take him seriously enough and let their guard down. He thought back to the two women and how "off" they'd seemed. He glanced across the room at the corpse of one of them and felt a fresh stab of fear in his stomach. He silently chastised himself. Did he expect the woman to rise from the dead and attack again?

He nearly jumped out of his skin again at a gentle knock on the door. Simion answered the knock, exchanged a few words with the servant, then returned with a pitcher and a steaming mug of cider.

"Thank you, Simion," Cravel said, accepting the mug.

"The warmth will do well to still your nerves, sir."

"I mean, *thank* you, my friend," Cravel repeated.

Simion bowed. "Of course, sir. So long as I can lift a single finger, it will be in your protection."

Cravel creased his lips into a smile and gave Simion a pat on the arm. He'd hired Simion over ten years ago as his bodyguard disguised as personal servant. That relationship had grown into friendship a long time ago. "Thank goodness for those two women and that man. We might both be dead, otherwise."

To Cravel's surprise, Simion's expression went chillingly sober; more than usual. "You've had a unique experience, sir."

Cravel's heart pounded in his chest, now. "How so, old friend?"

The master servant took a large cloth napkin off the dining table and used his hands and teeth to tie it around his forearm. Once he finished, he pulled up a chair beside Cravel and sat. Despite the fact that Cravel had never required him to do so, Simion had always asked permission to sit when in his presence. That the master servant had done so without asking told Cravel just how exhausted the man was.

"You, sir," Simion answered, "are one of the few who have received a visit from the khamra and remain among the living."

SELVETAR

Selvetar couldn't remember the last time he'd experienced anxiety about anything. Making his way through the halls of the magi fortress, however, he'd found himself reacquainted with the feeling.

An interesting visitor. Those were the words the aspirant had been given by Vladrick to relay to Selvetar. Those words, and that Selvetar was to cease whatever he was doing and come at once.

The first magus narrowed his eyes. Under normal circumstances he might have taken his time, for despite Vladrick's rank as magi master, Selvetar "hopped-to" for no one. Given his suspicion that they had an unwelcome guest in the Tower of Magi, and this recent "interesting visitor", Selvetar found himself sweeping down the halls with haste.

Aspirant, acolyte, and magi alike gave him a wide berth. Perhaps Selvetar's face reflected his mood, but he didn't care. If this Demerog droughtlord had indeed infiltrated the fortress, things were about to become a lot more interesting.

As soon as the door attendant spotted Selvetar rounding the corner to the hallway, he knocked, waited, then went inside. He'd stepped back out by the time Selvetar reached the door and gave a respectful bow as he opened it.

Selvetar responded with a nod as he passed. The moment he stepped into the magi master's private meeting room, Selvetar felt energy buzzing in the air. The two men sitting opposite each other looked in his direction and stood.

As usual, the powerful magi leader stood resplendent in his white robes, the color representing the unity of all four sects of the Order of Magi. Of like color, his long hair fell well below his shoulders and blended with his robes. The sides of his icy blue eyes creased when he smiled. "First Magus."

Selvetar offered a bow to his superior. "Magi Master."

Vladrick indicated the visitor with an open hand. "I give you Jyrin Maslyn. We've only had a short time to speak before your arrival, so I've not had the chance to inquire about his lack of sect robes."

Selvetar offered a polite nod to the visitor and they sat. As Vladrick went into introductions and Jyrin caught Selvetar up on the conversation, the first magus studied the man. Gray hair, green eyes, smile creases. He sat with his hands folded in his lap, erect posture and softly-spoken. His hand gestures were subtle, rather than sharp; an open hand rather than a pointing finger. Even his scent was decidedly neutral yet not so, like a perfume covering up another odor.

Everything about Jyrin's outward appearance indicated a kind and gentle soul, but something was off about him. Selvetar thought perhaps it was his recent studies about Demerog that had him on edge, but he dismissed the notion. Being able to read people was a reliable skill he'd honed over many years. He wasn't about to start doubting it now.

"… and as to my robes," Jyrin continued. "Well, I've not lived among magi in a very long time, and as such, have no sect of allegiance."

"Easy enough to find," Vladrick replied. "As I'm sure you well know."

Jyrin inclined his head. "I try to be well-rounded."

"An ability shared by few," Vladrick persisted. "Such balance of the essences is akin to being ambidextrous, Jyrin. Do you imply to being such?"

"Merely my aspirations of being such," Jyrin parried. "My pursuit for perfect balance with the essences is ongoing."

The magi master leaned back in his chair and studied the man. "An admirable life goal. And while I would like to further learn of your origins, I must instead ask about the purpose of a man claiming to be a magus without a sect, showing up at our door. What brings you here, Jyrin Mylan?"

Jyrin spread his hands. "I have traveled across Marai and beyond its borders. I've a love for learning of different places and peoples." He made an effort at an embarrassed grin that Selvetar didn't buy for an instant. "Though I hesitate to admit that I've never once visited the seat of magi power. I wished to rectify that."

The three men sat through a few moments of silence. Vladrick rubbed his chin while watching at the man. Jyrin met his gaze unflinchingly. Selvetar continued his silent observation of the visitor above his steepled fingers.

"And now that you've arrived," Vladrick finally said. "What is your impression of the seat of magi power?"

"I stood in awe of this fortress the moment it came into view," Jyrin said. "There is no structure like it in the world. At least, not that I've seen. Altarra itself is an impressive city made more so by the Tower of Magi."

Vladrick leaned forward in his seat. "Jyrin Mylan. I do not make it a practice of entertaining every magi visiting Altarra or the Tower of Magi. I would struggle to get anything done. So tell me, why have I made this exception for you?"

"I bring knowledge and experiences from distant lands," Jyrin replied. "Including those west of our borders. I have skills with the essences that might be a boon to the Order. The Khatala are far more dangerous than Marai realizes. The situation could escalate to a calamitous result much faster than most realize."

"You've shot a bit west of the mark," Vladrick said. "The king of Marai resides in Castle Jietar, east of here."

Jyrin nodded. "Yet a great source of his collected wisdom resides in the Tower of Magi, and sits before me."

For the first time since Amoura Xanna had disappeared, Selvetar found himself wishing his student were here. Frosty and recalcitrant though she may be, Amoura had a way of feeling things that he'd not seen in any other magus, himself included. Almost as if she could feel when someone was summoning or utilizing essence. Of course, if this man were using the power, even subtly, the telltale *arah* would have lit his eyes, even if only for an instant.

Selvetar considered all that as the two men continued their exchange. Was it possible to hide one's *arah*? That seemed unlikely, considering the nature of the power and how it was wielded. None of the ancient texts spoke of such a thing, but that wasn't much to go on. Magi knowledge of the immortals spoke of abilities present-day essence wielders could only dream of.

This man was off. Selvetar had no doubts about that. Whether or not it was Demerog who sat in their midst, he could only guess. But the timing of this mysterious guest's arrival and Selvetar's recent discovery about the droughtlord seemed too suspicious to ignore.

"What say you, First Magus?" Vladrick asked, interrupting his musings.

Selvetar didn't move a muscle, only cut his eyes toward the question. He looked back at Jyrin, who smiled at him, then lowered his steepled fingers. "I struggle to find a flaw in welcoming a knowledgeable and powerful ally. Though both attributes are subjective in nature. Still, I find you interesting, Jyrin Mylan of Nowhere."

Jyrin inclined his head again. "I only hope my claims meet the expectations I may have created."

"Indeed," Selvetar replied. "Especially considering such dark times to come. One might even say that with such happenings in the world, we're headed toward a blight."

Vladrick arched an eyebrow at that, while Jyrin's left eye twitched. "May I inquire of your meaning of that, First Magus?" the latter asked.

The moment between the question and awaited answer stretched for eternity. No stranger to the feeling, Selvetar could sit in the thickening tension indefinitely. He finally responded with his signature cutting smile. "Forgive my dramatization. The war has everyone on edge, and it sometimes leads me to sarcasm."

The palpable tension faded with Jyrin's responding chuckle. "Of course. We all cope with stress in our own way, don't we?"

"Indeed," Selvetar said.

Vladrick pursed his lips as he considered the visitor. "I admit you have my interest, Jyrin. You've come to us with claims of obscure knowledge of the essences, and knowledge gained through worldly travels and experiences. Whether this gains you a place in the Tower of Magi remains to be seen, but for now, be welcome."

Jyrin smiled as he inclined his head. "My thanks, Magi Master Vladrick. I could ask for no more. After so many years of wandering, I find it refreshing to be among those like myself."

"Let us speak again soon," Vladrick said. He stood, and Selvetar and Jyrin rose with him. "I've much to do with this day yet, so I bid you a pleasant day. Enjoy your stay with us. I'm sure First Magus Selvetar will answer any questions you may have."

Selvetar's eyebrow twitched in irritation. "Of course."

Vladrick turned away and strode toward his desk, a clear indication the discussion was at its end.

Jyrin followed Selvetar to the door and into the hallway. The first magus never broke stride, but continued on his way, to where, he wasn't yet certain.

"An amazing piece of architecture, this place," Jyrin said. He leaned back to marvel at the carved walls and columns towering overhead, and the stained-glass windows filtering sunlight into the shapes of the artwork they depicted.

A group of gray-robed acolytes hovered unsteadily overhead between two instructors as they struggled to control *air* while also manipulating *water,* using its physical namesake to clean the glass. "An efficient way to teach," Jyrin said.

Selvetar followed the visitor's gaze to the ceiling high above, where the students cleaned under the watchful eyes of the instructors. "The smarter acolytes appreciate this practice. The cleaning and maintaining of the Tower of Magi is a chore shared by all, whether on one's free time or during instruction."

"How many instructors are there?" Jyrin asked.

Selvetar noted a subtle shift in the man's tone. His eyes moved here and there, taking everything in, studying. "Have you an interest in joining their ranks?"

Jyrin's gaze flicked over to the first magus, and he responded with his disarming smile. "I'm not sure I would so highly regard myself as able to walk in and begin instructing students, First Magus."

"Yet you've already spoken of your possession of knowledge and techniques little known by the essence-wielder population at large."

"Knowledge and ability hardly denote teaching ability," Jyrin countered.

Selvetar conceded that truth with a nod and pointed ahead to the right. "You will find the dining halls there." A few moments further down the hall, Selvetar stopped and faced the other man. "This is where we part ways for now, Jyrin Mylan. Should you wish, seek out a resident magus to assist you in acclimating to your new surroundings. You may find this fortress rather large."

Jyrin inclined his head. "My thanks, First Magus. Though I confess my hopes to have enjoyed a tour with the second in command of this mighty seat of magi power, you are no doubt too busy and too important to serve as tourguide."

Selvetar refrained from letting his face tighten at the mention of his status. While the man obviously had meant it as a show of respect, as any other in the fortress would, it served as a prodding reminder that Selvetar sat below a man he did not see as the leader the order needed.

He turned down the opposite hallway of Jyrin, blue and silver robes swishing behind him. "Be welcome in the Tower of Magi, Jyrin of Nowhere."

"I hope to see you again very soon, First Magus Selvetar," came the distant reply.

Selvetar turned the corner and made straight for his office. He hadn't realized just how quickly he walked until the third acolyte practically dove aside and plastered himself against the wall to be out of the way. The more he thought about it, the more Selvetar disliked this new development. He couldn't remember the last time something had made him this uneasy. The mere presence of the man just felt … wrong.

He reached the fork in the hallway and started down the corridor leading to his office. A few steps in, he stopped and went back to the left hallway. Aspirants and acolytes moved up and down the path, books in hand or wrapped in arms as they conversed about the day's lessons or gossiped about whatever students gossiped about.

Everyone parted ways and stepped against the wall when Selvetar came near. Even those whose backs were to him seemed to feel his presence and move aside. The first magus spared them no thought, other than to wonder how well these fresh pupils would fair against the powerful foe roaming in their midst.

He reached a door with an eye-level insignia of a flame. He rapped twice and started to open the door, as was his right. He stopped halfway reaching for the handle, and instead tucked his hands in his sleeves.

After a few moments, the door opened and a curiously frowning Red filled the doorway. "If you're knocking, you're not a Red. Why are you here?" The boy stood easily head and shoulders above Selvetar. The hardness in his face and jaw smoothed out when he recognized the visitor. The fierceness in his blue eyes flickered out as he shrank in on himself and stepped aside. "Oh, I … First Magus." He bowed several times as he opened the door wider. "My deepest apologies, First Magus. I didn't know it was you. Of course, you needn't have knocked—"

"Of course I didn't," Selvetar cut in. "But we must observe the proper courteousness, shouldn't we?"

The red magus bowed again. "Of course, First Ma—"

"Where is Agra Red?" Selvetar glanced around at the other five standing Magi, couch, chairs, and textbooks all abandoned upon his entrance.

"I, er, I can only guess, First Magus," the boy said.

"And, that guess would be…" Selvetar noted that everything in the room seemed to favor the color red. The drapes, the furniture, red apples in a red bowl on a little round table by the window. It reminded him of his time as a student, many years ago, and how he'd wondered why the more senior magi were rarely found in the lounge. The easiest way to spot a new magus was the amount of color they wore in alignment with their sect. Red, Blue, Silver, or Brown. Monochromatic. Tacky.

"The sparring chamber," came a reply from behind. "Advanced Thermal Projection ended over an hour ago, First Magus. He sometimes goes to the sparring chamber to apply the day's lessons."

Selvetar responded with a downturned smile and nodded. "As every devoted pupil should." The downcast eyes of half the room indicated who the strewn textbooks *didn't* belong to.

"Should I retrieve him for you, First Magus?" the boy asked.

Selvetar started to reply in the affirmative, then thought better of it. "I will go to him." He turned on his heel and swept out the door. The expressions he left behind surely turned to gossip the moment the door closed. Children.

He sped through the halls once more, annoyed that he felt compelled to rush, yet unable keep from doing so. His ego held far less sway than the coming Ruination.

Selvetar swallowed at the realization he'd just accepted that it was indeed the Ruination upon the world. He shoved the thoughts aside before they could take root, but he would have to deal with them later. So be it.

He reached what the students called the sparring chamber, though no melee ensued behind the walls. This time, he didn't bother to knock, but quietly slipped inside.

The circular training room held six figures, and in the middle of the room, a single pinprick of red light flared. Agra raised his hand with the finger upon which the glowing essence ring sat. Flames appeared in the air in front of him and funneled toward his opponent.

The boy across from him grasped *fire* as well, his own essence ring glowing in with the telltale red *arah*. He drew his hand back and bellowed as he thrust it forward. A cone of flame somewhat smaller than Agra's streamed out. A splash of sparks lit the room as the two flaming funnels met.

Selvetar gave a tiny nod of appreciation. Resplendent in his dark red robes contrasting starkly with his pale complexion, Agra cut a fairly intimidating image. While his dramatic opponent exerted so much energy with swinging and thrusting gestures, Agra stood tall, staring the other boy down as he gradually overpowered him.

Of course, Agra also suffered from a degree of dramatics. Selvetar grinned at the forward-leaning stance, fingers curled like claws, and the tooth-bearing snarl underneath the narrowed, glaring eyes. The other boy was clearly no match for Agra, yet the more experienced magus enjoyed making a show of his superiority in front of their two watching peers.

Agra's opponent squared his sideways stance and balled his ring hand into a fist. "Yeeeaaaah!" He thrust his fist out. Shards of fire formed in the air and sped toward Agra.

To Selvetar's amusement, and disappointment, Agra hadn't expected such a creative twist. He threw himself aside and rolled gracelessly out of the way. With even less grace, he scrambled to his feet, slid a hand through his hair, and scowled.

Agra snarled and threw his arms out at his sides while his suddenly—foolishly—confident opponent stalked toward him. The other four young magi noted Selvetar's approach, and he held up a hand to indicate they remain silent.

A thin line of flame appeared in front of Agra and grew vertically until it became a wall. Agra smirked as he made the wall wider while pushed it toward his opponent. The boy on the other side braced himself as his ring flared blue. He yelled in defiance as he produced a wall of water. Agra laughed when the walls collided and his opponent's simply sizzled into steam.

The younger magus's eyes widened in panic. He couldn't possibly run to either side fast enough before the fire reached him.

Selvetar never broke stride as his ring flared silver. Agra's wall of flame rapidly shrank and died. The last sparks faded away less than a few feet from the crouched boy, who had his arm up protectively over his head.

So engrossed in his "sparring" match, Agra hadn't noticed Selvetar's presence. "I don't know how you did that, but let's see how much luck you've got left." Arms still out at his sides, Agra bent as though flexing his nonexistent muscles. He produced a bigger wall of flame but before he could send it at his opponent, another wall of flame several times taller and thicker appeared in front of his own.

Agra cried out and fell back as the new wall expanded to engulf his own and continued to grow. He tried to retreat, but a wall of ice appeared at his back. Agra skittered away until his back hit the ice wall. His smug superiority turned to terror as he could do nothing but watch the fire approach to consume him.

"Power is as intoxicating as it is sobering," Selvetar said as the fire wall disintegrated and the wall of ice evaporated.

Agra gasped at the sound of Selvetar's voice and spun to face him, mouth agape.

"The might that one feels in defeating another," Selvetar continued, "is equaled by the diminishment of the defeated." He gestured to the beaten boy across the room. By now, he and the other magi—Agra included—had turned to bow to him. "How powerful you must have felt, Agra, when dominating your foe. How did you feel when dominated by but a flake of my use of the power?"

He stopped in front of the humbled boy and stared at him. Agra slumped and cast his gaze at his feet. "Not powerful, First Magus," he mumbled in a tiny voice.

Selvetar waited until the arrogant boy finally lifted his gaze. "The way of power is a path lined with mirrors." He turned away. "Come." He exited the training room, Agra in tow.

"Er, First Magus?" Agra ventured. "I am honored by your presence and your lesson, but may I ask the purpose of your visit? You have a task for me?"

"In time, Agra." Selvetar said no more and fortunately the boy knew better than to press the issue.

When they reached his office, Selvetar entered and channeled *fire* to light the wall candles. He gestured to one of the cushioned seats near the hearth and took the one opposite Agra. He used *fire* to light the fresh logs, and sat for a while, fingers steepled, the only sound being that of the crackling flames. Agra fidgeted, focusing on anything to avoid meeting the first magus's intense gaze.

"We have a visitor," Selvetar said, eliciting a sigh of relief from Agra. "His name is Jyrin Maslyn, and he proclaims to be a powerful and knowledgeable magus who has traveled the world, though he claims no sect. Find him and express your interest in learning from him."

Agra bowed in his seat. "Yes, First Magus."

"Do not speak of me," Selvetar continued. "Do not speak of knowing me, nor confirm it if he asks. Report back to me after each visit with him, but he is not to know of this. You are to use the utmost discretion, Agra. This is important."

Agra's mouth opened wider and wider with every word until he realized it and snapped it shut with a click of his teeth. Selvetar waited patiently while the boy struggled to find words. "I … this sounds serious, First Magus. What's happening?"

If it had been Amoura who'd been sitting across from him, he'd have not thought twice about divulging the situation in its entirety. The young woman disliked him, which concerned Selvetar not at all. But she was honest, brave, and intelligent, qualities that were weak in the magus sitting before him. But the one quality Agra had that Amoura lacked, was loyalty to Selvetar. Loyalty, and a willingness to do whatever it took to prove he was worthy of the position Amoura once held.

"Concern yourself with the task I've assigned you. You sit here, now, because I'm confident you'll not fail me."

Agra dipped into a bow so low his chest pressed against his lap. "Of course! Of course, First Magus. As always, you can depend on me for anything. I will find this man and find out everything I can about him. There's no one better for this job, First Magus."

Selvetar responded with a nod and said no more.

Agra rightly took the gesture as his dismissal. He stood and bowed. "I will report to you tomorrow, First Magus." He straightened and left Selvetar with his thoughts.

In the flickering light of the fireplace and surrounding candles, Selvetar recalled the conversation with Jyrin. The man wasn't what he projected himself to be, that much was obvious. The real question lay in his real identity. Was he truly Demerog, or another droughtlord? Perhaps an underlord, or a droughtlord hopeful? Or, was all of his research making Selvetar a touch paranoid? Perhaps this Jyrin was an ambition essence wielder looking to enter the ranks of the Order.

Deep down, Selvetar knew the latter scenario unlikely. He needed to know more, and unfortunately Agra was his best option. He needed to find a replacement for Amoura. He needed to step up his ambitions to leave Altarra and start his own, more focused faction of magi. The traditional method of teaching that the Order employed was simply too slow and riddled with fluff. Considering what Selvetar was convinced was coming, now more than ever existed the need to develop more focused, battle-ready magi.

Amoura would have been an excellent example for his future organization to follow. But she was gone; likely thrown into some distant place by the very man he had just sent Agra to investigate.

The smell of burning wood found his nostrils, complimenting the warmth of the fire. Selvetar allowed the sensations to wrap about him like a blanket while he fell deeper into his thoughts. The Ruination was coming and he had to assume the Tower of Magi was compromised.

Discretion was quickly becoming a luxury Selvetar could ill afford. He'd have to be more aggressive in searching out magi to join him, which would almost certainly make an enemy out of Vladrick. But Selvetar knew the man. He'd scoff at the notion of the coming Ruination.

Selvetar used *air* to suck its namesake out of the flames, as he did with Agra's wall of fire. For a long time, he sat bathed in darkness, fingers steepled in front of his face.

NANDI

The balmy late spring day might have been enjoyable if not for the company. Nandi cut her eyes left and right at her captors. Myleshia and Laryn sat on the porch on either side of her, watching the girls tending the garden at the back of the house.

No matter how much she tried, Nandi couldn't avoid the occasional glare thrown her way by one of her toiling peers. Every other girl had started the day with a long run around the village with no breakfast. Now they labored in the garden before being allowed lunch. Another girl glared across the rows of cabbage at her. Nandi hadn't much spoken to the girl, but she thought her name might be Clairese.

Nandi kept her sigh inside her mind. She wouldn't give these women the satisfaction of seeing her squirm under the animosity of the other girls who worked and sweated in the fields while she'd had a hearty breakfast and sat in the shade. She tried not to think of that cold, thick, and chewy porridge, lest she grow nauseous and bring it back up onto the patio floor. It might have been disgusting and hard to swallow, but it was food.

She felt her strength returning even as she sat between these sour women. How could they do such a thing to her and these other girls? They themselves weren't laborwives, but surely they knew what that meant. If Nandi knew, they had to.

Questions to ponder after she put many miles between herself and this terrible place. *Focus, Nandi.*

"Enjoying your break?" Myleshia asked.

"No, House Mistress."

"Why not?" she asked, as if she didn't already know. Nandi shrugged. "Don't lie to me, girl," Myleshia pressed. "You're comfortable here on the patio. Why wouldn't you enjoy your break?"

Nandi rolled her eyes, which earned her a smack on the thigh with Laryn's switch. "Mind your expressions, child. However you've been raised, you *will* learn proper manners."

Nandi swore that if this woman questioned her parentage one more time, she'd make her pay for it.

"I don't think she much liked that," Myleshia said to her subordinate. "Look at that anger."

Nandi realized her arms and fists were so tense they were shaking. She relaxed.

"Is the mention of your past life painful, Tyshia?" Myleshia asked. "Is that why you react so angrily when it is mentioned?"

"I don't like you mentioning it because it feels like you're mocking me." Nandi felt her discretion slipping. She knew they were prodding her, but she was starting to care less and less by the moment. Probably what they wanted. She reached for the essences and felt them drawn to her call. Good.

"No one is mocking you, child," Laryn snapped. That one was the harshest of the three with her words, but Myleshia served out the worst punishments. "You are here to learn how to be a proper lady. That mouth and ruggedness of yours must be smoothed out if you're to be a proper lady and a proper wife one day."

Nandi felt fire shoot from her chest straight into her head. Her whole body went hot. She took a long deep breath and pushed it out. Soon. Her opportunity would come soon enough. She'd endure these women today, and tonight she'd gather Ailith and any of the other girls who wanted out of this hole, and they'd escape into the night with Sama.

SMACK!

Nandi hopped out of her seat when the switch struck her thigh, much harder this time. Despite the throbbing pain, she spun on her heels and stared right into the assistant house mistress's eyes. Laryn's mouth slowly opened as she took in Nandi's baleful glare. She slowly rose out of her chair to tower over Nandi, switch clenched in her right fist.

Nandi craned her head back to look up at her. If only the woman knew how much effort she exerted into not losing control of herself at that moment.

"You have a lot of fire, girl," she heard Myleshia say from above her shoulder.

Nandi turned to see the other woman was standing as well. She turned her back to the fields so that both women were in view. *Not now. Can't do this now.* The situation was slipping out of her control, if she ever had the situation in control to begin with. Obviously these women had been in the business of training slave wives for years, so no behavior Nandi exhibited could be new to them.

"Your attitude will be your undoing, little girl," Myleshia continued. "You will not disgrace the House of Valraga with such behavior."

"That's okay. If I'm not up to your standards, cast me out into the wild where you found me and I'll be along."

"You will not be leaving this place, girl," Laryn stated while Myleshia scrutinized her. "This is your home, Tyshia, and you will learn your place until the time comes—"

"To sell me off as a slave wife?" Nandi cut in and instantly regretted it.

"What did you say?" Laryn asked in a quiet voice. Her eyes flicked past Nandi in the direction of the field.

Nandi looked over her shoulder to see a handful of the girls watching, their work forgotten. She turned back just in time to see Myleshia's hand before it struck the side of her face.

Before she registered what had happened, Nandi found herself on the floor of the patio, trying to ignore the stars dancing in her vision. She felt *fire* practically begging for her call. She took several deep breaths and pushed it away. She wanted to be free, not to burn anyone. Laryn was right about one thing; Nandi did need to reign in her temper or something bad would happen. She could easily see herself burning both these women and the house into cinders, and the thought horrified her.

Laryn misunderstood her expression and nodded in approval at Myleshia. The house mistress, however, didn't look at Laryn. She continued to stare at Nandi as if she were a puzzle whose solution eluded her.

"Get up, Tyshia," Myleshia ordered. When Nandi complied, she continued to study her. "You don't fear us at all, do you?"

Nandi wasn't sure how to answer that question. The honest answer was no, she didn't. Even without the essences, she didn't fear these women or their punishments. Not after all she'd been through in the months leading to her arrival here. She might have laughed at the question if she hadn't been so angry.

"That was a question, Tysha." Nandi looked up from the ground to see Laryn staring at her. "The headmistress just asked you a question. Do you require the urging of my switch to answer?" The switch made a whisking sound in the air when she snapped it.

"I'd really just like to be released and left alone," Nandi said. "I was fine before those men kidnapped me."

"Nonsense, child," Laryn snapped. "You were fending for yourself in the dangerous wild. How much longer ..." she trailed off at Myleshia's upraised hand.

"You truly believe you'd be better off out there, don't you?" Her blonde locks spilled behind her head when she tilted it to study Nandi. "You would actually go back out into those dangerous woods if we let you. Do you know how many predators live out there?" She pointed in the direction of the wooded lands, and blessed freedom.

"I've had many opportunities to meet a lot of predators," Nandi said.

"And yet you'd rather the possibility of meeting more of them?" Myleshia asked.

"If it's a choice between them and …" Nandi bit off that last part, but the women's frowns said that she might as well have finished the thought.

"You need time to think yourself over," Myleshia said. "You are possessed of no manners, no gratitude, and set a terrible example for the other girls, many of whom are younger than you. Perhaps a few weeks of work and sleep by yourself will be enough time to contemplate your attitude and reform yourself."

A few weeks! Nandi's mouth fell open.

Laryn opened her mouth and nodded at Myleshia. "Ah, so she doesn't like being alone." She turned her smug expression on Nandi. "Well, perhaps if you behave yourself—"

"I'm not staying here a few more weeks." This was enough. Daylight might not be ideal, but she wasn't going to be put in some solitary confinement where Sama might not be able to find her. It would have to be now. She reached for the essences and smiled when they came to her call.

Laryn chuckled. "Is that so? I didn't realize you were in charge, now." With a flick of her hand, she struck Nandi on the arm with her switch. "Get *in* the house and see Headmistress Jasindi. Now!"

Nandi felt the welt growing on her arm. She delved *fire* and focused it on the switch.

Laryn looked into Nandi's eyes, first with curiosity, then shock when she no doubt saw the red *arah* in her eyes. Her shock had barely turned to horror when she cried out at the suddenly flaming switch in her hand. She dropped it and stepped back. The assistant house mistress stared wide-eyed at the burning switch, then looked at Nandi.

After the many days she'd spent surviving out in the wild, Nandi's instincts had sharpened. She backed away a couple steps to make sure neither woman could slip out of her field of vision. The essences would do her no good if Myleshia knocked her unconscious from behind.

Laryn took another step back. "Wilder," she breathed.

Myleshia had also taken a few steps away. "She's not a wilder. She looks nothing like them.

"She carries no ring, yet she uses the power." Laryn looked at Nandi as if she were a poisonous snake. "One of her parents must be a wilder. Her uncontrollable temper and use of essence proves it."

"Do not mention my parents ever again," Nandi warned.

The two women looked at each other, then back at Nandi. They were going to try to grab her. She delved *air* just as they lunged. Nandi buffeted the women with a powerful gust of wind that hurled them backwards. They crashed into the patio wall and crumpled to the floor.

She heard several gasps of astonishment and turned to see the girls gaping at her. Gardening implements fell from trembling hands that rose to cover open mouths. "She's a wilder," Nandi heard. "She's dangerous," others said. "Uncontrollable. She'll burn us all to a crisp. She'll burn the whole village!"

Nandi hopped down off the porch. "I'm not a wilder, but I can help us all get out of here! We don't have to be sold as slave wives!"

"Don't burn me," one girl cried. Nandi thought her name was Janice. "Please."

"I'm not going to burn anyone. I just want to go—"

"Then leave," another girl said. "Just don't kill us all."

Nandi looked from face to face, searching for an ally. She found none. A groan from behind turned Nandi around to see

Myleshia stirring. She turned back. "Last chance! I don't want to leave any of you but I'm not staying—"

"You think we'd chance leaving with a wilder and being burned alive?" said a girl Nandi didn't know. "I'd rather take my chances with a jarku!"

That hurt, but the prospect of being stuck here dulled the bite of the remark. Nandi sighed in resignation and started to walk away when a shock of red hair came bouncing around a clump of girls. "You better *not* leave without me!"

Nandi's heart leapt when she saw Ailith trotting past several incredulous girls. Behind her, Nandi heard Myleshia climbing to her feet.

"We had a deal, remember?" Ailith said. "I figure our chances are all the better if you can throw essences around like that. Let's get outta here!"

"You are going nowhere!"

Nandi froze. That wasn't Myleshia or Laryn. She turned and looked in the direction of Jasindi's commanding voice. The woman stood in the doorway of the patio glaring down at them. Her green eyes bore into the two girls. Nandi felt a cord of fear tracing down her spine, for on the ring finger of Jasindi's left hand glowed the brown *arah* of her essence ring.

That's a problem. Nandi considered her situation. How powerful was this woman? She would be more experienced than Nandi, but how much power could she wield? If she was powerful, wouldn't she have become a magus?

Jasindi stepped away from the door and knelt to check Laryn, who began to stir. She stood, looked to Myleshia, who glowered at Nandi, then moved to the top of the steps. "A little essence wielder. No fear of punishment, lack of respect, this explains a lot. You're clearly not a wilder, though. That's puzzling."

"All I want is to leave," Nandi said. "I don't want to make trouble for you or anyone else. I'd have been long gone by now if those men hadn't brought me here."

Jasindi laughed. "Oh, no, child. You're going nowhere. Maybe you'll not be a laborwife, but I'm sure the Order of Magi would take an interest in you."

Nandi frowned in disbelief. "Is that all you do? Sell people off as a business? You're no better than the people paying you."

Jasindi's ring flared brown. The ground in front of Nandi erupted, and the blast threw her back in a shower of rock and soil. She curled into a ball to protect her eyes and face. She felt the essences slipping away and grasped desperately for them. This was her only chance.

She sprang to her feet, delved *air*, and sent gust of wind at Jasindi, who drew up a protective wall of rock between herself and the assault. She then leaned around the wall and held her fist up. Her ring glowed brown again, and the ground around Nandi burst into another shower of earthy debris.

Nandi forced herself not to drop and curl into a ball out of reflex. She squinted and held her hand over her brow while focusing on Jasindi. She reminded herself that she was an asset, and so the woman was trying not to kill her.

She delved *fire* and sent a quick spout of flame at Jasindi. "Ah!" The headmistress ducked behind her protective wall, as Nandi had intended. She delved *earth* and blasted the wall apart.

Jasindi cried out in surprise again and covered her face with her arm. Nandi delved *air*, then *water*. She threw the latter's freezing namesake into the woman. The cold water drenched the headmistress and set her shivering. The glow of her essence ring dimmed and began to pulsate.

Nandi realized she'd caused Jasindi to lose her concentration and redoubled her efforts on *air* and *water*. She intensified her freezing assault on the woman, then spotted the other two women trying to approach. She broke off part of her assault on Jasindi and sent another blast of air into Myleshia and Laryn. Once again the women careened into the wall of the patio and spilled to the floor, wet and shivering.

Jasindi's lips were turning blue. Maybe if Nandi could get the woman close enough to unconsciousness—

Someone shouted from behind. "Hey! Get your hands off me you little rat!"

Nandi stole a quick glance over her shoulder to see Nimi, far too close for comfort, struggling to wrench her arm free of Ailith's grasp. The head girl had a rock in her hand; a large rock.

"You weren't going to hit my friend over the head with that, were you?" Ailith asked. She reached up and caught the taller girl's wrist when Nimi tried to bring it down on her head.

"Let … go!" Nimi twisted and pulled, but Ailith held on.

"You really are kind of weak for someone your size," Ailith growled. "Probably because we do all the work out here while you play with your dress all day." She stomped on Nimi's foot and when the girl screamed and bent forward, Ailith laid her low with a right hook punch to the jaw.

All around the garden girls gasped. Nandi didn't have time to watch the rest. She threw her focus back at Jasindi. The head-mistress was trying to climb back to her feet, but her shivering body betrayed her. She clenched her eyes shut and her essence ring tried dimly glowed to life again. She pushed a shaking fist toward Nandi.

The ground rippled away from Jasindi in a direct line toward Nandi. She threw herself aside and kept rolling. When she finally stopped, Nandi looked at the upturned scar of earth that ended a little past where she'd stood. Not once had Jasindi fought with the other three essences. Why? That ring gave her access to all four parts of the power, not just one.

The four girls closest to Nandi scampered away; all except one. Ingris stood as if her feet were fixed to the ground. She stared at Nandi with an unreadable expression and whispered something.

"What?" Nandi whispered loudly. She leaned forward. "What?"

Ingris's eyes darted left and right, and she whispered again. "Be*hind* you!"

Nandi's eyes went wide. She spun around just in time to see Jasindi up to one knee, focusing directly at Nandi while rubbing her hands over her arms to warm them. Her pulsating ring glowed brown.

Nandi delved *air* and *water* again, and sent another arctic blast of air into the headmistress.

Jasindi lifted her fist and her ring weakly glowed red. A flickering wall of flame appeared between her and Nandi. The wall started to expand, but then it wavered before growing solid again.

She's stronger with earth, Nandi realized. *And she's weak.* Nandi walked toward the kneeling, shivering headmistress, all the while assaulting her flimsy wall of fire. She thought about her kidnapping and subsequent captivity in this village. She remembered Nimi's condescending speeches, the punishments, the stinging swat of the switch. She thought about how these women had taken her freedom away and decided her life would be what they wanted.

Nandi used it all, every memory. She drew more essence and intensified her freezing assault. Ice crystals formed on Jasindi's hair. Myleshia and Laryn had curled into shivering balls as well, and Nandi realized she'd expanded her offense to include them. Good.

She reached the patio and ascended the steps. Her feeble fire barrier long defeated, Jasindi could do no more than remain on her knees, shivering with her arms wrapped around her torso. Her skin had taken on a blue shade, and her teeth chattered so loudly Nandi thought they might break.

Nandi lessened her assault as she stepped around the back of the trembling woman. Her essence ring had gone dormant. *You took my freedom from me. I'll take my payment.* She grabbed Jasindi's wrist and pulled at the ring. The woman groaned and tried to pull away. Nandi felt a sliver of the woman's strength returning.

Shen had to get that ring off. She'd beaten Jasindi with the element of surprise, but wasn't about to try her luck.

She clasped the essence ring between her fingers, closed her eyes, and reached inside the ring. She found the primal sentience that she somehow knew was present in all things, whether rock or tree or blade of grass. She touched that sentience and grew familiar with it. She then delved *air* and sucked a tiny bit of it from Jasindi's lungs.

The headmistress's eyes bulged so wide they looked like they would fall from their sockets. She unwrapped her arms from her body and began clasping at her throat. Preoccupied with trying to breathe, Jasindi didn't notice that Nandi was still holding her essence ring between her fingers.

It slipped right off and Nandi stepped away and slipped it onto her finger. The ring was too big, so she closed her fist to keep it in place. Nandi delved *air* and pushed Headmistress Jasindi away from her. She crashed into the other two women and all tumbled away in a tangle of limbs and dresses.

Nandi kept her eye on them as she backed away, but none of the women moved. She turned and trotted down the patio steps to where Ailith waited.

Green flames of excitement danced in the girl's eyes. "That was amazing, Nandi! I've never seen anything like that."

"Let's talk about it later." Nandi looked at the watching girls scattered about the garden and saw a mix of fear, apprehension, hesitance, and indecision. Some of them might be convinced to come with her and Ailith, but she didn't have time to convince them. "One last chance," she said. "You know they're prepping you to sell you off as laborwives. It's just another word for slave wife. Is that what you want?"

"What's happening over there?" a voice demanded from several houses down. "Why aren't you girls working?"

Nandi looked in the direction of voice, then back to the girls.

"It'll be dangerous out there, but I've survived fine. Better out there than what's waiting for you here."

No one said a thing. They just stood where they were, staring at her. Ailith grabbed her arm and started to pull her away. Nandi looked from face to face. How could they choose the fate awaiting them over freedom over their own lives? She looked at Ingris and saw something there.

"Ingris," Nandi said quietly. "You can come."

"C'mon, Nandi," Ailith pleaded. "They're coming!"

Nandi glanced down the road. Several men and a few women were marching toward the house. They didn't look happy. She looked back to Ingris. "C'mon. You can come with us. We'll look after you."

Ingris stood frozen, only her eyes moving left to right, taking in the other girls in her periphery. She half turned her head and saw the rapidly approaching adults. Her back went rigid, her face frozen in fear. "C ... come back for me. Just come back. Please." She spun and ran back into the garden and between the cornstalks.

Nandi shook her head as she turned away. Ailith tugged at her arm. "You're going to fool around and get us caught again. Let's *go*."

"We're going," Nandi said.

They sprinted around the side of the house and across the road and between two houses. "I'll take the lead," Ailith said, not even winded. To her surprise, Nandi found she wasn't short of breath either. All that running and labor had brought some benefit, at least. "We can make for the north border and into Nashma ..." she trailed off when Nandi shook her head.

"No. We go east. A friend is waiting for me. After that, we're going southeast. You're welcome to join us.

"Southeast?" Ailith frowned. "Why would ..." She held up a hand. "Later. Come. We'll go east as you say. But we'll have to take a roundabout path. We can hide in the high grass and make our way around."

Nandi followed Ailith between the houses, passing a barn and stable, then peeking out at the road to ensure it was clear. By now they heard the distant shouts of men. Pursuit wouldn't be far off.

Ailith kept them moving between structures and out of sight. It would have been quicker to just make straightaway out of the little town, hopping fences and crossing the roads, but that would have put them out in the open.

After several close calls and subsequent redirects, the high grass fields were finally in view. Crouched beside her fire-haired friend, Nandi gazed out at the grassy mounds with longing. The endless fields of four-foot tall grass swayed invitingly in the breeze, beckoning them into the embrace of freedom.

They started to slip out across the road, but ducked back at the sound of thundering hooves. The distant whinny of galloping horses drew closer from behind.

"We'll have to make a break for it," Ailith said. "They're closing in."

"If we step out on that road we'll be caught."

"You got an idea, then? Because they're about to be right on top of us and there's nowhere else to go."

Nandi looked around. They were huddled between two buildings whose windows were far too high to reach. The path back the way they'd come carried the sound of approaching horses, as did the road to the left. If they went out and turned right, they'd be spotted.

She rifled through every memory she had of the various ways she'd used the essences since learning she could delve. *Fire* wouldn't help, unless she planned to set a building on fire. She didn't want to do that. Surely there were good people to be found in this backwards town. And she might accidentally kill someone or an animal if she did that.

Earth and *water* seemed of little help, either, and she couldn't think of anything to do with *air* ...

"That's it!" she whispered.

"That's what?" Ailith growled. "I hope you've figured something out, because they're almost here.

"Hold on." Nandi closed her eyes and concentrated on *air*. She thought about when she'd accidentally hidden herself and Amiya from the murderous four-armed monsters back home in Vyne. She remembered that she had delved *air*, that day.

Nandi called to the essence and found it came more readily than she'd ever experienced. The essence ring. She clenched her fist and concentrated on weaving the essence around them. She remembered how her surroundings had taken on the blue tinge of dawn, as if the actual colors of the world were softened through a colored lens.

She opened her eyes at the sound of Ailith's gasp and smiled in satisfaction. The world looked like a soft tinted version of itself. Nandi looked down at Jasindi's essence ring. *Her* ring, now. It glowed silver.

Ailith's mouth fell open in awe as she looked up and all around. When she looked at Nandi, her green eyes widened. "Your eyes!"

"Silver," Nandi confirmed. "Yes, I know. A magus I'd learned from for a while called the color an *arah*."

Ailith whirled at the sound of nearby hoofbeats. "Does all this mean they won't see us or something?"

"I think so." In truth, she had no idea if this would work. Maybe those monsters saw differently than humans.

"We're about to find out." Ailith shrank back against the wall.

Nandi huddled next to the girl, baffled at the nearly identical situation she'd found herself in with this girl, so similar to her sister.

Two men on horseback appeared at the end of the alley in front of them. One of them looked in Nandi and Ailith's direction, then right past them and shook his head. He looked further down the alley and shouted, "you see anything?"

"Nothing," came the answer from farther behind. "Must be hidin' in a house somewhere."

"Must be," the man in front of them said. "No way they could've got onto the road without us seeing 'em." He raised his voice again. "Keep lookin'!"

The girls waited several moments after the men rode off before Ailith finally chanced a peek out of the alley. "They're gone. Let's go."

As cautious as field mice in a den of barn owls, the two girls crept out of the alley, then sprinted for the wooden fence. They vaulted over the fence and ran into the tall grass and crouched low.

"I think I saw something!" they heard in the distance. Both girls held their breath, expecting any moment for a hunting party to surround them. No hunting party came, however. They waited a while after, neither girl wanting to chance a move.

Ailith looked to Nandi. "Best you take a peek. My flaming locks'll give me away for sure against all this green."

"Good idea." Nandi raised her head just high enough to peek out of the tall grass. A few riders stood together nearby, one of them pointing in several directions. A few moments passed, and the riders disbursed. "They're splitting up," she said. "Probably going to gather a few more riders to look for us."

"They're going to pull out the hounds," Ailith said. For the first time since she'd met the fiery girl, Nandi saw fear in her eyes. "The hounds are big, Nandi. Really big. And they bite. They'll tear the arm right off you if their handler lets them."

"We need to get moving, then," Nandi replied. "We can make our way around to the east."

"There's no time to search for your friend. Once those hounds catch our scent, we'll never lose them short of finding a river to ride down."

"We won't have to look. She'll find us, trust me. With her help, we'll get away."

"I hope you're right. Now that I've tasted freedom, I'll sheath a sword in my chest before being taken again."

"We're not getting caught," Nandi said. "We just need to get around the other side of this village and we're on our way …" she trailed off at the sound of a raspy voice.

"Nandi girl never sticks to her own plan."

AMOURA

I mprisoned though she may be, Amoura Xanna couldn't help but appreciate the sanitary conditions of her cell. The royain of Shiedra didn't seem an unkind woman, despite the false accusations about Amoura's identity and apparent murder of her husband.

No matter how she mulled that over in her mind, Amoura couldn't imagine who these people had seen that would make them think it was she who'd committed the act. How many dark-skinned women with gray eyes walked the land of Marai? She'd never met one, and from the common reactions she received during her travels, no one else had, either.

There seemed only one explanation, but that was impossible. Her sister was long dead, killed in a violent battle between the king's forces and a band of Khatala. Perhaps it was some rare trait few people shared?

She sat cross-legged against the wall and let her head fall back against it. Whatever the mystery of this situation, she needed to figure something out, or she'd likely find herself facing a headsman's block, an archer's wall, or a stake upon which to burn. All prospects she had no intention of visiting.

Lief climbed through the barred window of her cell. The little tinfar woman took a careful survey of the surroundings and hopped down.

Amoura watched her in silence. "Hello, Lief," she said when her companion sat down beside her. "Here to keep a condemned soul company?"

Lief raised her eyebrows. "A rare bit of humor? There may be hope for you yet."

Amoura ran her tongue along the inside of her cheek with a little nod. "What makes you think I was being humorous?"

Lief let her eyelids droop. "Because you don't believe you're condemned any more than I do. However Amoura Xanna leaves this world, it won't be execution due to mistaken identity."

No lie, there. Amoura lifted her knees and wrapped her arms around them. "I'm open to any ideas you might have. I'd prefer a diplomatic resolution to this little problem, but you're right; I have no intention of being executed by mistake."

"I spoke with some *et'a* tinfar that live in the area," Lief said. "They didn't much like the deceased royain, but they're rather enamored of the royana. Lindra, they said her name is."

Amoura nodded again. "Yes. Her name is Lindra. She strikes me as a fair and just woman, whatever her husband was like."

"That's what Cemeradiut said."

"Ceme," Amoura blinked. "Who is this?"

"Ceme*radiut*," Lief repeated with a touch of impatience. "Why can't humans just listen and repeat. It's a skill that even a parrot can master. And they have beaks."

"They also require hearing things many times in order to repeat them, rather than my needing to hear Ceme*radiut* twice," Amoura countered. "Perhaps you'll forgive me. It is not a name one of human lineage would hear."

"That's fair, I guess," Lief allowed.

Amoura smiled. "It appears I incorrectly assumed all tinfar have short names, like you."

Lief held up her hand to muffle her laughter. "Depends. *Et'a*

Tinfar who live in the region you call Vyne, the region I'm from, have names like mine; short and simple. Those from this region you call Nashma have long names."

Amoura listened patiently through the explanation while refraining from interrupting. "Mind telling me what I said that was so funny?"

"Hm?" Lief blinked. "Oh." She chuckled again. "I'm sorry. I know you're trying. It's just that when you try to be friendly in the traditional sense, it doesn't quite work."

Amoura looked away from her "cellmate" and went back to staring across the room. "I see."

"Oh, Amoura, don't take what I said badly. I didn't mean it that way. I know you're trying to appear more friendly, but you don't need to go the extra bit. Trust me, when you're not so hard, you're quite lovely, smile or not. I'm sure others would agree."

Amoura's mouth fell open. Lief bounced her clay-colored eyebrows. The magus responded with a crinkled smile. She and Lief stared at each other for a moment before the magus broke into laughter.

Lief watched her with a genuine smile of her own, then stood to leave. "I'll keep my eyes and ears open and help wherever I can." She stopped at the bars and turned back. "Oh, and he's doing fine."

Amoura opened her mouth to respond, but held back. Just before Lief disappeared out the window she spoke up. "Lief."

The tinfar turned back. "Yes?"

"Thank you."

Lief responded with a wide smile. "You're welcome. I'll see you soon."

Alone with her thoughts again, Amoura found her heart lifted. Lief's visit had helped more than she would have expected. Through a lifetime of training, Amoura could remain composed under the most strenuous of circumstances, but it didn't mean she felt nothing on the inside.

She wondered how Emiel was holding up. Bone would doubtlessly have found some way to annoy any nearby guards, but what of the spicetrader? He'd overcome a lot of personal fears and fatal inadequacies over their travels together. She no longer had any doubts of his personal strength. But he was most certainly at his wit's end worrying about his daughters. She could see it in his face when they were on the move. Confined to a cell with no forward movement, he was probably on the verge of madness. She imagined she'd be the same in such a circumstance.

Best I worry about my own situation, she reminded herself. Given the royana's appearance of being levelheaded, Amoura figured there would be a trial. That would be the best scenario. No matter what Royana Lindra's soldiers thought they saw, there was no proving Amoura had been where they claimed she was.

Her thoughts drifted to the question of who would want a royain dead in the first place. What could the man have been or done that was so extreme to have spurred someone to have taken his life? The darker question, however, was who could have been skilled enough to accomplish such a feat? A royain might not be a king, but the leader of an entire province was no insignificant figure. He'd have a personal guard at all times, wouldn't he?

She lifted her head at the sound of creaking heavy doors followed by bootsteps. The click of a lock, and another. "Hey there," she heard Bone say. "Come to play a little game of chase the rodents?"

"There are no rodents in here, boy," a man's voice said.

"Eh, true. But most dungeons have rodents, so I thought I'd throw in a little tradition."

"If you'd like the traditional discomfort that comes with it," the soldier said, "that can be arranged. For now, kindly shut up and turn around."

Bootsteps approached Amoura's cell. The lock on the door clicked, and latches were pulled. A soldier pulled the cell door open, turned aside, and saluted. A heartbeat later, the armored woman who had shoved Amoura into her cell appeared in the doorway.

Amoura rose and faced the soldier. She stood with her helm under her arm as before, dark green eyes boring into Amoura's. She met the intense gaze as long as the soldier intended to hold it. She didn't fault the woman her anger, even if it was misplaced.

The soldier's face hardened even more. "You're a confident one, aren't you, Magus? Even without your toy on your finger, you still believe you hold power. Does your order teach courses on arrogance?"

"Yes, soldier," Amoura replied. "We hold courses on arrogance among many other mental trappings that accompany power."

"That you can more effectively exert your will over others."

"That we can avoid doing so," Amoura corrected.

The soldier looked as though she wanted to spit again. "Yet, here you are."

Amoura inclined her head. "Indeed."

The woman looked like it took every ounce of restraint not to draw her sword and run Amoura through. Given her situation, there wasn't much Amoura could have done to stop her. "Turn around."

Two words delivered with icy calm. Amoura silently complied. She felt the anger wafting from the woman. This soldier was a hair's breadth from ending her life and accepting the consequences later. Shiedra truly loved their royain.

The soldier grabbed her wrists, yanked them behind her back, and secured them together. A strong hand clamped Amoura's arm hard enough to elicit a wince, then spun her around. The woman stepped so close the tips of their noses nearly touched. "Understand this right now, assassin. The *instant* you are pronounced guilty, the last thing you will hear is song of my sword sliding free of its sheath just before separating your head from your shoulders."

Green fire. The woman's eyes were green fire, blazing so

angrily in Amoura's face she could practically feel the heat. "And if I'm proven innocent, soldier?"

In response, she grabbed Amoura's arm in that same vice-like grip and muscled her across the cell and out the door. Tomorrow she'd have a bruise on that arm for sure. Given the barely restrained rage in the woman marching her through these hallways, Amoura wondered if the soldier would strike her down whether pronounced innocent or not.

The silent walk to the outside world went quickly. Soon, Amoura found herself standing beside Emiel, Bone on the other side of the spicetrader.

Bone looked around. "Nice place they've got here. I really like the colored rock and cacti … ah!" He half turned to glare over his shoulder at the soldier behind him. "Mind telling me what I did to deserve that?"

"Shut your mouth," the soldier said.

Bone looked like he had a retort on the tip of his tongue, but he bit it back. He stole a glance at Emiel, then Amoura, then faced forward again. They passed a small number of residents who stopped what they were doing to stare openly at the prisoners.

Amoura ignored the many glares focused on her. These people were loyal to their royain. How else would they react upon seeing his supposed killer brought to justice?

"Isn't this rather an indignity, considering we've not been found guilty of anything yet?" Emiel asked.

"Only by the royana's order are we walking you through the quieter avenues and not parading you out in the open," a soldier answered. "You've exhausted your questions. Walk in silence or be carried unconscious."

The trio did as ordered. Amoura noted the red, downward-curved tile roofs atop soft-colored yellow, orange, and red adobe structures. Beautiful multi-colored stone walkways stretched in every direction, and small and large cacti grew, surrounded by smooth colored stones in neatly tended yards. Shiedra was unlike any city Amoura had ever been to. She wished she were here under better circumstances.

They entered a building with two ten-foot statues standing on either side of the front portal. The left statue was that of a woman holding a large tome in her arms. On the right, another woman held a sword. The statues were facing each other.

As they passed between the statues, the captives looked up at each. They appeared to be staring at one another, as if in challenge.

The walk to their destination went by in a blur, as Amoura was wrapped in her own thoughts. They entered a round chamber that could have easily fit two of the homes outside within. A raised semicircular bench greeted them, as did three stern faces that studied the trio from each side of the bench as they passed between.

Royana Lindra sat in the left of the two seats at the head of the desk, the right one empty. Where her appearance had been softened the previous day by her comfortable attire, now she cut a commanding figure.

Behind her left shoulder stood a woman with long wavy black hair tied back from her face. A tiny black mole dotted her cheek underneath the left of two sparkling green eyes. When she looked into Amoura's eyes, something passed between them that caught the magus off guard. It felt as though the woman had just read her, somehow.

On the royana's other side stood an older, stern-looking woman. Her hair was tied into a tight bun at the back of her head. As with most people in Shiedra, Amoura noticed, this woman also had green eyes, and they were hard. Not unkind, but hard.

The soldiers halted the captives, then boxed them in so close that Amoura could see nothing but the back of Bone's head, who she presumed could only see the back of Emiel's. The men and women on either side of the bench were completely obscured from her vision. The soldier beside Amoura moved away to be replaced by the woman who had cuffed her wrists. She grabbed Amoura by the arm and snatched her out of place, marching her up to the front of the line and placing her in front of Emiel.

"I assure you there is no need to exert such energy," Amoura quietly said.

"I assure your regret if you speak another word to me."

"That's enough," Lindra said to the soldier. "I expect better, Officer Taiyana."

Officer Taiyana snapped to attention and bowed. "Of course. My apologies, Royana."

The Royana shifted her attention from the volatile officer to Amoura. "I assume you understand why you've been brought here?"

"I do, Royana," Amoura replied. Her two companions replied the same.

The woman at Lindra's right shoulder leaned down and whispered into her ear. The royana nodded in response. "Captain Adolphus."

The captain stepped forward and executed a precise bow. "Excellency."

"Bring in the witnesses," Lindra ordered.

Blind on all sides except for her view of Lindra, Amoura heard footsteps as the supposed witnesses were brought in.

Royana Lindra's voice dominated the court hall when she spoke. "You are brought before this hearing today because you are accused of the assassination of Royain Dimitri Arella of Shiedra. I, Royana Lindra Arella of Shiedra will oversee this hearing as head of the council."

"These witnesses," the royana continued, "claim to have encountered you on the night of Royain Dimitri's assassination. They claim that it was you who struck the mortal blow, ending the life of the esteemed leader of Shiedra and all of Nashma, as well as a father of two sons, and I, his wife."

Amoura felt genuine regret for the woman and her sons, as well as for Nashma. The people here seemed to genuinely love their

Royain. She spared some of that concern for herself as well. However much she might empathize with these people's loss, she didn't intend to own it.

One by one, the witnesses stood and spoke of their experience. It turned out that all but the stately man were city guards. Amoura listened in utter bewilderment as each man and woman described her almost exactly. As the last testimony was given, Amoura understood the purpose of the soldiers crowding tight around her and the others. Her suspicion proved correct when the last person finished their testimony and the guards stepped back to the sound of gasps by the witnesses.

Amoura remained still, but swept her gaze over the three men and women seated on either side of the encompassing bench. The last man in the row on the right had the look of a dignitary. Beside the last witness on either side, the council did a fair job of keeping their expressions a blend of impersonal and mild hostility.

The collection of witnesses stiffened at the sight of Amoura, but when the more professional man got a good look at her, the lump in his throat bobbed up and down several times. He and Amoura locked gazes for several heartbeats before he looked away.

From the corner of her eye, Amoura saw one of the guard witnesses lean forward as if she were about to stand. His nostrils flared as he stared right at Amoura. She looked back at him, directly into his eyes, and watched the fires of rage slowly diminish. His lips parted ever so slightly, and a tiny frown creased his brow. He broke off contact and looked away.

"Is this the woman you saw?" Royana Lindra asked them.

One by one, the witnesses confirmed Amoura's identity; all but the two men who had actually looked her in the eye. The woman at Lindra's left looked at the two men for a heartbeat, then her eyes cut back to Amoura.

Royana Lindra's gaze snapped to the two men who still had not spoken. "Mr. Diega? Ambassador Tobain? You seem uncertain, yet you've described the accused accurately without seeing her until this moment."

The more plainly dressed man Amoura guessed to be Mr. Diega bowed. "Apologies, my Royana, but ..." He looked at Amoura again, and again, Amoura met his gaze. "My ... my Royana," Mr. Diega stammered. "She has the same thinly braided black hair, the same hue of skin, the same eyes, and of similar height, but I cannot say it is her."

Royana Lindra leaned back in her chair and appeared to mull that over. "What of you, Ambassador Tobain?"

Ambassador Tobain rose. For several long moments he stood quietly scrutinizing Amoura. She felt his gaze boring into the side of her head. When she looked at him, into his eyes, he gasped.

Officer Taiyana's iron-like fingers snaked around Amoura's arm and clamped down. When Amoura turned her head from the ambassador to the woman on her right, Taiyana held her gaze with icy contempt. She spoke in an equally cold voice. "Intimidation won't work here, assassin. Face forward."

"No." Royana Lindra's iron voice unclasped Taiyana's grip on Amoura's arm as if it had been physically removed. The royana took her turn in staring into Amoura's eyes. She seemed to come to a decision. "Witnesses. Rise. Step down from the bench and form a line."

Amoura heard Emiel and Bone muttering something behind her, followed by the sound of hands smacking backs, and the mercenary's responding curse.

The witnesses were lined up, and Lindra ordered them one by one to stand before Amoura and look her in the eye directly. "Study her face," the royana ordered. "Have a good look, as long as you need. Be absolutely certain this is the woman you fought that night. Do not give this council an answer you believe us to want, or that even you want. Give the answer that springs to you immediately."

One by one, the witnesses stepped in front of Amoura and

looked into her face, her eyes. Every encounter began with a look of hostility and ended in a mix of confusion or apprehension.

Lastly, Ambassador Tobain stepped in front of Amoura. Though she didn't enjoy the way he looked her over, there was no lewd intent. He took in her height, her face, her hair. "May I see her hands."

"I do not recommend this, Excellency," Captain Adolphus said. "All accounts speak of her having hands too fast to follow."

Tobain turned around to address Lindra. "My Royana. If this is the attacker, she could have killed me that night, but she did not. If I am to give you my proper answer, I must see everything about her I saw then."

Royana Lindra looked past the ambassador to Adolphus. "Remove her restraints, Captain."

Adolphus wanted to argue, Amoura saw it in his face and the way he looked at her. His inner turmoil flashed across his eyes in less than a heartbeat as he stepped behind the magus without another word. As he unclasped her wrist, however, he whispered into Amoura's ear. "Flex a muscle, twitch a finger, and my sword will find your lung."

There was no threat in the captain's words, only promise. Amoura slowly brought her hands up so that Tobain could see them.

The man swallowed. "Please, turn them." Amoura complied. "Thank you." He stepped aside. "Excellency," he closed his eyes and took a long, deep breath. "This is not the woman."

A quiet settled over the small assembly so heavy that it felt as though a pall had been thrown over it. Hands back at her sides, the statuesque Amoura cut her eyes left and right, taking in every face in her line of sight. The other witnesses looked at the floor in front of their feet. Telling, that they hadn't responded to the ambassador's words.

The woman standing at Lindra's left shoulder had been watching Tobain during their entire interaction. She'd been staring into the man's eyes through every word he spoke. While the royana had done the same, this was somehow different. When she turned her attention back to Amoura, the two locked gazes for what seemed forever. Again, the magus felt like this woman read everything about her through her eyes. Unnerving as it was, she met that green gaze as long as the woman held hers.

Royana Lindra leaned forward. "You're sure, Ambassador?"

"I wish it were otherwise, Excellency. I wish this was the woman who took our Royain and your husband from us, but it is not."

"Could your memory be fragmented by the trauma of the encounter?" one of the councilmen asked. "You stated in interview that it was dark in your house when the attack occurred. Might it be that you did not get a good enough look?"

Ambassador Tobain didn't hesitate in his answer. "It is not, Councilman. The memory of that night is forever burned into my mind and my occasional nightmares." He faced Amoura again as he spoke. The woman who attacked me looked very much the same as this woman. The same eyes, hair, skin. But the assassin's hands were calloused, while this woman's are not. The assassin was about the same height, but I remember the flex of her muscled arm when she overpowered me.

"I mean not to be rude," he said to Amoura. "But this woman's arms are not so muscled. She also looks somewhat younger."

"What of her eyes, Ambassador," Lindra asked. "Of all the characteristics of the assassin, her eyes have been described as the most striking.

Once more, Tobain looked into Amoura's eyes. "Her eyes are the same, Excellency."

The councilman who'd spoken earlier stood and leaned on the bench. He held out a hand in Amoura's direction. "Then, you've marked her as the assassin, have you not? Muscle can shrink away. Callouses can heal, be smoothed. A struggle in near darkness can obscure vision—"

Tobain nodded through every word. "You may be right in all of these things, Councilman, though I have little knowledge in muscle anatomy or skin conditions. But this woman's eyes, while the same *color* as the assassin's, are *not* the assassin's. I will never forget, nor could I ever mistake the hardness in that woman's eyes. I remember a voice of iron as sharp as any sword. Her words slid into my mind as though a blade through the heart. Every word I remember."

The councilman looked to Lindra at the head of the U-shaped bench. "If the ambassador has such a memory of this event"—he looked down at Tobain again—"surely he can recite the words spoken to him that night."

Royana Lindra looked at Tobain. "Ambassador?"

Tobain looked hesitant, which Amoura found puzzling. "Excellency. I might summarize—"

"Her words as you remember them," Royana Lindra commanded. "Look at me, Ambassador." Tobain complied. "Every word as you remember them. If you speak a lie or omit any bit of the truth, I will see it and I will not be pleased."

Amoura watched the exchange with mounting confusion as the man sagged underneath the royana's heavy gaze. Something sat beneath the surface of this situation that went beyond the attack.

"Looks like somebody's trying to come up with a lie," Emiel whispered under his breath.

Amoura didn't think so. This man looked as though he were about to say something he'd rather not.

Tobain's entire presence seemed to deflate. He kept his eyes on his royana as if pleading with her for something. But what?

"Excellency. Council. When I struggled with the assassin, she incapacitated me with little effort. She could have murdered my entire family, starting with myself."

"We know that already, Ambassador," the councilman snapped.

"But when she held back any number of killing blows she

could have delivered upon my person, she said these words to me." He took a deep breath.

"'Your work is good, but it is run over by those with more influence. You clean the mess of those more powerful than you. You act for life, and so yours continues. I am the result of the actions that have brought me here. The royain has been visited by his actions and intentions, this night. Walk the right path.'"

"What treason is this?" Captain Adolphus demanded. "How dare you speak of your royain—"

"Captain, enough," Lindra ordered.

Adolphus turned his thunderstruck expression on the royana. "Excellency, surely you cannot let this stand—"

"*Enough*, Captain." Royana Lindra stared at the captain until he bowed in apology.

What is this? Amoura looked from face to face until her gaze settled over the head of the bench. Royana Lindra did not look outraged or offended, nor did she even look angry. She held her composure well enough that most wouldn't see the flicker of weary acceptance in her eyes, but Amoura saw it. *Interesting.*

The man Amoura now believed to be the head of the council stood again, placed his hands on the desk and leaned forward. "Ambassador. I believe I needn't tell you that the words you've just spoken carry treasonous implications."

"If there were any other words I could have spoken, councilman," Tobain replied, "I would gladly have done so."

"The words of an assassin do not reflect the sentiment of the one who repeats them here," Lindra said. "I bade you to repeat the words the assassin spoke to you and you did so."

One of the guard witnesses opened her mouth, then closed it. The royana looked at her. "Speak now, if you've something to add."

"My Royana," she said. "The assassin who singlehandedly defeated all of us had eyes like this woman's in color only. They weren't just the color of steel, they *were* steel."

Amoura thought she could hear Officer Taiyana's teeth grinding. For her part, this whole ordeal had Amoura's head in a spin.

Lindra turned her attention to Amoura. "Have you anything to say in your defense, Magus?"

"Only that which I've already said, Royana," Amoura replied. "My companions and I had stopped at a nearby lake to rest our mounts before continuing on to the very city in which we found ourselves imprisoned. We were greeted by a mounted patrol that drew arms and arrested us as soon as they saw me. We have no knowledge of the curious and unfortunate events that befell this great city."

"What business brought you to Shiedra?" Lindra asked.

"The library," Amoura answered, to the sound of scoffing disbelief.

The Royana quieted the murmurs with an upraised hand. "The library?"

Amoura inclined her head. "My research determined the library in Altarra inadequate."

Lindra arched an eyebrow. "That is a statement I'd never expect to hear."

"It is a complicated matter, Royana."

Lindra sat erect in her chair, scrutinizing Amoura for many long and tense moments. Amoura endured it as long as need be. "Does the council have any further questions?" Lindra asked.

The three council members on the right looked to each other, as did the left. The head of the council stood. "The council has no further questions, Excellency."

The royana of Shiedra stood. "I've heard all that I need to hear." She looked to the witnesses. "You have the gratitude of the council and the royana for reliving that night and your testimony today. You are dismissed."

While her two companions murmured about the confusing situation and what it all meant, Amoura remained quiet and thoughtful. She faced forward, not looking at anyone, but listening to their reactions, catching snippets of whispered conversation where she could.

"Ambassador Tobain," Lindra called just as he stepped through the door.

The ambassador turned and bowed. "Excellency?"

"I would trouble you to remain a while longer, if you would be so kind."

"Of course, Excellency," Mr. Tobain replied. "It is no trouble at all." He started toward his seat, but the royana signaled for him to take the floor to the side of the captives. Amoura felt her wrists being grabbed and pulled behind her back while the restraints were applied again.

Royana Lindra looked from Amoura to the ambassador several times. "The other witnesses encountered the assassin in combat, that night. By all accounts, the woman was fast, fierce, but silent. Your encounter, frightening as it must have been, was the closest. You saw her face, her eyes, and heard her voice.

"Can you look upon this woman again? We must be absolutely certain. Your words may well exonerate or condemn her."

"I can, Excellency," Tobain said. Taiyana repositioned Amoura so that she stood facing the ambassador, but in full view for the royana and council. "Would you speak with me?" he asked.

"If it pleases the Royana, the council and yourself," Amoura replied, "yes."

"She may speak," Lindra said.

"My full name is Lyle Tobain," the ambassador began. "I have worked for the Royana and Royain of Shiedra for over ten years, now. The assassination of our esteemed Royain has left Shiedra and all of Nashma reeling, as I'm sure you gather by now."

Amoura listened, not quite sure where he was going with this. "I have gathered as much, Ambassador Lyle Tobain."

"Please, tell me a bit about yourself," he asked.

Amoura opened her mouth to speak when a council member

stood and waved her hand at the floor. "Excellency. Is this necessary? Why are we listening to a conversation?"

"Let us listen and find out," Royana Lindra replied. "Ambassador. Continue."

"Thank you, Excellency." Lyle indicated for Amoura to continue.

"My name is Amoura Xanna. My companions and I have traveled many miles and endured many challenges and dangers to reach this impressive city of Shiedra to visit its library. As I'm sure the Royana is aware, there have been attacks on a number of Marailander cities by four-armed creatures with skin like lava rock. These monsters wield terrible weapons to swift and brutal effect, all the while spitting curses in a language no one can identify."

Lyle Tobain squinted through her every word, though he only occasionally looked at her when she spoke. He was listening to her voice and the cadence in which she spoke, Amoura realized.

"It was my belief that I would find more answers in the formidable library of Shiedra," she continued. "Thus our presence in Nashma."

"And these two men who accompany you," Lyle said. "You've hired them?"

"I have not hired them, Ambassador. Unless the Royana commands otherwise, I would leave them to best explain their presence here." *Best wrap this up, Ambassador.* A palpable agitation and impatience hung in the air. She could feel the barely restrained anger in Officer Taiyana, standing only a few feet away. That woman desperately wanted to sheathe her sword into a vital organ in Amoura's body.

Royana Lindra must have felt it, too. She looked about the room, then addressed Tobain. "Your time is nearly expired, Ambassador."

Lyle Tobain chewed his bottom lip as he stared at Amoura. She watched the conflicting emotions play across his face. It would be so easy and satisfying to all if he were to simply declare her the assassin. From what Amoura knew of the assassin's, so long as Royana Lindra and Lyle Tobain continued working for the good of the people and not their own self-interest, there would be no additional visits from the Khamra.

With a great exhale, Ambassador Tobain turned to the royana. "Excellency." Another deep breath. "I maintain my previous statement." He half turned to look at Amoura as he spoke. "This is not the woman." He lifted his voice above the resulting murmurs of dissent. "The likeness is uncanny, as is her voice. But I heard the assassin's words very close to my ear. This is not her."

Another council member stood. "If what you say is true and this is not the assassin, then she must be a relative. Based on every account we've heard, the two are similar enough of feature and voice that they must certainly be of relation to one another."

"Which means if we detain one, we can reach the other," another council member added.

"Or perhaps both are complicit," added a third council member. "If they are in fact related, it isn't implausible."

The royana listened as everyone had their say. Amoura saw the well-hidden pain in her eyes. She wanted more than anything for Amoura to be the assassin who'd taken her husband's life, but she knew the truth of it every bit as much as her ambassador, if not for different reasons.

When the arguments died down, Royana Lindra held up a hand. The room fell silent, all eyes turned to the head of the bench. Amoura watched as Lindra gathered her thoughts and her resolve. Despite her certainty that the royana knew or at least felt sure that Amoura was not in fact the assassin, that didn't mean she wouldn't rule to that effect just to placate her people. Amoura had never been to Shiedra. She didn't know Lindra or her people.

"Never have I been more conflicted than at this moment," she began. "To have the Royain's murderer brought before me to face justice is a moment I've hoped for every day." She paused and looked each of the assembled captives in the eye, her gaze finally lingering on Amoura. "Yet the circumstances and witness accounts have made this a difficult situation of which neither solution will be celebrated.

"In truth, I'm at a loss of what to do with you, Magus. You come to Nashma with the face of an assassin, yet not so. I find it difficult to believe there is another woman with such similarities to you, and you are not related. However, I also see no lie in your eyes and hear none from your insistence that you have no such sibling. I've known Ambassador Tobain for many years. He is a good and honest man when others are not." Amoura thought she heard a tinge of disappointment in her tone.

"So, what to do with you? Nashma is still in mourning, and the execution of the royain's assassin would bring closure to the matter. However …" Lindra let out a great sigh. "I'll not condemn an innocent person to provide false closure for myself or anyone else."

To her side, Amoura heard Taiyana's long, slow and angry exhale. That one would never be convinced of Amoura's innocence, regardless of the facts.

"I find the thought a skilled assassin committing the act, defeating a team of guards, and escaping without a trace only to return with two companions to be found at a lake outside Shiedra, absurd. I also see none of the body composition in you that would have been necessary to defeat so many foes at once. I mean no offense in that, Magus."

Amoura inclined her head. "Your meaning is well understood, Royana."

Lindra looked to the rest of the bench. "It is the job of the ruling council to base our decisions on the facts presented, absent emotion or person desires. We are here to make the best judgment within our power. What is the verdict of the council?"

The head councilman stood. "Vote of innocent!" On the left side of the bench, one hand rose. On the other side, three. "The council shows four votes for innocent!" the head councilman stated. "Vote for guilty!" Two hands rose on the left side. The head councilman turned to Royana Lindra. "The council votes four to two, innocent."

Amoura heard Emiel's relieved sigh. The depth of her appreciation for that surprised even her.

Royana Lindra stood. "My vote as well; innocent. Captain Adolphus. Release them at once."

"Yes, Excellency." He and another officer went about unbinding Emiel and Bone, while Taiyana grudgingly released Amoura.

When the bounds were removed, Amoura refrained from rubbing her wrists just as she had the first time they'd been removed at the ambassador's request. She turned around and found herself facing the officer. Taiyana took one step forward, placing herself only inches in front of the magus.

Amoura looked into the fire dancing in the woman's eyes. She didn't believe for a moment that Amoura was innocent and there was nothing short of bringing in the real assassin that could convince her otherwise.

"One wrong step," Taiyana whispered. "Just one, I beg you."

"Step back and stand down, officer!" Adolphus commanded.

"Every *breath* you take while in Shiedra will be known to me." Taiyana stepped back and saluted her captain.

Bone and Emiel moved forward to stand on either side of her. "What's her problem?" Emiel asked, rubbing his wrists. "You've been proven innocent."

The mercenary snorted. "Like that means anything. She may be innocent, but I'm sure that officer has seen a guilty criminal or two go unpunished due to lack of proof."

"Regardless of that," Emiel replied. "If she's that angry in spite of her leader and council's ruling, she displays doubt in the system she serves."

"Don't be naive, spicetrader," Bone said. "You already forget about your friend back in Vyne who set your grand adventure in motion?"

"Details, mercenary," Emiel replied dryly. "You need to listen to details. I said she *displays* doubt in the system. In certain professions it's wise not to display such feelings openly, whatever you might think in private." He gave the young man a sidelong glance. "And how could I forget about that. You're standing right next to me."

The council had filed out of the hall. Emiel and Bone falling in behind them. The spicetrader turned back when he noticed Amoura not following. "Everything okay?"

"Everything is fine, Emiel," Amoura replied. She even offered a partial smile.His reciprocating smile far eclipsed her own. "I will meet you outside."

Emiel's smile faded when he looked at the guards. "You sure about that?"

"I'll be fine, Emiel."

Emiel hesitated and she saw the concern in his genuine brown eyes. "All right."

Amoura watched until they were gone, all but the royana's personal guard, Captain Adolphus, and Officer Taiyana.

"Is there something more, Magus?"

Amoura turned to face the royana, who still sat at the head of the bench staring back at her. "If it's your ring that concerns you, it will be returned to you shortly."

The magus inclined her head. "I appreciate your reassurance, Royana, but it is another matter. Given the circumstances, I understand it is much to ask, but I'd have a word, if you're willing." Amoura ignored the increasing hot anger radiating from Taiyana with every word she spoke.

Royana Lindra tilted her head, while the woman at her right simply watched Amoura, seeming not at all surprised. "Yes, that is an odd request, given the circumstances, but I have a small amount of time before I must see to other obligations. Very well." She rose and stepped down from the bench. Before Lindra and her two companions came within ten feet of the magus, her personal guard was there.

Despite the numerous hands gripping sword hilts and the lack of her essence ring, Amoura kept her features neutral. The Royana emitted the same poise and grace as she had on their first and less formal meeting. Amoura saw a hint of curiosity mingling with apprehension.

"Be assured that our conversation remains in this room, now and always," Lindra said when she noticed Amoura looking at the guards. "But you'll have to tolerate the presence of my personal guard."

She should have known better. How could she not assume the royana's personal guard would remain with her at all times given recent events? Now, standing here with these people who would happily remove her head from her shoulders right now, there wasn't a chance she could ask the questions she wanted to.

"You must have a rather sensitive subject to discuss with me," Lindra remarked, reading the hesitation in Amoura's face. "Magi are ever the mysterious type. Come." She started toward the door, Amoura, the two women, and her guard falling in around her.

"Believe it or not," Lindra said. "A magus once served as advisor to myself and the Royain. When the conflict between Marai and the west began to heat up, your Order sent representatives to offer guidance in dealing with the "untrained essence wielders, or wilders", as most refer to them."

"Rylden Silver," Amoura said. "I know of him."

"A good person. Though I found his general mistrust of the westerners unfair and problematic, I understand it is a deeply engrained way of thinking."

"A way of thinking that must change," Amoura agreed.

On the royana's other side, the woman she'd whispered with in the hearing room walked in silence. Amoura had no doubt the woman was listening intently, though she gave no indication.

"Excellency," the stern woman said. "If you would excuse me, I've my tasks to attend to."

"Of course, Adviasar," Lindra replied. "We will speak soon."

Through many turns down various hallways, the royana made idle conversation about Nashmarese—mostly Shiedran—history. She shared tidbits of historical information about various stone busts of former dignitaries, and the traditional matriarchal Shiedran leadership.

Amoura listened through it all, even asking questions occasionally so as not to let on that she knew the woman was trying to distract her from knowing her way around the building.

Lindra brought them to a stop down a long hallway with no windows. Her personal guard surrounded them but discretely faced away, while Captain Adolphus stood beside Lindra, his officer next to Amoura.

She couldn't fault their caution. From everything Amoura had heard about the assassin, if they were anything beyond a step away from the royana, the woman could have had her dead before they could lift a hand to stop it. Judging from the look on Captain Adolphus's face, he knew it too.

"Thank you for suffering me a while longer, Royana," Amoura said. "I cannot relate to how difficult this has been for you, but I can appreciate it."

"You are welcome, Magus. I doubt I'm going to like your question, but what is it you would ask of me that requires such confidence?"

Amoura took a measured breath. "You will not like my question, Royana, but I must ask. It is about the royain." Lindra's eyebrow twitched, but Amoura pushed on. "Everything I've heard suggests your great city was visited by a member of the Khamra. Are you familiar with them?"

"I am," came the pained response.

Amoura waited until the woman trusted her voice not to shake before continuing with so delicate a topic. "I wonder that they could have been mistaken, Royana. Everyone here seems to hold much love for him." Though her back was to the officer, Amoura cut her eyes to the side as though looking over her shoulder. "Some, very much so."

Lindra let out a heavy sigh. "The people of Nashma and especially Shiedra did indeed hold a great deal of esteem for their royain. And yes, some more than others. You must excuse Officer Taiyana. Royain Dimitri played an influential role in the lives of many in Shiedra."

"I see."

"No, you do not." Lindra stared off into a faraway place. "The royain placed the good of the Nashma above all else. His commitment to the prosperity of this great province was undeniable."

Amoura waited patiently for the other shoe to drop. *But?*

The quiet woman at Lindra's side clasped her hands together and gave the faintest of nods. Interesting.

"But, the Khatala conflict and correspondence between Shiedra and the crown have been complicated."

It looked like Lindra would say more, but she went silent. They held each other's gaze for several long moments. It seemed that Lindra was practically willing her to understand the unspoken. Finally, the woman exhaled a frustrated sigh. "Captain Adolphus."

The captain took one step to the side, faced Lindra, and bowed. "Excellency?"

"I require a few moments of privacy."

The muscles in the captain's jaw clenched. "My Royana—"

"I know what you would say, my Captain," Lindra cut in, "but this is my wish."

"My Royana, as captain of the Shiedran armed forces it is my duty to ensure your protection. If you require discretion, at least allow *me* to remain at your side."

"That won't be necessary, Captain," Lindra replied, never breaking eye contact with Amoura. "I understand your wariness, regardless of mine and the council's verdict, but it has been given."

Adolphus started to argue, but Royana Lindra broke off contact with Amoura to look the captain in the eye. "Make no mistake, Captain Adolphus. Your many years of service to Shiedra are without equal and have been greatly valued by the Royain and myself. However, as royana of the land of Nashma, I like to believe I'm somewhat competent in judgement."

"I … of course, Excellency. I would never insinuate—"

"Of course you wouldn't, Captain," Lindra cut in. "Please take my personal guard and your officer and wait further down the hall. I assure you, I'll be fine."

Captain Adolphus looked from the royana to Amoura several times. For a moment, Amoura thought he might refuse, but eventually he executed a stiff bow and ordered the soldiers to move away.

Beside Lindra her attendant maintained a neutral expression that likely mirrored Amoura's own.

"I appreciate the trust you've placed in me, Royana," Amoura began.

Lindra gave a subtle nod in response. "Perhaps when our conversation is done, you might speak to your Order on my behalf. I suspect I will have need of the services of the Order of Magi soon."

"Of course, Royana."

"The royain," Lindra began, cutting straight into the matter, "often executed his ambitions at a cost many others bore. Despite my disapproval of his alignment with King Alyn in the ensuing battle with the Khatala, Royain Dimitri overrode my wishes and entered Shiedra into the conflict."

A tiny frown creased Amoura's brow. "The battle between Jietar and the two Khatala nations is not of a scale that requires Shiedran aid. The west does not see all of Marai as an enemy. It is not their way."

"Our king has made persuasive offers to leaders across Marai," Lindra said. "And the Khatala would pay the bill in blood." The royana watched patiently while Amoura took a moment to digest that. She looked into each of Amoura's eyes as if willing her to understand something she didn't want to say, and still wasn't sure she should. "It has been made clear, Magus, that *all* of Marai stands to gain from a single act of unity."

By the Creator Himself. Amoura thought she'd understood Lindra's need for confidence, but it went far beyond her husband's questionable decisions. *Alyn would unite all of Marai to sweep the Khatala from the land. From every land.* This must be a mistake. Nothing that happened between Khatal and Marai warranted such extreme action.

She remembered a conversation with dear Hashma. *If you want to know the way of men and power, child, think on this; the borders of Marai did not always stretch so far.*

Standing in front of the troubled royana and her mysterious attendant, Amoura reflected on those words with a growing sense of dread. If Lindra's words proved true, King Alyn had placed a number on the breaths he drew.

EMIEL

When Amoura appeared at the top of the steps, Emiel felt a wave of relief. Considering her brush with possible execution, he couldn't imagine why she'd have wanted to remain in that building any longer than need be.

As she drew near, concern gradually took the place of relief. Something had shaken her. To anyone who didn't know the woman as well as he did, she would appear contemplative at most. Whether it was a trait of all magi or just Amoura, the woman had mastered the art of being unreadable.

Emiel knew her better, though. Her too-perfect posture as she descended the steps spoke of a distracted nervousness he remembered when they'd found themselves stuck in The Maze. "What's going on? You don't look too happy."

"When does she ever?" Bone remarked.

If Amoura had heard the mercenary's good-natured jab, she gave no indication. She seemed to be searching for the right words. "I need to get to the library. Royana Lindra's official pardon grants me access to the entire city, now. The library is why we came."

"Maybe keep a low profile on that city access part," Bone said. He eyed a few nearby soldiers who openly glared back. "Pardon or not, I think there's a lot of people carrying pointy objects looking for an excuse for you to breathe wrong. And by extension, us as well."

"Your point is well taken," Amoura replied.

Emiel noticed her rubbing her ring finger. "When are they going to give it back to you?" He nodded at her hand.

Amoura looked down at her fingers and stopped. "I don't know. Perhaps it will be delivered to my room."

Bone blinked at her. "You just had a conversation with her and didn't think to ask about your essence ring? Am I wrong in thinking those things are extra important to you magi?"

Amoura stared off into the distance. "The library is in that direction, I'm told." She pointed past a cluster of buildings. "Northeast of this spot." She started walking.

Emiel and Bone shared a look then fell in behind her. They gone perhaps a dozen steps before someone called from behind.

"Magus Amoura."

The group turned back to see the mysterious woman who'd been in the hearing walking toward them. "She nodded to Emiel and Bone before dipping into a bow and addressing Amoura. "Magus, apologies for the interruption, but may I have a word?"

"Of course," Amoura replied.

"She wears that Magus facade well, eh spicetrader?" Bone remarked.

"Hardly that, if you ask me," Emiel replied. He watched as the two women conversed across the street. The woman handed Amoura something and bowed again. "I've met a fair number of people in my travels and that isn't a facade."

"Maybe I used the wrong word. It's just so typical of magi to have this …" Bone waggled his fingers in front of his face and straightened his back. "This poise they always walk around with. Seems like they're putting on airs. She might not be *quite* as bad, but most of them walk around with their chins up in the air, looking down on everybody."

"You think so?" Emiel asked. "I don't have a lot of experience with them, but the few I've met didn't strike me that way. They just seem more, reserved. Maybe ... stately?"

"Airs," Bone reiterated.

Emiel thought about how he'd felt about magi before coming to know one. He thought about how heavy responsibility weighed on him just being a father, much less wielding the sort of power a magus did. For one with any sort of moral code, he imagined it would be an enduring battle against the ego for some, and the struggle to rise to the necessities of such a station for others. His gaze dropped to the ground. Being a father. A great responsibility indeed, and one he was failing at the longer he took to find his ladygirls.

"Not airs," Emiel said. "But the understanding of where they stand in a world that fears the power they have."

From the corner of his eye he saw Bone roll his eyes. "That was insightful, spicetrader. Maybe you should find a gaggle of vagabonds and start a philosophy club."

Emiel frowned. "*What?*"

Amoura returned and moved past them. "I have clearer directions to the library. We should get going."

"What's the rush?" Bone said as he trotted to catch up. "That royana give you a time limit for being here or something?"

"I would think you'd share Emiel's urgency to be done and away," Amoura replied. Her brisk pace hardly slowed when she turned a corner, purple robes swishing behind her.

"Oh, right." Bone turned an apologetic look in Emiel. "Didn't mean to forget about that."

Emiel gave the young man a pat on the back of the shoulder. Bone reciprocated, along with a half grin and a nod. "We'll find 'em, spicetrader. We'll find 'em and get back to Marai and deflate that blowfish."

Really? Emiel looked over at him, but Bone was already waving his unspoken question away. "Look, I know what you're thinking, because I've been thinking a lot about it too, all right? I was hired to drag your arse to Altarra and was paid well for it. Being a mercenary means being ruthless, especially because of my age and smaller stature."

Bone ran a hand through his short blonde hair and slapped his chest with his fist. "Gotta be tough out in the world or it'll break you. I've hunted down and dragged men and women back to their own executions for crimes big and bigger. There's people sitting in jails right now because I ignored their pleas that they had a good reason to steal what they stole. Never much sweated a job, before."

This was the most Bone had ever spoken about himself or his past. Emiel listened patiently while the young warrior came to his point.

"When that archminister hired me, he didn't give me too many specifics other than a certain resident in his city was giving him a lot of problems. I was hired to deliver a recalcitrant spicetrader to Altarra where he would go about serving whatever tasks he was to do there in repayment for the problems he'd caused."

Bone went silent for a while, and Emiel could see the unpleasant memories reflected in his hardening face. "What the big blowfish *didn't* tell me was that he'd actually kidnapped your girls."

Emiel started to remind him of their first conversation, but Bone beat him to it.

"Yes, yes, I remember you telling me you'd been separated from your kids. But a bounty is reliable for doing a number of things, including lying or offering a bigger bounty to free them. At that time, you were no different to me."

"And now is different," Emiel said.

Bone nodded. "Now is different. I don't think you did a *thing* to deserve what Decius ordered me to do, which means he lied and manipulated me. He put me, you, and my reputation at risk, and that doesn't sit well with me, you know?

"So, the way I figure it? I'm gonna help you get your kids

back. Considering the effort that's gonna take, I figure I'll return to Vyne, shove Decius's payment down his gullet, then take what I'm owed."

Emiel kept his smile inward. Bone still talked like a mercenary, but the meaning underneath the words carried a tone of honor and morals. He gave him another pat on the shoulder. "Well, *I* figure by the time we get my girls back and return to Vyne, we'll have to draw straws on who deals with him first."

Amoura stopped in front of a building of beautiful gray and brown stonework with a tiled roof. Balconies stretched around every side of the building on each of its three floors, where people relaxed while engaged in conversation or reading.

"I've never seen anything like this," Emiel said. "Looks like a bibliophile's paradise."

"That's a pretty big word, spicetrader," Bone said, reverting back to his usual sarcasm. "Getting into the spirit before we enter?"

"Yeah, maybe," Emiel replied. "I'll be sure to find you a book of definitions so you can look it up."

The sight and smell of thousands of books greeted them when they stepped inside. Nearly every wall held rows of books as thin as the side of a hand to as thick as a leg. Rows of huge stone columns lined the open gallery, each one holding rows of books as high as a tall person could reach.

Emiel marveled at the polished stone floors and stairs as he followed Amoura across the gallery. Even the ceiling was impressive, displaying beautiful works of art. How did they get people that high to do that?

Amoura spotted a librarian and went straight for him. When he noticed the magus approaching, he bent into respectful bow and smiled. "Welcome to the library of Shiedra, Magus," the softy spoken man said. "How may I assist you?"

"Good day to you," Amoura replied. "I need to visit your historical works."

The librarian nodded thoughtfully. "A rather large section. "Is there something more specific that I might narrow your search?"

"There is," Amoura replied in a quieter voice. "I wish to find works regarding the Ruination."

The librarian blinked several times. "A rather grim, topic, but one the library of Shiedra can supply. If you'll follow me?" He led them out of the gallery and down a quiet side corridor.

"Feels like they're leading us to another dungeon," Bone muttered, his voice seemingly swallowed up in the book-lined halls.

"I thought a building filled with books *was* a dungeon for you," Emiel replied.

"Only if it's filled with endless rambling about spice combinations."

Emiel chuckled. When the librarian finally halted, it was in front of a thick wooden door with iron hinges. Emiel thought it *did* look somewhat like the door to a dungeon.

The unfriendly door groaned as the librarian leaned into it and pushed it open. "Please." He indicated the room with an open hand. "Come with me."

The chamber was larger than Emiel had guessed, housing ten rows of bookshelves before he stopped counting. He wondered if the library had been an old building that had been maintained and eventually added to. While the open gallery sported polished stone floors and columns, with detailed painted ceilings, this room was dim, visibly old, and carried the thick smell of ancient books collected over centuries.

The room even felt ancient. The few patches of conversation drifting about the place here little more than whispers. The inhabitants handled the books with care, gingerly creaking open tomes and flipping pages with delicate care.

The librarian led them to a row at the back of the room and stopped at the farthest corner. He turned aside and indicated a section at the end above eye-level. "You will find these books cover your chosen topic, Magus."

"My thanks," Amoura said.

The librarian started away but stopped after only a few steps. "Apologies, Magus, but might I inquire about something?"

"Ask your question, sir," Amoura replied.

"In my years working in this library, I've had but two other instances of someone seeking information on the Ruination. The first was thirty years ago, and she was an historian. The second time—" The librarian frowned in thought. "The second time was little more than perhaps six months ago. Is there a reason behind this sudden interest in such a dark topic?"

A tiny frown creased Amoura's brow. "Is it not excessive to call two instances in the last thirty years a "sudden interest", sir?"

The librarian bowed his head. "I'm sure you are right, magus. I'll leave you to your studies."

Emiel watched him go. "He didn't believe that at all."

"No, he didn't." Amoura's braids fell away from her face as she perused the tomes overhead. Emiel busied himself looking as well. The quicker they found what the magus needed, the sooner they could be gone.

Amoura stretched up to her toes and slid a large blue book free, then the one next to it. Emiel found an interesting book on the War of the Immortals. He creaked the book open, wondering how Lief was, and what she might be doing. Usually she would have found him by now. He hoped something hadn't happened to his tinfar friend.

"This one's interesting," Bone said. "Talks about the beginning signs of the coming of the Ruination, and the various changes the earth goes through during the transition."

Emiel peered over the mercenary's shoulder and placed a finger on a part of the page. "The Ruination, the Confrontation, the Redemption."

"You already know of the Ruination," Amoura said, still buried in her own book. "The Confrontation seems self-explanatory on the surface, but there's more to it. 'Upon the coming of the Ruination, humankind will reach a point when it must confront itself, and the darkness within. Conflicts will escalate due to the very nature of the evil germinating in the world. The coming of the Fallen will force essence wielders, magi or not, to confront their inner selves in order to confront their greatest enemy.'"

She stopped reading and stared into the book. "The Illuminarians would confront the Fallen, as they have in all of history. But while we know the Fallen are returned simply by the nature of their imprisonment with Shurza, we don't know the fate of the Illuminarians."

"Which means it'll fall to the Order of Magi to confront the Fallen," Emiel surmised. A shadow passed across Amoura's face and she nodded.

"That doesn't sound like such a bad scenario," Bone said. "There's a whole lot of you and only a handful of them."

"Armed with knowledge of the essences that the most powerful magi today could only dream of," Amoura replied. "I wouldn't wish to be among an army of magi battling a handful of Fallen."

"Well, that bodes ill for the future," Emiel said. "Sounds like a battle that can't be won, yet one that's coming anyway. What hope is there, then?"

"The Illuminarians," Amoura answered. "They alone are capable of defeating the Fallen and preventing Shurza's full return."

Shurza. Emiel ran a hand over his clean-shaven head. All the talk about the Fallen, and he'd forgotten about the actual bringer of the Ruination. "Full return. So that thing is already out in the world in some capacity?"

"The appearance of drauk," Amoura said, "was the first sign that it has entered this world. While we were in Altarra, I found every book I could on the subject. Unfortunately, there is little to be found about the Underworld or the Ruination. At least, not in the Altarra library."

"So, you hope to piece it all together from one library to the next," Bone said. "Or at least enough to figure out what's going on, what's going to happen, and how to stop most of it from happening."

"Correct," Amoura replied. "The appearance of the drauk herald the Ruination. There is no doubt in that. What remains undecided is where the immortals are, and what state they are in. There's apparently some kind of connection between the Fallen and their monster, but I haven't found it yet."

Emiel thought on that as he flipped through his book. "Maybe if the Fallen can be found and put back wherever they came from, we might be rid of this Shurza thing?"

"Or at the very least," Amoura replied, "keep it from reaching its full power."

Bone smirked. "That all? Finding the Fallen and the Illuminarians, yatta yatta yatta. I was starting to think this would be hard."

"Meanwhile," Emiel said in a dry tone, "we've got the ole king of Marai waging battle against the Khatala over some slight that happened enough years ago to be forgotten."

"Strike a deadly blow to your enemies while they're fighting each other," Bone said. "Somewhere, I'm sure the Fallen are laughing at us."

Amoura and Bone continued bouncing information back and forth while Emiel focused on his book. He found the names of the various monsters they'd fought, and what would happen to the parts of the world where Shurza passed over. The world would gradually darken, little by little as Shurza grew in power.

This is interesting, he thought upon reaching another section. The coming of the Illuminarians would combat the darkness of the blight essence. He took that to be Shurza, but there seemed to be a darker implication to that reference. He reached one section that sent a chill through his body.

... ability inherent in the Fallen and the Illuminarians to wield the power of the essences through body and stone alike. It seems as though the Creator Himself foresees the coming tragedies that befall the earth. One fact shared throughout the ages is that while it is assured that the immortals would return in the advent of Ruination, it is not, however, assured that the condition of the Illuminarians upon awakening would be of sound mind and body.

In every age and subsequent coming of the Ruination, a person or persons are born with an echo of the abilities the immortals command. One who would wield the power of the essences through body and stone are born to battle Shurza and its minions. The role of such hybrid essence-wielders remains shrouded in mystery. The patterns suggest the possibility of replacing an immortal who might have died or gone mad under the conditions of their entrapment with the Fallen and the blight essence.

Hybrid. Emiel looked up from the book. He'd heard that word before, in Altarra. The magi master, Vladrick, had referred to Emiel as such, and had alluded to Amiya and Nandi sharing his "abilities". Emiel couldn't think of a worse possibility. He needed to find them and get them as far away as possible from ... where?

He tried to slow his increasingly pounding heart. It seemed like this Ruination would cover the world over, so where could he take the girls and hide? Could he? Would they willingly do so? He knew his girls well enough that they would rail against such a notion. Nandi would reason that they'd need to figure out a way to stop this, and that hiding would be pointless. Amiya would argue the same, only pointing out that it would be better to fight now, than let the fight come to them.

They would both be right, and that scared Emiel all the more. He didn't fear dying in itself—aside from being eaten alive—but the thought of harm coming to his girls terrified him. He glanced at Amoura and Bone who still conversed over their own various findings. If the magus knew about this bit of information and how it related to himself and possibly the girls, how would she react?

Would she try to force Emiel to train for this impending doom? Would she try to force it on his daughters as well?

He wanted to scoff at the idea. Amoura wouldn't have helped him escape Altarra and vow to help him find Amiya and Nandi only to turn on him in such a way. Or perhaps she already knew and was trying to lead him to the very information he had just read?

Emiel gave his head a mental shake. *That's paranoia.* But was it? He hadn't met many magi in his life, but one thing they had a reputation for was throwing their weight and influence around. He thought back to every instance he could remember of Amoura's interactions with people over their travels together. Ever had the magus been respectful of each individual she encountered, excluding himself. Well, in the beginning, anyway.

He didn't believe Amoura Xanna would force him and the girls to become magi and fight, but he didn't *want* to believe it, either.

"I think our esteemed spicetrader has found something," Bone quipped.

"What?" Emiel turned to see Bone and Amoura staring at him.

"You've got a guilty look about you," Bone replied. "Like you just found out something and are debating if you're going to tell us."

"Have you found something, Emiel?"

The lack of at least a little steel in Amoura's tone surprised Emiel. They'd read him as easily as the books they studied. "Just trying to think things through. It's all a lot to take in." It was true enough.

"All knowledge has value," Amoura said. "More so amidst a collective effort to solve a problem."

Emiel sighed and was about to hand over the book when the ground vibrated.

The trio froze and listened. The ground vibrated again, followed by a distant boom. Emiel's heart didn't know whether to race or sink. *Not again.*

"Cursed luck of the bloody Fallen," Bone swore. "Carlayn and now here? Are the blasted things following us?"

Amoura closed her book and slipped it back onto the shelf. "No. This will spread across the land and grow in frequency as the time nears."

"Fantastic," Bone said. "And just like in Carlayn, the fools took my sword and I haven't gotten it back."

"Then just like in Carlayn," Amoura replied, "you will retrieve it."

Bone grumbled as they swept down the row towards the door. A series of thuds vibrating the ground stopped them short. The sounds of infernal cursing preceded the screams of the dying.

"They must be after us," Bone said. "Otherwise why attack a library?"

"You think there's some logic to those things?" Emiel asked. Beside him, Amoura's ring came to life in a silver glow, while her eyes changed from their natural silver to bright blue.

Emiel glanced at her hand. When had she gotten her ring back? Must've been that mysterious woman who flagged the magus down while they were leaving.

"Libraries hold knowledge," Amoura said in answer to Bone's question. "Exactly why we're here, and exactly why the Fallen would want it destroyed."

Bone flexed his fists and looked around. "No armor, no weapon, no chance. This is great."

"Guess you'll have to depend on us," Emiel said. He focused on the essences and felt the power acknowledge him. The sensation made him shudder. It felt like calling to an immeasurable sentience that became aware of him. Part of Emiel felt the need to ask permission. He nearly gasped when he felt a response to the stray thought. *Permission granted? Am I going insane?*

Emiel riffled through his thoughts on the monsters they were about to fight. He remembered what the drauk were made of, and focused on water first, then air. The essences came to his call.

Bone slipped around to the side, staring at Emiel the whole time. "Looks like you're getting the hang of this. Get me to my stuff so I can contribute, yeah?"

The thuds grew louder. The thin braids about Amoura's head drifted in the air as she commanded its elemental namesake. The first impact on the door nearly buckled it. Dust and dislodged mortar hissed as it fell from the hinges and the top of the doorway. Amoura's robes drifted in the air as she continued to draw upon the essences.

The sound of rapid whispering and chairs flipping over broke the quiet of the study hall. Visitors scurried away from the door, hiding under desks and in aisles. Many concerned gazes alternated from trio to the doorway.

Emiel felt the power building in him. His fluttering heart slowed, his nerves stilled, and he felt a sense of calmness that lasted until the door exploded and the first four-armed monstrosity crashed in.

Amoura struck before Emiel could even think about it. Freezing air mingled with moisture formed a huge icicle that shot into the drauk with such force, its feet swept up from the ground as it flew back out the door.

Another took its place. The cursing underworld beast broke the doorway apart and headed straight for them. This time Emiel struck. He sent a barrage of ice spears into the monster while buffeting it with freezing air. The red veins of lava coursing about its body hissed in protest while it swung its arms against the frozen projectiles.

As bits of its rocky skin crumbled away, Amoura struck the final blow. She hit the monster with a stream of freezing water that rapidly cooled the lava rock skin and hardened the tiny molten veins all over its body. As its body cooled and it turned a charcoal color, it fell to its knees and broke apart.

Terrified screams followed the trio out of the room. Emiel forced himself not to look at the dismembered corpses strewn about the floor of the corridor on their way out. He kept his focus on the essences, remembering that only *air* and *water* could kill the things.

By the time they reached the main gallery, the screams ceased. *All dead,* Emiel realized. Anyone who hadn't gotten out of this area had been killed.

The entrance to the library had been destroyed. Now, a huge section of the front wall lay in a carpet of rubble, underneath and upon which lay more of the slain.

They raced outside the building and into chaos. Drauk were everywhere, chopping with crude lava rock swords and pounding with clubs of the same material. They cursed and spun, dashed and chopped. Four soldiers had surrounded a drauk and it cut them all down in short order.

Emiel, Amoura, and Bone fought their way through the streets, the former using *air,* and *water* to dispatch drauk wherever they found them.

Bone tried to lift a giant drauk sword, but barely budged the thing. "Fallen curse it. Thing's heavier than it looks. I need my gear!"

"Only place I can imagine it'll be is the barracks," Emiel said.

"It's in the same place it was taken off of you!"

Emiel and Bone turned to see Captain Adolphus and three bloodied soldiers jogging in their direction. "The attack happened earlier," he said. "They're just now reaching the interior of Shiedra." He looked at Amoura, who'd just finished off the last nearby enemy and turned back. "Now's a good chance to prove you're a friend, magus. Help us deal with this."

"I've already begun, Captain," Amoura replied. She pointed at the mercenary. "We need his armor."

"The jails," Adolphus said to one of his soldiers. "Get him there!" He looked back to Amoura. "I need your help out here. There's fighting everywhere and my soldiers can only be in so many places at once. Those things are cutting us apart."

Amoura looked at Emiel, and he read her intent. "I'll get him there," he said.

She responded with a firm nod. "Remember what you've learned." She and the captain moved toward the sounds of fighting, while his soldier led Emiel and Bone in the opposite direction.

Further down the avenue, two drauk dispatched seven soldiers and three civilians with little effort. Emiel forced down the queasiness he felt at seeing the raw brutality and focused on the essences. One of the monsters spotted the trio and tore down the street toward them. A second drauk noticed them as well, but it continued in a different direction.

Emiel hit it in the face with a spear of ice, then in the lower torso with another. It batted aside a third spear, but not without flinching away from the frozen projectile. He continued the assault with a stream of smaller icicles between the heavier barrage. They left the defeated monster in a steaming heap and continued around the corner.

"Straight ahead and left," the soldier called. "After the bend, fifty feet!"

Emiel took the lead. Sweat trickled down the side of his face from the effort of holding a continuous swirl of *air* and *water*, ready to blast anything not human.

They rounded the corner and saw only a section of the jail standing sentry over the remaining rubble. The soldier pointed to a smaller pile of stone and wood. "That's where we keep confiscated gear and weaponry. Your armor would be crushed under that."

"Not likely," Bone said. "I just need to get to it."

"Not likely?" The soldier backpedaled when a drauk suddenly crashed through a nearby wall and took a swing at him. He ducked the rocky sword and sliced the beast from its groin to the opposite side of its waist. If it were human, it would have been left to bleed to death on the ground. The drauk didn't react at all to the sword's bite.

Growling curses in its infernal tongue, the drauk backhanded the soldier with the club of a lower limb. His sword flew from his grasp and hit the wall of a building across the street. The man fell to the stone ground in a heap and didn't get up.

Emiel focused *water* and sent its physical namesake streaming into the drauk. It thrashed in vain against the cold water while inching its way closer. Eventually, the drauk's rocky skin cooled and started to break apart.

The four-armed monster had hardly toppled over and started to crumble when Emiel raced over to the downed soldier. Bone felt his neck. "He's got a pulse, at least."

"Best thing that can happen is these things think he's dead." Emiel hoped the man would be all right, but there was no time to worry about it.

They ran to the pile of rubble that had been the confiscation armory and Bone threw up his hands. "I know my stuff isn't broken, but I can't get to it."

Emiel focused on *earth*. The rubble shifted slightly, but fell back into place. He tried again to similar effect.

Bone looked up and down the street. "Try harder, man. Focus!"

"I'm doing my best to lift several tons of rock, Bone!" Emiel snapped. He tried again, but only managed to shift a few of the massive bricks.

The mercenary cursed something unintelligible as he retrieved the downed soldier's sword. Three drauk were running in their direction, shouting curses and weapons poised to strike.

"I don't know how it works but I've seen you do worse with the ground, spicetrader," Bone hollered. "Do something and do it fast!"

Emiel strained to use *earth* to clear away the rubble, but he couldn't. It was too heavy. He was about to say as much when the rock suddenly lifted into the air and sped down the street to crash into the drauk.

"He's right Emiel." Lief! "Its weight doesn't matter."

While Bone sprinted for the rubble and began digging, Emiel

kept watch while Lief assisted in clearing away the heavy stone. "Got it!" Bone proclaimed. Several moments later he appeared at Emiel's side, fastening the last straps and clips of his nearly indestructible teliak bone armor.

"Let's collect your magus and get out of here," Bone said. "And I'd like not to repeat this experience again wherever we end up next!"

Lief knelt and touched the ground. After a moment, she pointed. "This way!"

Emiel trotted after her. "*My* magus?"

Lief led them down street after street, and not once were they challenged. Emiel could only guess that the tinfar could feel where the fighting was through the ground and avoided it. Likely what she'd done to figure out where Amoura was.

When Amoura finally came into view, it was in the middle of chaos. The magus fought alone against a group of rampaging drauk in the most amazing and terrifying display Emiel had ever seen. Her ring and her eyes shifted between silver, blue, and brown, each color heralding the attack that followed. Such a color shift might be a warning to an attentive foe, but the magus struck so quickly it didn't matter.

Ice spears impaled two drauk while three more fell under the weight of a section of collapsed building. Freezing water cooled and crumbled a few more.

Emiel focused on *air* and *water* again. Lief struck with stalagmites shooting from the ground to impale her targets while Emiel formed a storm of ice shards. Bone raced in behind the horizontally raining shards.

The drauk were caught by surprise and lurched in what seemed like pain. With their backs arched, they made easy targets for Bone. The mercenary leapt mid-stride and beheaded the nearest monster. He rolled past the falling headless torso and came up running.

More drauk crashed through walls and ran toward the defenders. Archers appeared on rooftops and rained arrows down on the underworld monsters. The missiles skipped harmlessly off their rocky skin, while the enraged creatures lifted heavy pieces of rubble and sent them hurtling toward the archers.

Several were hit so hard they flew off their perches, while others cried out and threw themselves out of the way.

"Emiel, watch out!"

Lief's warning saved his life. Without thinking, Emiel dropped to the ground and felt the swoosh of a swinging sword that had nearly taken his head. He rolled onto his back and tried to focus on an essence. *Water* came to his call, but not fast enough.

The curses of the fearsome drauk froze the pit of his stomach, as did the hateful red-eyed glare it cast down on him as it brought both weapons of its upper arms down for the killing blow. Emiel shouted in defiance and struck out. The attack was too slow and too weak. Rocky skin sizzling, the drauk continued its downward stroke.

Emiel thought surely his life at its end when he saw a flash of green hair and a raspy-voiced growl.

The drauk stumbled aside but managed to stay upright. Emiel scooted backwards before scrambling to his feet. He quickly looked around. Another drauk was moving in his direction. Bone had engaged another of the monsters while Amoura finished off several more. Soldiers fought and died, but managed to bring down a couple of the beasts as well.

Emiel struck the approaching drauk with freezing water. It cooled and crumbled apart mid-stride. When he looked back, he saw the most curious of creatures fighting and actually beating a drauk back. A girl that looked no older than his daughters, with green hair and strange gray skin. Her eyes were as black as night, and her snarl looked animalistic.

What in the name of the Fallen is that? He summoned the essences again, but they fell away when he spotted two more girls, one with flaming red hair that made Bone's look almost dim. The other, though. The other had hair braided in cornrows. Her skin was just a bit darker than his, as were her eyes. Darker like his beloved dead wife, Aunya.

"Sama!" the girl yelled in dismay when the girl with the green hair received a backhand by a large club.

Emiel winced. He summoned *air* and *water* again, thinking to avenge the dead girl, for surely she had been killed by such a heavy blow by a creature likely five times her weight. To his disbelief, however, the girl groaned and climbed to her feet. She took a few wobbly steps forward and collapsed.

Emiel barely saw it, so focused was he on the other girl, *his* girl. He could tell by the way she'd yelled out the green-haired girl's name that it was Nandi he saw. His little ladygirl, taller now, with arms sporting tiny muscles.

"Get away from her!" Even Nandi's voice sounded a little deeper. Had it truly been that long?

Emiel snapped out of his stupor. He started to shout her name, but it seemed he was due another shock. Before his very eyes, Nandi created a spear of ice and sent it speeding into the back of the drauk. The ice started to melt as it pierced the monster's body, but she fed it a constant stream of freezing water to maintain its size.

The drauk arched its back and roared as the spear of ice passed through its body. Steam rose up around it, and it fell to its knees and disappeared into the cloud. A heartbeat later, an explosion of ice and rock flew out of the steam.

Emiel shielded his eyes with his forearm against the debris, then looked on his daughter in amazement. She hopped down off a pile of rubble and ran to the girl with the green hair. The redheaded girl ran just behind her.

"Nandi," he breathed. "NANDIIIII!"

"Dad?" She finally spotted him. "Dad! What are you doing here?"

A huge tentacle punched through the stone street and swept across the ground. It knocked several soldiers screaming into the air. Nandi's eyes glowed brown. Chunks of earth exploded around the tentacle until she revealed part of a huge upside-down nautilus-shaped body.

Somewhere behind him, Emiel heard Amoura grunt. He was still running for Nandi when she noticed him, then looked upward past him. "Dad, stop!"

He didn't stop. He sprinted harder. He had to reach her. She was right there, nearly in reach. Hopefully Amiya was nearby, but Nandi was right here.

"Dad. Stop!" Her eyes glowed silver just before she hit him with a gust of wind that knocked him sideways.

Emiel hit the ground rolling. When he finally stopped, he gave his head a shake and looked up. A tall bipedal creature with leathery yellow skin and spikes on its elbows and knees stood in the middle of a small crater. Leaper. If Nandi hadn't knocked him aside, it would have killed him.

The girl with the green hair barely scrambled to her feet and dove aside as another leaper crashed into the ground where she'd been. The impact launched her several feet into the air. She hit the ground and bounced into a wall where she lay gritting her teeth, her arm wrapped around her ribs.

Bone sprinted toward the leaper nearest the green-haired girl. When the monster swung one of its disproportionately long arms at him, Bone dropped and slid underneath it. He came up to one knee, drew his sword and severed the leaper's nearest leg.

While the mercenary set about finishing off the injured monster, a stalagmite burst out of the ground and impaled the one nearest Nandi. It happened an instant before Emiel hopped to his feet and ran towards it, spears of ice forming at his sides. He feathered the leaper with a dozen frozen missiles.

The monster's body jerked this way and that as the sharp ice cut through it, but it couldn't fall over. Lief drew another stalagmite from the ground to impale the leaper from the front and finally it hung limp, suspended in death.

Long waving appendages crashed into the ground around them. Emiel cursed as he was forced to dive aside to avoid being crushed. Not far away, Nandi did the same. She moved so quickly, now. How had she grown so much?

The questions came in a relentless torrent as Emiel watched Nandi hop back to her feet and freeze one of the swatting appendages. The redheaded girl picked up the largest rock she could find and slammed it down on the frozen tentacle. She hit it again and again until small fractures snaked away from the point of impact.

The massive creature screeched and tried to pull free, but a piece of the damaged appendage cracked and broke free, sending the monster into a frenzy. More of its bulk rose out of the ground and it pounded its tentacles at any target within reach.

Captain Adolphus and Officer Taiyana arrived in that moment with another contingent of soldiers. Both drew up short and stared in horror at the massive beast.

Scratched up and bleeding from several places, Amoura gathered herself and ran in front of the newly arrived forces. She spread her arms wide, her eyes and essence ring glowing red. The magus released a cone of flame that spiraled into sky and arced down onto the top of the monster.

The beast screeched as its outer shell and tough hide blistered under the intense heat. Amoura's ring flared sliver while her eyes glowed blue. Freezing water blasted into the boiling hot monster, and its screams turned into high-pitched wails.

Its outer shell cracked apart and Nandi bombarded it with boulders of ice and flaming rock. She was so focused on the giant nautilus-like creature she hadn't noticed a pair of drauk bearing down on her.

Bone intercepted one and cut it across the midsection. What should have been a fatal cut merely drew its attention. The other drauk kept running. Emiel was on the move. He screamed Nandi's name but she didn't hear. He wouldn't make it in time. His daughter was about to die right in front of his eyes.

To the blasted underworld of the Fallen. I'll rip you apart with my bare hands. Without a thought about what he was doing, Emiel created a gust of air that swept the drauk not away from his daughter, but toward himself. At the same time, Emiel jumped, power tingling in his hand. He drew his fist back and punched the monster with all his strength.

The drauk exploded into a shower of lava rock. Emiel landed awkward and fell into a sideways roll. Steaming chunks of the beast fell in a shower over him.

A violent quake shook the ground and nearly knocked him over. Emiel looked around and saw the same frantic expressions on the soldiers faces. *What now?*

In its final death throes, the nautilus creature swatted the ground near Nandi and her two companions. The impact launched the redheaded girl into the air, while the ground around Nandi and the other girl collapsed.

Emiel screamed. He scrambled to his feet and ran towards her, but Nandi disappeared; fell away before his eyes. A pit of ice froze his stomach and the chaos around him faded into the periphery. This wasn't happening. No. She wasn't gone. She couldn't be; not this close.

Everything seemed to happen in slow motion. Soldiers and drauk cut each other down, the nautilus monster pounded the ground around its body, and Amoura practically glided across the distance and reached for Nandi.

Emiel skidded to ta stop at the to the edge of the chasm. Down below, Amoura looked to have slowed the descent of the two girls. As if gravity itself mocked him, the three disappeared down the chasm, pulling them away. The sound of battle continued behind him, but he didn't care. All he could think about was his little girl falling into that black chasm.

Amoura held on to a broken piece of ledge, Nandi's ankle

gripped in her other hand. Nandi hung upside down, swinging back and forth. She and the green-haired girl held on to each other's wrists. All three hung suspended over a gaping black hole of nothingness.

"Hold on!" he called. "I'll get you out!"

"There's no time, Emiel," Amoura called back. "Get to Bone and find your other daughter."

Emiel slowly shook his head. "Don't do it, Amoura. DON'T YOU DARE LET GO!"

Amoura looked into his eyes and time came to a standstill. "Survive, Emiel."

She lost her grip. He heard Nandi's scream. He saw Amoura's eyes glow silver just before the black pit swallowed them all.

NANDI

On the run again. Nandi was beginning to think this was the new normal for her life. They'd run through the day and into the night, chased every step by the Valragan "kidnap patrol", as Nandi called them.

They'd first tried to run southeast to Altarra. Nandi still held some hope that she might find Dad there. To her immense frustration, the Valragans seemed to have known they'd try to run that way. A party of trackers had been deployed to swing around to the southeast and had been waiting on them.

Nandi had wanted to blast them aside, but she couldn't control the power well enough to do it without causing severe injury or death to the riders or—more importantly to Nandi—their horses.

How she loathed the Valragan people for their slavery practices under the guise of "training to be a good wife". She would return one day and free the other girls. Then she would burn that house to the ground.

Having been chased north instead of making their way southeast, the girls crept through the tall grass, practically sliding on their bellies like lizards. The tracking party was still out there, she knew. She could smell them, their horses, and their dogs. Another new thing Nandi had learned while wielding the power. After having stumbled on the technique of using *air* to wash away their scent, she realized she could use the power to bring smells to her as well. Now, the dogs had been much slower in tracking them. She couldn't throw them off completely, as the dogs had powerful noses, but it was enough to keep her and her friends ahead, at least.

She took a deep breath. Horses, dogs, and musty men. Though they were several hundred yards away, it smelled like they were right next to her. A useful tool she wouldn't forget. Nandi wondered what else she could do with the essences besides using them like a weapon.

She crept behind Sama, Ailith close behind. The two hadn't gotten off to a good start. Ailith had yelped and nearly attacked Sama when the tatamble had crept up on them unawares. Nandi had hopped between them before things went bad before they started. She had no doubt about her new friend's ability to defend herself from someone their own age, at least. But Sama would have crushed the girl.

For now, they fled together with Nandi still between them and each side-eyeing the other. Time. They just needed time.

"Psst. *Psssst!*"

Nandi looked over her shoulder. Ailith's green eyes looked back at her. She pointed at herself, then jabbed her finger ahead. Nandi responded with a nod, then held out her hand for her to wait. "Sama," she whispered. "Sama."

"Sama hears sister Nandi."

"Ailith knows the way," Nandi said. "She can lead us through the woods and past the border, out of their reach."

"Sister Nandi trust too much, girl with fire hair."

Nandi shook her head, though the tatamble girl wasn't looking. "I've told you. Sister Sama was so quiet that she startled Ailith. Fire-hair girl is our friend, Sama. I promise."

The silence stretched for so long, Nandi thought Sama wasn't going to reply. "If sister Nandi promise, Sama will allow. But Sama will watch."

She couldn't ask for more than that. It was a great deal of progress from the previous day. She looked back over her shoulder to see Ailith rolling her eyes. She signaled for the girl to take the lead.

Ailith crept forward, stopping beside Nandi just long enough to whisper, "I hope that thing doesn't take a bite out of me."

"Maybe Sama use fire hair to cook girl with bad mouth," came the response from ahead, "and then take bite."

Nandi covered her mouth to stifle her giggling while the growling Ailith moved ahead.

They continued their careful progress forward, stopping occasionally to peek out of the grass to make sure they hadn't been spotted. The riders had spread out and were trying to cover as much ground as possible. Nandi had managed to blow their scent in another direction to throw the dogs off, but it only lasted so long before they caught the right direction again.

Nandi wiped sweat from the side of her face. She'd never delved the power for such a prolonged period of time and found it tiring. She focused, though, and held on. Eventually they reached a rocky hill where the grass thinned out in every direction.

"There's nothing else to hide in from this point forward," Ailith called back. "We'll have to make a run for it."

"You're sure?" Nandi whispered back.

"Aye," came the response.

Nandi took a deep breath. "Okay. We'll move slow and low to the ground. Maybe they won't spot us."

"The Nashma border is over the hill," Ailith said. "We reach the border and there'll be a border patrol to chase away those rats."

"Then, let's get there," Nandi said. Maybe the people in charge of Nashma might help her get to Altarra and look for Dad.

Ailith led them out of the tall grass and toward the hill. They kept low, only Sama managing to be virtually invisible, as she'd shifted her hue to match the color of the ground. About halfway up, Nandi heard the shouts. All three girls turned to see their mounted pursuers racing toward them.

They ran up the rocky hill, darting between large rocks and boulders. The gravelly terrain made their progress slower than desired, but it also slowed the horses. The dogs, however, had no such trouble.

"Keep going," Nandi shouted. "I'll be right behind you!" She shifted her focus from *air* to *water.* Once she had a full grasp of the essence, she turned and created a stream of water that she focused on the ground and spread out to the sides.

Gravely dirt terrain quickly became mud that eroded under hoof and paw alike. The tracking hounds slipped and fell more than they moved forward, while the horses stumbled in the slick mud. Nandi winced and continued on. She hoped none of the horses would break a leg.

She reached the top of the hill where Sama and Ailith waited, and the three of them ran down the other side and continued across the open field. They'd put only a few hundred feet behind them when the first of their pursuers crested the hill.

"The Nashma border's just ahead!" Ailith called.

"Do they know that?" Nandi asked.

"Yes," came the reply. "That's why they're trying so hard to get to us now. They'll chase us until they see the patrol."

"Great," Nandi said, seeing no signs of any such thing. The sun had just crested the eastern horizon and cast its morning glow over the land. "Is the patrol hiding somewhere?"

"I don't know," Ailith finally answered. "We're in their territory and might have already crossed in. We should see someone by now!"

Nandi heard the thundering hoofbeats as the horses drew closer. They were in an open field with nowhere to hide and nowhere to climb. There was no question that they'd be caught.

"It's gonna be a fight," Ailith called from up ahead. "Might as well get ready for it."

"We've got no weapons," Nandi replied.

"Then it's going to be a choice for each of us." Ailith slid to a stop and turned. She picked up a handful of rocks and waited. "I've got nothing but this, but it'll have to do. I'm not going back without a fight, and I'll fight till they kill me!"

Sama turned, as did Nandi. The tatamble bared her teeth and flexed her long-nailed fingers. "Sama will fight. Even with fire-hair girl."

"We might just be friends yet," Ailith replied.

Nandi swallowed the dread in her stomach and made her decision. If it cost lives, she would have to live with it. They weren't taking her back, either, and they weren't taking her friends. "Everyone just keep running. They're not taking us anywhere."

She delved *fire*. The essence leapt to her call, and she remembered the essence ring on her finger. It flared red. Beside her, Ailith gasped. "What?" she asked.

"Your eyes," Ailith said. "They're glowing as red as your ring."

"Get going," Nandi said. "I'm going to delay them and I'll be right behind you."

The other girls wasted no time and took off. Nandi called *fire* to her command and used its physical namesake to surround her body in a swirling globe. It came so readily to her call she barely had to concentrate. Was this how the rings worked for all magi? Nandi had to remind herself of the danger, lest she fall into reveling in the power.

The horses whinnied and pulled up, much to the frustrated curses of their riders. "She's wielding the power!" one of them shouted.

"How is that possible?" yelled another. "She's just a girl."

"She stole the headmistress's essence ring!"

"That doesn't mean she should be able to use it," another yelled back.

Nandi made the fiery globe expand, sending tendrils of flame spewing at the horses and dogs. *Just to scare them.* She turned and ran. Every so often she sent a flare of fire out behind her and heard the whine of the dogs or the terrified whinnies of the horses.

Despite her efforts to intimidate them, the dogs and riders bore down on her. She had to try something else. Then it came to her. A barrier. Nandi re-focused the essence and sent a wide flare out in front of her. The riders fought with their mounts while the dogs flinched away from the flames crackling the burning grass. She started to create a wall of fire but realized they'd just go around it.

Instead, Nandi encircled the pursuers in flame. The horses screamed in terror while the dogs barked but backed away. The men were forced to dismount and hold the reins of their panicked mounts. Soon the entire group were huddled together, encircled by a ten-foot-high cylinder of fire.

Satisfied they wouldn't die of the heat, but not get away to pursue either, Nandi ran on. Without understanding how, she knew she'd put just enough power into the flames for them to last long enough for her and her friends to be far within Nashma's borders and hopefully found by the patrol.

Nandi continued to glance back until the circle of flames were little more than a red dot on the horizon. Ailith announced that they were well within the Nashmarese border, yet no patrol had found them.

"I don't understand," Ailith breathed once they stopped to rest. "We're almost to Shiedra. They should have found us a long time ago." She looked back the way they'd come. "How long're those flames gonna last?"

"They should have died out by now." Nandi looked over her shoulder as well.

BOOM.

They whirled in the direction of the distant sound.

BOOM.

Nandi, Sama, and Ailith looked at each other. *BOOM.* They looked back toward the sound. Northeast.

The pit of Nandi's stomach sank. "Dad always says when things are going wrong, they tend to pick up speed."

Ailith nodded, the fluffy curls of her unwieldy red hair bouncing with the movement. "Aye. My da used to say somewhat the same."

"I don't want to be anywhere near whatever that sound is," Nandi said after another distant boom.

"I don't think we have much choice," Ailith said. She looked back to the south as if she could see the Valragans coming. "We're close to Shiedra. Whatever's going on there, I'd rather gamble with that, than be captured again. Or," she pointed west, "we head to New Dama if you want another several days on the run. That's the closest civilization besides Shiedra, and it's not close."

Just the thought of trekking all the way to New Dama had Nandi walking toward Shiedra. The others fell in step beside her. Soon they were jogging toward the Nashmarese capital.

Nandi tried to let herself enjoy the crisp morning air and clear blue sky, but as they neared the city, the sounds of what surely must be some sort of battle grew louder.

"Well, now we know why no patrol found us," Ailith remarked. "What's going on over there?"

Nandi had a sinking feeling she knew exactly what was going on. By the time they reached the capital of Nashma, there could be no doubt that it was indeed a battle. Other sounds rose above the cacophony.

"What in the name of the Fallen is that?" Ailith asked. She stared at the distant explosions. "Did you hear that? Some strange language I've never heard of. And they sound angry."

"Those things," Nandi said. "It's those things again." Beside her, Sama hissed.

Ailith looked at them both, then back to Shiedra. "You know what that is?"

Nandi nodded. "Four-armed monsters with clubs and swords made of lava rock. They're big and fast, and spit curses in a language no one understands, but is without a doubt evil."

"Great," Ailith said. "Maybe New Dama isn't so bad an idea."

"I'd like to bypass this," Nandi said. "But if I can help, I have to."

Ailith groaned. "Of all the girls to escape with, it had to be the suicidal hero type. Fine. If you're going in there, I'm with you. You broke me out of Valraga and I'll not be soon forgetting it, don't doubt."

"Sama will never leave sister Nandi." The tatamble girl turned her determined coal black gaze on Nandi. "Sama will go."

Nandi looked at them both and felt awash in gratitude and determination. With these two at her side, all they needed was to find her sister, and nothing would stop them from finding Dad. "All right. We're doing it." They trotted toward the embattled city. "Ailith, do you know how to use any kind of weapon?"

"Aye," the Border Highland girl replied. "My da taught me the sword. My ma taught me to throw a punch. Same punch what near knocked my da out when he first tried to touch her without askin'."

"How fire-hair girl's parents not kill each other if they fight?" Sama asked. Nandi looked at her, but the tatamble was genuinely curious. "Sama not understand how girl's parents fight but later join to make fire-hair girl."

Ailith giggled. "You've never been to the Border Highlands, have you, lass?"

"What is lass?" Sama asked.

"It's what we call a girl or a young woman in my homeland," Ailith explained.

"So, Sama is lass because Sama has no mate?" She jabbed a finger into Nandi's side.

"Ouch!" Nandi rubbed her side. "You trying to ram that stone finger through my ribcage?"

"Sister Nandi is lass, too?" She tried to poke Ailith as well, but the girl saw Nandi's pain and hopped out of reach. "Ailith girl, too?"

"Er, ya," Ailith replied while trying not to laugh. "Me, Nandi, and Sama girl, all are lass because we are young and not married."

"What is girl when she has mate?" Sama asked.

"You'll have to finish this later," Nandi interrupted. She'd been using *air* to listen farther ahead, and heard the infernal curses of the four-armed monsters. She heard something else, too. It sounded as though it might be tunneling or breaking through the ground. Nightmarish memories of her, Amiya's, and Joga's escape from Vyne rushed back. The fear invoked by the huge creature froze the pit of her stomach. She forced herself to acknowledge the feeling so she could banish it. She was able to delve the essences and she had a ring to augment her abilities. Dad would do the same if he were here.

Shiedra must have been a beautiful place if not for the wanton death and destruction. One in four colorful and vibrant flowerbeds, rock and cactus gardens and reddish-brown adobe buildings lay in ruin. Blood of the slain soaked into the soil and stained the flat stone avenues.

The three girls crept along the streets, and Nandi led them past the broken remains of a four-armed monster. Steam still rose from its rapidly cooling body.

Nandi let go of *air* to keep from gagging on the intense coppery smell of blood, as well as the scattered remains of the dead, some not whole.

Beside her, Ailith lurched to the side and emptied her stomach into a flowerbed. Nandi clamped her eyes shut against the nauseating sound, but it got the better of her stomach. She dropped to her hands and knees and heaved up every bit of food she'd eaten in the last day. Just the sensation and sound of it made her vomit until she her body simply locked up.

She knew she was extremely vulnerable, but it took several moments before the muscles in her stomach relaxed enough for her to stand again. She looked around until she found a nearby fountain.

Nandi ran to the fountain and dipped her hands in, then sipped and rinsed out her mouth. Ailith had come in right beside her and done the same while Sama stood to the side, watching for danger.

"Okay," Nandi croaked. "Let's keep moving."

"Sister Nandi and fire-hair girl eat something bad? Sama not feel it."

"Yeah, sure," Nandi lied. "Something we ate. Let's go—"

They heard the thudding footfalls only a moment before the four-armed monster rounded a corner and spotted them. Pure evil radiated from its narrow red glare to match the unintelligible curses it spewed.

Nandi remembered the creatures' hot rocky skin and delved *air* and *water*. Beside her, Sama hissed. The tatamble took off toward the stomping monster.

On her other side, she heard Ailith yell a stream of curses that were very much understandable, and would have had Dad coating her tongue with soap.

Sama and the rocky creature met in a flurry of swinging clubs and chopping swords. Although terribly fast for its size, the creature remained one step behind the tatamble. Sama slipped around every weapon despite there being four of them. She struck kicks and openhanded strikes that actually caused the beast to stumble.

As soon as she found an opening, Nandi struck with a freezing blast of water. In a few heartbeats, the monster fell apart in a little more than a steaming pile of rubble.

"Girl's got a good punch," Ailith remarked.

Nandi found herself agreeing with equal surprise. She'd known Sama was strong for her size, but she'd never seen the girl fight like she had just now.

"You hear that?" Ailith asked.

Nandi strained to listen above the clamor. At first all she heard was screaming, dying, and the curses of the monsters. But then she heard what sounded like a soldier shouting orders. She *delved* air and tried to keep it focused on her ears and not her nose. The sounds became so clear it felt like the soldiers were all around her. "It's coming from that way." She pointed toward a walkway on the other side of the fountain.

It didn't take long before they found the soldiers as well as the source of the explosions. Several units of soldiers struggled against four veritable whirlwinds of death that were the four-armed beasts. They tried to form up ranks and fight with some semblance of tactic, but the cursing monsters just spun and chopped, spun and stabbed. One heavy blow from an upper or lower arm was enough to send a soldier flying, or shear through the sword of an ill-angled block.

A man in the strangest armor Nandi had ever seen battled two of monsters at once. He probably received more hits than he took, but to Nandi's eyes, the man—the young man—seemed to know which blows his armor could absorb in order to position himself for a better strike.

A single woman battled five at once. Her purple robes swished about as she moved here and there, blasting with shards of ice, jets of freezing water or air, stalagmites bursting from the ground.

Magus. Nandi started in her direction when Sama growled and took off toward a monster bearing down on a man who scooted away. The tatamble leapt straight at the beast and barreled into its side. She threw herself at the stumbling creature while Nandi tried to find an opening.

The man who'd nearly been killed scrambled to his feet and hit another monster with a jet of water. Another magus? Nandi frowned. Through the chaos she couldn't clearly make him out, but he didn't seem to be dressed like one.

Sama's raspy grunt tore her attention from the curious man. "Sama!" The monster had dealt her a heavy backhand that sent her friend flying into a pile of rubble. That blow would have killed an unarmored man, and likely injured an armored one. "Get away from her." Nandi delved *air* and *water*. She created a giant spear of ice and sent it speeding into the back of the monster.

It roared to the sky when the ice punched through its back and out of its chest. Nandi narrowed her eyes in focus. The ice began to melt upon contact with the heat of the beast's burning lifeblood. She continued to feed the ice spear freezing air and water, maintaining it as she pushed it farther through the monster's torso.

When it dropped to its knees, Nandi drew both ends of the ice in on itself and focused it into the center of the lava rock monster. Somehow, she knew how to do it, knew what she would do next. The more she delved, the more Nandi could feel how the essences worked.

Once she had the ice focused inside the core of the monster, she thrust a massive amount of *air* into it. The resulting explosion left little more of the creature than scattered rubble.

"NANDIIII!"

What? Nandi spun in the direction of the voice. Dad's voice. "Dad?" How could it be possible? "Dad! What are you doing here?"

They made eye contact. Nandi couldn't believe it. Dad. It *was* him! But how? Why here? *Later.* She started to run to him but a giant tentacle burst out the ground. *No, no, NO!* She would not be separated from Dad just after finding him again. *No!*

At a loss, the soldiers tried to form up ranks to figure out how to deal with this new threat. The four-armed monsters were all but destroyed, only a few left being dispatched by the magus. Another tentacle burst free and pounded the ground.

Nandi's essence ring flared brown as she delved *earth*. She focused on the ground around appendages where she guessed the body would be. Bit by bit she lifted and crushed rock and soil until the body came into view. Hopefully it would give the soldiers and the magus a target.

From the corner of her eye, Nandi saw Dad running toward her. When she looked in his direction, something else caught her eye from high in the sky. She looked up and her heart lurched in fear. A leaper. She remembered the terrible things out in the wilds during their flight from Vyne. Tall, yellow monsters with red slits for eyes and no mouth. Just as she remembered, the thing used the leathery membrane in the pit of its arms to guide its descent, which was in a straight line for Dad.

"Dad, stop. STOP!" Nandi pushed her hands toward him in a warding gesture, but he ignored her. He was so focused on getting to her, he completely blocked out everything else around him.

Nandi looked up again. The leaper was about to crash on top of him. Her essence ring flared silver as she delved *air*. She focused a burst of the essence's namesake and hit him from the side. The force knocked him sideways and sent him rolling over a dozen feet away. *Sorry, Dad. You're alive to forgive me later.*

The impact from the leaper's landing shook the ground and sent chunks of earth flying. Before Nandi could think about dealing with it, she saw Sama dive to the side just before a second leaper crashed into the ground where she'd been. The impact lifted her off the ground. Nandi gritted her teeth when she saw Sama bounce across the broken street and hit a wall. The tatamble scrambled to her feet, however, and remained crouched with her hand pressed to her ribcage.

Suddenly, the boy in the strange armor was there. He went at the leaper with fury, ducking under the swipe of a long arm and eventually severing one of its legs. Nandi felt confident he would finish it off and returned her attention to the leaper that was now stalking towards her. She started to delve again when a stalagmite burst out of the ground and impaled it. Nandi frowned and looked about. Dad ran toward the leaper, teeth bared in fury. She'd never seen him angry like that.

Razor sharp shards of ice formed around him and sped away. They zipped across the distance between them and took the leaper in the joints, neck, and abdomen. Nandi swallowed hard at the precision of the attack. The leaper's body jerked under the force of the impacts, but the stalagmite held it upright as it died.

The monster with the waving tentacles swatted the ground again. Nandi dove aside when another struck the ground nearby. She hopped to her feet, delved *air*, and focused a freezing blast on the appendage. It tried to rise again, but she froze it solid. The limb fell back to the ground with a heavy thud.

Ailith was there in an instant. The girl had found a big rock somewhere and gritted her teeth as she struggled to lift it over her head. She slammed it down on the frozen appendage, then lifted it again.

She's going to drop that thing on her head. Nandi used just a bit of *air* to help Ailith lift the rock, then focused more to strengthen her downward swing. This time the rock hit the frozen tentacle with enough force to break it apart, which sent the monster into a raging fit. Soldiers threw themselves out of the way as it slammed the ground with its remaining tentacles.

A violent quake shook the ground so violently Nandi lost her footing. She cut her leg on a piece of rubble, but the adrenaline pumping through her body dulled the pain. She scrambled upright again and tried to shake off the disorientation, but another crash hit the ground nearby, and she was suddenly falling.

Nandi didn't know up from down. One moment she knelt at the base of a pile of rubble, then next, she was falling headfirst into a gaping hole of nothing. She heard Sama's raspy cry of dismay. On pure instinct she looked up—which was down—and stretched out her arm. Sama reached for her and the two grabbed each other's forearms.

Their hands slid down until they were now holding each other's wrists. So preoccupied with holding on to Sama, Nandi didn't realize someone held on to her ankle until she heard Dad's voice.

She looked in the direction of her feet and saw that it was the magus who held her ankle. The woman held on to a blasted ledge with one hand, and Nandi—and by extension, Sama—with the other. Dad's panicked face appeared over the side of the ledge, much too far above to reach them.

"Don't do it, Amoura," she heard him yell. "DON'T YOU DARE LET GO!"

A brief silence followed, then the magus named Amoura said something in a soft tone that Nandi couldn't hear, and they fell.

ONE MOMENT she was hanging upside down, holding on to Sama, the next, they were falling. The rush of air and darkness swallowed Dad's horrified screams. She tried to focus on delving *air* to slow their descent, but it slipped away again and again. She clamped her eyes shut and strained to grab hold of the power.

Several heartbeats later they began to slow, though Nandi had no better a grip on *air* than she had in her previous efforts. She opened her eyes and looked around. Two silver orbs glowed at her from a few feet away. The glow illuminated the magus's face, giving her features both a majestic and eerie appearance. "Focus and assist me," she said.

"I can't delve enough to go upward," Nandi replied.

"There are no known essence wielders who can fly," the woman said. "Assist me in bringing us all down safely. Calm yourself and focus."

Nandi took a deep breath and concentrated on *air* again. Like a skittish deer, the essence finally came to her call, and she channeled it underneath them. Everyone jerked and tumbled in the open space. Somewhere behind her, Sama grunted nervously.

The magus quickly regained control and their rapid descent continued. "Focus on a heavy wind blowing from below. Like a powerful gust of air underneath you."

"I understand," Nandi replied, and tried again. This time, she channeled the essence downward, then in an upward sweep. After a few more jerky moments, they steadied out and their descent slowed.

"Good," Amoura said. "You learn fast. Are you Nandi or Amiya?"

"Nandi," she answered. "You must know dad."

"I do. We've been traveling together for some time now, trying to find you and your sister."

Nandi looked up at the quickly diminishing light above. Dad was up there. So close but so far. "Since you had to ask my name, I guess you haven't found Amiya."

"Unfortunately we haven't, but if she is as powerful as you are, I fear little for her safety until your father finds her."

"When does falling stop," a panicked Sama said from somewhere nearby. "Sama does not like floating with no sight."

Nandi saw the magus's curious expression and remembered the first time she'd heard the tatamble's voice. She looked down at the blackness below, then back to Amoura's silver glowing eyes. "I think I agree. This makes me nervous."

"I don't know how far down this goes," the magus replied. "But it seems a long way." She nodded approvingly at Nandi. "Your control is good." She then looked down at Nandi's finger where the essence ring glowed as silver as the magus's eyes. "Where did you get that?"

Nandi raised her hand and looked at the ring. "It's a long story."

"You clearly don't need it," Amoura said. "The *arah* in your eyes speaks of your ability to control the essences without use of the ring."

"It helps me have more control," Nandi admitted. "But don't you already know that? All magi use the ring this way, don't they?"

"No," Amoura replied. "Magi use the ring as their sole tool to control the essences."

Nandi frowned. "But you're delving without needing the ring, too. Your eyes glow with the silver *arah*. You have that same glow in your eyes."

The magus looked away. "That is a matter of training. I was trained in the more ancient way of wielding the power. Not many magi learn that way anymore."

"Oh," Nandi said. "How many?"

"I know of none other than myself, though I haven't traveled to every corner of the world."

Nandi thought that, along with this woman's reaction, odd. She looked down again. "We've got to be close to the bottom. How far down *is* wherever we're going?"

"Sama does not like this! Sama wants back on the ground."

"Be patient, child," Amoura replied. "We will eventually reach the bottom."

"Woman who steals Mother's power and keeps it as her own tells Sama to wait."

Nandi expected Sama to spit after growling out that statement. The two glowing essence rings and Amoura's glowing eyes lit just enough of the magus's face for Nandi to see her questioning expression. "Her kind don't take kindly to essence wielders," she explained. "Give it time. She'll warm up to you."

"Her kind?" Amoura asked. "Is she from some distant part of Marai?"

"Oh, she's from Marai," Nandi answered. "But she's a tatamble."

If the magus knew what a tatamble was, her expression gave no indication one way or the other. "We are doing our best to get safely to the ground, Sama," she said. "I am a friend."

Sama growled something unintelligible behind Nandi, who looked at Amoura and shrugged.

After what seemed like hours, they exited the darkness into a massive open space lit by glowing plant life Nandi had never seen before. Glowing blue and green moss-like plants clung to monstrous stalagmites and stalactites scattered throughout the cave. Could she even call it a cave? The place was so huge Nandi couldn't see the end of it in any direction. Even Sama briefly forgot about her mistrust of the magus and stared openmouthed at the colorful glow.

As they drifted ever downward, the shadows of towering carved stone edifices came into view. "By the Creator," Nandi breathed. "People live down here?"

"That is a good question," Amoura replied. "If so, let's hope they're friendly."

"Do you hear that?" Nandi strained to listen. "Sounds like running water."

"Very interesting," the magus said. "A running stream. If so, it might lead us back to the surface."

"A long, long way from here," Nandi replied. "Judging from how long we've been falling." She looked at the woman's glowing eyes again. "Thanks. Nothing would have been left of us once we hit down there."

Amoura's lips pressed together in a conservative smile. "You're welcome, Nandi." Her long thin braids fell over her face when she looked down. "I suspect you'd have had enough time in your fall to regain control enough to save yourselves."

Nandi doubted that, but she appreciated the confidence. "Maybe."

Finally they landed. Sama scampered away and crouched a good distance from the other two. Nandi stumbled through her landing, while the magus settled to the ground with admirable grace. She pretended not to watch the woman from the corner of her eye while she tried to comfort Sama. How long had Dad been traveling with her? She seemed nice enough, if reserved. She also seemed to have some sort of affection for him. Nandi had picked that up in the woman's tone when she'd said whatever she said to Dad.

Nandi shoved all that away for later. "She's a friend of my

father's, Sama. She was helping him to find me and she just saved our lives."

The tatamble kept her wary glare on the magus, who made no move to come closer. "Human steals Mother's power and uses as weapon. Sama saw."

"Have you already forgotten brother Joga?" Nandi asked the girl. "Khatala man borrows Mother's power to do good, too."

Sama's black-eyed stare flickered from Amoura to Sama. She could practically see the tatamble girl coming to the conclusion that her logic was defeated. "Humans care nothing for Mother. Humans only want Mother's power."

Nandi held her hands to her chest. "Sister Sama hurts Nandi. We come so far together. Nandi never steals from Mother."

"Sister Nandi, sister Amya and brother Joga different," Sama responded, somewhat weaker.

"Not all humans steal," Nandi pressed. "Many love and respect Mother like Sama; like all tatamble."

Sama peeled her gaze away from Nandi to look at the magus again. Amoura stood patiently to the side, looking about the area with the interest of a scholar. "Sister Nandi is sure?"

Nandi crouched in front of the girl. "Sister Nandi's father is a good man. If he trusts that woman, Nandi trusts her."

Sama growled petulantly, but stood, Nandi straightening with her. "If sister Nandi trust, Sama will trust. Will watch, but will trust."

It was as good as she was going to get. Nandi looked around the massive cavern. The glowing moss lit the cavern floor wherever it grew, but it didn't shine nearly bright enough to illuminate even a fraction of the place.

They followed the magus to a wide set of stone steps leading up to a stone structure that stretched so high it disappeared into the darkness above. Nandi looked to the side and saw what looked like a sconce on the five-foot tall pillar at the base of the steps. She stretched up onto her toes and looked inside. It was made of some kind of metal. She then looked at the shoulder-high wall connected to the pillar that led up the steps.

A groove had been carved into the top of the wall, and upon closer inspection, she thought she saw some sort of liquid. *What is that?* Nandi wished she had a torch, then thumped the side of her head when she remembered the essences.

She delved *fire*, and created a small globe of its physical namesake. She leaned forward to look into the groove but when she brought the globe too close, the liquid ignited.

"Aah!" Nandi fell onto her backside. When she heard the whoosh of the fire, she looked up to see the flames traveling up and down both lengths of the wall. The metal sconce lit into a large flame, while the fire traveling up the other end of the wall lit another sconce further up.

She watched in amazement as the fire traveled along an intricate path up the facade of the stone structure, lighting sconces as it passed. Soon, the entire structure was visible.

"Wow." Nandi craned her head back to take in the immensity of it. "Who did all this?"

The structure had been carved straight out of the cavern wall. Open windows sat agape, some beside balconies or connecting walkways bridging one to another. Statues dotted the inner courtyard, some in the form of people, others in the form of various animals, while others still in the form of humans astride horses.

"My guess," Amoura answered, "would be master stonemasons like none the world has seen for millennia or more. I've not ever heard of such a place."

Nandi realized Sama had gone quiet. She tore her gaze away from the sight to see that she was also staring wide-eyed at everything. She looked back to the steps as curiosity took hold. What might be inside this place?

They ascended the steps and looked through the windows at the glow of flickering firelight illuminating the rooms within. Nandi couldn't fathom the planning it must have taken to design and carve out a path for the fire to travel in order to light this entire structure. And, how had they done it in the dark? *Had to have been essence wielders*, she surmised. *How else?*

"Most interesting," the magus remarked.

"What?" Nandi said. "Other than your seriously understating how great this all is, what are you talking about?"

"It seems to be deserted," Amoura said. "Yet there isn't a sign of any previous life. Either every soul moved away from this place, or they would have lived out their lives and died here."

"No remains," Nandi surmised. "No skeletons or clothes or anything." She looked at the magus. "Maybe there's a cemetery around?"

"Maybe." Amoura inspected the walls. "There." She pointed to a stone staircase. "Let's see if we can get a higher point of view."

"Place too quiet," Sama said from behind. "No life, no death, air is not good for breath."

"Stale," Nandi agreed. "The air *is* a kind of stale down here."

"We're fortunate there is air down here at all," Amoura replied. "Come."

They followed Amoura up the steps, the magus slowly creeping up, her eyes and essence ring glowing a dim red. Nandi guessed she must be holding the power ready to strike, much like a soldier held her sword at the ready. She delved for *fire* as well, and held it ready.

The second floor was much like the first in that it was devoid of any indications of recent habitation. But the room they passed through on their way to the next set of steps housed a stone slab with tattered blankets, rotted over time. *A bed*, Nandi realized. That gave her a bit of comfort. At least she knew someone human, or at least resembling a human, had lived here. But where had they gone?

"Sama," Nandi called back. "Do you smell anything?"

"Nasty air," came the reply.

"No," Nandi restrained her giggle. "I mean, do you smell anything living. Is anything alive in this place other than us?"

The tatamble sniffed loudly several times. "Sama smells only rodents and bugs. Bats live here, but not inside. Nothing else in here alive."

Amoura glanced over her shoulder at Nandi. She gave the woman a confident nod. "If something was in here waiting on us, she'd smell it a long way off."

The magus didn't exactly stride up the steps with alacrity, but she did relax just a bit. As they continued their climb ever higher, the muscles in Nandi's legs started to burn. "We going all the way to the top?"

"Yes," Amoura said. "But we will rest a moment."

That was a surprise. Nothing in the woman's tone indicated she'd needed a break. Maybe she figured Nandi needed one.

"Sama will look ahead." The girl bounded past them and disappeared around the bend to the next floor.

"I wish I had her strength," Nandi said.

"Perhaps in time," Amoura replied, but Nandi was already shaking her head.

"No, it's actually not possible." She jerked her chin in the direction Sama had gone. "She *looks* like a girl my age. Might even be my age. But she's at least as strong as an adult."

Amoura arched an eyebrow at that. "Oh?"

Nandi nodded. "Trust me, you don't want to be on her bad side."

"Sounds like I nearly was, earlier."

Nandi shrugged. "She's mistrustful of anyone who wields the power. I think maybe all her people are."

"And who might "her people" be?"

"They're called tatamble. They live in the wilds, far away from humans."

"Fascinating," Amoura said. "I've never heard of a tatamble before."

"They avoid us. They don't trust any of us, not Marailander or Khatala."

The magus stood and straightened her purple robes. "They aren't alone in that sentiment."

Nandi waited for the woman to elaborate, but she said no more. They continued up the steps, reaching the top, crossing through a bedroom or social room of some sort, time and again. When they finally reached the top of the last set of stairs, they found Sama staring curiously at another metal sconce.

Upon closer inspection, Nandi saw that it was connected to yet another wall with a groove filled with the flammable liquid. The wall stretched up into the darkness. "I wonder what that'll light."

"Why not find out?" Amoura said.

Remembering what happened last time, Nandi took a step back before creating a globe of flame. She concentrated on the fire and willed a tiny stream straight into the sconce. Flames lit in the sconce and traveled up the wall, lighting the darkness as it went.

They waited in silence, hearing the occasional whoosh when another sconce lit. Nandi nearly jumped out of her skin when she heard Sama's frightened hiss. "Flames light the sky in fire!"

Nandi and Amoura followed the tatamble girl's gaze into the distance where a tiny red line traced a distant wall and traveled upward. Nandi's heart pounded in her chest when she saw what looked like spiderwebs of fire streaking across the ceiling of the great cavern. They ended at the hole where they'd entered, likely the ceiling had collapsed some long time ago. Nandi tried not to think about such an event happening again while they were down here. "Whoever lived down here, how in the name of the Creator did they do all this? Where did the liquid come from that lights from fire, and how did they get it up there?" She shook her head. "It's impossible."

"I know this place," Amoura said.

"You do?" Despite only having known the magus in the brief

time since their fall, Nandi found herself surprised to hear such awe in the magus's voice.

"I know *of* it," Amoura clarified. She pointed out at portion of the cavern now fully lit.

Nandi's mouth fell open. The area Amoura had pointed out could easily hold all of Vyne. "What *is* this place?"

The magus's answer shattered her awe. "We've found a place thought not to exist by some, and forever buried and lost to the world by others. What you see ahead is the Chamber of the Immortals."

AMIYA

"Where're we going?" Amiya massaged the bits of exposed scalp between her cornrow braids. The headache had mostly gone, but every so often a throb would hit. It felt like her heart was beating in her skull.

"Did you not insist that your father resides in Jietar?" Estrella replied.

"Mmph." Amiya could kick herself. Apparently she'd called out to Dad and Nandi during her wild episode in the Shattered Lands, and of course, Estrella hadn't missed it. She pressed her hand to her forehead and prayed to the Creator these occasional pains would cease. "I'd call it being held in Jietar more than residing. How long have we been walking?"

"Not long," came the reply. "Perhaps an hour."

"An hour and I don't know where we're going?" Amiya shook her head, then winced. She glanced at the sky and glared in the general direction of the torturous sun. "Why's it have to be so blasted *bright* right now?"

"The headaches have already become infrequent. As quickly as you've recovered, I think they should completely subside in less than another hour."

Amiya wanted to ask questions but she settled for walking in silence until the blasted throbbing in her head went away again. By midday the landscape changed from flat and barren, to rocky and sprinkled with cacti.

"Mind telling me what you did to me, back there?" she asked during another headache hiatus.

"I didn't do a thing to you, little one."

"I gotta disagree," Amiya argued.

Estrella smiled. "What I did was allow you to feel true power."

"And what's that supposed to mean? True power."

"How is your head?"

Amiya's frown deepened. "What? What's that got to do with—"

"I will not explain while you are preoccupied with your headache. If you would understand the experience I've gifted you with, I would have your undivided attention." She spared Amiya a violet-colored glance. "Preferably uninterrupted."

"All right, I get it. My head's fine and I'll keep my mouth closed."

"Good." Estrella's expression grew distant. "There is more than one way to experience the power. Magi have a pedestrian method with which to experience the power.

"The Khatala westerners, wilders, as Marailanders call them, have a deeper connection to the power. Because they access the essences through their own being, their understanding is more intuitive and deep, less academic. They can feel the power, become part of it to a degree. Their experience of the essences enables them to wield the power in what could be perceived as a more creative manner."

Amiya opened her mouth to ask a question, then remembered her promise. Estrella noticed, however. "Speak, little one, lest your question distract you from my words."

"How is it the Khatala are so different from Marailanders? They might be bigger, but they're not different otherwise, that I can see. Wouldn't magi wish to be able to access the power in a deeper way like this?"

"Superstition drifts along the currents of the ages, girl. Marai-landers at large may view essence wielders with suspicion, but the Order of Magi is little better."

"Wow," Amiya said. "You seem to love the Order of Magi *so* much."

Estrella smirked. "I have some experience with them. Children playing with tools they barely understand."

"But you do," Amiya said. "You know more about the essences than an entire organization of people who've dedicated their lives to studying them."

"Have care with the questions you ask, little one," Estrella warned. "You may not be prepared for the answer."

Amiya rolled her eyes. "Ah. So, we're doing riddles now? Gotcha. You gonna share some children's fables with me? Maybe give me a soft lecture on power and responsibility? I mean, I wooooaaaah!"

One moment Amiya had been walking beside Estrella, the next she was in the sky, falling. Amiya barely heard her own screams as the wind roared in her ears. The sky and ground flipped as she tumbled end over end. When she finally stopped rolling, Amiya looked down at the ground below. Far below. She was higher than the trees and hills, higher than the mountains!

She tried to wipe the tears streaming from the corners of her eyes and looked around. She was higher than the clouds! She might have enjoyed the beauty of it if the intensity of the wind weren't rippling the skin on her face, and she wasn't about to die a terrible death. She'd hit the ground and nothing would be left of her but a stain. Amiya tried to ignore the thumping in her chest as her heart threatened to beat right out of it. *Air.* She needed to use *air* to slow down.

Amiya closed her eyes and tried to focus through her terror. *If you don't get this right, you're dead.* Her hands shook but she kept her eyes closed. If she couldn't see her impending doom, she could concentrate.

When *air* finally came to her call, Amiya grasped it like a life-line and focused on gathering it beneath her and sending a blast upwards. She slowed down, but she hadn't balanced it right. The blast hit her off center and sent her cartwheeling and falling as fast as before.

The world spun and turned, and her stomach threatened to empty itself. She tried to focus again, but it was too much. She was dizzy, nauseous, and scared. The earth below still seemed very far away, but she could tell it was getting closer.

As abruptly as she found herself falling through the sky, she jerked to a stop. The sudden and jarring cease of movement made her stomach lurch again. She hung in the air, nothing but her eyes moving as she looked about. *I didn't do that.* Amiya closed her eyes, took a deep breath, and opened them again. "Okay," she yelled. "You can put me back on the ground, please. I get it."

Estrella gently floated into view from above. Her dark blue dress drifted in the breeze as she stopped in front of Amiya. "Have I your attention, little one?"

Amiya swallowed and bobbed her head.

"What is the extent of your experience with magi?" she asked.

"Um." Amiya swallowed again. "Every once in a while, one or two would stop through Vyne for whatever reason. They didn't exactly parade their abilities around town."

"Did you ever see them wield essence?"

"No." She shrugged. "Not much, anyway. I've seen them create fire and water, cause fast winds, that sort of thing."

"That sort of thing." Estrella stared at her. Amiya still found it difficult to meet the woman's violet eyes. "Consider this, little one. I've lived more years than you would think. Many more. I've experienced enough conversations to read a lie when I receive one."

You're no older than Dad, Amiya thought. "Okay."

"Given that," Estrella continued. "How easy do you think it would be for me to read a lie from someone of your age?"

Amiya shrugged. "I dunno." She looked away, studying the distant land below, stretching into infinity.

"No?" Estrella gave her a frosty grin.

Amiya was falling and screaming again. She tried to delve for *air*, but she couldn't focus through her terror. She fell through a patch of clouds and when she came out, the land below was much closer. "Okay!" she shouted. She was practically blind, now, through the tears streaming out of her eyes. "Okay, Estrella! You can stop me now."

She didn't stop. Amiya kept falling, speeding toward the ground and imminent death. Oddly enough, her panic started to ebb. She saw cottages and small towns dotting the landscape. Horse-drawn carriages and carts lumbered down dirt roads that snaked from one end of the horizon to the other. She saw the tell-tale rows of tilled soil indicative of farms and orchards.

It all looked so small from this high up. Everything seemed so small. Animals that easily outweighed her ten times over seemed like ants. How tiny everything sitting on top of such a vast world seemed from up here.

When she realized Estrella had no intention of stopping her this time, Amiya focused on *air* again. She closed her eyes and tried to visualize slowing herself down so that she could land softly. This time, her descent slowed a bit, but not enough. It was a start, however.

Amiya took a deep breath and tried again. Once more, her fall slowed a bit, but it wasn't enough to save her. As the ground rushed up to meet her, Amiya clamped her eyes shut. No point in seeing herself splat on the ground. Though, would she really see anything upon impact?

When her body jerked to a stop, Amiya said a silent prayer of thanks to the Creator and opened her eyes. Her heart nearly stopped when she saw that she floated less than a dozen feet above the earth. She began to lower slowly until her feet touched the sweet, soft grassy earth. Never had standing on solid ground felt so good. Amiya could have dropped to her hands and knees and kissed it, if the very concept of pressing her lips to grass and soil didn't sound disgusting.

Amiya forced herself not to look when Estrella floated down beside her. They stood beside each other but neither looked at the other.

"I believe our last conversation ended on the subject of lying," Estrella said, "and how those who aren't proficient are best served avoiding it?"

"I don't remember you saying that," Amiya replied, and instantly regretted it.

"Perhaps another type of lesson would make the subtlety apparent?"

"Selvetar!" Amiya blurted. "Look, his name is Selvetar, all right?" Amiya didn't know why she didn't say so earlier. It's not like the man didn't give her the creeps, anyway. "He taught me…" She noticed Estrella arch an eyebrow, "… *Us*." She sighed. "He taught *us* how to access the power."

"You and your sister?" Estrella said.

"Yes. He said he saw potential in us, wanted to teach us about the power. He let us delve using his ring."

"Interesting," Estrella said. "And how long did your tutelage under this Selvetar endure?"

Why do you talk so weird? "I'm not sure. A few weeks. Maybe a month. Before he came to see us, the most we could do was spin a flat rock in our hands as a game. Now I know that we were using the *air* essence to do it, but we didn't know what we were doing back then."

Estrella nodded thoughtfully. "And your education had been brought to an untimely end when the drauk attacked."

"Is that what those ugly things are called?" Amiya asked. She remembered all that horrible shouting and growling in a language she'd never heard before. She just *knew* those things were uttering foul words that would have Dad washing her mouth out with a bar of soap. "Well, yeah, that ended our lessons. After the drauk attacked, we were more concerned with not being cut to ribbons, and escaping Big Belly's house."

Estrella looked down at her with an amused expression. "Big Belly?"

"Yeah." Amiya snarled. "It's what I call that bloated sow who kidnapped us and forced our dad to run some stupid errand to get us back. He's the archminister of Vyne, and just about nobody likes him." Amiya fell in beside Estrella when she started walking again.

"You have quite a way with your words, little one."

"Yeah," Amiya muttered. "Nandi sometimes tells me my mouth will get me into trouble."

Estrella chuckled. "Everything has a use. The meaning delivered by certain words can vary depending on the time and context." She gave Amiya a sidelong glance. "Of course, when two words like big and belly are strung together, there is little variance in meaning. Learn to use that viper's tongue tactically. You will be interested in the results."

Mmm'kay? Amiya figured she'd chew on that a little more instead of asking what in the name of the Fallen this woman was talking about. She seemed the type you didn't exactly ask "what do you mean by that?" to. Maybe she meant Amiya shouldn't necessarily stop talking the way she did, but maybe pick different times to say what she did.

I'm not gonna stop calling that wild boar "Big Belly", though, she decided. *It'd be different if he was a nice person instead of a pile of smoldering mountain mole dung.*

She mentally winced at her own thoughts. Dad most certainly wouldn't have approved of that. As much as he loathed the archminister of Vyne, he never tolerated her insults of the man, though she had caught him trying not to laugh on occasion. "That's disrespectful," he'd say. "Even if it's a horrible person like Decius.

What if some nice person Decius's size hears you? Your words might be meant to cut at the archminister, but they might cut someone else as well."

Amiya remembered the lecture. She'd agreed and stuck to insulting the man when Dad wasn't around. Maybe he had a point, though. Amiya might not be as tactful as her sister, but she didn't want to go around indirectly insulting people, either.

"If you wrap yourself any tighter in your thoughts, you'll walk off another cliff."

Estrella's voice snapped Amiya out of her distraction just in time to not stumble over a slope. It wouldn't have been a fatal fall, more than an embarrassing roll to the bottom. "Uh, thanks."

Estrella pointed ahead. "There. Mt. Blood awaits."

"Mt. Blood?" Amiya peered into the distance and saw the red dots at the base of the mountain ahead. "I remember Dad's stories about that mountain."

"Please share," Estrella said.

"You seem to have a lot of experience in life. You've probably already heard it lots."

"Indulge me."

Amiya waited for the expected sarcasm, but Estrella walked on in silence, waiting. "Okay. The story goes that everything was fine in the First Age. There was either no evil during that time, or there was so little of it that there was no fighting. No wars, no weapons, no aggression of any kind. Essence wielders used the power to heal, assist in building grand structures and civilizations, things like that. The end of the First Age came when just enough evil crept into the world that men became angry and violent. They started making weapons out of tools. Eventually, essence wielders learned how to use the power as a weapon."

Amiya pointed at the distant mountain. The war of the First Age shed so much blood on that mountain that it soaked into the rocks and soil, and the rain couldn't wash it away. Some say the Creator kept it there as a reminder."

"What do you think?" Estrella asked.

Amiya shrugged. "Maybe He did, Maybe He didn't. I've never seen the Creator inflict any atrocities on people; they're too good at doing it to themselves. And maaaybe the soil on that mountain is just red, so they named it Mt. Blood."

They heard a distant boom, followed by a flicker of light from an explosion. Amiya's heart skipped a beat. "What was that?"

"More blood for the soil of Mt. Blood."

"Okay, so, can we go a different way? You can create that opening in the air and we can go anywhere, right?"

"It is called bridging. It can be done to transport oneself safely anywhere you've already been."

"I'm guessing since we're not already in Altarra, that you've never been there?" Amiya ventured.

"Though it has been a great many years, I've been there."

Amiya's mouth fell open. "I told you I was looking for my dad. Why didn't you just transport us there?"

"I recall that," Estrella said. "But I don't recall saying that *I* was looking for your father."

Amiya wanted to argue, but the truth was, this woman didn't owe her that. In fact, if anyone owed anyone, it would be Amiya's debt to Estrella for saving her life."

Estrella looked down at her with an unreadable expression. "Everything happens for a reason, little one. Your separation from your father and eventually your sister, our fateful meeting, everything." She waved a hand in the direction of Mt. Blood and the apparent battle happening. "Our arrival to this place where people are ending each other's lives."

"Sounds beautiful," Amiya replied dryly.

"The way of humankind, Amiya. Tell me what you would do if you found your father in Altarra right now."

"Easy," Amiya said. "We'd start searching for my sister."

"Where would you start?"

Amiya opened her mouth and closed it. Where *would* she start?

"Maybe retrace my steps from where we were separated." The answer sounded weak to her own ears, but what else could she do?

"Does your sister share your ability to bridge?"

Amiya shrugged. "If she does, she probably doesn't know it. I didn't know it either until I showed up on your mountain serving myself up on a platter for those cat monsters."

Estrella grinned. "I understand your urgency to find your family, little one. But consider the passage of months, as you've told me, since your father was forced to depart your home. Likely he's completed his task and returned home to find you not there. He would doubtlessly be on the move to find you. Your sister would not have remained where you were separated and is very likely looking for you both as well."

Amiya's heart sank as she listened to the undeniable logic. The world was a big place. They could be anywhere. Amiya thought about her own situation. The last place she figured she'd be at this moment was in northeast Marai, walking toward Mt. Blood and some sort of battle. She stared straight ahead without seeing anything. "Thank you."

Estrella tilted her head. "For what?"

"For not saying the other things that might have happened." She swallowed a lump building in her throat.

"That is indeed a possibility ..." Estrella trailed off when Amiya's shoulders bounced as the first tremors of grief hit.

Amiya tried to fight her emotions. The last thing she wanted was to cry in front of this woman. She was a total stranger, for Creator's sake! She took another lurching step, before grief overpowered her, and she dropped to her hands and knees. The world disappeared into a blurry stream of tears. "I can't ... I just ... they can't be ..." She couldn't bring herself to say it. They were all right. They *had* to be. Deep down, somehow, she would have known if something had happened to Nandi. That didn't make it any less painful that they were separated, likely by hundreds of miles. But Dad. She had no idea if Dad was okay, and just thinking of the possibility of him not being so felt like a hand crushing her heart.

She felt an arm wrap around her and help her to her feet. Amiya wiped her tears with her fists. So stupid, crying in front of this woman like that! She mumbled something incoherent and wrapped her arms around the woman before she knew what she was doing. She felt Estrella's hand touch the middle of her back, somewhat stiffly. A moment later Estrella pressed her close.

"All will be fine if you are strong, little one."

Amiya thought she heard something akin to affection in her voice. It sounded like it was as unfamiliar to Estrella as it was unexpected to Amiya. She released the woman and stepped away. She rubbed her eyes again. "M'sorry about that." She sniffed. "Don't know what's wrong with me. Just got overwhelmed. Lot happening and they're gone, and I was alone and … we've never been apart and Dad … and," she sniffed again. "It's always just been the three of us. Just us."

"Of course." Estrella's tone gave Amiya the impression of someone trying to use a finely honed sword that had seen many battles to cut a block of butter. "Your family could be anywhere. If you are to find them, you must survive. Understand?"

Amiya sniffed and nodded. "Yeah, you're right." When her tears were finally cleared enough that she could see again, she gazed into the distance and changed the subject. "You think that's the fight going on between the Khatala people and the king?"

"Children," Estrella said in a low voice Amiya wasn't sure she was supposed to hear. "I suspect that may indeed be the case. Let us see what we may see."

"You gonna do that bridge thing again?" Amiya asked, and Estrella nodded. "Mind teaching me?"

Estrella's grin answered the question as surely as if she'd spoken. "Come."

The woman's eyes flickered silver the moment before the air rippled and Amiya found herself suddenly on the slope of Mt.

Blood, amidst crimson rocks and boulders. She gasped and covered her ears with her hands when a deafening explosion hit further down the mountain.

"It looks like you're correct," Estrella said. "The king wages his war still."

"What a stupid reason to kill each other. Over a misunder-standing."

"Misunderstanding?" Estrella asked.

"You *must* know about that," Amiya said. "Everyone knows they're fighting because of the misunderstanding when the Khatala greeted them."

"Oh, that is the story most believe, but it goes back farther than that, little one. And the motivations of your king extend as far beyond a simple misunderstanding as the history of hostilities between the two peoples."

"You sound like Dad." Amiya doubled over and covered her ears when another explosion hit. "He says it's money," she said once the ringing in her ears subsided. "He says not even Big Bel … not even the archminister of Vyne would have been foolish enough to wage a war over something so small. He thinks the Khatala people have something King Alyn wants."

Estrella nodded. "Indeed. What do you think, Amiya?"

Amiya thought about it, but raised her hands and let them drop. "I don't know enough about it other than rumors and theories. I've only ever known one person from the west, and he's a really nice man. He never talked much about the tensions between our people, though. He did say that his people would normally consider the conflict restricted between Alyn and the nation he fought with."

"I suspect that would change if your king decided to unite Marai against them."

That gave Amiya pause. "You think he'd do that?"

"It's a natural progression. There is something of the Khatal or their homeland that your king wants. He can't remove them alone, so he would need to unite Marai against them."

"How do you know that?" Amiya asked, "and why do you keep calling him *my* king? He's yours too."

"I've seen this kind of thing play itself out far too many times not to recognize it."

"Okay," Amiya said. "And my other question?"

"The answer to that is a bit more complicated." Estrella pointed down the mountain. "A more important question faces us."

"It does?" Amiya looked in the direction the woman pointed. She stole a glance at Estrella and saw a flicker of excitement in the woman's violet eyes. It sent a chill down her spine.

"What to do about that?" Estrella said. "The king of Marai claims to defend you against a larger and stronger people who wield the essences without the use of corlite. Wilders. He and the Order of Magi consider the people of Khatal to be a reckless danger to the world with their undisciplined use of the power.

"The Khatala," she continued, "refuse to back down, and see Marai's actions as a threat to their way of life. Until now, only a small number of them fight. But, if all of Khatal unites against Marai, the result would be undesirable."

"How in the name of the Creator do you know all of this?" Amiya asked. "I've never heard anyone talk about all of Khatal fighting together, and even if they did, I can't imagine it being as grim as what you're saying. Wouldn't they just beat the king's forces back and make them leave Khatal alone?"

"Would that it were so simple," Estrella said. "Your king, Alyn, his name is? He carries the same torch of ambition as his predecessors."

"So, you're saying we should do something to help the Khatala, down there?" Amiya's heart picked up speed. It was one thing to use her power trying to keep monsters from killing her. There were only ever a few of them at a time. But to use the power against not just a human, but an entire force of them? That was different. Monsters came at you without much thought beyond killing you for food, or whatever reasons monsters killed people for. Humans were a different matter.

"Should we?" Estrella asked. "What if your king Alyn is defending Marai against an angry incursion of wilders carrying an age-old grudge? Perhaps the key to defeating them lies in the land of Khatal, and that is why he tries to push them back into their own lands."

"Are you *trying* to scramble my brain?" Amiya asked.

"Or, am I showing you how brain-scrambling it can be to decipher who, if anyone, is right or wrong?"

"I've got an idea. How about we just leave and let them keep at it?"

"What if we had the power to stop them?"

Amiya looked at her as if she'd gone mad, but the expression on Estrella's face made her wonder if either the woman was indeed insane, or did she actually possess the ability to do just that. "Um—"

"Well?"

Amiya looked down the mountain again. "This reminds me of when I was younger. I used to like watching ants. I was amazed at how they'd lift a dead insect or twigs or a small branch many times their weight and carry it up a tree.

"One time I saw two different groups of ants attacking each other. More started coming, so I took a stick and dug a deep line in the dirt between them. I couldn't do anything about the ones already tangled together fighting, but I tried."

She looked up at Estrella, expecting the woman to think her story was stupid. The woman returned her gaze, fully interested. "Well," she continued. "All I did was make them climb down into the line and fight in there until they piled up enough for both sides to walk across on top of *them* to get to each other."

"Hmm. So you believe that nothing we could do here would deter them from fighting, unless we somehow removed their will to fight each other?"

"Probably something like that."

She watched Estrella gaze back down the mountain. Something in the woman's face made her feel even more nervous. It seemed she knew a lot more than she let on. Amiya wondered what, but she wasn't sure she wanted to ask.

"Perhaps we will move on," Estrella finally said. "They will soon discover how petty their little feud truly is."

JOGA

oga found himself unconsciously backing away from the distant but rapidly closing teliak. They didn't normally roam out in the open like this. Something was wrong.

"I wish you had a weapon, Khatala," Nyimbe said. She turned and ran. "Remain if you must. I'll not be joining you. Kokunde!"

The hackles on the darkwood cat's arched back stood at attention. It growled and snapped its teeth at the air. "Kokunde," Nyimbe called again. "There will be many opportunities to fight. Now isn't the time. Come!" The giant cat hesitantly backed away before turning and bounding after the woman.

Joga ran after them. He followed behind Nyimbe and her feline companion, making straight for the cover of the woods. He looked to the east, where Altarra sat. The girls would be going that way to find their father. Joga gritted his teeth. It seemed all of creation itself aligned against him keeping his promise to them.

"Run, Khatala," Nyimbe called from up ahead. "Teliak's are fast, but we might make it."

Joga had never seen a teliak beast before, but the stories and appearance of those who had told him enough that he had no intention of meeting one now.

The shrill cry of the beast raised the hairs on the back of his neck. Joga looked over his shoulder and caught sight of the thing, and it was far too close. It lowered its plate-armored elongated head and looked directly at him. Joga looked into a set of orange eyes nearly as large as himself. Its eyes had a wild look, as though the beast had been driven insane.

When it opened its long maw to hiss at him, Joga saw row upon row of serrated teeth. He turned back, lowered his head, and sprinted for his life. His longer stride quickly brought him beside Nyimbe. She'd strapped her spear across her back, and now only her legs and arms pumped as she ran full out. Joga realized if the woman was just a little taller, she would have easily outrun him.

On her other side, Kokunde skidded to a stop and spun around. His tail bristled, as did the hackles on his heavily muscled back. The cat growled and snapped at the air.

"It's too close now," Nyimbe said, and she, too, stopped and turned.

"Cat fights to buy us time, no?" Joga asked, hesitantly stopping as well. He looked from Nyimbe—who'd started unstrapping her spear from her back—to the giant cat, to the massive armor-plated lizard practically gliding toward them.

Despite its size, the swing of the beast's thick legs made its footfalls soft and light. Joga could imagine how easy it would be for it to sneak up on prey with steps that quiet.

"Do what you must and live with it, Khatala," Nyimbe replied. "Kokunde and I fight together."

The teliak's red scales glistened under the brilliant sun, and as it drew closer, Joga saw that there were long thin spikes nearly as tall as a man protruding between the corners of the armor plates. It was less than a few hundred feet away and closing fast.

Joga looked north to the woods, then east to Altarra, then back at the crazed monster. He thought he saw something detach from its back and fall to the ground. Joga ignored it, squared himself, and delved for the aspects. They came readily to his call and he prepared himself, linking his consciousness to the power.

He nearly lost the aspects to his own terror when he saw Kokunde off to the side. The sickening sound of bone and joints popping, breaking, and reforming hit his ears with a resounding crack. Still on all fours, the darkwood cat lurched forward and convulsed, its mouth opening and closing.

Its hind legs buckled, then extended, as did its forelegs. Its already large back flattened and arched as new muscle formed. The guttural sound coming from the beast sent a chill down Joga's spine.

Hruh, hruh, hruh. Kokunde rose up on his hind legs and towered over the two humans, Joga's height and half again taller. Kokunde held his large paws out at his sides as they elongated into fingers equipped with knife-like claws.

The muscles in his furry striped chest flexed and knotted, as did the muscles in his former forelegs that were now arms. Kokunde flexed his curled fingers and took a half step forward, staring murderously at the approaching terror. Hruh, hruh, HRUH, HRUH, HRRAAAOOOOOOOOOOOO! Kokunde threw his wolfish head back and howled to sky above, then charged.

Joga swallowed hard and looked at Nyimbe. "Why you not hold that thing back? Should fight defensive."

Nyimbe kept her eyes on the teliak. "I have no influence over him in that state."

Joga watched the charging darkwood cat in disbelief. It was every bit the monster as the teliak. "How you fight with him?"

"I fight where he doesn't." Nyimbe took off after her horrifying companion.

Joga took a deep breath and ran after the strange woman. Fear diminished with every step; apprehension evaporated with each measured breath. The time for fear and flight had passed. Joga shed his gentle nature and became a living weapon. "Alyu mo Illyu mo Salah mala HAAA! Alyu mo Illyu mo Salah mala HAAA!" There was no time to dance the jahaka before this battle, but he said the words, became one with the words of power, the words of the jahaka. The four aspects of Mother *Illyu* swirled around him, ready for his guidance, ready to unite with him.

The teliak snapped its jaws at the transformed cat. Kokunde hopped far to the side, easily out of reach of the crushing bite, and leapt back in to deal a cutting swipe across the side of the plated head.

It sounded like two swords grinding together as the darkwood cat's claws slid across the plated scales. The teliak hissed and curled its body around to get a better angle at the threat. Kokunde bounded to the side and leapt in again. He scratched, slashed, and savaged the side of the giant reptilian monster's head.

The teliak swatted at the beast with one of its foreclaws and connected with Kokunde's side. The bipedal beast tumbled and bounced away, hopped back to his feet, and charged again.

As Joga and Nyimbe reached the embattled monsters, he filled himself with *olayem*, what the easterners called *earth* essence. Huge chunks of rock and clay lifted from the ground around him. He guided the *olayem* aspect, compressing the chunks of earth and elongating them into giant rocky spears. It wasn't a method typical in how Khatala wielded the aspects, but Joga saw the usefulness in it even if he was less proficient than a magus in this skill.

He delved *tinu* and used the *air* essence to guide the spears into position careful to avoid hitting Kokunde. Once an opening presented itself, Joga let fly.

The spears of rock exploded against the hard armor of the teliak, but struck with enough force to knock the monstrous lizard off balance. Kokunde roared and threw himself into the teliak. The darkwood cat hit the lizard with enough force to knock it on its side just as Nyimbe reached it.

With a screaming battle cry, the woman sprinted alongside its exposed underbelly and stabbed. Sharp as her spear was, it did little more than draw a pinprick of blood. She yanked the spear free and kept moving. The spear whirled in her hands and she stabbed again, then dragged it along the less-armored belly.

Nyimbe ducked a kicking hind leg, then rolled aside when the beast began to right itself. She jumped back in and stabbed her spear into an exposed gap in the scales.

While the teliak hissed and turned toward her, Joga delved *tinu* and *ushaa*. He molded the two aspects into a storm of ice shards as long as Nyimbe's spear. The bombardment forced the teliak to hunker down under the weight of the blows while Kokunde circled behind it.

"Concentrate on its face, Khatala!" Nyimbe called. "Try to blind it while we attack!"

Joga delved *naara* and created a thin stream of fire that he sent straight into the monster's face. The teliak threw its head side to side and charged him. Joga backpedaled while continuing his assault. This wasn't right. Teliak or not, no creature of the natural world would sustain an attack under constant bombardment like this. And especially if dealt injury. Only extreme hunger or a threat to its home or offspring would draw out such persistence.

Nyimbe and Kokunde hit it from the sides and the back, but the teliak had focused its attention on Joga, now. He prayed to Creator *Amyadali* to lend him strength. It seemed he must send this creature to the True Home, today. He delved *olayem, ushaa,* and *tinu.* While he retreated, Joga balled his left fist as a solid layer of hard stone formed and solidified around his hand and forearm.

On his right arm, Joga focused *ushaa,* and *tinu* to create warm, moist air around the lower part of his arm and fist. On his upper arm, he focused on creating cold, moist air.

The Teliak quickly closed the distance between them. It stretched its neck out and turned its head sideways, gaping maw closing in to swallow him whole. Joga skidded to a stop, channeled *tinu,* and gave himself a quick burst of air as he jumped straight up.

With the aid of *tinu,* Joga leapt above the snapping maw. Fist above his head, Joga brought it down like a hammer as he landed on the side of the monster's head. Chunks of rock covering his fist broke apart, but he managed to dent a few of the plated scales. Despite the weight behind the mighty blow, the teliak barely stumbled. Still, when it lifted its head and shook it side to side, Joga knew he'd hurt it.

While the lizard tried to shake off the pain, Kokunde leaped onto and ran the length of its tail, zigzagging between the spikes on its back.

Nyimbe followed right behind until she found a favorable spot and began stabbing her spear in the vulnerable areas between the hard-plated scales.

From tail to muzzle, the great lizard was as long as several village huts side by side, and three times as tall. Nyimbe's efforts did little more than irritate the massive beast, but Joga soon realized that that was her plan. Nyimbe drove her spear into one spot, and when the lizard turned, she moved to another. She focused on its joints while Kokunde raked and stabbed like a whirlwind of death.

With the beast occupied with his allies, Joga sprinted in. While his right arm tingled with static energy, he drew his left arm back, and punched its nearest foreleg. Though he'd hit it with all his strength, it did nothing more than get the monster's attention. Joga twisted away as the teliak turned toward him. His right arm trembled as the building electric energy buzzed up and down its length. Once the teliak swung its head into position, Joga gritted his teeth and swung his fist around in an uppercut augmented by a burst of lightening.

The impact lifted the teliak off its forelegs and launched Joga in the opposite direction. The ground shook when the beast crashed to the ground. Joga landed and rolled several dozen feet away. He tried to scramble back to his feet, but his body trembled from the shock.

Barely fazed by the sudden lurch of the reptile, Kokunde continued to savage the lizard's back and managed to tear off a piece of plated scale. While the bloodlusting darkwood cat ravaged the wound, Joga delved again. He'd begun to once again armor his arms with the power of the aspects when he heard Nyimbe's cry of surprise.

Nyimbe lifted into the air and flew away from the beast. She hit the ground hard and skidded to a stop, but didn't get back up. Kokunde roared in anger as he, too, lifted into the air. But instead of flying away, he floated sideways until he hovered over one of the lizard's spikes. Joga yelled in helplessness as all he could do was watch the beast drop onto one of the spikes. The impaled cat howled, kicked, and scratched, but it found no purchase.

Aspect wielder.

Joga looked around. Who was that? While the teliak slowly overcame the lightening blow, Joga searched for the unseen adversary. He spotted a tiny silver glow several hundred yards behind the teliak.

From the corner of his eye, Joga saw Nyimbe stir, and relief flooded him. Somehow, the fully suspended and impaled Kokunde continued his frenzy. The cat was every bit the monster the teliak was, and seemed as enraged as he was mortally wounded.

Joga moved to the side while delving again. He would fight from a distance and keep this new enemy in sight. He sent forth a storm of ice shards, spears of rock, and jets of fire toward the cowardly enemy.

The projectiles exploded before they got close, but he continued the assault. From the corner of his eye, Joga saw the teliak finally recover and turn its focus on him. He delved *olayem* and tore free a large chunk of earth. He molded it into a huge ball and launched it at the head of the beast while still focusing his assault on the other enemy.

The rock hit the teliak in the side of the head. The lizard stumbled sideways just as Kokunde somehow managed to snap the spike off that had impaled him. The darkwood cat wrapped its long, clawed fingers around the spike. With a screeching howl of agony, he pulled the piece of spike out of his torso and rammed it into the open wound where he'd torn off a scale.

For the first time, the teliak had been dealt a real injury. It bucked and squirmed and threw Kokunde from its back. The darkwood cat scratched and slashed at empty air as it flew away, while Joga redoubled his efforts as he ran toward the new enemy. *She must be controlling the beast.* He filled himself with the aspects and struck with all of them, at once.

Shards of ice and balls of fire streaked through the air. Stalagmites burst out of the ground. Though his strikes were inferior to that of a fully trained magus, his strength and speed with the aspects compensated. The woman fought off the assault for a time, but started to give ground. Joga drew chunks of earth from the ground, broke them apart, and sent them speeding in freezing blasts of air at his enemy.

She defeated everything he threw at her with ease, but he gave her no time to form an offense. He knew he'd caught her by surprise. She'd no doubt recognized his inferiority in wielding the aspects this way, but she hadn't expected his speed.

Joga threw everything he had at her from every direction. She easily picked off his attacks, but the effort had her focused in every direction. In the middle of a rain of ice spears, he set stalagmites bursting out of the ground all around her and finally one struck home. The woman grunted when a rocky spear stabbed up and into her side. She grabbed hold of the rock and tried to pull herself free, but eventually gave up and slumped at an awkward angle.

Joga finally reached her and she glared at him with unnaturally dark eyes. They reminded him of Sama's black orbs. But where the tatamble's eyes were black by nature, and possessed of no malice, this woman's eyes were a reflection of her soul, he knew.

Her skin was gray and lined, like a valley of cracked earth that had been parched from the power of Father *Alyu.* "*Dazra,*" he whispered.

She glared at Joga and gritted her teeth. "A wilder. Curse my luck."

"Who are you?" Joga demanded. "Why attack? And what have you done to that animal?" She kept pushing to free herself from the rock as if she hadn't heard the question, bits of blood trickling between her gritted teeth. "Will help you if you answer question," Joga said. "Why attack us?"

The woman with the lined, cracked skin looked into Joga's eyes. They locked stares for a few heartbeats before Joga's instincts screamed and he threw himself aside.

Had he been a little slower, the stalagmite that dropped from the sky would have driven through his skull and into the ground. Joga rose and started to delve when he saw the teliak turning in his direction. With an agonized groan, the *dazra* woman pulled free of the stalagmite.

One hand pressed to the wound, she fell to her knees, but Joga knew she was delving, though no *arah* shone in her eyes. The teliak started towards him, but stopped and shook its head.

Joga struck with ice shards, but she countered just as quickly with a funnel of fire. Joga delved *olayem*. A wall of earth burst up from the ground just in time to shield him from being incinerated.

The *dazra* half-limped half-ran behind the teliak and struggled her way up its tail. "You're formidable, wilder," the woman said once she'd reached its shoulders. She winced as she settled down between two spikes, on hand holding a spike, the other pressed to her rapidly healing side.

Joga backed away while delving all four of the aspects. He saw Nyimbe from the periphery, struggling to stand. Not far from her, Kokunde leaned against a tree, long-fingered claw clamped against the hole in his midsection. Joga couldn't fathom how the beast still lived.

"Make yourself servant to faithless, who serve mgomu." Joga bared his teeth as he drew upon the power, filling himself with it.

"You don't know a thing about power," the woman said. "You

play it, mumbling your little songs to the earth as if that is the way. You haven't any idea how badly you will be crushed in the days to come."

For the first time Joga spotted her pulsating essence ring. It glowed silver, the same pinprick glow he noticed in the middle of the teliak's eyes. The glow pulsated between silver and red. Did she somehow control the thing through *tinu* and *naara*?

He continued to back away while the teliak matched him. Joga didn't know why the woman didn't urge it to run him down, but he certainly wasn't about to ask. He struck with balls of ice and fire, created spears of ice and sent them speeding toward his enemy.

As powerful with the aspects as Joga was, his grasp of it in the way of magi was sorely deficient against this foe. The *dazra* countered his efforts with an efficiency that spoke of a deeper knowledge of the aspects. They exchanged volley after volley, canceling out each other's efforts while the *dazra* gradually overwhelmed him.

From the corner of his eye, Joga saw Nyimbe circling behind the teliak and to the left. She cocked her arm back, lining up her spear. It seemed too far a throw just to reach her target—who sat perched atop the moving reptile—let alone with any sort of accuracy.

Joga kept his eyes on the *dazra* astride her monster. He struck again, and again, but she defeated his offence and countered. He made sure to continue backing away in a direction that kept the teliak moving in a straight line, as that would make for an easier throw for Nyimbe.

The bloody Kokunde pushed away from the tree and staggered toward the giant lizard. He flexed his claws and lowered himself to all fours, shoulder-blades moving up and down as he stalked toward the teliak.

Nyimbe paced the great lizard, keeping her torso and arm still as a statue, only her legs moving to maintain her distance and position. Joga struck with fire. Nyimbe let fly. Kokunde bounded forward.

Everything happened at once. The *dazra* redirected Joga's speeding flames using *tinu*. The flames arced in front of the woman and curled around back toward him. Joga growled and drew up a wall of earth. The flames crashed into the stone slab and he felt the heat from the other side.

The heat and the flames suddenly winked out and he heard the woman's scream. Joga dropped the wall just in time to see Kokunde make a great leap forward. He reached the *dazra* just as she grabbed at Nyimbe's spear lodged in the back of her shoulder. The savagery of the darkwood cat combined with the human-like way in which he used his claws and upper body made Joga thankful the monster was a "friend".

The lupine beast crashed into the *dazra* and both tumbled over the other side of the teliak. Kokunde roared, snatching the spear out of her shoulder as if it were nothing. He tossed it aside during their descent from the back of the lizard and curled that same arm back, razor claws lined up and ready to drive into the woman's chest.

A flicker of silver passed across the woman's black eyes and a hard gust of air hit Kokunde from the side. He let out a loud grunt as the air was no doubt blasted from his lungs.

The *dazra* landed on her back, equally winded from the impact, and rolled onto her side. The teliak shook its head and hissed at Joga, but it didn't attack. It looked around as if in confusion, then took a half step towards him, mouth agape, thick forked tongue flicking in and out. It shook its head again, then charged.

Joga ran while summoning *olayem*. A chunk of earth burst out of the ground and stuck the teliak in its lower foreleg. He ran in an arc around the side as the great lizard stumbled. He spotted Nyimbe sprinting toward the downed essence wielder. She reached the woman fast, and fell upon her.

Nyimbe sat astride the woman and rained heavy blows down

on her. In a blur of elbows and fists she quickly had the woman bloodied and beaten. She lifted the *dazra* by the neck of her cloak and her head fell back. Nyimbe punched her in the face again, and the other woman's nose flattened in a gush of blood.

Joga reached them just as Nyimbe drew her fist back and lifted the woman up again. "Is done!" He yelled. "Is finished—"

"*She's* finished," Nyimbe cut in. "I'll not have her heal and hunt us down with her monster.

As if mentioning the teliak had drawn its attention, the great lizard turned in their direction and hissed. Nyimbe dropped the unconscious woman and stood beside Joga as they backed away. The beast took a step toward them, then suddenly lifted into the air and crashed hard to the ground.

The resulting tremor nearly knocked Joga off his feet. He stared wide-eyed, his heart nearly stopped at the seemingly impossible sight. The teliak hissed and tried to stand, but it lifted into the air and crashed to the ground again. Its head bounced when it finally collapsed onto it side.

What in the name of Creator Amyadali? Joga ran to the great beast and crept beside its head. He listened near its head and heard the telltale hollow rumble of its breath. He sighed in relief.

"That is foolish, Khatala."

Joga backed away from the unconscious teliak and looked in the direction of the speaker. A man leaned with his arms crossed against the same tree Kokunde had hit earlier. He stepped away from the tree and walked toward the unconscious *dazra*.

"Is not evil." Joga said. "Even if you do something to twist its mind, beast is not evil like her." He jerked his chin at the *dazra*.

The cloaked man laughed at him. "As you say." He knelt beside the woman and made a "tut tut" sound and shook his head. He looked up at Joga. "Impressive. Syalera is no easy foe."

"What is that?" Nyimbe whispered.

Joga studied the man. He wore a brown cloak similar to the woman's, only a shade darker. The cowl sat only partially on his head, so his cracked and lined face was fully visible. "*Dazra*," he answered. "In this land you call them droughtlord." Joga delved and filled himself with the power.

The man regarded Joga as one would an amusing child. "I imagine at this moment you're filling yourself with the essences. What do you call them, boy?" He touched a finger like parched leather to his cheek as if in thought. "Yes, that's right. Aspects." He nodded with a downturned smile of appreciation. A smart thing to do, since I *am* going to kill you." He offered a rather exaggerated grin. "Unless you join with us."

Joga snarled. "Will never destroy my soul and become like you, serving faithless—"

The man's laughter cut through Joga's retort. He waved a placating hand. "Please, Khatala, please stop. I fear my humor has failed to translate. I've no intention of truly bringing you to my side. The only real offer I have for you today is a quick death. You've proven yourself a worthy opponent to have so challenged Syalera. I owe you that much."

"Mmrg, he caught me off guard, Dycerin." Syalera groaned. She offered nothing else, just lay there with her eyes closed.

"Of course he did," Dycerin responded in a patronizing tone. "I'm impressed," he said, this time looking at Nyimbe. "You've really hurt her, haven't you?"

"Prepare, Nyimbe." Joga said a silent prayer to *Amyadali* for forgiveness, as did he apologize to the Ancients for what he was about to do. Though it had been by accident, he remembered all those many months ago the way he'd dropped himself in the middle of Vyne. He didn't bring the power fully to himself, yet, lest the *arah* in his eyes give him away. He held the power ready and kept his mind fixed on his destination.

Dycerin's expression showed little more than boredom. He gave Joga a onceover, then created and struck with a storm of ice shards and flying stalagmites, any of which could have cut Joga to ribbons.

The attack came so quickly that Joga barely had enough time to draw upon *olayem* and create a wall of earth between himself and the assault. "I'll just play along and pretend I can't send death arcing around that wall, Khatala," he heard Dycerin taunt. "How long do you think it will hold?"

Hidden from the *dazra's* sight, Joga seized the opportunity and created a *bridge*. The air warped around him as he stepped forward from the place he'd been standing, and into a new place.

To his credit, Dycerin possessed a keen sense of awareness. He detected the threat behind him just as Joga struck with *naara*. He heard the other man holler more in anger than pain as he quickly formed a barrier of ice close around his body and began to expand it.

Joga threw everything he had into drawing more of the power of *naara* and focusing it on his adversary.

Dycerin's barrier of ice looked nearly like a second skin, so close was it to his body. Silver continuously flickered across his black eyes. "I see why you had so much trouble with him, Syalera. He is powerful. Limited, but powerful."

"He's crafty and lucky," Syalera croaked. She rolled over to her hands and knees, touched her face, and winced. She glared over her shoulder at Nyimbe just in time to see the woman take her final running stride and kick her square in the face.

Syalera fell over back into unconsciousness, but the sound of her face breaking under the force of Nyimbe's kick drew Dycerin's attention. He tried to track her movement, but the woman was quick.

Nyimbe closed the distance and jumped toward Dycerin. She tucked her feet in close and kicked out toward his face. "Ah!" She fell flat on her back, but rolled away. Once she'd put some distance between them, Nyimbe began rubbing her suddenly blue feet.

Joga took advantage of the distraction and threw everything he had into a surge of *naara*. Flames erupted around him. He funneled as much of the power at the *dazra* as his body could bear. He pushed to the limits of his endurance and strength, walking a narrow line of obliteration. If his distraction flickered for even an instant, he would incinerate himself.

Dycerin offered no more sarcasm or smirks of superiority. Joga had his full attention, now, and the *dazra* exerted considerable will not at trying to attack, but simply hold off the raging inferno blowing into him. From somewhere seemingly far away, he thought he heard Nyimbe shout, but Joga dare not lose his distraction.

Through ice and fire Joga and the *dazara's* eyes met. Joga saw pure malice in those infinitely black orbs. He threw another surge of fire, which drew an angry snarl. Dycerin surged back with an equally powerful blast of freezing air. The hot and cold flames collided in a wall that pressed and shrank back from one side to the other in a battle of wills.

Sweat trickled down Joga's brow. He continued to stare into the black dots of hatred glowing at him through silver and red flames. This was a servant of the faithless and a minion of the void aspect *mgomu*. He couldn't die, here.

Nyimbe slowly circled behind the *dazra*. She'd retrieved her spear but wisely waited. If she let fly, now, the missile would either be frozen or burned to ashes. Farther back, Kokunde had finally awoken. The darkwood cat lowered himself to all fours and watched with the eyes of a predator, waiting for the opportunity to strike.

A few feet to Dycerin's side, Syalera's leg twitched as she slowly came back to consciousness. Time was running out.

"Alyu mo Illyu mo Salah mala, HAAA! Alyu mo Illyu mo Salah mala, HAAA!" The tips of the flames around Joga shifted blue. *"ALYU MO ILLYU MO SALAH MALA, HAAA!"*

The world disappeared in blue-tinged fire. The black pinpricks that were Dycerin's eyes flew to the left and disappeared. Joga drew the flames backwards, a wave drawing back to the ocean and ready to wash the beach. *Naara* roared within him, demanding to be released as he searched for his foe. They were gone. Dycerin and Syalera were nowhere to be found. He held on to *naara* a bit longer, hoping to *Amyadali* Herself that the flames he held wouldn't immolate him where he stood.

Joga felt his strength rapidly diminishing but still he held the flames raging and ready to strike. He saw Nyimbe shouting at him, but no sound could penetrate the roar of *naara* in his ears. She held her hands out in what looked like a warding gesture and pointed to the spot the two *dazra* had been.

Joga felt he understood and released the power. The flames winked out, and he staggered a bit before starting toward Nyimbe. The woman said something, but it all sounded muffled. Joga took another step and nearly fell over. He steadied himself and looked looked toward the short Marailander, who was now running towards him. Joga took one final wobbly step forward, then his legs gave out. The last thing he heard was Nyimbe shouting his name as the ground rushed up to meet him, and then there was darkness.

AMIYA

etty feud. Estrella's words echoed in Amiya's mind while she watched the conflict below, hearing the screaming and dying. The forces of Jietar far outnumbered that of the Khatala, but the western warriors gave no ground and fought without fear.

Amiya searched the fields for magi and found few. The king's ground soldiers represented the bulk of the forces. Even from this far up, she could hear the Khatala's booming Jahaka chant. Warriors at the front fought while those at the back kept up the chant. After some time, a rotation would occur. She felt a prickling on her arms and raised one to see tiny bumps and the hairs standing on end.

"The energy generated by their dance and their chant," Estrella explained. "It is a powerful thing. Far more so than what you see there."

"Really?" Amiya looked the battlefield over again. The king's forces looked much larger than the Khatala, and the magi unit, which numbered perhaps a quarter the Khatala force. "They should be able to run over the westerners. What's keeping them back?"

"An understanding of their enemy," Estrella answered. "Likely due to the magi bolstering the army."

A Khatala woman leaped high above the embattled mass and landed in the middle of the front lines of the Jietari forces. She pounded the ground with a thunderclap that blasted nearby soldiers into the air. She'd barely straightened when a magus hurled a shard of ice in her direction. The Khatala woman rolled aside barely in time to avoid being impaled. The ground exploded underneath her when another magus struck wielding *earth*. The magus who'd attacked with the ice shard drew upon *fire* and sent its namesake funneling at the airborne warrior. A weak stream of freezing water shot from the Khatala force and collided with the fire, barely turning it aside.

Amiya watched the battle with growing confusion. While each side attacked and defended, surged and retreated, neither seemed to gain the advantage. She also noted something else that gave her pause. "They're not using weapons." She frowned at the oddity until she remembered her travels beside Joga. "The Khatala don't use weapons."

"That is because they are their own weapons, little one," Estrella replied. "Their relationship with the essences, aspects, as they call them, is more similar to that of the immortals." She shrugged a shoulder. "If somewhat rudimentary."

Amiya turned her puzzled expression on the woman. "You don't seem bothered by any of that. Do you even care?"

Estrella considered the question for longer than Amiya felt should have been necessary. "A good question, child."

"Good *question*?" Amiya stared into Estrella's otherworldly violet eyes. "Seems like an easy one to me."

"Before I answer that, indulge me, if you will."

Amiya cut her eyes back to the battlefield, then to Estrella again. "Ooookay. I'm indulging."

Estrella spread a hand to encompass the battlefield below. "This conflict has existed on and off for generations with little, if any, progress toward a resolution. The fool king of Marai and the

Ancients of the Khatala carry their ages old grudge into each generation."

Amiya hopped into step beside Estrella when she started walking. The air around them rippled ever so briefly, and Amiya now found herself standing in a decrepit town with old rundown buildings. Estrella led her through the crumbled stone streets, passing men and women squatting against buildings asking for spare coins.

A variety of smells populated the air, including rotting wood, livestock, and manure. The smell of roasting meat and baking bread mingled with the other odors, and Amiya's stomach didn't know whether to rumble or heave.

An old man swept the front of his store with a splintered broom. He looked Estrella up and down with a none too kind expression, then spared Amiya a similar look before returning to his chore. They received similar looks ranging from unwelcoming curiosity to outright hostility.

"Friendly," Amiya remarked.

"We are strangers, here. Our dress and appearance mark us as Marailanders, who don't often visit."

"Um," Amiya's eyes darted left and right, taking in everything. "We're not in Marai?"

"Nogth," Estrella answered. "Far south of Marai."

Amiya's eyes nearly bulged out of her head. "Far south? As in beyond the Southern Serpent?"

"Well beyond those Frostland mountains and across the strait separating the two lands," Estrella confirmed. "This town is one of the poorest of the region. While it produces a fair amount of the region's rice and herbs, it remains at the bottom of Nogth's wealth."

Amiya listened to it all in bewilderment. "Why did you bring me here?" She nearly jumped out of her skin when she heard a boy's frantic screams of protest. His voice choked off to the sound of muffled cries, skidding footfalls and what she was sure were the thuds of blows raining down on a body. She heard the sound again and took off down the street and rounded the corner. If it were Dad, he would have run behind her while yelling at her to stop. Estrella said nothing, and probably kept her normal walking pace.

She turned the bend just in time to see a larger boy kick a smaller one in the stomach. The boy doubled over and dropped to his knees. "Hey!" Amiya yelled.

The taller boy straightened and looked at her. A predatory smile crept across his face and he fully turned to face her.

Amiya swallowed, but took a deep breath to keep her nerves in check. She'd learned how to fight long before she'd leaned how to delve. He was taller and stronger. She could see in his eyes that he thought this would be fun.

"Well, this is different, yep?" He nudged the curled-up boy with his toe. The boy groaned in response. "You planning to defend Booper's honor, yep?"

Amiya didn't answer. She walked toward him, ignoring the verbal barbs.

"You ain't for sure from 'round uh here," the boy continued. He squared himself, grin trembling as if he were trying to keep from laughing. "What're you, M'rai gall? Y'come your rich highness here to start makin'—"

"How 'bout you shut up and leave him alone or I'll push my fist between your ribs?" Amiya cut in.

"Woah ho ho hooo! You hear that, Booper?" He gave the boy another little kick. "She *is* gonna defend your honor, yep?"

While the boy was busy taunting his victim, Amiya lunged the last few feet between them. The boy reacted quickly and swept an arm out to grab her, but Amiya easily ducked under while at the same time punching him in the stomach will all her strength.

That drew a heavy grunt, but he still managed to wrap his arm around her neck. Amiya knew she had to be fast or she was in trouble. She pushed forward and began thrashing.

When the boy widened his stance to steady himself, she

stomped on his foot, then punched him in the groin. His arm immediately slackened around her neck. When she slipped out of his grip, the doubled-over boy reached out weakly and tried to grab her. Amiya grabbed one of his fingers, twisted, and pulled it backwards.

"Arryargh!" The boy limped forward as she pulled. "L'mme go!"

Amiya flipped his hand so that his palm was up and bent his finger further back. The boy somewhat stood, the pain in his groin preventing him from fully straightening. He tried to grab at her with his free hand, but she kept circling away, forcing him to turn in her direction while trying to reach across his other arm.

"Ah!" He gritted his teeth when she bent his finger back so hard it creaked in her grasp. "You're gonna break it. You're gonna *break* it!"

"Nah." Amiya waited for an opening and kicked him in the groin again.

The boy let out an agonized squeak and lifted up on his toes. Amiya finally let go of his finger and he immediately clamped his hands over the afflicted area as he fell forward. Amiya stepped past the groaning boy as he curled up and back and forth on the ground. She jerked her chin at him. "Why don't you just lay there a bit, *yep*?"

She reached out her hand to the other boy on the ground. "You all right?"

"M'fine," the boy said. "M'fine, okay? Just need a minute. I can take a punch just fine, okay? Just … he's bigger."

When the boy didn't take Amiya's proffered hand, she lowered it. "All right, then. What's your name?"

The boy looked up at her and snarled. "Probably gonna come down harder on me next time, you know. 'Specially since some girl," he gave her a once over, "some M'rai girl helped me."

Amiya's face hardened. "Okay. Fine." She turned away. "I'll keep being some girl from Marai and leave you to keep taking punches." She saw an amused Estrella watching from the corner of the street.

"Booray," came the answer from behind. Amiya stopped and turned back. The boy shrank away from her glare but quickly straightened and tried to stand tall. "M'name's Booray." He looked down at the taller boy who had stopped groaning. He curled his legs up in an attempt to roll over onto his knees.

The boy snarled again, this time down at his assailant. "Been calling me Booper for a long time. Never leaves me alone." He drew his foot back and kicked the downed boy in the face.

Amiya flinched. Booray returned her wide-eyed expression with a sneer that he leveled over the bloody-nosed bully. He kicked him in the face again. "Maybe you won't be punching me anymore, okay?"

"Maybe you should stop," Amiya said.

Booray ignored her and kicked him again, then lifted his foot and stomped on the taller boy's head. Booray stomped his head into the ground again, then again. With each stomp his face twisted a little more into a crazed excitement.

"I said STOP!" Amiya delved *air*. She hit Booray with a quick gust and sent the boy tripping and tumbling away.

When he finally stopped, he looked up at her with eyes wide and filled with terror. "Power witch!" He pointed a trembling finger. "Power witch!"

"Power what?" Amiya took a step back, then nearly jumped out of her skin when she heard Estrella's voice right behind her.

"I think our time here is done, little one. Come." Estrella placed a hand on her shoulder and turned her away.

Two steps later and Amiya found herself standing on a polished stone pathway snaking between towering buildings made of smooth stone and gardens packed with fragrant flowers and roses. Men and women dressed in what looked like little more than expertly tied linen sheets sat in pavilions, talking or walking the smooth clean pathways.

"Let me guess," Amiya said. "You've shown me the poor, now you show me the rich?"

"I show you the various forms of human civilization and allow you to form your own opinions of what people manifest for themselves and others."

Most of the people they passed ignored them, while some few looked them over, *then* ignored them. They stepped onto a bridge leading to another section of the city, divided by a ridge hundreds of feet deep. Amiya looked out at the open land stretching below and gasped. "We're in the mountains. High in the mountains." She turned to Estrella. "Where are …" She trailed off when she noticed the woman's eyes. They were no longer violet, but a deep green.

Estrella fluttered her eyelashes and grinned. "Most would find my eyes unnerving."

"You never hid their color from me."

"You've a strength about you that's difficult to miss."

Amiya didn't know what to say to that, so she looked back out at the view. "Where are we?"

"The Creator's Vision, as named by the ever-so humble Nogthi ruling class," Estrella said. "This city rests in the lap of the highest mountains of Nogth and boasts views to compliment it."

"Creator's Vision." Amiya laughed. "Okay, then."

"Nogthi elite believe themselves the true children of the Creator," Estrella explained. "All others are merely the seeds dropped from the branches of the original tree."

Amiya made a disgusted face. "Yuck."

That drew a soft chuckle from her tall companion. "In all fairness, not all Nogthi believe this." She waved her hand at the encompassing city. "But you'll find the most vehement believers here."

"Can't imagine why," Amiya muttered.

"This is also why Nogth is among the few places in the world who utilize slave labor, including laborwives."

Amiya turned away from the view to look over the city. Her

teeth clenched together as Estrella educated her on a place she liked less by the moment. "How can Khatal and Marai be fighting when there's a place like this, just south of the mountains across the strait?"

Estrella arched an eyebrow. "You would have the king and the Ancients attack this land unprovoked?"

"Unprovoked?" Amiya took an unconscious step away. "You just told me they keep slaves. Isn't that reason enough? Or do you condone—"

"Calm yourself, little one," Estrella said. "One cannot fight everyone they disagree with." She held up a hand when Amiya started to argue. "And before you begin cursing my soul, no, I do not agree. Were I given the power, I would see the ruling class of this land subjected to twice that of their slaves. But the rulers of the lands north of Nogth must employ diplomacy wherever possible. Otherwise it can be seen by some as a slippery decline to warmongering. Might other lands whose practices we don't like, see our attack on another as a future threat, should we view their lifestyles as an affront to their sensibilities?"

"If they do things like this place, they *should* be afraid."

"And thus, the world falls to an endless cycle of one land attacking another," Estrella said. "Over a thousand years ago, parts of Marai participated in the slave market. It was through the moral vision and diplomacy of Shiedra that many such places were shown the error of such practices. As a result, the province of Nashma lives without the animosity of conquered neighbors, little more than a border away."

"Some people don't respond to talking," Amiya said.

Estrella conceded the point with a nod. "That is when harsher methods could become necessary."

They crossed the bridge and came to a pond with a smaller bridge arching over it. The bridge ended in a multi-colored stone pathway leading to a white structure with two robed figures standing on either side of the entrance. They had their hands raised, palms facing upwards, as if receiving something from above. "Reminds me of the temples of the Brotherhood of the Source," Amiya said, looking up at the towering stone figures as they passed.

"Light of the Law of Truth," Estrella said. "It bears similarity to the Brotherhood of the Source, but with a Nogthi slant."

"They teach about the Creator's favoritism to this land and its people, and that the rest of us are heathens," Amiya replied dryly.

"Very good," Estrella said.

A man in wide-legged flowing trousers resplendent in yellow and orange flowers and matching tunic stepped forward. He had his hands clasped behind his back, feet shoulder-length apart. His long brown hair was tied away from his face and hung nearly to his waist. He looked them over, head to toe. "Greetings. Rare is it do we receive visitors from the north. Rarer still, within the walls of the Light of the Law of Truth. If you seek to become civilized and perhaps submit to labor for your sins, be welcome—"

"I'll stop you, now," Amiya said, holding up a hand.

Mouth still open, the man tilted his head and regarded Amiya with a curious expression that he then turned on Estrella, who offered a slanted smile. "I wasn't aware that the sins of the north have so deepened that they allow children to interrupt their betters."

"*Betters*," Amiya echoed, leaning her head back in mock surprise. "I wasn't aware that the arrogance of this land has become so putrid that you offer insult and expect no reprisal. Mind stepping aside, Mr. Pants?" Beside her, Amiya heard the faintest flicker of a laugh.

Red crept up Mr. Pants's neck and traveled up to cover his face. "You are a recalcitrant little weed, aren't you?" He looked to Estrella. "I assume you've taken authority of this urchin, as your heritage obviously doesn't speak to her parentage."

Amiya balled her fists. She barely had to think about it for *fire* to come readily available. "Speak another word about my parentage, Pants. One more."

"I believe we've all had enough conversation for today," Estrella intervened. "Perhaps step aside, good monk, that we may continue on."

"You clearly jest if you believe—"

"Step *aside*, good monk." Whether it was Estrella's tone or something else, the monk shrank away and shuffled aside.

"What'd you do to him?" Amiya asked, still half turned and staring at the monk as they continued on.

"You heard," Estrella replied. "I told him to step aside."

"Yeah, but what did you do to him to make him step aside?" Amiya pressed. "I need some of that."

"You need more lessons in diplomacy, little one. If you make an enemy of everyone you don't like, you'll find yourself swimming in them."

An occasional monk turned down the walkway headed toward them. Every time, they would stop as if about to challenge the pair, and every time, Estrella simply told them to step aside. Amiya stole a peek at the woman's eyes. No *arah* shone in them, so she wasn't using essence.

"Should we have allowed him to insult us all the way to the laborwife quarters?" Amiya asked a while later. "That first monk when he came in?"

"Do you believe it's possible he could have done that?"

"Probably not."

"Then what did his words matter?" Estrella said. "He is a little man of no importance or great importance, depending on where life leads us. Perhaps one day you will encounter him again after he's seen the error in his thinking. Or you may see him amidst an opposing force on a battlefield. None can know."

"I doubt that ugly mountain mole's backside will ever change."

"Because you doubt it doesn't eliminate the possibility," Estrella said.

Amiya looked around at the endless walls of paintings depicting monks, both men and women, performing various tasks. Given what she was learning about Nogth, it all looked nauseating. "Nothing he said bothered you at all?"

She laughed. "Dear child, why would it?"

Amiya thought on that. Why *would* the man's words have affected Estrella? Despite having not truly witnessed the woman's abilities, Amiya didn't doubt Estrella could have brought the monk's life to an abrupt halt in a number of ways she likely couldn't imagine.

"Would the hostile squeak of a mouse trouble you?" Estrella asked.

"I see your point. Why waste the energy on him."

"You're learning well."

"Mind telling me why we're here?" Amiya asked.

"For that." Estrella pointed at a balcony to the side of the walkway.

Amiya looked over the edge. Men and women sat cross-legged on large pillows on a carpeted floor. At the head of the room, a man lectured on the medicinal properties of various types of plants, herbs, and fungi. "... given a medium-sized dose that greatly reduced the labor pains of a delivering woman, that we could assist in a complicated birth that might have killed mother, child, or both."

The man's voluminous sleeve fell past his elbow as he pointed a wooden stick at a scrawling board for all to see. "There is a tiny village in the mountains in southeast Marai. In my travels, I encountered a child at the edge of death. A snake had bitten him only hours before my arrival. My knowledge of the local plants of the same class as those native to Nogth allowed me to heal the child, who would otherwise have succumbed to the venom."

A student raised his hand. The teacher indicated he speak. "Was it not his destiny as an uncivilized to die of his affliction? If he were of the Truth, would his parent's not have already possessed the knowledge and skills to save him?"

"Not so," the teacher replied. "It is true that the people of this village did not possess the knowledge to save the child from the bite, but they had plenty to offer me. For instance." He produced a root Amiya knew well. "This is a root from a northern plant called Sumrick. When boiled it releases nutrients into the water to produce a broth that when ingested, combats the effects of poison, including venom. The effect is uncanny, as it causes the afflicted to sweat, but most profusely in the area where the poison is concentrated. As long as the victim is kept from moving, the broth will cause the body to effectively cook the venom out of it."

Try as she might, Amiya didn't quite get what Estrella was after. The whole business with the root might come in handy if she ever got bit by a snake, but what did that have to do with why they were here?

"The mass sum of humanity is frustratingly diverse," Estrella explained. "If all behaved in the same manner, even consistent with their own regions or upbringing, taking a side in Alyn's fight would be simple."

"But there are good and bad people on every side," Amiya added, catching on.

"Most of the time. There have been moments throughout history when one side of a conflict was undeniably wrong. Here," she indicated the lecture hall below, "is an example of a single person in a society of elitists with cruel leanings, teaching greater morals to receptive minds. Might that instructor have changed the boy's mind about those who aren't Nogthi? Perhaps, perhaps not. But in that room of students, I would wager at least one mind entertained his words."

Amiya thought she understood. She didn't know much about anything regarding the conflict between Marai and Khatal. How awful would it be to take a stand and make a difference on the wrong side? But then, why was she standing here contemplating this to begin with? Dad and Nandi were her priority. Why did this woman have her contemplating matters that had nothing to do with her, anyway?

"Still wearing your thoughts on your face, little one?" Estrella asked. "You wish to expend your energy solely on finding your loved ones, but perhaps there is wisdom in fortifying yourself for what is to come."

"Okay?" Amiya looked up at her. "What *is* to come, Estrella?"

"Life," came the answer. "The world and everything in it."

"What in the name of the Fallen is *that* supposed to mean?" Amiya nearly took a step away when Estrella's visage darkened. It was there and gone in a flash, but she saw it. "Sorry."

"Narrow your focus to only your immediate goal at your peril," Estrella answered. "You think your time is best spent solely on finding your family, but as with you, they may well be scattered across Marai, and with any host of deadly terrain and adversaries, human or beast, between you."

Amiya watched her move close to the rail and look down at the lecture. Did the woman ever even *lean* on anything? "There are some from times of history," Estrella continued, "who attained great power through a narrow focus."

"And, it led to their undoing?" Amiya guessed.

"It led to the undoing of many around them," Estrella corrected. "It led to the undoing of their peers, those closest to them, and nearly the world. The ramifications of their focus are still felt today, and likely will be forevermore."

Amiya whistled through her teeth. "You really know how to go dramatic."

Estrella looked over her shoulder back the way they came. A moment later, Amiya heard lots of footsteps coming towards them.

"Our welcome has expired," Estrella remarked.

"I don't think we ever had a welcome." Amiya delved for the power. Like a sentient being, it acknowledged her call. *This gets easier every time*, she noticed. Beside her, Estrella half turned to look at the group of men dressed like the first man that had "greeted" them.

"You are trespassing in the sacred Temple of Law of Truth," stated a spectacled man at the front of the procession. "Submit yourself for arrest and be judged before the law of the Creator."

Amiya didn't draw upon the power just yet. She remembered what Estrella had said about diplomacy. When she looked up at the woman, she saw … boredom?

"Be assured, good monk," Estrella replied. "There will be no need for arrest nor judgement before your idea of the Creator. We shall be on our way."

"Submit by your will or ours," the monk demanded. Every monk had a stone glowing with a silver or blue *arah*.

"Looks like it's going to get bad," Amiya said. She summoned *fire* and kept it just out of reach, prepared to melt any hard ice projectiles hurled their way.

"Hardly," Estrella said. She still hadn't bothered to fully face them.

"Submit *now*," the lead monk boomed, his voice amplified no doubt by *air*.

Estrella blinked slowly in response.

The lead monk held his stone out. The air in front of him misted as a forearm-length spear of ice formed. The other monks did the same until each of the group stood behind a floating spear aimed at Amiya and Estrella. Amiya looked at it all, wondering if she could wield enough *fire* to stop all that by herself. "This is your final warning," the monk said. "Submit or be broken into submission."

"There was a time I would have responded to your threat in kind, monk," Estrella said. The words slid from her tongue like a sword from its sheath. "Instead, I will leave you with a lesson, this day. It will be painful."

The monks loosed their missiles.

Fire sprang to Amiya's call, but she needn't have bothered.

With a casual wave of Estrella's hand, the spears entered a rippling patch of air in front of them and exited several patches of waving air behind the monks.

Amiya's eyes widened, then she looked away from what surely would be a group of people sliced to ribbons. Out of sheer dignity, she refrained from covering her ears and prepared herself for the awful sound of sharp objects cutting through flesh. She clamped her eyes shut as the cries of agony still penetrated her hands covering her ears.

When she finally opened her eyes, she saw the monks to a man, lying on the ground holding legs punctured with an ice spear. Despite their painful injuries, Amiya knew the truth of it as soon as she saw it. If Estrella had wanted to kill them, she could have easily done it with their own missiles turned against them. They might bear permanent scars, possibly permanent injuries, but they were alive.

"Step back, little one," Estrella said.

Amiya didn't even think about heeding or refusing the order. As if her body had obeyed for her, she took a shaky step back. The world rippled around her, and a heartbeat later she found herself standing amidst broken, crumbled buildings, and ripped up earth. Craters large enough to fit several houses dotted the blasted town, as well as long wide strips of ground sliced open like scars.

Skeletons lay strewn about, some leaning against rubble with their bony mouths hanging open as if smiling, others facedown or in pieces. "What is this place?" Amiya looked to Estrella, who stood unaffected in her survey of the destroyed town. "Why did you bring me here?"

"Ever will Light and dark exist opposite each other," Estrella answered. "Humans will fight and kill and die. They will love and hate, help and hinder. And, it is all infinitely small by comparison to the forces they play with; forces that could obliterate them with less than a thought. I bring you here to show you the horror we are capable of and that it is nothing, compared to the blight."

33

EMIEL

It all meant nothing. The explosions, the writhing tentacles blasting the earth apart. The few remaining drauk battling the Shiedran soldiers, the war cries, the infernal curses, the shouts and screams. It all blurred and muffled in the background of Emiel's disbelief as he stared into the giant hole his daughter had fallen into.

She'd been right there. Right in front of him. After months of searching, surviving, worrying about his daughters and what had happened or was happening to them, Nandi had found him. And he'd lost her.

The breath nearly left Emiel when someone tackled him. His shock gave way to jarred panic, and he started to fight back until he realized it was Bone. "You wanna snap out of it, spicetrader? I can't fight these Fallen-cursed things and protect *you* too. It'd surely be helpful if you get yourself together!"

Emiel heard it all in a daze. He looked at Bone but saw his daughter's ankle in Amoura's grip just before they fell into the black pit.

Another ground-shaking rumble snapped him out of his stupor.

Emiel saw past Bone, another tentacle flatten a soldier. That had been the thing that opened the hole and lost his daughter to him.

He felt himself go cold, then raging hot. Another underworld monster. The blasted things were showing up everywhere, killing and maiming. And now, Emiel didn't know if Nandi was alive or dead. Whatever the answer to that, something would die, today.

Bone had still been talking, but trailed off when he looked into Emiel's eyes. The boy got off and moved away.

"Thank you." Emiel stood and faced the giant monster. Serai, he thought he remembered it being called. It was fully exposed, now, thanks to his powerful daughter.

Emiel strode toward the monster, heavy appendages crashing on the ground all around him. *Air, fire, water,* and *earth* swirled around his body like a second skin, ready for his call, eager to express his will.

A tentacle raised up in front of him and sped for his head. Emiel never broke his stride, didn't so much as react. He barely registered it at all. His body erupted in flames that engulfed the tentacle as if it had been doused in flaming pitch. It writhed in the air as it burned to ashes.

Another appendage swept toward him, and a sheet of ice formed in front of it. The edge was so thin and honed that the sweeping appendage sliced itself in half right across it. Blue-black ichor spouted from the waving, severed limb. The monster moaned loudly and shuffled its bulk away.

"Oh, no. You're not hurt, yet," Emiel said quietly. The thing swatted at him again and lost another appendage. It turned as if to move away, but a wall of ice as thick as a house formed in front of it. The beast pounded against it, but it may as well have hit the side of a mountain.

Stone steps emerged from the side of the mini crater, and Emiel descended and walked right up to the beast. With an expression as cold as the wall of ice trapping the serai, he placed his hand on it.

The flesh felt like dozens of layers of boiled leather armor. He placed his other hand on it. *Fire* flowed from his left hand while *air* flowed from his right. The giant beast tried to move away, tried to curl inward and grab at him with its shorter nautilus-like appendages.

The monster's body lit with a red inner glow, while its leathery hide looked as if it were freezing over. The large milky eyes simply melted, then the ooze froze on the sides of its head. In the span of but several heartbeats the monster simultaneously froze and melted.

Emiel heard the curse of a drauk. He turned, found the monster charging a cluster of soldiers, and summoned *earth*. A huge stalagmite burst from the ground, angled toward the sprinting monster. It impaled the drauk and lifted it from the ground as it rose. The four-armed monster hung suspended two dozen feet above the ground. It hadn't stopped squirming to free itself when two large balls of ice collided with either side of its head in an explosion of rock and lava-like blood.

From the bottom of the crater, Emiel stared up at the thing and wished there were more. That was the last of them, though. He heard a high-pitch voice screaming his name, but barely registered the sound. Bone suddenly appeared in front of him, shouting in his face. After a moment, Emiel blinked. The boy's distant voice came into focus.

"We've got to go!" Bone yelled. "People aren't much comfortable with essence wielders, and you don't have the ring or the magus robes to prevent both of us from being arrested, if we're lucky."

Emiel didn't need to ask about if they were "unlucky". Once they climbed back out of the crater, he looked at the giant hole again and started that way.

Bone grabbed him by the shoulders and forced Emiel to look at him. "Snap out of it, Emiel! Amoura's with her. You won't do any of them any good by dying here!"

All Emiel could do was nod. He followed Bone in a daze, barely seeing the carnage around them.

"Emiel?" It was Lief's voice. "Emiel? Are you okay? Please, snap out of it."

He looked down at his tinfar companion. "I'm fine. Let's just go."

"So," cough, "you're just gonna leave me, then?" a young girl's voice said from just ahead. "Uuurgh."

"Over there." Lief pointed at a redheaded girl trapped under a flat piece of rubble. Her brown eyes glowed as she delved *earth*. The girl scurried free as soon as the rock shifted.

"You've got my thanks," the girl said in an accent similar to Bone's when he turned it on. "Could'a right killed me if it fell just a little different."

Emiel stared at her until the girl took a step back. He blinked, then shook his head in apology. "You were with my daughter."

"How 'bout we have this discussion on the move." Bone grabbed him by the elbow and dragged him along, the others falling in step.

"Aye," the girl said. "Been a long way gettin' here, it was."

"Just a little farther," Bone said under his breath. "Just a little bit farther and we're—"

"HOLD!"

In front of Emiel, Bone's shoulders slumped and his head fell back. He heaved a great sigh, then turned around. Emiel turned with him to see a beaten and bloody, but very much alive Captain Adolphus making his way toward them. Emiel glanced down at his side, but of course, Lief was gone. He looked back up.

Adolphus limped toward them ahead of three other soldiers, Officer Taiyana at his side. He stopped right in front of them and looked Emiel and Bone in the eye.

Emiel had to admire the man. Despite having witnessed monsters he surely hadn't seen before and likely had never heard of, he seemed to be coping well.

The captain's hard, light brown eyes bore into Emiel with a no-nonsense intensity that demanded answers to questions he hadn't asked yet. "You fought well."

Emiel inclined his head silently, as did Bone beside him.

"Aye," the redheaded girl snapped. "And I suppose I didn't do a Fallen-blasted thing but sit on the ground and cry, then?"

Adolphus responded to that with frowning smile, then nodded in respect to the girl. Beside him, Officer Taiyana alternated her death stare between Emiel and Bone. All business, that one.

"As you're no longer prisoners of the Shiedra," Adolphus said, returning his attention to Emiel and Bone," I'm not ordering you to accompany me to see the Royana." He turned aside so that they could look with him at the surrounding devastation. "But, in spite of our initial meeting, I would appreciate it if you would come with us to speak with her nonetheless." He turned back. "I'm confident she'll want to hear anything you have to say."

"What makes you think we know anything more about this than you?" Bone asked.

Adolphus answered that with a long even look. "Son, I might have been otherwise engaged, but I've made a fair career for myself in being aware of my surroundings and those in them. Not a one of you reacted with surprise when those things, whatever they were, showed up. You also looked like you knew how to fight them. So if we can be finished with pretending not to know anything, let's get moving. If they struck once, I'm assuming it'll happen again and I'd rather be prepared."

They followed the soldiers through the wreckage, passing men and women digging themselves out of rubble. Many tears ran down dirt-covered cheeks as the living searched for survivors, or pulled free the dead.

Captain Adolphus ordered the soldiers remaining with him to assist in the recovery, leaving only himself and Taiyana. Emiel wished he'd ordered her away as well. The woman looked like she still wanted to sheathe her sword in his and Bone's chests. "I'm sorry about your companion," the captain said.

Emiel snapped out of his thoughts. "Pardon me?"

"Your companion, the magus," Adolphus repeated. "I'm sorry about her fall."

"Oh, thanks." Emiel struggled to hold back his emotions. Amoura was alive. He'd never met a tougher and more powerful woman aside from Aunya, though his beloved long dead wife hadn't any use of the essence power. No, Amoura survived, and if she survived, so did Nandi. He'd seen his little girl wielding the power with seemingly more competence than himself. They would work together.

Emiel grabbed hold of that lifeline of hope and forced his mind to see it as fact. He'd see them again. He would. If he allowed himself to consider anything else, it would destroy him. He owed his survival to Nandi and Amiya as well, whom he hadn't seen. Why weren't they together?

"You alright?" Bone asked.

Emiel looked at him. "Yeah, why?"

"You look pretty intense. Thinking about your love interest? Don't worry about her. She's a tough one. Gonna take a lot more than a fall to be rid of that one."

"Suren you're the sensitive one, then?" the redheaded girl said.

Bone looked down at her. "Where you be from, lass? You've the sound of the highlands on your tongue."

"North Highlands, aye," the girl said. "As you've got the sound of the East Highlands with that drawl."

"Drawl?" Bone jerked his head back. "You've quite the mouth on you, little lass."

"Says the one who's talkin' love interest to a man just found his daughter and she slipped away again."

Bone frowned at her, then looked at Emiel, who still struggled to hold himself together. The girl meant well, but her words were like salt in an open wound.

"Daughter?" Bone said in an uncharacteristic tone of kindness. "I … didn't know. My apologies, Emiel." He clenched his jaw. "But, I'm only sorry that you've been denied your reunion with your little girl. I saw her fighting. If Amoura's down there with her, you'd best be sure they'll find their way to safety together."

"Especially with that weird girl with the green hair," the redheaded girl said.

"Who?" Emiel asked.

"Maybe I'll tell you later, Mr. Nandi's Da."

That drew a bit of laughter from Emiel in spite of the situation. "You remind me of my other daughter—"

"Amiya," she finished for him. "Nandi told me all about her."

"What's your name?" Emiel asked.

"Ailith MacAra," the girl answered. "But I won't mind if you don't attach me surname every time you address me."

"Well then, Ailith MacAra," Emiel replied, still chuckling. "My name is Emiel Dharr. And you need not attach my surname either."

"Aye and well met, Mr. Emiel," Ailith said. She jabbed Bone in the hip with an elbow. He responded with an incredulous frown. "And what of yourself, Easterner?"

The mercenary shook his head. "Bone."

"*Bone*?" Ailith's shock of long curly red hair slid back away from her face when she looked up at him. "What kinda name is Bone? Your da not one for syllables, then?"

"I gave myself the name and it's all you need," Bone replied with a little more heat than Emiel thought necessary. "Easy enough, I'm thinkin'."

"Fair enough, 'Bone, I gave the name to myself and that's all you're gonna get,'" Ailith replied. "No need for all the extra huff."

Emiel wiped his face to keep from laughing. Even the perpetually grim Officer Taiyana looked to be holding back a smirk.

"Captain Adolphus!" A gray-haired and heavily muscled soldier trotted toward them. He stopped in front of Adolphus and saluted.

"Lieutenant Castilla," Adolphus replied.

"No further reports have come in, but my unit is combing Shiedra for survivors and any lingering hostiles." The man's booming voice filled the air between him. He looked like solid rock in uniform. "It appears to have been a random attack, but the Creator only knows what those things were and why they came here."

"We're working on finding that out now," Adolphus said. "Keep scanning until you've covered the whole of Shiedra. Send runners to nearby towns. Hopefully this was an isolated attack, but we need to know."

The lieutenant saluted again. "Yes, sir."

Emiel fought back his sense of urgency bordering on panic and tried to think things through. Nandi had exhibited some capabilities with the essences. Beside Amoura, she would be fine. Amiya was out in the world somewhere by herself likely looking for them both. Would she still be headed to Altarra? And, when and where had they been separated?Questions started piling up in his mind.

Four soldiers stood guard on either side of a fortified door. Upon seeing Adolphus, they saluted and the two closest to the iron door stepped aside. The smoldering remains of what looked to have been a single drauk lay to the side, near a handful of soldiers lining up and carrying off their injured and slain comrades.

Adolphus stopped in front of the guards. "What's the report?"

"The family and governing body is safe inside the compound, sir," a soldier replied. He drew the captain's attention to the scratched and dented iron door. "Only one attacked this location, sir."

Adolphus responded with a grim nod. "You were lucky." He led them through the fortified compound, past several patrol units stationed in the secured courtyard and up the steps beyond. Emiel couldn't imagine the planning it took to make an attack-resistant compound look and feel comfortable, but they'd done a fine job.

They found Royana Lindra amidst her court, who appeared to

be in heated discussion about who was behind the attack. The most common word Emiel heard was "wilders", but one person even suggested the distant land of Nogth to be the culprits.

"Ridiculous," Emiel muttered.

"Exactly what I need you to share with the Royana," Adolphus replied in an equally quiet voice. The man had excellent hearing.

Lindra noted their approach and gave a subtle nod to the captain while maintaining her attention on the rather energetic discussion happening between several men and women Emiel remembered from the hearing. While the council members were understandably unnerved by the attack, the royana oversaw the discussions with unwavering stoicism.

Emiel watched her with admiration. If Amoura was any indication of what magi were like, the royana would have made a good one.

They waited until Lindra was able to find an opening to excuse herself. She glided toward the group, all calm poise, unshaken by the horrific attack. "You have news, I hope." She looked over the group. "This should be interesting."

Emiel thought he detected the faintest quiver in her tone and found himself humbled. The royana was likely every bit as shaken by this attack as everyone else, but she remained strong for her people. How heavily must the recent events weigh on her? The loss of her husband, the royain, taking on the singular leadership of an entire province, and now an attack by monsters no one had likely ever seen before.

"I have soldiers scouring every inch of Shiedra, Excellency," Adolphus began. "I don't have an exact number, yet, but at least half a dozen of the creatures attacked the city, along with a bigger beast that struck from underground."

Lindra nodded and appeared to collect herself as she asked the next question. "Casualties?"

"Last report, forty-two soldiers and sixteen civilians, and that's before the underground beast struck. Several buildings were destroyed as well."

"Six unidentified monsters did that much damage." Lindra let out a heavy sigh. She looked to Emiel and Bone before turning a curious expression on Ailith. "I find myself surprised by your presence here."

"No more than our own," Bone said, then added, "Excellency."

"They're called drauk," Emiel spoke up. "They're creatures of the underworld and heralds of something much worse to come."

"That all sounds rather grim." She tilted her head. "Mr. Dharr, if I remember?"

"Emiel, if that's all right with you, Excellency," he replied. "And it's a lot more grim than you think."

"I suppose I should hear it, then." She looked them over again. "Where is your other companion?"

"She ..." Emiel took several steadying breaths until he trusted his voice not to crack. To his relief, the royana waited patiently for him to collect himself. "A beast known as a serai broke open a deep hole in the ground. She fell in."

Royana Lindra's sparkling green eyes softened. "I see. My condolences, Emiel. There is nothing I can say to soften the pain, but I offer you any help I can provide."

"Thank you, Excellency." Emiel told her and the captain everything he knew so far about the drauk and the ruination. Bone occasionally filled in any details he missed. The more he talked, the more incredulous Lindra and Adolphus grew. Even the ever stoic Taiyana twitched an eyebrow at some of the more outlandish details.

"If I have it right," Lindra said once he finished. "The attack on Shiedra was just one of several, and the monsters involved are some sort of herald to a dark force supposed to bring about a ruination? This sounds like a far reach, sir."

Emiel shrugged in agreement. "It sounds like a reach to my own ears, but I know what we've been through these past months, and everything Amoura Xanna has researched points to the same thing. All the books could be wrong, but whether they are or not, there are more cities than just Shiedra to account for the sudden appearance of hideous four-armed monsters."

Lindra suddenly looked like she felt every bit of the weight of her station and all that had happened these past months. "I don't discount your story, Emiel Dharr, but it is a lot to digest."

"Of course, Royana," Emiel replied. "I hope what I've given you will be of some use."

"I suspect it will," Lindra said. "What will you do now?"

"I have to find my daughters and my friend," Emiel said. "I nearly had one of my daughters back and she's lost to me again. I'll get them both back if I have to slaughter every drauk from one end of the world to the other, ruination be damned."

Lindra responded to that with a sagely nod. "I believe you, Emiel Dharr. May you find your daughters and your friend, and may you survive this coming doom, and whatever it brings."

Emiel bowed. "Thank you, Royana."

Despite his urgency to be away to Altarra, Emiel relented to Bone's insistence they take the royana up on her offer to house them for the night. They were both right, of course. Marching out with a full head of steam and no plan for the place he'd formerly been a prisoner wasn't the best strategy, but he needed to do something.

"Spend the night and think about all this," Bone said. "There'll be more opportunities for fighting than you can count, and far fewer to be able to avoid dying. Best not rush any of that if you can set out with at least your mind in the right place."

The mercenary had been right, of course. Now Emiel sat on the patio of his room in one of the inns that hadn't been damaged in the attack.

"We'll find them," Lief said. The tinfar had come as soon as he was alone in his room. "We will, my friend."

"Thank you." Two words. The only thing he could think to say.

Tomorrow would come soon, and one way or another, they'd be on their way. Nandi, Amiya, and Amoura were alive, he knew. His ladygirls were learning to survive in a world growing more dangerous by the day. If he wanted to survive to find them again, it was time he did the same.

MIKUNA

The *trogk* dropped to its knees, tiny streams of its lava-like lifeblood pouring out of dozens of wounds. Its lower set of hands held it up to a kneeling position while it tried to strike out at Mikuna with a weapon in one of its upper hands.

Mikuna called to *olayem, tinu,* and *ushaa.* The aspects sprang to her call. She formed a light coating of mud and rock around her hands and forearms and solidified it. She then formed a wide shard of ice as long as a sword over each arm.

The *trogk* growled and swung its club. Even at its kneeling position the beast was at eye-level with Mikuna. She whipped her left arm up in an outward arc to meet the swinging club. Her shard-arm sliced cleanly through the rocky club while at the same time Mikuna thrust her right arm straight.

With all her strength behind the stab, the honed tip of her right shard-arm slid into the *trogk*'s rocky chest. Mikuna quickly retracted just as the ice started to sizzle. She stepped backwards and lunged her body to the right, bringing her left shard-arm around and down. The *trogk*'s incoming rocky sword split in half around the razor sharp ice weapon.

Mikuna never stopped moving. Before the top half of the

trogk's sword thumped to the ground, she brought her left shard-arm up and across its throat. She followed the motion through and stabbed her right shard-arm through its face. The monster's curses died with it as it crumbled apart.

"Your back, *Asha!*" she heard Bayaku call from behind. Mikuna didn't take the time to turn. She delved *olayem*. A cluster of stalagmites burst from the ground and impaled the *trogk* rushing her from behind. The sharp stone raised the hulking beast into the air and held it aloft, thrashing and cursing until Akrim silenced it with a well placed ice spear through the neck. Its head fell free to join the crumbling body in a mess below.

Bayaku had been fighting two of the monsters at once. By the time Mikuna and Akrim had finished off their monsters, the veteran warrior had dispatched one of his enemies, and now battered the remaining one.

Despite the fast and relentless swings and spins, stabs and chops of the *trogk*, Bayaku always found a space around the weapon in each of its four hands. He dodged left and ducked low, straightened and leaned out of reach of a swinging rock sword. He continued to lean away until he lay flat on his back.

As Bayaku went down, the monster pursued with an overhead chop down that would have split the warrior in half while he lay on his back. But it was not Bayaku who would fall this day. With hands similarly encased in ice like Mikuna's, he brought them up in an inside to outside arc in front of his body. The maneuver cut apart the descending club aimed at his face.

Bayaku swatted the falling piece of club aside an instant before the ice fell away from his arms. The veteran warrior's eyes glowed brown and red. Mud covered his fists, then a layer of hard rock covered it. The outer layer of rock glowed red, then solidified into a metal many times harder than the lava rock sword descending toward him.

Fists protected by solid iron, Bayaku punched the sword from both directions and shattered it. He rolled sideways as the pieces of rock sword fell around him, and flipped up to his feet again.

The *trogk* stomped after him, but the Frostland warrior spun and dropped to one knee. Bayaku turned his torso into the punch and struck the pursuing underworld creature in the midsection. Its curses came to an abrupt end as it burst apart around the fist of iron.

Jista lowered herself to the ground and placed her ear to the earth. The tracker had collected an assortment of scars over the past few days, but so had they all. Despite Jista's formidable tracking and survival skills, the first attack two nights ago might have ended in disaster, had Bayaku not possessed such sensitive hearing and instincts. Every member of Mikuna's team was a highly capable warrior with abilities honed over a lifetime of training. But none of them were Bayaku.

Mikuna, Akrim, and Bayaku formed a triangle around the tracker as she listened to the ground. "More," Jista said. She pointed south. "Lots coming from that way." She then pointed northeast. "More that way, too, but fewer."

"Northeast, then," Mikuna said.

"More than enemies from the world below will challenge us if we venture too far from the Ridgeline," Bayaku said. His eyes glowed red, then brown. A moment later, the iron coating his fists softened and fell away. He flexed his fingers several times and dusted them off.

"I'd rather face an enemy we can reason with," Mikuna said.

"That could be argued," Akrim chimed in.

Mikuna set off at a fast jog, the others forming up around her. For a while they progressed uninhibited, but soon the *trogk* caught up. The hulking creatures didn't require rest, as they didn't tire. While Mikuna's band of warriors were well conditioned, they still had to run at a manageable pace. The *trogk* could sprint full speed, indefinitely, until they eventually ran the Khatala warriors down.

Long before the monsters reached them, Mikuna heard the

growling curses and thuds of their heavy footfalls. They couldn't continue like this. They had no way of knowing how many of the things roamed these lands, assuming there wasn't an infinite number of them to begin with.

"Here we go!" Akrim warned. He skidded to a stop and turned back. Eyes alight in with the *arah* of *olayem*, he summoned lance-like stalagmites out of the ground. He heaved one in each hand and let fly one after another, channeling *tinu* to speed the projetiles' flight. Several fell to the deadly missiles, but many more made it through. Akrim's eyes faded from brown, and lit silver. He blasted the sprinting monsters with a squall of freezing air.

Jista stepped beside him, her eyes also aglow with the silver *arah*. Though their abilities with the aspects in this way were less effective, their combined efforts slowed the *trogk* and cooled their bodies.

The first wave of the monsters finally succumbed and began to freeze. The charging monsters behind them, however, simply ran straight into and through their frozen comrades, blasting them to pieces.

"Gotta love that camaraderie," Akrim remarked.

Mikuna delved *olayem* and coated her hands and forearms in mud and rock, then solidified it. She then delved *tinu* and *ushaa*, creating finely honed ice shard weapons around her hands and forearms again. She charged the nearest *trogk* and slid on her side under a sweeping sword. She sliced through its leg, turned onto her back, and kicked her feet up. After flipping back onto her feet, Mikuna turned and jumped straight up. She tucked her knees up to her chest and the *trogk's* sweeping sword passed harmlessly under.

Mikuna delved *olayem*. A stalagmite burst from the ground underneath the *trogk's* chest. As the sharp rock impaled and lifted the monster up, Mikuna chopped her shard-arm down on its neck. The severed head bounced on the ground and rolled away as the body began to crumble. "We need to get out of the area, now!"

Bayaku punched a *trogk* in the leg with an iron-coated fist and shattered it. He ducked under a swipe at his head from behind, turned, and punched the other behind him in the hip. The monster fell over as chunks of its rocky body fell apart. Bayaku turned back to the first monster, iron-covered fist speeding in a right-handed punch straight for the injured *trogk's* face. Its rocky head exploded from the impact, lava rock flying everywhere.

Akrim ducked a thrusting rock sword and rolled to the side to avoid a swinging club. The second club of one of his enemy's lower arms grazed his shoulder and sent him spinning to the ground. Akrim kept his wits about him, however. He rolled with the momentum while delving *ushaa* and *tinu*. The Frostland warrior rolled up to a kneeling position and, with a *tinu*-enhanced throw, left fly a lance of ice.

The missile punched through the pursuing *trogk* and impaled the one behind it. The two underworld monsters thrashed and pounded at the ice until they broke it apart. But Akrim wasn't finished. He sent another lance speeding into his immediate adversary. The *trogk* spun and chopped its club down, shattering the projectile. Akrim launched another, and another, the *trogk* chopping and swatting in a continuous explosion of flying ice particles.

Akrim continued to give ground step by step while the underworld beast cursed and pounded through his assault. "You're a big tough tundra rat, aren't ya?" he said, still giving ground while the growling, cursing *trogk* spun, chopped, and pounded through the speeding ice. The sheer savagery of its movements would have sent any lesser person running. But Akrim was part of Mikuna's team for a reason.

"It's time," Akrim said. He broke off his assault and moved as if to flee. The unthinking savage immediately lunged into pursuit. Akrim knelt and delved *ushaa* and *tinu* once more, then thrust his hands out in front of him. The *trogk* had reached within a few feet of the kneeling warrior, but it wasn't quick enough.

Akrim slapped his hands together and created a cone of ice as large around as the *trogk*. It grew rapidly from his hands and slammed square into the monster. The *trogk's* body had been partially turned, and so two of its arms were forced against its body as the circular pillar of ice hit it. The impact shattered one of its arms as it flew backwards and crashed into another *trogk*.

Mikuna sliced clean through a rocky sword and ducked the followup swing of a club. Just fighting one of these things was a vicious dance, as there weren't two weapons to worry about, but four. She cut it across the leg, rolled past a descending club, and stabbed it in the side.

She retracted and used the momentum to spin herself around with a horizontal swing. The *trogk* behind her received a cut across the midsection that would have disemboweled a human. The monster barely reacted and kept coming. With a twist of her torso, Mikuna continued the swing of her right shard-arm while stabbing forward with her left.

The beast she'd cut across the abdomen had stupidly kept coming, and thus ran straight into her stabbing shard. The *trogk* behind her righted itself and started toward her again. Her other swinging shard-arm sheered through its leg.

Mikuna could feel the tremendous weight of the impaled *trogk* as it leaned forward on her left shard-arm. She yanked it free and fell into a backwards roll. The *trogk* had raised one of its clubs and had been swinging it down just as she pulled free. It stumbled forward and struck the other downed *trogk* on the top of the head. Mikuna rapidly stabbed it in the side with a series of one-two punches.

"*Tinu* glide! To the northeast." Mikuna delved *tinu* as she stepped back. The others broke off from their adversaries or finished off defeated foes. Together, they leapt toward the northeast.

Eyes flaring in the bright silver of the power of *tinu*, the Frost-land warriors glided high into the air. The *trogk* quickly diminished into dots on the ground as the four warriors flew away.

They glided a long way before their arc reached its height and they began to fall. Mikuna guided *tinu* into a continuous gentle gust of air that slowed her descent to the ground. The others did the same until they touched down far from the battle.

Again, they leapt into the air and glided far into the distance. In short order the team placed several leagues between themselves and the *trogk*. At the height of their assent, Mikuna saw pockets of fighting in the distance.

"By Creator *Amyadali*," Jista said from a few feet away as they started to fall again. "Have the eyes of *mgomu* itself turned to this land?"

"Every land," Mikuna answered. "The void aspect is awake and the sightless have returned. This will only get worse."

They landed and leapt again, looking into the distance. Mikuna spotted a lone figure leaping into the air. Not as high as she and her team, but higher than a jump unassisted by *tinu*. As she drew closer to the ground, she noted the distant figure's movements, which looked familiar. Someone fought with him; a much shorter person, even for a Marailander. A woman. And something else fought as well. An animal. A horribly savage animal.

By Creator Amyadali. "JOGA!" Mikuna would have willed her descent to quicken if she could. Her heart pounded with impatience as she helplessly watched her adoptive brother far in the distance, surrounded by *trogk* and what looked like a big bipedal monster.

As soon as they landed, Mikuna took off in a sprint and leapt again. She delved *tinu* and launched herself in an explosive burst of air. She shot into the sky like an arrow, quickly closing the distance. She reached the height of her arc and began her descent toward the tiny embattled figures below.

A couple hundred feet in the air, the distant sound of infernal curses found her ears. The little dots grew more detailed as Mikuna drew closer. She started to summon *naara* and incinerate the bipedal creature that got too close to Joga, but the beast not only struck down a *trogk* close to her brother, Joga struck out with a burst of freezing air at an enemy that leaped behind the wolfish beast.

There was no time to contemplate the oddity. She was nearly to the ground. She slowed her descent and drew upon *olayem* to coat her arms. Once she created the ice-shard blades around her arms, Mikuna used a quick burst of air to propel herself the last distance to reach the nearest enemy.

She hit the *trogk* in the back, shard-arms first. She might weigh much less than the monster, but her velocity more than made up for it. She knocked the *trogk* into a forward stumble. It caught itself with its lower arms, which bought it that instant it needed to get its upper hands down to keep from sprawling.

As soon as her blades pierced its back, Mikuna tucked her feet in and gave a quick push. The *trogk's* body might not be as scorching hot as lava straight from a volcano, but hot it still was. With a quick burst of *tinu* to aid her retreat, Mikuna kicked off of its back and avoided the burn.

She hit the ground amidst the chaos, stabbing out and sweeping her opposite arm. She stabbed one *trogk*, spun and dropped to a kneeling position, and dismembered another. She delved the aspects, used her meager distance abilities to keep them off balance, and while she went to work with her superior ice-shard arms. She stabbed and sliced, took an arm or a leg, and always kept moving.

A giant lance of ice burst through the back of a *trogk* and stabbed into the ground. A heartbeat later, Akrim touched down. Just past him, Bayaku struck the impaled *trogk* in the head with his iron-covered fists as he landed. The headless monster sagged on the lance and crumbled apart, while Bayaku went into a forward roll and came up fighting.

The skirmish ended with Mikuna, her team, and Joga and his companion panting as they scanned the battleground. The *trogk* lay in piles of rubble or falling apart. A few dozen feet away, the two-legged horror kept its yellow-eyed gaze on them as it stalked around the group and stopped behind the short dark-skinned woman. Where did it come from?

"Why are we not roasting that thing?" Akrim said.

"Speak words that I can understand," the woman beside Joga said.

Mikuna strained to remember her name. Nambe? Nimbay?

"Apologies," Akrim said, switching to the Marai tongue. "Was just expressing doubt about animal behind you."

"Kokunde is my friend," the woman said.

Nyimbe. That was her name. The others behind Mikuna must have looked as dubious as she felt, for the woman responded with a knowing grin.

"There would be no doubt if Kokunde was not a friend, Khatala."

"He is fireproof?" Akrim quipped.

"Long enough to get to the source and extinguish it," Nyimbe said.

Akrim chuckled uneasily. "Says you."

"Says many who witness the death of a fool at the jaws and claws of a tricoro," Bayaku remarked.

After a long pause, Akrim responded, "Oh."

"How find me?" Joga asked.

"Easier, since you travel in wrong direction, *yosha*," Mikuna said.

"So do you," Joga replied. "Are too far east."

"Chased here by *trogk*," Jista said. "Come from everywhere, it seems."

"Is why we are here," Joga said. "Well, part why we are here." He and Nyimbe shared a look.

Mikuna glanced from one to the other. "Would like to hear why."

"Will have to wait," Jista said.

Mikuna turned to see the tracker with her ear to the ground. "*Trogk*. Many of them."

"Which way they go?" Joga asked.

"Toward us," came the answer. "From south."

"Can distance ourselves from them like before," Akrim suggested.

Mikuna started to agree, then looked at Nyimbe. "Will not leave friends behind. Joga's friend is our friend," she added before Akrim could argue.

Before they could decide what direction in which to flee, the ground rumbled. The six warriors formed up into two back-to-back triangles while Nyimbe's fearsome four-legged monster stood several paces away from her, Joga, and Jista. It snapped its jaws at the air and lowered into a crouch.

An armor-plated leg burst out of the ground and spread its claws. The paw looked big enough to strangle a bear, with claws like daggers digging scars into the ground. It pulled itself out of the ground and leveled its crimson glare over them. Mikuna clenched her jaw. *Nokju.*

Several *trogk* burst out of the ground a heartbeat later and charged. The two groups engaged the *trogk*, the aspects aiding them against their unflinching, unfeeling enemies. Bayaku formed his iron fists again and Mikuna, her ice-shard blades.

Kokunde howled and charged the *nokju*. The darkwood cat leaped at the underworld beast, and the two monsters collided midair in a flurry of claws and teeth, biting and tearing. They hit the ground and rolled about, neither letting up.

Mikuna felled one *trogk* with a stab through the neck. The triumph cost her, for in a last effort, it swung one of its clubs at her side. She turned away to absorb the blow, but it still knocked her several feet away. She hit the ground in a dazed tumble and her ice weapons broke apart. Mikuna rubbed her right arm and winced. If it hadn't been protected by the ice, it would surely have been broken.

A *trogk* spotted her and charged. Mikuna struggled to stand, but a roar from the side alerted the beast to Joga's presence the instant before he crashed into its side.

Joga hit the ground in a roll when the monster fell. He created two spears of ice in his hands and rammed them into the monster's chest before it could stand. Standing again, Joga's eyes glowed brown as he delved *olayem*. A large chunk of the ground broke apart in front of him, and Joga gripped it on either side and lifted it over his head. The trogk had barely broken the second ice spear impaling its torso when the enraged Frostlander brought slammed the heavy chunk of earth down on top of it. The ground vibrated from an impact that left the monster scattered across the field.

Another *trogk* charged him from behind. Mikuna hopped to her feet and sent two spears of ice flying into the beast as she ran. Joga turned and saw the threat just before Mikuna reached it and punched his quickly formed shard-arm through its abdomen.

Mikuna nearly fell over as soon as she and Joga finished the beast. Her head still pounded, but her adrenaline kept her going. Akrim took a cut to the shoulder but peppered his adversary with ice lances that left it filled with holes before crumbling apart.

Bayaku, Jista, and Nyimbe fought together against two *trogk*, and had them down before Mikuna or Joga could assist. The short Marailander surprised her. She fought with an expertise that rivaled Bayaku's.

Kokunde and the *nokju* separated, both bleeding from many wounds yet showing no notice of it. They circled each other and charged in again. The *nokju* skidded to a stop and lashed out with one of the two waving appendages from each of its shoulders.

The darkwood cat dodged. When the tentacle drew back to lash again, Kokunde accepted the stinging blow that split the flesh in his shoulder. With a snarl, Kokunde bit down on the whip-like appendage and snapped it off. The *nokju* barked a growl and backed away as the darkwood cat spat the piece of its appendage on the ground.

It tried to circle the pursuing Kokunde until Joga formed a

spear of ice in his hand and threw it at the monster's head. His aim was slightly off, but the spear still punched into the monster's shoulder. It flinched away from the injury and tried to curl its body around to get at the weapon. Kokunde was there in a flash of fangs and biting jaws. The darkwood cat clamped onto the *nokju*'s neck and bit down with a resounding crack.

The monstrous cat backed away, arched his back, and howled at the sky.

"Makes you just want to run up and cuddle the thing," Akrim remarked when the darkwood cat turned toward them. He flicked his tongue out to clean his crimson muzzle.

Before the team could think of their next move, they heard the distant sound of growling curses. They turned to the south to see yet more *trogk* charging straight for them.

"Truly, we must be the saviors of the world," Akrim said. "Why else would the entire underworld open up and funnel all of its pets towards us?"

Without a word, Bayaku settled into a defensive stance. With weary sighs, the others did the same. If this didn't end, they would need to figure out a different strategy or they would drop from exhaustion before a *trogk* weapon sent them to the True Home.

"Look there." Jista pointed farther east where a force of mounted soldiers rode straight for the *trogk*. They drew swords and roared a battle cry moments before the two forces collided.

Akrim whistled through his teeth. "They need to learn how to fight these things."

Mikuna winced at the truth of Akrim's words. The soldiers fought valiantly and died. The *trogk* ran right through them, hacking and pounding, spinning, cursing, and stomping. For every *trogk* the soldiers felled, three or four men died. Sometimes more.

"Must help them," Joga said.

Beside Mikuna, Akrim let out a heavy sigh. "I'm sure they'll embrace us with love when it's done."

"What does *Asha* command?" Bayaku asked Mikuna, using her title with respect.

Mikuna felt mostly recovered now that her head had stopped pounding. There would be time to attend wounds later. She called to the aspects and felt them ready. "We fight."

THE NEARER THEY GOT, the clearer their view of the soldiers' livery became. They were Shiedran, which meant they must be close to Nashma's capital.

Once they noted the Khatala's approach, part of the Shiedran contingent formed up ranks to protect its flank.

"Do you know the *tinu* glide, *yosha*?" Mikuna asked Joga as she delved the aspect.

"No," Joga answered. "What is this?"

"We jump," Mikuna answered, "and *tinu* will carry us far. Delve the aspect and use a powerful gust of air to carry you high and far." Her eyes glowed silver as she explained. "Nyimbe, my friend. Stay to side of the fight. Warriors will not like companion."

Nyimbe said nothing, but she angled out to the far side of the fighting, Kokunde following.

"With permission, I will aid them," Bayaku said, for the duo would be very much alone amidst a host of rampaging trogk.

"Go," Mikuna ordered, and the veteran angled away after them.

With a burst of air, the Khatala leaped and glided in an arc, high over the defensive formation.

"This is amazing," Joga said from behind. "I could have used this technique early in the fulfillment of my bloodmark."

Aspect weapons at the ready, they descended out of their arc and crashed into the midst of the underworld creatures.

Fighting monsters of the underworld amidst potential enemies, the Khatala team were in a lethal situation. Still, with her brother fighting beside her, Mikuna felt a thrill that gave her speed and sharpened her senses.

Surrounded by a larger force and assaulted by a smaller one that knew how to fight them, the trogk began to fall. The underworld monsters fought without strategy. They simply growled their infernal curses, charged and attacked in every direction.

When the battle finally ended, pikes and arrows leveled at the Khatala. Mikuna let the ice shard blades fall apart from her arms and stood back to back with Joga, Akrim, and Jista. She looked over her shoulder, farther afield, but couldn't see the others.

A soldier walked his mount between two others and lifted his visor. He had a trimmed gray beard and a hard, scarred face. His green eyes smoldered as he looked upon the Khatala. "You are trespassing in the land of Marai, and by extension, the province of Nashma.

"Are welcome for help," Akrim muttered.

"Be silent, Akrim," Mikuna ordered.

The man she reasoned to be the leader turned to look at Akrim. "I don't recall sending for your aid."

Before Akrim could offer another quip and get them all in deeper trouble. Mikuna cut in. "Were chased into your territory. *Trogk* are everywhere. We fight all day."

"And came to our aid out of kindness," the Shiedran soldier replied dryly.

"Are not enemies," Mikuna said. "No matter what your king does, we do not quarrel with people of Marai."

"We're not going to debate your way of thinking versus ours, Khatala," the man said. "Your presence here can be considered an open act of hostility. However, your actions speak otherwise. You will be escorted to the Nashma border where you will be presumed to continue on back to your land."

A soldier to his side started to speak, presumably in protest, but a raised hand by the leader silenced him. "Do you understand?"

"Understand," Mikuna said. She glanced at Joga, who kept his expression neutral. They could discuss his goals later. "Will go."

They started to do just that when they heard a howl from further afield. Mikuna's heart sank.

"What in the name of the Creator was that?" the leader said. He turned to the man who'd tried to speak earlier. "Send a runner out there to find out—" he trailed off when a horse trotted through the ranks to reach him.

The soldier dismounted and saluted. "Sir. The monsters have been eliminated, but there's another problem.We surrounded a man, woman, and a beast that looks like a werewood cat. It seems to be the woman's companion, sir."

"Impossible," the lead soldier said. "You can't befriend those things."

"She's keeping herself between it and us, sir," the soldier went on. "It looks ready to attack at any moment."

"Then kill it," the leader said.

"Would not recommend," Joga spoke up from Mikuna's side. "If enemy, would have attacked your warriors, not *trogk*."

The lead soldier looked at Joga as if he'd forgotten they were there. "I'm not letting a monster like that roam our lands, Khatala."

"Helped destroy *trogk* that kill your people," Mikuna argued. "If was your enemy, would have killed many of your soldiers."

Joga turned to the dismounted soldier. "Did beast attack you?"

The soldier looked from Joga to his superior. "Not yet."

"Yet?" Mikuna gave him an incredulous look that she threw at the lead soldier as well. "How can say "yet" when no attack comes?" She indicated her group and waved in the direction of Bayaku's team. "Could have continued on. Could have left you to suffer more losses to *trogk* and kept ourselves out of danger. Now you treat us this way?"

The leader seemed to consider that before responding. "I recognize your aid, and I recognize that we benefitted from seeing how you fight them, which informed us how to better defeat the creatures ... *trogk*, you call them?" He pointed past them in the direction of Bayaku and the others. "But I'll not have a werewood beast roaming free in Nashma, slaughtering anyone it comes in contact with."

"Could have already done that!" Joga argued. "Enemy would not help you fight *trogk*."

Mikuna held up her hands in a peaceful gesture. "If let us go, will leave your land. All of us, with animal."

"Why are you here?" the soldier asked.

"Not intended to travel here," Mikuna replied truthfully. "Monsters chase us further inland. We kill them, but always more."

The lead soldier stared hard into her eyes as she spoke, his expression unreadable. "Did you know that the capital was attacked by the same monsters we just fought?"

The capital? Mikuna shook her head. "Did not know."

"Now you do," the soldier said. "Finding you within our borders with a weremonster in times of open conflict between the crown and your people is a hard coincidence to ignore."

Things were taking a negative turn, Mikuna knew. He was going to try to detain them and take them to Shiedra. Nyimbe's companion would likely be attacked, and she would die defending him. How many soldiers would die before they brought the thing down, she could only guess. Mikuna needed to make a hard decision, and quickly.

"I'm going to have to take you back to Shiedra," came the expected announcement. "Due to the nature of your arrival here and your aid in this battle, I will speak on your behalf before the Royana." He looked past them, and she saw a flicker of regret. "Your beast, however, will have to die. Whatever you think, a werewood cat is one of the most dangerous and unpredictable predators in the world. It cannot be trusted."

Mikuna glanced at Joga, who returned her gaze. She knew her brother well enough to know that his sense of loyalty and honor would never allow that to happen. Werewood cat or not, the monster fought beside them as an ally. Whether that was due to Nyimbe's presence or not mattered, Mikuna didn't intend to find out.

She looked back to the Shiedran commander. He'd watched her silent exchange with Joga and looked both of them in the eyes. This soldier had many years of experience. He knew what their answer would be.

"Before you respond, Khatala, let me warn you. My willingness to speak on your behalf is contingent upon your cooperation here and now. I would hope you wouldn't let a savage creature lead to the deterioration of this situation."

"No need for any of this," Mikuna tried one last time. "Will gladly leave your land. All of us."

"As Lieutenant of the Shiedran armed forces I am bound by the laws of Nashma to take you, who are in open conflict with our land, into custody and ensure the protection of those within our borders and by extension, the land of Marai." Mikuna could tell he wasn't enjoying any of this. "The choice isn't mine to make." He let out a deep breath. Mikuna heard a subtle note of pleading in his voice. "Do you submit?"

He didn't want to detain them, and she believed he didn't want to have Kokunde killed either. He was abiding the law of the land to which he was bound.

She delved for the aspects and held them ready. "No one must be harmed."

The lieutenant nodded. "Aside from your werebeast, unfortunately, none will …" he trailed off as he studied her eyes, then Joga's and Akrim's. "ARMS!"

Swords and pikes leveled toward Mikuna's team. The dismounted soldier stepped back and drew his sword as well.

"Don't do it," the lieutenant warned. "We *will* kill every last one of you if you attack—"

"Are good men," Mikuna said to her companions. "None must die."

The lieutenant swore as he snapped his visor shut. He'd barely gotten it down when the silver *arah* in Joga and Akrim's eyes flared. They delved *tinu*, as did she.

"As one!" Mikuna said, knowing her two companions were of the same mind. Together they let loose a powerful gust of air that caused the soldier's mounts to stumble away or fall over.

Some groaned under the weight of their heavy mounts, while others clenched broken legs and arms after being thrown from the saddle and landed wrong. A few recovered and charged, and Mikuna repelled them again with another mighty blast of air.

"*Tinu* glide!" Mikuna ordered, reverting to Khatalese.

Mikuna knelt just as the others lifted off. She heard Joga's cry of alarm as she delved *ushaa* and combined it to *tinu*. She pressed her palm to the ground and created a sheet of ice that rapidly spread under the nearby soldiers.

Horses and riders alike slipped and stumbled around her. Mikuna gave a great leap and, with a blast of air, lifted high and far into the air. She landed behind her companions as they fought to keep the Nashmarese soldiers from surrounding them.

They repeatedly blasted the soldiers with air, keeping them as far away as possible. Mikuna froze the ground in a wide radius around them again, then ordered their retreat.

Jista delved *naara* and melted a pathway out of the ice and they fled on foot, Kokunde reluctantly in tow. Nyimbe had shouted at the werewood cat several times not to attack, even placing herself in front of the fearsome monster. Mikuna could only shake her head at the courage of the woman.

They wouldn't get far on foot. Kokunde would have the only chance at outrunning the horses. She looked over her shoulder and saw the recovered Shiedrans fanning out and riding straight for them.

"Must use *tinu* glide," Jista suggested. "One of us can carry her." She jerked her chin at Nyimbe.

"Good idea," Akrim replied. "Who's going to carry that thing?" He nodded at Kokunde.

Mikuna couldn't disagree, she had no intention of having a werewood cat on her back, no matter how "friendly" it might be. Not that any of them actually could carry a several-hundred-pound cat. "Nyimbe. How fast your companion can run?"

"Not faster than a horse," came the answer. "Maybe close, but he's not that fast."

"We can spread out and repel them," Bayaku suggested, "while Nyimbe and the beast continue on. The *tinu* glide will carry us away once they've covered enough ground."

It wasn't perfect, but Mikuna couldn't think of anything else. "Fan out and hold them back. Retreat on my order. Nyimbe," she said, reverting back to Marai. "We will hold them back while you and your companion escape."

"I will not run and leave—"

"We can catch up with you. Must trust. Keep going!"

The woman growled but offered no more argument. "Kokunde!" The giant cat angled closer. Once it was within reach, to Mikuna and the other's shock, she grabbed a handful of coarse fur and vaulted onto his back. Short though she might be even by Marailander standards, Mikuna was still amazed that the werewood cat could carry her weight with little visible difficulty. Kokunde made a sound like a half bark half growl, and bounded away at a full run.

Mikuna wondered why the beast was called a "cat", when it looked more wolfish. A question for another time. She and her team fanned out and placed as much distance between themselves as they could within range of their power.

The Khatala warriors delved *tinu* and *ushaa*, and spread their arms wide. Their combined efforts created a freezing gale of wind while tiny hale pebbles pounded into the pursuing soldiers. They tried to angle out wide to get around, but Mikuna and Joga on each end extended the reach of their power out and toward the flanking riders.

Horses whinnied in protest against the freezing blast. Some soldiers were lifted out of the saddle and sent rolling away while their mounts fell over and scrambled to regain their footing. In the mass of chaos, Mikuna caught sight of the lieutenant leaning into his saddle, his muscly warhorse still trying to power forward. The horse finally faltered and reared onto its hind legs and fell over.

Mikuna almost lost her grip on the power when she thought the man had been crushed under his mount's weight, but he'd managed to bail out of the saddle at the last moment. He rolled away and struggled to a kneeling position.

Through the cluster of shivering, falling, and sliding soldiers, the Shiedran lieutenant partially raised his visor and looked straight across the field at Mikuna. She saw not anger or hostility in his belabored frown, but appreciation. His hard green-eyed stare held what looked like respect.

"Release *ushaa*," Mikuna commanded. Next to her, Jista repeated the order which carried down the line. They released the water aspect but continued to hold the force back with the raging gale-force winds. Once she was satisfied Nyimbe and Kokunde had gotten a safe distance away, she called for *tinu* glide, and the Khatala leaped far into the air.

From her vantage point high above, Mikuna could see that the lieutenant had called off pursuit. Many armored faces looked in their direction as the Khatala glided half a league away. Though she couldn't make him out from this distance, Mikuna imagined the lieutenant as well, watching their escape. She respected the man as a soldier doing his duty. Hopefully if they met again, it would be to bring about a truce that would lead to peace between their peoples.

They found Nyimbe and her monster waiting not far away from where they touched down. The woman crouched beside the were-wood cat and seemed to be inspecting his underbelly.

"That is a tough animal," Joga remarked as they approached. "Very tough."

Mikuna didn't disagree. She looked at the pair and shook her head. On four legs, the beast stood nearly as tall as Nyimbe.

"There are few things I'd rather not fight than a werewood cat," Bayaku said in a casual tone that belied the gravity of the statement.

Akrim laughed. "That, from you, Bayaku? What's worse, then. A teliak? Mulgin?"

"I'd like to know how she came to be friends with such a thing," Mikuna said. "Their reputation isn't a friendly one."

"It's a darkwood cat, not a werewood," Joga said, taking the lead until they'd gotten close enough that Kokunde took note. The darkwood cat curled his head around and looked at them. Though the monster's yellow-eyed gaze was fixed on Joga, Mikuna still felt a chill. "Careful, *yosha*," she said.

"We fought a teliak together not long ago," her brother replied, to her astonishment. "A *dazra* had been controlling it."

"A what?" Akrim replied. "You fought a teliak? A teliak *and* a *dazra?*" He waved a hand at the pair ahead. "And only with those two?"

"It wasn't fun," Joga said.

"Oh really? How not?" Akrim replied, laughing.

When Kokunde started to turn towards them, Joga stopped and held out his hands. "Want to help him," he said, reverting to his accented Marai.

"He's not very trusting," Nyimbe replied. "The wound has mostly closed, but we've been constantly on the move, as you know. The exertion over the past few days hasn't given him the proper time to fully heal."

"A formidable animal. I can try help him heal faster."

Nyimbe responded with a doubtful expression. She looked to Kokunde, who had turned to fully face Joga.

Mikuna nervously watched the exchange. She had all four of

the aspects ready, as she knew the others did as well. If the thing attacked her brother, she would destroy it.

The darkwood cat turned its attention from Joga to the other Khatala. Its upper lip curled back to display a set of impressive fangs as it growled at them. It snapped its jaws, then lowered into a defensive crouch.

"Your friends aren't helping," Nyimbe said.

Mikuna stared at the woman. Did she know they were delving?

"Let go of the power." Joga looked over his shoulder at Mikuna. "Will be fine, *yisha*. But when you delve, he doesn't like."

"Wouldn't want that," Akrim muttered.

The giant cat turned his head and looked at Akrim, who held his hands up in a placating gesture and apologized. He frowned as if wondering why he'd said the words. "Damned monster."

"He may not speak all of our words," Nyimbe said, "but he understands some of them. He also understands inflections and intent." She placed a hand on the darkwood cat's back. "I would do as Joga says, if I were you."

Mikuna looked to Joga. Her brother responded with a reassuring nod. She took a deep breath and let the power go. The others must have as well, for the werewood cat relaxed, if only a bit.

After some coaxing and very slow actions, Joga placed his hands on the beast and explained to Nyimbe his intent. The woman did her best to comfort the pained Kokunde while he worked.

Joga finally stood and wiped the perspiration from his brow. "All I can do, with healing knowledge I have. Wound is still fragile, though."

"Let me try," Mikuna said.

"You sure about that?" Jista asked. "That thing doesn't know you, *asha*."

"Helped us fight," Mikuna reminded.

"Because of its friend," the tracker countered.

Mikuna shrugged, still walking forward. Slowly. "Does it matter?"

"Yes," the other woman replied.

"Have more knowledge in healing," Mikuna said. "Can try."

It took some coaxing, but Nyimbe finally got Kokunde to relax enough for Mikuna to get close. The thing had a strong musty odor, like fur, woods, and sweat. Whether it was due to the exertion of the day or its normal scent, Mikuna still committed the smell to memory while hoping never to experience it again with a similar—and unfamiliar—beast.

She first placed a hand on his upper side and felt solid muscle bunch underneath the coarse fur at her touch. She looked him in the eye and nodded. "Want to help, Kokunde."

He held her in his intense yellow stare for many heartbeats before finally relaxing and turning aside. Nyimbe, watching the exchange from the side, nodded to Mikuna.

She knelt next to the cat and gently worked her way to the wound. It looked like a large and grievous puncture. Had the beast been stabbed? Mikuna closed her eyes and delved *naara* as she explored the clotted area.

With a prayer to *Amyadali* for guidance, she channeled gentle warmth into and around the wound, seeping in tiny amounts of *tinu* and *ushaa*. Once she'd done everything she could internally and superficially, she delved *olayem* and broke free a piece of nearby ground. She dug below the surface crust until she came to clay-like earth.

Once again, she delved *naara* and burned away any persistent germs or tiny forms of life that might cause infection, then coated it over the wound. With one last gentle wave of heat, she solidified the clay in a thin layer over the wound.

She stood and exhaled a satisfied breath. "Wound was already clotted. Did my best inside, and clay will provide extra protection against reopen."

Nyimbe nodded and gave Kokunde's back a satisfied pat. "Our sincere thanks, Khatala ... Mikuna," she said. "There will be no sign of the injury in another day. Two at most."

"What happened?" Mikuna asked. "Wound looked like might have been deep."

"Impaled on the spike of a teliak," Nyimbe said. And so she and Joga took turns telling them of their encounter with the mighty reptile and the *dazra*—droughtlord, she called them—that controlled it.

Mikuna listened while making an effort not to let her mouth hang open. Akrim occasionally responded with his usual incredulous laughter, while Jista whistled through her teeth.

Bayaku had been standing with his back to them, watching the east for pursuit. Even the veteran warrior, legendary among the Frostlands gave an occasional grunt of appreciation.

At Bayaku's suggestion, they turned west. The Shiedran lieutenant might not have given immediate pursuit, but that didn't mean he wouldn't show up with reinforcements, or that the Khatala party wouldn't encounter another Nashmarese patrol.

"New Dama," Joga said.

Mikuna noted ruefulness in her brother's tone. When she looked at him, she saw the clear regret on his face. "The twin balls of flame around you," she said, referring to the prophetic dream she'd shared with him what seemed so long ago, now.

Joga nodded. "Were separated. Don't know where they are, now."

Mikuna noted his broken Marai and remembered Nyimbe. She reverted back to the easterner language for her benefit. "Have any idea where they may be?"

"Back the way we've come, but south. Last place were together. Now." He shrugged helplessly. "Cannot know. Could be halfway around world or only a league away."

Mikuna desperately wanted her brother to remain at her side, but she knew he'd made a promise to his young Marailander friends. "Will do what, now?"

"Don't know," Joga answered. "Don't know where to go, where to look. Have failed them."

"Will find them," she said. "Or they find you."

Joga turned his hopeful expression on her. "Have dream?"

Mikuna looked ahead. She could just barely see the distant hazy image of the volcano near New Dama. "No dream, but I just know. Creator *Amyadali* tests us hard for a merciless world. She will test girls hard, that they will survive."

"Pray Creator *Amyadali* tests us all hard and often," Bayaku said in his usual baritone rumble. "There can be no doubt. The *trogk* have come, so the void has awakened. The sightless will bring the *Abliviar*.

EMIEL

Sleep, it turned out, did indeed change Emiel's mind. Not for the second or even third time this morning did he change his mind on how he would proceed. Amiya hadn't been with Nandi. She could be anywhere. Emiel clenched his jaw. And, she *was* somewhere. There wasn't anything else to consider. His girl might be fighting to survive or she might have come across some nice folk to take care of her until he found her. Either way, Amiya was out there somewhere.

That Nandi had fallen into the giant hole in the ground with Amoura helped to keep him together. Amoura wouldn't let his girl die. The magus possessed a great many skills in her essence repertoire. She would have found a way to save them both.

He leaned forward in his chair and stared out at the city below and the far distant mountains. Amoura would have set a course on finding a way out of that gigantic pit, but in the meantime Emiel would find a way down there to them.

Lief leaned against his leg. His dear little friend had felt no end of guilt that she wasn't able to lift Nandi and Amoura out. It was just too deep, she'd told him. The tinfar had stood next to him while he knelt in front of the hole, maybe even trying, herself, to will them up, as he'd been doing.

His breath misted much less in the morning air, today. Spring had begun to wane as summer gradually moved in. Another month or two and the nights would be nearly as warm as the days.

"You're sure," Lief said from beside his leg.

Emiel inhaled the crisp morning air and blew it out through his mouth. "I can't bring myself to leave, Lief. She was right there, and for all I know, they might be down there right now trying to get back out. Amoura might even be gathering herself to lift them out as I sit here."

When Lief didn't respond, he looked down at her and saw the dubious expression on her face. He stared at her for a long time but she didn't meet his gaze. "What, Lief? I know you're thinking something you figure I won't like, but I'd hear it anyway." Did he really want to, though?

The confliction in Lief's dark, earthy brown eyes had Emiel forcing himself not to look away. "Emiel, I don' think they're down there like you think."

He held up a hand. "Lief, they're alive. I don't even want to—"

"That isn't just a big hole, Emiel," Lief continued. "It's more than that. From as early as before your First Age, there have been endless underground places large enough to fit your human cities. I'm certain that's what that is. They've probably gone from the place they landed."

Mouth still half open in silenced protest, Emiel closed it and thought on that. "But ... why wouldn't Amoura lift them back out?"

Lief's responding sigh sounded tired. "My friend, the drop could have been as deep as a mountain is tall. We don't know. There are places underground that are hundreds of feet deep. There are ancient human civilizations down there. I think that might be what's beneath this city."

Emiel shook his head. "How hasn't Shiedra not fallen through?

If that tunneler was able to knock open that hole, the ground must not be that thick."

"One thin section of crust," Lief answered. "The tunneler hit a weak point that may have remained closed otherwise. There are many places like that. They open up when a violent quake happens, or some similar event, like with the tunneler."

"So, the hole is deep," Emiel said. "Really deep. She still can't lift them out?"

"I don't know the magus's affinity for *itsya*."

"Eets …" Emiel frowned. "Eets what?"

"*Itsya*," Lief repeated slowly. "What you call the *air* essence."

"I see," Emiel said. His face brightened. "Wait. I remember you telling me that there are four types of your people. One for each of the essences? Do you think …" he trailed off as Lief shook her head.

"I'm sorry, Emiel. *Itsya* Tinfar live in the highest places in the world. They live in the tallest trees on the tallest mountains and fly high in the air. I wouldn't be able to reach one unless I knew where to look. Then I would have to get their attention. They tend to be rather on the go, flying everywhere."

Emiel's heart sank back into place again. "Tell me more about the other types of tinfar. I need to get my mind off this, at least for a while."

"Well," Lief began. "*Matyu* tinfar live mostly in the ocean, though some are found in lakes. Only the largest lakes, though, since it reduces the chances of contact with"—she glanced up at Emiel—"um, other things."

"Humans," Emiel finished for her. "I'm not offended, Lief. I get it."

Lief gave his leg a little pat. "If you think *Matyu* tinfar are hard to reach, *y'maya* are the hardest and least approachable of us."

"Toward humans, you mean," Emiel said.

"Mostly," Lief agreed. "But they're not exactly outgoing. Of us all, they kind of like you the least."

"Yeesh. Would they attack me if I stumbled across one?"

"You've probably done just that and never known," Lief answered. "We're kind of everywhere and you just don't know it. If you did somehow come across one out in the open, they'd try to move away unless cornered. Then you'd have a problem. A big one."

Emiel imagined she was referring to being burned alive and silently agreed. "I'll remember to turn the other way if I come across any two-foot-tall people around fire or flying around."

"Unlikely," came the reply, "but a good idea."

They fell into silence again, Emiel wrapped in his thoughts about what he could do—if anything—to find his daughters, and Lief absently patting his leg.

"I don't know what to do, Lief," he finally said. "Amiya could be anywhere, and Nandi is down there with Amoura and that odd green-haired girl."

Lief perked up at that. "Green hair?"

Emiel nodded. "I didn't give the girl much thought because I was focused on getting to Nandi, but now that I think about it, she looked strange. She could have been the same age as Nandi and her new friend, Ailith, but I doubt it. She knocked over one of those drauk like she was its size. *I* couldn't have done that."

Lief stared right through him with a distant expression. Emiel looked at her with growing concern. "Should I be worried about that?"

The tinfar snapped out of her trance. "The green-haired girl fought beside your daughter?"

"I think I saw Nandi trying to protect her when a drauk nearly got hold of the girl. So I think they were friends. What is it?"

"Describe her," Lief said. "What you remember of the girl."

With growing concern, Emiel did as she asked. A frown creased Lief's brow as she listened, occasionally nodding at certain details. It was his turn to frown at her soft laughter once he'd finished.

"*Na 'ta* Corlyss wonders why I find humans so interesting," she said, and Emiel wondered if she was talking to him or herself. She gave his leg another pat and gave him a smile that eased his nerves, though he wished she'd let him in on all this. "Your Nandi has somehow managed to befriend a tatamble."

"A *what*?"

"Tatamble," Lief repeated. "If you think tinfar are reclusive and mistrusting, tatamble are far more so. They keep their distance, but are far more likely to attack you if you come across one. They mostly live in the mountains and certain forests. They're strong for their size and are fierce fighters. They also have the unconscious ability to shift the hue of their skin to blend with their environment, like a chameleon." She shook her head. "I don't know how your daughter managed to make a friend out of a tatamble, but that is no small thing."

"So, it's a good thing, then?"

"It's a very good thing," Lief said. "To have a tatamble as a friend is to have a loyal and fearsome ally. If Nandi travels beside that girl and Amoura, I'd not worry much at all about her, my friend."

Her words bought a measure of relief, though it would be impossible for Emiel to stop worrying. He worried about them when he used to leave for the day on a spice trade. He didn't know how he hadn't gone mad with worry, by now.

"Good to know," Emiel said. "Is there any way for you to determine which way they might have gone? Any way to find what direction and how far that place might go?"

Lief frowned in thought. "I'd have to find ask *e 'ta* tinfar local to the area. They might know."

"I'd appreciate it, my friend." Emiel stood and stretched, and his stomach growled. "Guess it's time to eat." He didn't really feel like it, but he'd force himself to eat. No good would come of starving himself.

"I'll search out an *e 'ta* clan and find you," Lief said. She climbed onto the balcony rail and looked back over her shoulder. "Whatever Amoura taught you while you were together, practice it as much as you can, okay?"

"That sounds ominous," Emiel replied with a nervous chuckle.

Lief said no more. She placed a hand against the adobe wall and seemed to step inside of it.

Emiel blinked. He walked over to the spot and touched it. He rapped his knuckles on the spot, expecting it to feel hollow, but it was solid. Shaking his head, he sighed and left for the dining hall.

He found Bone and Ailith at a table, the former devouring enough food for the both of them, the latter nearly as much. The girl's shock of red curls bounced when she whipped her head around and waved to him.

"Planning a part time job as a scullery boy to pay for all this?" Emiel said, sweeping his hand over the empty dishes. "Last I checked, our coin was running thin."

"Oh yeah," came the food-muffled reply. He reached behind his back and fiddled with something, then tossed a small sack at Emiel.

He caught it and untied the drawstring, then sucked air through his teeth when he looked inside. "What is this and where'd you get it from?" he whispered, glancing left and right.

"Relax, spicetrader. One of the royana's people showed up at my door with a couple sacks of coin. Payment for our assistance in the defense of Shiedra, she said." He shrugged. "Personally, I was fightin' more to keep from gettin' hacked to pieces than defending this place. But I'll gladly take it."

Heartlessly pragmatic as the comment was, Emiel couldn't honestly say his intentions hadn't been any less selfish. He'd been more concerned first with survival, then getting to Nandi. When the server arrived, he ordered a hot bowl of stew and cider.

"So, what's yer plan, then?" Ailith asked looking from Bone to Emiel. "Nandi and Sama and that power woman are down there."

"Power woman?" Emiel said.

"Ya, power woman."

"It's what we call them in the Highlands," Bone explained. "Over here in Marai, they call 'em magi," he said to Ailith. "Magus in the singular, understand."

"Sure," Ailith replied, then turned her expectant expression back to Emiel. "How we gonna get 'em out?"

"They might have moved on," Emiel said. "Apparently it might not be just a big hole."

"Apparently," Bone repeated. "Lief?"

Emiel nodded. "She says there are places deep underground that stretch for many miles. She thinks Nandi, Amoura, and the girl with the green hair—"

"Sama," Ailith interjected.

"Sama," Emiel added, "fell into one of those underground places. She says there might even be an ancient civilization down there."

"Lief," Ailith said. "Yer talkin' about that little short woman? She don't look human to me. I mean, she does, but not really."

"She's a tinfar," Emiel explained. "I'll leave it to her to fill you in on the rest." He looked across the table at Bone. "She's off to find an *earth* tinfar clan to see if she can find out about the place they fell into. If she can discover what direction it stretches, we'll know which way to go and hopefully find another way in further down."

"Seems a stretch," Bone said, "but I guess we don't have anything else to go on."

Emiel hadn't realized how hungry he was until the food came. He'd finished half the stew and a large roll before stopping to talk again. "Until we know for sure what direction they went in, I'm thinking it best to stay here. If Nandi came all this way from home, that means Amiya isn't likely to be in Vyne either."

Bone looked as if he wanted to say something, but didn't. Emiel had come to know the pragmatic mercenary long enough to know what that expression meant. "Look, whether or not you believe in parental intuition, you'll just have to trust me on this. Amiya is alive, somewhere, and looking for me and Nandi. If you don't believe me, I appreciate you not voicing as much. And if you think it's a lost cause and a waste of time, I'll not begrudge you leaving."

To his surprise, Emiel found himself hoping the young man didn't decide to do just that. This same person who had knocked him unconscious and taken him away from his home and his daughters so long ago had become something like a friend. To be fair, the boy *had* helped them escape Altarra and the magi master at no small risk to himself.

"Of course he believes you," Ailith said, elbowing Bone in the ribs.

"Ow!" Bone protested. He shoved the girl, who promptly shoved him back.

The side of Emiel's mouth twitched. Those two were like brother and sister, and the girl was like a Highlands version of Amiya.

"Yeah, yeah," Bone grumbled. "They're alive if you say they're alive. We'll find 'em."

Ailith responded with a decisive nod. "So, we're waitin' for that short lady to come find us before we go lookin'?"

"That's about where we're at," Emiel said. "Otherwise we're just wandering the world hoping to find them on one random guess to the next."

Ailith propped her elbows on the table and cupped her chin in her hands. "I remember Nandi tellin' me you were taken to Altarra, and that's where she and her sister had been goin'."

"Not much chance she's going that way, now," Bone said. "Only place she and Amoura are going is the exit to wherever they are, and wherever that leads to. Hopefully your little two-foot girl-friend can find out."

Ailith, spat half her watered-down ale back into her mug.

"It'd be nice if you quit saying that," Emiel said, thankful he'd finished his stew now that ale mist had entered his bowl. He looked at Ailith, now wiping her chin with a handkerchief. "We should probably think about getting you back home to your parents."

Ailith's face darkened at that. "Not sure I'd remember if we tried. I was taken from my parents when I was but a wee little thing. I remember my da teachin' me the sword and my ma teachin' me the bow. I remember other things, but not as much as I'd like." She glared down at the table. "I'll always remember how to get back to Valraga, though. I gots some revenge to take back there one day."

Emiel watched the girl's hands ball into fists. What had happened to her during her captivity in this Valraga? What had happened to Nandi while *she* had been there? He pushed that thought from his mind before it went down a dark path. He'd find out after he found his girls.

"Yer not leavin' me here, are you?" Ailith asked them. "I got nobody else. Nandi and Sama are my friends. We escaped Valraga and survived together to get here. She didn't leave me behind when she could have. I ain't for leavin' her behind, now."

Emiel noticed Bone looking at him. The mercenary must have seen the doubtful look on his face. "A little advice, Emiel. A Highlands woman makes up her mind about something, you're best going along with it. The girls aren't much different, especially at her age."

"What's with the Marailander accent, then?" Ailith asked Bone. "You sound like one of 'em."

"You talk around 'em and find yerself repeatin' yerself long enough, lass," Bone replied, "you'll be takin' on the accent just to avoid pullin' yer hair out. Now, about that sword and bow. Which one'r you feelin' better about?"

"Both," Ailith replied.

"Ain't got coin enough for gettin' you both," Bone said, now fully descended into his Highlands speech. "You're gonna have to pick one for now. Might have an easier time findin' a bow, since yer a bit short in the legs yet for a sword the right length."

"Hand me a sword and I'll give you short legs."

"Right, then," Bone said. "A bow it is."

Ailith gave a curt nod. "Maybe I'll find me a sword on the next person I sprinkle arrows into."

Emiel watched the exchange in amusement. He'd traveled a fair bit of distance across southern Marai and even into lands just south of Carlayn. The Highlands were a place he'd only heard about in conversation or seen on a map.

Seeing these two going on as they were, he wondered what people from other parts of the world were like. Had Amiya found a friend of vastly different background as Nandi had? Whoever that person might be, Emiel hoped for his beloved daughter's sake that the friend was at least as tough as this little ball of fire sitting across from him.

Their meal finished, the trio stepped out into the crisp spring air and started in the direction of the open market. According to Bone, a weapons shop lay just beyond. Emiel didn't know how well he felt about arming a girl no older than the twins, but he recognized the dangers in the world that were only getting worse.

When they reached the weapons shop, Emiel started to follow the others in when he heard Lief softly calling his name. He stopped and tried to inconspicuously look around.

"Emiel. Around the corner."

He walked to the side of the building and peeked around the wall. Lief waved at him from behind a wooden crate.

"There's not much time," she said.

"What?" Emiel's heart thumped in his chest. "What's going on? Are they—"

"I'm sorry, Emiel," Lief went on. "I wasn't able to get much information on the underground caverns, but your daughter and the others might be safer where they are, than here."

"Safer?" Emiel looked around the dingy alley as if the answers lay in the weeds and pebbles. "What are you talking about?"

"There's a large number of drauk heading for Shiedra," Lief said. "Maybe as many as fifty. They'll be here before the day is out."

Emiel knelt in front of her. "Does the Shiedran army know? Their force is many times that number."

"You've seen what just one of those things can do to a handful of armed and competent soldiers, Emiel," Lief said.

He didn't miss the flicker of disappointment in his friend's voice. He sighed. It wasn't like he wanted to run away and abandon these people. Well, if he was honest with himself, he would rather be someplace else, but he needed, *needed* to find the girls.

His daughters could be anywhere. It seemed the harder he tried to find them, the more fate pushed them away from each other. Was this by the Creator's design? Emiel tried not to spare a curse for Him if that was indeed the case. "What could I do against fifty rampaging drauk, Lief?"

"You can use the power."

"I can barely us it," Emiel argued.

"Which is probably more than anyone else in this city," Lief countered. "I haven't seen a single magus under the royana's employ, have you? Will you run and leave this human city to see more of its people die when you might help?"

"I don't need you to tell me what's right," Emiel snapped. He felt even more awful when the tinfar flinched away from the unintended sharpness in his tone. "All that matters to me is finding my girls."

She crossed her tiny arms and leaned on one foot, tapping the other. She may only be two feet tall, but the weight of her disapproving stare might as well have belonged to a giant. "If you keep ignoring everything around you like this, you'll find your girls and be together to watch the world burn. Would they want you to do that, Emiel? Would they do the same?"

Emiel knew she was right. He reminded himself that his tinfar friend was trying to help him remember what was right. He tried to care about what was right. As much as he knew the right thing to do was to help defend Shiedra, his mind remained singly focused on Amiya and Nandi.

He never should have let any of this happen. He should have taken the girls with him on his spice trades; kept them with him when he went out on the road. Absurd as he knew such notions to be, he still had them. Kneeling in the dusty alley, he stared absently at the ground while wrestling with his emotions.

A little hand rested on his shoulder. He looked into Lief's compassionate eyes. "You know what's already happened here, and what's about to happen. It's spreading, Emiel. Your Amiya and Nandi have surely faced similar trials as us."

Emiel nodded. He'd seen the way Nandi wielded the essences against the drauk. He hadn't noticed before, but now that he thought about the events of the previous day, he realized that Nandi hadn't been surprised or even afraid by the attack.

"They're learning and fighting, and surviving," Lief said. "You saw that with your own eyes."

Emiel took several deep breaths and wiped the moisture filling in his eyes. He would never stop searching for them, but he had to do what was right. If he didn't grow in his use of the essences and learn how to survive, he wouldn't be too effective in protecting the girls. Worse yet, he might not survive to find them. "Okay." He stood. "I'll do my best."

"You casting stones to read the future, spicetrader?" Emiel heard from behind. "Or dicing with yourself."

When Emiel stood and stepped aside to give Bone a view of Lief, the mercenary turned and glanced over his shoulder before entering the alley. "Should have known."

"You're pretty," Ailith said to the tinfar.

Lief tilted her head and smiled. "Well, thank you, little lady."

"Little," the Highland girl echoed dryly.

"Quite the mouth for such few years lived," Lief replied to the thinly veiled sarcasm. She placed her hands on her hips and somehow managed to look down her nose in disapproval at the taller girl. Ailith's red eyebrows raised into her hairline, but she offered no retort.

"Are the Fallen-blasted things following us, then?" Bone said after Emiel explained the situation. "If we're quick, we can be gone before …" he trailed off at Emiel's expression, then rolled his eyes. "I'm guessing you're going to have another go at getting yourself killed?"

"You already know the answer, Bone," Emiel answered. "And—"

"I know, I know." The mercenary patted the air between them. "And I'm free to go with no hard feelings if I decide to. Thanks for your understanding, but I'll not have the historians and arttellers recording that I ran away while a foolhardy spicetrader stayed to fight alongside people he hardly knows against ridiculous odds."

"Hardly ridiculous," Emiel said. "I've a powerful *e'ta* tinfar and the blade of a skilled mercenary with me."

Bone responded to that with a flat look and turned away. "I'm getting my Fallen-blasted armor before the Fallen-blasted things get here and I'm skulking around a warzone to get to it. Again!"

"Sure that I must be invisible, then," Ailith said as they followed the grumbling Bone out of the alley. Lief disappeared again, as always, preferring not to be seen by humans. "Yer talkin' about this great fight to come and don't give meself a second thought."

"Quite the opposite, actually," Emiel said. "I have no intention of you being anywhere near that battlefield. Rather," he quickly added before the girl's face could boil any more red, "you'd be effective with the archers, don't you think?"

The girl stared skeptically at him before replying with a firm nod. "Aye."

Emiel doubted Captain Adolphus would allow such a thing, but he'd rather an angry Ailith than a dead one.

They made it only a few paces down the street before Bone detoured them to the weapons shop to find some sort of protection for Ailith. The shop owner gave them a disapproving look, but found the smallest boiled leather top and bottom he could find. The man still ended up cutting it down to fit the girl. It wasn't the neatest work, but they needed it in a hurry and it would be serviceable enough.

It took Emiel only a short time to change into his own boiled leather armor, and he and Ailith waited for Bone to return to the front of the inn. A short while later, the mercenary once again stood resplendent in his polished teliak bone armor.

"That's the strangest getup I've ever seen," Ailith remarked. "That stuff really gonna turn aside a blade or arrow?"

"Won't find a bit of armor better at doin' just that, lass," Bone replied.

"Mind if I give it a try?" came the cheeky reply.

Having been there a couple times, now, they easily found the Shiedran barracks. The men standing guard barred them entry, but after hearing their story and remembering their visit with Adolphus after the attack, they sent word to the captain.

Adolphus looked none too pleased to see them again. After they explained the situation, the captain ran a hand through his black and gray-sprinkled hair. "Why is it that every time I see you, I can assume I won't like what follows?"

"Figure we might as well be consistent," Bone replied, to which the captain leveled an unappreciative glare his way.

"I'm supposed to act on your word, with no proof? How do you know this?"

"There isn't time to go into that, Captain," Emiel said.

"Give me the abridged version, then." When Emiel started to

argue, Adolphus held up a hand. "You're asking me to mobilize the entire Shiedran armed forces. Answer the question."

Emiel took a deep breath. "Just as you're now discovering monsters in the world that want to kill you, there are others that share this world who mean us no ill will."

Captain Adolphus stared at him for several tense heartbeats, clearly unimpressed with the cryptic response. "You've seen what those things can do, Captain," Emiel pressed. "They're likely charging toward Shiedra right now."

The captain growled a curse and turned to one of the gate guards. "Get word to Lieutenant Castilla. I want every soldier in Shiedra on high alert. Go!"

He turned back when the soldier ran off. "I'd say I hope you're right, or I'll look the fool, but I'd rather look the fool than you being right about this."

"We're here to help," Emiel said.

Adolphus looked them over, his gaze lingering doubtfully over Ailith. "I've seen you in battle," he said to Bone. "I'd happily have your blade on Shiedra's side." He looked at Emiel. "I don't much care for essence wielders, especially the non-magi type, but I'll take all the help I can get. You, girl. You'll be safe in the barracks surrounded by—"

"I'm not fer being carted off to cower in some musty war-man house," Ailith interrupted.

"War-man?" Captain Adolphus looked to Emiel and Bone, who both shrugged helplessly. "This is adult business, girl." He signalled to the other guard.

"Yer not tellin' me to go … hey! Let me go ya stinkin' Fallen-cursed oxen's dung!"

"That one has quite the mouth," Adolphus said as the poor soldier dragged off the kicking and cursing girl. Having had enough, the man threw her over his shoulder and stomped off.

"She's a Highlander," Bone replied as the flailing girl's red curls bounced out of sight.

The three men turned in the direction of a blaring horn. "That's the east wall," Adolphus said.

They rushed to the guard towers inside the east gates just as they were being pulled closed. All around, civilians rushed about at the guidance of soldiers directing them.

"What news?" Adolphus asked when a woman rushed up and removed her helm to salute.

"Same things as the ones that attacked us yesterday, Captain," the woman said. Her green eyes smoldered with determination. "They're marching straight for us."

"Marching?" Emiel and Bone said in unison.

The soldier glanced at them while Adolphus turned aside to look them both in the eye. "What do you know? What's the significance of them marching?"

Emiel shook his head, a sense of dread creeping into the pit of his stomach. "They don't normally march. They run."

"More like sprint," Bone added.

"Yeah," Emiel said. "Tearing up everything in their path, including the ground. And the growling, shouting language they curse in is enough to give you the chills."

Helm tucked under her arm, the soldier shook her head. "I remember the curses from yesterday, but those things are marching in formation."

Emiel looked at Bone and saw concern on the young man's face. "I have a feeling we won't like this."

"If they're not running, that gives us a little more time," Adolphus said.

"We need to have a look," Emiel said, starting toward the ladder alongside the parapet. When the soldier moved to stop him, Adolphus nodded his consent.

When the reached the top of the parapet and peered into the distance, Bone whistled through his teeth. "I don't know how to feel about that."

Emiel felt the same. What looked like fifty drauk marched

silently and purposefully toward the eastern walls of Shiedra. He'd never seen the creatures not in a berserk state. As he watched the approaching monsters, a figure caught his eye, right in the center of the cluster. A lone man.

As the realization dawned on him, Emiel felt cold dread wash over him. "I'm not going to be much help against the drauk," he said to Bone.

Bone didn't answer right away, but when he did, his tone spoke of the same dread Emiel felt. "Aye, spicetrader. You'll be too busy trying not to die." He placed a gloved hand on Emiel's shoulder and gave it a squeeze. *"Alspied 'n' struntha frin din Creator."* When Emiel looked at him in confusion, he clarified. "A saying, from my homeland. All speed and strength to you from the Creator."

"This will be bad," Adolphus said, "but there's not enough of them to win the day. We will destroy them all."

Emiel heard the words and no one could have wished them true more than he. But that man walking in the middle of those drauk… He shook his head again. "I wish it were only those things to worry about, Captain."

Adolphus turned a puzzled look on him, and Emiel pointed at the marching cluster of monsters and the man in the middle. "The drauk aren't charging because they're being controlled by him."

The captain frowned. "I see him. But, who's *him*? And how could anyone control those things?"

Emiel reached to the essences, a simple touch to comfort himself that they were there. *Looks like my first test. Creator see me through this. My girls need me.* "Someone powerful enough to destroy all of them by himself," he said to Adolphus, "A droughtlord."

AMOURA

Chamber of the Immortals. Well, they weren't actually *in* the chamber, but Amoura was sure it was here somewhere. She rifled through memories of her studies back in Altarra. The classes only glanced over the history involving the Illuminarians and the Fallen. At that time, when Amoura was no more than an acolyte, and hadn't questioned why none of her courses covered much of anything regarding the two factions.

Her independent studies gave her a theory and lessened her respect for her Order. Fear. Fear of a split happening again. The last thing the Order of Magi wanted was for its ranks to pursue the greater powers and understandings of the essences.

She didn't blame them for being wary of such a possibility. If enough magi attained such great and terrible power, they could well break the world. Everything she'd read about the immortals suggested this. The fact that they had attained immortality through their knowledge of the essences was in itself, an amazing feat.

For a long time, Amoura scanned the enormous cavern. Buildings carved into the walls, stone sculptures, and pathways filled with flammable oil that lit large sconces all about the cavern to produce enough brilliant golden light to make the place navigable.

Beside her, Nandi shifted from foot to foot. "Um, you said this was the Chamber of the Immortals. Kinda big. Maybe we should have a look around and see if one's in here. Maybe they can help us get out."

"Patience," Amoura replied. "We must know what we're about before we proceed."

To her surprise, the girl straightened her back and assumed a posture not unlike Amoura's. "You're right, of course. We should be careful."

Amoura spared a sidelong glance at the girl. Was Nandi teasing her? "If the books are correct, this is a cavern that houses a chamber where rests a sleeping immortal."

"Then perhaps we should try to find this chamber and awaken the immortal," Nandi said in a rather stately tone. Was the girl imitating her? And, did Amoura really sound like that?

"Why sister Nandi talk so different, now?" Sama said from a few paces away. "Why stand so stiff and talk like woman who steals power from mother?"

Amoura kept her features neutral, though her mouth twitched. She saw Nandi watching her before turning to her strange companion.

"I'm just trying to help figure out the situation, Sama," the girl said, still formal. Amoura did *not* sound like that! "If there is an immortal here, we must find them."

"What is this ammortal sister Nandi and woman talk about? Does ammortal steal power from earth mother like woman?"

"She doesn't steal the power, sister Sama," Nandi said. In her exasperation she reverted back to her normal self. "She borrows the power just like sister Amiya and brother Joga."

Sama responded with a noncommittal grunt, but said no more.

Nandi straightened her back again. "Should we not work together to find and awaken this immortal, that they may aid us in leaving this place?"

"We must," Amoura cleared her throat. "I think first, we should consider the implications ... the consequences, of doing that, should we attempt it." She did *not* sound so formal.

"Why so?"

"If there is a sleeping immortal in this place, we don't know how they'll receive us," Amoura explained. "They all had quite different personalities ranging from mild to volatile. They may not want to be awakened, and we must be prepared for whatever their reaction might be, should we do so."

"With all those monsters roaming the land," Nandi said, "we need them."

You have no idea how right you are, girl. She led them, or rather, Nandi, along the center of an avenue between the stone buildings on either side. The incredible cavern was every bit as large as any city she'd seen on the surface. That fact alone made it ten times more impressive.

The one major difference she noticed were the homes. Instead of individual houses, a certain number of the stone buildings carved out of the wall were reserved for homes, as they'd seen in the first building they'd entered to get a better view.

"Amazing," Nandi breathed. "How could anyone have done all this?"

Amoura had no answer. It was indeed amazing. The avenue they walked was wide enough for two carts to pass each other. Stone statues sat at the base of steps leading up to building entrances, as well as the occasional statue in the middle of the pathway.

"All this incredible work," Nandi said, "but where are the people?"

"Where, indeed," Amoura replied, for that was exactly the question in her mind. Had something driven the inhabitants off? Had they migrated to another home?"

Nandi looked up at her. "You don't think something bad happened here, do you?"

"You mean something that might have killed everyone?"

Amoura asked. The girl nodded. "Doubtful." Amoura returned her gaze to their surroundings. "If the first building is any indication, there may have been some sort of exodus."

"Why woman say words Sama doesn't understand?" the tatamble complained. "What is this nexodus?"

"Exodus," Amoura corrected. "It means the departure of a large number of people. Judging by the emptiness of this great city, its entire population seems to have left."

"I want to know why," Nandi said, "but I'm nervous about what the why might be, and what it means for us."

"You are smart to feel that way," Amoura said as they started an uphill hike toward another section of town. "People rarely leave their homes en mass"—she cleared her throat—"in large numbers like this, unless there is a very good reason. I suspect that reason carried negative implications."

"Might it have been some sort of physical threat?" Nandi suggested. "Like the collapsing of part of this cave as what led to our arrival here? Perhaps the indursion of some sort of malevolent life forms?"

"The in*cur*sion of a malevolent force could have been the catalyst for their flight, but I've seen no signs of struggle or death. There is no destruction that isn't erosion due to time." She swept a hand out at the ancient city before them. "If it was a threat large enough to cause an entire city's population to uproot and flee, there would be signs."

"Mayhap they discovered the converging threat long enough before it arrived that they were already gone," Nandi said.

Amoura was positive she'd never used the word "mayhap" in her life. Where had this girl heard that? "Perha …" She glanced at the girl. "Maybe so."

They made their way down the central avenue, Nandi turning about and gazing in awe at the magnificent underground city. Despite her general dislike of anything connected to humans, the tatamble girl looked at least interested, though she hid it behind quick glances that lingered longer if she thought the others weren't watching.

Amoura found herself impressed as well. She would never have guessed something like this existed. Though in the back of her mind sat the reminder that millions of tons of rock lay over-head between them and the surface, the splendor of this under-ground city couldn't be denied.

"What's that murky pond over there?" Nandi pointed to a black pond to the side of the road. It sat alone in a bare patch of land, the nearest structure of any kind no closer than fifty feet.

Amoura considered it for a while before finally moving closer. When Nandi started to walk faster, she held the girl back with an outstretched arm. "We don't know the nature of this place. Be careful."

Nandi straightened her back and gave a curt nod. "I don't know of what I was thinking. You're correct, of course."

Amoura kept most of her sigh inward as she carefully made her way to the black pond. She sniffed the air but noticed no smell. "Hmm." Her essence ring emitted a soft glow as she reached for the power and knelt beside the black pond. "This is the same liquid used to light the sconces. A thick, flammable liquid of some sort."

"So, don't go delving *fire*," Nandi said. She seemed to catch herself again. "It would be a most unfortunate thing to light this entire city afire."

"That it would," Amoura agreed.

Nandi ran a hand over her cornrow braided hair. "Ugh. They're fraying. I'll need to redo them soon. I wish Amiya was here. We do each other's hair."

"New growth," Amoura said. She figured they could use a brief rest, having been on the move for hours now. With no sunlight, there was no way to tell how long they'd been down her. Had a day already passed? Two? "Come." She led the girl to a stone bench and pointed at a large wooden block. "Bring that over here."

Nandi first tried to lift it, then resorted to sliding it over until

Sama came over with a confused expression, and simply lifted it and carried it over. "Showoff," Nandi grumbled.

Amoura smiled as she patted the wooden block in front of her. Sama hopped up on the far side of the stone bench and squatted beside Amoura, watching as she unravelled Nandi's thick, braided hair. She wished she had a comb, but she could make do without.

"How many immortals do you think are down here?" Nandi asked.

Amoura gathered the girl's long thick hair and separated it in sections. "I don't know. I also don't know if we'll find the immortals we want, or what state they'll be in when we do. So much time has passed."

"I hope it's Illuminarians down here," Nandi said. "I can't think of why they'd be anything other than happy we've awakened them, when we do."

"Not necessarily." Amoura gripped Nandi's long puffy hair into her hand and began sliding it through her fists. She picked out a small section and separated it. With agility borne from a lifetime of experience, her fingers moved of their own accord as she wove the hair between and around her fingers, braiding it close to the girl's scalp.

"Wait." Nandi held up a hand and twisted around to look at her. Could you do it like yours?"

Amoura smiled and nodded. When the girl turned back, she undid the first section of the first row, then separated it into a square plait. More familiar with this pattern, Amoura's fingers worked even quicker. "The immortals have been asleep for hundreds of years, Nandi. It's possible that some of them were imprisoned in the void with Shurza."

"With what?" Nandi asked.

"Shurza. It is the name of the void essence created by the Fallen. It is not only the absence of life, but the opposite of it. It was created as a weapon to defeat the immortals by simply canceling out the essences as soon as the wielder drew from them.

"But, they were too ambitious. What was originally supposed to be no more than a cloud of anti-essence, it collected and devoured the power and became sentient."

"How is that possible?"

Beside Amoura, Sama growled in irritation. "Humans play and don't understand. This is why tatamble avoid. Humans would break the world."

"That's pretty grim, Sama," Nandi said.

"She is correct," Amoura said, though it pained her to admit it. "Before the Illuminarians and the Fallen had become such, they were simply two factions of magi well-learned in all things relating to the power. Unfortunately, in their single-minded goal of defeating their age-old enemies, one faction devised the idea of creating the cloud of anti-essence.

"What they'd forgotten, was that the essences are a part of the earth itself, an elemental power borne from a sentient being, and possessed of a form of sentience in itself. In the presence of that cloud, created with a powerful negative intent by seven powerful magi, Shurza took form and became aware."

She finished the last of the braids and gently slid her hands down the sides of Nandi's head, smoothing down the braids. "There."

The braids whipped about her face as she turned her head from side to side. "Thanks." She ran her fingers through her thin braids and slid them along the rows of scalp between the square plaits. "I love it."

Amoura gave Nandi's shoulder a little pat, smiling wistfully at her handywork. Might it have been like this between herself and her older sister, had she been alive? "You're welcome."

Nandi stood and shook her head again, her smile so wide Amoura couldn't help but smile back. "You should do this, Sama," Nandi said to the tatamble girl. "It'd look good on you."

Sama touched her long green locks as if she'd forgotten they were there. "Why Sama would do this? Sama's hair is fine and free."

Nandi shrugged. "Suit yourself."

Sama suddenly hissed and stood up, staring into the distance.

"What is it, Sama? Do you see something? Hear something?"

Sama pointed. "Something that way. Something not good. Stay far away, Sama would."

"Sounds fine to me," Nandi said. "Dad always says if you get a scent of trouble, move in the opposite direction."

Amoura grinned. "That sounds like your father."

Nandi searched Amoura's eyes. "How is Dad? You with him for long? How was he doing?"

Such simple questions, yet it sent Amoura's mind racing back to when first she'd met Emiel. The spicetrader and his then kidnapper, Bone, had been surrounded by a pack of jarku. How long ago that seemed. She hadn't been particularly enamored of the man, not because of anything he had done, but because of the situation.

"You look like you're remembering something nice," Nandi observed. "Do you and my dad like each other, or something?"

Amoura blinked several times as she fought back the heat rising to her face. "He is a kind man. I think very highly of him, yes."

Nandi's lips twitched to the side of her face. "So, which one are we gonna do, have a look at what Sama's talking about, or leave?"

Amoura looked to Sama. The girl definitely held a bias toward an essence wielders she didn't know personally. Could it be her kind could feel the presence of the power in use? Was an essence wielder nearby, holding the power and watching them? "We will be careful, but we will have a look. Please show us the way, Sama."

The tatamble looked at Nandi who nodded encouragingly. Grumbling the whole way, Sama led them to the base of a set of stone steps wider than the road they'd been walking. They ascended the steps and came to what looked like a raised rectangular platform.

As they drew closer, Amoura saw someone lying on their back atop a platform of some kind. A man. "Wait here," she told the others. Essence ring emanating a soft glow as she was ready to bring the power to bear, Amoura approached the platform and looked down at the man lying upon it.

The moment she laid eyes on the clean-shaven head and face of the dark-skinned man, Amoura felt a chill. Though the texts didn't go deep into specifics, they supplied enough description of each of the immortals for her to recognize this man. "Malkiem," she breathed.

"Who?" Nandi asked.

So entranced was she by the sleeping Illuminarian, the girl's voice startled Amoura out of her reverie. "Malkiem," she said more loudly. "Leader of the Illuminarians."

"So, one of the hibernating Illuminarians you've been telling me about," Nandi said.

Sama kept her distance and just offered the occasional hiss.

Amoura shared the tatamble's hesitance. She had no idea what this man would do if or when she awakened him. Assuming she knew how.

"What now?" Nandi asked.

After staring at the man for several moments, Amoura gave a slow shake of her head. "I don't know."

"Shouldn't we wake him up?"

Amoura wasn't sure she knew the answer to that, either. "Perhaps."

"From everything you've told me and everything I've learned since leaving Vyne," Nandi continued, "I think we should wake him. This Shurza thing sounds bad. The Illuminarians are probably the only thing that can destroy it."

She couldn't deny the girl's logic but Amoura felt a deep hesitation. Still, the fact they'd stumbled upon a sleeping immortal, and not just any, but the leader of the Illuminarians, couldn't be ignored. The Fallen and their droughtlords were no doubt awake and roaming the lands by now. Shurza was free, and it was a matter of time before it came to full strength. They needed all the help they could get.

Nandi shifted impatiently while Amoura studied the sleeping immortal. "Can't we just give him a gentle shake and wake him up?"

Amoura responded with a slow shake of her head. "No."

"Why not?"

Slowly and gradually, Amoura inched her hand toward the unconscious man. "Would you lie down to sleep atop a platform like this, in the open, for any kind of danger to befall you?"

After a brief pause, Nandi answered, "No. I suppose not. Perhaps Malkiem implemented a force or barrier to protect his person while he sleeps."

"Perhaps," Amoura replied to the once again formal girl. She waved her hand near him, then closer. Once her hand came to within a few inches of the sleeping Illuminarian, Amoura felt a buzz of energy. It felt like a sentient thing coiled like a snake ready to strike.

Her essence ring emitted a soft red glow as she reached for a small bit of *fire*. Amoura sent a tiny spark of fire across Malkiem's chest and toward his far shoulder. It should have struck the platform right next to his arm, but instead, the fire seemed to have been devoured by a black cloud.

Amoura noticed the glow of her ring die away, and she looked at it in puzzlement, then back at the unconscious man. Beside her, Nandi gasped. "What is it?" she asked the girl.

"Something just sucked up the essence you held from your ring. It felt like it sucked it right *out* of your ring, but I don't know how that's possible. You don't actually store essence inside the ring, you just channel it, Don't you? Like a conduit."

At the mention of her ring, Amoura noticed the ring on the girl's finger for the first time. Nandi dropped her hand at her side.

"You felt it draw the power out of my ring?" she asked the girl.

"Mhm."

"All of the essences?"

"No, just *fire*. Didn't *you* feel it?"

Amoura frowned and looked back to Malkiem, wondering if some force surrounding him had absorbed the tiny bit of *fire* she'd drawn. She reached for *air* and tried to open herself to any such sensations. As soon as she sent a spike of cold air at the sleeping man, another black cloud swirled over the spot she'd focused on and swallowed it. Amoura flinched away when this time, she also felt the *air* essence being sucked out of her ring.

"It happened again!" Nandi said. The girl took a wary step away; Amoura didn't blame her.

Behind them, Sama hissed. "Sleeping man is evil and should be left sleeping. Out of him shadows come creeping."

Amoura frowned at the girl and her randomly strange way of speaking. Were all tatamble like this? "I felt it a little, this time."

"A little?" Nandi replied. "It felt so heavy. Like the air we're breathing was sucked away."

Amoura wondered if it was one of the girl's hybrid traits that lent her the ability to feel it so strongly. At some point she'd need to test Nandi's abilities.

"Whatever's swirling around that guy," Nandi said, "I think it'll suck in anything we throw at it. It feels like some sort of hungry, empty space that'll eat up any essence we put in."

"Like a void," Amoura murmured. Once again, she revisited the texts, remembering every snippet of the battle of the immortals she'd found in her research. The black cloud's name was Shurza, but the texts described it as the blight essence. She'd also come across one other name for it; void essence.

"So, what are we supposed to do with him?" Nandi asked. "We can't use any essences to get rid of whatever's swirling around him, and I don't know about you, but I'm not touching him."

"No, we're not touching him."

"Then must leave him and go," Sama said.

"I know you think he's evil, Sama," Nandi said. "But he isn't. He helped save the world a long time ago."

Sama responded with little more than a skeptical grunt but said no more.

Once again Amoura fell back on her studies. The void essence ate any of the power thrown into it, yet it didn't consume the whole world. How, and why? Perhaps the world was too large to consume all at once, and so Shurza would simply drink from it like one would with a straw from the ocean. But unlike a person drinking such, the insatiable Shurza would grow larger and more powerful with every sip.

"Three were trapped in the void with Shurza and the Fallen," she whispered.

"But, that doesn't make sense," Nandi said. "If that thing is a void, how could it be trapped in a void?"

"A good question," Amoura replied. She pressed her finger to her cheek as she stared at Malkiem. "Unlike a normal void, like a space with no air to breathe or no light, the void essence is a living, sentient thing. All living things need something to feed it."

"We cut off its food supply, then?" Nandi asked.

"That would seem to be the case. But, if we're trying to free him—"

"We have to get rid of the prison he's trapped in. The one he's trapped in with that thing."

Amoura frowned. "I believe so."

"But, it's already free, isn't it?"

"It is. But it isn't fully grown, or the world would have already perished." That last bit she wasn't completely certain about. No one truly knew what would happen, should Shurza reach its full potential, but a dead world seemed like a certainty. And if not that, the world would likely wish it was dead.

"If that's true," Nandi said. "Then we should leave him asleep. It sounds like part of Shurza is wrapped around him. If we break that, it'll probably go and find the rest of itself."

Amoura nodded in appreciation of the girl's wit. "We may have no choice. If we leave him, Shurza may eventually find this part of itself and kill him to take it back."

"I don't like this bargain at all," Nandi said. "We need him to fight the thing, but to get him free, we have to make it stronger."

"That seems the inevitable conclusion," Amoura said. She straightened, now positive she knew what to do, yet dreading it all the same. "The Fallen are free and are compelled to serve the void essence. They will strengthen it, and as they do, it will grow and seek out its missing parts. When that happens, he and the other two who were imprisoned with Shurza will die or possibly be subverted."

"Oh, no." Nandi shook her head, her new skinny braids smacking against her face. "We don't need more Fallen than there already are."

"No, we don't," Amoura agreed. "I wish I had more time to teach you, but this is the moment we've arrived at. Step away from this platform and prepare yourself as best you know how. Be ready to wield the power, but do not call upon it yet. Just be ready to defend yourself if I fall."

"Don't say that. You're not going to *fall*, and leave us here by ourselves."

"I assure you I have no intention of dying, this day," Amoura replied as she stared down at the Illuminarian. "But the possibility remains. Now, step away."

Amoura spread her robes away from her shoulders and held her hands out in front of her. She scanned the man's body not so much to detect the threat, which was all around him, but in thought. Malkiem, or rather, his soul, had been trapped in a space devoid of the essences. If she understood correctly, Shurza being set free meant Malkiem hadn't been trapped with the whole of the void essence, but only part of it in a separate void. She had so many questions.

"Remember what I said, Nandi." She reached for the power. "Draw upon the essences only to defend yourself. Don't feed it."

As quickly as she could, Amoura drew the four essences through her ring. She sent as much of *air* into the void as she could. The black cloud appeared and concentrated on the area she hit. Amoura continued to send as much of the power into it as she could, then channeled *water* into a different place. The black cloud appeared there, as well.

She changed tactics and moved *water* to attack the same spot as *air*. The black cloud ate hungrily from that spot. She did the same with *fire*. The black cloud devoured everything she threw at it, showing no indication of filling up or even that the essences were even there. They simply ceased to be as soon as they hit.

Sweat trickled down the side of her face as Amoura concentrated all her effort into attacking that one spot. Her strength was starting to ebb. Hoping she was right about her hunch, she sent an experimental stream of water at his head.

The cloud ate it, but this time, a few droplets landed on his face. Amoura channeled all the power she could wield into the spot at his feet, the ravenous cloud eating it up.

Howling wind and the roar of a river and flames filled her ears. Her thin braids and robes whipped in the tempestuous wind, but she held her course. "Nandi! Bring forth *air*. Send it to his head."

"What?"

"Do as I say!"

The powerful response surprised Amoura, for a physical blast of the essence's namesake nearly knocked her over as it punched through the black cloud and hit the Illuminarian's face. *The girl could effectively battle a full magus*, she thought.

A frown creased Malkiem's brow.

"Don't stop," Amoura yelled. "Hold on as best you can!"

"Trying!" the girl shouted through the roar of essence power.

Malkiem's frown deepened. His lips moved, just a bit.

Amoura's strength was draining. *Wake up!*

His fingers moved, then a foot. A burst of searing light flooded the cavern.

Amoura realized she was flying backwards. Before she could think to right herself, she hit the ground on her back with a heavy grunt as the wind blasted from her lungs.

She fell into a fit of coughing and wheezing inhalations while rolling onto her side. After a few moments, she propped herself up on her elbow and looked around.

Nandi lay on her side as well, while Sama was on hands and knees, green hair hanging over her face.

Amoura looked back up the steps to see Malkiem lying on the platform as though nothing at all had happened. With a disappointed sigh, Amoura lifted herself up. She froze when Malkiem turned his head in her direction.

Time may well have stopped as she and the Illuminarian locked gazes, neither uttering a word or making a move. His body heaved once, as if a great breath escaped him.

Amoura slowly rose, but remained where she stood. "Malkiem? Malkiem of the Illuminarians. You are freed—"

The leader of the Illuminarians narrowed his eyes. "What have you DOOOOOOOOOOOOOOOOOONE!"

A blast of air more powerful than anything Amoura had ever felt crashed into her like a tsunami. It lifted her from the ground as though she were a leaf and hurled her away. Nandi, Sama, the altar and the enraged Illuminarian rapidly diminished as Amoura flew backwards at a such a speed she knew nothing would be left of her when she eventually hit a cavern wall.

She tried to reach for *air*, tried to counter the power speeding her to her death. She might as well have tried to push over a boulder with her bare hands. The power of the Illuminarian was too great, too awesome for her to even approach.

The far cavern wall rushed towards her. She clamped her eyes shut just before impact but her body jerked to a stop. Amoura barely had time to take a shaky breath when she suddenly sped back in the opposite direction, rushing toward the standing Illuminarian.

As she flew back to Malkiem, she saw a black cloud with outstretched arms and claws take form behind him. It flew up and away just before she reached the immortal.

Once again, her body jerked to a stop. She hovered above the ground, high enough that he had to look up at her. A great weight pressed in on Amoura's body. She gritted her teeth, focusing through the pain. She reached for the essences and barely found them. Her ring emitted a dim, pulsating glow, indicating her tenuous grasp on the power.

Eyes aglow with a silver *arah*, Malkiem looked at her finger, then slid his enraged gaze back up to her face.

"Malkiem," Amoura groaned through the strangling pressure. "I am … Amoura … Xan, ugh! Amoura … Xanna … of the Order of Mag, ah!"

"Magi." The word eased from his mouth like lava seeping through a thin layer of crust.

Amoura let out a high-pitched groan when the pressure intensified. She needed to stop him before he crushed her. She struggled for any essence to throw at him, but she barely caught a wisp.

He looked at her ring again, and his silver eyes flared.

The essence ring on Amoura's finger exploded. She looked down in dismay as the fragments of her essence ring fell to the ground and scattered.

Amoura closed her eyes and fought through her fear. She forced herself to look at the man. She saw no satisfaction in his face, no sense of superiority of one who took pleasure in defeating his adversary. He'd simply done what he'd done, and now he would kill her. She had no doubt about that.

Malkiem's hands clenched into fists, his teeth bared. His *arah* shifted, all the colors of the essences combining as he drew massive amounts of the power to obliterate her.

37

RAYNE

Rayna sipped her hot spiced tea, gazing over the top of the mug at the grinning Eryn Tolen. The Shetaran advisor sat erect in his chair, legs crossed, left eyebrow perpetually lifted as he raised his own mug of tea to his lips. His green doublet was of the Shetaran style, the left side stopping at the middle of the ribcage while the right side reached to the waist. His matching breeches were fitted, with a spiraling design on the left leg.

During this, her third meeting with the man, Rayna struggled as best she could to find something, anything redeemable about the man. Perhaps he didn't understand the situation between Alyn and the Khatala, as many didn't. Maybe he was misinformed about some crucial detail leading to his own ill-informed advice to the Shetaran prime minister.

As with the first two friendly meetings with the man, Rayna became more certain that whatever Eryn Tolen might be, misinformed did not number among his attributes.

She leaned back in her chair and feigned a contented smile as she gazed at the brick and mortar buildings with their sloping roofs. Despite the steepness of the slopes, a soft-soled shoe could find purchase so long as they were traversed at a proper angle. Some of the homes and buildings sat so close together that one could almost step from one roof to the other.

Rayna looked at the multi-colored plants and bushes, the distant trees and other plants native only to this region so near to the great volcano that sat on the border of Shetar and New Dama. It was a beautiful place, to be sure.

"For such a dainty, lovely lady, you have a lot of interest in this war, Lady Tana," Tolen said. "Though I never tire of such fascinating discussions, it strikes me as rather odd."

"It isn't war itself that I find so interesting," Rayna said, "but the stakes."

"Oh?" Eryn's raised eyebrow twitched. "What stakes might those be?"

"Well, do they ever change?" Rayna asked. "I mean, that age old grudge about a misunderstood tradition can only stretch so far."

"I wouldn't be so sure," Eryn Tolen said, taking another sip. "There are peoples in many places around the world with rather strong-willed perspectives on life, and firmly held traditions. I once had to profusely apologize because I scratched the underside of my nose with my finger during a trade meeting with a Nogthi."

"What's so terrible about that?" Rayna asked innocently.

"Only that in Nogthi culture. To touch anywhere on the underside of the nose during a conversation indicates that the words of the person you're talking to, well, to put it crudely, stink."

Rayna's eyes widened. "Really? I would never have thought something like that. It seems an easy thing to accidentally offend, once you travel outside your homeland."

Tolen took another sip and lowered the mug. "It can be, my dear. This is why I hire a local to consult beforehand, and accompany me on foreign deals whenever possible. In some places a cultural offense can have rather … dire, consequences."

"Such as a war lasting many years?"

Tolen shook his head with a chuckle. "Hardly a war, Tana, though many call it that. No, my dear. If this were a true war, more than just Jietar and two Khatala nations would be involved."

Rayna raised her mug to that. "Pray to the Creator things don't devolve to that state, then."

The advisor responded with a noncommittal shrug. "As with most things in life, some good could come of it."

Rayna painted an incredulous expression on her face. "I can't imagine how so, Eryn. People are already dying on the battlefield, and many more wounded. The earth is torn up and soaking with blood. And for what?"

Eryn chuckled through it all. "You've a flair for the dramatic, I see." He opened a hand towards her. "While, yes, there are people perishing in battle, it isn't nearly as many as you might think.

"And, the earth is rather resilient. There isn't any lasting damage being inflicted on that patch of land. This enduring conflict is two sides holding their ground while trying to figure out a way past it."

"Seems a long time in figuring out a way past it." She frowned as if remembering what he'd said a moment earlier. "And, what do you mean by "some good could come of it?" How could anything good come out of something like that?"

Again, Tolen shrugged. "Sometimes it takes a situation to escalate in order for both sides to see their folly. Sometimes that escalation has to reach near catastrophic conditions for that realization to occur.

"And, sometimes the defeat of one side leads to the wealth of another, while the defeated returns to their home, whichever side that may be. Other times, such a conflict can unite what were formerly divided sections of one land and its people, thus strengthening the region as a whole."

Rayna maintained her facade of superficial interest but listened carefully. Her mind worked quickly as she unpacked the advisor's words as he spoke them. He most certainly wouldn't speak openly about Jietar's plans for Khatal to a stranger he'd only had tea with three days in a row. The man would have to be a fool to do such. "Are you hungry, Mr. Tobain?"

"Eryn," he insisted. "And now that you mention it, I could have a meal."

"I would recommend somewhere to dine," Rayna spread her hands, "but I confess, this is my first visit to Shetar."

"I know a place," Eryn said. "I've a meeting after I leave you. We can go after."

He told Rayna the place and time for them to meet, promising fine food and finer drink, which Rayna hoped would be quite potent. After a lingering hug that left a smile on Eryn Tolen's face, they parted ways.

Rayna walked away without looking back. As soon as she stepped around the wall of a store, she slipped a brown headscarf out of her shoulder bag, quickly tied it around her head so that only her face was visible, and adjusted the single strap of the bag to tie around her waist.

When she slipped around the building again, she wove between the throngs, her sharp eyes searching and finally picking out the green doublet that spoke of even greater wealth among a clearly wealthy populace.

She tailed him to what she learned two days ago to be his home. It sat at the edge of a cluster of other homes, housing Shetar's wealthiest. Having searched around the outside of the house over the past two days, she knew he had a personal maid that lived in the house.

A carriage waited by the house, and when the advisor arrived, the driver hopped down, knocked on the door, and opened it. Out stepped a man with thick arms and legs, and an even thicker midsection. Rayna judged him to be close to three times her weight, and while a good portion of it wasn't muscle, a decent bit was.

Falling upon years of experience, she took a guess and made her way around to reach the side of the house, then skulked alongside it until she reached the cliff upon which the house's back patio overlooked.

Rayna carefully made her way over the side of the cliff. Little more than protruding rocks and shrubbery growing out the side of the cliff wall served as handholds, but it was enough. She climbed sideways until she came underneath the thick wooden beams supporting the overhanging balcony.

Six beams as large around as her body extended out from solid ground, and three lay sideways across them, the flat foundation of the balcony sitting atop the sideways beams. There was just enough space between the crisscrossing beams for Rayna to slip between. She picked a spot right near the edge of the balcony and lay silently, waiting.

A short while later she heard the soft footsteps that would be the maid. Dishes clinked as they were placed on a table, followed by the sound of liquid being poured. The soft footsteps receded, and two sets of heavier footsteps thumped the floor almost immediately after.

Eryn Tobain and his guest conversed for a time on many trivial subjects ranging from the view from his patio, to trade between their two provinces and Nashma, which separated them.

"Tell me, Advisor. Where does the mind of your prime minister sit with the state of the wilder conflict?"

"Perfect choice of word, Rogyn," Eryn scoffed. "Conflicted. That would describe the indecisive man's mind. King Alyn's promise of a share of the spoils near the Shattered Lands tugs just hard enough that Zachryn considers the offer. The man continues to waver on making a decision, but he may yet be persuaded.

"I must ask, however. Why wouldn't King Alyn have already taken that corlite deposit? It's not in Khatal or near its borders."

Rogyn grunted. "The wilders aren't just big dumb animals, no matter how much some wish it so. If there's one thing they know how to sniff out, it's a corlite deposit. There's a sizable number of them guarding it."

"A sizable number," Eryn replied dubiously. "How so? The Shattered Lands are far into Marai. Not only that, I can't imagine so many of them huddled around the deposit that Alyn couldn't send a force to chase them off. He takes the deposit, sends it to Shetar as a gift with promise of a full share upon entering the battle, the problem begins to erode."

Emissary Rogyn's baritone rumble of a laugh set Rayna on edge. "You ever seen a wilder fight, my good man?"

After a lengthy pause, Eryn replied, "can't say that I have."

"Pray you never do. Doesn't matter if it's women or men, they'll put pain on you like you've never experienced."

"There are female warriors across Marai."

"Not like the westerners," Rogyn said. Rayna could imagine him shaking his head against the advisor's logic. "You've not seen them, Eryn. The shortest woman is taller than most Marai men, and just as strong. The men," a silent pause. "Let's just say that as strong as they are in their particular use of the essences, they're just as strong physically."

Rayna heard a slurp from a mug, then the man named Rogyn spoke again. "And in answer to your other question, the wilders know how to be discrete when they want to. How they managed to get so far northeast into Marai without being noticed, I don't know. But they did. Word of them squatting in the Shattered Lands around that deposit came in not long ago."

"This gets ever more interesting as time moves on," Eryn said. "Jietar seems to be doing well in the battle near Mt. Blood."

"The Jietari forces are impressive for sure. But the Khatala have no true taste for blood in this fight. As hard as this may be to wrap your mind around, their stake in this fight is only an apology from Alyn for the wrongs done all those years ago, and Marai rolling back its borders to what they once were."

"That's rather simplistic."

"They are a simple people," Rogyn replied. "Frustratingly so, when you consider the wealth in corlite they're sitting on. Alyn understands what the westerners are capable of more than most think. If the other nations enter the conflict, it will become a full-on war. The physical and elemental prowess of the wilders is not to be underestimated."

"Which is why he needs Marai unified against them," Eryn said. "And with those corlite deposits—"

"He can not only fuel the war effort indefinitely," Rogyn added, "but make it practically impossible for Altarra to ignore it."

"Altarra meaning the Order of Magi."

"Now you have it."

"Well, then." A brief moment of silence passed that Rayna guessed was Eryn sipping his drink. "If he manages to get the entire Order of Magi behind him, that would give even the wilders pause."

"Indeed," Rogyn said. "As you may have guessed, we've had a setback in Shiedra."

"The assassination," Eryn said, a note of anxiety in his voice.

"Yup. And his widow has been far less than cooperative, given she doesn't share her dead husband's ambitions."

"Perhaps her perspective would change once she sees Shetar's take of that corlite deposit."

"That's the idea, Advisor," Rogyn said. "Which is why I'm here in Shetar. Alyn hopes for the two of us to persuade your Prime Minister of the merits of an alliance."

Rayne closed her eyes and breathed deeply. She'd heard enough several minutes ago, and had already reached under her pant legs and slipped off both vambraces, securing them to her arms. She methodically checked every weapon about her person, ensuring they were secure, then began to make her way toward the edge of the balcony.

"All this talk is making me want to be away from here," she heard Eryn say. The man sounded nervous.

"What for?" Rogyn asked. "Surely you're not expecting an assassin visit. Your patio overlooks a sheer cliff."

"The royain's bedroom was similarly difficult to reach."

Rayne heard chairs shuffling as the men stood. She reached the edge of the patio and hung by her hands, her body dangling over what must be a hundred-foot drop or more.

She concentrated on her corlite beads, lightening her body-weight. Hanging by just her hands, Rayne noted where she'd heard the sounds of chairs pushing back and the relative position of the voices. The lean corded muscles in her arms bunched as she pulled with all her strength.

She silently flew straight up and over the rail. The two men had their backs to her and were oblivious to Rayne's ascent.

Mid-air, Rayne threw herself into a forward flip, while slipping free a dagger from each side of her waist. The instant before her foot touched the floor, she whipped both hands out. The daggers sped as silently through the air as her landing, and her aim was true. Both missiles punched into the backs of her targets.

"Agh!" Eryn Toben arched his back, while Rogyn growled and half turned half lurched around.

Rayne was already on the move. Having slightly turned and gotten a look at her, the emissary stumbled aside by the time she reached them. Toben, however, had arched his back in reflex, which placed his neck in a perfect position.

In one maneuver, the assassin yanked the blade from his back while wrapping her arm arm around his neck. She noted the man's shock of recognition just before she opened his throat.

"Khamra … cowards," Rogyn gasped. His gaze fell over Eryn Toben who lay still in his rapidly pooling lifeblood. He struggled upright, then winced.

Bloody dagger in hand, Rayne circled the much bigger man, then circled back, forcing him to move to keep her in his line of vision. The fact that the man was standing at all made her all the more careful. He would have been formidable uninjured, but she made no mistake that he was still dangerous.

"Waiting … for my strength … to drain … away … coward?" Rogyn grunted.

Rayne flipped her dagger in her hand. Once, twice, a third time. The site of a bloody dagger flipping like that would illicit fear in a normal target, fatally drawing their attention to the weapon for her to strike, fast as a cobra. This man was made of stronger stuff.

"You gonna … make the … first … move, assassin?" He kept his hateful glare on Rayne while still keeping her in front of him. "This little … toothpick isn't … gonna … kill me."

Rayne launched her remaining dagger at the emissary and sprinted right behind it while drawing another from behind her lower back.

Rogyn swatted at the dagger and barked a pained curse. He leaned to one side as if fleeing the agony in the middle of his back, where the blade remained. He managed to knock the flying dagger aside but the missile still cut his forearm. Right behind the deflected weapon, Rayne sliced him across the forearm when he raised it to block the blade, aimed for his throat.

The large man surprised her with a fast backhand of the same arm. Rayne hadn't expected him to still be able to move that fast, but her reflexes had her under the backhanded swing before it reached her. With a flick of her wrist, the concealed blade in her vambrace sprang free and into her grasp.

She rose and stabbed the blade toward Rogyn's midsection. He powered through the attack and bulled into her. His shoulder smashed into her chest and he wrapped his thick arms around her.

Rayne's feet left the floor when the man easily lifted her. Having aimed for his abdomen, she felt her dagger skip off of one of his ribs. Rogyn grunted, but held on. Rayne still had a grip on her weapon and drove it into his side repeatedly. She had to get free before he slammed her to the floor and crushed her or hurled her over the side of the balcony.

Every time she drove the blade into him, the big man grunted but still he didn't let go. Rayne tried to drive her knee into his groin, but now he was running, albeit clumsily under the weight of his injuries. She realized that only a mortal blow would stop him, as the big man was functioning on pure adrenaline.

Rayne felt herself being lifted higher. Rogyn bellowed in her ear as he lifted her up and tossed her over the rail. As she went up and out, Rayne flicked her wrist and her remaining blade sprang into her grasp. As she turned end over end, she focused on the emissary, now leaning on the rail. Her body sideways in the air, Rayne let fly. The dagger whipped through the air just as Rogyn tried to straighten. His hands went to his throat to grasp the handle of the embedded dagger.

The last thing Rayne saw before she fell below the balcony was the emissary yanking the blade out and his throat, lifeblood gushing free.

RAYNE THREW ALL her focus into the corlite beads at the tips of her braids, whipping about her face as she plummeted more than a hundred feet toward certain death.

She concentrated first on lightening her bodyweight, then focused on slowing her descent. Her descent gradually began to slow, but she was still falling too fast. Rayne sank back into a lifetime of training and meditation. She'd grown to become the best of the Khamra even before learning that she had use of corlite.

The endless hours of mental training kept panic from her mind. As the ground rushed to meet her, she threw all her focus and energy into further slowing her fall and lessening her bodyweight.

Less than a few heartbeats later and she knew her efforts wouldn't be enough. As the ground sprang up to meet her, Rayne stretched out her body as much as she could, and at the moment of impact, threw herself into a forward roll. Explosions of pain burst into her ankles, her right shoulder, and her hips.

She didn't know how long she lay broken on the ground, but the intensity of the pain from her crash flowed through her body like her own lifeblood.

Rayne focused on her breathing, but even that hurt. She waded through an ocean of agony, parting the waves and making her way to internal organs, joints, and ligaments.

Once again, she called upon her corlite beads. Warmth gradually spread through her body. She might have saved herself an instant death on impact, but she'd still die if she didn't repair herself.

She closed her eyes and increased the healing warmth flowing through her body like a fog rolling across the land. Every breath came accompanied by a ripple of pain. She focused on her lungs and felt something stabbing into one.

Rayne sent the healing warmth into that area. She detected a broken rip that had punctured her lung. She gritted her teeth and focused on the broken bone. Gradually it withdrew from the wound and began to knit back together. She divided her attention between that and sealing the puncture, lest she bleed to death internally.

In the back of her mind, Rayne knew that if word got to the right people quickly enough, they would find her here, vulnerable. If night fell, they would likely find what was left of her, as some nocturnal predator may well happen upon her, if a carrion crow didn't peck her to death first. She needed to heal and be gone. Long gone.

But this. Rayne thought she'd known pain before, but she hadn't. Both her ankles and her right foot were broken. She'd dislocated her shoulder, for the pain was far worse than if it were broken. Her hips had also either broken or dislocated. She couldn't tell, for every part of her body burned in agony.

Through some miracle, her lung was the only internal organ to have sustained any damage, and she'd mostly sealed up the wound.

Her rib had knitted back together as well. She concentrated first on her ankles. She needed to be able to walk. She could focus on her wrists while she moved.

The pain pounded her like a stomping teliak. Rayne felt her grasp on consciousness slipping. *No. No!* Steady breaths. One at a time. She felt the bones in her ankles struggling to repair while the ligaments reattached. The tiny bones in her right foot slowly knitted back together and reconnected.

Once her ankles and foot were healed, she focused on her hips. The wave of agony that washed over her nearly knocked Rayne unconscious. Her breaths started to speed up, and again, she forced them to steady.

A beetle scurried past her face. For some reason, the randomness of it made her laugh, then suck in a breath from the resulting stab of pain. She could smell the dust on the ground, feel the small pebbles sticking into her from underneath. A breeze blew over her, and even that hurt.

When Rayne heard the first distant bark of a jarku, she knew she was in trouble. She focused on her hips, throwing everything she had into healing the cartilage and ligaments, popping everything back into place. This time she did cry out. Loudly. The pain was so intense she didn't care if someone from above heard. The world fell away and there was only agony.

Her ribs were healed but tender, the hole in her lung closed, but fragile. Rayne rolled over onto her stomach and propped herself up on her forearms. She worked her knees under her, clenching her teeth so hard she thought they too might break.

Finally, Rayne stood and began walking. Her right foot and ankles protested, her hips flared with white-hot fiery agony, and her newly healed rib creaked with every step. She continued her jerky, stumbling walk, not sure where she was going, but anywhere away from here. If she could find a copse to shelter and hide in, or even a single tree to get off the ground …

Her vision blurred, the world grew ever darker, and suddenly she felt something hit the right side of her body. Pain exploded in her many wounds again. She blew out a heavy breath and saw a cloud of dust through her slitted eyes. She was on the ground again.

The last thing Rayne heard before she surrendered into nothingness was the creaking sound of wooden wheels.

38

AMIYA

Death. It greeted them around every corner, up and down every street, inside every house and through every window. Well, the windows in houses that still stood.

Amiya's heart pounded. The place even smelled dead. And the quiet. She hummed just to remind herself that she hadn't gone deaf. The quiet hung thick like a quilt. "Right. You're showing me the horror we're capable of and that it's nothing compared to the void. Got it." She looked over her shoulder at Estrella. "Can we go, now?"

The tall woman stood at ease, wrapped in her dark blue cloak like an ominous statue. In the drab mix of gray and brown that colored this dead town, Estrellas violet eyes practically glowed.

"Um ... how about it?" Amiya tried again. "I get your meaning. Humans destroy stuff, but we're much smaller than we think, in the grand scheme of things, right? Maybe we can talk about all this over a meal? I know a good place back in Vyne."

Estrella looked past her but said nothing. Amiya turned to follow her gaze but saw nothing but more crumbled buildings and scattered bones. Were there even any rodents or bugs in this place?

"Do you know what an imprint is, little one?" Estrella returned her frightening violet gaze to Amiya.

"Imprint?" Amiya frowned. "I'm not sure I know what you mean."

"The Illuminarians defeated Shurza by cutting off its nourishment." She made a sound that could have been a huff of laughter. Brief and quiet. "Ironically, they created a void of essences to trap the blight, or rather, void essence itself. They also managed to seal away the Fallen with it, given they were tethered to their own creation. An unexpected and crafty maneuver."

Amiya had no idea where this was going, so she just listened. What else could she do?

"The souls of the Fallen drifted in the void with Shurza for time immeasurable. No up or down, left or right. No tangibility or even sight. Just floating in nothingness with an immense presence of malevolent power all around you."

"That sounds almost as bad as dying."

"One could argue such an existence is worse," Estrella replied. She indicated their surroundings. "An imprint is a place where the souls of the dead are tethered to the place they perished. Only through a great knowledge of the essences and a twisted misuse of that power could tether a soul to a place."

"But, if someone had that much knowledge of the power? Wouldn't they know better?"

"Having knowledge and abilities does not denote the proper sense of whether that knowledge and ability should be employed," Estrella answered. "The ability to wield the power isn't exclusive to Magi, as you well know. What these other essence wielders don't have, however, is access to the vast well of knowledge of the Order of Magi."

"So, what? They tried something big and blew themselves up?"

Estrella chuckled this time. "I'd wager they would have found that outcome more preferable. No, they sought to bend the essences and twist them into their own creations." She walked by, and Amiya followed her to the end of the street where a brown stone statue lay halfway inside the broken wall of a house.

Amiya squinted at it. "How can a statue look like that?" She pointed at its limbs. "It looks like it fell. Like, it was walking, and it fell."

"An essence golem," Estrella explained. "Made completely of corlite, and highly durable."

"Wow." Amiya took a tentative step forward and touched the tip of its foot. A buzzing power sprang into her fingers and she snatched her hand back as if she'd been shocked.

"You felt something?" Estrella asked.

Amiya nodded as she backed away. "Yeah. Like the Shattered Lands but stronger."

"Corlite's value rests in its malleability and that it is a conductor of the essence power," Estrella said. "It really is up to your knowledge and imagination as to what you can do with or through it." She grinned. "Or what you put *into* it."

Amiya's mouth fell open. Before she realized it, she was standing behind Estrella. She shuffled back around to the woman's side. "You're not telling me that someone's soul is in that thing. How?"

"Not all of them."

"*All*?" Amiya stared at the statue as if it might stand up right then. "You mean, there were more than this one?"

"There were many. Large, lumbering, and strong. While most were given life through essence, some were inhabited by human souls. When the golems were destroyed, those souls remained tethered here, in this place.

"Llasram was once a city of great power, but also paranoia. In their desperate race to become a greater power in the world, the leaders of this place enlisted the skills of essence wielders to create the essence golems. Powerful and uneducated, these non-magi made rather ... grievous mistakes." She waved a hand. "Here, you see the result."

"Ugh." Amiya frowned at the thing. "I'd really rather be gone from here."

"So would they," Estrella said. "Well, some of them, anyway. Do you not feel it?"

"I don't want to feel it." If Amiya knew how to *bridge*, she would have done so at that moment.

"Why do you wish to go?"

Amiya looked at her as though she'd lost her mind. "Because that thing scares me. This whole town scares me."

"No better reason to stay, little one." Estrella stepped forward, knelt, and touched the foot of the golem. Several heartbeats passed before she stood again.

"What'd you do that for—" Amiya's eyes widened when the huge stone foot, half as tall as her body, shifted. "What's your Fallen-blasted problem?" Amiya asked as she backed away.

Dust rained off the body of the golem as it slowly climbed to its feet. The rest of the house crumbled around it as it broke through the hole in the wall. Glowing brown eyes in an otherwise featureless head glowed at Amiya and Estrella.

"Why would you wake it?" Amiya demanded. "We could have just left the blasted thing alone—" The sound of crumbling stone and splitting wood sent a chill down Amiya's spine. Heart pounding in her chest, she turned to see three more of the things lumbering toward them.

"You wake us to remind us of our endless torment."

Amiya spun a circle. The voice had no source. "I didn't do anything." She pointed at Estrella. "Your friend, there, woke you up, but maybe just lie back down and relax. Go back to sleep and we'll leave."

"You mock our torment by awakening us. You will suffer eternity with us."

Amiya looked expectantly at Estrella. "You wanna fix this? You woke them up and made them mad."

Estrella smiled affectionately at Amiya, then took a step backwards. The air around her warped, like a body of water around a stone cast into its surface.

For several heartbeats Amiya stared at the empty space. She bit her lower lip and nodded. *Okay.*

Four towering golems converged on her from every direction. They must have been ten feet tall, but to Amiya, who hadn't quite reached five feet yet, they seemed like walking mountains.

"You take me all over the place, from Marai to that Nogth place, then bring me here and drop me off." Amiya nodded again. "All right. You'd better hope I die, here, Estrella. You'd better pray to the Creator that I don't make it out of here."

She stood still and turned a circle, analyzing each of the corlite constructs. What else could she do? Amiya reached for the essences. *Fire* came readily to her call, and she launched a stream of its physical namesake into one of the approaching golems.

It walked right into the flames and kept coming, never breaking stride.

Amiya reached for *air*. The essence came to her, albeit hesitantly. She created a powerful gust of air and continued to build it. All around her the wind started to howl. Wooden debris and bone fragments skipped across the torn streets.

When she could contain the power no longer, Amiya released it in a howling windstorm directed at the two golems in front of her. While she achieved the desired effect in that the corlite constructs stumbled aside, the power of her own blast threw her backwards.

As she flew away, Amiya realized how lucky she was. Neither she nor the golems behind her had expected the result, and so they didn't react fast enough to catch her when she zipped between them.

When Amiya finally hit the ground, she skipped and tumbled over broken stone, crashing through several skeletons and scattering the bones. She felt nicked and bruised in a dozen places at least. When she finally skidded to a stop, she had to force herself not to reach down to touch her bleeding, skinned knees.

On reflex alone she delved *fire* and let fly twin cones of flames funneling into the corlite golems. The lumbering giants walked through the fire like before.

That doesn't work, stupid, she chastised herself. She released the essence and delved *water* and *air*. She backed away from the advancing golems, struggling to concentrate on combining the two essences. Why couldn't they be made of ice? She could have melted them in short order.

She heard the distant sound of crumbling wood and stone and sighed. *I'm just gonna assume that's more.* Several moments later she saw that she'd assumed correctly. Four more golems appeared. They made a straight line for Amiya, walking through anything in their path, whether it be a pile of rubble, skeletons, or a standing wall.

Amiya looked in every direction, taking count. *Five, six, eight ... TEN?* Her heart started to thump in her chest. "Ten?" she whispered aloud. "I can't destroy *one* of these things."

One of the original four golems grabbed a nearby chunk of broken wall and hurled it at her. Amiya screamed and dove aside. The missile barely missed her. She felt the ground vibrate when the piece of wall hit, even as she rolled and scrambled to her feet.

She'd lost her grip on the essences in trying not to be crushed, so Amiya reached for the power again. *Air* and *water* came easier to her call, this time. She struggled to combine them once more, growling in frustration. She needed to be faster at this. The ground thudded rapidly with each step of the ten golems closing in around her.

Desperation slithered up her back like a snake, threatening to strangle the courage from her. She threw what little effect she'd created from the combined essences at the nearest golem. The freezing ice shards shattered against the walking stone construct like raindrops on steel.

She delved *earth* and found it the most hesitant to heed her call. She groaned in concentration, willing, *pleading* with the essence to come to bear. A large chunk of broken street slowly rose into the air. Amiya focused it on a golem and let fly.

The chunk of street glided lazily through the air toward her target. The corlite golem barely regarded the incoming missile. It punched a huge fist into the stone chunk and it burst into hundreds of pieces. It and the other nearby golems walked through the rain of debris, continuing their steady advance.

Another golem picked up a chunk of rock and hurled it at her. Then another. Amiya dove to the side and kept rolling as rock projectiles exploded all around her. A piece of debris flew away from a shattered wall and clipped her across her cheek. Amiya felt blood trailing down the side of her face.

She rose on wobbly legs and tried to take stock of where all the lumbering giants were. Amiya felt a thud so heavy she knew one was right behind her. She dropped to her stomach and rolled to the side. Her guess saved her life. A massive foot crunched into the ground where she'd been standing. It sank several inches into the hard-stone street as if the golem had just stepped into a patch of mud.

Amiya swallowed. *Gotta keep moving.* She scrambled up and forward, very much aware that the thing might still be on her back. The resulting tremor and rain of debris confirmed it. They were all around her, now.

She ran straight for a golem and slid between its legs. She delved *air* and *water*, climbed to her feet, and froze the ground underneath the stone monster. It turned and took a step towards her; the thick sheet of ice broke apart underneath its heavy footsteps.

"Die and remain for eternity."

"That's pretty dramatic, sir," Amiya replied. "Or ma'am. Or whatever you are." Remembering her fight with the drauk and the tunneler, she delved *earth* and tried to raise herself out of the stone giants' reach. Slowly the ground underneath her shifted, and she rose into the air.

Beads of sweat collected on her forehead. The strain of working with the essence she had the least affinity for took more time and energy. Amiya rose six feet into the air and kept rising. Or tried to.

A golem reached her platform and punched into it. Amiya screamed as she suddenly found herself falling. Her teeth chattered as the platform broke apart under her and she bounced atop it. A giant hand slapped at her and she rolled out of the way just in time.

The impact still sent her flying to the side amidst dirt, soil, and rock. When she hit the ground—rather painfully—Amiya curled into a ball, arms over her head as the earthy rain fell over her.

Another golem closed in and raised its foot. Amiya barely skittered backwards to avoid being crushed. She looked around and her heart leapt when she spotted a gap between the converging stone monsters. She hopped to her feet and ran straight for it, ignoring the tiny fires of pain wracking her body. With a cry of triumph she outpaced the golems and made it clear.

She kept running, determined to put as much distance between herself and that cursed town as possible. Her progress began to slow as the effort to move forward grew more difficult. Bleeding legs pumping with as much strength as she had left, Amiya put her head down and pushed on. She ran so hard she was nearly out of breath, but despite her effort, she felt herself sliding backwards. *What in the name of the blasted Fallen? What's happening to me?*

"You will not escape our torment," the voice said. No, not one voice, but many. *"You will die, here. And remain forevermore."*

"So, we've moved from ... eternity to ... forevermore," Amiya panted.

The invisible force lifted her and pushed her straight back to the town and the waiting golems. *"You will remain here with those you mock by your very existence."*

This wasn't playing fair. She'd escaped those things and they were throwing her right back in? "You're mad at me because *you* messed up and tied yourself here? That's *your* fault, not mine!"

Helplessly suspended above the ground, Amiya sped back toward the golems. The nearest one raised its giant fist, ready to pound her into oblivion as soon as she reached it.

Amiya's lips wrinkled as her anger grew. They were taking their frustration and rage out on her. How was it her fault they did what they had to imprison themselves here? No. She would *not* die and sit here as some imprisoned soul, sulking in a rubble and skeleton-infested town with dumb stone people walking around.

Through her anger she felt the anger of the souls sending her back to their corlite creations. They were there, all around her. She didn't know how, but she could feel them.

In a fleeting moment of clarity, Amiya remembered when she'd touched the boulders in the Shattered Lands, and the intense feeling when she'd touched the foot of the golem. The corlite golem.

Magi use corlite to wield the essences. Can I be any stupider? Amiya's face lit in a wild grin. She focused on the nearest golem and drew essence through it. A massive surge of the power sprang to her call and she almost lost her grip on it from the shock.

The corlite golem lurched and dropped to a knee. The force propelling Amiya toward it fell away, but before she hit the ground, she used *air* to slow, then stop her fall.

Aware of the other advancing constructs, Amiya took her time to walk up to the nearest kneeling golem. She placed her hand on its bulky arm and tore every flicker of essence out of it. The stone monster pulsated in the four colors of the essences before falling over in a heavy, dusty crash. It lay still, like an emptied vessel.

Amiya turned to face the other nine golems. She opened her arms. "I'm right here." Never had she felt so confident, so *powerful*.

If the golems heard her, they gave no indication, only continued their steady advance. Amiya delved *air* and lifted a golem high into the air. It waved its arms and legs as if trying to balance itself while she moved it over the head of another.

Amiya didn't let it drop, but instead thrust it downward with every ounce of her strength. The golem crashed down on its comrade and both burst apart in a deafening explosion. Amiya didn't need to shield her eyes from the flying shrapnel. With little more than a thought, she created a barrier of *air*.

She walked towards the golems, fragments of the two she destroyed bouncing off her shield. She saw another one to the side and began drawing the power out of it. Created out of corlite and animated with the essences, these things were nothing more than gigantic essence rings!

The power flooded to her call and swirled around her. She reveled in the immensity of it all, basking in the ocean of power in which she swam. It was then she felt a tug of resistance.

Having dropped to its knees, the golem rose again as the essences returned to its body.

"What?" Amiya looked around. She took a step back as her confidence wavered. "What happened?"

"The power of the golems is not yours to command."

Amiya struck out fast and hard at the remaining golems. *I'd better finish them off while I've got all this power.*

She drew all four of the essences, ready to do just that, when she felt them being sucked away. Amiya's body jerked as if she'd been shoved. "What?" The power was gone. All of it.

"You know nothing of the power you play with. What you have can be taken."

"Yeah?" Nandi had always told her she thought fast when she was angry. Now her mind raced through many possibilities. Whoever these things were, they had the ability to pull the essences away from her. If they could do it, so could she.

She backpedaled as the golems advanced until her back hit an invisible barrier. *Going to play like that, are you?* Amiya's anger lit like a torch. She began to draw essence out of the nearest golem again.

As expected, the unseen speaker stopped her and began to pull it back to the stone construct. This time, Amiya reached out to her invisible enemy. With her senses, she sought out any indication of the power flowing through her adversary. She found it and immediately began drawing the essences from the unseen enemy as it had done to her.

She didn't hear the cry of fear with her ears, but she felt it with her mind. She drew the power out of her adversary while it pulled back. The golems hesitated briefly, then began their advance again.

"You are powerful but we are more."

"So there's more of you after all." Amiya let herself go, opened herself to her anger and the power she fought wrestle from her enemy. She felt its fear, then its sense of triumph just before another player entered the fight.

Amiya stumbled and fell onto her backside when the force of a second presence hit her. Then another, and another. They surrounded her as surely as she could see the golems doing the same. Then she noticed the eyes of the corlite monsters. Most of them stared lifelessly at her, but three looked at her with more purpose than an animated object.

"If you're not gonna play fair, you're gonna play without your toys." She focused on the three inhabited golems and attacked. As she drew the essence from them, she felt them fighting back. More souls joined in the fight, quickly overwhelming her.

Amiya's eyes widened. "How …" Her mouth fell slack as she realized that she could not only feel their emotions, ranging from anxiety to pure malice, but also their knowledge. She could read what they knew of the essences, their successes and failures, their mistakes and accomplishments. Everything.

She allowed them pull the essences away from her. So distracted were they in defeating her efforts, they didn't realize that she siphoned not the power of the essences from them, but their knowledge of it. It entered her mind and she drank it, as thirsty for the knowledge as a flower in a sun-parched valley.

Comprehension of the essences flooded into her. Not just one lifetime, but several lifetimes of research and understanding, diverse perspectives and approaches to the use and wielding of the power. She learned what they did to create the golems, the mistakes they made in thinking they could use the essences internally to enhance their physical prowess. Every bit of understanding they had of the essences were now hers.

She sensed that one of them finally realized what she was doing. They used *air* to push her the remaining distance toward the golems.

"Oh, no." Amiya laughed. "You can't really attack me. All you've got left is manipulating what's around you. Powerful ghosts. That's about all you are, isn't it?"

With a thought, she cut off the force propelling her, then drew the essences out of the nearest golem. It fell face first into the ground. She emptied another, then another. The souls of the dead howled at her, tried to stop her, but Amiya held the knowledge of every one of them. While they each had their own understandings of the essences, she had all of it combined.

They tried to pull the power away from her and she laughed. "Should'a let me go, like I *asked*." Her enemies tugged at power flowing to her grasp. Amiya held onto it as if holding her end of a rope, while the souls held onto many parts of the other end.

She yanked that rope of power out of their insubstantial grasps and was rewarded by their collective gasp. *"This is not possible. She is a child."*

"Oh, so you realized I'm a child and *still* tried to kill me?" Amiya struggled to contain her rage. She wanted to obliterate them all. They were evil. The world would be better off without them. If these souls were willing to murder a child, what else were they capable of?

"I could destroy you all," Amiya said. "You know that, now, don't you?" She felt their mingled anger and fear. Yes, they knew.

The three inhabited golems rushed her. Amiya first struck them with a punch of air, which knocked them back. "Hmm." As she'd done with the essence animated golems, she reached into the three inhabited by the evil spirits.

As one, the corlite constructs stopped mid-step. If they'd had human bodies, Amiya figured they'd be trembling. They should be, for they knew what she'd just learned. As all the collective knowledge of these souls swirled in her mind, she had a new realization.

Amiya's eyes widened with the realization that she could destroy their very being and assimilate it into herself. All of their once physical abilities with essences would be hers. Not only would Amiya possess their knowledge, but she would have all their experiences and abilities inside her as if they were her own. Many lifetimes of experience with the power.

"No! You know not what you do! It is abomination!"

"Says the one who just tried to kill me and now doesn't want to die."

"We are already dead, girl," the souls pleaded with her. *"This is worse than death."*

"Sad for you, then," Amiya said, already pulling the three spirts out of the golems and beginning to crush them. It almost felt like chewing a piece of food. Grind it up to bits and swallow. Somewhere in the back of her mind, a flicker of revulsion sparked. She shoved it back and kept going.

"Worse than death not just for us, but for you!"

"You'll say anything to get out of this," Amiya said. "It'll be over soon. Say night-night—"

"STOP, NOW!"

Amiya flinched. "What—"

The space in front of the three golems warped, and Estrella stepped in front of them. Without even looking back she whipped her arm backwards. All three golems shattered. The spirits inhabiting the golems shrank away in terror.

Amiya glared at her. "Oh, you're back. I'll deal with you, too. In a moment." She continued pulling at the now frantic spirits who knew they could do nothing to prevent their impending annihilation.

"Fool child!" Estrella severed the link between Amiya and the spirits as though with a knife.

The jarring effect of the separation nearly knocked her off her feet. Amiya struck out with a massive amount of all four essences at once. How easily they came to her call, now!

A horizontal storm of ice shards rained down on Estrella. Cones of fire and exploding earth and thrusting stalagmites assaulted her.

The ice shattered before it touched Estrella. The stalagmites burst apart, while the fire engulfed her, but did not burn her flesh.

Amiya had just enough time to frown in confusion when a shockwave of energy surged from the woman and hit her like the fist of a hundred golems combined.

The power was wrenched from her grasp as surely as she'd done to the golems and the evil souls. Her body lifted into the air and sped straight for the waiting Estrella.

Amiya jerked to a stop right in front of Estrella's angry violet glare. Her hand snapped up and gripped Amiya's chin. It was the first time the woman had ever touched her. She had a painfully powerful grip.

"You would destroy yourself and sully your very soul, idiot girl."

"Thanks for the warning," Amiya tried to answer, her voice muffled due to her cheeks being compressed. Her body still floated in a constant flow of *air*.

Estrella let her go, simultaneously releasing *air*. "Oomph!" Amiya hadn't expected the abrupt release and fell onto her still stinging backside.

"You would have made yourself a monster." Estrella turned away, walked a few steps, then turned back. "What you almost did is worse than anything the souls imprinted in this land could have dreamed of in their worst nightmares!"

Amiya felt the agreement of the invisible souls. She wanted to rage at them, hurt them, but the tiny part of her mind that had rejected what she'd almost done grew stronger. Estrella was right, she knew.

"Destroying the spirit of another and devouring it is the worst crime of nature you could commit. Such heinousness is worthy of *it*."

"It?" Amiya stood. "What's *it*? And how do you know? Have you done it before? If you have, how can you judge—"

"No, fool girl. I have not, nor would I ever. As rightfully reviled as the Fallen are, even *they* would not commit such an atrocity." Her anger seemed to dim at that. "Though they created the one who would—and will do just that."

Amiya stared at her. "What are you talking about? How do you know so much about what the Fallen would or wouldn't do? You talk like you know them. You seem to have all this vast knowledge. Did you collect it over thousands of years? What are you, an Illuminarian?" She said the last word with more than a little sarcasm to hide her fear.

A flicker of something unreadable crossed Estrella's violet eyes. "Yes, little one. I have collected knowledge and experience over thousands of years. But I am not an Illuminarian."

Amiya stood frozen; her fear as bright as the midday sun.

39

SELVETAR

Over a hundred pairs of eyes focused on Selvetar. Of the hundred, perhaps half held promise. Not the promise of acolytes becoming magi, and magi rising in the ranks, but the promise of becoming powerful to his needs.

The class of acolytes and new magi—for Selvetar did not teach aspirants—sat rapt on his every word. It wasn't often the first magus taught a class, but when he did, only students with the most promise were approved to attend.

"Corlite," he said, pointing to a diagram of the valued stone. "The conduit through which the essences flow is made up of literally thousands of minerals. It is a stone unlike any other in the world not simply because of its properties in relation to the essences, but because of its very makeup.

"It is as hard like any typical stone yet is the most malleable. Despite thousands of years of working with the stone, we still do not know all its uses. There are some historical claims that corlite was even used in the creation of large objects or even articles of clothing."

He scanned the classroom after that last statement. Expressions ranged from neutral, to intrigue, to apathy. At the front of the class,

Agra leaned forward. The boy's hunger practically shouted through his wide-eyed stare. That one would make a lover out of power itself, given the chance.

"The essences can be wielded in a myriad of ways we know of, but many more that have been lost to time. An example being that during the brutal wars of the First Age, magi had learned the technique of warping the space around themselves to step into a location as close as a few feet, or to as far as another part of the world."

Though they dare not scoff in his presence, many shifted in their seats, some going as far as to wipe a hand over their face or look down at their desk. Of course not all would believe. Not a single living magus that anyone knew of exhibited this capability.

He noticed that a good handful of students were still taking notes, however. They didn't look as eager as Agra, whom Selvetar suspected might start watering at the mouth, but they were focused. Many of these young and future magi studied without the need of homework. They spent as much time in the library as they did in their own rooms.

Selvetar looked them over with a mental nod of approval. He'd kept an eye on every student in this class. Of the lot, thirty already possessed as much knowledge in the essences as a five-year magus. They learned quickly, and exhibited a strong ability to absorb lessons and make adjustments.

The trait that most interested Selvetar, however, was each student's grasp with the essences. Each still had an affinity for a particular essence, but their proficiency with the other three was powerful enough that they could challenge a fellow magus of a different affinity.

"It is my intention to teach another class in a week's time," Selvetar said. "Should there be interest. How many present are interested?"

Every hand in the classroom rose into the air.

Selvetar nodded. "Your studies for the next week will center on the underworld, the immortals, and the war of the immortals."

That drew hushed gasps all around. All except the students of interest, though they, too, looked taken aback. "For those of you truly focused," he continued, "I would be interested to know what tunnels your studies lead you through. The Order of Magi is possessed of a rich and sprawling history."

He looked the class over for several moments. The students sat quietly, trying not to squirm when his gaze fell over one after another. "Dismissed."

Agra immediately came up and bowed. "Thank you for the privilege, First Magus," he groveled. "Your vast knowledge and perspective is unmatched in all the Order. I only wish to one day—"

"You have many hours of study ahead of you, Agra Red," Selvetar interrupted. "I expect nothing short of a mind filled to the brim with new insights gleaned through the short time you have allotted to you."

Agra bobbed into a bow again. "Of course, First Magus."

The boy swept out of the room in a swirl of red robes, leaving fifty students still writing notes. Selvetar stood at the head of the classroom, watching. Just his mere presence would have sent aspirants flying for the door upon class dismissal, and acolytes bobbing in apology on their way to the door. This group never looked up from their note-taking.

"I don't believe I said so much during the conclusion of this class that warrants such feverish recording," he said to the remaining group.

The students practically looked up as one. They looked from Selvetar to the door, wondering if he wanted them to leave.

Selvetar said nothing. He stood perfectly still, his iron gaze sweeping over the classroom. One by one, books gently closed, notes were folded and put away, and chairs emptied.

He watched twenty students move for the door, giving no chastisement or offer to stay. When the last student left, Selvetar looked to the remaining group of interest. All thirty waited in their seats.

Apprehension shown on their young faces, but the thirst for knowledge overrode any fear they might have of irritating him.

Selvetar smiled and went to close the door. "Now that only my true students are all present, let our lesson begin."

&

"GREETINGS AGAIN, SENIOR BROTHER," Selvetar said.

Brother Amerus Layun looked no happier to see Selvetar now than he ever had. He unsettled the man, who already held a distrust for magi in general.

Hands clasped behind his back, Amerus stood at the rail on the third-floor bridge, watching the team of singers below practicing songs and hymns in the Grand Choir Hall. "Greetings, First Magus. What brings you from your warm and cozy tower to my church?"

"How fares the archminister?" Selvetar asked.

"He's very happy with himself, as usual." Amerus answered. "Why have you come, First Magus? After the events of your last visit, I would have thought you'd be in the Altarra library, buried in books."

The choir hit a high note, their voices ringing throughout the hall and drifting up to the two men to envelope them like a warm quilt.

"You're not far wrong, Senior Monk ..." Selvetar blinked when the man's expression soured.

Amerus didn't seem to notice Selvetar had gone silent until several moments passed. The monk looked into Selvetar's questioning gaze, then back down at the choir. "It seems that title may not apply to me much longer."

Interesting. Selvetar arched an eyebrow.

Layun stared down at the singing choir, their soft but powerful voices rising and falling to the conductor's tempo. The thin baton bobbed and twirled in the conductor's delicate grasp, the unified voices of the choir dancing along.

After a while, Amerus glanced sidelong at Selvetar. "Abbot Bemious is growing old. I am being strongly encouraged to submit myself for the role of his replacement."

"This is not good news?" Selvetar asked.

"I'd rather not." Amerus's tone matched his expression. "My place is among the brothers, out in the world being of service." He waved a hand at the beautiful stained windows depicting various canonized and holy figures, blazing suns, and other works of art that cast their splendor upon the floor of the grand hall by the light of the sun. "Not doling out orders surrounded in opulence."

"Is that what your current abbot does? Dole out orders while surrounded in opulence?"

Amerus opened his mouth, then closed it again.

For a while they said nothing, just watched the choir and conductor. The choir finished their hymn and moved on to a livelier song. Selvetar watched with a tiny grin of appreciation. The voice of the choir buzzed with energy and sent it crackling throughout the hall, penetrating every corner, every inch of the place. Even two floors up, Selvetar felt the energy of their song flow through him.

The muscles in Amerus's jaws protruded, so tightly were his teeth clenched. "I would never suggest such a thing." He glanced at Selvetar again, and visibly relaxed … a bit. "But your point is well-taken. I do not want this responsibility."

"Some of the best leaders in history came to their station hesitantly."

Amerus snorted. "Your words are true, even if you do not share the sentiment, First Magus."

Selvetar's low, quiet laughter startled Amerus, who raised his eyebrows in surprise. The first magus spread his hands. "Is anyone without fault, soon-to-be-Abbot?"

Amerus responded with a long heavy sigh. "Why are you here, First Magus?"

Selvetar folded his hands in his voluminous sleeves and looked down at the choir, who were in the final notes of another song. "Have you ever thought about the similarities between the Brotherhood of the Source and the Order of Magi?"

"I try not to," came the short response.

"Why is that? It hasn't escaped my attention that your Brotherhood mistrusts the Order, yet you employ the same power as we."

"Not entirely," Amerus countered. "We of the Brotherhood do not wear the powerful tools of the Creator upon our person like a coveted bauble, nor do we use the power to suit our own agendas. We wield the power of the Creator sparingly, and with great care."

And far less effectively. Selvetar nodded slowly. "Given that, Brother Amerus Layun, what do you believe the Order of Magi actually does? Do you think we travel the world, confiscating corlite to augment our power? Do you see us huddling in the Tower of Magi and our other branches across the world, amassing wealth and power for the sake of it, or for some future agenda?"

"I don't know what you do, First Magus," Amerus replied tightly.

"If you know not what we do," Selvetar ventured, "then I feel compelled to ask why you so mistrust the Order of Magi?"

"You hold far too much power."

"Does the Brotherhood not hold as much?" Selvetar asked.

"Different. You use your corlite rings to devastating effect. Your knowledge of the essences is a vast resource you do not share."

Selvetar chuckled at the absurdity of that. "You would have us share our knowledge openly, with every person who comes knocking at our door?"

"Of course not. Discretion is ever a virtue. But your Order is secretive and secluded within itself, First Magus. Even in the middle of a vast city, you are distant and separate."

Selvetar responded with a faint nod. "There was a time when the Order of Magi mingled about the people. We served as advisors to ruling bodies and monarchs. We bolstered military efforts, assisted in healing."

"And yet, now you do so little."

"That is an unfair assessment, Brother Amerus. Though our regression is undeniable, it was necessary."

"I doubt that. The Brotherhood of the Source has remained to be a beacon of light and hope to the world through every age, through times light and dark."

"The Brotherhood provides a vastly different service than the Order," Selvetar said. "You are a man of intelligence. You know this. The presence of a number of magi in any civilization sowed seeds of jealousy and in some cases, paranoia in neighboring lands. Desperation can lead to disastrous consequences, Senior Brother. How many wars have been fought since the Order of Magi withdrew its influence?"

"Withdrew your influence?" Amerus gave him a dubious look. "Ever has your order flexed a great deal of influence over everything, First Magus."

"But not overtly," Selvetar argued. "Our folly was to stand tall and openly with the outside world, and it led to much difficulty."

At Amerus's impatient nod, Selvetar figured it was time to make his point. "The Brotherhood of the Source and the Order of Magi are not so different in our desire to serve the greater world. We both employ the essences through use of corlite to reach that end."

"Now we come to it," Amerus said. "What is it, then? Do you wish to negotiate with me about the stone? I assure you that we have little—"

"Your monks are proficient in its use and you employ your skills for the betterment of all," Selvetar pressed on. "My Order is no different. However …" He let the word hang until Amerus turned to face him.

"While I believe," Selvetar continued, "That the Order of Magi is best place is to exist alongside humanity and not in the middle of it, we are subtly moving away from that ideal. The enduring conflict between Jietar and the Teratoma and Dokayuk nations is gradually pulling us in.

"There are already magi, albeit a small number, sent by the magi master himself to assist the king of Marai. I find this concerning."

"And, you're telling me this why, exactly?" Amerus asked. "Are you planning to overthrow your magi master and wish for the Brotherhood to assist with your coup?"

Selvetar smiled fondly at that. "Of course not, Brother Amerus. I come to you as someone who values your insight and knowledge. The problems facing us are not confined to the Order's involvement in the conflict. There is a larger, darker matter that takes precedence."

He saw the subtle shift in Amerus's posture. The monk's eyes grew distant, as though Selvetar's words sent his thoughts some-place else.

"The Archminister swims in his pool of ignorance of what is coming," Selvetar continued. "I doubt not at all that Senior Brother Amerus, soon to be Abbot Amerus, if the church is smart, sees the truth of things.

"From Carlayn to Shiedra to your very own Vyne, comes news of rampaging four-armed monsters with skin like jagged rock lined with outer veins of lava. My studies inform me that these creatures are called drauk, and they are the heralds of—"

"The Ruination," Amerus said, his voice barely a whisper.

Selvetar nodded. "Jietar and the two Khatala nations battle each other over matters of practically no consequence given what's coming. The leader of my own Order has dipped his hand into the conflict, while all our efforts are best served preparing."

"Your words ring true," Amerus said. "But what is the purpose of them?"

"Merely that we work together, Brother Amerus. The Brother-hood of the Source and the Order of Magi have ever existed in a passively adversarial relationship, but we aren't so different that we cannot combine our efforts for the sake of humanity."

"Most would argue we are quite different, First Magus. I'm inclined to count myself among that number. Even our use of the corlite is different."

"Barely so."

"The most powerful brother with the stones might provide a challenge for one of your acolytes, maybe," Amerus admitted, not bothering to hide a sour expression. "Our entire focus with the stones and the power through which it flows bears similarity at best. Little more."

"All the more reason to aid each other, Brother Amerus. If we were the same, we would be exactly that, two heads of the same body. But our differences would complement each other."

Amerus narrowed his eyes. "What is your game, First Magus Selvetar. Are you in the midst of a power grab and wish to draw upon the power and credibility of the Brotherhood?"

Selvetar let his annoyance play across his face, just a quick flicker. It was enough.

The monk bowed his head in apology. "I retract—"

"It isn't an unreasonable suspicion, Brother Amerus, and not completely off the mark. The answer to your question is no. I am not planning to overthrow the magi master in a power grab. I am, however, displeased with his actions and his failure to heed my warnings.

"I still plan to serve as best I can, the Order of Magi, but I will do more. Through my own experimental curriculum, I've confirmed that the time it takes to properly train someone from aspirant to full magus can be greatly reduced."

"And this pertains to me, how?" Amerus asked.

"Magi do not train in physical combat. The Brotherhood does not train in advanced essence combat, but mostly defense and healing."

"You wish to marry the two? Did you not just say that if we were the same, what would be the point?"

"Not marry the two," Selvetar clarified. "Work together. Dark days are in our future, good Brother Amerus. Seeing monks of the Source and magi of the Order, side by side in our battle against a common foe will not only bring hope to the masses, but embolden them in the fight that will come to us all. The Ruination has no singular target other than the world itself."

"You propose an aggressive plan, First Magus."

Selvetar spread his hands. "No magus will interfere in any way with your discipline, just as I'm certain you would not interfere with ours. What I suggest is an alliance that would endure to ensure our survival of the coming war for the world itself. If that alliance survives into something lasting, all the better.

"What we can be certain about is that the destroyer and its Fallen are upon the world once more, and they will wipe us from existence if we do not stand together against them."

He waited patiently in the stretched silence as Amerus digested it all. The choir had finished its daily training and the hall attendants lit incense throughout the hall. The thick sweet scent drifted through the space, making its way up to the two men.

Amerus leaned on his elbows on the rail. "What you suggest has appeal, but I don't imagine your magi master would be any more willing to invite the monks into your tower as the Brotherhood would your magi."

Selvetar reached into a pocket in his robes and handed the monk a map. "There is a place marked where I and a number of students will train. We welcome the opportunity to do so alongside the Brothers of the Source.

"Staging a coup would be a potently stupid action to take," Selvetar said. "Only a fool would create conflict and divide resources when the blight is upon us. Many do not know, believe, or wish to believe what is coming. Nevertheless, we must prepare, and quickly. The darkness gathers itself. So too, must we."

NANDI

Nandi opened her eyes to a throbbing headache made worse by the violent shaking. Strong and none-too-gentle hands gave her another rough shake.

"Sister Nandi must wake up," Sama hissed in her ear. "Sister Nandi must wake up. *Now*."

The girl shook her again. Nandi's head felt like it would explode. She gritted her teeth and tried to push Sama away. "I'm awake, Sama. You can stop shaking me."

Nandi rubbed her forehead. Where was she, and what happened to knock her out? She rolled over onto her side and saw Amoura hovering in front of a man who stood with fists clenched so tight the veins in his arms bulged. His nostrils flared below his baleful stare; a stare directed at her. Everything came rushing back to Nandi in that moment.

Maybe Nandi should have taken Sama's cue and whispered her response instead of talking so loudly.

The Illuminarian, Malkiem, looked at her with a curious expression while Amoura stared at him. Floating above the ground like that, the magus looked as stiff as a board and very uncomfortable. Her robes were pressed against her body, and every so often she would wince.

Malkiem looked back to Amoura, his face a mask of anger. "Are you an underlord? A droughtlord? Or a magus turned from the light?" Amoura offered a strangled response that Nandi couldn't hear. Malkiem bared his teeth, and Amoura gasped.

"Hey!" Nandi shouted. "How about you put her down and we can talk about this like we're at least trying to be civilized."

"Quiet, child!" Malkiem barked.

"Put … her … down."

The Illuminarian looked at her with even more curiosity. "You will be *quiet*. You do not understand—"

"I said put her DOWN!" *Air* sprang to her call and she hit the Illuminarian with all of it.

Clearly he hadn't expected an essence attack, especially one so powerful. Malkiem's eyes widened. He reacted just quick enough to shield himself from the mass of air that plowed into him with the force of a charging elephant.

Amoura fell to the ground in a coughing, gagging heap as the man slid backwards. He looked at Nandi in appreciation. "Impressive, girl. I don't believe I've ever heard of so young an essence wielder with such power." He looked down at Amoura. "Clever."

Nandi's hear went out to Amoura, who struggled to gather herself. "She's not a droughtlord, or any of those other things you called her. She's a magus."

"Little better," the Malkiem snarled.

Nandi blinked. "What's that supposed to mean? You're on the same side—"

"You have no idea what you're talking about!" His voice boomed through the underground city, bouncing off stone walls and roaring through the vacant homes and buildings. "Just as you are a child, playing at what you hardly understand, so too, are they." He stabbed a finger at Amoura, who had managed to rise up to one knee.

"Look," Nandi said. "Whatever problem you have with magi, it has nothing to do with her. So why don't you calm down and we can talk."

"You freed part of Shurza," he said to Amoura, ignoring Nandi. "Have you any *idea* what that means? What age is this? Do magi no longer know the history? Do you not know of my fate? Mycia's? Typhirelli's? We paid a heavy price to seal that thing away from the world, and you just freed part of it! Do you not think it will find its other parts? It doesn't rest. It doesn't sleep. It will search until it merges with its other parts and becomes whole again!"

"We believe … that most … of it is already … free," Amoura gasped. She pushed herself to stand on wobbly legs. "Drauk have appeared. Tunnelers, serai. Cities have been attacked—" She stopped talking at the sight of his increased anger. "Illuminarian," Amoura said. "We don't yet know who set it free—"

"It was one of YOU!" Two huge cones of fire formed in the air, arched upwards, and crashed into either side of Amoura.

Nandi cried out when Amoura disappeared amidst the raging flames. One moment the magus had been standing there, the next, gone, incinerated. Nandi bared her teeth, her hands balled into fists at her side.

She delved all of the essences. Aided by the essence ring she'd taken from Jasindi, the power came more readily to her call than ever before. Spears of ice formed in the air in front of Nandi and sped toward Malkiem. Stalagmites thrust out of the ground, lifted into the air, and chased after the ice.

Malkiem barely gave her efforts a thought. The ice and rock burst apart before they got close. "I appreciate your power at such a young age, young lady, but you do not know what—"

"Neither do you!" Nandi shouted. Her essence ring flared brown and red. "You've been asleep down here while we've been up there fighting!" A huge chunk of earth broke free of the ground and hovered before her, broke apart and reformed into a spear, then lit afire. The flaming spear shot through towards the Illuminarian.

Malkiem arched an eyebrow. He turned his head toward the fiery spear and the oddest thing Nandi had ever seen, happened. One of his eyes glowed blue, while the other glowed silver. Two *arahs*?

The flames engulfing the rocky spear died as it broke apart. By the time it reached the Illuminarian, the missile was little more than airborne gravel. The gravel floated in the air and began to combine into much larger rocks.

Nandi took an unconscious step back as a cluster of rocks on the right turned to ice while the cluster on the left lit on fire. Behind the floating rock stood Malkiem, one eye now glowing a mix of silver and blue, the other, red.

She concentrated on *air* and *fire* as dozens of rocks of ice and fire flew towards her. She hit each with the opposite essence, hoping to burn away the ice and freeze and erode the fire rock like Malkiem had done. Her efforts did nothing. The missiles flew towards her uninhibited.

Nandi ran and threw herself aside. Ice and flame rained down around her. She curled into a ball and wrapped her arms over her head as fire roared in her ears and ice struck the ground in deafening, high-pitched explosions. When all finally went quiet, Nandi cracked her eyes open.

Malkiem stared at her, nodding in satisfaction. "Now be still, child. I will get you out of this place and from there, you are on your own."

So focused on Nandi was he, that the Illuminarian hadn't noticed the kneeling, flame-engulfed silhouette of Amoura Xanna.

Eyes pressed closed, teeth gritted, her thin braids whipping about her face, she had her arms crossed over her chest, curled fingers facing away from her body. She was keeping the flames at bay, without her ring!

Malkiem noticed Nandi's distraction and looked back to the

mini inferno he'd created as if he'd forgotten it was there. When he saw Amoura struggling not to be burned alive, he tilted his head. "This is a surprise." Once again, both his eyes glowed as red as the lava in the lavakhan's chamber Nandi had been in, so long ago now it seemed. "The Order of Magi has grown weaker with every passing age. I'd expected barely a sliver of the power to come to your call *with* your ring. Yet here you resist me without one."

Having blended with her surroundings, Sama crept behind Nandi and whispered in her ear. "Sama and Nandi must go. Must get away."

"We can't leave her to die," Nandi whispered back. "She saved our lives, Sama." She heard a plaintive growl, but nothing more. As quietly as she could, Nandi rose and delved again.

Malkiem frowned. "Enough, child!"

Nandi's essence ring burst apart while at the same time a chunk of the ground broke free. It burst into hundreds of pieces that flew toward Nandi and crashed against her. They stuck in place, combining with each other as though forming a second skin. They covered all of her body up to her face, solidifying until she stood encased in rock and unable to move.

"The Order of Magi began its downward spiral even before the last age in which we fought the blight. Your Order became infested with underlords and droughtlords, biding their time while breaking apart the Order of Magi from the inside. Only a droughtlord or a fool would have released the Shurza again. A shame you've turned to the blight. Only a hybrid wielder has a chance to defeat the incursion."

Nandi watched helplessly as Malkiem's body lit in flames larger than those engulfing Amoura. The flames rose nearly to the ceiling of the underground cavern.

Limited as her experience with the power was, Nandi couldn't have imagined the essences used this way, let alone so much of it. She delved again, knowing it would be harder now that her ring was destroyed. The power came to her call, though she didn't know what she could do with it to free herself.

She riffled through every memory she had of Selvetar's teachings and what she'd seen and experienced of wielding the power. She remembered sucking some of the air out of Jasindi's lungs to weaken her so that she could get her ring.

Nandi flinched away from that terrible thought, but forced herself through the memory anyway. All their lives were at stake. She focused on *water* and increased the moisture in the rock.

The roar of the gigantic torch that was Malkiem filled her rock-covered ears. Despite the immense power he wielded, the man seemed hardly to be exerting himself. Were the Fallen this powerful?

Amoura started to slump. She must be reaching the limits of her ability while Malkiem hadn't even gotten started yet.

Nandi felt the rock soften. Soon she felt the moisture on her skin. She flexed her arms and felt the wet earth give. While still concentrating on her task, Nandi opened her senses and felt Malkiem's power. She gasped, breathless as the immense power almost overwhelmed her.

She felt scratching from behind, then felt air on her back as Sama managed to dig part of her out. "Sister Nandi cannot defeat him. Will all die."

"I don't expect you to die with us," Nandi replied. "But I'm not leaving her." Sama's only response was to keep digging. Finally, the rock crumbled apart around her.

As soon as she was free, Nandi focused on the flames around Amoura and tried the same tactic she had against Jasindi. It worked too well. The fire flew away from the beleaguered magus and sped straight for her.

"Uh oh." Eyes wide as saucers, Nandi delved *air* and redirected the flames around her body. She remembered a time when Dad had taken her and Amiya with him on a spicetrade. They'd stopped to cook a meal, and when he finished, Dad had thrown dirt over the fire.

"Suffocates it," Dad had said. "Even fire needs to breathe air."

Still wielding *air*, Nandi once again drew upon the undesirable memory of her fight with Jasindi. As she had done with the flames assaulting Amoura Xanna, Nandi focused on the air feeding the fire. The flames died away.

"You're straining my patience, girl."

Nandi didn't know how his voice could be audible through that roaring fire. "You started it." She focused on *air* again and began pulling away the air feeding the Illuminarian's fire.

Malkiem's confused expression turned to one of appreciation. He simply watched as Nandi gradually killed the towering flames. Sweat trickled down the sides of her face. The effort took a lot more out of her than she'd expected.

Through force of will alone, she remained standing—albeit on wobbly legs—when the last of Malkiem's flames died away. The Illuminarian stared at her for a long time, then laughed and clapped. "Well done, little essence wielder. Well done." He bowed.

In front of her, Amoura was on hands and knees, head hanging as she struggled to catch her breath.

"Where did you learn such a thing?" Malkiem asked.

"You think I'm going to tell you that?" Nandi replied. "I don't think people normally give tips to the person trying to kill them."

"I'm not trying to kill you."

"Fine." Nandi indicated Amoura who was finally lifting herself up. "You're trying to kill *her*." Malkiem's face darkened, but before he could respond, Nandi pressed on. "I know you think she's a drought-lord or whatever that other thing was you said, but she's not. She saved our lives and battled a bunch of four-armed monsters with us."

Malkiem seemed to consider that. He looked at Amoura. "What age is this? The Third?"

Amoura held the man's gaze for a long time before answering.

"The Third Age passed while the Immortals and Shurza slept. You would call this the Fourth Age."

Her voice sounded strained. Nandi didn't know how Amoura was still conscious after that assault.

"Fourth Age," Malkiem breathed. "What must the world look like, now? What civilizations are left? Where are the others?"

Nandi glanced at Amoura, but the magus just watched the Illuminarian as he seemingly asked himself a stream of questions.

He finally looked at Amoura again. "You're sure? This is the Fourth Age?"

Amoura didn't answer, though her face tightened. Even from her distance, Nandi would have shriveled away from the woman's angry steel-colored gaze. Malkiem seemed not to notice.

He rubbed his chin and turned away from Amoura, walked a few steps, then turned back. "If your words are true and the Shurza is mostly free, there isn't much time."

"I tried to tell you that." Amoura's every word came out in a dangerously even tone.

Nandi watched her. Amoura stood still as a statue and clearly furious. But the magus said and did nothing. Just watched the distracted Malkiem as he paced back and forth.

"I'm free. The Shurza looms. The incursion is upon us." He stared hard at Amoura, then at Nandi. "As is the emergence." He started pacing again.

Figuring they were safe enough now that the man had calmed down, Nandi moved to stand beside Amoura. "He seems insane. Maybe we should just leave him."

"Being imprisoned with Shurza for hundreds of years would have destroyed anyone but an Illuminarian," the magus replied. "And even then …" she went quiet for a moment. "He isn't insane; but he is damaged."

"… battle the incursion, but the cost. The cost is so great. We barely sealed it away, last time." He looked back at Amoura and Nandi, then looked past Nandi, his expression curious. "A tatamble?" He bowed again. "I've made a grave error, it seems. If the elusive tatamble journeys by your side, you must indeed be of honor."

"We must return to the surface," Amoura said. "As you've said, there isn't much time. We must fortify for what's to come."

Malkiem looked at her. Had he heard a word the woman said? "What of the others? Mycia, Typhirelli, Dirge, Zeraphal, Amadon? Are they awake?"

"We don't know," Amoura admitted. "We found you by accident." She pointed back the way the came. "A tunneler destroyed a section of the ground at the other end of this cavern. We fell through and came this way."

Malkiem looked the way she pointed, then toward the ceiling of the cavern. "A long way to fall. Magi have actually mastered flight?"

"No, not flight—" Amoura tried to answer.

"You must know the history if you came this way and found me."

"I am not capable of—"

"Perhaps I've underestimated magi in this age." He looked at Amoura, then past her. "I must find the others before they do, or before the incursion." He walked past them.

"Hey!" Nandi snapped. "You gonna help us get out of here? We just—"

"There may yet be time for you to learn all you must," Malkiem said. "But that will wait. I must find the others ..." He stopped walking.

Several paces behind him, Amoura stopped and held her arm out protectively across Nandi.

"The Storm Swirl."

"The what?" Nandi asked. "Hey, wait!"

Malkiem took off in a run, jumped impossibly high into the air, and hovered several dozen feet above. "Only the hybrids can defeat the Shurza," he said. "We will need you."

They watched as the man glided away to the spot they had entered and lifted up and out of sight.

"That's great," Nandi said. "We free him and he leaves us down here." She looked at Amoura. "I hope there's a way out. I don't want to die in a cave, ancient and beautiful or not."

She stared at the magus, who apparently had contracted Malkiem's affliction of ignoring people. Amoura continued to look in the direction the man had gone. She looked at her hand, and the finger that had once held her essence ring and whispered a single world. "Hybrid?"

EMIEL

Emiel slid his hand over his torso, protected by boiled leather that would do nothing to protect him against the thrusting rock sword of a drauk. He looked down at the helm under his arm. That would do nothing at all to prevent the swing of a drauk's club from crushing his head or breaking his neck.

"Giving up already?" Bone teased when Emiel sat the helmet on the floor of the parapet.

"What good'll it do? Even you're teliak helmet won't stop a descending club from pushing your head down between your shoulders.

A couple soldiers laughed nervously. Bone shrugged. "True."

Emiel mentally ran through everything he'd ever seen Amoura do with the essences. He thought back to his time in the Maze, and his desperate fight with the bearverine.

"Soldiers of Shiedra!" Adolphus bellowed. "These are not human foes. They are not possessed of remorse or empathy. You've fought these things before. They have not flesh and blood like ours, but that of hot rock, and blood like lava. That blood is not hot enough to melt your weapon if you pull it free fast enough. The skin will turn aside a slicing blade, but it can be pierced.

"They move with purpose because they are controlled by the man walking in the center. Archers! Focus your fire on him only. I don't know where these things come from, but we'll leave it to the Creator to sort them out, once we send them to Him."

Emiel didn't know if it was a good thing or not that the drauk moved more controlled under the power of the droughtlord. *Not a good thing*, he decided.

"Most of you have seen what these things are like," Adolphus went on. "Slashing and swinging motions, turning in every direction. They fight with a brutish craze none of us can match. Remember your training and use your mind to defeat a stronger, faster foe."

The enemy came to within a couple hundred feet of the wall and stopped. The droughtlord looked up at them and Emiel ignored the chill he felt. That was his enemy. No one else here would be able to fight him. All these soldiers, and even Bone, could do was hold off the Drauk in hopes that Emiel could defeat the droughtlord. *No pressure.*

Bone leaned close. "You ready for this?"

Emiel took a deep, steadying breath and nodded. "As ready as I can be." To his surprise, the mercenary patted him on the shoulder.

"You've had many days around that grumpy woman. You'll do fine." He shrugged again. "Or we'll all die. Either way, it'll happen as it does."

"Thanks," Emiel said dryly.

"I'm with you, Emiel."

"Lief?" Emiel glanced about while trying not to look conspicuous. "Where are you?"

"Don't worry about that," came the reply. "I'm here."

"Thank you," he whispered.

Adolphus walked up to him and gripped the side of his shoulder. "You ready, young man?"

"I'm ready."

The Captain looked him hard in the eye, then gave a curt nod.

"Good. Fight wherever you're best of use but stay out of the way of my men." He turned away and started down the ladder where the bulk of the Shiedran force waited.

"What about you?" Emiel asked Bone, while Adolphus gave his speech to the soldiers below.

Bone jabbed a thumb over his shoulder. "You think I'm going down there to get stuffed in with that lot?" He shook his head. "Nope. As much as it makes me queasy to admit, you're our best bet of beating that guy. And since you couldn't swing a sword to save your life, it's left to me to babysit you out there."

"You're melting my heart, mercenary."

"Eh." Bone shrugged again. "Plus, we've got to find your family."

The gates opened and the Shiedran troops poured out. Adolphus stood at the center of the formation, barking orders and organizing the troops. There was no banner man, as this was not a battle against a human force.

"They're all on foot," an archer beside Emiel noticed.

"Riding out on horses would only get the animals slaughtered," Emiel said. "And the riders right along with them. Best to be able to maneuver with your feet on the ground."

Adolphus worked his way to the front of his ranks and drew his sword. The sound of hundreds of swords sliding from sheathes rang in Emiel's ears. The captain of the Shiedran armed forces led his force in a steady march toward the advancing drauk.

Emiel wiped sweat from his brow, then his face as more sweat formed. He was nervous, but not *that* nervous. He looked around to see everyone else sweating as well, then looked up at the cloudless sky. Spring had not yet fully waned. How could it be this hot?

He looked back at the once again steadily advancing drauk force, or more specifically, the droughtlord at its center. "Nice play."

"What?" Bone asked, he shifted a bit, the only indication from the stoic young warrior that he too felt the uncomfortable heat.

Emiel delved for *air* and *water*. After a few moments, the essences came fully to his call. He'd need to be faster once the fighting started, but he still found the power faster now than before.

Once he had the two essences fully available Emiel focused on the immediate area. A chilling breeze countered the stifling heat. He held to it until he was sure everyone wasn't about to drop from heat exhaustion, then intensified his efforts, concentrating on the droughtlord.

Emiel focused on his enemy and sent freezing rain showering over them. The drauk didn't seem to like that, as they roared and cursed. He felt the droughtlord countering his efforts, but he pushed harder. Soon the freezing rain turned to hail.

The man stopped walking, his surrounding force of monsters stopping with him. The hooded figure looked straight at the parapet and Emiel could swear the man looked directly at him.

A few heartbeats later a jolt of electricity confirmed his suspicion. Emiel flew backwards and would have plummeted over twenty feet to the ground below if Bone hadn't had such quick reflexes. The mercenary snapped his hand out and grabbed Emiel's ankle as he lifted off the ground. "Urgh. You're heavy, spicetrader. Get back up here and stop playing around."

Emiel hung upside down, teeth chattering as his body involuntarily convulsed through the electric shock. He tried to clamp his teeth shut to keep from biting off part of his tongue.

He started to curl himself up to grab hold of the ledge to help Bone, but his muscles wouldn't obey him. Once his mind started to clear, he delved *air*, and created a steady gust of wind to help the mercenary lift him over the edge.

Emiel rolled onto his side and watched as the archers let fly. They fired volley after volley, but he knew it would do no good. He'd barely finished that thought when the archers threw themselves to the floor an instant before a storm of shards crashed against the wall and whizzed overhead.

Next the heat returned, hotter this time. Emiel balled his fist and banged it on the parapet floor as he pushed himself upright. *Let's see what I've got.*

He peeked out of one of the embrasures and saw that the drauk had begun running toward the Shiedrans. Pikemen took the front and second row of the line, while swordsmen and women waited behind them.

The archers went back to their stations at the arrow loops and launched another volley. The missiles burned in the air before they got anywhere near the droughtlord.

Emiel delved *air* and *water*. He created dozens of arm-length ice shards and set them hovering beside the nervous archers, who eyed them and Emiel with apprehension. He gave them a reassuring nod, then focused back on the droughtlord. Sweat poured down the side of his face. He needed to stop this heat.

The archers let fly again, as did Emiel. He set a good bit of energy behind the missiles, and the ice shards sped ahead of the arrows. While the droughtlord destroyed the projectiles, Emiel delved *earth*. Stalagmites burst out of the ground, impaling several charging drauk. Only three of the creatures hit the sharp rock hard enough to be stopped. The others were delayed only long enough to snap the stalagmites apart and keep running.

He delved *fire* and sent a swirling cone of flame speeding toward his target. The droughtlord lifted his hands and created a stream of water that collided with the fire.

After several heartbeats they broke off their attacks. Emiel started to delve again when the sound of zapping electricity preceded several archers flying away from the parapet. Unlike Emiel, the soldiers had no one to grab hold of them. They fell convulsing in mid-air, plummeting over twenty feet to the ground.

Emiel cringed. The fall might not kill them, but it put them out of the fight. He turned back to look out the embrasure just as a flaming ball of fire hit the wall beneath where he, Bone, and two archers stood. The impact shook the parapet, and the afflicted section broke apart beneath them.

Something inside Emiel awoke. His instincts came alive, and he, Bone, and the screaming archers slowed in their descent until the touched down on the grassy field.

Several hundred soldiers blocked his view from the droughtlord, but it hardly mattered. The forty-seven remaining drauk and a single droughtlord could decimate ten times their number.

"Stay here," he said to the archers, and started walking.

"Feeling tough?" Bone asked, walking beside him.

Emiel's response surprised himself as much as the mercenary. "Yep."

He heard the indecipherable curses of the drauk over the ringing of steel and the screams of the dying. "Those things'll probably wipe Adolphus's soldiers out before the droughtlord has to lift a finger," Bone said.

"I need to get there faster," Emiel said. His voice sounded oddly calm to his own ears. "I can't wait, Bone. You'll have to reach me."

"Like you can really run faster than me, spicetrader ..."

Bone's voice fell away as Emiel jumped and delved *air*. Whether he wielded the power was some sort of instinct or something else, Emiel simply lifted high into the air and arced over the soldiers still not engaged with the drauk. He glided over the embattled soldiers being cut and beaten down by the four-armed heralds of the ruination.

The droughtlord was watching him, and as he began his descent, Emiel saw the intrigue on the man's cracked and leathery face.

A storm of ice spears sped towards Emiel. He blasted them apart with a burst of air. A wall of fire rose in front of him, and Emiel sent a geyser of water funneling into it, then delved air and pushed the steam toward the droughtlord.

While his adversary used *air* to easily defeat the skin-melting steam, Emiel landed and struck with ice, fire, and rock. He hurled frozen and stone spears, and rolling waves of fire. The droughtlord countered and struck back.

Back and forth the two fought, wielding the four essences to devastating effect. The earth rumbled as they broke apart sections of the ground and formed them into heavy weapons. A speeding shard of ice narrowly missed Emiel's midsection. It dealt him a stinging slice across his hip, and another nearly took him in the shoulder.

He fell onto his side, rolled back to his feet, and struck with *earth*. He felt the presence of another wielding the same essence, augmenting the effect of his attack. Lief.

The rolling quake hit the droughtlord as if it came from the ocean. "Together, my friend." Though he didn't get a response, he knew she heard him.

The ground around the droughtlord exploded, re-formed into boulders, and fell upon him. He broke them apart only for them to combine again into smaller rocks.

Emiel struck with stinging frigid wind followed by gouts of flame. The droughtlord defended himself through it all, but he started to give ground. From behind, Emiel heard cursing drauk and fighting soldiers. He half turned to pick out his targets, and sent several giant lances of ice speeding into the backs of seven drauk.

He turned back to the droughtlord to see his adversary creating two opposing walls of ice. The cloaked man with the sun-parched skin slapped his hands together, and the walls of ice closed in to crush Emiel.

Once again, an instinctive knowledge of the power came to him. Fire erupted around Emiel's arms and hands, and he thrust them out at his sides. The ice walls rapidly melted around his fiery limbs. Emiel kept his arms out at his sides then, as his adversary had done, clapped his hands together in front of him.

A thunderous wave of fire shot toward the droughtlord. The

arah in his eyes glowed silver, then blue as he tried to counter the attack but there was too much power behind it.

The man lit up like a torch, but even as he screamed in agony, the man kept his mind about him enough to douse the flames using *water* to create its physical namesake.

Emiel used the same water his enemy created and froze it. Caught unaware, the man dropped to the ground, the heavy ice sheets crashing on top of him. Emiel created ice sheet after ice sheet, each no less than two feet thick, and dropped them on top of the droughtlord.

He created huge boulders of stone and dropped them on his enemy. The ice shattered under the weight of the stone.

The droughtlord lay on his back, blood staining the corner of his mouth. He had his hands out in front of him as he kept a steady flow of wind to hold back the crushing assault.

Emiel thought of how he'd used the man's delving of *water* against him. He reached out as if with his own hand, and grabbed hold of the power. The droughtlord's eyes widened when *air* was suddenly yanked away from him. Emiel hit him with a wall of its namesake, then hit him with a wall of *earth*.

The droughtlord skidded across the ground, only to be lifted by a sudden plateau of ground springing up beneath him. When the lift stopped, he kept going up. Now mid-air, the droughtlord managed to twist his body toward Emiel and hit him with a jolt of electricity.

With a steady flow of air, he righted himself and leveled an angry snarl Emiel's way.

All Emiel could do was endure the convulsions as the electricity coursed through his body. Through the pain of his seizing muscles, he felt the energy around him, felt the humid resonance from the electric shock the droughtlord had created in the air.

Though his mind couldn't explain it, Emiel felt in his body what his enemy had done, and his body committed it to memory. He stopped convulsing and rolled onto his hands and knees. When he looked up, the droughtlord—having finally landed—stood a couple dozen feet away. The man's murderous glare bordered on madness.

Emiel launched a barrage of ice spears, then stone spears. He sent a blast of water toward his adversary, and the man created a shield of air around himself. With new muscle memory similar to a swordsman who'd trained for years on a single stroke, Emiel delved *air* and *water*.

The droughtlord continued to resist the watery blast, the bombardment of rock, and the flying shards. Emiel sent forth a bolt of electricity that lit the flow of water from himself straight into the *air* barrier.

A crackling explosion threw the droughtlord from his perch and shook the ground. Emiel felt the buzzing electricity in his teeth, but it was small enough that he could shrug off. He ran toward the droughtlord, holding all the essences ready. His right arm lit afire while rock lifted and formed around his left.

Still shaking, the robed droughtlord struggled to hands and knees and created a wall of ice between them. Emiel struck the wall with a fist made of stone, then struck it with fist made of fire. Several one-two punches and the ice wall broke apart even as it melted.

Emiel saw the red glow of the droughtlord's *arah*, and he held his forearm out in front of him. A large stone shield formed on his arm that nearly caused him to topple over. *Too heavy*. He dropped to a knee and made himself as small as possible just as a wave of fire fell over him and blasted around the sides and top of the shield.

He delved *air*. With a steady flow swirling upwards underneath the stone shield, Emiel was able to lift it and move forward. The raging flames whooshed around him. If the flames themselves didn't kill him, surely this oven-like heat would.

The fire abruptly winked out, and Emiel heard a loud grunt. When he looked around the stone shield, he saw the droughtlord picking himself up off the ground. A patch of crumbled earth lay behind him. Lief.

Emiel threw another electric shock into the man, sending him into uncontrollable spasms. He delved *air* and hit him with its namesake. After being thrown into the air, tumbling and convulsing, the effects of the shock finally started to wear off.

For a while, the droughtlord didn't move, and Emiel thought the fight might be over. He signed when his enemy stirred, then rose again.

Emiel growled a curse that would have had his daughters' hands on their hips, glaring at his hypocrisy. He set a towering cylinder of fire swirling around the droughtlord. The man looked about himself, then back at Emiel.

"I can't imagine why you're looking at me like that," Emiel said. "We didn't attack you. *You* came *here*."

"Do you think this little fire will hold me?" The droughtlord's voice sounded like stone grinding against stone. Through the fire, Emiel saw his cracked and leathery skin. So many lines crossed his face that it looked like a map. "You will die here, and this city will serve the Fallen."

"Nobody's serving anybody. You're beaten. Yield and you'll be taken—"

A sudden whoosh of freezing air hit the fire. Emiel fell back. The cold was so intense that it burned his skin. The cylindrical barrier stood now as flames frozen solid. It would have been beautiful if not for the evil inside of it.

Emiel shielded his eyes with his forearm when the ice exploded. The fragments slowed to stop, gathered together into a long shard of ice and sped toward his heart. Emiel barely threw himself aside in time.

The shard struck the ground with such force, soil washed over him. He stood and swiped a hand over his face. "You're seriously trying to kill me?"

Head tilted to the side, the droughtlord looked at him as if he'd lost his mind. "Stand right there, fool, and I'll confirm your question." His eyes glowed red, but they flickered out when a chunk of earth struck him from behind.

"You can't reason with him, Emiel!" Lief again. Emiel looked around. Where was she? "I know you don't want to, but you have to stop him no matter what that means."

Emiel delved again. *Maybe I can injure him. Knock him unconscious.* He struck out with a thrust of air equal to the punch of someone twice his height. He threw chunks of rock large enough to deal great injury.

The droughtlord defeated his efforts all while staring murderously into his eyes. He hurled a wave of fire, then created a shard of ice larger than his body and sent it speeding towards Emiel.

Great amounts of power flowed between and around the two of them. The bombardment grew so intense that Emiel now functioned on instinct alone. He broke apart rock, shattered ice projectiles, froze fire, and marched toward his adversary.

He could feel everything the man was doing, and every time he launched an attack, a tiny reflex in Emiel's mind urged him to snatch the power out of the air and use it. He kept trying to understand, which kept him on the defensive even as he moved ever closer.

A boulder hit the ground beside him and lifted Emiel into the air. The droughtlord laughed while breaking apart a rocky spear—obviously created by Lief—aimed at his head. While Emiel was still airborne, the droughtlord formed a giant blade of ice. The blade shot straight for his chest.

With his death speeding towards him, Emiel's mind shut down and instinct took over. His body and the blade stopped moving at the same time. Emiel's body turned until he floated upright, and the giant blade of ice rotated until its tip aimed at the droughtlord.

Emiel and the blade sped toward his adversary. Stone broke away from the ground in every direction. The chunks of rock lifted into the air and gathered around Emiel. Balls of fire lit in the air and followed the stone and ice.

The droughtlord fought off the wave of ice, fire, and stone. He created a shield of air and Emiel pounded it relentlessly. The ground beneath his adversary exploded.

When the droughtlord tried to use *air* to right himself, a storm of giant rocks flew in and exploded all around him. The concussive force of the blasts left the man in a semiconscious daze. Ears and nose bleeding, the droughtlord tried to lower himself while offering some meager offense, but Emiel swatted his efforts aside.

"You will not win." The grayish, leather-skinned man looked at Emiel, blood seeping through his clenched teeth. "The blight will take you and everything and everyone you love."

Amiya, Nandi, and Amoura's faces flashed before Emiel's eyes. A stalagmite burst out of the ground angled for the drought-lord's back. It ran through his back and out of his chest, lifting him off the ground even as a spear of ice took him in the neck.

As he hung there suspended while his life drained away, the man slowly turned his head toward Emiel and opened his mouth.

Before they could make eye contact, Emiel delved a massive amount of *fire* and swept it over the droughtlord. In the span of several hammering heartbeats, the fire died away and all that remained was a scorched stalagmite.

Emiel stared at it for a long time. He'd killed a man. No matter the circumstances, he had ended another person's life …

The clang of steel, Shiedran battle cries, and the curses of the drauk filled his ears. Emiel turned and ran toward the battle. Several drauk in front of him spun circles, hacking and clubbing, stomping, cursing. Dead soldiers lay all around them while others darted in from the side or behind to strike a blow, then retreat.

Emiel lifted the nearest drauk into the air and feathered them with spears of ice. By the time the monsters fell back to the earth, they'd already crumbled apart.

Having seen what he'd just done, the soldiers parted for him.

Emiel jogged through the Shiedran force, dispatching the heralds of Shurza as he went. Somewhere along the way he heard Bone's voice, and the young mercenary appeared at his side. The boy yelled something, likely a sarcastic quip, but Emiel didn't hear.

He felt the power coursing through the drauk. He felt the heat flowing from the tiny rivulets of lava coursing through the inner and outer veins of rocky bodies. He felt the power in the stone that sustained them.

There's an easier way. Emiel sucked the lava out of several drauk as soon as he reached them. The monsters, all mid-attack, simply slowed and fell over. Emiel passed as they broke apart.

On he went, dispatching the horrid creatures, Bone at his side, a contingent of Adolphus's forces surrounding him. They were near the wall when he came to the last remaining drauk; he dispatched three of the four with little effort.

The fourth struggled to push forward despite two pikemen having run their weapons through its midsection, and a third through its back. A bloody Captain Adolphus sheathed his sword and held out his hand. A soldier stepped forward and handed him her pike.

Captain Adolphus charged in and ran the pike into the drauk's side, between its upper and lower arms. The thing cursed and turned about, dragging the soldiers with it. Another pikeman stabbed it from the other side.

Adolphus set his feet and with an effort, yanked the pike out of the rocky creature. "Retract!" The soldiers pulled their weapons free, then on Adolphus's order, they stabbed again. Chunks of the thing fell off its body and its movements greatly slowed. Finally, it fell to its knees, and Captain Adolphus released the pike, drew his sword, and stepped in. The drauk suddenly lunged to sweep its huge rocky sword at the captain. Its head suddenly snapped back, and when it came forward again, Emiel saw an arrow sticking out of one of its eyes. He looked toward the wall to see the short figure with flaming red hair standing on top of one of the embrasures.

Ailith lowered her bow and stared at an approaching archer until he stopped and backed off.

"Feisty," Emiel said.

"You've no idea," Bone replied.

Adolphus moved in before the barely affected drauk could attack. He swung his sword into its throat, pulled it free and chopped again.

The sound of steel sliding on stone rose above the cheers of the Shiedran soldiers until finally the rocky head fell from it shoulders and thumped on the ground.

All watched as the last drauk crumbled apart. Emiel and Adolphus locked eyes, and the captain walked over and grabbed his shoulder. The man had an iron grip.

"Well done," Adolphus said. He turned to look over his battered troops. News of the battle's conclusion had already begun to spread. Medics and civilians poured out of the once barricaded city walls to tend the injured and carry off the slain. "Back to Shiedra!" Adolphus ordered.

"Thank the Creator there weren't more of those things," he said in a quieter voice to Emiel and Bone.

"We were lucky," Emiel replied. "We've seen several types of monsters attacking cities. I don't understand why they only sent this kind."

"Maybe they thought the presence of the droughtlord would be enough," Bone suggested.

"Who're *they*?" Adolphus asked.

"The Fallen." The captain's brow creased at that. "It's true," Emiel said. "These monsters," he indicated the crumbled remains about the field. "Drauk, are the beginning. A blight has been unleashed on the world, and these things are the heralds. It's going to get a lot worse."

Adolphus's stony face hardened even more. He pulled aside two passing solders. "You," he said to one of them. Report to the royana, now. I'll be there soon." The soldier saluted and ran off as

Adolphus turned to the second. "Lieutenant Braga should be back or returning soon with his force. Find him and tell him to begin fortifications, then report back to me." He turned back to Emiel and Bone. The man was not happy.

"What is it?" Emiel asked. "Things are sure to get worse, but why the urgency now?"

"That was a test," Adolphus answered. "If what you say is true, the Fallen or whoever sent those things to us were testing our defenses, our force, our numbers."

Emiel nodded as he came to understand. "Then, do what needs doing, Captain."

"What of you?" Adolphus asked. "Your aid was instrumental, today."

Emiel felt regret as he shook his head. "I can't remain. I have—"

"Son," Adolphus interrupted. "I know your story, and I appreciate it. The Creator Himself knows I do, as I've children of my own. But until you discover where they are, you're roaming the lands without direction and doing no one, not even yourself, any good. Stay and fight with us. You're new to wielding that power of yours? Hone it here."

Emiel sighed. The man was right. His ladygirls and Amoura were lost to him. Until he found any scent of their trail to follow, he could well be moving away from them instead of towards.

"Whatcha got, spicetrader?" Bone asked him.

Emiel looked at the scuffed and bloodied mercenary. Could Bone even call himself that anymore? A true mercenary would have long ago left or offered his services for a high price. "Stay and fight."

Adolphus nodded and gave his shoulder another squeeze, then turned away. As the clinking of the captain's armor diminished, Emiel and Bone looked out over the battlefield. Soldiers and civilians respectfully lifted their slain comrades and carried them back to the city while others chased away opportunistic carrion crows.

"I know you want to find them, Emiel," Lief said. Emiel looked down to see his tinfar companion standing beside him. She looked up into his eyes, her clay-brown orbs so sincere. "It must be terribly heartbreaking not to search for them, but you must continue to learn and grow in your power for what's to come."

"I know," Emiel said. The monsters of the supposed underworld were only part of the problems ahead. He'd have to deal with the Order of Magi at some point. Once word spread across the land and people began to accept the reality of what was coming, Shiedra and every other city in Marai would call to the Order to bolster their forces.

Somewhere out in the world, Nandi and Amoura looked after each other. Though he'd never stop worrying, he knew his daughter couldn't be in better company. He said a silent prayer to the Creator that Amiya was equally lucky. Having not seen his other daughter with Nandi tore at Emiel's heart, but she was alive, he knew it. Though a large part of it was desperate hope, he knew deep in his heart that Amiya was still alive.

EPILOGUE

Dan Petrie sat down on the cold stone floor of the underground cavern. From the stale air, to the darkness, to the areas where sound traveled no farther than arm's length then echoed through an open space, so much of this place reminded him of where it all began. *Where we began it all*, he reminded himself.

Just thinking about that terrible, fateful day when he, Jack, and Mick stumbled upon the chamber of evil made him want to empty his stomach on the ground. A simple dig, and now the world might end.

Dan looked down the trail. Seven torches lined the snaking pathway leading uphill to his position. The men and women were exhausted, as was he. But unlike the others, guilt pushed Dan beyond his fatigue. Every day he pushed them to their limits, hiking on for hours against their protests until Anglyn had advised him to be easier on the others. "You keep pushing this hard, you'll be doing this by yourself," she told him.

He looked down the trail at the tall woman. She sat cross-legged on the stone floor as well, torch leaning against a nearby piece of elevated stone while she ate a snack. She was right, of course. Just because Dan felt the crushing weight of responsibility for what he and his dead companions had set upon the world didn't mean he should run his team into the ground.

The torches started moving in his direction again. Dan waited until they reached him, then called for them to gather around. Flickering torchlight danced across seven dirty faces. Anglyn stood to one side as she always did, judging the mood of the group.

"I know I've promised you all a lot," he began.

"A *lot*," one of the gathered grumbled. A few murmurs of agreement floated about the team.

Dan held up a hand. "I know your frustration, believe me. But we must be careful."

"Because we don't want to set more evil out in the world," came the sarcastic response. A round of chuckling ensued.

Dan didn't bother trying to convince them. These men and women were here because the potential to make a rare discovery held more sway than their skepticism or outright disbelief of his claims. "Let's just get moving," he said.

The procession continued their uphill hike, slowing when they came to a long stone bridge with nothing but a black, infinite drop on either side. Who built this? How?

At the end of the bridge, the path snaked downwards, then across waist-high water under a low stone ceiling. Several hours and several breaks later, all of Dan's research and preparation paid off.

The pathway ended at two sets of steps leading to a platform. The torchlight didn't reach far enough to see the full size of it, but even the bit Dan could see looked quite large.

"Dan, look."

He turned to see Anglyn pointing at a sconce set in a towering stone pillar.

"There's some sort of oil in this. It will probably burn."

"What makes you think that?" another digger asked.

"It's in a sconce obviously made for fire," she explained. "Might as well try it."

"Might as well," Dan agreed, nodding at the sconce.

Anglyn tilted her torch into the sconce. Flames danced in the iron sconce for several heartbeats, then a trail of fire climbed a tiny, narrow stone bridge that had been concealed in the darkness. Another sconce lit at the top of a stone pillar on the other side of the platform.

"Nicely done," Dan said as he moved to another pillar. He lit the sconce attached to the side, which lit the pillar in the distance. He went to that pillar while Anglyn went to the one opposite hers. They each lit the sconces, which in turn lit the first two.

Four streams of fire traveled overhead to the middle of the dark platform and lit a massive sconce held aloft by larger versions of the fire bridges attaching the pillars.

As soon as the fire collected in the giant sconce, the firelight illuminated a woman floating upright in the center of the platform. She drifted up and down as if floating on a lazy breeze.

Dan's eyes widened while his mouth fell open. He shouldn't be surprised. Every bit of his extensive studies in every library he'd visited spoke of chambers that housed the Illuminarians. No, not surprised. Awestruck and terrified.

Anglyn's voice stopped him mid-step as he began up the stairs. "Are you sure, Dan? Are you absolutely sure?"

Dan looked over at her, still standing next to the pillar thirty feet away. He looked across the platform to see the cluster of diggers all huddled together, staring awestruck at the floating woman. "What choice is there?"

"You said that three, or maybe more, were trapped with that thing," Anglyn said.

Well, looks like she believes me, now. Dan looked from her back to the other diggers. Likely they *all* believed him now. Whatever smug satisfaction he might have had couldn't take hold in the face of what he was about to do. Or try to do.

He approached the floating woman. Her short black hair shimmered in the torchlight, giving her sleeping, youthful face a serene look. If she were standing, Dan didn't think the woman's head would even reach his shoulder. Such a short and fragile-looking woman; an Illuminarian?

Dan swallowed his doubt. What else would she be? All the books and notes, the historical texts and accounts of the end of the last Battle of the Immortals left trails of clues to where each of the sleeping Illuminarians resided.

"I can't believe it's really her," Anglyn whispered.

Dan's heart nearly stopped at the sound of her voice, right next to him, now. He looked at her, then back to the floating Illuminarian. "Mycia," he breathed.

Anglyn gripped his arm. "Don't the historical accounts speak of her being somewhat passionate?"

"Passionate." Dan snorted. He walked a circle around the floating woman and stopped in front of her again. She looked so serene, as if in a blissful rest. Her legs and arms hung bent and lax, her head just slightly lowered.

"You falling in love?" Anglyn teased.

Dan blinked, then felt heat rising to his face. He hadn't realized he'd been staring. "Passionate puts it mildly. By all accounts, this woman is—"

"Volatile?" Anglyn offered. "Harsh? Sharp? Relentless? Crazed?"

Dan patted the air through every word. "I really hope she can't hear you, Anglyn."

"She's asleep." Anglyn waved a dismissive hand. "Are you sure about this? She may be an Illuminarian, but everything we've studied about them suggests she was extreme in every way. And she was one of the three trapped with that *thing*."

Anglyn still couldn't bring herself to speak Shurza's name. Dan didn't blame her for that. Just thinking it made him uneasy. "What choice do we have? The Fallen are free and so is … that thing. If we don't find and free the Illuminarians, the world will end."

"Kinda dramatic, don't you think?" one of the other diggers called from across the platform.

Everyone started moving closer, but Dan held out his hand. "Stay away. The last thing we need is for her to wake up surrounded." The diggers all looked at each other and moved back.

"How do you plan to do this?" Anglyn asked.

Dan knelt and shrugged off his travel pack. He fished around in one of the pockets until his fingers closed around a rough piece of stone.

Anglyn pressed a hand over her mouth to muffle her gasp. "Is that what I think it is?"

"Corlite," Dan said.

"Where'd you get that?"

Dan shrugged. "What does it matter?"

Anglyn chuckled uncomfortably. "What does it matter? You mean aside from the fact that it's a crime against the crown?"

"You think they go to every household checking, Anglyn?" Dan raised the stone in front of his face. "There's no choice in this. We need to wake them. All of them. What King Alyn does or doesn't want will be irrelevant if the Fallen find them and kill them in their sleep."

He held the stone with his thumb and forefinger and moved it closer to the floating woman. Once the stone came to within a foot, a black cloud swirled around her body and accumulated in the space in front of the stone.

Dan tried to shrug off his growing fear but pulled the stone back. He, Mick, and Jack had already freed most of the creature. His two companions had paid for that mistake with their lives. Did he really want to free another piece of the thing? Would it kill Dan and everyone else here? *What choice is there?*

He moved the stone closer again. The black cloud formed around her as if trapped in an invisible globe, and once again concentrated on the space where he held the corlite.

"It wants the stone," Anglyn observed. "If you touch it with the stone, you'll feed it and make it stronger."

Dan thought about that. As a digger, he'd studied up on the precious stone. Corlite didn't necessarily hold essence, but was instead, a conduit. In his studies, however, Dan had begun to suspect that the stone could also be imbued with the power.

He looked at the piece of corlite in his fingers. Not having any affinity with the essences, he had no idea if this stone contained any of the power or not. If this cloud—presumably a piece of Shurza—reached so eagerly for it, did that mean it contained some bit of essence? Or was it merely that the stone had the potential?

Mycia's hand twitched and both Dan and Anglyn jumped back. Across the platform, the other diggers called over with loudly whispered questions.

"We're fine," Dan called back.

"This is enough for me," one of the diggers said. Tek. He'd been apprehensive from the start. "We should get out of there. Maybe contact Altarra and they can send some magi down here to deal with this. They're at least qualified."

An increasing murmur of agreement broke the eerie silence of the cavern. Dan and Anglyn shared a look. The team stood on the verge of leaving, and he could see in Anglyn's eyes that she might be losing her nerve as well.

"It's not an unreasonable idea," she said. "Magi would know better about how to deal with this than us."

Dan shook his head. "I've traveled across a good deal of Marai, and talked to a handful of magi, Anglyn. From my conversations I'm not even sure they teach the history about the Immortals." He turned back. "And we don't have time."

"How do you know, Dan? How?"

"I … just do." Dan walked up to the floating immortal and held the stone in front of her. The black cloud tracked his movements again, but he steadily moved it closer.

Mycia's fingers moved ever so subtly. Dan moved it in front of her face and watched. One of her closed eyes twitched. The black cloud dissipated for a moment, then returned. When Dan moved it down to her hand again, this time she lifted it, just a bit.

Her lips parted, but she said nothing. Dan looked her over with a growing sense of curiosity and apprehension. The cloud kept thickening and thinning. It would grow bigger, then fade into almost nothing.

"Interesting," Dan breathed. Was there some sort of battle being waged between the Illuminarian and the piece of Shurza with which she was trapped in this floating invisible bubble? Would the stone aid her?

He held the corlite in front of her hand. Energy radiated from the invisible field and set the tiny hairs on his arm on end. Mycia's hand flexed again, and she lifted it toward the stone.

Dan nearly screamed when he looked up at her face to see her eyes open and staring at him. He held her gaze, but she didn't blink, didn't give any indication she even saw him. And her eyes were an endless void of blackness. Maybe this wasn't a good idea …

Mycia's hand lifted a bit more, and Dan felt the stone trying to pull away. He looked down at it, then back up. The woman stared right at him, now. Cold fear gripped his stomach and spread around to creep up his spine.

He started to back away when the stone glowed red. The piece of corlite suddenly turned scorching hot. Dan cursed and dropped it, shaking his burned hand.

The corlite stone floated in front of him for a several fluttering heartbeats, then floated closer to Mycia. Her eyes began to flicker between black and green, which Dan presumed to be her normal eye color. The black cloud swirled violently around her, as if agitated.

Several moments passed during what Dan believed to be some internal struggle. The stone suddenly lit with a searing white light that filled the entire cavern and the pathway below.

Dan shielded his eyes against the sudden brilliance. He hadn't realized he'd been backing away until he nearly fell down the steps. When he finally lowered his forearm from his face and opened his eyes, he saw Mycia standing on the platform, looking up at a floating black cloud.

Whatever fear Dan had felt before gave way to outright panic. He looked left and right only to see Anglyn with a similar look of terror, and the other diggers across the platform, seemingly frozen with fear.

Mycia tilted her head as she looked up at the floating cloud. "How long has it been?" Her voice sounded soft and innocent, almost like a child's. "How long have we existed together in the void, little Shurza?"

She rolled the stone around in her fingers as she spoke. In front of her face, two glowing purple slits opened. Eyes?

"Oh, little Shurza," Mycia cooed. "How you've tried to destroy me over and over again, for, what? A millennia? Two? Ten? How long have you hunted my very existence in the confines of this essence void you pulled me into, that long ago fateful day? Or was it not that long ago?"

As quietly as he could, Dan took a careful, slow step back.

"Take not … another … step," Mycia ordered in such a soft tone, she could have been speaking to an infant. She didn't even look at him. Didn't take her eyes off the cloud. "You wish to flee to the rest of yourself, don't you, Shurza child? You wish to be made whole?" She tilted her head in the opposite direction. "Aw. That is endearing. But you cannot. Not while I hold you in the void."

She held up the stone. "Ironic. Through your endless years of hunting me down to destroy me, you've revealed your very nature. I will not be as cruel as you, Shurza child. I will not torment you endlessly."

The narrow slits in the trapped cloud narrowed even more. Mycia's laugh sounded like honey on the tip of a sword as it slowly entered flesh. "Do not be afraid. I will release you, little Shurza child." She blew it a kiss. "Go. Be one with oblivion."

She gripped the stone in her fist. Brilliant white light shined through her fingers and surrounded the piece of Shurza. The insubstantial creature let out an unearthly wail that made Dan want to end his own life rather than endure it any longer.

The white light surrounded and diminished the black cloud, then sucked it into the stone. Mycia looked at the stone as if it were the most curious thing in the world, then clamped her hand shut and shattered it.

White light flooded the cavern again. Raging funnels of broken earth and fire, water and howling wind swirled around the woman. Mycia floated in the middle of it all, her jubilant laughter riding the cacophony like life astride death.

ALSO BY RAMÓN TERRELL

World of a Broken Age:

Echoes of a Shattered Age

Legends of a Shattered Age

Heroes of a Broken Age (forthcoming)

Hunter's Moon:

Running from the Night

Hunter's Moon

Darkness of Day

Revenire

The Fairies:

Out of Ordure

Saga of Ruination:

Unleashed

Emergence

ACKNOWLEDGMENTS

No book is created alone. I would like to first thank my lovely wife, Tanya Terrell who has endured many a night of my sitting in the office working after I've gotten home from the job, working on my day off, working whenever I can fit it in.

Thank you to my editor, Michelle Dunbar. You've greatly helped Emergence to be the best it can be.

Thank you, Flora Samuelson, for always being there to help with comments and proofreading. You've been here since day one and I can't begin to tell you how much I appreciate it.

Thank you, Cat Lee, for running anchor with proofreading. Simply put, you rock!

And finally, THANK YOU, to all of the fans who have put up with this long delayed timeline, stuck by me when things were going more difficult than usual, and have cheered me every step of the way. This book and every other, always, is for you.

Ramón Terrell